Wieland;
or
The Transformation.
An American Tale

with Related Texts

Charles Brockden Brown

WIELAND;

or

THE TRANSFORMATION.
AN AMERICAN TALE

with Related Texts

Edited, with an Introduction and Notes, by
Philip Barnard and Stephen Shapiro

Hackett Publishing Company, Inc.
Indianapolis/Cambridge

For further information, please address:

Hackett Publishing Company, Inc.
P.O. Box 44937
Indianapolis, IN 46244-0937

www.hackettpublishing.com

Cover design by Abigail Coyle
Text design by Carrie Wagner
Composition by Macmillan Publishing Solutions
Printed at Sheridan Books, Inc.

Library of Congress Cataloging-in-Publication Data

Brown, Charles Brockden, 1771–1810.
  [Wieland]
  Wieland, or, the transformation : an American tale, with related texts / Charles
Brockden Brown ; edited, with an introduction and notes by Philip Barnard and
Stephen Shapiro.
     p. cm.
  Includes bibliographical references.
  ISBN 978-0-87220-974-9 (pbk.)—ISBN 978-0-87220-975-6 (cloth)
  1. Gentry—Pennsylvania—Fiction. 2. Brothers and sisters—Fiction.
3. Ventriloquists—Fiction. 4. Tricksters—Fiction. 5. Religious fanaticism—
Fiction. 6. Murder—Fiction. 7. Pennsylvania—History—Colonial period,
ca. 1600–1775—Fiction. I. Barnard, Philip, 1951– II. Shapiro, Stephen, 1964–
III. Title. IV. Title: Wieland. V. Title: Transformation.
  PS1134.W5 2009
  813'.2—dc22
                                                            2008052828

CONTENTS

ACKNOWLEDGMENTS

We thank the Department of English, University of Kansas, and the Department of English and Comparative Literary Studies, University of Warwick, for support throughout the preparation of this volume. The staffs of the University of Kansas libraries and The Spencer Research Library rare book collection have been generous sources of textual materials. Richard Clements, recently of the Spencer Library, has provided valuable support with ongoing work on Brown, facilitating access to materials that have contributed to this volume and related work for the Charles Brockden Brown Scholarly Edition.

For access to their digitized texts of the first editions of *Wieland* and *Memoirs of Carwin*, we acknowledge and thank the University of Virginia libraries and their Early American Fiction Collection project. The analysis of textual data provided by S.W. Reid in the 1977 Kent State Bicentennial Edition of the novel has been a basic source of information for our work.

Anthony Corbeill at Kansas has been very generous with advice and insights concerning Cicero and Brown's use of Latin texts. Heide Crawford at Kansas and Helmut Schmitz at Warwick have likewise provided consultation and textual expertise on Schiller and C. M. Wieland. The Warwick Research Collective's work on world literature has been inspirational. The translation work of Joerg Meindl at Kansas and Anne Schwan at Napier University in Edinburgh made it possible for us to include C. M. Wieland's "Answers and Counter-Questions" in this edition's Related Texts.

We are thoroughly indebted to the community of scholars who work on Brown and early modern culture, and to colleagues in the Charles Brockden Brown Society, whose insights and advice have helped form our ideas about and approach to this and other writings by Brown. Mark Kamrath and Bryan Waterman, in particular, have offered insightful comments and consultation on the novel and other materials used here. The Related Text of Brown's letter to Samuel Miller draws on John R. Holmes and Edwin Saeger's invaluable work on Brown's correspondence, as well as from ongoing work with Mark Kamrath and Elizabeth Hewitt for the upcoming volume of Letters for the Brown Electronic Archive and Scholarly Edition project.

For guidance and support with the editorial process at Hackett, we thank Rick Todhunter, still an extraordinarily supportive editor after three close encounters. Carrie Wagner, Christina Kowalewski, and Abigail Coyle, once again, have made essential contributions to the book's design and the quality of its text.

Personal thanks and Woldwinite relations of reason and desire link us to Anne Schwan, Cheryl Lester, and Julia Barnard.

INTRODUCTION

I realize more and more that poetry is the common property of mankind, and that it appears everywhere and at all times in hundreds and thousands of men . . . each one must tell himself that the poetic gift is not such a rare thing, and that nobody has a particular reason to pride himself for having written a good poem. But of course, if we Germans do not look beyond the narrow circle of our own environment, we all too easily fall into this kind of pedantic arrogance. Therefore I like to look around in foreign nations and advise everyone to do the same on his part. National literature means little these days; the epoch of world literature is at hand, and everybody must endeavor to hasten its coming.

—Goethe, *Letters to Eckermann* (1827)

Wieland as World Literature

As the aging writer Goethe, one of the most celebrated figures of his time, surveyed the literary scene of the 1820s, he argued that all cultural artifacts are products of global conditions and that all belong to a shared environment. In rejecting Romantic era claims for the heroic status of individual genius, the primacy of the aesthetic over the social and political, and the priority of national identities, the eminent German powerfully turned back many of the positions that his own long artistic career had been taken to exemplify. Goethe's insistence on a properly international horizon appeared as the negative effects of provincial patriotism were beginning to be revealed, but his global perspective had already been articulated and affirmed in the 1790s by a spectrum of writers that included the Philadelphia novelist Charles Brockden Brown.

Brown's first book-length fiction, *Wieland; or the Transformation. An American Tale* (1798)[1] was, for many decades, presented and labeled as the first American novel

---

[1] *Wieland* was the first of Brown's book-length fictions to see publication. A previously written novel, *Sky-Walk; or, The Man Unknown to Himself* was completed by March 1798 and partially typeset before being lost in a series of mishaps after printer-publisher James Watters died in that year's Philadelphia yellow fever epidemic. *Wieland* was first published in New York, on September 14, 1798, printed by T. & J. Swords for publisher Hocquet Caritat.

and Brown as the "father" of a national literature.[2] Since the 1980s and an often feminist-inspired scholarship that drew attention to earlier and female-authored works, such assertions of Brown's genetic or foundational significance have largely vanished.[3] Yet because of the novel's second subtitle, "An American Tale"—possibly related to the exchange in Chapter 4 about the validity of using a single family to represent an entire nation—and because Brown sent a presentation copy of the novel to Thomas Jefferson, then vice president and leader of the opposition Democratic-Republican Party, it is still a widely circulated commonplace that Brown's novel is primarily concerned with the nature of a unique national identity in the wake of American independence.[4] In what follows, our presentation of the novel will suggest that making Americanness or American identity the primary perspective from which to understand the novel fundamentally mistakes Brown's purpose and significantly distorts the conceptual and historical contexts that Brown openly and insistently provided for his readers.

Although *Wieland*'s preface recalls a shocking 1781 family murder in upstate New York, as well as similar incidents,[5] Brown locates these events within interpretive claims and generic narrative assumptions that largely belong to a well-developed set of concerns about society and politics raised by a group of English progressive writers (William Godwin, Mary Wollstonecraft, Thomas Paine) and within the plot devices of the German fantastic or gothic literature that was being translated and widely circulated in the 1790s. The international or, to use Goethe's phrase, world-literary core of Brown's novel is both obvious and obviously ignored by many commentators. The fiction is named after a family that claims a close relation to Christoph Martin Wieland, the prolific German novelist, playwright, and journalist, who was not only still alive when Brown's novel appeared, but was routinely considered by Anglophone reviewers as the preeminent German writer of the age, a figure comparable to Voltaire in the pantheon of Enlightenment artists. In the years immediately prior to the publication of *Wieland*, C. M. Wieland's work was increasingly available in English translations, and individual volumes of his collected writings in German were reviewed in major London publications to make Anglophone readers aware of their importance. Other characters in Brown's novel, such as Henry Pleyel and his fiancée Theresa de Stolberg, are similarly given the names of then widely known writers and musicians from German culture. At a key point in the novel, Clara Wieland alludes to the contemporary vogue for thrilling ballads such as *Lenore,* the gothic poem by Gottfried Bürger that caused tremendous interest among English poets

---

[2] Fred Lewis Pattee's "Introduction" to his 1926 edition of *Wieland,* for example, the standard twentieth-century edition until the 1970s, asserts that "the term 'Father of American literature' belongs unquestionably to Charles Brockden Brown" (ix).

[3] For the opening of the contemporary horizon on early American Republic writing, see Davidson, *Revolution and the Word.*

[4] See, for example, Fussell, "*Wieland*: A Literary and Historical Reading"; Budick, *Fiction and Historical Consciousness*; Fliegelman, *Prodigals and Pilgrims*; and Elliott, *Revolutionary Writers.*

[5] See the accounts of the Yates and Beadle family murders in Related Texts.

at the same time Brown was composing *Wieland,* and the Wieland family are presented reading this kind of sensational work in the original German for their group amusement.[6] Few other American-produced novels so consciously recall and insert themselves within a contemporaneous internationalized literary realm. The recovery of this environment and aspects of its significance, which have been something of a lost world for American Studies, is one purpose of this introduction.[7]

Largely because of a posthumous biography by Brown's close friend, William Dunlap, who labored to obscure Brown's progressive and cosmopolitan concerns as he attempted to secure Brown's reputation in a time of increasingly conservative and nationalist orthodoxy in the 1810s,[8] Brown was long regarded as a careless writer whose speed in composition resulted in distracting and confusing subplots, merely ornamental references, disconnected plot points, and other compositional problems. But in fact, Brown's complex back stories and subplots are remarkably coherent and precise; they develop well-informed networks of allusions and historical reference points that educated readers of Brown's time could recognize. Perhaps in part because the later template for interpreting pre-twentieth century U.S. gothic writing has been Edgar Allan Poe, whose international allusions tend toward ironic ornaments or pastiche counterfeits, scholars have largely tended to overlook the rich web of Brown's references, back stories, and telegraphed contexts, and have not developed the ways that this information supports and furthers his literary purposes.

For example, *Wieland*'s use of confusion created by ambivalent and indirect, ventriloquized speech has often been interpreted in primarily epistemological terms to mean that Brown wants to illustrate the fragility of language and meaning, or asserts a skeptical position on the basic potential of truth claims.[9] That is, many critics argue that Brown is primarily interested in abstract questions about how we perceive and know, rather than concrete questions concerning social and political circumstances.

---

[6] See the William Taylor version of *Lenore* in Related Texts.

[7] For an early but isolated attempt to develop this context, see Harry R. Warfel's "Charles Brockden Brown's German Sources." (1940). Besides the discussion developed here, see also the excerpts from and discussions of Wieland, Bürger, Schiller, and other figures associated with the German literary wave of the 1790s in Related Texts. Brown's circle not only translated German texts, but were active readers of a wide spectrum of English magazines (*Monthly Review, Monthly Magazine, Analytical Review*) that were themselves dedicated to commenting on continental European events, as well as the findings of the Irish and Scottish Royal Academies. Additionally, they were keen readers of French newspapers and publications.

[8] Dunlap's 1815 biography and miscellany of uncollected writings, *The Life of Charles Brockden Brown*, has a complex history and exerts a powerful influence on the direction of subsequent commentary on Brown. For discussions of the ways that Dunlap developed his biographical commentary from the previously existing, unfinished draft by Paul Allen, and of the pressures that Brown's family exerted on the final product, see the introductions to two facsimile editions of the Allen version of the biography by Bennett, and by Hemenway and Katz.

[9] See, for example, Hagenbüchle, "American Literature and the Nineteenth-Century Crisis in Epistemology"; Russo, "The Chimeras of the Brain: Clara's Narrative in *Wieland*"; Seltzer, "Saying Makes it So: Language and Event in Brown's *Wieland*"; and Voloshin, "*Wieland*: 'Accounting for Appearances.'"

In keeping with the English radical writings aforementioned, however, it may be more accurate to say that Brown understands ambiguity as a result and corollary of particular configurations of social power and political conditions, not as an inherent feature of language or of differences between written and oral media. Further, the tension of "double-tongued" speech seems to result in Brown's fictions from the collision of different sociolinguistic registers resulting from an imperial power's efforts to subjugate weaker regions. *Wieland* and Brown's other fictions repeatedly refer to a set of contested geographies: Saxony, the Languedoc region in Mediterranean France, Lombardy, Ireland, and Pennsylvania. All are regions that have been formed (and repeatedly reformed, over centuries) by imperial and dynastic conflicts, and by the subsequent collision of regional dialects with the standardizing, centralizing languages of imperial authorities. Readers today might not immediately think of Pennsylvania as belonging to this list, but Brown experiences this Mid-Atlantic state and its Philadelphia port as territories that were still British colonial outposts when he was born there in 1771. Brown's Pennsylvania and Mid-Atlantic region was forged through frontier disputes with native Americans and between European powers (these disputes are at the center of his 1799 novel *Edgar Huntly*, for example) and appears functionally, in his novels, as a focal point for global imperial-commercial networks (familiar to him through his family import-export business) that are populated by frequently displaced immigrant groups from a variety of linguistic and ethno-national backgrounds (vividly dramatized in the novels *Ormond* and *Arthur Mervyn*).

Rather than understanding Pennsylvania or the United States as existing only in opposition to Great Britain or as fundamentally separate from it, Brown is fascinated by the ways that similar regional subunits function as transistors of global pressures that produce local conditions as parts of a world-system in conflict throughout the eighteenth century. Seemingly isolated and individual disturbances, in Brown's fictions, are local effects of larger historical conflicts, and language is the medium through which worldwide conflicts—over territory, between classes and other status groups, and among religions—are articulated.

As Brown suggests in his essays on novel writing, the purpose of literature is to help individuals navigate within changing historical conditions. With its tale of a family's changing attitudes over three generations, *Wieland*'s theme is the dynamics, promises, and pitfalls of social change. Brown's argument, as he develops that theme, is that social conditions change, but they change in both directions, both toward progressive Enlightenment and back away from it. Whereas "revolution" is often used in modern parlance to mean irreversible change, Brown and his period can still hear the word's more literal and early-modern sense of a cyclical motion revolving back to its starting point. Coming of age in a time when once triumphant and confident political progress was being contained by resurgent conservatism (or, as some social historians see it, by the birth of a modern, postrevolutionary form of conservatism as a fundamental sociopolitical orientation)[10] Brown may intend the novel's subtitle,

---

[10] For the development of modern, postrevolutionary ideological orientations, see Wallerstein, *After Liberalism*.

"the Transformation," to identify the contemporary wave of counterreform or counterrevolution under which he lived and wrote. The novel's depiction of its characters' dizzying oscillations between confident equipoise and anxious self-doubt may suggest Brown's larger purpose of investigating the roots and results of the dramatic turn away from modern equality that took shape at the end of the 1790s. At its heart, *Wieland* explores the relative stability of Enlightenment-era social and political agendas, and the causes for their demise.

Brown's Life and the Context of the 1790s

Brown was born into a Philadelphia Quaker merchant family on January 17, 1771. Philadelphia, the capital of the newly formed United States during the 1790s and then the largest, wealthiest, most culturally and politically diverse city in North America, was his home for most of his life. Beginning in the mid-1790s and particularly during the intense 1797–1800 period when he was writing his novels, however, Brown also lived in New York and moved in a cosmopolitan circle of young upper-class intellectuals who circulated and debated the latest medical-scientific, political, and cultural information and produced writings on a wide variety of subjects.

Growing up a Philadelphia Quaker (members of The Religious Society of Friends are commonly known as "Quakers" or "Friends"), Brown was shaped by that community's history of dissenting relations to mainstream Protestant and Anglo-American culture, and by Philadelphia's importance as both a political center and a major port connected with Atlantic and global mercantile networks. Brown had a classical education at the elite Friend's Latin School in Philadelphia and seems to have taught briefly at the Friends' Grammar School in the early 1790s, but, unlike his male friends in the New York circle, did not attend a university, since many Quakers and other dissenters in the U.S. and England did not patronize the educational institutions that served dominant Protestant groups. Although Brown's adult years led him from his Philadelphia origins to the intellectual world of the radical Enlightenment, his Quaker background nonetheless marks his development in fundamental ways. Quaker traditions and doctrines concerning egalitarianism and equal authority for women in the Quaker community contributed to Brown's lifelong commitment to women's education and equality.[11] Similarly, Quaker leadership in antislavery organizations is part of the background for the implicit and explicit reflections on slavery in the novel *Arthur Mervyn* and other writings. Interestingly, after having grown up as Quakers in the increasingly diversified Philadelphia of the late eighteenth century, Brown and all his siblings but one married non-Quakers (Brown's youngest brother, Elijah Jr., remained unmarried), an increasingly common trend for Quakers at this time. Consequently, Brown was formally dissociated from the Quaker meeting in Philadelphia when he married Elizabeth Linn, daughter of a Presbyterian minister, in 1804.

---

[11] See Fleischmann, *A Right View of the Subject: Feminism in the Works of Charles Brockden Brown and John Neal.*

Growing up the fourth of five brothers and seven surviving siblings in a merchant family,[12] Brown's life was shaped by the mercantile culture of Philadelphia during the Revolutionary era. The merchant careers of Brown's father and four brothers made him intimately familiar with the circum-Atlantic import-export commerce that was the main business of Philadelphia's port.[13] Brown's father Elijah came to Philadelphia as a young man from Chester County, Pennsylvania, and had a checkered business career mainly as a conveyancer, a broker and manager for real estate, mortgage, and other transactions. In 1777–1778, during the American Revolution, he was arrested and interned in Virginia as one of a group of Quakers deemed "dangerous to the State" because they refused on religious grounds to sign oaths of allegiance. In 1784, he was humiliatingly imprisoned for debt. Through all this, the father struggled to continue in business, partly sustained by the real-estate holdings and financial interests of Brown's maternal aunt, Elizabeth Armitt.

Although his family intended for him to become a lawyer, Brown abandoned his Philadelphia law apprenticeship in 1793, complaining that the language of law existed to deny rather than enact justice, and moved toward the circle of young, New York-based intellectuals who helped launch his literary career and, with Brown as one of their group, enacted progressive Enlightenment ideals of conversation, intellectual inquiry, and companionship.[14] The New York group included a number of young male professionals who called themselves The Friendly Club, along with female relatives and friends who were equally invested in progressive intellectual exchange and enlightened models for same-sex and other-sex companionship. This progressive model of companionship based on "reason and desire" expressed through a "republic of letters" is a crucial context for Brown's astonishing burst of novel writing between 1798 and 1801. The key figure in this group was Elihu Hubbard Smith (1771–1798), a Yale-educated physician and writer who met Brown in Philadelphia in 1790 and played a crucial role in encouraging his literary ambitions. Aspects of Smith's life, from his abolitionism and Deism[15] to his

---

[12] Kafer, *Charles Brockden Brown's Revolution*, provides the numbers we use here, i.e., five brothers and two sisters who survived to adulthood, plus three siblings who died at birth or in early infancy (45, 210, n36, 221n25).

[13] See the accounts of Brown family business interests in Warfel, *Charles Brockden Brown: American Gothic Novelist*, 16–18, 23, 204; Clark, *Charles Brockden Brown: Pioneer Voice of America*, 108–09, 194–95; and Kafer, 26–37, 45–46, 162, 214n15. Brown's older brothers, particularly Joseph, voyaged throughout the Atlantic world.

[14] For discussions of this circle, see Waterman, *Republic of Intellect* and Teute, "A 'Republic of Intellect':" and "The Loves of the Plants." The diaries of William Dunlap and Elihu Hubbard Smith provide detailed records of Brown's activities and relations within this circle.

[15] "Deism" is a progressive eighteenth-century response to Christianity. It affirms the existence of a "supreme being," but rejects revelation, supernatural doctrines, and any notion of divine intervention in human affairs. Reason and science, rather than scripture and dogma, are the basis for religious belief. Late-eighteenth-century writers often adopt a deistic stance as part of their general secular and rationalist critique of earlier institutions. Deism is associated with "natural religion" and the well-known metaphor of the deity as a "clock-maker" who creates the universe but makes no further intervention in it. Many leaders of the American Revolutionary generation were deists, notably Benjamin Franklin and Thomas Jefferson. See Walters, *Rational Infidels: The American Deists*.

efforts to treat yellow fever victims and other progressive political and social positions, figure as models for characters and events in Brown's novels *Edgar Huntly* (1799) and *Arthur Mervyn* (1799–1800).

As one of this circle, Brown developed his knowledge of like-minded British radical-democratic writers of the period—above all William Godwin and Mary Wollstonecraft (whose books were already in Brown's household as a youth, before he met Smith)—as well as medical and physiological claims drawn from the Scottish Enlightenment (notably Erasmus Darwin), the French Naturalists, and other streams of continental Enlightenment thought. The circle was committed to abolitionist activism and many of the male members of the group were officers in abolition societies. The circle's interest in similar groups of progressive British thinkers was strong enough that they established contact through correspondence with scientist Erasmus Darwin (via Smith), novelist Thomas Holcroft, and Godwin himself (via Dunlap and Godwin's ward Thomas Cooper, an actor who emigrated to the U.S. and moved in Brown's circles). Thus Brown's interest in European developments led him to participate in a network of like-minded endeavors, but his progressive, modernizing ideals meant that he felt little or no need to emulate Europe or the past as superior cultures.

If Brown's intellectual circle in New York constitutes one part of the context for his burst of novel writing, the other crucial element in this context is the explosive political atmosphere of the revolutionary 1790s as it culminated in the antirevolutionary backlash of 1797–1800. Throughout the decade, events and discussions in New York and Philadelphia were closely intertwined with the ongoing processes of the French Revolution (1789–1798), the Haitian Revolution (1791–1804) and events leading to the Irish uprisings of 1796–1798. Refugees and participants from these revolutionary events filled the streets of 1790s Philadelphia and New York with émigrés of every stripe and color, from Royalist French aristocrats and planters from the Caribbean fleeing ongoing revolutions, to enslaved "French negroes" or "wild Irish" revolutionary activists and intellectuals. By the end of the decade a severe reaction against the progressive ideals of the revolutionary era spread through the Atlantic world and was especially powerful in England, Germany, and the recently formed United States. During the administration of the second U.S. president, John Adams (1796–1800), the ruling Federalist Party presided over a partisan and repressive response to real and imagined threats of revolutionary subversion and potential conflict with France.[16] Enacting the now-infamous Alien and Sedition Acts (1798), for example, Federalists made it illegal to criticize the Adams administration and legitimated the arrest and deportation of those deemed enemies of the state (i.e., French and Irish radicals). Paranoid countersubversive fantasies about conspiracies led by mysterious groups like the Illuminati (a secret society ostensibly plotting to overthrow church and state

---

[16] See the discussions of this backlash and its implications in Cotlar, "The Federalists' Transatlantic Cultural Offensive of 1798 and the Moderation of American Political Discourse"; Elkins and McKitrick, *The Age of Federalism*; Fischer, *The Revolution of American Conservatism*; Miller, *Crisis in Freedom: The Alien and Sedition Acts*; and Tise, *The American Counterrevolution.*

institutions), as well as elite panic about newly articulated ideals of universal democracy, including female equality and slave emancipation, contributed to this crisis. Traces of the Illuminati scare are evident in both *Wieland* and its "prequel" *Memoirs of Carwin the Biloquist.*[17] Although these excesses led to the Federalist's defeat and the election of their Democratic-Republican opponent Jefferson in the 1800 election, the conservative wave announced by this convulsion helped put an end to the Revolutionary era and laid the foundations for the more staid cultural order of the early nineteenth century.

Brown's efforts to establish himself as a writer in this period were impressive indeed. After several years of experimentation with poetry and literary narratives that remained unfinished, Brown's novelistic phase began with the 1798 feminist dialogue *Alcuin* and continued unabated through the composition of eight novels by late 1801. Throughout this period, in addition to work on these novels, Brown was editing the New York *Monthly Magazine* (April 1799–December 1800) and publishing numerous essays, tales, and reviews. As noted earlier, the four "gothic" novels for which Brown is best known—*Wieland, Ormond, Arthur Mervyn,* and *Edgar Huntly*—were all published between September 1798 and September 1799 (*Mervyn, Second Part* appeared in September 1800), and there was a period in 1798 when all four were under way at once. Although Cold War-era commentators often presented Brown as a writer who renounces his literary and progressive political ideals when he stops publishing novels in 1801, a more plausible explanation for his subsequent shift toward other forms of writing is that his novels did not make money, the particular conditions that fueled the intense novelistic burst from 1798 to 1801 changed (who could sustain such a rhythm of production?), and he became interested in new literary outlets. Like his older counterpart Godwin in England, Brown moves away from the novel because he feels it no longer offers an effective mode of argumentation in the increasingly conservative cultural and political environment that emerges after 1800. Had Brown lived longer, he might conceivably have returned to novel writing, as Godwin did in the later 1810s.

Brown's later literary career builds continuously on the novels and earlier writings. Between 1801 and his death from tuberculosis in 1810, Brown edited two important periodicals: *The Literary Magazine* (1803–1807), a literary and cultural miscellany that renewed his experience with the earlier *Monthly Magazine* and that he filled with his own essays and fiction; and *The American Register* (1807–1809), a historical and political periodical that featured Brown's "Annals of Europe and America," a comprehensive narrative of Napoleonic-era geopolitics. In addition, he undertook a novel-length historical fiction known as the *Historical Sketches* (1803–1806) that was published only posthumously, a now-lost play, and several lengthy, quasinovelistic pamphlets on expansion into the Louisiana territory and Jefferson's embargo policies (1803, 1809). These writings continue Brown's career-long concern with the link between historical and fictional ("romance") writing, and extend the earlier program of "reason and desire" that makes writing an instrument of progressive, educational

---

[17] For more on the Illuminati scare see the discussion in Related Texts.

principles in the public sphere. Rather than dramatizing the ways individuals are shaped by social pressures and crisis contexts, as he did in his novels, the later Brown explores forms of historical narrative and the larger historical world that made up the allusive backdrop of the earlier fiction. The critical perspective on global webs of imperial warfare, colonialism, and political-religious conflict that figures in the Wieland family history, for example, becomes explicit and is explored in detail in the later historical writings and essays.[18]

The Woldwinite Writers and Brown's Novelistic Method

The world of *Wieland* and Brown's other novels, with their gothic emotional intensities, disorienting psychological and social violence, and embedded back stories and subplots, may be difficult to sort out on first encounter. Understanding some basics about Brown's primary intellectual and political sources, and his well-defined novelistic method, however, can help the reader understand features of his novels that might otherwise seem difficult to grasp.

Unlike many authors of eighteenth-century fiction, Brown had a well-developed methodology and set of themes for writing novels. His method draws on and further

---

[18]In his June 1803 letter to Samuel Miller, Brown writes:

The *reformation* in religion, as it is called, was one of the most important revolutions which has occurred in Europe since the fall of the Roman Empire.

The destruction of this empire, was, indeed, rather nominal than real, since the Bishop of Rome succeeded the ancient emperors in one of their most important attributes or characters, that of the Pontifex Maximus, & since, in this character, they exercised a much more absolute authority over more extensive & distant regions than was ever exercised by Trajan, Constantine or Justinian. The Reformation may be considered as the defection of certain provinces of this empire & the effort by intrigues, arms & controversial writings, of Rome & her votaries to regain these provinces, which began in the Sixteenth, were far from having terminated at the opening of the Eighteenth century. The western nations of Europe were, at this period, engaged in a ruinous war, in part of the consequence of this great scism. The great object which ingaged the attention of speculative men was the merits and demerits of different schemes of christianity, & kings & ministers were fully occupied in destroying or supporting the claims to civil authority founded upon these differences.

In the progress of this century, things insensibly assumed a new appearance. The mind of man is ever restless & each successive age producing a new object to exercise ambition & curiosity. Having exausted the great questions which divided protestants & Romanists, a controversy gradually arose as to the truth of religion, & more especially of Christianity itself. As the inhabitants of Europe were engaged in other earlier ages, & in discussing the respective merits of christianity & paganism & afterwards of the merits of different schemes or systems of Christianity, they came, in the Eighteenth century to discuss the truth of any form whatsoever of religion. In place of ancient denomination, mankind began to assume the distinctions of christians & infidels, or religionists & atheists. From enquiring how the scriptures ought to be interpreted, & which among the successors of christ deserve to be held in reverence as infallible teaching, the questions now were whether Christ himself ever existed; whether the history of his life possessed any historical credibility, & even whether there were any grounds for the existence or commonly recieved attributes of GOD himself.

develops the ideas of the British radical-democratic writers of the period. Brown's enthusiastic reception of these Woldwinite[19] ("Anglo-Jacobin") writers—above all Mary Wollstonecraft, William Godwin, Thomas Holcroft, Robert Bage, and Thomas Paine—undergirds his entire literary project after the mid-1790s. The British "Dissenter" culture of highly educated middle-class professionals and the clubs and academies from which these writers emerged was the wider context of Brown's own Philadelphia Quaker community. Brown was exposed to the Woldwinite writers through his father's copies of their works even before he moved into the New York circle and explored their writings in greater detail.[20]

The Woldwinite agenda rests on three basic arguments that draw together the main strands of knowledge and critique in the late, radical Enlightenment. Drawing on well-established eighteenth-century arguments and themes such as associative sentiment (the idea that emotions are communicated from one individual to another and may be used to encourage constructive, progressive behavior), these arguments sum up this group's rejection of the prerevolutionary order and their conviction that social progress may be achieved by altering dominant ways of thinking through peaceful cultural means such as literature. First, the social order of the old regime (monarchy and feudalism) is to be rejected because it is artificial and illegitimate, violating the natural equality of humanity by imposing coercive hierarchies of caste and faith. Second, given that the old regime maintained its domination through an obscurantist mythology of territorialized race, priestly tricks, and a politics of secret plots, conspiracies, and lies, a new social order will require the development of more rational, constructive, and transparent institutions and practices. Third, the illustration of progressive behavior, in print and other media, will multiply to generate larger social transformation because society works through chains of associative sentiment and emulation. These cultural relays will generate progressive change as the illustration of virtuous behaviors and results spreads through imitation, with each individual learning and transmitting new and improved ways of acting by observing others. Proceeding from these assumptions, the Woldwinites' critique leads to their antistatism, their distrust of institutions, and to their use of cultural forms such as literature to advance their program. Because they believed in the natural propulsion

---

[19] We use the term Woldwinite to highlight, through an abbreviation of Wollstonecraft and Godwin, this group's special place among the British radical democrats of the 1790s. The term "Godwinians" erases the crucial role of Wollstonecraft and other women in this group, a role that was particularly important for Brown and many other writers. Similarly, these British writers are also discussed as "Jacobins" or "Anglo-Jacobins," a name used by opponents to link them to the most authoritarian and partisan faction of the French revolution, but the group explicitly rejected the "Jacobin" position in favor of its own distinct set of cultural-political positions. For studies of literary Woldwinism, see: Clemit, *The Godwinian Novel*; Kelly, *The English Jacobin Novel 1780–1805* and *English Fiction of the Romantic Period, 1789–1830*; Butler, *Jane Austen and the War of Ideas*; and Tompkins, *The Popular Novel in England, 1770–1800*.

[20] For the Woldwinite writings in Brown's household, see Warfel, 17–18, 27; Clark, 16; Kafer, 46, 66–72.

of cooperative behavior and the guidance of critical reason, these writers see social change as resulting from the amplification of transformed local, interpersonal or intersubjective relations.[21] Thus, as we say today, the personal is political.

In their assumption that global historical change begins from the bottom up with the premeditated transformation of relations among a small circle, the Woldwinites are an early instance of the belief in a cultural avant-garde that aims to develop means of worldly social revolution through arts and manners rather than political parties or state institutions. In contemporary terms, the Woldwinites introduce a relatively straightforward, albeit limited idea of environmental or social construction, the notion that individuals are shaped or conditioned by their social environments and circumstances. Their ideas about social construction are limited in that they position themselves as innocent participants and do not always recognize the dilemmas implicit in their own social program (particularly its assumptions about sentiment, benevolence, and associative imitation), and insofar as they direct their critique mainly at the hierarchical inequalities of the old regime while neglecting new modes of inequality that are part of the emergent structures of liberal capitalism. Brown adopts their environmentalist argument but also, as a second-wave Woldwinite, recognizes that their ideas about social construction and action are incomplete. His fiction attempts to think through their limitations and implications in ways that we will explore in greater detail when we turn to the plot of *Wieland* in what follows.

Building on these basic Woldwinite ideas, Brown's fictional method is articulated in several key essays on narrative technique and the social role of the novel that appear at the height of his novelistic phase, notably "Walstein's School of History" (August–September 1799) and "The Difference between History and Romance" (April 1800).[22] To summarize this method, we can say that Brown's novels combine elements of history and fiction, placing his characters in situations of social and historical distress as a means of engaging a wider audience into considerations of progressive behavior. His novels explore how contemporary subjects—whether relatively elite actors such as Clara Wieland or relatively disempowered, lower-status individuals like Frank Carwin—respond to damaging social conditions caused by defects in dominant ideas and practices. Through their interconnected patterns of socially conditioned behavior, dramatic suspense, and gothic intensities, Brown's fictions urge readers to reflect on how to overcome corruption in order to construct a more "virtuous," more equal and fulfilling society.

This approach begins with Brown's understanding of the relation between historical and fictional ("romance") writing. History and fiction, he argues, are not different because one deals with factual and the other with fictional materials. Rather, they are intrinsically connected as two sides of one coin: history describes and documents the results of actions, while fiction investigates the possible motives and circumstances that cause and explain these actions. Fictions are thus narrative experiments that tease out possible preconditions for historical events or behaviors, and that reason

---

[21] For more on Godwin, see the excerpt in Related Texts.

[22] These essays are included in this volume's Related Texts.

through social problems presented as hypothetical situations; they are a form of conjectural or counterfactual history. Whereas history describes events, romance analyzes and projects the probable causes, conditions, and preconditions of events. The "Walstein" essay builds on this distinction and develops a three-fold plan for novel writing, providing a fuller account of the rationale and essential themes that inform Brown's fiction. "Walstein" is presented in a narrative frame that alludes to Friedrich Schiller and other figures associated with the same German literary wave of the 1790s that is also registered on several levels in *Wieland*, most obviously in the way that central characters' names reference well-known figures of contemporary German literature and culture.

In the essay, the historian Walstein combines history and romance in such as way as to promote "moral and political" engagement while rejecting universal truths, stressing the situatedness of engaged political response in noble and classical figures such as the Roman statesman Cicero. Walstein's pupil Engel then modernizes and develops the theory by adding that a romance, to be effective in today's world, must be addressed to a wide popular audience and draw its characters not from the elite but from the same middling and lower-status groups that will read and be moved by the work. History and romance alike must address issues and situations familiar to their modern audience, notably the common inequalities arising from relations of sex and property. Thus a modern literature will insert ordinary individuals such as Clara Wieland or Frank Carwin, rather than elite actors like Cicero, into crisis situations in which they must negotiate contemporary conflicts involving social status and property, and erotic desire or gender relations. Finally, a thrilling style and form are crucial, since a romance capable of moving its audience to considerations of progressive action must "be so arranged as to inspire, at once, curiosity and belief, to fasten the attention, and thrill the heart." In this manner, Brown's method uses the twists and turns of his intentionally challenging plots, as well as dramatic phenomena such as family murders, mental illness, or ventriloquism, as ways to illustrate and think through interrelated social problems and encourage an engaged response to them.

Sincerity: The Foundation for Political Change

In reading *Wieland*, our starting point will be the call for sincerity announced by the title page's prefatory quatrain. Sincerity is a keyword at the heart of the Woldwinite model for social transformation. In their usage it means much more than simply speaking honestly as an individual, although this basic injunction is intended as well. Sincerity is a multi-leveled political agenda that seeks to remove an entire standing order of political and religious imposture: the sly ambiguities of politicians who hide the intentional effects of policies and laws behind falsehood and propaganda; a culture of governmental secrets and covert surveillance of the citizenry; willful obstruction of access to education and other forms of opportunity; and the mystification of empirical science by agents of institutionalized religion who fear that it will remove the tissue of superstition used to dominate the laity. The Woldwinites understand sincerity, on all levels, as a practice that will germinate to undermine vested, self-serving interests and replace them with a more equal and transparent society.

Sincerity's power and transformative potential are generated in the context of the intimate discussion group or conversation between friends, not in individual meditation or in public debates between ostensibly anonymous interlocutors. Unlike Descartes and the tradition of early modern rationalism that descends from him, which emphasizes the thinking processes of the isolated individual, the Woldwinite writers see autonomous ratiocination as unregulated and thus liable to idiosyncratic excess and error. They recognize that humans are social creatures who develop in and through a culture of interaction. Therefore, the Woldwinites favor the hygiene of group dialogue, in which individual ideas or positions are exercised and modified through collective consideration. They do not, however, idealize entirely "open" or public (print) debates, which they see as easily degenerating into bullying or posturing, and into manipulation by special interests masquerading as a univocal general will or acting through charismatic invocation of simplistic but appealing sophistries. Private or semi-public dialogue between friends or within a salon-like group is the Woldwinite's ideal form because it rescues the individual from the errors of lonely thought, but also provides an arena outside the dominant *status quo* in which individuals can be comfortable enough to present their assumptions or behavior for comment and questioning.

The conversational circle also provides a living, experiential context for the transmission and enactment of ideas that the printed page cannot. The Woldwinites are acutely aware that most people find the contemplation of political philosophy or the evaluation of analytical propositions intolerably dull and unengaging. At the same time, they understand that these matters are too important to be left lying between the covers of unopened books moldering on shelves, and that abstract or abstruse questions need some enticing or thrilling presentational format in order to seize attention and magnetize the mind. The conviviality of group discussion and debate helps lubricate the flow of ideas as people naturally enjoy moments of congeniality.

Once an individual gains experience in sincere intercourse within one group or setting, the Woldwinites anticipate that she or he will increasingly expect and enact transparency in others. The communication of this ideal is intended to expand and saturate all aspects of civil society. Eventually despotic forms of government and faith will fade away without the need for violent confrontation, since the legitimacy of these institutions will have been so thoroughly eroded by encircling demands for transparency as to make the violent spasms of revolution unnecessary. As previously mentioned, the personal is political here, in that personal interactions will cascade to alter the political environment. The converse is likewise understood to be true; a corrupt political society corrupts its inhabitants even within their daily actions. Insincerity is not simply the absence or tactical omission of truth; it is a poison that destroys relations as people increasingly adjust to and replicate the dominant order's silences and moments of blocked communication, which are as damaging as outright lies. Consequently, Woldwinite fictions are replete with images of knowledge cloistered or trapped in locked chests and libraries or hidden rooms. Beyond being mysterious in an immediate sense, such hidden knowledge and secreted information symbolize the entire apparatus of corrupt misrule, associated with aristocratic and priestly regimes that use magical aura and prestige to block rational inquiry into the legitimacy of their rule.

Brown and his associates were perhaps as centrally fascinated by the promise of sincerity's enactment through conversation as by any other single aspect of the Woldwinite program. They also worried about the damage caused by the strategic delay or willful omission of transparent communication. In a tale like "A Lesson on Concealment; or, Memoirs of Mary Selwyn," Brown relates how an avalanche of tragic events is set off less by outright falsehoods, than by personal guardedness and an inability to communicate.[23] On the other hand, Brown's Wollstonecraftian *Alcuin; A Dialogue* dramatizes the benefits of speaking truthfully and openly, even if such frankness initially produces awkward moments.

From *Wieland*'s title page, with its cautionary verse about straying from virtue into mazy paths of ambiguity, to its concluding reflection on the Conway subplot, the importance of sincerity is presented as a key theme. In the attendant *Memoirs of Carwin*, this concern appears with the unpalatable Ludloe, who professes to seek human enlightenment but is deeply engaged in schemes of deception. Likewise, Carwin's dubious uses of ventriloquism seem to appear as a form of unlocatable and often self-interested, hence inauthentic and insincere voice. From the moment of Carwin's first appearance to Clara on the grounds at Mettingen, he is encoded with allusions to the classical god Hermes or Mercury, a trickster figure of double meanings. Carwin's shadiness, often literalized as he hides in closets and natural enclosures, is figured in glimmering or flitting light associated with his movements. His masquerades in different identities, his reluctance to speak openly about his past and present, and his ambiguous answers all damage the fabric that forms the social safety net protecting against rule by violence.

Ludloe's plotting and Carwin's impostures are intentionally easy to deplore and condemn. Taking this concern a step further, however, it seems clear that Brown develops *Wieland* in such a way that all of its primary characters share culpability in performances of double-tongued insincerity. In a key discussion of the mysterious voices in Chapter 8, for example, Theodore Wieland hastily forecloses discussion of events, suggesting a lack of intellectual rigor and weakness of mind that presages later developments. Implicitly, the elder Wieland's religious conversion in Chapter 2 and Theodore's exaggerated adulation of Cicero in Chapters 3 and 4 are criticized for the narrowness of their construction and for the absence of comparative evaluation achieved through dialogue. By holding their ideas in private contemplation, insulated from discussion and debate, the Wieland patriarchs effectively enact insincerity. If Brown's novel develops a critique of religious enthusiasm and the spirit of revelation, it is that such positions are functionally insincere insofar as their proponents insist on the private, isolated nature of their claims.

---

[23] "A Lesson on Concealment; or, Memoirs of Mary Selwyn," in *Monthly Magazine* 2.3 (March 1800), 174–207. Reprinted in Brown, *Somnambulism and Other Stories*, 53–102.

Similarly, Pleyel's claims to transparent rationality are undermined by his manipulation of Carwin to test Clara, his covert surveillance of Clara that includes creeping into her room to read her diary unobserved, and his refusal to consider contrary evidence when he suspects Clara is promiscuous. Clara herself enacts insincerity when she keeps silent about her unspoken but deeply engrained suspicions concerning Theodore's latent aggression and emotional health, expressed in fantasies in which he lures her on to destruction, and thus never reveals her experience of the mysterious voice that interrupts her dream in Chapter 7. In other words, the novel seems to be constructed in such a manner as to suggest that nearly all of the novel's tragic events might arguably have been avoided or moderated if Mettingen's inhabitants had practiced group sincerity in the sense that Brown and the Woldwinites understand it. They do not, however, and gothic consequences seem to unfold swiftly.

Wieland is not simply didactic, despite the moralizing hints in the quatrain that prefaces the novel.[24] Developing a detailed historical context within the novel and drawing on related literary currents of the Revolutionary era, Brown explores the structural pressures that create effects of insincerity, rather than focusing primarily on personalized "faults" in isolated individuals. Rather than simply repeating the Woldwinite dogma about insincerity, he tests this set of ideas by probing further into the originating causes that generate insincerity, exploring the social roots of a problem that was imperfectly or incompletely pursued by the earlier writers, and examining issues that their political philosophy did not because their narrative-analytical framework was not capable of doing so.

To gain leverage on the English progressive thinkers, Brown turned to generic conventions then mainly associated with the 1770s and 1780s German *Schauerroman*, the "shudder" or "horror" novel of gruesome events and mysterious appearances. Although examples of this fictional subgenre are often assumed to be straightforward homologues or equivalents of English gothic fiction, the German horror tales have different emphases and implied goals than their English-language counterparts. With its suicidal gloom, spectacular destructions, insinuations of rape, covert spying, secret rooms, and familial violence, *Wieland* draws from a catalogue of features then more common in German than in English writers, until Matthew Lewis's *The Monk* (1794), which itself was deeply influenced by the German horror wave and related French elements. While the Woldwinites, in works such as Godwin's *Caleb Williams* or Wollstonecraft's *Maria, or The Wrongs of Woman*, often cast their fictions in general gothic modes, they did not seem to recognize as completely as Brown what cultural purposes and complaints gave rise to the German gothic-sensational writing, nor how those codes might be imported and used to construct a mode of critical Anglophone fiction. For the German wave arose as a structure of feeling[25] in which

---

[24] For the argument that Brown's intentions in writing the novel were fundamentally didactic, see, for example, Tompkins, *Sensational Designs*.

[25] Raymond Williams uses "structure of feeling" to convey the phenomenon that occurs when a cultural form is used to express emergent social experiences that otherwise lack the forms of their own representation. See Raymond Williams, *The English Novel from Dickens to Lawrence*.

the charnel and the grotesque are used to convey frustration at incomplete modernity and unrealized Enlightenment, frustration with the thwarted promise that intellectual freedom could be transmuted into political and social equality.

The German Horror Novel and the Critique of Enlightened Absolutism

Throughout the 1790s, Anglophone readers consumed German sensational fiction and poetry with a passion. Contemporary journalistic complaints about these literary imports often combine aesthetic condemnation or mockery with the assertion that these German forms were intrinsically associated with the period's revolutionary energies.[26] Contemporary reviewer William Preston, for instance, complained that in the "gloomy and disgusting pictures" drawn by German sensational fiction, "every motive is inculcated, which may induce men to be discontented, with the government under which they live, or, indeed, with any government, and to become active partizans of anarchy and disorder."[27] But while rants by the period's conservative commentators often made for good press, their sound and fury ought not to be taken as generally representative of the time. European sensational fiction was popularly read by a wide spectrum of Anglophone readers, and mainstream reviews carefully distinguished between subvarieties of the genre and gave serious consideration to examples they felt were more skillfully made. Further, English reviewers often exaggerated the equation of culture and politics, since the nations that actually did experience revolutionary processes, like France, produced comparatively less horror fiction.[28] The primary production of and market for gothic representations seems to have been located in regions just beyond the borders of the Revolution, mainly Germany and England.

In a description useful for considering the significance of this "uneven" cultural geography of late-eighteenth-century horror fiction, Leon Trotsky (1879–1940)

---

[26] The overall Anglophone German wave of the 1790s, in most accounts, extends from 1788 to about 1802. The two commonly cited reference points are Henry Mackenzie's forward-looking Royal Society of Edinburgh lecture on German Drama in 1788 and William Preston's nationalistic and xenophobic rejection of the period's German imports in 1802. The peak years 1796–1800 are marked by the much-commented vogues for Bürger's *Lenore* (1796) and the dramatist Kotzebue (1798–1800). For more on the German wave and its cultural politics, see Mortensen, *British Romanticism and its Continental Influences: Writing in an Age of Europhobia*; Maertz, "The Importation of German and Dissenting Voices in British Culture: Thomas Holcroft and the Godwin Circle"; Skokoe, *German Influence in the English Romantic Period, 1788–1818*; and Herzfeld, *William Taylor of Norwich: A Study of the Influence of Modern German Literature in England*.

[27] William Preston, "Reflections on the Peculiarities of Style and Manner in the late German Writers, whose Works have appeared in English; and on the Tendency of their Productions," *Edinburgh Magazine* 20 (1802), 353–61, 406–08; 21 (1802), 9–18, 89–96 (1803): here 11–12.

[28] For a French perspective on the horror genre and its historical development in relation to the Anglophone wave, see D.A.F. Sade, "Reflections on the Novel" ("*Idée sur les romans*"), as well as Paulson, *Representations of Revolution, 1789–1820*.

developed the idea of what he called combined and uneven development.[29] When a highly developed region forcefully incorporates a less powerful region within its sphere of influence and the capitalist world market, by overwhelming that region's weak middle class, Trotsky argues that characteristic consequences develop. In the absence of control by its own middle classes, the region responds to its experience of inclusion within imperial market networks by resuscitating obsolete narrative devices and behavioral practices, and presenting these cultural forms as authentic expressions of local identity. But since these representations, in fact, belong to obsolete or residual (outdated) social formations, they are necessarily reinvented in ways that meld ancient forms with the expression of modern concerns. New "traditions" are literally invented and circulated as modern products wearing the garb of the old. The archaic and residual elements in these modern representations do not represent any actual continuity with the past but, instead, function as a means of responding to sudden changes imposed by more powerful forces outside the dominated region.

Although Trotsky developed this idea as a way of understanding the appeal of folk customs and primitivism at the turn of the twentieth century, he identified a dynamic process that has recurred in many forms throughout the history of modern culture from the eighteenth century forward. Understanding this dynamic helps us see why horror fiction and related forms had greater impact in certain regions in the eighteenth century, and helps clarify the meanings the horrid tales tended to convey. In the last third of the eighteenth century, German writers began to produce forms that emphasized strongly felt emotions threatening to overwhelm Enlightenment rationality; these forms are often labeled as the writing of *Sturm und Drang* (storm and stress). Additionally, there began to be a profusion of what literary historian J.W. Appell called the genre of knights, robbers, and horror, with the latter becoming increasingly dominant as time went on.[30] These tales of a highly imaginary feudal world of bandits, blood trials of honor and revenge, and contrived spectacles of ghosts, spirits, and necromancy can be seen, in retrospect, as a cultural critique of Enlightened Absolutism, the historical development exemplified in the German-speaking world by the administration of Prussian statesman Frederick the Great (1712–1786) and the Hohenzollern dynasty.

Enlightened Absolutism was a project of nondemocratic social reform from above, which maintained existing political hierarchy and aristocratic privileges while promoting religious toleration and other limited forms of intellectual and civil rights. Various eighteenth-century European leaders flirted with the practice as a means of calibrating the pace of historical change so that there would be no revolutionary or truly democratic movement for emancipation. The contradiction inherent in this project was that while ruling aristocratic elites encouraged their subjects to think and

---

[29] See Trotsky, *The Permanent Revolution, and Results and Prospects*; and *History of the Russian Revolution*, Vol. 1: Appendix One.

[30] Johann Wilhelm Appell, *Die Ritter-, Räuber- und Schauerromantik. Zur Geschichte der deutschen Unterhaltungs-Literatur* (facsimile reproduction by Leipzig, Zentral-Antiquariat der Deutschen Demokratischen Republik, 1967; originally printed Leipzig, Engelmann, 1859).

question their experiences and beliefs, they insisted that the practice of rational skepticism and inquiry should not effect the mechanism of ruling power.[31] This strategy of separating the cultural practices of the Enlightenment from its political implications was a sociopolitical vision that the French Revolution of the 1790s would demolish. Napoleon's rise to power after 1798, in the wake of the French Revolution, subsequently revealed what was implicit in Frederick the Great's embodiment of enlightened despotism, namely, its ultimate reliance on militaristic imperialism to silence civilian desires for liberty, and its dependence on domestic State violence against citizens unwise enough to seek genuine emancipation.

Some regions, such as Saxony, emphasized in the background of the Wieland family, experienced these pressures with special intensity because they were at the crossroads of imperial frontiers and were scored with differences between Catholic rulers and Protestant civil populations. Here the German middle class was not strong enough to capitalize on these tensions to achieve the same social and political break that their French analogs would ultimately attain: the delegitimization and overthrow of the aristocratic and religious old regime. Frustrated in coming so close yet remaining so far from substantive change, Germans began to produce quasimedieval and horror tales as a means of signifying the nightmare of being unable to escape the premodern period. Hence the genre's reimagining of an obsolete feudal order whose actors are impatient to achieve true modernity, and hence the general symbolic violence imagined in gory tales, as if to overcompensate for the absence of a successful attack against the absolutist state and to lend terrorizing form to its real violence.

In this manner the German horror subgenre registers both frustration at blocked modernity—at the incomplete nature of Enlightened Absolutism and its unfulfilled promises—and an impatient desire to voice this anger, even if only symbolically. These impulses appear quite vividly in one of the period's most popular poems, Bürger's *Lenore*, included in this volume's Related Texts. *Lenore* tells the story of a woman waiting for her beloved knight to return from an imperial campaign. It emphasizes her grief at his absence and the foreclosure of her dreams, which cause her to embrace sacrilege and consider her world a living hell. Implored by her mother not to challenge the silent assumptions of the old order, she does so anyway. That night, her lover returns and takes her on a night ride, past a train of skeletons, only to reveal at midnight that he too is a skeletal apparition and that the marriage bed she anticipated has become a graveyard plot. The grotesque result of the woman's deep frustration, both erotic and social, can be read as a parable of anger at the failure to achieve truly substantive changes in Germany. The specter bridegroom's transformation exemplifies the perceived truth that the German regions were falling backward, cursed by Absolutist militarism, and failing to advance toward the modern age.

These tales were eagerly consumed in England during the 1790s for roughly similar reasons, as a fraction of the middle classes, often from nonconformist or dissenting religious backgrounds, found that their own sense of frustration with failure to achieve equality was, even if intuitively, well represented by the *Schauerroman*, the German

---

[31] For examples of this tension, see the excerpt from C. M. Wieland in Related Texts.

horror novel. As Anglophone writers both witnessed radical change occurring in France and experienced an increasingly repressive home government unwilling to even partially expand the enactment of democracy, they found that the restlessness exemplified in sensational German writing perfectly captured their own experience in ways that the local traditions of the novel or stage could not. Their increasing fascination with tales of secret societies also functions as a simultaneous recognition of and compensatory explanation for frustrated hopes of revolution and progress, since there must be *some* explanation for the absence of a successful bourgeois revolution. The idea of a manipulative secret society was an effective popular-culture substitute, in the absence of a more precise language of class interests. In a period that lacked a conceptual language and terminology for the political economy of classes, one important function of gothic literature was to supply a symbolic language for that missing function.

This proto-critique of incomplete modernity is arguably what attracted Brown to combine Woldwinite ideals with then-familiar devices from the German horror subgenre for his tale of traumatic events outside Philadelphia. For Brown, crafting *Wieland* in the form of a German novel also speaks to what simultaneously made it "An American Tale." In the late 1790s, the groups who had benefited most from leadership in the early Republic, congealed in the ruling Federalist Party and the party interests of the New England clerics who controlled the universities, later known as the Ivy League, were increasingly reluctant to acknowledge the implications of democracy, namely, that political power flows from the citizenry. Accustomed to a quasifeudal sense of entitlement, these U.S. political and religious leaders enacted conditions and contradictions that were similar to those of Enlightened Absolutism. From this perspective, we can understand that Brown calls *Wieland* an "American Tale" not because he feels that its events are particularly "American" in any essentialist sense, but rather because they represent local American instances of global phenomena that take place in analogous regions throughout the world, particularly in other similarly contested regions such as Saxony, Languedoc, Ireland, and so on. Hence, perhaps, the logic of Brown's three-part title, which presents a German reference associated with the culture of Absolutist Enlightenment, a noun indicating the politics of counterenlightenment, and finally a regional occurrence of this contradiction. The domestic expression of a global history informs Brown's purpose in relating the tale of the Pennsylvania Wielands and their ensuing traumas.

"The House and Name of Wieland": Exploding the Old Order

Wieland's narrative involves three distinct segments:[32] the brief but, in informational terms, extremely rich back story concerning the Wielands' paternal family history

---

[32] Our discussion in what follows draws from Shapiro, *The Culture and Commerce of the Early American Novel.*

two generations back (through the father and grandfather's generations) and events in Saxony, London, and Pennsylvania (Chapters 1–2); the main segment treating the life of the Wieland and Pleyel siblings in the late 1760s, and their encounter with Frank Carwin, on the family estate Mettingen just outside Philadelphia (Chapters 3–26); and the final narrative coda that treats Clara's return to Europe, her relocation from Mettingen to the Languedoc region of southern France with her maternal uncle, the surgeon Thomas Cambridge (Chapter 27). Although of uneven length in narrative terms, this segmentation seems to provide an allegorical and historical schema that helps us better understand the novel's arguments about social and historical change. Each of these segments, on examination, utilizes similar narrative devices, which Brown seems to use to represent sequential historical phases of social organization, each with its own characteristics and contradictions. These epochs are, roughly: 1) an early modern stage of rule by aristocratic State and religious authorities; 2) the eighteenth century's spirit of Enlightenment, and; 3) a more recognizably modern or allegorically postrevolutionary stage looking to the onset of the nineteenth century's rule by the commercial middle classes, with their associated legal and medical professionals. Brown seems to inscribe the differences between these periods by characteristic changes, ending each phase with the death of a representative father by a blow to the side. The tensions in each of the three periods appear in conflicts between at least two different kinds of language or speech in each case, as well as in references to iconic foundational texts and knowledges that seek to explain the origin of violence and conflict within the terms and conceptual framework that exemplify each period.

The story of what Clara refers to at the end of Chapter 16 as "the house and name of Wieland" begins with an initial effort to overcome the caste differences of the feudal period and its codes of rule by power and justice by force. Clara and Theodore's grandfather was the second son of a Saxon noble family, who fell in love with and married a Hamburg merchant's daughter. The misalliance between a minor aristocrat and a child of the rising mercantile middle class, sketched out in Chapter 1, typifies a new outlook on personal relations, in which marriage is not arranged to consolidate feudal alliances between noble families, but as an affirmation of affectionate love and the individual's right to structure their life outside of ancient regulations. After Wieland's family disowns him, he attempts to survive on the practical merit of his (artistic) skill, rather than by the ascribed status of his bloodline. Rejecting Latin, the consecrated language of elite communication, he writes in the Saxon dialect, a modernizing language comprehensible to a wider and more popular audience. The grandfather's attempt to enter the modern period fails, however, as the man and his wife soon die and their orphaned son is apprenticed to a London trader.

Stuck in a foreign country and in the humiliating conditions of bound labor, the son of this couple, who will become Clara and Theodore's father, is trapped in a wretched situation somewhat akin to slavery, with little hope for escaping a life of constant physicalized work and miserable living conditions. In this jail-like scenario, the youth discovers a book explaining the origins and beliefs of the Camisards, an apocalyptic, visionary sect from the Cévennes Mountains of southern France, which led a rebellion in the first decade of the eighteenth century, in desperate response to religious persecution and economic deprivation. The Languedoc-Cévennes region, named for its own Occitan language (the Langue d'oc or "language of Oc"), experienced the full weight of the counterreformation, the Catholic Church's efforts to contain or crush Protestant threats to its long-held authority. After Louis XIV revoked the Edict of Nantes in 1685, abandoning a forward-looking measure that had given religious freedom to France's minority Protestant population, and amidst worsening economic conditions, the Camisard revolt arose and continued from 1702 to 1710. This uprising of mostly farmers and artisans was led by visionary "prophets," often young and frequently including women, who delivered apocalyptic and millenarian revelations, usually in standard French, rather than in their local Occitan, as part of ecstatic trances.

After the rebellion was brutally suppressed, some of the Camisards fled to England under the leadership of Elias (Élie) Marion and other so-called "French Prophets" and continued to spread their doctrines from south London.[33] Marion preached a coming apocalypse and warned his followers to prepare for emigration from England and a war of vengeance against the earthly representatives of Satan. Attracting English followers among London's artisans, Camisard doctrines were translated and published in books like Maximilien Mission's *A Cry From The Desert: Or, Testimonials of the Miraculous Things Lately Come to Pass In The Cevennes* (1707), and Marion's own *Prophetical Warnings* (1707). When "English Prophets" also began to produce apocalyptic and ecstatic revelations, London authorities criminalized the group and Marion and his followers left England.

When the elder Wieland discovers a French Prophet text and becomes enraptured by its emphasis on individual, nonscriptural, divine revelation (what the period's commentators called "enthusiasm"), he takes up a religious movement that was generated as a response to social prejudice and economic deprivation. Since his current condition as a belabored expatriate and child of disinherited and absent parents corresponds to many of the structural pressures that gave rise to the Camisard movement, the youth has good reason to be attracted by its rhetoric of personal redemption and punishment against worldly evil. Following the Prophets' call to emigrate, the elder Wieland leaves England and, after an unsuccessful attempt to convert Native Americans, purchases and settles at Mettingen, an estate worked by African slaves. There he builds a temple for his ascetic prayers, while his unnamed wife is identified as a follower of a religious group called the Moravians, a German Pietist movement that also emphasized internal revelation unmediated by ministers or scriptural education. In Chapter 2, after some years of comfort, he has a presentiment of divine punishment and feels scorching heat in his body. After appearing to undergo spontaneous combustion in his temple (his clothes are burnt), he claims to have felt as if a club struck his right arm. His brother-in-law, the surgeon Thomas Cambridge, who

---

[33] For more on the Camisards and French Prophets, see the excerpts from Marion's *Prophetical Warnings* in Related Texts.

witnessed the event from a spot nearby, doubts his claims of spontaneous combustion, and Clara and Theodore's father dies quickly from the effects of his injuries.

Brown uses this short but highly sensational account of the elder Wieland's death to represent the mental state of an older order based on the absolute power of the divine and implicitly regal state. In this lifeworld,[34] authority rules through coercive violence and the psychological trauma of shock and awe. The subject must submit to the capricious despotism of an omnipotent, wrathful ruler, and implicitly to the authority of his earthly representatives. Such an image for the power of the absolutist State was characterized by early modern English political philosopher Thomas Hobbes as a Leviathan, an arrangement in which the total power of the king can repress any activity of his subjects under the justification of maintaining the "natural" order of status hierarchies. The elder Wieland's "scorched and bruised" body suggests that every individual is isolated before the terrific judgment of a divine ruler who "enforces, by unequivocal sanctions, submission to his will." Yet, for Brown, this grim lifeworld is less the continuation of medieval tenets than a response, albeit extreme, to the failure of initial efforts toward a more democratic society, and a consequence of the grandfather's failure to use the modern arts to completely escape the caste bigotry of his family. The grandfather's proto-Enlightenment imagination has been unable to survive, and this failure of opportunity opens the door to a painful experience of aggressive frustration, resentment, and internalization of betrayal. When the elder Wieland combusts, it is not just Brown's figurative suggestion that the premodern world is literally "exploded" or made obsolete in the modern age, but also, seemingly, a suggestion that progressive change is not securely acquired or cemented, for what has also disappeared in the explosion is the Saxon grandfather's initial, youthful attempt to break free from the strictures of an unequal and oppressive past.[35]

Declaring a New Order: The Wielands' Age of Enlightenment

After their father's shocking death and their nameless mother's swift disappearance in the aftermath, a now orphaned Theodore and Clara Wieland find themselves emancipated from the dictates of older authorities. Raised by an aunt, but liberated from the "corruption and tyranny" of schools, the siblings can shape their interests and influences as they wish. They are free to construct a new and enlightened social system. Coming of age, they return to Mettingen and seek to enact this ideal. The Wieland siblings have a cosmopolitan worldview and read widely in several European

---

[34] "Lifeworld" describes the way that the combined force of social and cultural institutions and their associated practices create a shared world of common sense and perceived reality. Roughly speaking, our "lifeworld" is the sum of the assumptions, meanings, and norms that we absorb from our social environment.

[35] For two discussions that develop implications of the back story concerning Saxony, see White, "Carwin the Peasant Rebel" and Doyle, *Freedom's Empire*.

languages. The father's grim temple of worship is redecorated as a summerhouse intended to host convivial discussion and intellectual-aesthetic performances. Although Theodore would traditionally exercise undivided authority over their father's property and over his sister, he divides the patrimony, or paternal inheritance, with his sister, and Clara lives in and manages her own home on a separate part of the estate. With the addition of Theodore's wife Catharine, a childhood playmate, and frequent visits by Catharine's brother Henry Pleyel, the Wieland-Pleyel circle leads a cloistered but comfortable life of elite leisure, overseeing their properties and children, and improving their minds with reading, music, conversation, and intellectualized landscaping. Theodore has four children, but his model of fatherhood is very different from the elder Wieland's austere and self-absorbed patriarchy. Theodore ostensibly abandons his patriarchal privilege (the *patria potestas* of Roman and medieval law), the gender equivalent of aristocratic birth, and acts in a more fraternal and congenial fashion that initially appears to be a form of benign paternalism.

Within this world, the nightmare of history, history as a record of crimes committed in common, seems to have been overcome or least held in check. Mettingen functions as a pastoral, well-regulated community, where Theodore, Clara, and Pleyel can each exemplify a particular strand of Enlightenment era emphases. Theodore upholds an ideal of elite, leisured republicanism. In this view, the management of society should not be left to aristocrats or religious officials, who offer little but their bloodlines and medieval standards of blind obedience, but to more rational actors and managers, those whose wealth allows them to be free of economic pressures that corrupt decisionmaking.[36] This version of republicanism should not be mistaken as democratic; in no sense does it imply that the people (the *demos*) should exercise political power (*kratos*). Elite republicanism affirms the notion of citizenship, the idea that noble blood should not be a distinguishing feature in political activity, but it also makes an immediate distinction between "active" and "passive" citizens, granting the right to vote and take part in the political process only to male property owners above a certain degree of wealth, and consequently excluding women, workers, and nonwhites.[37] This elite and exclusionary version of republicanism consequently tends to idealize the gentry's countryside estates as scenes of elevated and rightful deliberation, far from the confusing din and demotic, plebian energies of the city.

Brown encodes this version of republicanism at Mettingen not only by giving the estate particular features of elite republican or "Augustan" organization such as its elaborate, botanically organized gardens, but also by having Theodore idealize the Roman statesman and orator Cicero, at this time a primary icon for elite republicanism. Theodore literally puts Cicero on a pedestal, installing a bust of the orator in the temple that the elder Wieland had designed for divine communion, and studying

---

[36] For a discussion of civic republicanism and its relation to other republican and more radical orientations during the Revolutionary period, see Kramnick, *Republicanism and Bourgeois Radicalism: Political Ideology in Late Eighteenth-Century England and America.*

[37] For the concept of citizenship and the historical distinction between "active" and "passive" rights in the Revolutionary era, see Wallerstein, "The Bourgeois(ie) as Concept and Reality."

Cicero's writings with the kind of devotion that religious scholars bring to sacred texts. As Brown made clear in a series of texts on Cicero and contemporary Cicero-worship, he takes a critical position in the eighteenth century's long tradition of coded political debates concerning this figure.[38] Although Theodore never demands the patriarch's dictatorial right, the unspoken assumption of the pastoral republican order that he oversees is that Theodore's judgment will always be the first and ultimately, perhaps, the only one considered.

Clara embraces the period's belief in the outlook known in the eighteenth century as sensibility or sympathy. Sensibility and sympathy were widely used keywords in the period, and generally involve the notions that knowledge and the subsequent relations based on it are "naturally" and spontaneously formed as the body responds to environmental influences. In the model of interaction and association provided by sensibility, there is an innate virtue within us that spontaneously reacts without the need for reasoning, formal training by masters, or analytical deliberation; sensibility's effects are generated and communicated through social contact or association; and a damaged sensibility results in vicious acts, bodily dysfunction, or a combination of the two. Even though it does not emphasize a concept of reason and may be elaborated in such a way as to bring out "irrational" potentials, the complex of ideas associated with sensibility and sympathy is generally a feature of the bourgeois-led Enlightenment. Sensibility removes the need for our relations to be mediated and organized by intermediary religious or political authorities, and against the old regime holds out the promise of more spontaneous and egalitarian modes of relation and interaction. Rather than imagining a severe and judging God, whose obscure intentions must be explained to the laity by priests, for example, religious thought developed in accordance with sensibility allows for the individual to "feel" the divine directly, and its predicates inform a variety of the period's Protestant and dissenting religious outlooks, from Methodism, German Pietism, and Quaker "inner light" to Deism's protoatheist notion of a god detached from worldly affairs and uninterested in the routine of omniscience and omnipotence. Like republicanism, the politics of sympathy has divergent meanings that are modernizing in some senses and limiting in others. Sensibility replaces the exceptional or unique body distinguished by noble blood with a universal and expansive body, for all individuals share and may relate to one another with the power of sympathy. Yet because the proper display and manifestation of sensibility can easily be converted into restrictive codes of bourgeois refinement or aesthetic distinction, sensibility can also become a way of rejecting the feudal old regime for a new one that is still hierarchal and fundamentally exclusionary in its effects.[39]

---

[38] For more on Brown's Cicero writings, see "On the Merits of Cicero," "Ciceronians," and "Death of Cicero, A Fragment" in Related Texts.

[39] For the concept and culture of sensibility, see Barker-Benfield, *The Culture of Sensibility: Sex and Society in Eighteenth-Century Britain*; Barnes, *States of Sympathy: Seduction and Democracy in the American Novel*; Jones, *Radical Sensibility: Literature and Ideas in the 1790s*; and Mullan, *Sentiment and Sociability: The Language of Feeling in the Eighteenth Century*.

Clara identifies herself with the rhetoric of sensibility, for example, when she explains in Chapter 3 that the family's religious practice was "excited by reflection on our own happiness, and by the grandeur of external nature" rather than "the dissection of creeds" and that, unlike their father, Clara and Theodore rarely pray aloud. Similarly, when Clara considers the cause of her father's spontaneous combustion at the end of Chapter 2, she discounts the idea that the blow was caused by the "vindictive and invisible hand" of a "Divine Ruler [who] interferes in human affairs" and enforces "submission to his will." Instead, she offers the materialist explanation that her father's disordered mental and emotional state led to internal friction and combustion. As Clara understands it, God has not intervened in past events at Mettingen and need not be feared in the present. When foreboding events do occur, Clara's first impulses are usually to try and restore her sympathetic balance by trying to regulate the flow of visual and aural sensations that might disturb her equipoise; her fainting at key scenes acts as a circuit breaker that stops the influx of sensations and allows her to regain psychic and embodied balance.

Henry Pleyel, finally, appears as the advocate of an elite rational and skeptical outlook that, like republicanism and sensibility, holds out both promise and limitations. While Brown has Clara, perhaps partly due to her infatuation with him, present Pleyel as a forthright "champion of intellectual liberty" who rejects "all guidance but that of his reason," he also emphasizes Pleyel's ties to declining and implicitly inadequate forms of dynastic and regal, Absolutist Enlightenment. It is Pleyel who urges Theodore to claim a late-feudal inheritance in the German territory Lusatia in Chapter 5, and who marries (and presumably inherits the patrimony of) the German noblewoman Theresa de Stolberg before joining Clara and her uncle Thomas Cambridge in Chapter 27 after this aristocratic wife's death in childbirth.

As we will note in what follows, Pleyel's claims of intellectual liberty never extend to any affirmation of social liberty, and his claims to exercise reason, when confronted with a crisis, are more dogmatic than analytical or thoughtful. Certainly Pleyel's version of reason does not seem to include self-analysis: throughout the novel his actions imply an undisturbed assumption of elite privilege. Pleyel participates in a cosmopolitan culture of enlightenment along with Theodore and Clara, and displays a Voltaire-like humor and wit that provide a foil to Theodore's morose religiosity. But like his peers, Pleyel is the product of an exclusionary world of estates and servants, and empowers himself through imperial networks of wealth and status hierarchies.

In the persons of Theodore, Clara, and Pleyel, then, Mettingen offers a spectrum of lower-gentry and bourgeois Enlightenment beliefs and outlooks that were part of the period's larger effort to emancipate humanity from the constraints of the feudal and early modern period. When mysterious voices presaging death, rape, and murder begin to be heard at Mettingen, Brown seems to be putting these ideas or positions on trial in order to test them either individually or as a collective set of beliefs that together summarize a patrician view of Enlightenment. As events descend into a spiral of confusion, blame, and violent madness, Mettingen's ideals seem to fail that test. Brown's interest in staging the collapse is not simply to create sensational thrills, however, but, as his essays on novel writing indicate, to dramatize the hidden causes or springs of his characters' behaviors, to cast light on the intrinsic contradictions of Mettingen that may allow the reader to decipher the elements of a larger problem involving the fragility of a society built on these claims.

To highlight the keyword from the novel's subtitle, we can say that the "transformation" of individual characters may be understood as one way that Brown emphasizes the contradictions of the new social order. The dramatic transformation that occurs in multiple forms over the course of the novel, within individual characters and, in a more allegorical sense, between different generations of the Wieland family, may arguably be read as Brown's term for something like counterenlightenment, counterreformation, or, more simply, political reaction. What circumstances and forces lead to the collapse of Mettingen's aspirations toward the progressive ideals of Enlightenment? In essence, this is the larger question that Brown's novel poses about the durability, or lack thereof, of the Enlightenment's social and political implications at the end of the eighteenth century and its revolutionary phase.[40]

Clara: The Obstacle of Gender

Brown's response to the paradoxes of this version of the Enlightenment begins with Clara's introduction to *Wieland*. When we first encounter Clara Wieland, she appears to be an empowered, confident woman. *Wieland* is Clara's narrative, told from her perspective and in her voice.[41] Although the novel takes the form of an extended letter or memoir recounting her perspective on traumatic events, she maintains control of the communication and its form. Clara tells, so to speak, but she is not told about. Unlike many of the period's other fictions about women, Clara's narrative is not mediated for the reader by a framing voice, an editorializing narrator, or a monitorial correspondent, and thus her tale is mostly free from interruption, even when she incorporates reported speech.[42] The sole exceptions are the embedded court testimony

---

[40] For more discussion of the novel in terms of debates about U.S. Enlightenment, see Christophersen, *The Apparition in the Glass*; Elliott, *Revolutionary Writers*; Hinds, *Private Property*; Looby, *Voicing America*; and Ruttenberg, *Democratic Personality*.

[41] For commentary that develops implications of Clara's centrality, see Barnes, "Loving with a Vengeance: *Wieland*, Familicide and the Crisis of Masculinity in the Early Nation"; Dill, "The Republican Stepmother: Revolution and Sensibility in Charles Brockden Brown's *Wieland*"; Hinds, *Private Property*; Samuels, *Romances of the Republic*; Schreiber, "'The Arm Lifted Against Me': Love, Terror, and the Construction of Gender in *Wieland*"; and Vickers, "Patriarchal and Political Authority in *Wieland*."

[42] For examples of the way eighteenth-century female-focused narratives may be framed, mediated, or prefaced by other (male or female) voices that underwrite but implicitly delimit and control the relevance of their female's subject's experience, see, for example, Defoe's *Moll Flanders* (1722); or Anne Radcliffe's *The Italian* (1797). Editorializing narrators or monitorial correspondents often function to oversee and otherwise moralize about female behavior; this is a well-developed feature of the period's third-person and epistolary novels from Samuel Richardson's *Clarissa* (1748; featuring the monitorial Anna Howe) to later U.S. examples of the seduction genre such as Susanna Rowson's *Charlotte Temple* (1794, in which an intrusive narrator instructs the reader); or Hannah Foster's *The Coquette* (1797, featuring the monitorial interlocutors Lucy Freeman and Julia Granby).

of her brother, given to her by Thomas Cambridge and quoted in Chapters 19 and 20, and a short note from Carwin in Chapter 15.

Clara's exceptional control over her story seems matched by her special status at Mettingen. Despite Theodore's new, relatively enlightened model of paternalist authority, Mettingen maintains strong gender divides, often split along the lines of cultured reason versus sympathetic emotion. While the men debate the meanings of classical texts, Theodore's wife, Catharine, sits by the margins, busy with traditional women's work such as sewing. While the men debate each other, it is the women—Clara, Catharine, and the adopted Conway girl Louisa—who seem to have strong nurturing bonds with one another, which exist alongside, but separate from, their ties with the men. Catharine's marriage to Theodore, for example, is celebrated by Clara as much for cementing her life-long proximity to Catharine (and her brother Henry) as for providing for her brother's happiness.

Between Clara's control over her own property and tale, and the bonds of emotional warmth tied to a collective female sphere, Clara initially seems to bridge the gender divide as she attempts to enjoy the benefits of both masculinity and femininity. Theodore and Pleyel include her in their intellectual considerations in the early chapters and, after the novel's crisis, she is allowed to see the carnage in Chapter 17 by her maternal relative Mr. Hallet, when he assumes that she is emotionally and morally capable of withstanding its horror. Carwin begins his tricks against Clara partly to test her reputation for courage, which is reputed to be above that of other women. Yet despite Clara's apparent rise above the status of a *feme covert*, a woman who cannot own property or make legal decisions on her own behalf,[43] she never attains actual equality in Mettingen. The men continue to assume their prerogative to judge her actions and their right to invade her personal space. Pleyel admits to being insincere about his old acquaintance Carwin, for example, in order to examine Clara's reaction to the newcomer. When Pleyel slyly creeps into Clara's room while she is writing in her diary, he both misinterprets what she has written, giving it the most damaging construction, and assumes that *his* understanding, the rationality he dogmatically claims, cannot be mistaken and must be superior to Clara's account of her own behavior. Likewise, even though Carwin lacks the family relation that Pleyel might claim in defense of his voyeurism, he assumes the same prerogative to spy on Clara, as if such a privilege belongs to any man over any woman. Even Theodore, who should presumably know and care for his sister more than any other, is very reluctant to accept her self-"vindication" over the testimony of men.

---

[43] Under the laws of "coverture," part of Anglo-American common law in this period, women had no legal personhood or formal, statutory independence. A woman's legal identity (and consequently her right to own property, sign contracts, and so on) was absorbed into or "covered" by that of her father, husband, or other male guardian. In the Anglo-Norman legal terminology of this system an unmarried woman was a *feme sole* (a woman alone), a married woman a *feme covert* (a covered woman). Although it abolished titles and primogeniture, the American Revolution did not change these laws concerning women's subordination. For a discussion of coverture and its relation to the period's U.S. reading culture, see Kerber, *Women of the Republic: Intellect and Ideology in Revolutionary America*; and Davidson, *Revolution and the Word*.

Nowhere is the implicit inequality within Mettingen more telling than with the matter of violence. When physical aggression threatens, the implied and actual victims are only the novel's women and children. The mysterious voices unnerve and confuse the men, but they announce and inaugurate fatal effects against the women.

Clara herself answers the riddle of what lies at the root of the obstacle facing female equality: the ideologies governing female desire and the limitations surrounding the cultural script of virtue as it applies to women. Clara might be educated, self-reliant, property-owning, and exceptionally resilient in the face of extreme challenges, but even these individual advantages are not enough to overcome the larger social limitations surrounding women. The touchstone moment comes in Chapter 6 when Clara first sees Carwin on her property. His arrival at Mettingen creates for Clara the "first inroads of a passion incident to every female heart": erotic passion. Immediately after seeing and sketching Carwin, Clara falls into morbid contemplations, and entertains "ominous and dreary" anxieties concerning death. Attempting to shake off this mood, she turns to her grandfather's melody for a ballad about a German knight who dies in the First Crusade. Though Clara does not name the song, as noted earlier it suggests Bürger's *Lenore* (1773), the sensation of the late 1790s, which was the German ballad foremost in the minds of Brown's intended Anglophone readership. Beyond the basic parable of incomplete or frustrated modernity mentioned earlier, we can also note that the poem's historical narrative involves a further reference to gender inequality in recent dynastic struggles. We recall that the poem's original and most translations relate the story of a German woman waiting for her soldier lover's return from Frederick the Great's 1756 invasion of Prague, which touched off the Seven Years War and continued the Prussian-led War of Austrian Succession (1740–1748).

In connection with Clara's fate as a privileged yet structurally disempowered woman at Mettingen, we can also note that the ballad's military campaign was directed against Maria Theresa of Austria (1717–1780) and her efforts to control the Hapsburg empire, considered problematic because Salic law prohibited a woman from inheriting the throne. There are variations between the Crusader setting of the poem in the William Taylor translation likely invoked here and its Seven Years War setting in most versions (see the commentary in the Related Text on *Lenore* in this volume), but the well-known connection to the Seven Years War remains relevant here, given its significance as the most general context for the lives of the novel's characters, who comment on it in Chapter 7, typically failing to recognize its effects on their lives. In this strategically located allusion to *Lenore*, then, the suggestion may be that Clara, however unconsciously, links a woman's challenge to (male) authority with female destruction. If *Lenore* is the intertextual poem to which Brown alludes, then the reference foreshadows the outcomes of *Wieland*.

The gender disequilibrium brought to the novel's surface by the "amorous contagion" of love (Chapter 5) is not the only instance of Clara's inability to act outside customary constraints on women. Despite her supposed equality with her brother, throughout the novel she continually defers to his opinion, idealizes his actions, and defends him against accusations, long after it has been made clear, even by Theodore himself, that such defense is pointless. Throughout her tale, beginning with the dream about Theodore in Chapter 7, Clara senses that men are threatening her, metaphorically summoning her to fall into a "pit" or "abyss," a literalization of her subliminal recognition that an attempt to cross from the constraints of femininity to the freedom of masculinity, as the standard of equality, will result in her vertiginous demise. Even when Clara initially considers abandoning female passivity by encouraging Pleyel to propose to her, she reminds herself to "be regardful of insurmountable limits," acknowledging and naturalizing the social constraints placed on female equality in the consolidation of erotic partnership.

Following Mary Wollstonecraft's claim that women are subordinated to men by the social conditioning of gender, and not by the biological determination of sex, Brown suggests to his readers that Clara is held back in two related ways: by the implied resistance of men to grant her full equality on the one hand, but also by her own internalized deference to male authority and desire on the other. Throughout *Wieland*, Brown charts out the frequently unspoken limits to female emancipation that continue even beyond the legal boundaries of property and self-representation. Beyond the possibility of overcoming legal restraints, he seems to suggest, there remains the culture of gender inequality, both imposed by men and internalized by women.

Female inequality alone, however, seems clearly insufficient to account for the extent of the tale's ensuing tragedy. To understand a second major fracture line that shapes life at Mettingen, we need to look more closely at the more obvious outsider, Frank (or Francis) Carwin.

Carwin: Class and the Limits of Equality

As Clara discovers that gender inequalities exert a powerful force in Mettingen's enlightened social order, Carwin finds that class differences play a basic role there as well.[44] From the moment he arrives, Carwin's plebian or lower-class presence poses a challenge to the Enlightenment-era perspectives displayed by the three primary characters in Mettingen. How can Theodore's leisured republicanism, Pleyel's claims of rationality, or Clara's sympathetic or sensibilitarian model of association function with the removal of class hierarchies? Clara highlights these issues concerning class immediately on her first sighting of Carwin in Chapter 6. Carwin's initial appearance in worn and dusty clothing seems to mark him as a low-status rural worker or, even worse, an itinerant beggar. Such figures exist for Clara only in her social peripheral vision, barely noticed or acknowledged. Carwin's appearance is more noteworthy, however, because he seems to be admiring the estate's carefully designed botanical gardens, and thereby participating in the aesthetic refinement of its owners. The

---

[44] For commentary on Carwin, see Downes, "Constitutional Secrets: 'Memoirs of Carwin' and the Politics of Concealment"; Lyttle, "The Case Against Carwin"; Rosenthal, "The Voices of *Wieland*"; Ruttenberg, *Democratic Personality*; White, "Carwin the Peasant Rebel"; and Wolfe, "Ventriloquizing Nation."

erosion of the assumed boundary between low-status manual labor and more pres-
tigious mental or intellectual exertions disturbs Clara, and prompts her to wonder
about the actual stability of such status boundaries, and about what might happen
if the predicates of the Enlightenment were truly made universal so that illumination created a democratic sociopolitical order. The prospect of Carwin's equality
within her circle both intrigues and frightens her as she begins to wonder about the
actual implications of her leisured idealism concerning "the influence of progressive
knowledge" in dissolving the "alliance which commonly subsists between ignorance"
and field work (46). From an analytical perspective, we can say that, because Clara
apparently lacks an intellectual framework for thinking through the processes and
problems involved in social betterment, she experiences this question of boundary
blurring through the codes of sympathetic erotic desire and destruction. Yet she
cannot bring herself to fully imagine what her grandfather had enacted: love across
social strata.

Although Carwin temporarily joins Mettingen's conversational sphere, he fears—
rightly, as it turns out—that the group will not truly welcome him as an equal. What
the Wieland-Pleyel circle sees as his insincerity and unwillingness to speak openly
about his past and present activity outside Mettingen, Carwin sees as necessary protection against exclusion based on his class origins. Although Carwin gives in to his
curiosity and mischievous urges, his first use of ventriloquism at Mettingen, in Chapter
4, is a panicked response to Theodore's unexpected arrival near the "summer-house" at
the temple's base, where Carwin has been sleeping unbeknownst to the Wielands. After
this initial incident, Carwin subjects each of his three primary interlocutors to a specific
voice trial, often involving desire, as if to gauge their reactions as a way of testing the
social waters he has encountered on the estate. When Carwin ventriloquizes a rhetoric
of violence, his mimicry possibly echoes Mettingen's own intrinsic aggression.

What Carwin discovers at Mettingen is the deeply ingrained privilege and social
prejudices of the Wielands, which are especially visible in Clara, who automatically
assumes that lower-status individuals do not share the kind of individual complexity and worthwhile qualities she takes for granted in her peers. In Chapter 7, after
hearing a mysterious voice claim to protect her from "ruffians" who would harm
her, Clara wonders how this can be possible, since her charity in the neighborhood
causes the poor to admire and respect her, as if anger at systemic social inequalities
is inconceivable. The tenants who live at Mettingen are infantilized in Chapter 22
as "honest creatures" and remain nameless, without individuality. When Carwin
claims in the course of his confession (late in Chapter 22), that Clara's personal
servant Judith is promiscuous and sells herself, Clara fails to challenge the slur on a
lower-status woman, even though she aggressively defended herself against similar
accusations. Nowhere is Clara's refusal to leave her mental confines more apparent
than in the final bedroom confrontation with Theodore and Carwin in Chapters
24–26, where she insistently seeks to defend and exculpate her brother, long past the
rational point of deniability, and where she is at her most vengeful against Carwin,
as if his responsibility was intensified, or at least made imaginable, as a result of his
lower-status background.

While Carwin is initially described with images that refer to Hermes or Mercury, a trickster god associated with communication, his ambiguity expresses the double condition that he faces, the tension between his high intelligence and his birth into lower-class status. Like Clara, Carwin is best understood as embodying the paradoxes or contradictions of a society that claims to be based on democratic enfranchisement, but that in reality organizes itself for the benefit of elites. Carwin's lifeworld is thus formed by an ecology of frustration at being held back from rising status based on his merits. His experience seems to contradict the Enlightenment claim that talent or merit alone should determine an individual's opportunities and accomplishments. This theme of blockage within the rhetoric of equality is taken up with the *Memoirs of Carwin the Biloquist.*

Memoirs of Carwin the Biloquist

When Brown reached the last stages of work on *Wieland* in August 1798, even before the novel was finalized, he also began working on what is effectively a "prequel," *Memoirs of Carwin the Biloquist*, a narrative that develops Carwin's backstory before his arrival at Mettingen. Brown explained in a letter to his friend William Dunlap that work on this narrative ended by September 4, when Brown interrupted his literary work entirely because of the growing New York yellow fever epidemic of 1798.[45]

Five years later, in November 1803, as Brown was starting up his Philadelphia-based *Literary Magazine*, he returned to the as-yet unpublished *Memoirs of Carwin* and began to print it in monthly serial installments. The narrative was halted temporarily after the seventh installment in May 1804, possibly because Brown had reached the end of the previously written material. Since the manuscript does not survive, it is impossible to say exactly what portion of the narrative was completed in 1798, or what revisions Brown may have made to previously existing portions in 1803. The narrative was extended for three more installments (July 1804 and February–March 1805) before being abandoned after installment ten.

For readers today, the relationship between *Wieland* and *Carwin* is often uncertain. Because *Wieland* refers to the character Ludloe and to events in Spain that are only detailed in *Memoirs of Carwin*, Brown seems to have intended for the two tales to inform each other. On the other hand, the nature and extent of this link remains unclear, since *Memoirs of Carwin* remains unfinished. Students of *Wieland* also face an additional peculiarity due to the publication and reception history of the two narratives. *Carwin*'s first continuous publication was in William Dunlap's 1815 posthumous biography of Brown, a combined biographical sketch and literary miscellany that printed a large quantity of rare or uncollected material by Brown as a way to increase the book's interest and value. As a result of Dunlap's decision to publish the narrative, *Carwin* was also included in a British edition of Brown's minor works in 1822; once

---

[45] For more on the composition and chronology of *Memoirs of Carwin*, see the discussion in Related Texts and Cowie, "Historical Essay."

again separately from *Wieland*. After this printing, *Carwin* was not republished until the twentieth century, and was never printed along with the novel until Fred Lewis Pattee's 1926 edition of *Wieland*, which was the edition largely referred to until the 1977–1987 Kent State "Bicentennial" edition of Brown's novels. After Pattee, and especially after the 1977 scholarly edition, most major editions of *Wieland* publish *Carwin* in continuous form immediately following the text of the novel.

The primary consequence of *Carwin*'s late-twentieth-century prominence and wide availability after the 1970s to many readers who encounter Brown first as the author of *Wieland*, is that most academic commentary on *Wieland* and on Carwin's role in that novel takes the *Memoirs of Carwin* as an unspoken reference, even though few student readers are actually assigned *Carwin* as a supplemental text. Because the majority of readers newly encountering Brown do not actually read *Carwin*, there is an argument for considering *Wieland* simply on its own terms. On the other hand, *Carwin* may arguably be more representative of Brown's fiction and influences than *Wieland*. Whereas *Wieland* is unique among Brown's major narratives in certain ways, notably in its intensively developed relation to non-Anglophone literatures and emphasis on elite mentalities separated from the culture of commerce, *Carwin*'s tale of vengeful pursuit by an elite former patron highlights obvious links to William Godwin and to Brown's other fictions, since it develops plot points and arguments from Godwin's influential 1794 novel *Caleb Williams*. The generic model of a corrupt and vicious upper-class patron persecuting a lower status and younger assistant was one that Brown used and modified repeatedly, from the model fiction in his essay on novel writing, "Walstein's School of History" (see Related Texts), to his novels *Ormond, Edgar Huntly,* and *Arthur Mervyn,* all begun during the same period as *Wieland*, and all completed within two years of *Wieland*'s publication in September 1798.

Similarly, the suggestive hints about Ludloe's secret "fraternity" that surface in the final installments of *Memoirs of Carwin* are as explicit a development as Brown ever provides of the period's popular themes concerning conspiratorial secret societies. This theme looms large in German robber and horror fictions of the 1770s and 1780s (from Schiller's early play *The Robbers* to his later novel of state intrigue *The Ghost-Seer*) and was central to the well-known Illuminati panic that was occurring while Brown was writing *Wieland*.[46] It is notable, however, that Brown never uses the term Illuminati in *Wieland* or *Memoirs of Carwin* (or in any of his writings) and that his most evident and general response to the demonizing, ultraconservative narratives of the panic episode, in his fictions, is to dramatize and reject the local patterns of fearful xenophobia and scapegoating that were exploited and encouraged by the panic. That is, Brown's most general response to the Illuminati panic, which can be discerned throughout his novels, is to emphasize the behavioral logic of the panic (xenophobia, projection, scapegoating, and blame) by building these traits into many of his characters and clearly rejecting them, for example in Clara Wieland's vengeful

---

[46] For a fuller discussion of the Illuminati panic see the Dwight-Ogden debate in Related Texts.

eagerness to blame Carwin for atrocities committed by her elite brother. When Clara supposes that the lower-status interloper Carwin is a dangerous foreigner, despite his subsequently revealed local origins, absorbs misleading print material accusing him of crimes, and consistently and irrationally blames him for traumatic events even though more plausible scenarios are repeatedly offered by her uncle Thomas Cambridge, for example, one may plausibly read this aspect of the novel as an allegory critical of the elite panic that gives shape to the anti-Illuminati myths.

However one approaches *Memoirs of Carwin*, its differences from and connections to *Wieland* are certainly worth bearing in mind. For this reason, we include *Carwin* as a Related Text, reintroducing the section breaks of its original serialization in order to give the reader an idea of the only form in which Brown published it. Our discussion here approaches *Memoirs of Carwin* as a narrative in its own right, but also as a prequel that may clarify aspects of *Wieland*.

Somewhat like *Wieland*, which Clara writes to a close friend or family member who may use her tale to better understand the events she has undergone, Carwin's narrative takes the form of a personal memoir addressed to someone familiar with events at Mettingen, possibly the physician Thomas Cambridge. In Installment 5, Carwin assumes his addressee's intimate familiarity with the disaster at Mettingen, described as "what has happened to yourselves." The implication may be that Carwin's memoir, at least in part, is one element of wider attempts to understand the tragedy that occurred in the novel and a belated defense that he was not allowed to deliver earlier.

In basic ways, *Memoirs of Carwin* can be read as an inversion of the aspirational tale of uplift that is Benjamin Franklin's *Autobiography* (1793). Indeed, the name Frank Carwin can be heard as an echo of "Franklin." Franklin's autobiography presents his steady rise to fame and fortune as a model for other aspiring young men from nonelite backgrounds, who like him receive little family encouragement or support for their ambitions. Like the young Franklin, Carwin thirsts for learning and reveals an early talent for language and letters, but his advancement toward participation in an international Enlightenment is blocked by an abusive father and brother.

After experimenting with the production of echoes in a secluded glen, Carwin teaches himself the trick of ventriloquism, which he initially plans on using to frighten his father into allowing him to leave for Philadelphia, where he can depend on his wealthy aunt. Although Carwin hesitates to enact this scenario, its elements will be repeated again and again with ever-higher stakes. When Carwin becomes frustrated with his inability to achieve upward social progress, he frequently searches out "secret spaces," both natural and man-made, from the guarded libraries of the Escorial or Ludloe's Irish estate to the summerhouse at Mettingen, in the hopes that they will reveal secreted information or other mechanisms allowing him to elevate himself. The search for hidden resources or "tricks" seems to suggest Carwin's lack of faith in transparent opportunities for his intelligence and skill. Instead of pursuing a "forth-right journey" toward virtuous citizen status in the manner that Franklin claims all can achieve if they follow his steps, however, Frank Carwin's frustrations with this ideal's unfulfilled promise lead him in two directions, albeit negative or harmful ones, that seem to hold out the possibility of self-advancement even as they simultaneously negate possibilities for greater equality. This twofold contradiction seems to be a core insight developed or implied in *Memoirs of Carwin*.

The first and most obvious avenue of possibility open to Carwin is Ludloe's patronage and the secret society to which it is connected. Throughout his narrative Carwin becomes increasingly, and ever more ambivalently, dependent on his mysterious patron, who holds out continually delayed and increasingly dubious promises of a better future. Although Ludloe claims to embrace the language of radical enlightenment, his actions turn backward toward medieval or Inquisitorial spying networks on the one hand, and toward hierarchical, quasi-imperialist or Jesuitical precedents for colonizing non-European lands as controlled social or utopian experiments on the other. Although aspects of Ludloe's secret fraternity, particularly its surveillance practices, correspond to accounts of historical organizations, from State police networks to secretive brotherhoods like the Illuminati, his plans do not seem to involve attempts to subvert existing church or state institutions (distinguishing his actions from the scenarios of the 1797–1800 Illuminati scare).

Similarly, Ludloe's schemes, by contrast, primarily revealed in hints and details in Installments 6 and 9, involve possibly utopian colonization plans, apparently in south Pacific regions that were little explored at the early 1760s moment of the narrative.[47] Thus *Carwin's* plot developments move toward an interest in the creation or manipulation of wider cultural or belief systems, and toward the management of coercive systems that these new schemes seem likely to establish (exactly what purpose Ludloe envisions for Carwin's ventriloquial talents is never stated). While many of the German State Romance novels, such as Schiller's *Ghost-Seer* or Tschink's *The Victim of Magical Delusion* focus on anxieties about the nation–state, *Carwin's* scenario seems to go beyond a concern for the American state and towards an emphasis on thinking about the structural similarities of Western polities more generally. Brown develops this kind of wider, systemic vision of sociopolitical organization in a later letter he wrote to his friend Samuel Miller in June 1803, just months before he returned to *Memoirs of Carwin* and began publishing it in his *Literary Magazine*, and in fictional works such as the *Historical Sketches*.[48]

The second and perhaps less obvious path for Carwin's advancement and rise toward middle-class status takes the form of exploitation directed against the primary object of failed promises for middle-class enfranchisement: women. Using his familiarity with the gender critiques provided by the Woldwinite writers, which he highlights in his key essay on novel writing as the need to develop reflections on dominant systems of "sex and property,"[49] Brown develops the narrative in such a

---

[47] For commentary on this aspect of Carwin's narrative, see Hsu, "Democratic Expansionism in Memoirs of Carwin"; Kazanjian, "Charles Brockden Brown's Biloquial Nation: National Culture and White Settler Colonialism in *Memoirs of Carwin the Biloquist*"; and Leask, "Irish Republicans and Gothic Eleutherarchs: Pacific Utopias in the Writings of Theobald Wolfe Tone and Charles Brockden Brown."

[48] See the June 1803 letter to Samuel Miller in Related Texts; and Barnard, "Culture and Authority in Brown's *Historical Sketches*."

[49] For Brown's remarks on the centrality of "sex and property" to novelistic plots, see the second section of "Walstein's School of History" in Related Texts.

way as to demonstrate how the sense of betrayal that Carwin feels, as a class representative, becomes channeled into gender discrimination and actions against women. Throughout his memoir—from his early conflict with his aunt's servant Dorothy in Installment 3 to the final scheme to seek enrichment by marrying the widow Bennington in Installments 7–10—Carwin's anger at the coercive nature of existing society becomes translated into anger at women, who are presented as the persons in control of the wealth that might allow the youth to advance and rise in society. Carwin often seems afraid to confront the men with authority over him, beginning with his anxieties about tricking his father, but he is frequently put in the position of using or exploiting women, often by the very men that he ought to be challenging.

Violence against women in *Memoirs of Carwin* seems to occur because females are easier targets for blame and may be made to pay the price for anger aroused by elite refusal to allow for the realization and extension of democracy. In this manner, Brown's narrative reveals a structural cause for female subordination that even the Woldwinites may not have fully realized. On this reading, women's disempowerment is not simply the negative absence of education and of the right to make decisions for themselves. In Brown's narrative this disempowerment also has a positive or active, additive element tied to class conflict, as those in power displace challenges to their authority by redirecting and projecting anger caused by unrealized modernity onto women. The root of gender inequality, as Brown analyzes it, is the failure to extend democracy among men.

The Modern Age: New Models of Exclusion

Events at Mettingen end in catastrophic tragedy. Clara writes her account in the aftermath and initially claims that, like Bürger's Lenore, she is falling into her grave after a suicidal depression. This downbeat anticipation, which seems to establish an impending narrative resolution in Chapter 26, could have had much to recommend it as a convenient ending, albeit a pessimistic one, and could have provided a genre-appropriate "right feel" in concluding Clara's disastrous tale. Like the heroine of Samuel Richardson's *Clarissa* (1748), the familiar precedent at this time for narratives concerning a traumatized but virtuous female, a dying Clara would fit the period's conventions for a woman who alternatively resisted and capitulated to rogue male authority. This was not the ending that Brown wrote or wanted, however. Even under tremendous deadline pressure from his printer and after long conversations and suggestions from his friends about a suitable conclusion, Brown developed a final chapter that effectively negates the Richardson-style conclusion that might have been expected and, in its place, introduces a new, third phase for the Wieland family story.[50]

---

[50] The diaries of Brown's friends Elihu Hubbard Smith and William Dunlap provide records of multiple conversations on strategies for ending the novel. Smith's *Diary* for July 25, 1798 reports "Charles & I had a long conversation, chiefly on a suitable catastrophe to his tale" (on the same night the group was reading Christoph Martin Wieland's *Oberon*) and on September 5 notes "read Brown's conclusion to his 'Wieland.'" On September 6, Dunlap's *Diary* notes "read the additions . . . to his 'Wieland.'" For a summary and discussion of the novel's composition process, see Cowie, "Historical Essay."

This third phase is dominated by the arrival of a different kind of father and a different mode of knowledge, embodied in the persons of Clara's maternal cousin, the magistrate Mr. Hallet, and her maternal uncle, the physician Thomas Cambridge. Cambridge is a figure who oversees the novel's phase shifts; he was present at Mettingen on the night when the elder Wieland combusted and, in the wake of Theodore's breakdown, it was Cambridge's knowledge that provided a new narrative for the family: *mania mutabilis*, or transforming madness. Instead of citing the religious texts of the father or the Ciceronian legal speeches beloved by the son, Cambridge relies on the new medical and scientific knowledges exemplified by Erasmus Darwin, who sought to expand the classification of illness and understand its relation to larger systems in nature and society.[51] As a product of the discipline of medicine and newest kinds of knowledge it produces, Cambridge provides an explanation for events that suggests that madness, or situational emotional disturbances, run on both sides of the Wieland family. If that is the case, then the family's earlier concerns with religious obedience or aesthetic-intellectual virtue have been supplanted in a newer, forward-looking social order that now demands management by professionals who determine the course of action by reference to preexisting diagnostic codes. If Theodore's madness and the ambiguity surrounding Carwin exemplify the fundamentally contradictory nature of a society that maintains privilege while entertaining itself with the rhetoric of freedom, then the rise of Hallet and Cambridge, as legal and medical adjudicators,[52] suggests that Brown recognizes how the bourgeois-led modern period will respond to the popular disturbances of the Revolutionary era.

The replacement of Enlightenment decision making through collective conversation by the modern professional's authority to determine the course of events appears dramatically in Chapter 27's narrative coda, and in the very different, less congenial Clara who appears in this final chapter. Cambridge's desire for Clara to travel, in fact, beyond removing her from Theodore's reach, corresponds to Erasmus Darwin's clinical indications for the treatment of *mania mutabilis*. In the novel's final chapter, the tone of Clara's communication becomes more distant and imperious.[53] The news that she ultimately marries Pleyel is reported quickly and, surprisingly, without animation. The Clara of this third and final stage no longer seems to flourish in female community and seems to be wholly incorporated within a male world. Clara survives, but in a seemingly diminished and transformed state.

For many critics, the final chapter's return to the complicated subnarrative concerning Major Stuart and Louisa Conway appears as a significant "flaw" or violation of

---

[51] See the excerpt from Darwin's *Zoönomia; or, The Laws of Organic Life* in Related Texts.

[52] For juridical and legal categories in *Wieland,* see Korobkin, "Murder by Madman: Criminal Responsibility, Law, and Judgment in *Wieland*"; Edwards, *The Troubling Confessions of Charles Brockden Brown's* Wieland; and Schneck, "Wieland's Testimony: Charles Brockden Brown and the Rhetoric of Evidence."

[53] For an empirical study of the change in Clara's diction, see Stewart, "Charles Brockden Brown: Quantitative Analysis and Literary Interpretation."

dramatic economy, possibly indicating Brown's inability to maintain control of his narrative or develop a more appropriate conclusion. But just as Clara's earlier tendency to break out into forensic questioning of her choices was not a sign of Brown's inability to maintain narrative tension, but a feature of his literary method—which asks for readers to pause at moments of greatest excitement to consider the social pressures afoot—the Stuart-Conway subnarrative may have a clear meaning if we understand it in the context of Clara's psychological and social trajectory.

The novel ends with an intentional repetition and recollection of the moralizing quatrain from the title page, signaled by the symmetrical uses of the keyword "double-tongued," but it ends with a difference. Whereas the novel began with a general caution (applicable to all) that the self should not participate in equivocation, it ends with Clara's judgment against others who equivocate. This more judgmental and objectifying perspective seems to signal Clara's acceptance of a disciplinary attitude that classifies others, and her participation in a movement toward classification and rationalization through "disciplinary" knowledges that are embodied in her uncle (now her guardian and surrogate father) Thomas Cambridge. Rather than reflecting on the ways that gender, class, and other inequalities were part of the problem at Mettingen, Clara now reinforces the gap between her rationalization and those that it condemns, perhaps seeking to protect her posttraumatic security through a mindset of exclusion.

It is this rule-based attitude, perhaps, that explains why Clara returns to the story of Louisa Conway's mother, with its themes of seduction and masculine vengeance. Rather than emphasizing what might easily be understood as an example of backward-looking violence against women, Clara glosses the tale as a regulatory and cautionary parable to be used as a guide to future action. By the book's end, Clara's overall, somewhat disappointing conclusion seems to be that the cause of the Wieland family's (and the Stuart-Conway family's) self-destruction was their *personal* inability to use more than a single example to regulate their conduct. "If" individuals exercised more adequate foresight and framed their actions by more adequate principles, she suggests in the novel's final paragraph, "then" their actions would not produce such disastrous outcomes. The reader may find Clara's concluding, moralistic perspective a less than satisfactory explanation for all that preceded it, and ultimately one that appears to be as self-aggrandizing as Carwin's.

But Clara's narrow and predictably moralistic conclusions should not be conflated with Brown's goals in providing this willfully anticonventional ending. By returning to Europe, and relocating to the French Languedoc region of the Camisard revolt whose visions electrified her father, Cambridge and Clara have completed a revolution in the family's history, in the early-modern sense, returning to a transformed point of origin. But their relocation to Montpellier may implicitly acknowledge their failure to address the underlying causes and circumstances that led to the tragedy at Mettingen. With the introduction of a third and final stage in the history of the Wieland family, Brown seems to suggest that the postrevolutionary order following the Enlightenment and its state "revolutions" will not eliminate preexisting and underlying social modes of inequality so much as it will redefine them and provide new legitimation for them with new knowledges and technical rationales. Thus, as so many readers have noted, the novel seems to end on a very dark note.

Throughout the novel, the problem with the Wielands is not that they lack frames of reference or sources of certainty, but perhaps that they often fail to see what was in front of them anyway. Theodore idealizes Cicero's defense of a man accused of attempted murder within his family, but the defense is a problematic one at best, for Cicero later boasted of winning the acquittal by deception. By focusing the jury on the faults of a woman, the defendant's mother Sassia, Cicero gained an acquittal for the son Cluentius. When a similar character assassination is attempted against Clara, Theodore seems unable to notice the uncanny parallels. When the Wielands ask Carwin what he thinks about the mysterious voices, like Pleyel he provides a rationalist explanation that is basically accurate; but again, Theodore fails to pursue what otherwise might seem to be an obvious line of reasoning. Clara's first view of Carwin is prompted by his sympathetic appreciation of nature, which is much like her own, but even after watching him disappear into the copse near the summerhouse, she never considers that her favorite location might be favored by Carwin as well. As Brown relates it, the problem is not that the Wielands have no comparative model, but that they do not see or understand themselves in terms of their most basic relational ties to those around them. They remain isolated figures who understand their relations to others on the basis of bloodlines and status groupings: "the house and name of Wieland."

That the novel's most spectacular violence comes from the figure most centrally committed to the status quo of leisured rule—Theodore—also indicates Brown's awareness of the cause of the exaggerated fears of foreign subversion that circulated through America in 1798. For Brown, these fears are more comprehensible as a tactic employed by the standing order than as the consequence of genuine threats. Brown perceives the manner in which the ruling Federalist Party and associated clerical elites constructed a widespread fear of perceived foreign threats as a smoke screen intended to mystify the ruling order's refusal to risk more democracy and social justice. In this light, gothic themes both express a critique of thwarted enlightenment and point a mirror back toward the ruling authorities, so that they may see that the horror lies within, and that the heart of darkness does not belong to foreign influences, but to the revanchism or reactionary violence of existing elites facing the drumbeat of democracy. While some contemporaries rejected this social dynamic in direct and explicit forms, *Wieland* provides a related critique in a more allegorical and indirect form. Offering *Wieland* to his readers, Brown encourages us to relate our own unquestioned assumptions about comfort and liberty to the global network of structured inequality that produces these home conditions.

A NOTE ON THE TEXT

Wieland; or the Transformation. An American Tale was first published in book form on 14 September 1798. New York émigré bookseller Hocquet Caritat was the publisher, and T. and J. Swords (also used for many other publications by Brown's circle) the printer.

The Kent State "Bicentennial" edition of *Wieland* and *Memoirs of Carwin*, published in 1977, is the modern scholarly text of these two narratives and provides a "Textual Essay" and "List of Emendations" that document copy-text variants among early editions and provide a rationale for selecting between variants. The novel was translated into French in 1808 (*La Famille Wieland, ou les prodiges, traduction libre d'un manuscrit américain*; trans. M. Pigault-Mauxbaillarq; Calais: Moreaux, 1808) and apparently first published in England by Henry Colburn in 1811. A few records suggest a plan for a Minerva Press printing in London in 1803, but no copy exists and scholars regard this as an indication that the planned edition never materialized.

This Hackett edition uses the first, Swords printing as its copy-text, silently correcting that edition's obvious typographical errors. We regularize the first edition's irregular dashes and ellipses but otherwise make no modernization of alternative spellings or usage since these present no problem for the contemporary reader.

For *Memoirs of Carwin the Biloquist* and other texts by Brown, this edition uses the first printings from Brown's New York *Monthly Magazine* and Philadelphia *Literary Magazine* for copy-texts, as well as the initial text of "Death of Cicero" from the second printing of volume III of Brown's novel *Edgar Huntly*. We have presented *Memoirs of Carwin* in the serialized form in which it originally appeared, rather than in the continuous form that editors began to adopt after Brown's death. The installment numbers before each segment are our addition. More information on the publication history of these texts is available in the Related Text headnotes concerning them.

Similarly, the other Related Texts in this volume are drawn from first or, where indicated, other contemporary printings, and are not modernized. The copy-text for the translation of an excerpt from C. M. Wieland's "Answers and Counter-Questions" is the first printing in the *Teutsche Merkur* (some modern editions of this text alter its first paragraphs in significant ways).

For a full discussion of the novel's textual history, see the textual essay, notes, and appendices by S. W. Reid in the Kent State edition.

WIELAND;

OR THE

TRANSFORMATION.

AN

AMERICAN TALE.

—◆—

From Virtue's blissful paths away
The double-tongued are sure to stray;
Good is a forth-right journey still,
And mazy paths but lead to ill.[1]

—◆—

COPY-RIGHT SECURED.

NEW-YORK:

Printed by T. & J. Swords, for H. Caritat.
—1798.—.

---

[1] The quatrain is by Brown. It hints that the romance will moralize against "double-tongued" imposture which assumes that virtue or righteousness can occasionally or tactically dispense with sincerity.

ADVERTISEMENT

THE following Work is delivered to the world as the first of a series of performances, which the favorable reception of this will induce the Writer to publish. His purpose is neither selfish nor temporary, but aims at the illustration of some important branches of the moral constitution of man. Whether this tale will be classed with the ordinary or frivolous sources of amusement, or be ranked with the few productions whose usefulness secures to them a lasting reputation, the reader must be permitted to decide.

The incidents related are extraordinary and rare. Some of them, perhaps, approach as nearly to the nature of miracles as can be done by that which is not truly miraculous. It is hoped that intelligent readers will not disapprove of the manner in which appearances are solved, but that the solution will be found to correspond with the known principles of human nature.[1] The power which the principal person is said to possess can scarcely be denied to be real. It must be acknowledged to be extremely rare; but no fact, equally uncommon, is supported by the same strength of historical evidence.

Some readers may think the conduct of the younger Wieland impossible. In support of its possibility the Writer must appeal to Physicians and to men conversant with the latent springs and occasional perversions of the human mind. It will not be objected that the instances of similar delusion are rare, because it is the business of moral painters to exhibit their subject in its most instructive and memorable forms. If history furnishes one parallel fact, it is a sufficient vindication of the Writer; but most readers will probably recollect an authentic case,[2] remarkably similar to that of Wieland.

It will be necessary to add, that this narrative is addressed, in an epistolary form, by the Lady whose story it contains, to a small number of friends, whose curiosity, with regard to it, had been greatly awakened. It may likewise be mentioned, that these events took place between the conclusion of the French and the beginning of

---

[1] "Known principles of human nature": for Brown's views on romance or novel writing as the investigation of human nature for the purpose of creating a more just and beneficial society, see Related Texts "Walstein's School of History" and "The Difference Between History and Romance."

[2] "Authentic case": two incidents of patriarchal familicide, in which fathers killed their families during episodes of insanity, were familiar to Brown's readers in 1798. The widely publicized cases of James Yates and William Beadle, which occurred in 1781 and 1782, respectively, were still being reprinted and discussed in the late 1790s and 1800s. A key account of the Yates murders in rural, upstate New York was republished in a New York newspaper in 1796 and mentioned specifically in the long review of *Wieland*, probably by Brown's friend William Dunlap, that appeared in the New York *Monthly Magazine* (Jan. 1800), a periodical edited by Brown and his New York circle. For more on the Yates and Beadle murders, see the accounts here in Related Texts.

the revolutionary war.[3] The memoirs of Carwin,[4] alluded to at the conclusion of the work, will be published or suppressed according to the reception which is given to the present attempt.

C. B. B.

September 3, 1798.

---

[3] "Between the conclusion of the French and the beginning of the revolutionary war": between 1763 and 1775 or, in other words, between the end of the Seven Years War (1756–1763) and the onset of the American Revolutionary War (1775–1783). The Seven Years War (whose North American theater is the French and Indian War) was a global, worldwide war between the rival French and British commercial empires, and will form the general historical backdrop for the lives of the novel's characters, many of whom are functionaries or relatives of functionaries in the imperial administration of these territories and conflicts. For more on the novel's historical setting, see the Introduction.

[4] "Memoirs of Carwin": Brown did in fact go on to develop *Memoirs of Carwin the Biloquist* as a prequel to *Wieland*, beginning in August 1798, even before the completion of this novel. Although it was never finished, Brown eventually published it in ten installments in his *Literary Magazine*, from 1803 to 1805. For more, see this narrative in Related Texts.

WIELAND;
OR THE TRANSFORMATION.

Chapter I

I FEEL little reluctance in complying with your request. You know not fully the cause of my sorrows. You are a stranger to the depth of my distresses. Hence your efforts at consolation must necessarily fail. Yet the tale that I am going to tell is not intended as a claim upon your sympathy.[1] In the midst of my despair, I do not disdain to contribute what little I can to the benefit of mankind. I acknowledge your right to be informed of the events that have lately happened in my family. Make what use of the tale you shall think proper. If it be communicated to the world, it will inculcate the duty of avoiding deceit. It will exemplify the force of early impressions, and show the immeasurable evils that flow from an erroneous or imperfect discipline.[2]

My state is not destitute of tranquillity. The sentiment that dictates my feelings is not hope. Futurity has no power over my thoughts. To all that is to come I am perfectly indifferent. With regard to myself, I have nothing more to fear. Fate has done its worst. Henceforth, I am callous to misfortune.

I address no supplication to the Deity. The power that governs the course of human affairs has chosen his path. The decree that ascertained the condition of my life,

---

[1] "Not . . . a claim upon your sympathy": throughout the novel, narrator Clara Wieland invokes and often depends on eighteenth century codes of "sympathy" and "sensibility" in ways that foreground these concepts and their implications. At the outset of her narrative, speaking retrospectively, Clara invokes sympathy but also seems to distance herself from it as a possibly deceptive, unreliable mode of social relations. Sympathy and sensibility are key interrelated concepts that play an important role in Brown and throughout his period. They identify an immediate emotional-physical relation or response to other individuals, often celebrated as replacing older, prerevolutionary or aristocratic modes of deference with new, more modern and implicitly egalitarian models for interpersonal behavior and cooperation.

[2] "Duty of avoiding deceit . . . early impressions . . . erroneous or imperfect discipline": in the novel's first four paragraphs, Clara Wieland establishes a retrospective narrative frame and prepares the reader for her challenging narrative. In this first paragraph, she prefaces her story by asserting that it will have a "moral" concerning the importance of sincerity ("the duty of avoiding deceit") and that it will illustrate the ways that environment and circumstances shape behavior ("the force of early impressions"). Additionally, she notes that the reader and addressee must approach the narrative with an independent mind: "make what use of the tale you shall think proper." Implicitly, in these remarks, sincerity and insight are not something that we can automatically or naively achieve; they require discipline, learning, and practice. Clara's introduction tries to enact these values by refusing to seduce the reader via appeals to "sympathy," by warning us that the ensuing tale will be "incredible" and difficult to clarify, by supplying detailed historical background, and by asking us to analyze and learn from what we will read.

The fictional addressee of the narrative ("your request") is not clearly identified, although remarks in Chapters 25–27 suggest that a trusted family member or companion such as her maternal cousin, the surgeon Thomas Cambridge, is the likely candidate. See notes 25.1 and 26.3.

admits of no recall. No doubt it squares with the maxims of eternal equity. That is neither to be questioned nor denied by me. It suffices that the past is exempt from mutation. The storm that tore up our happiness, and changed into dreariness and desert the blooming scene of our existence, is lulled into grim repose; but not until the victim was transfixed and mangled; till every obstacle was dissipated by its rage; till every remnant of good was wrested from our grasp and exterminated.

How will your wonder, and that of your companions, be excited by my story! Every sentiment will yield to your amazement. If my testimony were without corroborations, you would reject it as incredible. The experience of no human being can furnish a parallel: That I, beyond the rest of mankind, should be reserved for a destiny without alleviation, and without example! Listen to my narrative, and then say what it is that has made me deserve to be placed on this dreadful eminence, if, indeed, every faculty be not suspended in wonder that I am still alive, and am able to relate it.

My father's ancestry was noble on the paternal side; but his mother was the daughter of a merchant. My grand-father was a younger brother, and a native of Saxony.[3] He was placed, when he had reached the suitable age, at a German college.[4] During the vacations, he employed himself in traversing the neighbouring territory. On one occasion it was his fortune to visit Hamburg. He formed an acquaintance with Leonard Weise,[5] a merchant of that city, and was a frequent guest at his house. The merchant had an only daughter, for whom his guest speedily contracted an affection;

---

[3] "Saxony": Clara begins by historicizing the events that have occurred, sketching the history of the paternal side of the family two generations back. Saxony refers generally to several territories in the southeastern region of Germany. The largest was the Electorate of Saxony, including the cities of Leipzig and Dresden along the Elbe River; this region was a center of German intellectual culture in the eighteenth century. Saxony included Wittenberg (where Martin Luther began the Protestant Reformation) and from 1517 through the Thirty Years War (1618–1648) was at the center of politico-religious wars of the Reformation. At this time the region was undergoing further conflicts as a result of limited reforms related to its regime of regal, Absolutist Enlightenment. For more on Absolutist Enlightenment and how the forms of fiction to which it gave rise influence Brown and *Wieland*, see the Introduction and Related Texts.

[4] "College": a secondary or preuniversity school.

[5] "Hamburg . . . Leonard Weise": Hamburg was an independent city-state, a mercantile center, and primarily Protestant. The name Leonard Weise seems to allude to the well-known 1779 play *Nathan the Wise* (*Nathan der Weise*) by Saxon writer Gotthold Ephraim Lessing (1729–1781). The play was famous for rejecting Christian prejudices against Jews, and Lessing based the character Nathan on Jewish philosopher Moses Mendelssohn (1729–1786), an important German Enlightenment figure born in Dessau, just north of Saxony. *Nathan the Wise* is set in Jerusalem during the Third Crusade and primarily stages an extended conversation between the Jewish merchant Nathan, the Muslim Sultan Saladin, and a Christian Knight Templar. It argues for religious tolerance, Enlightenment ideals of friendship and sincerity, and rational skepticism toward religious doctrines and beliefs in supernatural events like miracles. As the noble Wieland (the narrator's grandfather) marries the daughter of a merchant, he enacts the modern values called for in Lessing's play. The possibility that Wieland's wife may be ethnically Jewish raises questions that Brown introduces more obviously with the Jewish character Achsa Fielding in his novel *Arthur Mervyn* (1799–1800).

and, in spite of parental menaces and prohibitions, he, in due season, became her husband.

By this act he mortally offended his relations. Thenceforward he was entirely disowned and rejected by them. They refused to contribute any thing to his support. All intercourse ceased, and he received from them merely that treatment to which an absolute stranger, or detested enemy, would be entitled.

He found an asylum in the house of his new father, whose temper was kind, and whose pride was flattered by this alliance. The nobility of his birth was put in the balance against his poverty. Weise conceived himself, on the whole, to have acted with the highest discretion, in thus disposing of his child. My grand-father found it incumbent on him to search out some mode of independent subsistence. His youth had been eagerly devoted to literature and music. These had hitherto been cultivated merely as sources of amusement. They were now converted into the means of gain. At this period there were few works of taste in the Saxon dialect.[6] My ancestor may be considered as the founder of the German Theatre. The modern poet of the same name[7] is sprung from the same family, and, perhaps, surpasses but little, in the fruitfulness of his invention, or the soundness of his taste, the elder Wieland. His life was spent in the composition of sonatas and dramatic pieces. They were not unpopular, but merely afforded him a scanty subsistence. He died in the bloom of his life, and was quickly followed to the grave by his wife. Their only child was taken under the protection of the merchant. At an early

---

[6] "Saxon dialect": Clara identifies her family with modernizing trends away from Latin and toward cultural production in modern languages. Although the linguistic "low Saxon" of northern Germany (not used in Saxony) was dominant before the Reformation, Martin Luther's 1534 translation of the Bible into German (emphasizing central and southern dialects) gave new prestige to the dialects of Saxony, which by the eighteenth century developed into the dominant forms used for scientific and literary writings. This development was championed by Saxon political interests and spearheaded by Johann Adelung (1732–1806), principal librarian to the elector of Saxony, who argued that the upper-class dialects of his region should become standard. Christoph Martin Wieland's well-known debate with Adelung on this question began with his essay "On the Question: What is High German?" (1782). The question of a rural region's marginality or weakness as conveyed by the "double-tongued" difference between regional languages and protonational standards is also implicit in this chapter's later mentions of religious and civil strife in the Languedoc region of southern France.

[7] "Modern poet of the same name": several key names in the novel, above all Wieland, are associated with the progressively coded German literary wave of the 1790s. Brown, his circle, and the British writers they read followed Continental European cultural developments and debates closely, and published commentary on them. Late-eighteenth-century English critics considered Christoph Martin Wieland (1733–1813) the period's most significant German literary figure. At this time Wieland's reputation exceeded that of other German writers such as Goethe and Schiller, who are now considered more significant. As a prolific novelist, poet, dramatist, translator (especially of Shakespeare's plays), essayist, and editor of *Der Teutsche Merkur* (*The German Mercury*, 1773–1789), a periodical based in Weimar, he was received in Anglo-American circles as an influential proponent of progressive, but not radical, values, the promoter of an intensely cosmopolitan outlook, and a crucial figure in the circulation of late-Enlightenment ideas and cultural forms between England, Germany, and France, as well as a mediator of Eastern/Islamic literary themes for European readers. For more on Wieland and the 1790s German wave, see the Introduction and Related Texts.

age he was apprenticed to a London trader, and passed seven years of mercantile servitude.[8]

My father was not fortunate in the character of him under whose care he was now placed. He was treated with rigor, and full employment was provided for every hour of his time. His duties were laborious and mechanical.[9] He had been educated with a view to this profession, and, therefore, was not tormented with unsatisfied desires. He did not hold his present occupations in abhorrence, because they withheld him from paths more flowery and more smooth, but he found in unintermitted labour, and in the sternness of his master, sufficient occasions for discontent. No opportunities of recreation were allowed him. He spent all his time pent up in a gloomy apartment, or traversing narrow and crowded streets. His food was coarse, and his lodging humble.

His heart gradually contracted a habit of morose and gloomy reflection. He could not accurately define what was wanting to his happiness. He was not tortured by comparisons drawn between his own situation and that of others. His state was such as suited his age and his views as to fortune. He did not imagine himself treated with extraordinary or unjustifiable rigor. In this respect he supposed the condition of others, bound like himself to mercantile service, to resemble his own; yet every engagement was irksome, and every hour tedious in its lapse.

In this state of mind he chanced to light upon a book written by one of the teachers of the Albigenses, or French Protestants.[10] He entertained no relish for books,

---

[8] "Mercantile servitude": the orphaned son (Clara's father) is apprenticed to a trader in a standard seven-year contract. His status is like that of an indentured servant, not much higher than that of a slave. Like an indentured servant or enslaved African, the elder Wieland is worked hard, badly housed, and poorly fed, and these alienating circumstances lead to the "habit of morose and gloomy reflection" that Clara emphasizes shortly, which will play an important role in what follows.

[9] "Mechanical": a "mechanic" in this period is a specialized worker with an artisanal skill or craft trade, although the term still suggests repetitious and unthinking physical labor.

[10] "Albigenses, or French Protestants": the first of this chapter's many references to historical episodes of Christian religious schism and institutional violence. The passage combines references to two separate French episodes, repeating the Wieland family's indirect ties to the history of religious strife in Saxony. The Albigenses, also known as Cathars (Greek *katharoi,* "perfect ones"), were a Christian sect of the eleventh century in the Languedoc region of southern France. Named after Albi, a town in this region, the Albigensians developed a dualistic worldview. They believed in a stark opposition between ethereal love and material power as the creations of two different, opposing gods. Rex Mundi ("king of the world"), the divine presence of the Old Testament and essentially evil, had created the physical world and the body as prisons, and demanded obedience through shock and awe. An opposing god of love and peace, represented in the New Testament, was incarnate and immaterial. Their leaders practiced ascetic self-discipline and ecstatic rituals of inner experience. To crush the heresy, the Catholic Church launched the Albigensian Crusade (1209–1229), sparking a series of massacres and peasant revolts, ultimately resulting in the establishment of the Inquisition in Toulouse in 1229. Although often considered primarily in religious terms, the Albigensian movement was also a peasant revolt against centralized Church and aristocratic authority in a period of agrarian depression and rising taxes. Like Saxony, Languedoc was a region with its own dialect (the "langue d'oc" or Occitan) in conflict with standardizing national forms. As a nonnative speaker struggling under an oppressive living and work environment, Wieland seems drawn to the writings of those who shared similar conditions.

and was wholly unconscious of any power they possessed to delight or instruct. This volume had lain for years in a corner of his garret, half buried in dust and rubbish. He had marked it as it lay; had thrown it, as his occasions required, from one spot to another; but had felt no inclination to examine its contents, or even to inquire what was the subject of which it treated.

One Sunday afternoon, being induced to retire for a few minutes to his garret, his eye was attracted by a page of this book, which, by some accident, had been opened and placed full in his view. He was seated on the edge of his bed, and was employed in repairing a rent in some part of his clothes. His eyes were not confined to his work, but occasionally wandering, lighted at length upon the page. The words "Seek and ye shall find,"[11] were those that first offered themselves to his notice. His curiosity[12] was roused by these so far as to prompt him to proceed. As soon as he finished his work, he took up the book and turned to the first page. The further he read, the more inducement he found to continue, and he regretted the decline of the light which obliged him for the present to close it.

The book contained an exposition of the doctrine of the sect of Camissards,[13] and an historical account of its origin. His mind was in a state peculiarly fitted for the reception of devotional sentiments. The craving which had haunted him was now supplied with an object. His mind was at no loss for a theme of meditation. On days of business, he rose at the dawn, and retired to his chamber not till late at night. He now supplied himself with candles, and employed his nocturnal and Sunday hours in studying this book. It, of course, abounded with allusions to the Bible. All its

---

[11] "Seek and ye shall find": Matthew 7:7 and Luke 11:9.

[12] "Curiosity": curiosity is a keyword for Brown and often figures in his plots with an ambivalent meaning. It reflects the Enlightenment desire to learn, but can also lead to unchecked excess. This happens to the protagonist of William Godwin's novel *Caleb Williams* (1794), where the protagonist discovers secrets about his aristocratic employer by exploring his library and private papers. Clara's father and the character Carwin will be motivated by curiosity in this narrative and *Memoirs of Carwin* (see note 23.2).

[13] "The book . . . Camissards . . . origin": that the elder Wieland becomes a disciple of a sect that believes in apocalyptic, divine commandments received through ecstatic experiences of foreign and ancient languages foreshadows later events for his children. The Camisards were a Protestant (Huguenot) sect in the Languedoc-Cévennes region of southern France who launched a guerilla revolt in 1702–1710 against the French monarchy after twenty years of anti-Protestant persecution. Camisard is derived from *camise* (shirt or smock in the Occitan language), indicating the group's laboring-class, artisan, and peasant constituencies. The revolt took place in same territory as the Albigensian episode five hundred years earlier, and the French city Montpellier, where Clara relocates at the end of the novel (see note 27.1), is at the heart of the same Languedoc region where both revolts occurred.

A fraction of the Camisard Protestants, known in English as the "French Prophets" or "Cévenols" (from the Cévennes Mountains) fled to London in 1706 under the leadership of Elias Marion (1678–1713), where they published books like the one that Wieland seems to be reading here. The book Wieland discovers by chance is difficult to identify precisely but, given this history, it may have been something like Marion's *Prophetical warnings of Elias Marion*, etc. (1707) or other tracts by the group. For more on the Camisards and Marion, see the excerpts here in Related Texts.

conclusions were deduced from the sacred text. This was the fountain, beyond which it was unnecessary to trace the stream of religious truth; but it was his duty to trace it thus far.

A Bible was easily procured, and he ardently entered on the study of it. His understanding had received a particular direction.[14] All his reveries were fashioned in the same mould. His progress towards the formation of his creed was rapid. Every fact and sentiment in this book were viewed through a medium which the writings of the Camissard apostle had suggested. His constructions of the text were hasty, and formed on a narrow scale.[15] Every thing was viewed in a disconnected position. One action and one precept were not employed to illustrate and restrict the meaning of another. Hence arose a thousand scruples to which he had hitherto been a stranger. He was alternately agitated by fear and by ecstacy. He imagined himself beset by the snares of a spiritual foe, and that his security lay in ceaseless watchfulness and prayer.

His morals, which had never been loose, were now modelled by a stricter standard. The empire of religious duty extended itself to his looks, gestures, and phrases. All levities of speech, and negligences of behaviour, were proscribed. His air was mournful and contemplative. He laboured to keep alive a sentiment of fear, and a belief of the awe-creating presence of the Deity. Ideas foreign to this were sedulously excluded. To suffer their intrusion was a crime against the Divine Majesty inexpiable but by days and weeks of the keenest agonies.

No material variation had occurred in the lapse of two years. Every day confirmed him in his present modes of thinking and acting. It was to be expected that the tide of his emotions would sometimes recede, that intervals of despondency and doubt would occur; but these gradually were more rare, and of shorter duration; and he, at last, arrived at a state considerably uniform in this respect.

His apprenticeship was now almost expired. On his arrival of age he became entitled, by the will of my grand-father, to a small sum. This sum would hardly suffice to set him afloat as a trader in his present situation, and he had nothing to expect from the generosity of his master. Residence in England had, besides, become almost impossible, on account of his religious tenets. In addition to these motives for seeking a new habitation, there was another of the most imperious and irresistable necessity. He had imbibed an opinion that it was his duty to disseminate the truths of the gospel among the unbelieving nations. He was terrified at first by the perils and hardships to which the life of a missionary is exposed. This cowardice made him

---

[14] "His understanding had received a particular direction": Clara emphasizes the way her father's life was shaped by the "force of early impressions," a principle she noted at the outset of the story. See note 1.2.

[15] "Constructions . . . formed on a narrow scale": Clara notes that the "understanding" the elder Wieland derives from his Bible study is problematic because his interpretations are isolated from the implications of other readings. The comment also seems to reflect the Woldwinite lack of confidence in the isolated Cartesian ego's ability to produce rational truth; reasonable conclusions must emerge from the checks and balances of educated discussion in the context of social experience and intercourse.

diligent in the invention of objections and excuses; but he found it impossible wholly to shake off the belief that such was the injunction of his duty. The belief, after every new conflict with his passions, acquired new strength; and, at length, he formed a resolution of complying with what he deemed the will of heaven.

The North-American Indians naturally presented themselves as the first objects for this species of benevolence. As soon as his servitude expired, he converted his little fortune into money, and embarked for Philadelphia. Here his fears were revived, and a nearer survey of savage manners once more shook his resolution. For a while he relinquished his purpose, and purchasing a farm on Schuylkill,[16] within a few miles of the city, set himself down to the cultivation of it.[17] The cheapness of land, and the service of African slaves,[18] which were then in general use, gave him who was poor in Europe all the advantages of wealth. He passed fourteen years in a thrifty and laborious manner. In this time new objects, new employments, and new associates

---

[16] "A farm on Schuylkill": the Schuylkill River formed the western boundary of Philadelphia. Estates like the one established by the elder Wieland were situated along both banks of the Schuylkill and provided wealthy families with country seats near the urban center.

[17] "Set himself down to the cultivation of it": the narrative's details concerning the early development of the Wieland estate may build on some aspects of the history of Brown's maternal great-uncle and namesake Charles Brockden (1683–1769). In 1737, Brockden bought a twelve-hundred-acre country seat near what is now Williamstown, New Jersey, about twenty miles from Philadelphia. Like the Wieland home, Brockden's house looked to be of the prosperous new wealth, neither a possession of an older established Tory "gentleman" class, nor of common farmers. Brockden's land was worked by German and Swedish indentured laborers ("redemptioners"), and he owned at least one slave, although he eventually sold her to the Moravian community as a gesture of quasi-emancipation.

Like the elder Wieland, Brockden was a bit of a religious wanderer. He began life as an Anglican, but joined the Quakers for technical reasons after marrying his first wife, since Quakers were otherwise excommunicated for marrying outside their faith. After encountering the charismatic Moravian leader Zinzendorf in 1743 (see note 1.20 in this chapter for Zinzendorf), he joined that community and later debated the well-known Methodist revivalist George Whitfield on the relative merits of the period's competing Protestant sects.

[18] "African slaves": although this is the novel's only explicit mention of slavery on the Wieland estate, the detail is significant and ties the family's wealth and leisure to unfree labor and the dynamics of empire and colonialism. Combined with information about the elder Wieland's efforts to proselytize Native Americans, it implicitly acknowledges that the Wieland family's establishment in North America, like European settlement generally, was part of a larger, ongoing process of imperial expansion and colonial profiteering. Although Clara never mentions African slavery again, there is nothing in the rest of the novel to indicate that the Wielands ever stop owning slaves. Though not explicitly described as such, the inhabitants of the hut on their property may be (former) African slaves (see note 22.1). Indeed, in the preliminary "outline" of *Wieland*, the character that later becomes Theodore Wieland escapes from confinement and "kills a faithful Negro who withstands him."

Brown and his circle were abolitionists, and he develops critical reflections on slavery in his novels *Arthur Mervyn* (1799–1800) and *Stephen Calvert* (1799–1800), as well as in numerous essays. Partly because Quakers founded it, and because many Quakers were leaders in the Anglo-American abolition movement, Pennsylvania became the first state to abolish slavery in 1780, after the period of this novel's action. Even earlier, in 1758, practicing Quakers were forbidden on religious grounds from owning slaves. The Wielands are not Quakers, however, and thus throughout the period of the novel's action may still own slaves in Pennsylvania.

appeared to have nearly obliterated the devout impressions of his youth. He now became acquainted with a woman of a meek and quiet disposition, and of slender acquirements like himself. He proffered his hand and was accepted.

His previous industry had now enabled him to dispense with personal labour, and direct attention to his own concerns. He enjoyed leisure, and was visited afresh by devotional contemplation. The reading of the scriptures, and other religious books, became once more his favorite employment. His ancient belief relative to the conversion of the savage tribes, was revived with uncommon energy. To the former obstacles were now added the pleadings of parental and conjugal love. The struggle was long and vehement; but his sense of duty would not be stifled or enfeebled, and finally triumphed over every impediment.

His efforts were attended with no permanent success. His exhortations had sometimes a temporary power, but more frequently were repelled with insult and derision. In pursuit of this object he encountered the most imminent perils, and underwent incredible fatigues, hunger, sickness, and solitude. The licence of savage passion, and the artifices of his depraved countrymen, all opposed themselves to his progress. His courage did not forsake him till there appeared no reasonable ground to hope for success. He desisted not till his heart was relieved from the supposed obligation to persevere. With a constitution somewhat decayed, he at length returned to his family. An interval of tranquillity succeeded. He was frugal, regular, and strict in the performance of domestic duties. He allied himself with no sect, because he perfectly agreed with none. Social worship is that by which they are all distinguished; but this article found no place in his creed. He rigidly interpreted that precept which enjoins us, when we worship, to retire into solitude, and shut out every species of society. According to him devotion was not only a silent office, but must be performed alone. An hour at noon, and an hour at midnight were thus appropriated.[19]

At the distance of three hundred yards from his house, on the top of a rock whose sides were steep, rugged, and encumbered with dwarf cedars and stony asperities, he built what to a common eye would have seemed a summer-house. The eastern verge of this precipice was sixty feet above the river which flowed at its foot. The view before it consisted of a transparent current, fluctuating and rippling in a rocky channel, and bounded by a rising scene of cornfields and orchards. The edifice was slight and airy. It was no more than a circular area, twelve feet in diameter, whose flooring was the rock, cleared of moss and shrubs, and exactly levelled, edged by twelve Tuscan columns, and covered by an undulating dome. My father furnished the dimensions and outlines, but allowed the artist whom he employed to complete the structure on his own plan. It was without seat, table, or ornament of any kind.

This was the temple of his Deity. Twice in twenty-four hours he repaired hither, unaccompanied by any human being. Nothing but physical inability to move was allowed to obstruct or postpone this visit. He did not exact from his family

---

[19] "An hour at noon, and an hour at midnight were thus appropriated": these fixed times seem to be recalled by the elder Wieland's son Theodore during the novel's final confrontation in Chapter 25 (see note 25.5).

compliance with his example. Few men, equally sincere in their faith, were as sparing in their censures and restrictions, with respect to the conduct of others, as my father. The character of my mother was no less devout; but her education had habituated her to a different mode of worship. The loneliness of their dwelling prevented her from joining any established congregation; but she was punctual in the offices of prayer, and in the performance of hymns to her Saviour, after the manner of the disciples of Zinzendorf.[20] My father refused to interfere in her arrangements. His own system was embraced not, accurately speaking, because it was the best, but because it had been expressly prescribed to him. Other modes, if practised by other persons, might be equally acceptable.

His deportment to others was full of charity and mildness. A sadness perpetually overspread his features, but was unmingled with sternness or discontent. The tones of his voice, his gestures, his steps were all in tranquil unison.[21] His conduct was characterised by a certain forbearance and humility, which secured the esteem of those to whom his tenets were most obnoxious. They might call him a fanatic and a dreamer, but they could not deny their veneration to his invincible candour and invariable integrity. His own belief of rectitude was the foundation of his happiness. This, however, was destined to find an end.

Suddenly the sadness that constantly attended him was deepened. Sighs, and even tears, sometimes escaped him. To the expostulations of his wife he seldom answered

---

[20] "Disciples of Zinzendorf": Moravians. Czech Jan Hus (1372–1415) founded the Moravian Church in the late fourteenth century as a protest against the sociopolitical power of Catholicism. Hus was excommunicated and burned at the stake as a dangerous heretic, but the movement he founded is often considered the first Protestant episode, more than a century before Martin Luther began the Reformation in 1517 in Saxony. Clara's mother's adoption of elements from Moravian practices provides a final link in the chapter's lengthy set of allusions to insurrectionary Christian schisms.

After the Thirty Years War (1618–1648), the culmination of the wars of the Reformation, Hus' followers survived only in small numbers, scattered in underground pockets through Saxony and Silesia (present-day southeastern Germany and Czech Republic). In 1722, the arrival and settling of a few of these believers at the estate of Nikolaus Zinzendorf (1700–1760) at Herrnhut sparked a Moravian renewal. Like other "enthusiastic" Protestant sects, Moravians emphasized personal revelation, frequent prayer, ascetic communal living, and proselytizing missionary work. Zinzendorf was a Saxon-born Lutheran, but converted and became a leading figure in the Moravian movement. He traveled widely as the best-known Moravian missionary and visited North America in 1741–1742. In 1741, Moravians established two large communal settlements in Nazareth and Bethlehem, Pennsylvania, on land purchased from two of William Penn's sons; this is the area where the character Carwin will hide after the novel's crisis (see note 23.5). They concentrated on efforts to convert Native Americans, and their land transactions with the Lenni Lenape were less fraudulent than those of the Quakers. As noted earlier (see note 1.17), Brown's great-uncle and namesake Charles Brockden became a Moravian in 1743, in the aftermath of Zinzendorf's tour. Clara's later mention of people living at the "Hut" on the edges of her family's estate may also allude to the original settlement on Zinzendorf's estate (see note 22.1).

[21] "Tones . . . in unison": the bodily features of sensibility. Invoking eighteenth-century codes of physical sympathy and sensibility, Clara implies that the father's rational and emotional faculties are in harmony at this point of his story.

any thing. When he deigned to be communicative, he hinted that his peace of mind was flown, in consequence of deviation from his duty. A command had been laid upon him, which he had delayed to perform. He felt as if a certain period of hesitation and reluctance had been allowed him, but that this period was passed. He was no longer permitted to obey. The duty assigned to him was transferred, in consequence of his disobedience, to another, and all that remained was to endure the penalty.

He did not describe this penalty. It appeared to be nothing more for some time than a sense of wrong. This was sufficiently acute, and was aggravated by the belief that his offence was incapable of expiation. No one could contemplate the agonies which he seemed to suffer without the deepest compassion. Time, instead of lightening the burthen, appeared to add to it. At length he hinted to his wife, that his end was near. His imagination did not prefigure the mode or the time of his decease, but was fraught with an incurable persuasion that his death was at hand. He was likewise haunted by the belief that the kind of death that awaited him was strange and terrible. His anticipations were thus far vague and indefinite; but they sufficed to poison every moment of his being, and devote him to ceaseless anguish.

Chapter II

EARLY in the morning of a sultry day in August, he left Mettingen,[1] to go to the city. He had seldom passed a day from home since his return from the shores of the Ohio.[2] Some urgent engagements at this time existed, which would not admit of further delay. He returned in the evening, but appeared to be greatly oppressed with fatigue. His silence and dejection were likewise in a more than ordinary degree conspicuous. My mother's brother, whose profession was that of a surgeon,[3] chanced to spend this night at our house. It was from him that I have frequently received an exact account of the mournful catastrophe that followed.

As the evening advanced, my father's inquietudes increased. He sat with his family as usual, but took no part in their conversation. He appeared fully engrossed by his own reflections. Occasionally his countenance exhibited tokens of alarm; he gazed stedfastly and wildly at the ceiling; and the exertions of his companions were scarcely sufficient to interrupt his reverie. On recovering from these fits, he expressed no surprize; but pressing his hand to his head, complained, in a tremulous and terrified tone, that his brain was scorched to cinders. He would then betray marks of insupportable anxiety.

My uncle perceived, by his pulse, that he was indisposed, but in no alarming degree, and ascribed appearances chiefly to the workings of his mind. He exhorted him to recollection and composure, but in vain. At the hour of repose he readily retired to his chamber. At the persuasion of my mother he even undressed and went to bed. Nothing could abate his restlessness. He checked her tender expostulations with some sternness. "Be silent," said he, "for that which I feel there is but one cure, and that will shortly come. You can help me nothing. Look to your own condition, and pray to God to strengthen you under the calamities that await you." "What am I to fear?" she answered. "What terrible disaster is it that you think of?" "Peace—as yet I know it not myself, but come it will, and shortly." She repeated her inquiries and doubts; but he suddenly put an end to the discourse, by a stern command to be silent.

She had never before known him in this mood. Hitherto all was benign in his deportment. Her heart was pierced with sorrow at the contemplation of this change. She was utterly unable to account for it, or to figure to herself the species of disaster that was menaced.

Contrary to custom, the lamp, instead of being placed on the hearth, was left upon the table. Over it against the wall there hung a small clock, so contrived as to strike a

---

[1] "Mettingen": the name of the Wieland family's estate, presumably referring to the town of the same name in Westphalia, Northwestern Germany. The Battle of Mettingen, a significant clash between French revolutionary and Austrian forces, took place in 1796. Clara notes in Chapter 3 that the name was not chosen by the Wielands, but is the name of the property's first owner.

[2] "Shores of the Ohio": the Moravians were active in missionary work to convert Native Americans along the upper Ohio River, in western Pennsylvania and Ohio.

[3] "My mother's brother . . . a surgeon": Clara's maternal uncle, who witnesses her father's death, is Thomas Cambridge. This character will be named and play an important role later in the novel, beginning in Chapter 18.

very hard stroke at the end of every sixth hour. That which was now approaching was the signal for retiring to the fane[4] at which he addressed his devotions. Long habit had occasioned him to be always awake at this hour, and the toll was instantly obeyed.

Now frequent and anxious glances were cast at the clock. Not a single movement of the index appeared to escape his notice. As the hour verged towards twelve his anxiety visibly augmented. The trepidations of my mother kept pace with those of her husband; but she was intimidated into silence. All that was left to her was to watch every change of his features, and give vent to her sympathy in tears.

At length the hour was spent, and the clock tolled. The sound appeared to communicate a shock to every part of my father's frame. He rose immediately, and threw over himself a loose gown. Even this office was performed with difficulty, for his joints trembled, and his teeth chattered with dismay. At this hour his duty called him to the rock, and my mother naturally concluded that it was thither he intended to repair. Yet these incidents were so uncommon, as to fill her with astonishment and foreboding. She saw him leave the room, and heard his steps as they hastily descended the stairs. She half resolved to rise and pursue him, but the wildness of the scheme quickly suggested itself. He was going to a place whither no power on earth could induce him to suffer an attendant.

The window of her chamber looked toward the rock. The atmosphere was clear and calm, but the edifice could not be discovered at that distance through the dusk. My mother's anxiety would not allow her to remain where she was. She rose, and seated herself at the window. She strained her sight to get a view of the dome, and of the path that led to it. The first painted itself with sufficient distinctness on her fancy, but was undistinguishable by the eye from the rocky mass on which it was erected. The second could be imperfectly seen; but her husband had already passed, or had taken a different direction.

What was it that she feared? Some disaster impended over her husband or herself. He had predicted evils, but professed himself ignorant of what nature they were. When were they to come? Was this night, or this hour to witness the accomplishment? She was tortured with impatience, and uncertainty. All her fears were at present linked to his person, and she gazed at the clock, with nearly as much eagerness as my father had done, in expectation of the next hour.

An half hour passed away in this state of suspence. Her eyes were fixed upon the rock; suddenly it was illuminated. A light proceeding from the edifice, made every part of the scene visible. A gleam[5] diffused itself over the intermediate space, and instantly a loud report, like the explosion of a mine, followed. She uttered an involuntary shriek, but the new sounds that greeted her ear, quickly conquered her surprise. They were piercing shrieks, and uttered without intermission. The gleams which had diffused themselves far and wide were in a moment withdrawn, but the interior of the edifice was filled with rays.

---

[4] "Fane": temple.

[5] "Gleam": throughout the novel, important events will be presaged by this kind of intermittent, unexpected, or mysterious light.

The first suggestion was that a pistol was discharged, and that the structure was on fire. She did not allow herself time to meditate a second thought, but rushed into the entry and knocked loudly at the door of her brother's chamber. My uncle had been previously roused by the noise, and instantly flew to the window. He also imagined what he saw to be fire. The loud and vehement shrieks which succeeded the first explosion, seemed to be an invocation of succour. The incident was inexplicable; but he could not fail to perceive the propriety of hastening to the spot. He was unbolting the door, when his sister's voice was heard on the outside conjuring him to come forth.

He obeyed the summons with all the speed in his power. He stopped not to question her, but hurried down stairs and across the meadow which lay between the house and the rock. The shrieks were no longer to be heard; but a blazing light was clearly discernible between the columns of the temple. Irregular steps, hewn in the stone, led him to the summit. On three sides, this edifice touched the very verge of the cliff. On the fourth side, which might be regarded as the front, there was an area of small extent, to which the rude staircase conducted you. My uncle speedily gained this spot. His strength was for a moment exhausted by his haste. He paused to rest himself. Meanwhile he bent the most vigilant attention towards the object before him.

Within the columns he beheld what he could no better describe, than by saying that it resembled a cloud impregnated with light. It had the brightness of flame, but was without its upward motion. It did not occupy the whole area, and rose but a few feet above the floor. No part of the building was on fire. This appearance was astonishing. He approached the temple. As he went forward the light retired, and, when he put his feet within the apartment, utterly vanished. The suddenness of this transition increased the darkness that succeeded in a tenfold degree. Fear and wonder rendered him powerless. An occurrence like this, in a place assigned to devotion, was adapted to intimidate the stoutest heart.

His wandering thoughts were recalled by the groans of one near him. His sight gradually recovered its power, and he was able to discern my father stretched on the floor. At that moment, my mother and servants arrived with a lanthorn,[6] and enabled my uncle to examine more closely this scene. My father, when he left the house, besides a loose upper vest and slippers, wore a shirt and drawers. Now he was naked, his skin throughout the greater part of his body was scorched and bruised. His right arm exhibited marks as of having been struck by some heavy body. His clothes had been removed, and it was not immediately perceived that they were reduced to ashes. His slippers and his hair were untouched.

He was removed to his chamber, and the requisite attention paid to his wounds, which gradually became more painful. A mortification speedily shewed itself in the arm, which had been most hurt. Soon after, the other wounded parts exhibited the like appearance.

Immediately subsequent to this disaster, my father seemed nearly in a state of insensibility. He was passive under every operation. He scarcely opened his eyes, and was

---

[6] "Lanthorn": lantern.

with difficulty prevailed upon to answer the questions that were put to him. By his imperfect account, it appeared, that while engaged in silent orisons,[7] with thoughts full of confusion and anxiety, a faint gleam suddenly shot athwart the apartment. His fancy immediately pictured to itself, a person bearing a lamp. It seemed to come from behind. He was in the act of turning to examine the visitant, when his right arm received a blow from a heavy club. At the same instant, a very bright spark was seen to light upon his clothes. In a moment, the whole was reduced to ashes. This was the sum of the information which he chose to give. There was somewhat in his manner that indicated an imperfect tale. My uncle was inclined to believe that half the truth had been suppressed.[8]

Meanwhile, the disease thus wonderfully generated, betrayed more terrible symptoms. Fever and delirium terminated in lethargic slumber, which, in the course of two hours, gave place to death. Yet not till insupportable exhalations and crawling putrefaction[9] had driven from his chamber and the house every one whom their duty did not detain.

Such was the end of my father. None surely was ever more mysterious. When we recollect his gloomy anticipations and unconquerable anxiety; the security from human malice which his character, the place, and the condition of the times, might be supposed to confer; the purity and cloudlessness of the atmosphere, which rendered it impossible that lightning was the cause; what are the conclusions that we must form?

The prelusive[10] gleam, the blow upon his arm, the fatal spark, the explosion heard so far, the fiery cloud that environed him, without detriment to the structure, though composed of combustible materials, the sudden vanishing of this cloud at my uncle's approach—what is the inference to be drawn from these facts? Their truth cannot be doubted. My uncle's testimony is peculiarly worthy of credit, because no man's temper is more sceptical, and his belief is unalterably attached to natural causes.

I was at this time a child of six years of age. The impressions that were then made upon me, can never be effaced. I was ill qualified to judge respecting what was then passing; but as I advanced in age, and became more fully acquainted with these facts, they oftener became the subject of my thoughts. Their resemblance to recent events revived them with new force in my memory, and made me more anxious to explain them. Was this the penalty of disobedience? this the stroke of a vindictive and invisible hand? Is it a fresh proof that the Divine Ruler interferes in human affairs, meditates

---

[7] "Orisons": prayers.

[8] An imperfect tale . . . suppressed": Clara's uncle, a surgeon and man of science, is skeptical about the elder Wieland's story. He suspects that some element of the incident has been kept secret and that another explanation of the event, for example that Wieland was attacked for an unexplained reason, is more likely.

[9] "Insupportable exhalations and crawling putrefaction": the smell of the father's rotting flesh drives away most observers. Eighteenth-century accounts of spontaneous combustion commonly emphasized horrible odors.

[10] "Prelusive": anticipatory, preliminary, introductory. That the gleam was "prelusive" means that the light appeared just before the event.

an end, selects, and commissions his agents, and enforces, by unequivocal sanctions, submission to his will? Or, was it merely the irregular expansion of the fluid that imparts warmth to our heart and our blood, caused by the fatigue of the preceding day, or flowing, by established laws, from the condition of his thoughts[11]?*

*A case, in its symptoms exactly parallel to this, is published in one of the Journals of Florence. See, likewise, similar cases reported by Messrs. Merille and Muraire, in the "Journal de Medicine," for February and May, 1783. The researches of Maffei and Fontana have thrown some light upon this subject.[12]

---

[11] "The condition of his thoughts?": Clara's line of questioning, following her uncle's suspicion "that half the truth had been suppressed," suggests that she doubts a supernatural explanation for the mysterious events. Instead, she uses contemporary knowledges to interpret her father's apparent spontaneous combustion as a consequence of imbalanced sensibility. As her father experienced extreme emotional and mental stress, his body may have suffered internal irritation that caused it to explode in flames. Accounts of the 1776 incident that Brown refers to in his footnote, concerning an Italian priest named Bertholi who died in a manner "exactly parallel to this," provide all of the clinical details cited in the elder Wieland's death, and assign strictly physical and nonsupernatural causes to the phenomenon. Bertholi was praying alone when his cries called people to witness a light flaming around his body. He claimed he had felt the blow of a cudgel on his right hand, and his right arm was almost entirely separated from his body. He died four days later after his body began to disintegrate with a horrible odor. This account of the Bertholi incident was reprinted and circulated widely (see the next note on Brown's source).

It is notable that Brown makes no mention of alcoholism, then the most common explanation for supposed incidents of spontaneous combustion. Most fictional examples of combustion well into the next century, for example in Herman Melville's *Redburn* (1849) or Charles Dickens's *Bleak House* (1852), connect the phenomenon to solitary alcoholics. William Dunlap, one of Brown's closest friends, related the case of thirty-year-old New Yorker Hannah Bradshaw, who was supposed to have combusted on January 1, 1771, after a night of New Year's drinking, in his *A History of New York for Schools* (1837). He describes Bradshaw as "a woman of large dimensions, masculine person, coarse manners, and notorious in the neighborhood for her boldness, habitual intemperance, and the vices allied to, and engendered by it" (I.168). The passage goes on to claim that there are no instances of temperate people spontaneously combusting. Common opinion in this period also held that spontaneous combustion was more likely among older women then among men.

[12] "This subject": Brown's note apparently draws this series of authorities from the widely circulated account: "Letter respecting an Italian priest, killed by an electric commotion, the cause of which resided in his own body." The initial printing, which claims to be drawn from "one of the journals of Florence," is probably the version in the London *Literary Magazine and British Review* IV (May 1790), 336–39; this printing is referenced and quoted in the review of *Wieland* that appeared in the New York *Monthly Magazine* in January 1800, possibly written by Brown's friend William Dunlap. The same account was reprinted in the U.S., in the Philadelphia *American Museum, or, Universal Magazine* (April 1792), 11–14.

The names and accounts cited in Brown's note were discussed and quoted in English-language discussions of spontaneous combustion well into the nineteenth century. In "Sur un effet singulier de la combustion," Merille and Muraire give accounts of separate incidents of combustion from 1779 and 1782 in the Parisian *Journal de Médecine* LIX (February and May 1783), 140 and 440. Francesco Scipione, the Marquis of Maffei (1675–1755) wrote about a 1731 incident in Italy that was, likewise, cited and reproduced widely. Felice Fontana (1730–1805) was a leading naturalist and physiologist; the article Brown uses cites his *Ricerche filosofiche sopra la fisica animale* [*Philosophical Inquiries on Animal Physics*] (1775).

Chapter III

THE shock which this disastrous occurrence occasioned to my mother, was the foundation of a disease which carried her, in a few months, to the grave. My brother[1] and myself were children at this time, and were now reduced to the condition of orphans. The property which our parents left was by no means inconsiderable. It was entrusted to faithful hands, till we should arrive at a suitable age. Meanwhile, our education was assigned to a maiden aunt who resided in the city, and whose tenderness made us in a short time cease to regret that we had lost a mother.

The years that succeeded were tranquil and happy. Our lives were molested by few of those cares that are incident to childhood. By accident more than design, the indulgence and yielding temper of our aunt was mingled with resolution and stedfastness. She seldom deviated into either extreme of rigour or lenity. Our social pleasures were subject to no unreasonable restraints. We were instructed in most branches of useful knowledge, and were saved from the corruption and tyranny of colleges and boarding-schools.

Our companions were chiefly selected from the children of our neighbours. Between one of these and my brother, there quickly grew the most affectionate intimacy. Her name was Catharine Pleyel.[2] She was rich, beautiful, and contrived to blend the most bewitching softness with the most exuberant vivacity. The tie by which my brother and she were united, seemed to add force to the love which I bore her, and which was amply returned. Between her and myself there was every circumstance tending to produce and foster friendship. Our sex and age were the same. We lived within sight of each other's abode. Our tempers were remarkably congenial, and the superintendants of our education not only prescribed to us the same pursuits, but allowed us to cultivate them together.

---

[1] "My brother": Clara refers to her brother Theodore only as "my brother" or by the patronym "Wieland," emphasizing his role as family patriarch after their father's death. She never provides a first name for any of the three generations of male Wielands she discusses, presenting them only as representatives of a paternal line: "the house and name of Wieland," as she will put it at the moment of crisis in Chapter 16 (117). The first name Theodore appears only once in the novel, in the court papers cited at the beginning of Chapter 19. For Theodore's name, see note 19.1.

[2] "Pleyel": the name Brown selects for Catharine and her brother Henry evokes that of Ignaz Pleyel (1757–1831), a leading composer of the classical period. As he did with the Wielands, Brown uses the name of a widely known figure associated with the cultural movements of the Enlightenment and revolutionary era. Ignaz Pleyel was born and came to prominence in Austria, where he was first a student and later a friendly rival of Josef Haydn. By the 1790s and 1800s, after Haydn's retirement, Pleyel was perhaps the best-known composer in Europe. According to some sources, Pleyel's music was performed in North America in these years more frequently than that of any other composer. Brown and his friends, for example, were likely familiar with Pleyel's music for stage versions of the popular abolitionist drama *Inkle and Yarico*. After 1795, Pleyel established himself in Paris, where he became an important music publisher, impresario, and founder of the piano company that still bears his name at the beginning of the twenty-first century. The Salle Pleyel, an important recital hall in present-day Paris, also bears his name.

Every day added strength to the triple bonds that united us. We gradually withdrew ourselves from the society of others, and found every moment irksome that was not devoted to each other. My brother's advance in age made no change in our situation. It was determined that his profession should be agriculture. His fortune exempted him from the necessity of personal labour.[3] The task to be performed by him was nothing more than superintendance. The skill that was demanded by this was merely theoretical, and was furnished by casual inspection, or by closet study. The attention that was paid to this subject did not seclude him for any long time from us, on whom time had no other effect than to augment our impatience in the absence of each other and of him. Our tasks, our walks, our music, were seldom performed but in each other's company.

It was easy to see that Catharine and my brother were born for each other. The passion which they mutually entertained quickly broke those bounds which extreme youth had set to it; confessions were made or extorted, and their union was postponed only till my brother had passed his minority.[4] The previous lapse of two years was constantly and usefully employed.

O my brother! But the task I have set myself let me perform with steadiness. The felicity of that period was marred by no gloomy anticipations. The future, like the present, was serene. Time was supposed to have only new delights in store. I mean not to dwell on previous incidents longer than is necessary to illustrate or explain the great events that have since happened. The nuptial day at length arrived. My brother took possession of the house in which he was born, and here the long protracted marriage was solemnized.

My father's property was equally divided between us.[5] A neat dwelling, situated on the bank of the river, three quarters of a mile from my brother's, was now occupied by me. These domains were called, from the name of the first possessor, Mettingen.

---

[3] "Agriculture . . . personal labour": Clara's brother Theodore acts as a leisured, supervisorial farmer in roughly the same sense that George Washington, John Adams, or Thomas Jefferson oversaw agricultural production on their estates.

[4] "Minority": age before legal adulthood.

[5] "My father's property was equally divided between us": traditionally, property descended first to the eldest son (following laws of primogeniture, the right of inheritance by the first-born male descendent, which Clara will mention at the beginning of Chapter 5; see note 5.2). Under the laws of "coverture," part of Anglo-American common law in this period, women had no legal personhood or formal independence. A woman's legal identity (and consequently her right to own property, sign contracts, and so on) was absorbed into or "covered" by that of her father, husband, or other male guardian. Although it abolished primogeniture, the American Revolution did not change these laws concerning women's subordination.

The relatively equitable division of the Wieland patrimony between the siblings, by contrast, implies that Clara has a potential for freedom from the period's customary restrictions on women's behavior and status. As the novel develops, Clara experiences tremendous conflicts between, on the one hand, traditionalized restrictions on female behavior and her accustomed deference toward patriarchal authority and, on the other, her "modern" capacity for more independent thinking and action, and equal rights with men.

I can scarcely account for my refusing to take up my abode with him, unless it were from a disposition to be an economist of pleasure. Self-denial, seasonably exercised, is one means of enhancing our gratifications. I was, beside, desirous of administering a fund, and regulating an household, of my own. The short distance allowed us to exchange visits as often as we pleased. The walk from one mansion to the other was no undelightful prelude to our interviews. I was sometimes their visitant, and they, as frequently, were my guests.

Our education had been modelled by no religious standard. We were left to the guidance of our own understanding, and the casual impressions which society might make upon us. My friend's temper, as well as my own, exempted us from much anxiety on this account. It must not be supposed that we were without religion, but with us it was the product of lively feelings, excited by reflection on our own happiness, and by the grandeur of external nature. We sought not a basis for our faith, in the weighing of proofs, and the dissection of creeds.[6] Our devotion was a mixed and casual sentiment, seldom verbally expressed, or solicitously sought, or carefully retained. In the midst of present enjoyment, no thought was bestowed on the future. As a consolation in calamity religion is dear.[7] But calamity was yet at a distance, and its only tendency was to heighten enjoyments which needed not this addition to satisfy every craving.

My brother's situation was somewhat different. His deportment was grave, considerate, and thoughtful. I will not say whether he was indebted to sublimer views for this disposition. Human life, in his opinion, was made up of changeable elements, and the principles of duty were not easily unfolded. The future, either as anterior, or subsequent to death, was a scene that required some preparation and provision to be made for it. These positions we could not deny, but what distinguished him was a propensity to ruminate on these truths. The images that visited us were blithsome and gay, but those with which he was most familiar were of an opposite hue. They did not generate affliction and fear, but they diffused over his behaviour a certain air of forethought and sobriety. The principal effect of this temper was visible in his features and tones. These, in general, bespoke a sort of thrilling melancholy.[8] I scarcely ever knew him to laugh. He never accompanied the lawless mirth of his companions with more than a smile, but his conduct was the same as ours.

---

[6] "The product of lively feelings, excited by reflection on our own happiness, and by the grandeur of external nature . . . not . . . in the weighing of proofs, and the dissection of creeds": another passage in which Clara displays a Rousseauistic belief that she can guide her actions by the spontaneous effects of associative sympathy and sensibility, rather than rational investigation. Throughout the tale, as Clara experiences extreme anxiety and violent emotional shocks, she will repeatedly try to slow or block her sensations of nature by fainting or covering her eyes.

[7] "In calamity religion is dear": Clara's remarks suggest that theistic beliefs may be invoked as an emotional crutch in times of crisis, but have little meaning beyond creating a momentary and somewhat illusory sense of order and relief.

[8] "Somewhat different . . . thrilling melancholy": unlike Clara, but like his father the elder Wieland, Theodore's temperament is religious, morose, and preoccupied with death. Yet in contrast to his father, and more in keeping with the "enlightened" times in which he lives, his mind is "enriched by science and embellished with literature" (as Clara notes two paragraphs further on).

He partook of our occupations and amusements with a zeal not less than ours, but of a different kind. The diversity in our temper was never the parent of discord, and was scarcely a topic of regret. The scene was variegated, but not tarnished or disordered by it. It hindered the element in which we moved from stagnating. Some agitation and concussion is requisite to the due exercise of human understanding. In his studies, he pursued an austerer and more arduous path. He was much conversant with the history of religious opinions, and took pains to ascertain their validity. He deemed it indispensable to examine the ground of his belief, to settle the relation between motives and actions, the criterion of merit, and the kinds and properties of evidence.

There was an obvious resemblance between him and my father, in their conceptions of the importance of certain topics, and in the light in which the vicissitudes of human life were accustomed to be viewed. Their characters were similar, but the mind of the son was enriched by science, and embellished with literature.

The temple was no longer assigned to its ancient use. From an Italian adventurer, who erroneously imagined that he could find employment for his skill, and sale for his sculptures in America, my brother had purchased a bust of Cicero. He professed to have copied this piece from an antique dug up with his own hands in the environs of Modena.[9] Of the truth of his assertions we were not qualified to judge; but the marble was pure and polished, and we were contented to admire the performance, without waiting for the sanction of connoisseurs. We hired the same artist to hew a suitable pedestal from a neighbouring quarry. This was placed in the temple, and the bust rested upon it. Opposite to this was a harpsichord, sheltered by a temporary roof from the weather. This was the place of resort in the evenings of summer. Here we sung, and talked, and read, and occasionally banqueted. Every joyous and tender scene most dear to my memory, is connected with this edifice. Here the performances of our musical and poetical ancestor were rehearsed. Here my brother's children received the rudiments of their education; here a thousand conversations, pregnant with delight and improvement, took place; and here the social affections were accustomed to expand, and the tear of delicious sympathy to be shed.

My brother was an indefatigable student. The authors whom he read were numerous, but the chief object of his veneration was Cicero.[10] He was never tired of conning

---

[9] "Modena": an Italian city known for its marble quarries.

[10] "The chief object of his veneration was Cicero": as a mark of his cultivation and learning, Theodore idealizes Marcus Tullius Cicero (106–43 B.C.E.), the Roman orator and statesman who figured centrally in political struggles over the status of the Roman Republic during Julius Caesar's dictatorship and the civil wars that led to the Republic's end. Cicero's writings were an important focal point in elite eighteenth-century education (when rhetoric was still an essential part of training for political leadership) and debates about Cicero's character functioned as coded political arguments throughout the period. By installing a bust of Cicero on the temple mount, Wieland signals his rejection of his father's extreme Christianity in favor of a pagan icon of republican enlightenment. Yet the somewhat ironic manner in which Brown emphasizes Theodore's Cicero-worship (Clara jokes about "the divinity of Cicero" in this chapter's final sentence) seems to invoke the period's cultural and ideological debates.

By having Theodore idealize Cicero, literally putting him on a pedestal, Brown seems to link him with the type of Federalist or Augustan, conservative idealization of Cicero that was common

and rehearsing his productions. To understand them was not sufficient. He was anxious to discover the gestures and cadences with which they ought to be delivered. He was very scrupulous in selecting a true scheme of pronunciation for the Latin tongue, and in adapting it to the words of his darling writer. His favorite occupation consisted in embellishing his rhetoric with all the proprieties of gesticulation and utterance.

Not contented with this, he was diligent in settling and restoring the purity of the text. For this end, he collected all the editions and commentaries that could be procured, and employed months of severe study in exploring and comparing them. He never betrayed more satisfaction than when he made a discovery of this kind.

It was not till the addition of Henry Pleyel, my friend's only brother, to our society, that his passion for Roman eloquence was countenanced and fostered by a sympathy of tastes. This young man had been some years in Europe. We had separated at a very early age, and he was now returned to spend the remainder of his days among us.

Our circle was greatly enlivened by the accession of a new member. His conversation abounded with novelty. His gaiety was almost boisterous, but was capable of yielding to a grave deportment, when the occasion required it. His discernment was acute, but he was prone to view every object merely as supplying materials for mirth. His conceptions were ardent but ludicrous,[11] and his memory, aided, as he honestly acknowledged, by his invention, was an inexhaustible fund of entertainment.

His residence was at the same distance below the city as ours was above,[12] but there seldom passed a day without our being favoured with a visit. My brother and he were endowed with the same attachment to the Latin writers; and Pleyel was not behind his friend in his knowledge of the history and metaphysics of religion. Their creeds, however, were in many respects opposite. Where one discovered only confirmations of his faith, the other could find nothing but reasons for doubt. Moral necessity, and calvinistic inspiration, were the props on which my brother thought proper to repose. Pleyel was the champion of intellectual liberty,[13] and rejected all guidance but that of his reason. Their discussions were frequent, but, being managed with candour as well as with skill, they were always listened to by us with avidity and benefit.

---

among the U.S. elite during the 1790s. John Adams, for example, president of the U.S. and leader of the conservative, Anglophile Federalist party when *Wieland* appeared in 1798, famously regarded Cicero as the highest example of civic and patrician values. This kind of "Tory" presentation of Roman history was disputed throughout the century, however, and Brown echoes these debates with critical treatments of Cicero-worship in this novel and other writings. For more on Brown's Cicero writings and their relation to the period's cultural politics, see Related Texts in this volume.

[11] "Ludicrous": playful, witty, humorous.

[12] "The same distance below the city as ours was above": in Chapter 5, Clara will explain that Pleyel's land is near the point where the Schuylkill River joins the Delaware, about 2.5 miles south of central Philadelphia (see note 5.13), suggesting that Mettingen is near the area where the Wissahickon Creek meets the Schuylkill, about 2.5 miles north of Philadelphia's center.

[13] "Intellectual liberty": unlike Clara, who relies on reflexive, associative sympathy, or Theodore, who believes in supernatural guidance ("calvinistic inspiration"), Henry Pleyel champions skeptical Enlightenment rationality as his moral compass. Each of these ways of thinking will be put to the test in Mettingen.

Pleyel, like his new friends, was fond of music and poetry. Henceforth our concerts consisted of two violins, an harpsichord, and three voices. We were frequently reminded how much happiness depends upon society. This new friend, though, before his arrival, we were sensible of no vacuity, could not now be spared. His departure would occasion a void which nothing could fill, and which would produce insupportable regret. Even my brother, though his opinions were hourly assailed, and even the divinity of Cicero contested, was captivated with his friend, and laid aside some part of his ancient gravity at Pleyel's approach.

Chapter IV

SIX years of uninterrupted happiness had rolled away, since my brother's marriage. The sound of war had been heard, but it was at such a distance as to enhance our enjoyment by affording objects of comparison. The Indians were repulsed on the one side, and Canada was conquered[1] on the other. Revolutions and battles, however calamitous to those who occupied the scene, contributed in some sort to our happiness, by agitating our minds with curiosity, and furnishing causes of patriotic exultation. Four children, three of whom were of an age to compensate, by their personal and mental progress, the cares of which they had been, at a more helpless age, the objects, exercised my brother's tenderness. The fourth was a charming babe that promised to display the image of her mother, and enjoyed perfect health. To these were added a sweet girl fourteen years old,[2] who was loved by all of us, with an affection more than parental.

Her mother's story was a mournful one. She had come hither from England when this child was an infant, alone, without friends, and without money. She appeared to have embarked in a hasty and clandestine manner. She passed three years of solitude and anguish under my aunt's protection, and died a martyr to woe; the source of which she could, by no importunities, be prevailed upon to unfold. Her education and manners bespoke her to be of no mean birth. Her last moments were rendered serene,[3] by the assurances she received from my aunt, that her daughter should experience the same protection that had been extended to herself.

On my brother's marriage, it was agreed that she should make a part of his family. I cannot do justice to the attractions of this girl. Perhaps the tenderness she excited might partly originate in her personal resemblance to her mother, whose character and misfortunes were still fresh in our remembrance. She was habitually pensive, and this circumstance tended to remind the spectator of her friendless condition; and yet that epithet was surely misapplied in this case. This being was cherished by those with whom she now resided, with unspeakable fondness. Every exertion was made to enlarge and improve her mind. Her safety was the object of a solicitude that almost exceeded the bounds of discretion. Our affection indeed could scarcely transcend

---

[1] "Sound of war . . . Indians . . . Canada was conquered": the French and Indian War, the North American theater of the Seven Years War (1756–1763), has come to an end. British imperial forces have conquered all of New France, which covered the Mississippi valley, Great Lakes region, and eastern Canada. This historical reference point helps situates the main sequence of the narrative in the late 1760s.

[2] "A sweet girl fourteen years old": this is Louisa Conway, whose story develops into a complex seduction subplot involving the fate of Louisa's mother. Clara will return to the story of Louisa's family in her narrative coda in Chapter 27 (see note 27.5).

[3] "My aunt's protection . . . died a martyr to woe . . . rendered serene": "my aunt" is Mrs. Baynton, a family friend, first named two paragraphs further on (see next note). This explanation about the fate of Louisa Conway's mother will be an important detail in Chapter 14, when a newspaper article circulates an accusation that the character Carwin killed a Conway female who may be this woman. See note 14.4.

her merits. She never met my eye, or occurred to my reflections, without exciting a kind of enthusiasm. Her softness, her intelligence, her equanimity, never shall I see surpassed. I have often shed tears of pleasure at her approach, and pressed her to my bosom in an agony of fondness.

While every day was adding to the charms of her person, and the stores of her mind, there occurred an event which threatened to deprive us of her. An officer of some rank, who had been disabled by a wound at Quebec, had employed himself, since the ratification of peace, in travelling through the colonies. He remained a considerable period at Philadelphia, but was at last preparing for his departure. No one had been more frequently honoured with his visits than Mrs. Baynton,[4] a worthy lady with whom our family were intimate. He went to her house with a view to perform a farewell visit, and was on the point of taking his leave, when I and my young friend entered the apartment. It is impossible to describe the emotions of the stranger, when he fixed his eyes upon my companion. He was motionless with surprise. He was unable to conceal his feelings, but sat silently gazing at the spectacle before him. At length he turned to Mrs. Baynton, and more by his looks and gestures than by words, besought her for an explanation of the scene. He seized the hand of the girl, who, in her turn, was surprised by his behaviour, and drawing her forward, said in an eager and faultering tone, Who is she? whence does she come? what is her name?

The answers that were given only increased the confusion of his thoughts. He was successively told, that she was the daughter of one whose name was Louisa Conway, who arrived among us at such a time, who seduously concealed her parentage, and the motives of her flight, whose incurable griefs had finally destroyed her, and who had left this child under the protection of her friends. Having heard the tale, he melted into tears, eagerly clasped the young lady in his arms, and called himself her father. When the tumults excited in his breast by this unlooked-for meeting were somewhat subsided, he gratified our curiosity by relating the following incidents.

"Miss Conway was the only daughter of a banker in London, who discharged towards her every duty of an affectionate father. He had chanced to fall into her company, had been subdued by her attractions, had tendered her his hand, and been joyfully accepted both by parent and child. His wife had given him every proof of the fondest attachment. Her father, who possessed immense wealth, treated him with distinguished respect, liberally supplied his wants, and had made one condition of his consent to their union, a resolution to take up their abode with him.

"They had passed three years of conjugal felicity, which had been augmented by the birth of this child, when his professional duty called him into Germany. It was

---

[4] "Mrs. Baynton": when Clara stops in the city briefly in Chapter 12, on her way to find Pleyel, she will take refuge with this matron and family friend. Described here as "my aunt," in Chapter 15 her relationship to Clara will be "truly maternal." Although there is no clear reference to any historically attested figure, John Baynton (1726–1773) was a wealthy Philadelphia merchant exporter of this period, whose daughter Mary Baynton (1749–1825) was married in 1763 to his younger business partner George Morgan (1743–1810), a successful land speculator, gentleman farmer, and Indian trader for the Baynton firm in western Pennsylvania and along the upper Ohio River.

not without an arduous struggle, that she was persuaded to relinquish the design of accompanying him through all the toils and perils of war. No parting was ever more distressful. They strove to alleviate, by frequent letters, the evils of their lot. Those of his wife, breathed nothing but anxiety for his safety, and impatience of his absence. At length, a new arrangement was made, and he was obliged to repair from Westphalia to Canada.[5] One advantage attended this change. It afforded him an opportunity of meeting his family. His wife anticipated this interview, with no less rapture than himself. He hurried to London, and the moment he alighted from the stage-coach, ran with all speed to Mr. Conway's house.

"It was an house of mourning. His father was overwhelmed with grief, and incapable of answering his inquiries. The servants, sorrowful and mute, were equally refractory. He explored the house, and called on the names of his wife and daughter, but his summons was fruitless. At length, this new disaster was explained. Two days before his arrival, his wife's chamber was found empty. No search, however diligent and anxious, could trace her steps. No cause could be assigned for her disappearance. The mother and child had fled away together.

"New exertions were made, her chamber and cabinets were ransacked, but no vestige was found serving to inform them as to the motives of her flight whether it had been voluntary or otherwise, and in what corner of the kingdom or of the world she was concealed. Who shall describe the sorrow and amazement of the husband? His restlessness, his vicissitudes of hope and fear, and his ultimate despair? His duty called him to America. He had been in this city, and had frequently passed the door of the house in which his wife, at that moment, resided. Her father had not remitted his exertions to elucidate this painful mystery, but they had failed. This disappointment hastened his death; in consequence of which, Louisa's father became possessor of his immense property."

This tale was a copious theme of speculation. A thousand questions were started and discussed in our domestic circle, respecting the motives that influenced Mrs. Stuart[6] to abandon her country. It did not appear that her proceeding was involuntary. We recalled and reviewed every particular that had fallen under our own observation. By none of these were we furnished with a clue. Her conduct, after the most rigorous scrutiny, still remained an impenetrable secret. On a nearer view, Major Stuart proved himself a man of most amiable character. His attachment to Louisa appeared hourly to increase. She was no stranger to the sentiments suitable to her new

---

[5] "Westphalia to Canada": details here and in Chapter 27 suggest that Major Stuart, Louisa Conway's father, was involved in events leading to the Battle of Minden in the German region of Westphalia (August 1, 1759), where British-Prussian forces decisively defeated the French and their Saxon allies. Stuart is then transferred to another theater in the ongoing Seven Years War, and wounded in the Battle of Quebec (September 13, 1759; Clara noted this event three paragraphs earlier), another decisive victory for the British. Stuart's name suggests a Scottish origin, while his wife's maiden name (Conway) suggests Irish ethnicity on her side of their family.

[6] "Mrs. Stuart": Louisa Conway's mother. Louisa is known by her mother's maiden name, which the mother has presumably used to disguise her identity.

character. She could not but readily embrace the scheme which was proposed to her, to return with her father to England. This scheme his regard for her induced him, however, to postpone. Some time was necessary to prepare her for so great a change and enable her to think without agony of her separation from us.

I was not without hopes of prevailing on her father entirely to relinquish this unwelcome design. Meanwhile, he pursued his travels through the southern colonies, and his daughter continued with us. Louisa and my brother frequently received letters from him, which indicated a mind of no common order. They were filled with amusing details, and profound reflections. While here, he often partook of our evening conversations at the temple; and since his departure, his correspondence had frequently supplied us with topics of discourse.

One afternoon in May, the blandness of the air, and brightness of the verdure, induced us to assemble, earlier than usual, in the temple. We females were busy at the needle, while my brother and Pleyel were bandying quotations and syllogisms. The point discussed was the merit of the oration for Cluentius, as descriptive, first, of the genius of the speaker; and, secondly, of the manners of the times. Pleyel laboured to extenuate both these species of merit, and tasked his ingenuity, to shew that the orator had embraced a bad cause; or, at least, a doubtful one. He urged, that to rely on the exaggerations of an advocate, or to make the picture of a single family a model from which to sketch the condition of a nation, was absurd.[7] The controversy

---

[7] "Oration for Cluentius . . . absurd": this brief disagreement about the merits and implications of Cicero's forensic oration *Pro Cluentio* (*In Favor of Cluentius*; 66 B.C.E.) seems to reinforce the critical implications of Clara's earlier remarks on Theodore's Cicero-worship (see note 3.10). Since the case describes corrupt actions, Theodore and Pleyel disagree as to what the oration implies about Cicero, and as to whether the character of a single group can be taken to illustrate that of an entire society. Then as now, *Pro Cluentio* is a much-studied example of rhetoric and legal argumentation. Hugh Blair's *Lectures on Rhetoric and Belles Lettres* (1783), for example, the most influential rhetorical manual of Brown's generation, examines it as a preeminent example of "Eloquence of the Bar" (Chapter 27). It is the longest extant speech by Cicero, and is notable for its complex plot and tableau of social corruption, which implicitly involves Cicero himself since he boasted of misleading the jury. Like Brown's novel, the oration dramatizes intrafamily violence among rural elites and challenges the reader with an intentionally demanding plot.

The oration was Cicero's legal defense of Cluentius, accused by his mother Sassia of poisoning his stepfather, her third husband. Cicero's defense avoids the question of Cluentius' guilt and focuses instead on Sassia's low morals, starting with her decision to force her daughter to divorce a man so that she could take him as her second husband. Emphasizing family murder, bribery, poisoning, and corruption, the oration paints a very dark picture of Roman society and also, for commentators like Blair, provides evidence of Cicero's own vanity and other perceived character flaws, since in arguing the case he knowingly defended a guilty party and famously boasted of his success in gaining an acquittal by "throwing dust in the jury's eyes." If Theodore sees this speech as evidence of the "genius of the speaker . . . and manner of the times," this still leaves a great deal open to debate, for, in the terms of Enlightenment Cicero debates, the case shows the orator acting viciously, affirming reputational self-interest rather than seeking justice according to republican principles of disinterested virtue and the common good. Pleyel takes a skeptical position against Theodore's possibly naive celebration of Cicero and against the idea that a single group's behavior can be generalized to evaluate an entire society.

was suddenly diverted into a new channel, by a misquotation. Pleyel accused his companion of saying "*polliceatur*" when he should have said "*polliceretur*."[8] Nothing would decide the contest, but an appeal to the volume. My brother was returning to the house for this purpose, when a servant met him with a letter from Major Stuart. He immediately returned to read it in our company.

Besides affectionate compliments to us, and paternal benedictions on Louisa, his letter contained a description of a waterfall on the Monongahela.[9] A sudden gust of rain falling, we were compelled to remove to the house. The storm passed away, and a radiant moon-light succeeded. There was no motion to resume our seats in the temple. We therefore remained where we were, and engaged in sprightly conversation. The letter lately received naturally suggested the topic. A parallel was drawn between the cataract there described, and one which Pleyel had discovered among the Alps of Glarus.[10] In the state of the former, some particular was mentioned, the truth of which was questionable. To settle the dispute which thence arose, it was proposed to have recourse to the letter. My brother searched for it in his pocket. It was no where to be found. At length, he remembered to have left it in the temple, and he determined to go in search of it. His wife, Pleyel, Louisa, and myself, remained where we were.

In a few minutes he returned. I was somewhat interested in the dispute, and was therefore impatient for his return; yet, as I heard him ascending the stairs, I could not but remark, that he had executed his intention with remarkable dispatch. My eyes were fixed upon him on his entrance. Methought he brought with him looks considerably different from those with which he departed. Wonder, and a slight portion of anxiety were mingled in them. His eyes seemed to be in search of some object.

---

[8] "*Polliceatur . . . polliceretur*": two forms of the Latin verb *polliceor*, to promise. These are, respectively, the present and the imperfect tenses of the third person singular subjunctive form. The point of disagreement, in other words, is a grammatical detail concerning the tense of the verb. The first form (*polliceatur*), in fact, is the one that occurs in the text of *Pro Cluentio* 71, in a passage that jokes and puns about the way Cluentius' opponent bribed judges. The verb occurs twice in that passage, first as *polliceatur* and subsequently as *pollicetur* (the present indicative). The form suggested by Pleyel (*polliceretur*; the imperfect subjunctive) makes little sense in the passage and, to a knowledgeable Latinist, would suggest that Pleyel does not know Latin well, or as well as Theodore. In Theodore and Henry's discussion, larger sociopolitical and ethical issues seem to be sidetracked by a point of grammatical detail.

[9] "Monongahela": a river that runs through western Pennsylvania to meet the Alleghany River at Pittsburgh, where they form the Ohio. The Monongahela valley was the site of a major British defeat in the Seven Years War. In a battle that is referenced as an important element of historical context for Brown's novel *Edgar Huntly* (1799), the retreating army of British General Braddock was encircled and routed by French and Native American forces, suffering tremendous casualties. A professional soldier, Stuart may be combining natural observation with war nostalgia.

[10] "Alps of Glarus": in central Switzerland, frequently visited by wealthy travellers on the "Grand Tour," a journey that completed upper-class education in the early-modern Atlantic world and developed sensibility through tourism. Pleyel's knowledgeable comparison between American and European landscapes is another detail underscoring the elite experience and cosmopolitan perspective of the Wieland-Pleyel circle.

They passed quickly from one person to another, till they rested on his wife. She was seated in a careless attitude on the sofa, in the same spot as before. She had the same muslin[11] in her hand, by which her attention was chiefly engrossed.

The moment he saw her, his perplexity visibly increased. He quietly seated himself, and fixing his eyes on the floor, appeared to be absorbed in meditation. These singularities suspended the inquiry which I was preparing to make respecting the letter. In a short time, the company relinquished the subject which engaged them, and directed their attention to Wieland. They thought that he only waited for a pause in the discourse, to produce the letter. The pause was uninterrupted by him. At length Pleyel said, "Well, I suppose you have found the letter."

"No," said he, without any abatement of his gravity, and looking stedfastly at his wife, "I did not mount the hill."—"Why not?"—"Catharine, have you not moved from that spot since I left the room?"—She was affected with the solemnity of his manner, and laying down her work, answered in a tone of surprise, "No; Why do you ask that question?"—His eyes were again fixed upon the floor, and he did not immediately answer. At length, he said, looking round upon us, "Is it true that Catharine did not follow me to the hill? That she did not just now enter the room?"—We assured him, with one voice, that she had not been absent for a moment, and inquired into the motive of his questions.

"Your assurances," said he, "are solemn and unanimous; and yet I must deny credit to your assertions, or disbelieve the testimony of my senses, which informed me, when I was half way up the hill, that Catharine was at the bottom."

We were confounded at this declaration, Pleyel rallied[12] him with great levity on his behaviour. He listened to his friend with calmness, but without any relaxation of features.

"One thing," said he with emphasis, "is true; either I heard my wife's voice at the bottom of the hill, or I do not hear your voice at present."

"Truly," returned Pleyel, "it is a sad dilemma to which you have reduced yourself. Certain it is, if our eyes can give us certainty, that your wife has been sitting in that spot during every moment of your absence. You have heard her voice, you say, upon the hill. In general, her voice, like her temper, is all softness. To be heard across the room, she is obliged to exert herself. While you were gone, if I mistake not, she did not utter a word. Clara and I had all the talk to ourselves. Still it may be that she held a whispering conference with you on the hill; but tell us the particulars."

"The conference," said he, "was short; and far from being carried on in a whisper. You know with what intention I left the house. Half way to the rock, the moon was for a moment hidden from us by a cloud. I never knew the air to be more bland and more calm. In this interval I glanced at the temple, and thought I saw a glimmering between the columns. It was so faint, that it would not perhaps have been visible, if

---

[11] "Muslin": a light cotton fabric. Catharine is occupied with women's conventional work, sewing or embroidery.

[12] "Rallied": teased.

the moon had not been shrowded. I looked again, but saw nothing. I never visit this building alone, or at night, without being reminded of the fate of my father. There was nothing wonderful in this appearance; yet it suggested something more than mere solitude and darkness in the same place would have done.

"I kept on my way. The images that haunted me were solemn; and I entertained an imperfect curiosity, but no fear, as to the nature of this object. I had ascended the hill little more than half way, when a voice called me from behind. The accents were clear, distinct, powerful, and were uttered, as I fully believed, by my wife. Her voice is not commonly so loud. She has seldom occasion to exert it, but, nevertheless, I have sometimes heard her call with force and eagerness. If my ear was not deceived, it was her voice which I heard.

"'Stop, go no further. There is danger in your path.' The suddenness and unexpectedness of this warning, the tone of alarm with which it was given, and, above all, the persuasion that it was my wife who spoke, were enough to disconcert and make me pause. I turned and listened to assure myself that I was not mistaken. The deepest silence succeeded. At length, I spoke in my turn. 'Who calls? is it you, Catharine?' I stopped and presently received an answer. 'Yes, it is I; go not up; return instantly; you are wanted at the house.' Still the voice was Catharine's, and still it proceeded from the foot of the stairs.

"What could I do? The warning was mysterious. To be uttered by Catharine at a place, and on an occasion like these, enhanced the mystery. I could do nothing but obey. Accordingly, I trod back my steps, expecting that she waited for me at the bottom of the hill. When I reached the bottom, no one was visible. The moon-light was once more universal and brilliant, and yet, as far as I could see no human or moving figure was discernable. If she had returned to the house, she must have used wonderous expedition to have passed already beyond the reach of my eye. I exerted my voice, but in vain. To my repeated exclamations, no answer was returned.

"Ruminating on these incidents, I returned hither. There was no room to doubt that I had heard my wife's voice; attending incidents were not easily explained; but you now assure me that nothing extraordinary has happened to urge my return, and that my wife has not moved from her seat."

Such was my brother's narrative. It was heard by us with different emotions. Pleyel did not scruple to regard the whole as a deception of the senses. Perhaps a voice had been heard; but Wieland's imagination had misled him in supposing a resemblance to that of his wife, and giving such a signification to the sounds. According to his custom he spoke what he thought. Sometimes, he made it the theme of grave discussion, but more frequently treated it with ridicule. He did not believe that sober reasoning would convince his friend, and gaiety, he thought, was useful to take away the solemnities which, in a mind like Wieland's, an accident of this kind was calculated to produce.

Pleyel proposed to go in search of the letter. He went and speedily returned, bearing it in his hand. He had found it open on the pedestal; and neither voice nor visage had risen to impede his design.

Catharine was endowed with an uncommon portion of good sense; but her mind was accessible, on this quarter, to wonder and panic. That her voice should be thus inexplicably and unwarrantably assumed, was a source of no small disquietude. She admitted the plausibility of the arguments by which Pleyel endeavoured to prove, that this was no more than an auricular[13] deception; but this conviction was sure to be shaken, when she turned her eyes upon her husband, and perceived that Pleyel's logic was far from having produced the same effect upon him.

As to myself, my attention was engaged by this occurrence. I could not fail to perceive a shadowy resemblance between it and my father's death. On the latter event, I had frequently reflected; my reflections never conducted me to certainty, but the doubts that existed were not of a tormenting kind. I could not deny that the event was miraculous, and yet I was invincibly averse to that method of solution. My wonder was excited by the inscrutableness of the cause, but my wonder was unmixed with sorrow or fear. It begat in me a thrilling, and not unpleasing solemnity. Similar to these were the sensations produced by the recent adventure.

But its effect upon my brother's imagination was of chief moment. All that was desirable was, that it should be regarded by him with indifference. The worst effect that could flow, was nor indeed very formidable. Yet I could not bear to think that his senses should be the victims of such delusion. It argued a diseased condition of his frame, which might show itself hereafter in more dangerous symptoms. The will is the tool of the understanding, which must fashion its conclusions on the notices of sense. If the senses be depraved, it is impossible to calculate the evils that may flow from the consequent deductions of the understanding.[14]

I said, this man is of an ardent and melancholy character. Those ideas which, in others, are casual or obscure, which are entertained in moments of abstraction and solitude, and easily escape when the scene is changed, have obtained an immoveable hold upon his mind. The conclusions which long habit has rendered familiar, and, in some sort, palpable to his intellect, are drawn from the deepest sources. All his actions and practical sentiments are linked with long and abstruse deductions from the system of divine government and the laws of our intellectual constitution. He is, in some respects, an enthusiast, but is fortified in his belief by innumerable arguments and subtilties.

His father's death was always regarded by him as flowing from a direct and supernatural decree. It visited his meditations oftener than it did mine. The traces which it left were more gloomy and permanent. This new incident had a visible effect in augmenting his gravity. He was less disposed than formerly to converse and reading. When we sifted his thoughts, they were generally found to have a relation, more or less direct, with this incident. It was difficult to ascertain the exact species of impression which it made upon him. He never introduced the subject into conversation, and listened with a silent and half-serious smile to the satirical effusions of Pleyel.

---

[13] "Auricular": "perceived by the ear; audible" (*OED*).

[14] "Diseased condition of his frame . . . understanding": Clara worries that if Theodore's embodied sensibility is damaged, then so too will be his dependent reasoning; he may lapse into madness. This passage begins the narrative's steady development toward the breakdown that Clara foreshadows and fears.

One evening we chanced to be alone together in the temple. I seized that opportunity of investigating the state of his thoughts. After a pause, which he seemed in no wise inclined to interrupt, I spoke to him—"How almost palpable is this dark; yet a ray from above would dispel it." "Ay," said Wieland, with fervor, "not only the physical, but moral night would be dispelled." "But why," said I, "must the Divine Will address its precepts to the eye!" He smiled significantly. "True," said he, "the understanding has other avenues." "You have never," said I, approaching nearer to the point—"you have never told me in what way you considered the late extraordinary incident." "There is no determinate way in which the subject can be viewed. Here is an effect, but the cause is utterly inscrutable. To suppose a deception will not do. Such is possible, but there are twenty other suppositions more probable. They must all be set aside before we reach that point." "What, are these twenty suppositions?" "It is needless to mention them. They are only less improbable than Pleyel's. Time may convert one of them into certainty. Till then it is useless to expatiate on them."

Chapter V

SOME time had elapsed when there happened another occurrence, still more remarkable. Pleyel, on his return from Europe, brought information of considerable importance to my brother. My ancestors were noble Saxons, and possessed large domains in Lusatia.[1] The Prussian wars had destroyed those persons whose right to these estates precluded my brother's. Pleyel had been exact in his inquiries, and had discovered that, by the law of male-primogeniture,[2] my brother's claims were superior to those of any other person now living. Nothing was wanting but his presence in that country, and a legal application to establish this claim.

Pleyel strenuously recommended this measure. The advantages he thought attending it were numerous, and it would argue the utmost folly to neglect them. Contrary to his expectation he found my brother averse to the scheme. Slight efforts, he, at first, thought would subdue his reluctance; but he found this aversion by no means slight. The interest that he took in the happiness of his friend and his sister, and his own partiality to the Saxon soil, from which he had likewise sprung, and where he had spent several years of his youth, made him redouble his exertions to win Wieland's consent. For this end he employed every argument that his invention could suggest. He painted, in attractive colours, the state of manners and government in that country, the security of civil rights, and the freedom of religious sentiments. He dwelt on the privileges of wealth and rank, and drew from the servile condition of one class, an argument in favor of his scheme, since the revenue and power annexed to a German principality afford so large a field for benevolence. The evil flowing from this power, in malignant hands, was proportioned to the good that would arise from the virtuous use of it. Hence, Wieland, in forbearing to claim his own, withheld all the positive

---

[1] "Lusatia": a disputed province of Saxony on the border between present-day Germany and the Czech Republic, and the location of the estate where Zinzendorf, mentioned earlier (see note 1.20), sheltered the Moravians. As a border region, Lusatia was contested between Protestant-peopled but Catholic-ruled Saxony on one side, and Catholic Poland on the other. From the end of the Thirty Years War (1648) to the French Revolution and Napoleonic Wars (1789–1815), the region was continually embroiled in central European politico-religious wars and territorial struggles between Austria, Prussia, and Russia. These are the "Prussian Wars" mentioned in the next sentence and again at greater length in the third paragraph of this chapter.

[2] "Male-primogeniture": the feudal law establishing the right of inheritance of the first-born son, excluding other siblings or claimants, which was still extant in common law, although diminishing in Anglo-American practice, up to the time of the American and French revolutions. Clara's earlier remark about the equal division of family property between herself and her brother (see note 3.5) has already implicitly condemned this remnant of feudalism as an unenlightened relic of the old regime. Brown's reference to primogeniture in Saxony is accurate; disputes about the obligation of primogeniture were important in Saxony during this period and played along Protestant and Catholic fault lines, resulting in the fragmentation of the territory into increasingly petty Protestant duchies that were not reintegrated into a state until the Napoleonic period. See Sutter, *Protestantism and Primogeniture in Early Modern Germany.*

felicity that would accrue to his vassals from his success, and hazarded all the misery that would redound from a less enlightened proprietor.[3]

It was easy for my brother to repel these arguments, and to shew that no spot on the globe enjoyed equal security and liberty to that which he at present inhabited. That if the Saxons had nothing to fear from mis-government, the external causes of havoc and alarm were numerous and manifest. The recent devastations committed by the Prussians furnished a specimen of these. The horrors of war would always impend over them, till Germany were seized and divided by Austrian and Prussian tyrants;[4] an event which he strongly suspected was at no great distance. But setting these considerations aside, was it laudable to grasp at wealth and power even when they were within our reach? Were not these the two great sources of depravity? What security had he, that in this change of place and condition, he should not degenerate into a tyrant and voluptuary? Power and riches were chiefly to be dreaded on account of their tendency to deprave the possessor. He held them in abhorrence, not only as instruments of misery to others, but to him on whom they were conferred. Besides, riches were comparative, and was he not rich already? He lived at present in the bosom of security and luxury. All the instruments of pleasure, on which his reason or imagination set any value, were within his reach. But these he must forego, for the sake of advantages which, whatever were their value, were as yet uncertain. In pursuit of an imaginary addition to his wealth, he must reduce himself to poverty, he must exchange present certainties for what was distant and contingent; for who knows not that the law is a system of expence, delay and uncertainty? If he should embrace this scheme, it would lay him under the necessity of making a voyage to Europe, and remaining for a certain period, separate from his family. He must undergo the perils and discomforts of the ocean; he must divest himself of all domestic pleasures; he must deprive his wife of her

---

[3] "Enlightened proprietor": as he urges Theodore to leave his life in Pennsylvania for "large domains" in Lusatia, Pleyel implicitly wants him to assert Protestant rule in them, coded as "enlightened" reform and "freedom of religious sentiments." Theodore refuses the seduction of power and status as a "field for benevolence," however. For more on the ways that this dilemma connects with the novel's wider questioning about the difference between real and regal Enlightenment, see the Introduction.

With this dilemma concerning a creole American's return to claim a European inheritance, Brown may allude to Bernardin de Saint-Pierre's novel *Paul and Virginia* (1787), which relates how a happy utopia of friendship-based love in Mauritius is lost when Virginia travels to Paris to claim an inheritance and is overwhelmed by old-world, class-based corruption. The tale was widely translated and a favorite in Brown's New York circle in the years leading up to *Wieland*. Friedrich Schiller and William Godwin also addressed disillusionment about hopes of enlightened reform in Central Europe, in, respectively, *Don Carlos: Infant of Spain* (1783–1787, English translation 1798) and *St. Leon: A Tale of the Sixteenth Century* (1799).

[4] "Recent devastations . . . Austrian and Prussian tyrants": the "Prussian wars" that figure in the background of Pleyel's geopolitical calculations are generally known as the Silesian Wars (1740–1763). These conflicts strained Saxon alliances and overlapped with the German theaters of The Wars of Austrian Succession (1740–1748) and the worldwide Seven Years War (1756–1763) that forms a general backdrop for the lives of the novel's characters.

companion, and his children of a father and instructor, and all for what? For the ambiguous advantages which overgrown wealth and flagitious[5] tyranny have to bestow? For a precarious possession in a land of turbulence and war? Advantages, which will not certainly be gained, and of which the acquisition, if it were sure, is necessarily distant.

Pleyel was enamoured of his scheme on account of its intrinsic benefits, but, likewise, for other reasons. His abode at Leipsig made that country appear to him like home. He was connected with this place by many social ties. While there he had not escaped the amorous contagion. But the lady, though her heart was impressed in his favor, was compelled to bestow her hand upon another. Death had removed this impediment, and he was now invited by the lady herself to return. This he was of course determined to do, but was anxious to obtain the company of Wieland; he could not bear to think of an eternal separation from his present associates. Their interest, he thought, would be no less promoted by the change than his own. Hence he was importunate[6] and indefatigable in his arguments and solicitations.

He knew that he could not hope for mine or his sister's ready concurrence in this scheme. Should the subject be mentioned to us, we should league our efforts against him, and strengthen that reluctance in Wieland which already was sufficiently difficult to conquer. He, therefore, anxiously concealed from us his purpose. If Wieland were previously enlisted in his cause, he would find it a less difficult task to overcome our aversion. My brother was silent on this subject, because he believed himself in no danger of changing his opinion, and he was willing to save us from any uneasiness. The mere mention of such a scheme, and the possibility of his embracing it, he knew, would considerably impair our tranquillity.

One day, about three weeks subsequent to the mysterious call, it was agreed that the family should be my guests. Seldom had a day been passed by us, of more serene enjoyment. Pleyel had promised us his company, but we did not see him till the sun had nearly declined. He brought with him a countenance that betokened disappointment and vexation. He did not wait for our inquiries, but immediately explained the cause. Two days before a packet had arrived from Hamburgh, by which he had flattered himself with the expectation of receiving letters, but no letters had arrived. I never saw him so much subdued by an untoward event. His thoughts were employed in accounting for the silence of his friends. He was seized with the torments of jealousy, and suspected nothing less than the infidelity of her to whom he had devoted his heart. The silence must have been concerted. Her sickness, or absence, or death, would have increased the certainty of some one's having written. No supposition could be formed but that his mistress had grown indifferent, or that she had transferred her affections to another. The miscarriage of a letter was hardly within the reach of possibility. From Leipsig to Hamburgh, and from Hamburgh hither, the conveyance was exposed to no hazard.

---

[5] "Flagitious": "extremely wicked or criminal: heinous, villainous" (*OED*).

[6] "Importunate": persistent, troublesome.

He had been so long detained in America chiefly in consequence of Wieland's aversion to the scheme which he proposed. He now became more impatient than ever to return to Europe. When he reflected that, by his delays, he had probably forfeited the affections of his mistress, his sensations amounted to agony. It only remained, by his speedy departure, to repair, if possible, or prevent so intolerable an evil. Already he had half resolved to embark in this very ship which, he was informed, would set out in a few weeks on her return. Meanwhile he determined to make a new attempt to shake the resolution of Wieland. The evening was some-what advanced when he invited the latter to walk abroad with him. The invitation was accepted, and they left Catharine, Louisa and me, to amuse ourselves by the best means in our power. During this walk, Pleyel renewed the subject that was nearest his heart. He re-urged all his former arguments, and placed them in more forcible lights.

They promised to return shortly; but hour after hour passed, and they made not their appearance. Engaged in sprightly conversation, it was not till the clock struck twelve that we were reminded of the lapse of time. The absence of our friends ex-cited some uneasy apprehensions. We were expressing our fears, and comparing our conjectures as to what might be the cause, when they entered together. There were indications in their countenances that struck me mute. These were unnoticed by Catharine, who was eager to express her surprize and curiosity at the length of their walk. As they listened to her, I remarked that their surprize was not less than ours. They gazed in silence on each other, and on her. I watched their looks, but could not understand the emotions that were written in them.

These appearances diverted Catharine's inquiries into a new channel. What did they mean, she asked, by their silence, and by their thus gazing wildly at each other, and at her? Pleyel profited by this hint, and assuming an air of indiffer-ence, framed some trifling excuse, at the same time darting significant glances at Wieland, as if to caution him against disclosing the truth. My brother said nothing, but delivered himself up to meditation. I likewise was silent, but burned with impatience to fathom this mystery. Presently my brother and his wife, and Louisa, returned home. Pleyel proposed, of his own accord, to be my guest for the night. This circumstance, in addition to those which preceded, gave new edge to my wonder.

As soon as we were left alone, Pleyel's countenance assumed an air of serious-ness, and even consternation, which I had never before beheld in him. The steps with which he measured the floor betokened the trouble of his thoughts. My inquiries were suspended by the hope that he would give me the information that I wanted without the importunity of questions. I waited some time, but the confusion of his thoughts appeared in no degree to abate. At length I mentioned the apprehensions which their unusual absence had occasioned, and which were increased by their behaviour since their return, and solicited an explanation. He stopped when I began to speak, and looked stedfastly at me. When I had done, he said, to me, in a tone which faultered through the vehemence of his emotions, "How were you employed during our absence?" "In turning over the

Della Crusca dictionary,[7] and talking on different subjects; but just before your entrance, we were tormenting ourselves with omens and prognosticks relative to your absence." "Catharine was with you the whole time?" "Yes," "But are you sure?" "Most sure. She was not absent a moment." He stood, for a time, as if to assure himself of my sincerity. Then, clenching his hands, and wildly lifting them above his head, "Lo," cried he, "I have news to tell you. The Baroness de Stolberg[8] is dead!"

This was her whom he loved. I was not surprised at the agitations which he betrayed. "But how was the information procured? How was the truth of this news connected with the circumstance of Catharine's remaining in our company?" He was for some time inattentive to my questions. When he spoke, it seemed merely a continuation of the reverie into which he had been plunged.

"And yet it might be a mere deception. But could both of us in that case have been deceived? A rare and prodigious coincidence! Barely not impossible. And yet, if the accent be oracular—Theresa is dead. No, no," continued he, covering his face with his hands, and in a tone half broken into sobs, "I cannot believe it. She has not written, but if she were dead, the faithful Bertrand would have given me the earliest information. And yet if he knew his master, he must have easily guessed at the effect of such tidings. In pity to me he was silent."

"Clara, forgive me; to you, this behaviour is mysterious. I will explain as well as I am able. But say not a word to Catharine. Her strength of mind is inferior to your's. She will, besides, have more reason to be startled. She is Wieland's angel."

Pleyel proceeded to inform me, for the first time, of the scheme which he had pressed, with so much earnestness, on my brother. He enumerated the objections

---

[7] "Della Crusca dictionary": the Academia della Crusca published this authoritative Italian dictionary beginning in 1612. In the 1790s the name also evoked associations with Della Cruscan poetry, a subgenre of sensibilitarian poetic exchange between friends in mixed-sex conversational groups like that formed by the Wielands and Pleyels. "Della Crusca" was the pseudonym of the movement's leading figure, British poet Robert Merry (1755–1798), and his poetic exchanges with "Anna Matilda" were widely reprinted and well-known to Brown and his friends, who practiced this sort of poetry themselves. For more on this genre and its significance in the Revolutionary era, see McGann, *The Poetics of Sensibility*.

[8] "Baroness de Stolberg": the seat of the Counts of Stolberg in the Harz Mountains was part of Saxony. Thus, if Pleyel married the Baroness and Wieland asserted his lineage claims, both would be minor Saxon nobility. Additionally, as he did with the names Wieland and Pleyel, Brown invokes a name that was known to contemporary readers and associated with the period's German literary wave. The writings of Friedrich von Stolberg (or Friedrich Leopold, Count Stolberg, 1750–1819) were widely circulated in English in this period. His *Travels through Germany, Switzerland, Italy, and Sicily* was translated in 1796–1797 by Woldwinite writer Thomas Holcroft and praised in the same periodicals that Brown's circle followed most closely. Brown's friend Smith speaks of reading this work in his diary. As editor of the New York *Monthly Magazine* and the later Philadelphia *Literary Magazine,* Brown published excerpts from Stolberg's *Travels* (for example, "Sketch of Modern Manners of Rome" in *Monthly Magazine,* August 1799) and numerous articles on German literature that discuss him. Friedrich's brother Christian (1748–1821) and sister Catherine (Katharina) von Stolberg (1751–1832), were also widely published writers, although less prominent in Anglophone circles.

which had been made, and the industry with which he had endeavoured to confuse them. He mentioned the effect upon his resolutions produced by the failure of a letter. "During our late walk," continued he, "I introduced the subject that was nearest my heart. I re-urged all my former arguments, and placed them in more forcible lights. Wieland was still refractory. He expatiated on the perils of wealth and power, on the sacredness of conjugal and parental duties, and the happiness of mediocrity.[9]

"No wonder that the time passed, unperceived, away. Our whole souls were engaged in this cause. Several times we came to the foot of the rock; as soon as we perceived it, we changed our course, but never failed to terminate our circuitous and devious ramble at this spot. At length your brother observed, "We seem to be led hither by a kind of fatality. Since we are so near, let us ascend and rest ourselves a while. If you are not weary of this argument we will resume it there."

"I tacitly consented. We mounted the stairs, and drawing the sofa in front of the river, we seated ourselves upon it. I took up the thread of our discourse where we had dropped it. I ridiculed his dread of the sea, and his attachment to home. I kept on in this strain, so congenial with my disposition, for some time, uninterrupted by him. At length, he said to me, 'Suppose now that I, whom argument has not convinced, should yield to ridicule, and should agree that your scheme is eligible; what will you have gained? Nothing. You have other enemies beside myself to encounter. When you have vanquished me, your toil has scarcely begun. There are my sister and wife, with whom it will remain for you to maintain the contest. And trust me, they are adversaries whom all your force and stratagem will never subdue.' I insinuated that they would model themselves by his will: that Catharine would think obedience her duty.[10] He answered, with some quickness, 'You mistake. Their concurrence is indispensable. It is not my custom to exact sacrifices of this kind. I live to be their protector and friend, and not their tyrant and foe. If my wife shall deem her happiness, and that of her children, most consulted by remaining where she is, here she shall remain.' 'But,' said I, 'when she knows your pleasure, will she not conform to it?' Before my friend had time to answer this question, a negative was clearly and distinctly uttered from another quarter. It did not come from one side or the other, from before us or behind. Whence then did it come? By whose organs was it fashioned?

"If any uncertainty had existed with regard to these particulars, it would have been removed by a deliberate and equally distinct repetition of the same monosyllable, 'No.' The voice was my sister's. It appeared to come from the roof. I started from my seat. Catharine, exclaimed I, where are you? No answer was returned. I searched the room, and the area before it, but in vain. Your brother was motionless in his seat. I

---

[9] "Mediocrity": "a moderate fortune or condition in life" (*OED*). This positive use of the term, in formulations such as "a fortunate mediocrity" or Clara's "happiness of mediocrity," was common in the period. Again, Wieland is reluctant to trade his "moderate" fortune and republican leisure in Pennsylvania for feudal domains and aristocratic rank in Saxony.

[10] "Obedience her duty": here and again at the end of the paragraph, Pleyel articulates the period's conventional assumptions concerning the "duty" of the *feme covert*, a woman who has no legal personhood and will presumably defer in significant decisions to the male who has authority over her.

returned to him, and placed myself again by his side. My astonishment was not less than his."

"'Well,' said he, at length, 'What think you of this? This is the self-same voice which I formerly heard; you are now convinced that my ears were well informed.'

"'Yes,' said I, 'this, it is plain, is no fiction of the fancy.' We again sunk into mutual and thoughtful silence. A recollection of the hour, and of the length of our absence, made me at last propose to return. We rose up for this purpose. In doing this, my mind reverted to the contemplation of my own condition. 'Yes,' said I aloud, but without particularly addressing myself to Wieland, 'my resolution is taken. I cannot hope to prevail with my friends to accompany me. They may doze away their days on the banks of Schuylkill, but as to me, I go in the next vessel; I will fly to her presence, and demand the reason of this extraordinary silence.'

"I had scarcely finished the sentence, when the same mysterious voice exclaimed, 'You shall not go. The seal of death is on her lips. Her silence is the silence of the tomb.' Think of the effects which accents like these must have had upon me. I shuddered as I listened. As soon as I recovered from my first amazement, 'Who is it that speaks?' said I, 'whence did you procure these dismal tidings?' I did not wait long for an answer. 'From a source that cannot fail. Be satisfied. She is dead.' You may justly be surprised, that, in the circumstances in which I heard the tidings, and notwithstanding the mystery which environed him by whom they were imparted, I could give an undivided attention to the facts, which were the subject of our dialogue. I eagerly inquired, when and where did she die? What was the cause of her death? Was her death absolutely certain? An answer was returned only to the last of these questions. 'Yes,' was pronounced by the same voice; but it now sounded from a greater distance, and the deepest silence was all the return made to my subsequent interrogatories.

"It was my sister's voice; but it could not be uttered by her; and yet, if not by her, by whom was it uttered? When we returned hither, and discovered you together, the doubt that had previously existed was removed. It was manifest that the intimation came not from her. Yet if not from her, from whom could it come? Are the circumstances attending the imparting of this news proof that the tidings are true? God forbid that they should be true."

Here Pleyel sunk into anxious silence, and gave me leisure to ruminate on this inexplicable event. I am at a loss to describe the sensations that affected me. I am not fearful of shadows. The tales of apparitions and enchantments did not possess that power over my belief which could even render them interesting. I saw nothing in them but ignorance and folly, and was a stranger even to that terror which is pleasing. But this incident was different from any that I had ever before known. Here were proofs of a sensible and intelligent existence, which could not be denied. Here was information obtained and imparted by means unquestionably super-human.[11]

---

[11] "By means unquestionably super-human": despite her skepticism, Clara begins to consider the possibility of supernatural agency. Throughout the remainder of the narrative, at her moments of greatest uncertainty and desperation, Clara will waver between rational analysis and anxiety or fear-driven suspicions of supernatural agency.

That there are conscious beings, beside ourselves, in existence, whose modes of activity and information surpass our own, can scarcely be denied. Is there a glimpse afforded us into a world of these superior beings? My heart was scarcely large enough to give admittance to so swelling a thought. An awe, the sweetest and most solemn that imagination can conceive, pervaded my whole frame. It forsook me not when I parted from Pleyel and retired to my chamber. An impulse was given to my spirits utterly incompatible with sleep. I passed the night wakeful and full of meditation. I was impressed with the belief of mysterious, but not of malignant agency. Hitherto nothing had occurred to persuade me that this airy minister was busy to evil rather than to good purposes. On the contrary, the idea of superior virtue had always been associated in my mind with that of superior power. The warnings that had thus been heard appeared to have been prompted by beneficent intentions. My brother had been hindered by this voice from ascending the hill. He was told that danger lurked in his path, and his obedience to the intimation had perhaps saved him from a destiny similar to that of my father.

Pleyel had been rescued from tormenting uncertainty, and from the hazards and fatigues of a fruitless voyage, by the same interposition. It had assured him of the death of his Theresa.

This woman was then dead. A confirmation of the tidings, if true, would speedily arrive. Was this confirmation to be deprecated or desired? By her death, the tie that attached him to Europe, was taken away. Henceforward every motive would combine to retain him in his native country, and we were rescued from the deep regrets that would accompany his hopeless absence from us. Propitious was the spirit that imparted these tidings. Propitious he would perhaps have been, if he had been instrumental in producing, as well as in communicating the ridings of her death. Propitious to us, the friends of Pleyel, to whom has thereby been secured the enjoyment of his society; and not unpropitious to himself; for though this object of his love be snatched away, is there not another who is able and willing to console him for her loss?[12]

Twenty days after this, another vessel arrived from the same port. In this interval, Pleyel, for the most part, estranged himself from his old companions. He was become the prey of a gloomy and unsociable grief. His walks were limited to the bank of the Delaware. This bank is an artificial one. Reeds and the river are on one side, and a watery marsh on the other, in that part which bounded his lands, and which extended from the mouth of Hollander's creek[13] to that of Schuylkill. No scene can

---

[12] "Console him for her loss?": the first admission (to the reader, retrospectively, but not to those around her at the time) that Clara is romantically attracted to Pleyel. Throughout the narrative Clara will simultaneously try to observe and subvert elite codes of female behavior that limit her willingness to acknowledge her desires and other "passions."

[13] "Hollander's creek": a creek that ran from the Delaware river west toward the Schuylkill, about 2.5 miles south of central Philadelphia in this period. If Pleyel's "lands" border on the Delaware and the marshy area below Hollander's Creek, this means his home is on the low-lying, unattractive land that is today occupied by the Philadelphia Naval Shipyards, the southernmost tip of the peninsula where Philadelphia is located. The "unwholesome airs" and unhealthy situation of this then-marshy land, discussed in the next two paragraphs, are the reason Pleyel will become a guest of the Wielands two paragraphs further on.

be imagined less enticing to a lover of the picturesque than this. The shore is deformed with mud, and incumbered with a forest of reeds. The fields, in most seasons, are mire; but when they afford a firm footing, the ditches by which they are bounded and intersected, are mantled with stagnating green, and emit the most noxious exhalations. Health is no less a stranger to those seats than pleasure. Spring and autumn are sure to be accompanied with agues and bilious remittents.[14]

The scenes which environed our dwellings at Mettingen constituted the reverse of this. Schuylkill was here a pure and translucid current, broken into wild and ceaseless music by rocky points, murmuring on a sandy margin, and reflecting on its surface, banks of all varieties of height and degrees of declivity. These banks were chequered by patches of dark verdure and shapeless masses of white marble, and crowned by copses of cedar, or by the regular magnificence of orchards, which, at this season, were in blossom, and were prodigal of odours. The ground which receded from the river was scooped into valleys and dales. Its beauties were enhanced by the horticultural skill of my brother, who bedecked this exquisite assemblage of slopes and risings with every species of vegetable ornament, from the giant arms of the oak to the clustering tendrils of the honey-suckle.[15]

To screen him from the unwholesome airs of his own residence, it had been proposed to Pleyel to spend the months of spring with us. He had apparently acquiesced in this proposal; but the late event induced him to change his purpose. He was only to be seen by visiting him in his retirements. His gaiety had flown, and every passion was absorbed in eagerness to procure tidings from Saxony. I have mentioned the arrival of another vessel from the Elbe.[16] He descried her early one morning as he was passing along the skirt of the river. She was easily recognized, being the ship in which he had performed his first voyage to Germany. He immediately went on board, but found no letters directed to him. This omission was, in some degree, compensated by meeting with an old acquaintance among the passengers, who had till lately been a resident in Leipsig. This person put an end to all suspense respecting the fate of Theresa, by relating the particulars of her death and funeral.

---

[14] "Agues and bilious remittents": shivering and vomiting fevers.

[15] "Horticultural skill . . . honey-suckle": botany and gardening were highly valued in late-Enlightenment culture, commonly understood as gentlemanly pursuits related to progressive sensibility and sociability in works such as Erasmus Darwin's *The Botanic Garden* (1791), which was carefully read and reprinted in New York by Brown's circle in 1798 (with the same publisher who handled *Wieland* and many of the group's other publications). Theodore's horticultural interests echo this set of concerns. More locally, Clara describes a style of gardening and landscaping that was quite familiar to Brown. Many of the country homes outside Philadelphia on the scenic stretch of the Schuylkill River where Mettingen is located featured elaborately landscaped ornamental and botanical gardens that were open to strolling visitors. This is the context in which Clara will first glimpse the character Carwin in the next chapter, strolling on the carefully tended grounds of the Wieland estate. See note 6.1 for Clara's reflections on Carwin's first appearance in this setting.

[16] "Elbe": the main river running through Saxony, connecting Leipzig and Hamburg with the North Sea.

Thus was the truth of the former intimation attested. No longer devoured by suspense, the grief of Pleyel was not long in yielding to the influence of society. He gave himself up once more to our company. His vivacity had indeed been damped; but even in this respect he was a more acceptable companion than formerly, since his seriousness was neither incommunicative nor sullen.

These incidents, for a time, occupied all our thoughts. In me they produced a sentiment not unallied to pleasure, and more speedily than in the case of my friends were intermixed with other topics. My brother was particularly affected by them. It was easy to perceive that most of his meditations were tinctured from this source. To this was to be ascribed a design in which his pen was, at this period, engaged, of collecting and investigating the facts which relate to that mysterious personage, the Dæmon of Socrates.[17]

My brother's skill in Greek and Roman learning was exceeded by that of few, and no doubt the world would have accepted a treatise upon this subject from his hand with avidity; but alas! this and every other scheme of felicity and honor, were doomed to sudden blast and hopeless extermination.

---

[17] "Dæmon of Socrates": "daemon" is a Greek term for a supernatural being or spirit, and Socrates alludes to a personal or guardian daemon in several Platonic dialogues. The concept is translated into Latin as a person's "genius" and in early Christian tradition as both protective "angel" and threatening "demon." After her own experience of the voices, Clara will begin to speculate about a watchful "genius," "angel," and "guardian" in later chapters. Socrates' daemon was widely discussed by writers in classical antiquity and the romantic period. He mentions this daemon in numerous passages as a prophetic inner voice or sound that warns him when he is about to make a mistake: see *Phaedrus* 242b–c, *Alcibiades I* 106a, *Euthydemus* 272e, *Euthyphro* 3b, *Republic* 496c, *Theatatus* 151a, and *Theages* 128d–129c.

In the *Apology*, one of the charges against Socrates is that he believes in invented beings aside from the official gods, namely his daemon. He acknowledges and defends his experience of a divine "omen" or "sign" (*daemonion*) before being judged guilty and condemned to death (27b–e, 31d–32a, 40a–c). In the *Symposium,* Socrates explains that the priestess Diotima told him that Love is neither mortal nor immortal but an intermediate daemon who is poor, ugly, homeless, and a master of artifice and deception, somewhat like the itinerant figure Carwin who will appear in the next chapter: "he is always poor, and anything but tender and fair, as the many imagine him; and he is rough and squalid, and has no shoes, nor a house to dwell in; on the bare earth exposed he lies under the open heaven, in the streets, or at the doors of houses, taking his rest; and like his mother he is always in distress. Like his father too, whom he also partly resembles, he is always plotting against the fair and good; he is bold, enterprising, strong, a mighty hunter, always weaving some intrigue or other, keen in the pursuit of wisdom, fertile in resources; a philosopher at all times, terrible as an enchanter, sorcerer, sophist" (203d; B. Jowett tr.).

Chapter VI

I NOW come to the mention of a person with whose name the most turbulent sensations are connected. It is with a shuddering reluctance that I enter on the province of describing him. Now it is that I begin to perceive the difficulty of the task which I have undertaken; but it would be weakness to shrink from it. My blood is congealed: and my fingers are palsied when I call up his image. Shame upon my cowardly and infirm heart! Hitherto I have proceeded with some degree of composure, but now I must pause. I mean not that dire remembrance shall subdue my courage or baffle my design, but this weakness cannot be immediately conquered. I must desist for a little while.

I have taken a few turns in my chamber, and have gathered strength enough to proceed. Yet have I not projected a task beyond my power to execute? If thus, on the very threshold of the scene, my knees faulter and I sink, how shall I support myself, when I rush into the midst of horrors such as no heart has hitherto conceived, nor tongue related? I sicken and recoil at the prospect, and yet my irresolution is momentary. I have not formed this design upon slight grounds, and though I may at times pause and hesitate, I will not be finally diverted from it.

And thou, O most fatal and potent of mankind, in what terms shall I describe thee? What words are adequate to the just delineation of thy character? How shall I detail the means which rendered the secrecy of thy purposes unfathomable? But I will not anticipate. Let me recover if possible, a sober strain. Let me keep down the flood of passion that would render me precipitate or powerless. Let me stifle the agonies that are awakened by thy name. Let me, for a time, regard thee as a being of no terrible attributes. Let me tear myself from contemplation of the evils of which it is but too certain that thou wast the author, and limit my view to those harmless appearances which attended thy entrance on the stage.

One sunny afternoon, I was standing in the door of my house, when I marked a person passing close to the edge of the bank that was in front. His pace was a careless and lingering one, and had none of that gracefulness and ease which distinguish a person with certain advantages of education from a clown.[1] His gait was rustic and aukward. His form was ungainly and disproportioned. Shoulders broad and square, breast sunken, his head drooping, his body of uniform breadth, supported by long and lank legs, were the ingredients of his frame. His garb was not ill adapted to such a figure. A slouched hat, tarnished by the weather, a coat of thick grey cloth, cut and wrought, as it seemed, by a country tailor, blue worsted[2] stockings, and shoes fastened by thongs, and deeply discoloured by dust, which brush had never disturbed, constituted his dress.

---

[1] "Clown": a laboring-class rural person, a rustic, a farmhand. The next three paragraphs develop an extended reflection on Clara's surprise at seeing what appears to be a laboring-class person strolling through the estate, rather than members of an educated elite who presumably contemplate and respond aesthetically and intellectually to the gardens and landscaping. For the initial description of the grounds, see note 5.15. For Carwin's retrospective comments on the pleasure he took in walking here, see note 22.7.

[2] "Worsted": woolen.

There was nothing remarkable in these appearances; they were frequently to be met with on the road, and in the harvest field. I cannot tell why I gazed upon them, on this occasion, with more than ordinary attention, unless it were that such figures were seldom seen by me, except on the road or field. This lawn was only traversed by men whose views were directed to the pleasures of the walk, or the grandeur of the scenery.

He passed slowly along, frequently pausing, as if to examine the prospect more deliberately, but never turning his eye towards the house, so as to allow me a view of his countenance. Presently, he entered a copse at a small distance, and disappeared. My eye followed him while he remained in sight. If his image remained for any duration in my fancy after his departure, it was because no other object occurred sufficient to expel it.

I continued in the same spot for half an hour, vaguely, and by fits, contemplating the image of this wanderer, and drawing, from outward appearances, those inferences with respect to the intellectual history of this person, which experience affords us. I reflected on the alliance which commonly subsists between ignorance and the practice of agriculture, and indulged myself in airy speculations as to the influence of progressive knowledge in dissolving this alliance, and embodying the dreams of the poets. I asked why the plough and the hoe might not become the trade of every human being, and how this trade might be made conducive to, or, at least, consistent with the acquisition of wisdom and eloquence.[3]

Weary with these reflections, I returned to the kitchen to perform some household office. I had usually but one servant, and she was a girl about my own age. I was busy near the chimney, and she was employed near the door of the apartment, when some one knocked. The door was opened by her, and she was immediately addressed with "Pry'thee, good girl, canst thou supply a thirsty man with a glass of buttermilk?"[4] She answered that there was none in the house. "Aye, but there is some in the dairy yonder. Thou knowest as well as I, though Hermes[5] never taught thee, that though every

---

[3] "Progressive knowledge . . . wisdom and eloquence": Clara indulges a brief local fantasy about progressive enlightenment, which in this period was often allegorized as paternalist agrarian or pastoral independence, represented in the figure of the virtuous citizen as "yeoman farmer." Insofar as this novel rejects this image of the paternalist republican gentry farmer, it can be read as response to its other appearances in key texts of the period, such as Crèvecoeur's *Letters from an American Farmer* (1784) and Jefferson's *Notes on the State of Virginia* (1784).

[4] "A glass of buttermilk": Carwin's question and riddle about milk, addressed to the female servant identified later in this chapter as Judith, involve double entendres and may euphemistically allude to breast milk. During Carwin's confession in Chapter 22, he claims that he and Judith are either already engaged in a sexual affair at this time or will be shortly (see note 22.8).

[5] "Hermes": the larger allusion suggests that Carwin should be seen as an ambiguous, slippery figure whose words need to be regarded skeptically. The Olympic god Hermes is associated with cattle and breast milk in several legends. In one, the Milky Way originated when Zeus tricked the goddess Hera into nursing his illegitimate son Hermes (in some accounts this incident concerns Hercules). Realizing that she was nursing a child not her own, Hera pushed Hermes away from her breast and the milk that spilled out created the milky band of stars across the sky. In other episodes, Hermes is commonly represented as a cowherd because he stole Apollo's cattle on the day he was born, and because he was sent by Zeus to save the heifer-nymph Io (who had been disguised to protect her from Hera's jealousy).

dairy be an house, every house is not a dairy." To this speech, though she understood only a part of it, she replied by repeating her assurances, that she had none to give. "Well then," rejoined the stranger, "for charity's sweet sake, hand me forth a cup of cold water." The girl said she would go to the spring and fetch it. "Nay, give me the cup, and suffer me to help myself. Neither manacled nor lame, I should merit burial in the maw of carrion crows, if I laid this task upon thee." She gave him the cup, and he turned to go to the spring.

I listened to this dialogue in silence. The words uttered by the person without, affected me as somewhat singular, but what chiefly rendered them remarkable, was the tone that accompanied them. It was wholly new. My brother's voice and Pleyel's were musical and energetic. I had fondly imagined, that, in this respect, they were surpassed by none. Now my mistake was detected. I cannot pretend to communicate the impression that was made upon me by these accents, or to depict the degree in which force and sweetness were blended in them. They were articulated with a distinctness that was unexampled in my experience. But this was not all. The voice was not only mellifluent[6] and clear, but the emphasis was so just, and the modulation so impassioned, that it seemed as if an heart of stone could not fail of being moved by it. It imparted to me an emotion altogether involuntary and incontroulable. When he uttered the words "for charity's sweet sake," I dropped the cloth that I held in my hand, my heart overflowed with sympathy, and my eyes with unbidden tears.

This description will appear to you trifling or incredible. The importance of these circumstances will be manifested in the sequel. The manner in which I was affected on this occasion, was, to my own apprehension, a subject of astonishment. The tones were indeed such as I never heard before; but that they should, in an instant, as it were, dissolve me in tears, will not easily be believed by others, and can scarcely be comprehended by myself.

It will be readily supposed that I was somewhat inquisitive as to the person and demeanour of our visitant. After a moment's pause, I stepped to the door and looked after him. Judge my surprize, when I beheld the self-same figure that had appeared an half hour before upon the bank. My fancy had conjured up a very different image. A form, and attitude, and garb, were instantly created worthy to accompany such elocution; but this person was, in all visible respects, the reverse of this phantom. Strange as it may seem, I could not speedily reconcile myself to this disappointment. Instead of returning to my employment, I threw myself in a chair that was placed opposite the door, and sunk into a fit of musing.

My attention was, in a few minutes, recalled by the stranger, who returned with the empty cup in his hand. I had not thought of the circumstance, or should certainly

---

Legends generally present Hermes (Latin Mercury) as a mischievous trickster and thief; as messenger of the gods, he is associated with language, eloquence, deception, and communication. Hence "Mercury" was a common name for early modern newspapers. Hermes is also represented as a protector of herds and as *psychopompos,* or the deity who guides souls to the place of the dead; Carwin begins life as a cowherd in the prequel *Memoirs of Carwin,* included in Related Texts.

[6] "Mellifluent": sweet or musical to hear.

have chosen a different seat. He no sooner shewed himself, than a confused sense of impropriety, added to the suddenness of the interview, for which, not having foreseen it, I had made no preparation, threw me into a state of the most painful embarrassment. He brought with him a placid brow; but no sooner had he cast his eyes upon me, than his face was as glowingly suffused as my own. He placed the cup upon the bench, stammered out thanks, and retired.

It was some time before I could recover my wonted composure. I had snatched a view of the stranger's countenance. The impression that it made was vivid and indelible. His cheeks were pallid and lank, his eyes sunken, his forehead overshadowed by coarse straggling hairs, his teeth large and irregular, though sound and brilliantly white, and his chin discoloured by a tetter.[7] His skin was of coarse grain, and sallow hue. Every feature was wide of beauty, and the outline of his face reminded you of an inverted cone.

And yet his forehead, so far as shaggy locks would allow it to be seen, his eyes lustrously black, and possessing, in the midst of haggardness, a radiance inexpressibly serene and potent, and something in the rest of his features, which it would be in vain to describe, but which served to betoken a mind of the highest order, were essential ingredients in the portrait. This, in the effects which immediately flowed from it, I count among the most extraordinary incidents of my life. This face, seen for a moment, continued for hours to occupy my fancy, to the exclusion of almost every other image. I had purposed to spend the evening with my brother, but I could not resist the inclination of forming a sketch upon paper of this memorable visage. Whether my hand was aided by any peculiar inspiration, or I was deceived by my own fond conceptions, this portrait, though hastily executed, appeared unexceptionable to my own taste.

I placed it at all distances, and in all lights; my eyes were rivetted upon it. Half the night passed away in wakefulness and in contemplation of this picture. So flexible, and yet so stubborn, is the human mind. So obedient to impulses the most transient and brief, and yet so unalterably observant of the direction which is given to it! How little did I then foresee the termination of that chain, of which this may be regarded as the first link?

Next day arose in darkness and storm. Torrents of rain fell during the whole day, attended with incessant thunder, which reverberated in stunning echoes from the opposite declivity. The inclemency of the air would not allow me to walk out. I had, indeed, no inclination to leave my apartment. I betook myself to the contemplation of this portrait, whose attractions time had rather enhanced than diminished. I laid aside my usual occupations, and seating myself at a window, consumed the day in alternately looking out upon the storm, and gazing at the picture which lay upon a table before me. You will, perhaps, deem this conduct somewhat singular, and ascribe it to certain peculiarities of temper. I am not aware of any such peculiarities. I can account for my devotion to this image no otherwise, than by supposing that its properties were rare and prodigious. Perhaps you will suspect that such were the first inroads of a passion incident to every female heart,[8] and which frequently gains a footing by means even more slight, and more improbable than these. I shall not

---

[7] "Tetter": a general term for skin eruptions, "eczema, herpes, impetigo, ringworm, etc." (*OED*).

[8] "First inroads of a passion incident to every female heart": in other words, erotic desire.

controvert the reasonableness of the suspicion, but leave you at liberty to draw; from my narrative, what conclusions you please.

Night at length returned, and the storm ceased. The air was once more clear and calm, and bore an affecting contrast to that uproar of the elements by which it had been preceded. I spent the darksome hours, as I spent the day, contemplative and seated at the window. Why was my mind absorbed in thoughts ominous and dreary? Why did my bosom heave with sighs, and my eyes overflow with tears? Was the tempest that had just past a signal of the ruin which impended over me? My soul fondly dwelt upon the images of my brother and his children, yet they only increased the mournfulness of my contemplations. The smiles of the charming babes were as bland as formerly. The same dignity sat on the brow of their father, and yet I thought of them with anguish. Something whispered that the happiness we at present enjoyed was set on mutable foundations. Death must happen to all. Whether our felicity was to be subverted by it to-morrow, or whether it was ordained that we should lay down our heads full of years and of honor, was a question that no human being could solve. At other times, these ideas seldom intruded. I either forbore to reflect upon the destiny that is reserved for all men, or the reflection was mixed up with images that disrobed it of terror; but now the uncertainty of life occurred to me without any of its usual and alleviating accompaniments. I said to myself, we must die. Sooner or later, we must disappear for ever from the face of the earth. Whatever be the links that hold us to life, they must be broken. This scene of existence is, in all its parts, calamitous. The greater number is oppressed with immediate evils, and those, the tide of whose fortunes is full, how small is their portion of enjoyment, since they know that it will terminate.

For some time I indulged myself, without reluctance, in these gloomy thoughts; but at length, the dejection which they produced became insupportably painful. I endeavoured to dissipate it with music. I had all my grand-father's melody as well as poetry by rote. I now lighted by chance on a ballad, which commemorated the fate of a German Cavalier, who fell at the siege of Nice under Godfrey of Bouillon. My choice was unfortunate, for the scenes of violence and carnage which were here wildly but forcibly pourtrayed, only suggested to my thoughts a new topic in the horrors of war.[9]

---

[9] "Ballad . . . Godfrey of Bouillon . . . horrors of war": Clara identifies this ballad as her grandfather's work, but the details she provides, drawn from several sources, seem to allude primarily to the Gottfried Bürger's *Lenore*, a hugely popular and influential literary phenomenon of the late 1790s. Clara's remarks about the ballad in this strategically situated paragraph—between her sudden, eroticized, and ominous fascination with Carwin and her first terrifying experience of the "mysterious voice"—implicitly tie the period's "terror" aesthetics, based on a sensational use of language to create emotional effect, with the reverberations of imperial aggression and religious conflict.

First published in Germany in 1773, the ballad became a literary sensation in 1790s Anglophone circles. Four major versions were translated and published in 1796 alone, all well known to Brown and his circle. The poem conveys a terrifying tale of a bride-to-be who longs for her soldier-lover after he departs for battle. Distraught when he does not return, Lenore renounces god and wishes for death. Unexpectedly the lover reappears that night and carries her away on horseback. Ghosts appear around them as they ride and, instead of a bridal chamber, the pair arrive at a tomb where

I sought refuge, but ineffectually, in sleep. My mind was thronged by vivid, but confused images, and no effort that I made was sufficient to drive them away. In this situation I heard the clock, which hung in the room, give the signal for twelve.[10] It was the same instrument which formerly hung in my father's chamber, and which, on account of its being his workmanship, was regarded, by every one of our family, with veneration. It had fallen to me, in the division of his property, and was placed in this asylum. The sound awakened a series of reflections, respecting his death. I was not allowed to pursue them; for scarcely had the vibrations ceased, when my attention was attracted by a whisper, which, at first, appeared to proceed from lips that were laid close to my ear.

No wonder that a circumstance like this startled me. In the first impulse of my terror, I uttered a slight scream, and shrunk to the opposite side of the bed. In a moment, however, I recovered from my trepidation. I was habitually indifferent to all the causes of fear, by which the majority are afflicted. I entertained no apprehension of either ghosts or robbers. Our security had never been molested by either, and I made use of no means to prevent or counterwork their machinations. My tranquillity, on this occasion, was quickly retrieved. The whisper evidently proceeded from one who was posted at my bed-side. The first idea that suggested itself was, that it was uttered by the girl who lived with me as a servant. Perhaps, somewhat had alarmed her, or she was sick, and had come to request my assistance. By whispering in my ear, she intended to rouse without alarming me.

Full of this persuasion, I called; "Judith," said I, "is it you? What do you want? Is there any thing the matter with you?" No answer was returned. I repeated my inquiry, but equally in vain. Cloudy as was the atmosphere, and curtained as my bed was, nothing was visible, I withdrew the curtain, and leaning my head on my elbow, I listened with the deepest attention to catch some new sound. Meanwhile, I ran over in my thoughts, every circumstance that could assist my conjectures.

My habitation was a wooden edifice, consisting of two stories. In each story were two rooms, separated by an entry, or middle passage, with which they communicated by opposite doors. The passage, on the lower story, had doors at the two ends, and a stair-case. Windows answered to the doors on the upper story. Annexed to this, on

---

the bridegroom's armor and flesh fall away to reveal a deathly skeleton. In Bürger's original and most English versions, the lover is a cavalier who falls in a battle during the Seven Years War, but the William Taylor translation favored by Brown's circle makes the specter bridegroom a knight from the First Crusade (1096–1099). Clara's reference ("Godfrey of Bouillon") is to the Third Crusade, but seems to connect this invented ballad to *Lenore* and to other "terror" novels of the period that utilize these Crusader settings.

Whatever version of *Lenore* is referenced, Clara's remarks seem to evoke a woman's refusal of divine authority in favor of love with a spectral figure who portends catastrophe. If this is so, then Clara's ballad prefigures her future while allusively acknowledging her desire for the mysterious stranger. For more on *Lenore* and its significance for Brown and his circle, see the Introduction and Related Texts.

[10] "Clock . . . signal for twelve": as Clara points out, this is the same clock that her father, the elder Wieland, consulted in his daily regimen of religious devotions, and which is associated with his mysterious death. The same timepiece will figure in the final confrontation in Chapter 25. See note 25.5.

the eastern side, were wings, divided, in like manner, into an upper and lower room; one of them comprized a kitchen, and chamber above it for the servant, and communicated, on both stories, with the parlour adjoining it below, and the chamber adjoining it above. The opposite wing is of smaller dimensions, the rooms not being above eight feet square. The lower of these was used as a depository of household implements, the upper was a closet in which I deposited my books and papers. They had but one inlet, which was from the room adjoining. There was no window in the lower one, and in the upper, a small aperture which communicated light and air, but would scarcely admit the body. The door which led into this, was close to my bed-head, and was always locked, but when I myself was within. The avenues below were accustomed to be closed and bolted at nights.

The maid was my only companion, and she could not reach my chamber without previously passing through the opposite chamber, and the middle passage, of which, however, the doors were usually unfastened. If she had occasioned this noise, she would have answered my repeated calls. No other conclusion, therefore, was left me, but that I had mistaken the sounds, and that my imagination had transformed some casual noise into the voice of a human creature. Satisfied with this solution, I was preparing to relinquish my listening attitude, when my ear was again saluted with a new and yet louder whispering. It appeared, as before, to issue from lips that touched my pillow. A second effort of attention, however, clearly shewed me, that the sounds issued from within the closet, the door of which was not more than eight inches from my pillow.

This second interruption occasioned a shock less vehement than the former. I started, but gave no audible token of alarm. I was so much mistress of my feelings, as to continue listening to what should be said. The whisper was distinct, hoarse, and uttered so as to shew that the speaker was desirous of being heard by some one near, but, at the same time, studious to avoid being overheard by any other.

"Stop, stop, I say; madman as you are! there are better means than that. Curse upon your rashness! There is no need to shoot."

Such were the words uttered in a tone of eagerness and anger, within so small a distance of my pillow. What construction could I put upon them? My heart began to palpitate with dread of some unknown danger. Presently, another voice, but equally near me, was heard whispering in answer. "Why not? I will draw a trigger in this business, but perdition be my lot if I do more." To this, the first voice returned, in a tone which rage had heightened in a small degree above a whisper, "Coward! stand aside, and see me do it. I will grasp her throat; I will do her business in an instant; she shall not have time so much as to groan." What wonder that I was petrified by sounds so dreadful! Murderers lurked in my closet. They were planning the means of my destruction. One resolved to shoot, and the other menaced suffocation. Their means being chosen, they would forthwith break the door. Flight instantly suggested itself as most eligible in circumstances so perilous. I deliberated not a moment; but, fear adding wings to my speed, I leaped out of bed, and scantily robed as I was, rushed out of the chamber, down stairs, and into the open air. I can hardly recollect the process of turning keys, and withdrawing bolts. My terrors urged me forward with almost a mechanical impulse. I stopped not till I reached my brother's door. I had not gained the threshold, when, exhausted by the violence of my emotions, and by my speed, I sunk down in a fit.

How long I remained in this situation I know not. When I recovered, I found myself stretched on a bed, surrounded by my sister and her female servants. I was astonished at the scene before me, but gradually recovered the recollection of what had happened. I answered their importunate inquiries as well as I was able. My brother and Pleyel, whom the storm of the preceding day chanced to detain here, informing themselves of every particular, proceeded with lights and weapons to my deserted habitation. They entered my chamber and my closet, and found every thing in its proper place and customary order. The door of the closet was locked, and appeared not to have been opened in my absence. They went to Judith's apartment. They found her asleep and in safety. Pleyel's caution induced him to forbear alarming the girl; and finding her wholly ignorant of what had passed, they directed her to return to her chamber. They then fastened the doors, and returned.

My friends were disposed to regard this transaction as a dream. That persons should be actually immured in this closet, to which, in the circumstances of the time, access from without or within was apparently impossible, they could not seriously believe. That any human beings had intended murder, unless it were to cover a scheme of pillage, was incredible; but that no such design had been formed, was evident from the security in which the furniture of the house and the closet remained.

I revolved every incident and expression that had occurred. My senses assured me of the truth of them, and yet their abruptness and improbability made me, in my turn, somewhat incredulous. The adventure had made a deep impression on my fancy, and it was not till after a week's abode at my brother's, that I resolved to resume the possession of my own dwelling.

There was another circumstance that enhanced the mysteriousness of this event. After my recovery it was obvious to inquire by what means the attention of the family had been drawn to my situation. I had fallen before I had reached the threshold, or was able to give any signal. My brother related, that while this was transacting in my chamber, he himself was awake, in consequence of some slight indisposition, and lay, according to his custom, musing on some favorite topic. Suddenly the silence, which was remarkably profound, was broken by a voice of most piercing shrillness, that seemed to be uttered by one in the hall below his chamber. "Awake! arise!" it exclaimed: "hasten to succour one that is dying at your door."

This summons was effectual. There was no one in the house who was not roused by it. Pleyel was the first to obey, and my brother overtook him before he reached the hall. What was the general astonishment when your friend was discovered stretched upon the grass before the door, pale, ghastly, and with every mark of death!

This was the third instance of a voice,[11] exerted for the benefit of this little community. The agent was no less inscrutable in this, than in the former case. When I

---

[11] "Third instance of a voice": as Clara recalls at the end of this paragraph, the first was Theodore's experience of Catharine's voice in Chapter 4 (pp. 30–34); the second was the warning to Pleyel that Stolberg is dead in Chapter 5 (pp. 40–41).

ruminated upon these events, my soul was suspended in wonder and awe. Was I really deceived in imagining that I heard the closet conversation? I was no longer at liberty to question the reality of those accents which had formerly recalled my brother from the hill; which had imparted tidings of the death of the German lady to Pleyel; and which had lately summoned them to my assistance.

But how was I to regard this midnight conversation? Hoarse and manlike voices conferring on the means of death, so near my bed, and at such an hour! How had my ancient security vanished! That dwelling, which had hitherto been an inviolate asylum, was now beset with danger to my life. That solitude, formerly so dear to me, could no longer be endured. Pleyel, who had consented to reside with us during the months of spring, lodged in the vacant chamber, in order to quiet my alarms. He treated my fears with ridicule, and in a short time very slight traces of them remained: but as it was wholly indifferent to him whether his nights were passed at my house or at my brother's, this arrangement gave general satisfaction.

Chapter VII

I WILL not enumerate the various inquiries and conjectures which these incidents occasioned. After all our efforts, we came no nearer to dispelling the mist in which they were involved; and time, instead of facilitating a solution, only accumulated our doubts.

In the midst of thoughts excited by these events, I was not unmindful of my interview with the stranger. I related the particulars, and shewed the portrait to my friends. Pleyel recollected to have met with a figure resembling my description in the city; but neither his face or garb made the same impression upon him that it made upon me. It was a hint to rally me upon my prepossessions,[1] and to amuse us with a thousand ludicrous anecdotes which he had collected in his travels. He made no scruple to charge me with being in love; and threatened to inform the swain, when he met him, of his good fortune.

Pleyel's temper made him susceptible of no durable impressions. His conversation was occasionally visited by gleams of his ancient vivacity; but, though his impetuosity was sometimes inconvenient, there was nothing to dread from his malice. I had no fear that my character or dignity would suffer in his hands, and was not heartily displeased when he declared his intention of profiting by his first meeting with the stranger to introduce him to our acquaintance.

Some weeks after this I had spent a toilsome day, and, as the sun declined, found myself disposed to seek relief in a walk. The river bank is, at this part of it, and for some considerable space upward, so rugged and steep as not to be easily descended. In a recess of this declivity, near the southern verge of my little demesne, was placed a slight building, with seats and lattices. From a crevice of the rock, to which this edifice was attached, there burst forth a stream of the purest water, which, leaping from ledge to ledge, for the space of sixty feet, produced a freshness in the air, and a murmur, the most delicious and soothing imaginable. These, added to the odours of the cedars which embowered it, and of the honey-suckle which clustered among the lattices, rendered this my favorite retreat in summer.

On this occasion I repaired hither. My spirits drooped through the fatigue of long attention, and I threw myself upon a bench, in a state, both mentally and personally, of the utmost supineness. The lulling sounds of the waterfall, the fragrance and the dusk combined to becalm my spirits, and, in a short time, to sink me into sleep. Either the uneasiness of my posture, or some slight indisposition molested my repose with dreams of no cheerful hue. After various incoherences had taken their turn to occupy my fancy, I at length imagined myself walking, in the evening twilight, to my brother's habitation. A pit, methought, had been dug in the path I had taken, of which I was not aware. As I carelessly pursued my walk, I thought I saw my brother, standing at some distance before me, beckoning and calling me to make haste. He stood on the opposite edge of the gulph. I mended my pace, and one step more would have plunged me into this abyss, had not some one from

---

[1] "Prepossessions": "the condition of being favourably predisposed towards a person or thing" (*OED*).

behind caught suddenly my arm, and exclaimed, in a voice of eagerness and terror, "Hold! hold!"[2]

The sound broke my sleep, and I found myself, at the next moment, standing on my feet, and surrounded by the deepest darkness. Images so terrific and forcible disabled me, for a time, from distinguishing between sleep and wakefulness, and withheld from me the knowledge of my actual condition. My first panics were succeeded by the perturbations of surprize, to find myself alone in the open air, and immersed in so deep a gloom. I slowly recollected the incidents of the afternoon, and how I came hither. I could not estimate the time, but saw the propriety of returning with speed to the house. My faculties were still too confused, and the darkness too intense, to allow me immediately to find my way up the steep. I sat down, therefore, to recover myself, and to reflect upon my situation.

This was no sooner done, than a low voice was heard from behind the lattice, on the side where I sat. Between the rock and the lattice was a chasm not wide enough to admit a human body; yet, in this chasm he that spoke appeared to be stationed. "Attend! attend! but be not terrified."

I started and exclaimed, "Good heavens! What is that? Who are you?"

"A friend; one come, not to injure, but to save you; fear nothing."

This voice was immediately recognized to be the same with one of those which I had heard in the closet; it was the voice of him who had proposed to shoot, rather than to strangle, his victim. My terror made me, at once, mute and motionless. He continued, "I leagued to murder you. I repent. Mark my bidding, and be safe. Avoid this spot. The snares of death encompass it. Elsewhere danger will be distant; but this spot, shun it as you value your life. Mark me further; profit by this warning, but divulge it not. If a syllable of what has passed escape you, your doom is sealed. Remember your father, and be faithful."

Here the accents ceased, and left me overwhelmed with dismay. I was fraught with the persuasion, that during every moment I remained here, my life was endangered; but I could not take a step without hazard of falling to the bottom of the precipice. The path, leading to the summit, was short, but rugged and intricate. Even star-light was excluded by the umbrage, and not the faintest gleam was afforded to guide my steps. What should I do? To depart or remain was equally and eminently perilous.

In this state of uncertainty, I perceived a ray flit across the gloom and disappear. Another succeeded, which was stronger, and remained for a passing moment. It glittered on the shrubs that were scattered at the entrance, and gleam continued to succeed gleam[3] for a few seconds, till they, finally, gave place to unintermitted darkness.

---

[2] "Hold! hold!": Clara dreams that Theodore is beckoning her on toward disaster before she is saved by a mysterious intervention. When Carwin discusses this and other mysterious scenes with Clara at the end of Chapter 22, he explains that the phrase is drawn from *Macbeth* I.v.50–54 (see note 22.11). The same words will be used in the central scene in Chapter 16.

[3] "Gleam": Carwin's movements are often vaguely perceived by Clara and the others as transient gleams and flickers of light.

The first visitings of this light called up a train of horrors in my mind; destruction impended over this spot; the voice which I had lately heard had warned me to retire, and had menaced me with the fate of my father if I refused. I was desirous, but unable, to obey; these gleams were such as preluded the stroke by which he fell; the hour, perhaps, was the same—I shuddered as if I had beheld, suspended over me, the exterminating sword.[4]

Presently a new and stronger illumination burst through the lattice on the right hand, and a voice, from the edge of the precipice above, called out my name. It was Pleyel. Joyfully did I recognize his accents; but such was the tumult of my thoughts that I had not power to answer him till he had frequently repeated his summons. I hurried, at length, from the fatal spot, and, directed by the lanthorn which he bore, ascended the hill.

Pale and breathless, it was with difficulty I could support myself. He anxiously inquired into the cause of my affright, and the motive of my unusual absence. He had returned from my brother's at a late hour, and was informed by Judith, that I had walked out before sun-set, and had not yet returned. This intelligence was somewhat alarming. He waited some time; but, my absence continuing, he had set out in search of me. He had explored the neighbourhood with the utmost care, but, receiving no tidings of me, he was preparing to acquaint my brother with this circumstance, when he recollected the summer-house on the bank, and conceived it possible that some accident had detained me there. He again inquired into the cause of this detention, and of that confusion and dismay which my looks testified.

I told him that I had strolled hither in the afternoon, that sleep had overtaken me as I sat, and that I had awakened a few minutes before his arrival. I could tell him no more. In the present impetuosity of my thoughts, I was almost dubious, whether the pit, into which my brother had endeavoured to entice me, and the voice that talked through the lattice, were not parts of the same dream. I remembered, likewise, the charge of secrecy, and the penalty denounced, if I should rashly divulge what I had heard. For these reasons, I was silent on that subject, and shutting myself in my chamber, delivered myself up to contemplation.

What I have related will, no doubt, appear to you a fable. You will believe that calamity has subverted my reason, and that I am amusing you with the chimeras of my brain,[5] instead of facts that have really happened. I shall not be surprized or offended, if these be your suspicions. I know not, indeed, how you can deny them admission. For, if to me, the immediate witness, they were fertile of perplexity and doubt, how must they affect another to whom they are recommended only by my testimony? It was only by subsequent events, that I was fully and incontestibly assured of the veracity of my senses.

---

[4] "Exterminating sword": the connection of Clara's ominous dream about Theodore and the image of a fatal blade foreshadows later events.

[5] "Chimeras of my brain": chimera is a keyword for Brown throughout his writing, meaning "an unreal creature of the imagination, a mere wild fancy, an unfounded conception" (*OED*). In Brown's usage it refers to delusions resulting from incoherent and poorly rationalized ideas or, in essence, superstition.

Meanwhile what was I to think? I had been assured that a design had been formed against my life. The ruffians had leagued to murder me. Whom had I offended? Who was there with whom I had ever maintained intercourse, who was capable of harbouring such atrocious purposes?

My temper was the reverse of cruel and imperious. My heart was touched with sympathy for the children of misfortune. But this sympathy was not a barren senti-ment.[6] My purse, scanty as it was, was ever open, and my hands ever active, to relieve distress. Many were the wretches whom my personal exertions had extricated from want and disease, and who rewarded me with their gratitude. There was no face which lowered at my approach, and no lips which uttered imprecations in my hear-ing. On the contrary, there was none, over whose fate I had exerted any influence, or to whom I was known by reputation, who did not greet me with smiles, and dismiss me with proofs of veneration;[7] yet did not my senses assure me that a plot was laid against my life?

I am not destitute of courage, I have shewn myself deliberative and calm in the midst of peril. I have hazarded my own life, for the preservation of another, but now was I confused and panic struck. I have not lived so as to fear death, yet to perish by an unseen and secret stroke, to be mangled by the knife of an assassin, was a thought at which I shuddered; what had I done to deserve to be made the victim of malignant passions?

But soft! was I not assured, that my life was safe in all places but one? And why was the treason limited to take effect in this spot? I was every where equally defenceless. My house and chamber were, at all times, accessible. Danger still impended over me; the bloody purpose was still entertained, but the hand that was to execute it, was powerless in all places but one!

Here I had remained for the last four or five hours, without the means of resis-tance or defence, yet I had not been attacked. A human being was at hand, who was conscious of my presence, and warned me hereafter to avoid this retreat. His voice was not absolutely new, but had I never heard it but once before? But why did he prohibit me from relating this incident to others, and what species of death will be awarded if I disobey?

He talked of my father. He intimated, that disclosure would pull upon my head, the same destruction. Was then the death of my father, portentous and inexplicable as it was, the consequence of human machinations? It should seem, that this being is apprised of the true nature of this event, and is conscious of the means that led to it. Whether it shall likewise fall upon me, depends upon the observance of silence.

---

[6] "My temper was the reverse of cruel and imperious . . . sympathy . . . sentiment": Clara assumes that no one can think badly of her since she gives charity to the region's poor, invoking her elite per-formance of "sympathy" and "sentiment" as evidence of innocence and (civic) virtue. The passage, somewhat like her earlier thoughts on spreading republican virtue to the lower orders (see note 6.3) and other aspects of her narrative, implies her unquestioning assumption of class privilege and ideals of Enlightened Absolutism and the elite renovation of society.

[7] "Proofs of veneration": signs of respect or reverence.

Was it the infraction of a similar command, that brought so horrible a penalty upon my father?

Such were the reflections that haunted me during the night, and which effectually deprived me of sleep. Next morning, at breakfast, Pleyel related an event which my disappearance had hindered him from mentioning the night before. Early the preceding morning, his occasions called him to the city; he had stepped into a coffee-house to while away an hour; here he had met a person whose appearance instantly bespoke him to be the same whose hasty visit I have mentioned, and whose extraordinary visage and tones had so powerfully affected me. On an attentive survey, however, he proved, likewise, to be one with whom my friend had had some intercourse in Europe. This authorised the liberty of accosting him, and after some conversation, mindful, as Pleyel said, of the footing which this stranger had gained in my heart, he had ventured to invite him to Mettingen. The invitation had been cheerfully accepted, and a visit promised on the afternoon of the next day.

This information excited no sober emotions in my breast. I was, of course, eager to be informed as to the circumstances of their ancient intercourse. When, and where had they met? What knew he of the life and character of this man?

In answer to my inquiries, he informed me that, three years before, he was a traveller in Spain. He had made an excursion from Valencia to Murviedro,[8] with a view to inspect the remains of Roman magnificence, scattered in the environs of that town. While traversing the scite of the theatre of old Saguntum,[9] he lighted upon this man, seated on a stone, and deeply engaged in perusing the work of the deacon Marti.[10] A short conversation ensued, which proved the stranger to be English. They returned to Valencia together.

His garb, aspect, and deportment, were wholly Spanish. A residence of three years in the country, indefatigable attention to the language, and a studious conformity with the customs of the people, had made him indistinguishable from a native, when he chose to assume that character. Pleyel found him to be connected, on the footing

---

[8] "Valencia to Murviedro": from Valencia, a city on the Mediterranean coast of Spain, a short distance north to the smaller city, also on the coast. Murviedro was an eighteenth-century name for present-day Sagunto, called Saguntum by the Romans.

[9] "Roman magnificence . . . theatre of old Saguntum": descriptions of the Roman theater, aqueducts, and other antiquities of Sagunto were available in travel books and learned works on classical art. The theater, which could seat 4,000 spectators, was damaged by the Napoleonic army that captured Sagunto in 1812, and became the focus of a major restoration effort in the 1990s.

[10] "The work of the deacon Marti": Manuel Martí y Zaragoza (1663–1737), a Latinist and poet, dean of the College at Alicante, published his brief *Descripción del Teatro de Sagunto*, the book Carwin is reading, in 1705. This account of the theater's structure and function was republished and discussed through the century, and became a significant topos for thinking about Roman art and architecture. Brown probably draws his information about Marti's work from Irish antiquarian William Conyngham, *Observations on the description of the theatre of Saguntum, as given by Emanuel Marti, Dean of Alicant, in a letter addressed to D. Antonio Felix Zondadario* (Dublin: Royal Irish Academy, 1789), which provides a translation of Marti along with his architectural drawings and scenic plates of the theater, including the setting described by Pleyel.

of friendship and respect, with many eminent merchants in that city. He had embraced the catholic religion, and adopted a Spanish name instead of his own, which was Carwin, and devoted himself to the literature and religion of his new country. He pursued no profession, but subsisted on remittances from England.

While Pleyel remained in Valencia, Carwin betrayed no aversion to intercourse, and the former found no small attractions in the society of this new acquaintance. On general topics he was highly intelligent and communicative. He had visited every corner of Spain, and could furnish the most accurate details respecting its ancient and present state. On topics of religion and of his own history, previous to his *transformation*[11] into a Spaniard, he was invariably silent. You could merely gather from his discourse that he was English, and that he was well acquainted with the neighbouring countries.

His character excited considerable curiosity in this observer. It was not easy to reconcile his conversion to the Romish faith, with those proofs of knowledge and capacity that were exhibited by him on different occasions. A suspicion was, sometimes, admitted, that his belief was counterfeited for some political purpose. The most careful observation, however, produced no discovery. His manners were, at all times, harmless and inartificial, and his habits those of a lover of contemplation and seclusion. He appeared to have contracted an affection for Pleyel, who was not slow to return it.

My friend, after a month's residence in this city, returned into France, and, since that period, had heard nothing concerning Carwin till his appearance at Mettingen.

On this occasion Carwin had received Pleyel's greeting with a certain distance and solemnity to which the latter had not been accustomed. He had waved noticing the inquiries of Pleyel respecting his desertion of Spain, in which he had formerly declared that it was his purpose to spend his life. He had assiduously diverted the attention of the latter to indifferent topics, but was still, on every theme, as eloquent and judicious as formerly. Why he had assumed the garb of a rustic, Pleyel was unable to conjecture. Perhaps it might be poverty, perhaps he was swayed by motives which it was his interest to conceal, but which were connected with consequences of the utmost moment.

Such was the sum of my friend's information. I was not sorry to be left alone during the greater part of this day. Every employment was irksome which did not leave me at liberty to meditate. I had now a new subject on which to exercise my thoughts. Before evening I should be ushered into his presence, and listen to those tones whose magical and thrilling power I had already experienced. But with what new images would he then be accompanied?

Carwin was an adherent to the Romish faith, yet was an Englishman by birth,[12] and, perhaps, a protestant by education. He had adopted Spain for his country, and had intimated a design to spend his days there, yet now was an inhabitant of this district, and disguised by the habiliments of a clown! What could have obliterated the

---

[11] "*Transformation*": the only occurrence of the keyword from the novel's subtitle.

[12] "Romish faith . . . Englishman by birth": all of these suppositions and conjectures about Carwin turn out to be mistaken.

impressions of his youth, and made him abjure his religion and his country? What subsequent events had introduced so total a change in his plans? In withdrawing from Spain, had he reverted to the religion of his ancestors; or was it true, that his former conversion was deceitful, and that his conduct had been swayed by motives which it was prudent to conceal?

Hours were consumed in revolving these ideas. My meditations were intense; and, when the series was broken, I began to reflect with astonishment on my situation. From the death of my parents, till the commencement of this year, my life had been serene and blissful, beyond the ordinary portion of humanity; but, now, my bosom was corroded by anxiety. I was visited by dread of unknown dangers, and the future was a scene over which clouds rolled, and thunders muttered. I compared the cause with the effect, and they seemed disproportioned to each other. All unaware, and in a manner which I had no power to explain, I was pushed from my immoveable and lofty station, and cast upon a sea of troubles.

I determined to be my brother's visitant on this evening, yet my resolves were not unattended with wavering and reluctance. Pleyel's insinuations that I was in love, affected, in no degree, my belief, yet the consciousness that this was the opinion of one who would, probably, be present at our introduction to each other, would excite all that confusion which the passion itself is apt to produce. This would confirm him in his error, and call forth new railleries. His mirth, when exerted upon this topic, was the source of the bitterest vexation. Had he been aware of its influence upon my happiness, his temper would not have allowed him to persist; but this influence, it was my chief endeavour to conceal. That the belief of my having bestowed my heart upon another, produced in my friend none but ludicrous sensations, was the true cause of my distress; but if this had been discovered by him, my distress would have been unspeakably aggravated.

Chapter VIII

AS soon as evening arrived, I performed my visit. Carwin made one of the company, into which I was ushered. Appearances were the same as when I before beheld him. His garb was equally negligent and rustic. I gazed upon his countenance with new curiosity. My situation was such as to enable me to bestow upon it a deliberate examination. Viewed at more leisure, it lost none of its wonderful properties. I could not deny my homage to the intelligence expressed in it, but was wholly uncertain, whether he were an object to be dreaded or adored, and whether his powers had been exerted to evil or to good.

He was sparing in discourse; but whatever he said was pregnant with meaning, and uttered with rectitude of articulation, and force of emphasis, of which I had entertained no conception previously to my knowledge of him. Notwithstanding the uncouthness of his garb, his manners were not unpolished. All topics were handled by him with skill, and without pedantry or affectation. He uttered no sentiment calculated to produce a disadvantageous impression: on the contrary, his observations denoted a mind alive to every generous and heroic feeling. They were introduced without parade, and accompanied with that degree of earnestness which indicates sincerity.

He parted from us not till late, refusing an invitation to spend the night here, but readily consented to repeat his visit. His visits were frequently repeated. Each day introduced us to a more intimate acquaintance with his sentiments, but left us wholly in the dark, concerning that about which we were most inquisitive. He studiously avoided all mention of his past or present situation. Even the place of his abode in the city he concealed from us.

Our sphere, in this respect, being somewhat limited, and the intellectual endowments of this man being indisputably great, his deportment was more diligently marked, and copiously commented on by us, than you, perhaps, will think the circumstances warranted. Not a gesture, or glance, or accent, that was not, in our private assemblies, discussed, and inferences deduced from it. It may well be thought that he modelled his behaviour by an uncommon standard, when, with all our opportunities and accuracy of observation, we were able, for a long time, to gather no satisfactory information. He afforded us no ground on which to build even a plausible conjecture.

There is a degree of familiarity which takes place between constant associates, that justifies the negligence of many rules of which, in an earlier period of their intercourse, politeness requires the exact observance. Inquiries into our condition are allowable when they are prompted by a disinterested concern for our welfare; and this solicitude is not only pardonable, but may justly be demanded from those who chuse us for their companions. This state of things was more slow to arrive on this occasion than on most others, on account of the gravity and loftiness of this man's behaviour.

Pleyel, however, began, at length, to employ regular means for this end. He occasionally alluded to the circumstances in which they had formerly met, and remarked the incongruousness between the religion and habits of a Spaniard, with those of a native of Britain. He expressed his astonishment at meeting our guest in this corner of the globe, especially as, when they parted in Spain, he was taught to believe that Carwin should never leave that country. He insinuated, that a change so great must have been prompted by motives of a singular and momentous kind.

No answer, or an answer wide of the purpose, was generally made to these insinuations. Britons and Spaniards, he said, are votaries of the same Deity, and square their faith by the same precepts; their ideas are drawn from the same fountains of literature, and they speak dialects of the same tongue; their government and laws have more resemblances than differences; they were formerly provinces of the same civil, and till lately, of the same religious, Empire.[1]

As to the motives which induce men to change the place of their abode, these must unavoidably be fleeting and mutable. If not bound to one spot by conjugal or parental ties, or by the nature of that employment to which we are indebted for subsistence, the inducements to change are far more numerous and powerful, than opposite inducements.

He spoke as if desirous of shewing that he was not aware of the tendency of Pleyel's remarks; yet, certain tokens were apparent, that proved him by no means wanting in penetration. These tokens were to be read in his countenance, and not in his words. When any thing was said, indicating curiosity in us, the gloom of his countenance was deepened, his eyes sunk to the ground, and his wonted air was not resumed without visible struggle. Hence, it was obvious to infer, that some incidents of his life were reflected on by him with regret; and that, since these incidents were carefully concealed, and even that regret which flowed from them laboriously stifled, they had not been merely disastrous. The secrecy that was observed appeared not designed to provoke or baffle the inquisitive, but was prompted by the shame, or by the prudence of guilt.

These ideas, which were adopted by Pleyel and my brother, as well as myself, hindered us from employing more direct means for accomplishing our wishes. Questions might have been put in such terms, that no room should be left for the pretence of misapprehension, and if modesty merely had been the obstacle, such questions would not have been wanting; but we considered, that, if the disclosure were productive of pain or disgrace, it was inhuman to extort it.

Amidst the various topics that were discussed in his presence, allusions were, of course, made to the inexplicable events that had lately happened. At those times, the words and looks of this man were objects of my particular attention. The subject was

---

[1] "Same civil, and till lately, of the same religious, Empire": the Roman Empire. When Brown's friend William Miller asked him, in 1803, to summarize the most important transformations that occurred during the eighteenth century, Brown replied that these were the critique and rejection of theistic belief, and new stages of print culture and colonialism. Brown viewed these shifts in a long-duration sense and argued that they are the ultimate consequence of the Reformation and its religious wars, considered as the secession of Protestant countries from their original positions in the Roman (pagan, then Catholic) Empire. This is the same long view and empire-focused, nonnationalistic perspective on modern history that Carwin implies with his answer to Pleyel's question. For more, see this letter from Brown to Miller in Related Texts.

extraordinary; and any one whose experience or reflections could throw any light upon it, was entitled to my gratitude. As this man was enlightened by reading and travel, I listened with eagerness to the remarks which he should make.

At first, I entertained a kind of apprehension, that the tale would be heard by him with incredulity and secret ridicule. I had formerly heard stories that resembled this in some of their mysterious circumstances, but they were, commonly, heard by me with contempt. I was doubtful, whether the same impression would not now be made on the mind of our guest; but I was mistaken in my fears.

He heard them with seriousness, and without any marks either of surprize or incredulity. He pursued, with visible pleasure, that kind of disquisition which was naturally suggested by them. His fancy was eminently vigorous and prolific, and if he did not persuade us, that human beings are, sometimes, admitted to a sensible intercourse with the author of nature, he, at least, won over our inclination to the cause. He merely deduced, from his own reasonings, that such intercourse was probable; but confessed that, though he was acquainted with many instances somewhat similar to those which had been related by us, none of them were perfectly exempted from the suspicion of human agency.

On being requested to relate these instances, he amused us with many curious details. His narratives were constructed with so much skill, and rehearsed with so much energy, that all the effects of a dramatic exhibition were frequently produced by them. Those that were most coherent and most minute, and, of consequence, least entitled to credit, were yet rendered probable by the exquisite art of this rhetorician. For every difficulty that was suggested, a ready and plausible solution was furnished. Mysterious voices had always a share in producing the catastrophe, but they were always to be explained on some known principles, either as reflected into a focus, or communicated through a tube. I could not but remark that his narratives, however complex or marvellous, contained no instance sufficiently parallel to those that had befallen ourselves, and in which the solution was applicable to our own case.

My brother was a much more sanguine[2] reasoner than our guest. Even in some of the facts which were related by Carwin, he maintained the probability of celestial interference, when the latter was disposed to deny it, and had found, as he imagined, footsteps of an human agent. Pleyel was by no means equally credulous. He scrupled not to deny faith to any testimony but that of his senses, and allowed the facts which had lately been supported by this testimony, not to mould his belief, but merely to give birth to doubts.

It was soon observed that Carwin adopted, in some degree, a similar distinction. A tale of this kind, related by others, he would believe, provided it was explicable upon known principles; but that such notices were actually communicated by beings of an higher order, he would believe only when his own ears were assailed in a manner which could not be otherwise accounted for. Civility forbad him to contradict my brother or myself, but his understanding refused to acquiesce in our testimony.

---

[2] "Sanguine": hopeful or confident (here, confident that divine interference in human actions may account for the mysterious voices).

Besides, he was disposed to question whether the voices heard in the temple, at the foot of the hill, and in my closet,[3] were not really uttered by human organs. On this supposition he was desired to explain how the effect was produced.

He answered, that the power of mimickry was very common. Catharine's voice might easily be imitated by one at the foot of the hill, who would find no difficulty in eluding, by flight, the search of Wieland. The tidings of the death of the Saxon lady were uttered by one near at hand, who overheard the conversation, who conjectured her death, and whose conjecture happened to accord with the truth. That the voice appeared to come from the ceiling was to be considered as an illusion of the fancy. The cry for help, heard in the hall on the night of my adventure, was to be ascribed to an human creature, who actually stood in the hall when he uttered it. It was of no moment, he said, that we could not explain by what motives he that made the signal was led hither. How imperfectly acquainted were we with the condition and designs of the beings that surrounded us? The city was near at hand, and thousands might there exist whose powers and purposes might easily explain whatever was mysterious in this transaction. As to the closet dialogue, he was obliged to adopt one of two suppositions, and affirm either that it was fashioned in my own fancy, or that it actually took place between two persons in the closet.

Such was Carwin's mode of explaining these appearances. It is such, perhaps, as would commend itself as most plausible to the most sagacious minds, but it was insufficient to impart conviction to us.[4] As to the treason that was meditated against me, it was doubtless just to conclude that it was either real or imaginary; but that it was real was attested by the mysterious warning in the summer-house, the secret of which I had hitherto locked up in my own breast.

A month passed away in this kind of intercourse. As to Carwin, our ignorance was in no degree enlightened respecting his genuine character and views. Appearances were uniform. No man possessed a larger store of knowledge, or a greater degree of skill in the communication of it to others: Hence he was regarded as an inestimable addition to our society. Considering the distance of my brother's house from the city, he was frequently prevailed upon to pass the night where he spent the evening. Two days seldom elapsed without a visit from him; hence he was regarded as a kind of inmate of the house. He entered and departed without ceremony. When he arrived he received an unaffected welcome, and when he chose to retire, no importunities were used to induce him to remain.

---

[3] "In the temple, at the foot of the hill, and in my closet": this list of the mysterious voices omits the fourth event, at the beginning of Chapter 7, when Clara was in the grotto and dreamt that Theodore was luring her on toward an abyss. Clara has kept this instance secret during discussions of the voices. Although the voice commanded her to keep the incident secret ("divulge it not"), her continuing silence and reluctance to tell the others about it may also imply that she is anxious or in denial about an intuitive fear that Theodore is dangerous. Her anxiety about this intuition will continue to build in the next chapter.

[4] "Insufficient to impart conviction to us": Carwin has answered carefully but, when pressed, he sides with Pleyel against Theodore and Clara, suggesting that the mysterious voices can only be human tricks. The Wielands, nevertheless, reject the possibility of a rationalistic explanation.

The temple was the principal scene of our social enjoyments; yet the felicity that we tasted when assembled in this asylum, was but the gleam of a former sun-shine. Carwin never parted with his gravity. The inscrutableness of his character, and the uncertainty whether his fellowship tended to good or to evil, were seldom absent from our minds. This circumstance powerfully contributed to sadden us.

My heart was the seat of growing disquietudes. This change in one who had formerly been characterized by all the exuberances of soul, could not fail to be remarked by my friends. My brother was always a pattern of solemnity. My sister was clay, moulded by the circumstances in which she happened to be placed.[5] There was but one whose deportment remains to be described as being of importance to our happiness. Had Pleyel likewise dismissed his vivacity?

He was as whimsical and jestful as ever, but he was not happy. The truth, in this respect, was of too much importance to me not to make me a vigilant observer. His mirth was easily perceived to be the fruit of exertion. When his thoughts wandered from the company, an air of dissatisfaction and impatience stole across his features. Even the punctuality and frequency of his visits were somewhat lessened. It may be supposed that my own uneasiness was heightened by these tokens; but, strange as it may seem, I found, in the present state of my mind, no relief but in the persuasion that Pleyel was unhappy.

That unhappiness, indeed, depended, for its value in my eyes, on the cause that produced it. It did not arise from the death of the Saxon lady: it was not a contagious emanation from the countenances of Wieland or Carwin. There was but one other source whence it could flow. A nameless ecstacy thrilled through my frame when any new proof occurred that the ambiguousness of my behaviour was the cause.[6]

---

[5] "My sister was clay, moulded by the circumstances in which she happened to be placed": Clara's sister-in-law, Catharine. The remark suggests a Wollstonecraftian perspective on women's subordination and domestic "slavery," and reiterates Clara's emphasis, in the novel's first paragraph, on the ways that social environment shapes character (see note 1.2).

[6] "A nameless ecstasy . . . my behaviour was the cause": by having Clara take pleasure in the game of love and erotic manipulation, Brown seems to suggest another Wollstonecraftian reflection on the way she is acculturated to be preoccupied with love and romance. Clara recognizes female subordination in the behavior of her sister-in-law Catharine, but less so in herself. Love and fear alike are generating "passions" that connect Clara with the values of sentiment and sensibility, but that set her at odds with rational behavior. The passions and illusions of love are immediately put into question in the following chapter.

Chapter IX

MY brother had received a new book from Germany. It was a tragedy, and the first attempt of a Saxon poet, of whom my brother had been taught to entertain the highest expectations. The exploits of Zisca, the Bohemian hero,[1] were woven into a dramatic series and connection. According to German custom, it was minute and diffuse, and dictated by an adventurous and lawless fancy. It was a chain of audacious acts, and unheard-of disasters. The moated fortress, and the thicket; the ambush and the battle; and the conflict of headlong passions, were pourtrayed in wild numbers, and with terrific energy. An afternoon was set apart to rehearse this performance. The language was familiar to all of us but Carwin, whose company, therefore, was tacitly dispensed with.[2]

The morning previous to this intended rehearsal, I spent at home. My mind was occupied with reflections relative to my own situation. The sentiment which lived with chief energy in my heart, was connected with the image of Pleyel. In the midst of my anguish, I had not been destitute of consolation. His late deportment had given spring to my hopes. Was not the hour at hand, which should render me the happiest of human creatures? He suspected that I looked with favorable eyes upon Carwin. Hence arose disquietudes, which he struggled in vain to conceal. He loved me, but was hopeless that his love would be compensated. Is it not time, said I, to rectify this error? But by what means is this to be effected? It can only be done by a change of deportment in me; but how must I demean myself for this purpose?

I must not speak. Neither eyes, nor lips, must impart the information. He must not be assured that my heart is his, previous to the tender of his own; but he must be convinced that it has not been given to another; he must be supplied with space whereon to build a doubt as to the true state of my affections; he must be prompted

---

[1] "Zisca, the Bohemian hero": another allusion to the early Moravian movement and wild sectarian violence. Jan Zizka (Czech for "one-eyed"; 1360–1424) was a follower of Jan Hus, founder of the Moravian movement, and a legendarily ferocious warrior in the period's religious-political uprisings. In the 1790s, Zizka was still famous for his dying wish: he ordered his soldiers to flay his skin and use it to cover a drum, so that the sound of it would frighten their enemies. Thomas Carlyle sums up Zizka's reputation in his *History of Friedrich II of Prussia* (1858): "Zisca, stout and furious, blind of one eye and at last of both, a kind of human rhinoceros driven mad, had risen out of the ashes of murdered Huss, and other bad Papistic doings, in the interim; and was tearing up the world at a huge rate." Accounts of Zizka's exploits were available to Brown in histories such as William Gilpin, *The lives of John Wicliff; and of the most eminent of his disciples; Lord Cobham, John Huss, Jerome of Prague, and Zisca* (1766). For earlier references to the Moravians, see notes 1.17, 1.20, 2.2, 5.1.

[2] "A new book from Germany . . . terrific energy . . . dispensed with": Clara's paragraph-long evocation of a thrilling work of "adventurous and lawless fancy" presented in a "wild" and "terrific" style, is an apt description of *Wieland* itself and a knowing tip of the hat to the 1790s German wave of "horror" fiction (*Schauerroman*), as the Wielands read aloud this historical tale of early Protestant-Catholic conflicts for its aesthetic, rather than spiritual, effects. The work's "outrageous vehemence" will soon be rivaled by Clara's own experience. The group reads the text in the original German, excluding Carwin on the assumption he does not speak the language.

to avow himself. The line of delicate propriety; how hard it is, not to fall short, and not to overleap it!

This afternoon we shall meet at the temple. We shall not separate till late. It will be his province to accompany me home. The airy expanse is without a speck. This breeze is usually stedfast, and its promise of a bland and cloudless evening, may be trusted. The moon will rise at eleven, and at that hour, we shall wind along this bank. Possibly that hour may decide my fate. If suitable encouragement be given, Pleyel will reveal his soul to me; and I, ere I reach this threshold, will be made the happiest of beings. And is this good to be mine? Add wings to thy speed, sweet evening; and thou, moon, I charge thee, shroud thy beams[3] at the moment when my Pleyel whispers love. I would not for the world, that the burning blushes, and the mounting raptures of that moment, should be visible.

But what encouragement is wanting? I must be regardful of insurmountable limits. Yet when minds are imbued with a genuine sympathy, are not words and looks superfluous? Are not motion and touch sufficient to impart feelings such as mine? Has he not eyed me at moments, when the pressure of his hand has thrown me into tumults, and was it possible that he mistook the impetuosities of love, for the eloquence of indignation?

But the hastening evening will decide. Would it were come! And yet I shudder at its near approach. An interview that must thus terminate, is surely to be wished for by me; and yet it is not without its terrors. Would to heaven it were come and gone!

I feel no reluctance, my friends to be thus explicit. Time was, when these emotions would be hidden with immeasurable solicitude, from every human eye. Alas! these airy and fleeting impulses of shame are gone. My scruples were preposterous and criminal. They are bred in all hearts, by a perverse and vicious education, and they would still have maintained their place in my heart, had not my portion been set in misery. My errors[4] have taught me thus much wisdom; that those sentiments which we ought not to disclose, it is criminal to harbour.

It was proposed to begin the rehearsal at four o'clock; I counted the minutes as they passed; their flight was at once too rapid and too slow; my sensations were of an excruciating kind; I could taste no food, nor apply to any talk, nor enjoy a moment's repose: when the hour arrived, I hastened to my brother's.

Pleyel was not there. He had not yet come. On ordinary occasions, he was eminent for punctuality. He had testified great eagerness to share in the pleasures of this rehearsal. He was to divide the task with my brother, and, in tasks like these, he always engaged with peculiar zeal. His elocution was less sweet than sonorous; and, therefore, better adapted than the mellifluences of his friend, to the outrageous vehemence of this drama.

---

[3] "Add wings to thy speed . . . shroud thy beams": Clara lapses into the precious phraseology of sentimental love narratives to highlight her deluded state.

[4] "Perverse and vicious education . . . errors": like Wollstonecraft, but only in retrospect, Clara rejects the cultural common sense that preoccupies her with fantasies of romance and blinds her to what was occurring around her.

What could detain him? Perhaps he lingered through forgetfulness. Yet this was incredible. Never had his memory been known to fail upon even more trivial occasions. Not less impossible was it, that the scheme had lost its attractions, and that he staid, because his coming would afford him no gratification. But why should we expect him to adhere to the minute?

An half hour elapsed, but Pleyel was still at a distance. Perhaps he had misunderstood the hour which had been proposed. Perhaps he had conceived that to-morrow, and not to-day, had been selected for this purpose: but no. A review of preceding circumstances demonstrated that such misapprehension was impossible; for he had himself proposed this day, and this hour. This day, his attention would not otherwise be occupied; but to-morrow, an indispensible engagement was foreseen, by which all his time would be engrossed: his detention, therefore, must be owing to some unforeseen and extraordinary event. Our conjectures were vague, tumultuous, and sometimes fearful. His sickness and his death might possibly have detained him.

Tortured with suspense, we sat gazing at each other, and at the path which led from the road. Every horseman that passed was, for a moment, imagined to be him. Hour succeeded hour, and the sun, gradually declining, at length, disappeared. Every signal of his coming proved fallacious, and our hopes were at length dismissed. His absence affected my friends in no insupportable degree. They should be obliged, they said, to defer this undertaking till the morrow; and, perhaps, their impatient curiosity would compel them to dispense entirely with his presence. No doubt, some harmless occurrence had diverted him from his purpose; and they trusted that they should receive a satisfactory account of him in the morning.

It may be supposed that this disappointment affected me in a very different manner. I turned aside my head to conceal my tears. I fled into solitude, to give vent to my reproaches, without interruption or restraint. My heart was ready to burst with indignation and grief. Pleyel was not the only object of my keen but unjust upbraiding. Deeply did I execrate my own folly. Thus fallen into ruins was the gay fabric which I had reared! Thus had my golden vision melted into air!

How fondly did I dream that Pleyel was a lover! If he were, would he have suffered any obstacle to hinder his coming? Blind and infatuated man! I exclaimed. Thou sportest with happiness. The good that is offered thee, thou hast the insolence and folly to refuse. Well, I will henceforth intrust my felicity to no one's keeping but my own.

The first agonies of this disappointment would not allow me to be reasonable or just. Every ground on which I had built the persuasion that Pleyel was not unimpressed in my favor, appeared to vanish. It seemed as if I had been misled into this opinion, by the most palpable illusions.

I made some trifling excuse, and returned, much earlier than I expected, to my own house. I retired early to my chamber, without designing to sleep. I placed myself at a window, and gave the reins to reflection.

The hateful and degrading impulses which had lately controuled me were, in some degree, removed. New dejection succeeded, but was now produced by contemplating my late behaviour. Surely that passion is worthy to be abhorred which obscures our understanding, and urges us to the commission of injustice. What right had I to expect his attendance? Had I not demeaned myself like one indifferent to his happiness, and as having bestowed my regards upon another? His absence might be prompted by the love which I considered his absence as a proof that he wanted. He came not because the sight of me, the spectacle of my coldness or aversion, contributed to his despair. Why should I prolong, by hypocrisy or silence, his misery as well as my own? Why not deal with him explicitly, and assure him of the truth?

You will hardly believe that, in obedience to this suggestion, I rose for the purpose of ordering a light, that I might instantly make this confession in a letter. A second thought shewed me the rashness of this scheme, and I wondered by what infirmity of mind I could be betrayed into a momentary approbation of it. I saw with the utmost clearness that a confession like that would be the most remediless and unpardonable outrage upon the dignity of my sex, and utterly unworthy of that passion which controuled me.

I resumed my seat and my musing. To account for the absence of Pleyel became once more the scope of my conjectures. How many incidents might occur to raise an insuperable impediment in his way? When I was a child, a scheme of pleasure, in which he and his sister were parties, had been, in like manner, frustrated by his absence; but his absence, in that instance, had been occasioned by his falling from a boat into the river, in consequence of which he had run the most imminent hazard of being drowned. Here was a second disappointment endured by the same persons, and produced by his failure. Might it not originate in the same cause? Had he not designed to cross the river that morning to make some necessary purchases in Jersey? He had preconcerted to return to his own house to dinner; but, perhaps, some disaster had befallen him. Experience had taught me the insecurity of a canoe, and that was the only kind of boat which Pleyel used: I was, likewise, actuated by an hereditary dread of water. These circumstances combined to bestow considerable plausibility on this conjecture; but the consternation with which I began to be seized was allayed by reflecting, that if this disaster had happened my brother would have received the speediest information of it. The consolation which this idea imparted was ravished from me by a new thought. This disaster might have happened, and his family not be apprized of it. The first intelligence of his fate may be communicated by the livid corpse which the tide may cast, many days hence, upon the shore.

Thus was I distressed by opposite conjectures: thus was I tormented by phantoms of my own creation. It was not always thus. I can ascertain the date when my mind became the victim of this imbecility; perhaps it was coeval with the inroad of a fatal passion;[5] a passion that will never rank me in the number of its eulogists; it was alone sufficient to the extermination of my peace: it was itself a plenteous source of calamity, and needed not the concurrence of other evils to take away the attractions of existence, and dig for me an untimely grave.

---

[5] "Phantoms . . . imbecility . . . fatal passion": Clara assumes that her reverie about Pleyel's drowning is tied to an indulgence in erotic desires. She conjures a similar scene again in the next chapter; see note 10.9.

The state of my mind naturally introduced a train of reflections upon the dangers and cares which inevitably beset an human being. By no violent transition was I led to ponder on the turbulent life and mysterious end of my father. I cherished, with the utmost veneration, the memory of this man, and every relique connected with his fate was preserved with the most scrupulous care. Among these was to be numbered a manuscript, containing memoirs of his own life. The narrative was by no means recommended by its eloquence; but neither did all its value flow from my relationship to the author. Its stile had an unaffected and picturesque simplicity. The great variety and circumstantial display of the incidents, together with their intrinsic importance, as descriptive of human manners and passions, made it the most useful book in my collection. It was late; but being sensible of no inclination to sleep, I resolved to betake myself to the perusal of it.

To do this it was requisite to procure a light. The girl had long since retired to her chamber: it was therefore proper to wait upon myself. A lamp, and the means of lighting it, were only to be found in the kitchen. Thither I resolved forthwith to repair; but the light was of use merely to enable me to read the book. I knew the shelf and the spot where it stood. Whether I took down the book, or prepared the lamp in the first place, appeared to be a matter of no moment. The latter was preferred, and, leaving my seat, I approached the closet in which, as I mentioned formerly, my books and papers were deposited.

Suddenly the remembrance of what had lately passed in this closet occurred. Whether midnight was approaching, or had passed, I knew not. I was, as then, alone, and defenceless. The wind was in that direction in which, aided by the deathlike repose of nature, it brought to me the murmur of the water-fall. This was mingled with that solemn and enchanting sound, which a breeze produces among the leaves of pines. The words of that mysterious dialogue,[6] their fearful import, and the wild excess to which I was transported by my terrors, filled my imagination anew. My steps faultered, and I stood a moment to recover myself.

I prevailed on myself at length to move towards the closet. I touched the lock, but my fingers were powerless; I was visited afresh by unconquerable apprehensions. A sort of belief darted into my mind, that some being was concealed within, whose purposes were evil. I began to contend with those fears, when it occurred to me that I might, without impropriety, go for a lamp previously to opening the closet. I receded a few steps; but before I reached my chamber door my thoughts took a new direction. Motion seemed to produce a mechanical influence upon me. I was ashamed of my weakness. Besides, what aid could be afforded me by a lamp?

My fears had pictured to themselves no precise object. It would be difficult to depict, in words, the ingredients and hues of that phantom which haunted me. An hand invisible and of preternatural strength, lifted by human passions, and selecting

---

[6] "That mysterious dialogue": Clara's second experience of the mysterious voice, in Chapter 7, when it woke her from the dream in which Theodore beckoned her toward an abyss. Although she has not told her friends about this incident (see note 8.3), it continues to preoccupy her in moments of anxiety.

my life for its aim,[7] were parts of this terrific image. All places were alike accessible to this foe, or if his empire were restricted by local bounds, those bounds were utterly inscrutable by me. But had I not been told by some one in league with this enemy, that every place but the recess in the bank was exempt from danger?

I returned to the closet, and once more put my hand upon the lock. O! may my ears lose their sensibility, ere they be again assailed by a shriek so terrible! Not merely my understanding was subdued by the sound: it acted on my nerves like an edge of steel. It appeared to cut asunder the fibres of my brain, and rack every joint with agony.

The cry, loud and piercing as it was, was nevertheless human. No articulation was ever more distinct. The breath which accompanied it did not fan my hair, yet did every circumstance combine to persuade me that the lips which uttered it touched my very shoulder.

"Hold! Hold!" were the words of this tremendous prohibition, in whose tone the whole soul seemed to be rapt up, and every energy converted into eagerness and terror.

Shuddering, I dashed myself against the wall, and by the same involuntary impulse, turned my face backward to examine the mysterious monitor. The moon-light streamed into each window, and every corner of the room was conspicuous, and yet I beheld nothing!

The interval was too brief to be artificially measured, between the utterance of these words, and my scrutiny directed to the quarter whence they came. Yet if a human being had been there, could he fail to have been visible? Which of my senses was the prey of a fatal illusion? The shock which the sound produced was still felt in every part of my frame. The sound, therefore, could not but be a genuine commotion. But that I had heard it, was not more true than that the being who uttered it was stationed at my right ear; yet my attendant was invisible.

I cannot describe the state of my thoughts at that moment. Surprize had mastered my faculties. My frame shook, and the vital current was congealed. I was conscious only to the vehemence of my sensations. This condition could not be lasting. Like a tide, which suddenly mounts to an overwhelming height, and then gradually subsides, my confusion slowly gave place to order, and my tumults to a calm. I was able to deliberate and move. I resumed my feet, and advanced into the midst of the room. Upward, and behind, and on each side, I threw penetrating glances. I was not satisfied with one examination. He that hitherto refused to be seen, might change his purpose, and on the next survey be clearly distinguishable.

Solitude imposes least restraint upon the fancy. Dark is less fertile of images than the feeble lustre of the moon. I was alone, and the walls were chequered by shadowy forms. As the moon passed behind a cloud and emerged, these shadows seemed to be endowed with life, and to move. The apartment was open to the breeze, and the curtain was occasionally blown from its ordinary position. This motion was not unaccompanied with sound. I failed not to snatch a look, and to listen when this

---

[7] "An hand invisible and of preternatural strength . . . selecting my life for its aim": as her fear and anxiety build, Clara's imagination combines elements of her father's death and her more recent forebodings about Theodore, foreshadowing later events in her bedroom.

motion and this sound occurred. My belief that my monitor was posted near, was strong, and instantly converted these appearances to tokens of his presence, and yet I could discern nothing.

When my thoughts were at length permitted to revert to the past, the first idea that occurred was the resemblance between the words of the voice which I had just heard, and those which had terminated my dream in the summer-house. There are means by which we are able to distinguish a substance from a shadow, a reality from the phantom of a dream. The pit, my brother beckoning me forward, the seizure of my arm, and the voice behind, were surely imaginary. That these incidents were fashioned in my sleep, is supported by the fame indubitable evidence that compels me to believe myself awake at present; yet the words and the voice were the same. Then, by some inexplicable contrivance, I was aware of the danger, while my actions and sensations were those of one wholly unacquainted with it. Now, was it not equally true that my actions and persuasions were at war? Had not the belief, that evil lurked in the closet, gained admittance, and had not my actions betokened an unwarrantable security? To obviate the effects of my infatuation, the same means had been used.

In my dream, he that tempted me to my destruction, was my brother. Death was ambushed in my path. From what evil was I now rescued? What minister or implement of ill was shut up in this recess? Who was it whose suffocating grasp I was to feel, should I dare to enter it? What monstrous conception is this? my brother![8]

No; protection, and not injury is his province. Strange and terrible chimera! Yet it would not be suddenly dismissed. It was surely no vulgar agency that gave this form to my fears. He to whom all parts of time are equally present, whom no contingency, approaches, was the author of that spell which now seized upon me. Life was dear to me. No consideration was present that enjoined me to relinquish it. Sacred duty combined with every spontaneous sentiment to endear to me my being. Should I not shudder when my being was endangered? But what emotion should possess me when the arm lifted against me was Wieland's?

Ideas exist in our minds that can be accounted for by no established laws. Why did I dream that my brother was my foe? Why but because an omen of my fate was ordained to be communicated? Yet what salutary end did it serve? Did it arm me with caution to elude, or fortitude to bear the evils to which I was reserved? My present thoughts were, no doubt, indebted for their hue to the similitude existing between these incidents and those of my dream. Surely it was phrenzy that dictated my deed. That a ruffian was hidden in the closet, was an idea, the genuine tendency of which was to urge me to slight. Such had been the effect formerly produced. Had my mind

---

[8] "My brother!": Clara assumes that Theodore is hiding in her closet, waiting to attack and possibly rape her, acknowledging the suspicions and fears that have been felt but not articulated until this event. Since the implications of this dawning awareness are akin to the outrageousness of the German drama she described at the beginning of the chapter, perhaps, Clara shortly downplays it as a "frantic conception" and "infatuation."

been simply occupied with this thought at present, no doubt, the same impulse would have been experienced; but now it was my brother whom I was irresistably persuaded to regard as the contriver of that ill of which I had been forewarned. This persuasion did not extenuate my fears or my danger. Why then did I again approach the closet and withdraw the bolt? My resolution was instantly conceived, and executed without faultering.

The door was formed of light materials. The lock, of simple structure, easily forewent its hold. It opened into the room, and commonly moved upon its hinges, after being unfastened, without any effort of mine. This effort, however, was bestowed upon the present occasion. It was my purpose to open it with quickness, but the exertion which I made was ineffectual. It refused to open.

At another time, this circumstance would not have looked with a face of mystery. I should have supposed some casual obstruction, and repeated my efforts to surmount it. But now my mind was accessible to no conjecture but one. The door was hindered from opening by human force. Surely, here was new cause for affright. This was confirmation proper to decide my conduct. Now was all ground of hesitation taken away. What could be supposed but that I deserted the chamber and the house? that I at least endeavoured no longer to withdraw the door?

Have I not said that my actions were dictated by phrenzy? My reason had forborne, for a time, to suggest or to sway my resolves. I reiterated my endeavours. I exerted all my force to overcome the obstacle, but in vain. The strength that was exerted to keep it shut, was superior to mine.

A casual observer might, perhaps, applaud the audaciousness of this conduct. Whence, but from an habitual defiance of danger, could my perseverance arise? I have already assigned, as distinctly as I am able, the cause of it. The frantic conception that my brother was within, that the resistance made to my design was exerted by him, had rooted itself in my mind. You will comprehend the height of this infatuation, when I tell you, that, finding all my exertions vain, I betook myself to exclamations. Surely I was utterly bereft of understanding.

Now had I arrived at the crisis of my fate. "O! hinder not the door to open," I exclaimed, in a tone that had less of fear than of grief in it. "I know you well. Come forth, but harm me not. I beseech you come forth."

I had taken my hand from the lock, and removed to a small distance from the door. I had scarcely uttered these words, when the door swung upon its hinges, and displayed to my view the interior of the closet. Whoever was within, was shrouded in darkness. A few seconds passed without interruption of the silence. I knew not what to expect or to fear. My eyes would not stray from the recess. Presently, a deep sigh was heard. The quarter from which it came heightened the eagerness of my gaze. Some one approached from the farther end. I quickly perceived the outlines of a human figure. Its steps were irresolute and slow. I recoiled as it advanced.

By coming at length within the verge of the room, his form was clearly distinguishable. I had prefigured to myself a very different personage. The face that presented itself was the last that I should desire to meet at an hour, and in a place like this. My wonder was stifled by my fears. Assassins had lurked in this recess. Some divine voice warned me of danger,[9] that at this moment awaited me. I had spurned the intimation, and challenged my adversary.

I recalled the mysterious countenance and dubious character of Carwin. What motive but atrocious ones could guide his steps hither? I was alone. My habit suited the hour, and the place, and the warmth of the season.[10] All succour was remote. He had placed himself between me and the door. My frame shook with the vehemence of my apprehensions.

Yet I was not wholly lost to myself: I vigilantly marked his demeanour. His looks were grave, but not without perturbation. What species of inquietude it betrayed, the light was not strong enough to enable me to discover. He stood still; but his eyes wandered from one object to another. When these powerful organs were fixed upon me, I shrunk into myself. At length, he broke silence. Earnestness, and not embarrassment, was in his tone. He advanced close to me while he spoke.

"What voice was that which lately addressed you?"

He paused for an answer; but observing my trepidation, he resumed, with undiminished solemnity: "Be not terrified. Whoever he was, he hast done you an important service. I need not ask you if it were the voice of a companion. That sound was beyond the compass of human organs. The knowledge that enabled him to tell you who was in the closet, was obtained by incomprehensible means.

"You knew that Carwin was there. Were you not apprized of his intents? The same power could impart the one as well as the other. Yet, knowing these, you persisted. Audacious girl! but, perhaps, you confided in his guardianship. Your confidence was just. With succour like this at hand you may safely defy me.

"He is my eternal foe; the baffler of my best concerted schemes. Twice have you been saved by his accursed interposition. But for him I should long ere now have borne away the spoils of your honor."

"He looked at me with greater stedfastness than before. I became every moment more anxious for my safety. It was with difficulty I stammered out an entreaty that he would instantly depart, or suffer me to do so. He paid no regard to my request, but proceeded in a more impassioned manner.

"What is it you fear? Have I not told you, you are safe? Has not one in whom you more reasonably place trust assured you of it? Even if I execute my purpose, what injury is done? Your prejudices will call it by that name, but it merits it not.

"I was impelled by a sentiment that does you honor; a sentiment, that would sanctify my deed; but, whatever it be, you are safe. Be this chimera still worshipped;[11] I will do nothing to pollute it." There he stopped.

---

[9] "Some divine voice warned me of danger": like the Daemon of Socrates, mentioned at the end of Chapter 5. See note 5.17.

[10] "My habit suited the hour, and the place, and the warmth of the season": scantily dressed ("habit" here means clothing or outfit) and isolated in her bedroom, Clara assumes that Carwin intends to rape her. In the following exchange Carwin confirms that this is the most likely scenario in the circumstance.

[11] "Be this chimera still worshipped": the ideal of virginity as proof of virtue.

The accents and gestures of this man left me drained of all courage. Surely, on no other occasion should I have been thus pusillanimous.[12] My state I regarded as a hopeless one. I was wholly at the mercy of this being. Whichever way I turned my eyes, I saw no avenue by which I might escape. The resources of my personal strength, my ingenuity, and my eloquence, I estimated at nothing. The dignity of virtue, and the force of truth, I had been accustomed to celebrate; and had frequently vaunted of the conquests which I should make with their assistance.

I used to suppose that certain evils could never befall a being in possession of a sound mind; that true virtue supplies us with energy which vice can never resist; that it was always in our power to obstruct, by his own death, the designs of an enemy who aimed at less than our life. How was it that a sentiment like despair had now invaded me, and that I trusted to the protection of chance, or to the pity of my persecutor?

His words imparted some notion of the injury which he had meditated. He talked of obstacles that had risen in his way. He had relinquished his design. These sources supplied me with slender consolation. There was no security but in his absence. When I looked at myself, when I reflected on the hour and the place, I was overpowered by horror and dejection.

He was silent, museful, and inattentive to my situation, yet made no motion to depart. I was silent in my turn. What could I say? I was confident that reason in this contest would be impotent. I must owe my safety to his own suggestions. Whatever purpose brought him hither, he had changed it. Why then did he remain? His resolutions might fluctuate, and the pause of a few minutes restore to him his first resolutions.

Yet was not this the man whom we had treated with unwearied kindness? Whose society was endeared to us by his intellectual elevation and accomplishments? Who had a thousand times expatiated on the usefulness and beauty of virtue? Why should such a one be dreaded? If I could have forgotten the circumstances in which our interview had taken place, I might have treated his words as jests. Presently, he resumed:

"Fear me not: the space that severs us is small, and all visible succour is distant. You believe yourself completely in my power; that you stand upon the brink of ruin. Such are your groundless fears. I cannot lift a finger to hurt you. Easier it would be to stop the moon in her course than to injure you. The power that protects you would crumble my sinews, and reduce me to a heap of ashes in a moment, if I were to harbour a thought hostile to your safety.

"Thus are appearances at length solved. Little did I expect that they originated hence. What a portion is assigned to you? Scanned by the eyes of this intelligence, your path will be without pits to swallow, or snares to entangle you. Environed by the arms of this protection, all artifices will be frustrated, and all malice repelled."

Here succeeded a new pause. I was still observant of every gesture and look. The tranquil solemnity that had lately possessed his countenance gave way to a new expression. All now was trepidation and anxiety.

"I must be gone," said he in a faltering accent. "Why do I linger here? I will not ask your forgiveness. I see that your terrors are invincible. Your pardon will be extorted

---

[12] "Pusillanimous": cowardly, timid.

by fear, and not dictated by compassion. I must fly from you forever. He that could plot against your honor, must expect from you and your friends persecution and death. I must doom myself to endless exile."

Saying this, he hastily left the room. I listened while he descended the stairs, and, unbolting the outer door, went forth. I did not follow him with my eyes, as the moon-light would have enabled me to do. Relieved by his absence, and exhausted by the conflict of my fears, I threw myself on a chair, and resigned myself to those bewildering ideas which incidents like these could not fail to produce.

Chapter X

ORDER could not readily be introduced into my thoughts. The voice still rung in my ears. Every accent that was uttered by Carwin was fresh in my remembrance. His unwelcome approach, the recognition of his person, his hasty departure, produced a complex impression on my mind which no words can delineate. I strove to give a slower motion to my thoughts, and to regulate a confusion which became painful; but my efforts were nugatory. I covered my eyes with my hand, and sat, I know not how long, without power to arrange or utter my conceptions.

I had remained for hours, as I believed, in absolute solitude. No thought of personal danger had molested my tranquillity. I had made no preparation for defence. What was it that suggested the design of perusing my father's manuscript? If, instead of this, I had retired to bed, and to sleep, to what fate might I not have been reserved? The ruffian, who must almost have suppressed his breathings to screen himself from discovery, would have noticed this signal, and I should have awakened only to perish with affright, and to abhor myself. Could I have remained unconscious of my danger? Could I have tranquilly slept in the midst of so deadly a snare?

And who was he that threatened to destroy me? By what means could he hide himself in this closet? Surely he is gifted with supernatural power. Such is the enemy of whose attempts I was forewarned. Daily I had seen him and conversed with him. Nothing could be discerned through the impenetrable veil of his duplicity. When busied in conjectures, as to the author of the evil that was threatened, my mind did not light, for a moment, upon his image. Yet has he not avowed himself my enemy? Why should he be here if he had not meditated evil?

He confesses that this has been his second attempt. What was the scene of his former conspiracy?[1] Was it not he whose whispers betrayed him? Am I deceived; or was there not a faint resemblance between the voice of this man and that which talked of grasping my throat, and extinguishing my life in a moment? Then he had a colleague in his crime; now he is alone. Then death was the scope of his thoughts; now an injury unspeakably more dreadful. How thankful should I be to the power that has interposed to save me!

That power is invisible. It is subject to the cognizance of one of my senses. What are the means that will inform me of what nature it is? He has set himself to counterwork the machinations of this man, who had menaced destruction to all that is dear to me, and whose cunning had surmounted every human impediment. There was none to rescue me from his grasp. My rashness even hastened the completion of his scheme, and precluded him from the benefits of deliberation. I had robbed him of the power to repent and forbear. Had I been apprized of the danger, I should have regarded my conduct as the means of rendering my escape from it impossible. Such,

---

[1] "Conspiracy": the first hint of the pattern of allusions that will link Carwin to the contemporary Illuminati scare concerning a supposed conspiracy of secret societies to subvert established church and state institutions in the era of the French Revolution. For more on the Illuminati scare, see the Introduction and Related Texts.

likewise, seem to have been the fears of my invisible protector. Else why that startling intreaty to refrain from opening the closet? By what inexplicable infatuation was I compelled to proceed?

Yet my conduct was wise. Carwin, unable to comprehend my folly, ascribed my behaviour to my knowledge. He conceived himself previously detected, and such detection being possible to flow only from *my* heavenly friend, and *his* enemy, his fears acquired additional strength.

He is apprized of the nature and intentions of this being. Perhaps he is a human agent.[2] Yet, on that supposition his achievements are incredible. Why should I be selected as the object of his care; or, if a mere mortal, should I not recognize some one, whom, benefits imparted and received had prompted to love me? What were the limits and duration of his guardianship? Was the genius[3] of my birth entrusted by divine benignity with this province? Are human faculties adequate to receive stronger proofs of the existence of unfettered and beneficent intelligences than I have received?

But who was this man's coadjutor? The voice that acknowledged an alliance in treachery with Carwin warned me to avoid the summer-house. He assured me that there only my safety was endangered. His assurance, as it now appears, was fallacious. Was there not deceit in his admonition? Was his compact really annulled? Some purpose was, perhaps, to be accomplished by preventing my future visits to that spot. Why was I enjoined silence to others, on the subject of this admonition, unless it were for some unauthorized and guilty purpose?

No one but myself was accustomed to visit it. Backward, it was hidden from distant view by the rock, and in front, it was screened from all examination, by creeping plants, and the branches of cedars. What recess could be more propitious to secrecy? The spirit which haunted it formerly was pure and rapturous. It was a sane sacred to the memory of infantile days, and to blissful imaginations of the future! What a gloomy reverse had succeeded since the ominous arrival of this stranger! Now, perhaps, it is the scene of his meditations. Purposes fraught with horror, that shun the light, and contemplate the pollution of innocence, are here engendered, and fostered, and reared to maturity.

Such were the ideas that, during the night, were tumultuously revolved by me. I reviewed every conversation in which Carwin had borne a part. I studied to discover the true inferences deducible from his deportment and words with regard to his former adventures and actual views. I pondered on the comments which he made on the relation which I had given of the closet dialogue. No new ideas suggested themselves in the course of this review. My expectation had, from the first, been disappointed on

---

[2] "Perhaps he is a human agent": as Clara wonders whether her "invisible protector" is a "heavenly friend" or a benevolent man acting in secret, she never considers the possibility that Carwin is simply lying and pretending to be a threat.

[3] "Genius": a personal or attendant spirit that watches over a person from birth. This is the Latin version of the Greek "daemon" referenced earlier as a precedent for the experience of omens and mysterious voices.

the small degree of surprize which this narrative excited in him. He never explicitly declared his opinion as to the nature of those voices, or decided whether they were real or visionary. He recommended no measures of caution or prevention.

But what measures were now to be taken? Was the danger which threatened me at an end? Had I nothing more to fear? I was lonely, and without means of defence. I could not calculate the motives and regulate the footsteps of this person. What certainty was there, that he would not re-assume his purposes, and swiftly return to the execution of them?

This idea covered me once more with dismay. How deeply did I regret the solitude in which I was placed, and how ardently did I desire the return of day! But neither of these inconveniencies were susceptible of remedy. At first, it occurred to me to summon my servant, and make her spend the night in my chamber; but the inefficacy of this expedient to enhance my safety was easily seen. Once I resolved to leave the house, and retire to my brother's, but was deterred by reflecting on the unseasonableness of the hour, on the alarm which my arrival, and the account which I should be obliged to give, might occasion, and on the danger to which I might expose myself in the way thither. I began, likewise, to consider Carwin's return to molest me as exceedingly improbable. He had relinquished, of his own accord, his design, and departed without compulsion.

"Surely," said I, "there is omnipotence in the cause that changed the views of a man like Carwin. The divinity that shielded me from his attempts will take suitable care of my future safety. Thus to yield to my fears is to deserve that they should be real."

Scarcely had I uttered these words, when my attention was startled by the sound of footsteps. They denoted some one stepping into the piazza[4] in front of my house. My new-born confidence was extinguished in a moment. Carwin, I thought, had repented his departure, and was hastily returning. The possibility that his return was prompted by intentions consistent with my safety, found no place in my mind. Images of violation and murder assailed me anew, and the terrors which succeeded almost incapacitated me from taking any measures for my defence. It was an impulse of which I was scarcely conscious, that made me fasten the lock and draw the bolts of my chamber door. Having done this, I threw myself on a seat; for I trembled to a degree which disabled me from standing, and my soul was so perfectly absorbed in the act of listening, that almost the vital motions were stopped.

The door below creaked on its hinges. It was not again thrust to, but appeared to remain open. Footsteps entered, traversed the entry, and began to mount the stairs. How I detested the folly of not pursuing the man when he withdrew, and bolting after him the outer door! Might he not conceive this omission to be a proof that my angel[5] had deserted me, and be thereby fortified in guilt?

Every step on the stairs, which brought him nearer to my chamber, added vigor to my desperation. The evil with which I was menaced was to be at any rate eluded.

---

[4] "Piazza": a porch or, sometimes, a covered walkway between a main building and an outbuilding.

[5] "Angel": in this usage, another term for a guardian spirit.

How little did I preconceive the conduct which, in an exigence[6] like this, I should be prone to adopt. You will suppose that deliberation and despair would have suggested the same course of action, and that I should have, unhesitatingly, resorted to the best means of personal defence within my power. A penknife[7] lay open upon my table. I remembered that it was there, and seized it. For what purpose you will scarcely inquire. It will be immediately supposed that I meant it for my last refuge, and that if all other means should fail, I should plunge it into the heart of my ravisher.

I have lost all faith in the stedfastness of human resolves. It was thus that in periods of calm I had determined to act. No cowardice had been held by me in greater abhorrence than that which prompted an injured female to destroy, not her injurer ere the injury was perpetrated, but herself when it was without remedy. Yet now this penknife appeared to me of no other use than to baffle my assailant, and prevent the crime by destroying myself. To deliberate at such a time was impossible; but among the tumultuous suggestions of the moment, I do not recollect that it once occurred to me to use it as an instrument of direct defence.[8]

The steps had now reached the second floor. Every footfall accelerated the completion, without augmenting, the certainty of evil. The consciousness that the door was fast, now that nothing but that was interposed between me and danger, was a source of some consolation. I cast my eye towards the window. This, likewise, was a new suggestion. If the door should give way, it was my sudden resolution to throw myself from the window. Its height from the ground, which was covered beneath by a brick pavement, would insure my destruction; but I thought not of that.

When opposite to my door the footsteps ceased. Was he listening whether my fears were allayed, and my caution were asleep? Did he hope to take me by surprise? Yet, if so, why did he allow so many noisy signals to betray his approach? Presently the steps were again heard to approach the door. An hand was laid upon the lock, and the latch pulled back. Did he imagine it possible that I should fail to secure the door? A slight effort was made to push it open, as if all bolts being withdrawn, a slight effort only was required.

I no sooner perceived this, than I moved swiftly towards the window. Carwin's frame might be said to be all muscle. His strength and activity had appeared, in various instances, to be prodigious. A slight exertion of his force would demolish

---

[6] "Exigence": "an emergency; a difficulty, extremity, strait" (*OED*).

[7] "Penknife": in this period, a penknife is a small knife intended for preparing and sharpening quill pens, an ordinary part of the equipment used by writers.

[8] "Direct defence": in retrospect, Clara is amazed that, instead of defending herself, her impulse was to use the penknife to commit suicide as a way to avoid rape. The implication is perhaps not only that she was too frightened to think clearly but, more suggestively, that she was too conditioned in female passivity to act against a male. Clara has emphasized how other characters' upbringings and circumstances shape their behaviors, and now this passage makes a similar point with regard to her. Clara is aware of these constraints on one level, but finds it difficult to break with them and act "freely," outside the limitations they impose. For her somewhat different behavior in the novel's second bedroom assault scene in Chapter 25, see note 25.3.

the door. Would not that exertion be made? Too surely it would; but, at the same moment that this obstacle should yield, and he should enter the apartment, my determination was formed to leap from the window. My senses were still bound to this object. I gazed at the door in momentary expectation that the assault would be made. The pause continued. The person without was irresolute and motionless.

Suddenly, it occurred to me that Carwin might conceive me to have fled. That I had not betaken myself to flight was, indeed, the least probable of all conclusions. In this persuasion he must have been confirmed on finding the lower door unfastened, and the chamber door locked. Was it not wise to foster this persuasion? Should I maintain deep silence, this, in addition to other circumstances, might encourage the belief, and he would once more depart. Every new reflection added plausibility to this reasoning. It was presently more strongly enforced, when I noticed footsteps withdrawing from the door. The blood once more flowed back to my heart, and a dawn of exultation began to rise: but my joy was short lived. Instead of descending the stairs, he passed to the door of the opposite chamber, opened it, and having entered, shut it after him with a violence that shook the house.

How was I to interpret this circumstance? For what end could he have entered this chamber? Did the violence with which he closed the door testify the depth of his vexation? This room was usually occupied by Pleyel. Was Carwin aware of his absence on this night? Could he be suspected of a design so sordid as pillage? If this were his view there were no means in my power to frustrate it. It behoved me to seize the first opportunity to escape; but if my escape were supposed by my enemy to have been already effected, no asylum was more secure than the present. How could my passage from the house be accomplished without noises that might incite him to pursue me?

Utterly at a loss to account for his going into Pleyel's chamber, I waited in instant expectation of hearing him come forth. All, however, was profoundly still. I listened in vain for a considerable period, to catch the sound of the door when it should again be opened. There was no other avenue by which he could escape, but a door which led into the girl's chamber. Would any evil from this quarter befall the girl?

Hence arose a new train of apprehensions. They merely added to the turbulence and agony of my reflections. Whatever evil impended over her, I had no power to avert it. Seclusion and silence were the only means of saving myself from the perils of this fatal night. What solemn vows did I put up, that if I should once more behold the light of day, I would never trust myself again within the threshold of this dwelling!

Minute lingered after minute, but no token was given that Carwin had returned to the passage. What, I again asked, could detain him in this room? Was it possible that he had returned, and glided, unperceived, away? I was speedily aware of the difficulty that attended an enterprize like this; and yet, as if by that means I were capable of gaining any information on that head, I cast anxious looks from the window.

The object that first attracted my attention was an human figure standing on the edge of the bank. Perhaps my penetration was assisted by my hopes. Be that as it will, the figure of Carwin was clearly distinguishable. From the obscurity of my station, it was impossible that I should be discerned by him, and yet he scarcely suffered me to catch a glimpse of him. He turned and went down the steep, which, in this part, was not difficult to be scaled.

My conjecture then had been right. Carwin has softly opened the door, descended the stairs, and issued forth. That I should not have overheard his steps, was only less incredible than that my eyes had deceived me. But what was now to be done? The house was at length delivered from this detested inmate. By one avenue might he again re-enter. Was it not wise to bar the lower door? Perhaps he had gone out by the kitchen door. For this end, he must have passed through Judith's chamber. These entrances being closed and bolted, as great security was gained as was compatible with my lonely condition.

The propriety of these measures was too manifest not to make me struggle successfully with my fears. Yet I opened my own door with the utmost caution, and descended as if I were afraid that Carwin had been still immured in Pleyel's chamber. The outer door was a-jar. I shut, with trembling eagerness, and drew every bolt that appended to it. I then passed with light and less cautious steps through the parlour, but was surprized to discover that the kitchen door was secure. I was compelled to acquiesce in the first conjecture that Carwin had escaped through the entry.

My heart was now somewhat eased of the load of apprehension. I returned once more to my chamber, the door of which I was careful to lock. It was no time to think of repose. The moon-light began already to fade before the light of the day. The approach of morning was betokened by the usual signals. I mused upon the events of this night, and determined to take up my abode henceforth at my brother's. Whether I should inform him of what had happened was a question which seemed to demand some consideration. My safety unquestionably required that I should abandon my present habitation.

As my thoughts began to flow with fewer impediments, the image of Pleyel, and the dubiousness of his condition, again recurred to me. I again ran over the possible causes of his absence on the preceding day. My mind was attuned to melancholy. I dwelt, with an obstinacy for which I could not account, on the idea of his death. I painted to myself his struggles with the billows, and his last appearance. I imagined myself a midnight wanderer on the shore, and to have stumbled on his corpse,[9] which the tide had cast up. These dreary images affected me even to tears. I endeavoured not to restrain them. They imparted a relief which I had not anticipated. The more copiously they flowed, the more did my general sensations appear to subside into calm, and a certain restlessness give way to repose.

Perhaps, relieved by this effusion, the slumber so much wanted might have stolen on my senses, had there been no new cause of alarm.

---

[9] "His corpse": the second time Clara has imagined Pleyel's corpse after drowning. See note 9.5.

Chapter XI

I WAS aroused from this stupor by sounds that evidently arose in the next chamber. Was it possible that I had been mistaken in the figure which I had seen on the bank? or had Carwin, by some inscrutable means, penetrated once more into this chamber? The opposite door opened; footsteps came forth, and the person, advancing to mine, knocked.

So unexpected an incident robbed me of all presence of mind, and, starting up, I involuntarily exclaimed, "Who is there?" An answer was immediately given. The voice, to my inexpressible astonishment, was Pleyel's.[1]

"It is I. Have you risen? If you have not, make haste; I want three minutes conversation with you in the parlour—I will wait for you there." Saying this he retired from the door.

Should I confide in the testimony of my ears? If that were true, it was Pleyel that had been hitherto immured in the opposite chamber: he whom my rueful fancy had depicted in so many ruinous and ghastly shapes: he whose footsteps had been listened to with such inquietude! What is man, that knowledge is so sparingly conferred upon him! that his heart should be wrung with distress, and his frame be exanimated with fear, though his safety be encompassed with impregnable walls! What are the bounds of human imbecility! He that warned me of the presence of my foe refused the intimation by which so many racking fears would have been precluded.

Yet who would have imagined the arrival of Pleyel at such an hour? His tone was desponding and anxious. Why this unseasonable summons? and why this hasty departure? Some tidings he, perhaps, bears of mysterious and unwelcome import.

My impatience would not allow me to consume much time in deliberation: I hastened down. Pleyel I found standing at a window, with eyes cast down as in meditation, and arms folded on his breast. Every line in his countenance was pregnant with sorrow. To this was added a certain wanness and air of fatigue. The last time I had seen him appearances had been the reverse of these. I was startled at the change. The first impulse was to question him as to the cause. This impulse was supplanted by some degree of confusion, flowing from a consciousness that love had too large, and, as it might prove, a perceptible share in creating this impulse. I was silent.

Presently he raised his eyes and fixed them upon me. I read in them an anguish altogether ineffable. Never had I witnessed a like demeanour in Pleyel. Never, indeed, had I observed an human countenance in which grief was more legibly inscribed. He seemed struggling for utterance; but his struggles being fruitless, he shook his head and turned away from me.

My impatience would not allow me to be longer silent: "What," said I, "for heaven's sake, my friend, what is the matter?"

He started at the sound of my voice. His looks, for a moment, became convulsed with an emotion very different from grief. His accents were broken with rage.

---

[1] "The voice . . . was Pleyel's": Clara thought Theodore was in the closet, only to discover it was Carwin; she thought Carwin was in the next room, only to discover it is Pleyel, who has been a guest at her house ever since her first experience of the voices at the end of Chapter 6. This will not be the last time that Clara imaginatively circulates men as common antagonists.

"The matter—O wretch!—thus exquisitely fashioned—on whom nature seemed to have exhausted all her graces; with charms so awful and so pure! how art thou fallen! From what height fallen! A ruin so complete—so unheard of!"

His words were again choked by emotion. Grief and pity were again mingled in his features. He resumed, in a tone half suffocated by sobs:

"But why should I upbraid thee? Could I restore to thee what thou hast lost; efface this cursed stain; snatch thee from the jaws of this fiend; I would do it. Yet what will avail my efforts? I have not arms with which to contend with so consummate, so frightful a depravity.

"Evidence less than this would only have excited resentment and scorn. The wretch who should have breathed a suspicion injurious to thy honor, would have been regarded without anger; not hatred or envy could have prompted him; it would merely be an argument of madness. That my eyes, that my ears, should bear witness to thy fall! By no other way could detestible conviction be imparted.

"Why do I summon thee to this conference? Why expose myself to thy derision? Here admonition and entreaty are vain. Thou knowest him already, for a murderer and thief. I had thought to have been the first to disclose to thee his infamy; to have warned thee of the pit to which thou art hastening; but thy eyes are open in vain. O soul and insupportable disgrace!

"There is but one path. I know you will disappear together. In thy ruin, how will the felicity and honor of multitudes be involved! But it must come. This scene shall not be blotted by his presence. No doubt thou wilt shortly see thy detested paramour. This scene will be again polluted by a midnight assignation. Inform him of his danger; tell him that his crimes are known; let him fly far and instantly from this spot, if he desires to avoid the fate which menaced him in Ireland.[2]

"And wilt thou not stay behind?—But shame upon my weakness. I know not what I would say.—I have done what I purposed. To stay longer, to expostulate, to beseech, to enumerate the consequences of thy act—what end can it serve but to blazon thy infamy and embitter our woes? And yet, O think, think ere it be too late, on the distresses which thy flight will entail upon us; on the base, grovelling, and atrocious character of the wretch to whom thou hast sold thy honor. But what is this? Is not

---

[2] "Ireland": the first suggestion that Carwin has a history of trouble in Ireland. Pleyel earlier asserted that Carwin is "an Englishman by birth" (see note 7.12), but the reader later discovers that he is Pennsylvania-born. Besides the mystery about Carwin's background, however, the reference to Ireland also associates him with conservative fears about subversive intrigue and political conspiracy. Irish resistance to British rule developed into a failed revolution in the late 1790s and many refugees from these Irish uprisings were in Philadelphia and New York when *Wieland* was written. Like the revolutionary French and the imagined Illuminati conspiracies (with which Carwin will also be associated), Irish immigrants were one of the primary objects of scapegoating that culminated in Federalist-sponsored repressive measures such as the 1798 Alien and Sedition Acts. The Irish were feared and despised by the period's Anglo-identified elite, and this kind of stigma, beyond the immediate dramatic situation, may be what Pleyel invokes in the next paragraph when he describes Carwin as "base, grovelling, and atrocious." For more see the Introduction and Carter, "A 'Wild Irishman' under every Federalist's Bed."

thy effrontery impenetrable, and thy heart thoroughly cankered? O most specious,[3] and most profligate of women!"

Saying this, he rushed out of the house. I saw him in a few moments hurrying along the path which led to my brother's. I had no power to prevent his going, or to recall, or to follow him. The accents I had heard were calculated to confound and bewilder. I looked around me to assure myself that the scene was real. I moved that I might banish the doubt that I was awake. Such enormous imputations from the mouth of Pleyel! To be stigmatized with the names of wanton and profligate! To be charged with the sacrifice of honor! with midnight meetings with a wretch known to be a murderer and thief! with an intention to fly in his company!

What I had heard was surely the dictate of phrenzy, or it was built upon some fatal, some incomprehensible mistake. After the horrors of the night; after undergoing perils so imminent from this man, to be summoned to an interview like this; to find Pleyel fraught with a belief that, instead of having chosen death as a refuge from the violence of this man, I had hugged his baseness to my heart, had sacrificed for him my purity, my spotless name, my friendships, and my fortune! that even madness could engender accusations like these was not to be believed.

What evidence could possibly suggest conceptions so wild? After the unlooked-for interview with Carwin in my chamber, he retired. Could Pleyel have observed his exit? It was not long after that Pleyel himself entered. Did he build on this incident, his odious conclusions? Could the long series of my actions and sentiments grant me no exemption from suspicions so foul? Was it not more rational to infer that Carwin's designs had been illicit; that my life had been endangered by the fury of one whom, by some means, he had discovered to be an assassin and robber; that my honor had been assailed, not by blandishments, but by violence?

He has judged me without hearing. He has drawn from dubious appearances, conclusions the most improbable and unjust. He has loaded me with all outrageous epithets. He has ranked me with prostitutes and thieves. I cannot pardon thee. Pleyel, for this injustice. Thy understanding must be hurt. If it be not, if thy conduct was sober and deliberate, I can never forgive an outrage so unmanly, and so gross.

These thoughts gradually gave place to others. Pleyel was possessed by some momentary phrenzy: appearances had led him into palpable errors. Whence could his sagacity have contracted this blindness? Was it not love? Previously assured of my affection for Carwin, distracted with grief and jealousy, and impelled hither at that late hour by some unknown instigation, his imagination transformed shadows into monsters, and plunged him into these deplorable errors.

This idea was not unattended with consolation. My soul was divided between indignation at his injustice, and delight on account of the source from which I conceived it to spring. For a long time they would allow admission to no other thoughts. Surprize is an emotion that enfeebles, not invigorates. All my meditations were accompanied with wonder. I rambled with vagueness, or clung to one image with an obstinacy which sufficiently testified the maddening influence of late transactions.

---

[3] "Specious": "outwardly plausible or attractive, but of little real value" (*OED*).

Gradually I proceeded to reflect upon the consequences of Pleyel's mistake, and on the measures I should take to guard myself against future injury from Carwin. Should I suffer this mistake to be detected by time? When his passion should subside, would he not perceive the flagrancy of his injustice, and hasten to atone for it? Did it not become my character to testify resentment for language and treatment so opprobrious?[4] Wrapt up in the consciousness of innocence, and confiding in the influence of time and reflection to confute so groundless a charge, it was my province to be passive and silent.

As to the violences meditated by Carwin, and the means of eluding them, the path to be taken by me was obvious. I resolved to tell the tale to my brother, and regulate myself by his advice. For this end, when the morning was somewhat advanced, I took the way to his house. My sister was engaged in her customary occupations. As soon as I appeared, she remarked a change in my looks. I was not willing to alarm her by the information which I had to communicate. Her health was in that condition which rendered a disastrous tale particularly unsuitable.[5] I forbore a direct answer to her inquiries, and inquired, in my turn, for Wieland.

"Why," said she, "I suspect something mysterious and unpleasant has happened this morning. Scarcely had we risen when Pleyel dropped among us. What could have prompted him to make us so early and so unseasonable a visit I cannot tell. To judge from the disorder of his dress, and his countenance, something of an extraordinary nature has occurred. He permitted me merely to know that he had slept none, nor even undressed, during the past night. He took your brother to walk with him. Some topic must have deeply engaged them, for Wieland did not return till the breakfast hour was passed, and returned alone. His disturbance was excessive; but he would not listen to my importunities, or tell me what had happened. I gathered from hints which he let fall, that your situation was, in some way, the cause: yet he assured me that you were at your own house, alive, in good health, and in perfect safety. He scarcely ate a morsel, and immediately after breakfast went out again. He would not inform me whither he was going, but mentioned that he probably might not return before night."

I was equally astonished and alarmed by this information. Pleyel had told his tale to my brother, and had, by a plausible and exaggerated picture, instilled into him unfavorable thoughts of me. Yet would not the more correct judgment of Wieland perceive and expose the fallacy of his conclusions? Perhaps his uneasiness might arise from some insight into the character of Carwin, and from apprehensions for my safety. The appearances by which Pleyel had been misled, might induce him likewise to believe that I entertained an indiscreet, though not dishonorable affection for Carwin. Such were the conjectures rapidly formed. I was inexpressibly anxious to change them into certainty. For this end an interview with my brother was desirable. He was gone, no one knew whither, and was not expected speedily to return. I had no clue by which to trace his footsteps.

My anxieties could not be concealed from my sister. They heightened her solicitude to be acquainted with the cause. There were many reasons persuading me to silence:

---

[4] "Opprobrious": scornful, insulting, contemptuous.

[5] "That condition which renders a disastrous tale . . . unsuitable": in other words, Catharine is pregnant. A "disastrous tale" leads to a miscarriage at the end of Brown's novel *Edgar Huntly* (1799).

at least, till I had seen my brother, it would be an act of inexcusable temerity[6] to unfold what had lately passed. No other expedient for eluding her importunities occurred to me, but that of returning to my own house. I recollected my determination to become a tenant of this roof. I mentioned it to her. She joyfully acceded to this proposal, and suffered me, with less reluctance, to depart, when I told her that it was with a view to collect and send to my new dwelling what articles would be immediately useful to me.

Once more I returned to the house which had been the scene of so much turbulence and danger. I was at no great distance from it when I observed my brother coming out. On seeing me he stopped, and after ascertaining, as it seemed, which way I was going, he returned into the house before me. I sincerely rejoiced at this event, and I hastened to set things, if possible, on their right footing.

His brow was by no means expressive of those vehement emotions with which Pleyel had been agitated. I drew a favorable omen from this circumstance. Without delay I began the conversation.

"I have been to look for you," said I, "but was told by Catharine that Pleyel had engaged you on some important and disagreeable affair. Before his interview with you he spent a few minutes with me. These minutes he employed in upbraiding me for crimes and intentions with which I am by no means chargeable. I believe him to have taken up his opinions on very insufficient grounds. His behaviour was in the highest degree precipitate and unjust, and, until I receive some atonement, I shall treat him, in my turn, with that contempt which he justly merits: meanwhile I am fearful that he has prejudiced my brother against me. That is an evil which I most anxiously deprecate, and which I shall indeed exert myself to remove. Has he made me the subject of this morning's conversation?"

My brother's countenance testified no surprize at my address. The benignity of his looks were no wise diminished.

"It is true," said he, "your conduct was the subject of our discourse. I am your friend, as well as your brother. There is no human being whom I love with more tenderness, and whose welfare is nearer my heart. Judge then with what emotions I listened to Pleyel's story. I expect and desire you to vindicate yourself from aspersions so foul, if vindication be possible."

The tone with which he uttered the last words affected me deeply. "If vindication be possible!"[7] repeated I. "From what you know, do you deem a formal vindication necessary? Can you harbour for a moment the belief of my guilt?"

---

[6] "Temerity": unreasonable disregard for danger or opposition, "rashness, foolhardiness, recklessness" (*OED*).

[7] "If vindication be possible!": although "vindication" was in common usage in this period (Clara will use it several more times in the following chapters), the manner in which this passage repeats the word possibly seeks to recall Mary Wollstonecraft's landmark argument about women's social subordination in *A Vindication of the Rights of Woman* (1792). The *Vindication* was a key work for the period, and for Brown and his circle in particular. For more, see the Introduction.

He shook his head with an air of acute anguish. "I have struggled," said he, "to dismiss that belief. You speak before a judge[8] who will profit by any pretence to acquit you: who is ready to question his own senses when they plead against you."

These words incited a new set of thoughts in my mind. I began to suspect that Pleyel had built his accusations on some foundation unknown to me. "I may be a stranger to the grounds of your belief. Pleyel loaded me with indecent and virulent invectives, but he withheld from me the facts that generated his suspicions. Events took place last night of which some of the circumstances were of an ambiguous nature. I conceived that these might possibly have fallen under his cognizance, and that, viewed through the mists of prejudice and passion, they supplied a pretence for his conduct, but believed that your more unbiassed judgment would estimate them at their just value. Perhaps his tale has been different from what I suspect it to be. Listen then to my narrative. If there be any thing in his story inconsistent with mine, his story is false."[9]

I then proceeded to a circumstantial relation of the incidents of the last night. Wieland listened with deep attention. Having finished, "This," continued I, "is the truth; you see in what circumstances an interview took place between Carwin and me. He remained for hours in my closet, and for some minutes in my chamber. He departed without haste or interruption. If Pleyel marked him as he left the house, and it is not impossible that he did, inferences injurious to my character might suggest themselves to him. In admitting them, he gave proofs of less discernment and less candor than I once ascribed to him."

"His proofs," said Wieland, after a considerable pause, "are different. That he should be deceived, is not possible. That he himself is not the deceiver, could not be believed, if his testimony were not inconsistent with yours; but the doubts which I entertained are now removed. Your tale, some parts of it, is marvellous; the voice which exclaimed against your rashness in approaching the closet, your persisting notwithstanding that prohibition, your belief that I was the ruffian, and your subsequent conduct, are believed by me, because I have known you from childhood, because a thousand instances have attested your veracity, and because nothing less than my own hearing and vision would convince me, in opposition to her own assertions, that my sister had fallen into wickedness like this."

I threw my arms around him, and bathed his cheek with my tears. "That," said I, "is spoken like my brother. But what are the proofs?"

He replied—"Pleyel informed me that, in going to your house, his attention was attracted by two voices. The persons speaking sat beneath the bank out of sight.

---

[8] "You speak before a judge": Theodore's language introduces the thematics of courtroom testimony, foreshadowing later events.

[9] "Viewed through the mists of prejudice and passion . . . his story is false": throughout this passage and the following confrontation with Pleyel in Chapters 12–13, Clara rationally assesses the ways that "prejudice and passion" and complexities of evidence lead others (males to whom she must defer) to jump to conclusions and accept erroneous theories about her. All of these insights seem forgotten, however, when the tables are turned and she becomes a higher-status person in a position to "judge" Carwin's story (and his claims about her female servant) in Chapters 25 and following.

These persons, judging by their voices, were Carwin and you. I will not repeat the dialogue. If my sister was the female, Pleyel was justified in concluding you to be, indeed, one of the most profligate of women. Hence, his accusations of you, and his efforts to obtain my concurrence to a plan by which an eternal separation should be brought about between my sister and this man."

I made Wieland repeat this recital. Here, indeed, was a tale to fill me with terrible foreboding. I had vainly thought that my safety could be sufficiently secured by doors and bars, but this is a foe from whose grasp no power of divinity can save me! His artifices will ever lay my fame and happiness at his mercy. How shall I counterwork his plots, or detect his coadjutor? He has taught some vile and abandoned female to mimic my voice. Pleyel's ears were the witnesses of my dishonor. This is the midnight assignation to which he alluded. Thus is the silence he maintained when attempting to open the door of my chamber, accounted for. He supposed me absent, and meant, perhaps, had my apartment been accessible, to leave in it some accusing memorial.

Pleyel was no longer equally culpable. The sincerity of his anguish, the depth of his despair, I remembered with some tendencies to gratitude. Yet was he not precipitate? Was the conjecture that my part was played by some mimic so utterly untenable? Instances of this faculty are common. The wickedness of Carwin must, in his opinion, have been adequate to such contrivances, and yet the supposition of my guilt was adopted in preference to that.

But how was this error to be unveiled? What but my own assertion had I to throw in the balance against it? Would this be permitted to outweigh the testimony of his senses? I had no witnesses to prove my existence in another place. The real events of that night are marvellous. Few, to whom they should be related, would scruple to discredit them. Pleyel is sceptical in a transcendant degree. I cannot summon Carwin to my bar, and make him the attestor of my innocence, and the accuser of himself.

My brother saw and comprehended my distress. He was unacquainted, however, with the full extent of it. He knew not by how many motives I was incited to retrieve the good opinion of Pleyel. He endeavored to console me. Some new event, he said, would occur to disentangle the maze. He did not question the influence of my eloquence, if I thought proper to exert it. Why not seek an interview with Pleyel, and exact from him a minute relation, in which something may be met with serving to destroy the probability of the whole?

I caught, with eagerness, at this hope; but my alacrity was damped by new reflections. Should I, perfect in this respect, and unblemished as I was, thrust myself, uncalled, into his presence, and make my felicity depend upon his arbitrary verdict?

"If you chuse to seek an interview," continued Wieland, "you must make haste, for Pleyel informed me of his intention to set out this evening or to-morrow on a long journey."

No intelligence was less expected or less welcome than this. I had thrown myself in a window seat; but now, starting on my feet, I exclaimed, "Good heavens! what is it you say? a journey? whither? when?"

"I cannot say whither. It is a sudden resolution I believe. I did not hear of it till this morning. He promises to write to me as soon as he is settled."

I needed no further information as to the cause and issue of this journey. The scheme of happiness to which he had devoted his thoughts was blasted by the discovery of last night. My preference of another, and my unworthiness to be any longer the object of his adoration, were evinced by the same act and in the same moment. The thought of utter desertion, a desertion originating in such a cause, was the prelude to distraction. That Pleyel should abandon me forever, because I was blind to his excellence, because I coveted pollution, and wedded infamy, when, on the contrary, my heart was the shrine of all purity, and beat only for his sake, was a destiny which, as long as my life was in my own hands, I would by no means consent to endure.

I remembered that this evil was still preventable; that this fatal journey it was still in my power to procrastinate, or, perhaps, to occasion it to be laid aside. There were no impediments to a visit: I only dreaded lest the interview should be too long delayed. My brother befriended my impatience, and readily consented to furnish me with a chaise and servant to attend me. My purpose was to go immediately to Pleyel's farm, where his engagements usually detained him during the day.

Chapter XII

MY way lay through the city. I had scarcely entered it when I was seized with a general sensation of sickness. Every object grew dim and swam before my sight. It was with difficulty I prevented myself from sinking to the bottom of the carriage. I ordered myself to be carried to Mrs. Baynton's,[1] in hope that an interval of repose would invigorate and refresh me. My distracted thoughts would allow me but little rest. Growing somewhat better in the afternoon, I resumed my journey.

My contemplations were limited to a few objects. I regarded my success, in the purpose which I had in view, as considerably doubtful. I depended, in some degree, on the suggestions of the moment, and on the materials which Pleyel himself should furnish me. When I reflected on the nature of the accusation, I burned with disdain. Would not truth, and the consciousness of innocence, render me triumphant? Should I not cast from me, with irresistible force, such atrocious imputations?

What an entire and mournful change has been effected in a few hours! The gulf that separates man from insects is not wider than that which severs the polluted from the chaste among women. Yesterday and to-day I am the same. There is a degree of depravity to which it is impossible for me to sink; yet, in the apprehension of another, my ancient and intimate associate, the perpetual witness of my actions, and partaker of my thoughts, I had ceased to be the same. My integrity was tarnished and withered in his eyes. I was the colleague of a murderer, and the paramour of a thief!

His opinion was not destitute of evidence: yet what proofs could reasonably avail to establish an opinion like this? If the sentiments corresponded not with the voice that was heard, the evidence was deficient; but this want of correspondence would have been supposed by me if I had been the auditor and Pleyel the criminal. But mimicry might still more plausibly have been employed to explain the scene. Alas! it is the fate of Clara Wieland to fall into the hands of a precipitate and inexorable judge.

But what, O man of mischief! is the tendency of thy thoughts? Frustrated in thy first design, thou wilt not forego the immolation of thy victim. To exterminate my reputation was all that remained to thee, and this my guardian has permitted. To dispossess Pleyel of this prejudice may be impossible; but if that be effected, it cannot be supposed that thy wiles are exhausted; thy cunning will discover innumerable avenues to the accomplishment of thy malignant purpose.

Why should I enter the lists against thee? Would to heaven I could disarm thy vengeance by my deprecations! When I think of all the resources with which nature and education have supplied thee; that thy form is a combination of steely fibres and organs of exquisite ductility[2] and boundless compass, actuated by an intelligence gifted with infinite endowments, and comprehending all knowledge, I perceive that my doom is fixed. What obstacle will be able to divert thy zeal or repel thy efforts?

---

[1] "Mrs. Baynton's": this is the "worthy lady" and family friend first mentioned in Chapter 4, where she provided an initial connection to Major Stuart and the Louisa Conway subnarrative; see notes 4.3–4.4.

[2] "Ductility": flexibility, adaptability.

That being who has hitherto protected me has borne testimony to the formidableness of thy attempts, since nothing less than supernatural interference could check thy career.

Musing on these thoughts, I arrived, towards the close of the day, at Pleyel's house. A month before, I had traversed the same path; but how different were my sensations! Now I was seeking the presence of one who regarded me as the most degenerate of human kind. I was to plead the cause of my innocence, against witnesses the most explicit and unerring, of those which support the fabric of human knowledge.[3] The nearer I approached the crisis, the more did my confidence decay. When the chaise stopped at the door, my strength refused to support me, and I threw myself into the arms of an ancient female domestic.[4] I had not courage to inquire whether her master was at home. I was tormented with fears that the projected journey was already undertaken. These fears were removed, by her asking me whether she should call her young master, who had just gone into his own room. I was somewhat revived by this intelligence, and resolved immediately to seek him there.

In my confusion of mind, I neglected to knock at the door, but entered his apartment without previous notice. This abruptness was altogether involuntary. Absorbed in reflections of such unspeakable moment, I had no leisure to heed the niceties of punctilio.[5] I discovered him standing with his back towards the entrance. A small trunk, with its lid raised, was before him, in which it seemed as if he had been busy in packing his clothes. The moment of my entrance, he was employed in gazing at something which he held in his hand.

I imagined that I fully comprehended this scene. The image which he held before him, and by which his attention was so deeply engaged, I doubted not to be my own. These preparations for his journey, the cause to which it was to be imputed, the hopelessness of success in the undertaking on which I had entered, rushed at once upon my feelings, and dissolved me into a flood of tears.

Startled by this sound, he dropped the lid of the trunk and turned. The solemn sadness that previously overspread his countenance, gave sudden way to an attitude and look of the most vehement astonishment. Perceiving me unable to uphold myself, he stepped towards me without speaking, and supported me by his arm. The kindness of this action called forth a new effusion from my eyes. Weeping was a solace to which, at that time, I had not grown familiar, and which, therefore, was peculiarly delicious. Indignation was no longer to be read in the features of my friend. They were pregnant with a mixture of wonder and pity. Their expression was easily interpreted. This visit,

---

[3] "Witnesses the most explicit and unerring . . . fabric of human knowledge": in other words, the sense perceptions of a rational observer.

[4] "Chaise . . . ancient female domestic": a chaise is a light carriage. The method of travel and repeated dependence on servants or slaves (while fainting, bursting into tears, and otherwise performing her distress throughout this chapter) underscore the elite nature of Clara's somewhat ritualized behavior here.

[5] "Punctilio": excessive concern about small matters or technicalities. Clara will put aside customary formalities.

and these tears, were tokens of my penitence. The wretch whom he had stigmatized as incurably and obdurately wicked, now shewed herself susceptible of remorse, and had come to confess her guilt.

This persuasion had no tendency to comfort me. It only shewed me, with new evidence, the difficulty of the task which I had assigned myself. We were mutually silent. I had less power and less inclination than ever to speak. I extricated myself from his hold, and threw myself on a sofa. He placed himself by my side, and appeared to wait with impatience and anxiety for some beginning of the conversation. What could I say? If my mind had suggested any thing suitable to the occasion, my utterance was suffocated by tears.

Frequently he attempted to speak, but seemed deterred by some degree of uncertainty as to the true nature of the scene. At length, in faltering accents he spoke:

"My friend! would to heaven I were still permitted to call you by that name. The image that I once adored existed only in my fancy; but though I cannot hope to see it realized, you may not be totally insensible to the horrors of that gulf into which you are about to plunge. What heart is forever exempt from the goadings of compunction and the influx of laudable propensities?

"I thought you accomplished and wise beyond the rest of women. Not a sentiment you uttered, not a look you assumed, that were not, in my apprehension, fraught with the sublimities of rectitude and the illuminations of genius. Deceit has some bounds. Your education could not be without influence. A vigorous understanding cannot be utterly devoid of virtue; but you could not counterfeit the powers of invention and reasoning. I was rash in my invectives. I will not, but with life, relinquish all hopes of you. I will shut out every proof that would tell me that your heart is incurably diseased.

"You come to restore me once more to happiness; to convince me that you have torn her mask from vice, and feel nothing but abhorrence for the part you have hitherto acted."

At these words my equanimity forsook me. For a moment I forgot the evidence from which Pleyel's opinions were derived, the benevolence of his remonstrances,[6] and the grief which his accents bespoke; I was filled with indignation and horror at charges so black; I shrunk back and darted at him a look of disdain and anger. My passion supplied me with words.

"What detestable infatuation was it that led me hither! Why do I patiently endure these horrible insults! My offences exist only in your own distempered imagination: you are leagued with the traitor who assailed my life: you have vowed the destruction of my peace and honor. I deserve infamy for listening to calumnies so base!"

These words were heard by Pleyel without visible resentment. His countenance relapsed into its former gloom; but he did not even look at me. The ideas which had given place to my angry emotions returned, and once more melted me into tears. "O!" I exclaimed, in a voice broken by sobs, "what a task is mine! Compelled to hearken to charges which I feel to be false, but which I know to be believed by him

---

[6] "Remonstrances": strenuous objections or complaints.

that utters them; believed too not without evidence, which, though fallacious, is not unplausible.

"I came hither not to confess, but to vindicate. I know the source of your opinions. Wieland has informed me on what your suspicions are built. These suspicions are fostered by you as certainties; the tenor of my life, of all my conversations and letters, affords me no security; every sentiment that my tongue and my pen have uttered, bear testimony to the rectitude of my mind; but this testimony is rejected. I am condemned as brutally profligate: I am classed with the stupidly and sordidly wicked.

"And where are the proofs that must justify so foul and so improbable an accusation? You have overheard a midnight conference. Voices have saluted your ear, in which you imagine yourself to have recognized mine, and that of a detected villain. The sentiments expressed were not allowed to outweigh the casual or concerted resemblance of voice. Sentiments the reverse of all those whose influence my former life had attested, denoting a mind polluted by grovelling vices, and entering into compact with that of a thief and a murderer. The nature of these sentiments did not enable you to detect the cheat, did not suggest to you the possibility that my voice had been counterfeited by another.

"You were precipitate and prone to condemn. Instead of rushing on the impostors, and comparing the evidence of sight with that of hearing, you stood aloof, or you fled. My innocence would not now have stood in need of vindication, if this conduct had been pursued. That you did not pursue it, your present thoughts incontestibly prove. Yet this conduct might surely have been expected from Pleyel. That he would not hastily impute the blackest of crimes, that he would not couple my name with infamy, and cover me with ruin for inadequate or slight reasons, might reasonably have been expected." The sobs which convulsed my bosom would not suffer me to proceed.

Pleyel was for a moment affected. He looked at me with some expression of doubt; but this quickly gave place to a mournful solemnity. He fixed his eyes on the floor as in reverie, and spoke:

"Two hours hence I am gone. Shall I carry away with me the sorrow that is now my guest? or shall that sorrow be accumulated tenfold? What is she that is now before me? Shall every hour supply me with new proofs of a wickedness beyond example? Already I deem her the most abandoned and detestable of human creatures. Her coming and her tears imparted a gleam of hope, but that gleam has vanished."

He now fixed his eyes upon me, and every muscle in his face trembled. His tone was hollow and terrible—"Thou knowest that I was a witness of your interview, yet thou comest hither to upbraid me for injustice! Thou canst look me in the face and say that I am deceived!—An inscrutable providence has fashioned thee for some end. Thou wilt live, no doubt, to fulfil the purposes of thy maker, if he repent not of his workmanship, and send not his vengeance to exterminate thee, ere the measure of thy days be full. Surely nothing in the shape of man can vie with thee!

"But I thought I had stifled this fury. I am not constituted thy judge. My office is to pity and amend, and not to punish and revile. I deemed myself exempt from all tempestuous passions. I had almost persuaded myself to weep over thy fall; but

I am frail as dust, and mutable as water; I am calm, I am compassionate only in thy absence.—Make this house, this room, thy abode as long as thou wilt, but forgive me if I prefer solitude for the short time during which I shall stay." Saying this, he motioned as if to leave the apartment.

The stormy passions of this man affected me by sympathy. I ceased to weep. I was motionless and speechless with agony. I sat with my hands clasped, mutely gazing after him as he withdrew. I desired to detain him, but was unable to make any effort for that purpose, till he had passed out of the room. I then uttered an involuntary and piercing cry—"Pleyel! Art thou gone? Gone forever?"

At this summons he hastily returned. He beheld me wild, pale, gasping for breath, and my head already sinking on my bosom. A painful dizziness seized me, and I fainted away.

When I recovered, I found myself stretched on a bed in the outer apartment, and Pleyel, with two female servants standing beside it. All the fury and scorn which the countenance of the former lately expressed, had now disappeared, and was succeeded by the most tender anxiety. As soon as he perceived that my senses were returned to me, he clasped his hands, and exclaimed, "God be thanked! you are once more alive. I had almost despaired of your recovery. I fear I have been precipitate and unjust. My senses must have been the victims of some inexplicable and momentary phrenzy. Forgive me, I beseech you, forgive my reproaches. I would purchase conviction of your purity, at the price of my existence here and hereafter."

He once more, in a tone of the most fervent tenderness, besought me to be composed, and then left me to the care of the women.

Chapter XIII

HERE was wrought a surprizing change in my friend. What was it that had shaken conviction so firm? Had any thing occurred during my fit, adequate to produce so total an alteration? My attendants informed me that he had not left my apartment; that the unusual duration of my fit, and the failure, for a time, of all the means used for my recovery, had filled him with grief and dismay. Did he regard the effect which his reproaches had produced as a proof of my sincerity?

In this state of mind, I little regarded my languors of body. I rose and requested an interview with him before my departure, on which I was resolved, notwithstanding his earnest solicitation to spend the night at his house. He complied with my request. The tenderness which he had lately betrayed, had now disappeared, and he once more relapsed into a chilling solemnity.

I told him that I was preparing to return to my brother's; that I had come hither to vindicate my innocence from the foul aspersions which he had cast upon it. My pride had not taken refuge in silence or distance. I had not relied upon time, or the suggestions of his cooler thoughts, to confute his charges. Conscious as I was that I was perfectly guiltless, and entertaining some value for his good opinion, I could not prevail upon myself to believe that my efforts to make my innocence manifest, would be fruitless. Adverse appearances might be numerous and specious, but they were unquestionably false. I was willing to believe him sincere, that he made no charges which he himself did not believe; but these charges were destitute of truth. The grounds of his opinion were fallacious; and I desired an opportunity of detecting their fallacy. I entreated him to be explicit, and to give me a detail of what he had heard, and what he had seen.

At these words, my companion's countenance grew darker. He appeared to be struggling with his rage. He opened his lips to speak, but his accents died away ere they were formed. This conflict lasted for some minutes, but his fortitude was finally successful. He spoke as follows:

"I would fain put an end to this hateful scene: what I shall say, will be breath idly and unprofitably consumed. The clearest narrative will add nothing to your present knowledge. You are acquainted with the grounds of my opinion, and yet you avow yourself innocent: Why then should I rehearse these grounds? You are apprized of the character of Carwin: Why then should I enumerate the discoveries which I have made respecting him? Yet, since it is your request; since, considering the limitedness of human faculties, some error may possibly lurk in those appearances which I have witnessed, I will briefly relate what I know.

"Need I dwell upon the impressions which your conversation and deportment originally made upon me? We parted in childhood; but our intercourse, by letter, was copious and uninterrupted. How fondly did I anticipate a meeting with one whom her letters had previously taught me to consider as the first of women, and how fully realized were the expectations that I had formed!

"Here, said I, is a being, after whom sages may model their transcendent intelligence, and painters, their ideal beauty. Here is exemplified, that union between intellect and form, which has hitherto existed only in the conceptions of the poet.

I have watched your eyes; my attention has hung upon your lips. I have questioned whether the enchantments of your voice were more conspicuous in the intricacies of melody, or the emphasis of rhetoric. I have marked the transitions of your discourse, the felicities of your expression, your refined argumentation, and glowing imagery; and been forced to acknowledge, that all delights were meagre and contemptible, compared with those connected with the audience and sight of you. I have contemplated your principles, and been astonished at the solidity of their foundation, and the perfection of their structure. I have traced you to your home. I have viewed you in relation to your servants, to your family, to your neighbours, and to the world. I have seen by what skilful arrangements you facilitate the performance of the most arduous and complicated duties; what daily accessions of strength your judicious discipline bestowed upon your memory; what correctness and abundance of knowledge was daily experienced by your unwearied application to books, and to writing. If she that possesses so much in the bloom of youth, will go on accumulating her stores, what, said I, is the picture she will display at a mature age?

"You know not the accuracy of my observation. I was desirous that others should profit by an example so rare. I therefore noted down, in writing, every particular of your conduct. I was anxious to benefit by an opportunity so seldom afforded us. I laboured not to omit the slightest shade, or the most petty line in your portrait. Here there was no other task incumbent on me but to copy; there was no need to exaggerate or overlook, in order to produce a more unexceptionable pattern. Here was a combination of harmonies and graces, incapable of diminution or accession without injury to its completeness.

"I found no end and no bounds to my task. No display of a scene like this could be chargeable with redundancy or superfluity. Even the colour of a shoe, the knot of a ribband, or your attitude in plucking a rose, were of moment to be recorded. Even the arrangements of your breakfast-table and your toilet have been amply displayed.

"I know that mankind are more easily enticed to virtue by example than by precept. I know that the absoluteness of a model, when supplied by invention, diminishes its salutary influence, since it is useless, we think, to strive after that which we know to be beyond our reach. But the picture which I drew was not a phantom; as a model, it was devoid of imperfection; and to aspire to that height which had been really attained, was by no means unreasonable. I had another and more interesting object in view. One existed who claimed all my tenderness. Here, in all its parts, was a model worthy of assiduous study, and indefatigable imitation. I called upon her, as she wished to secure and enhance my esteem, to mould her thoughts, her words, her countenance, her actions, by this pattern.

"The task was exuberant of pleasure, and I was deeply engaged in it, when an imp of mischief was let loose in the form of Carwin. I admired his powers and accomplishments. I did not wonder that they were admired by you. On the rectitude of your judgment, however, I relied to keep this admiration within discreet and scrupulous bounds. I assured myself, that the strangeness of his deportment, and the obscurity of his life, would teach you caution. Of all errors, my knowledge of your character informed me that this was least likely to befall you.

"You were powerfully affected by his first appearance; you were bewitched by his countenance and his tones; your description was ardent and pathetic: I listened to you with some emotions of surprize. The portrait you drew in his absence, and the intensity with which you mused upon it, were new and unexpected incidents. They bespoke a sensibility somewhat too vivid; but from which, while subjected to the guidance of an understanding like yours, there was nothing to dread.

"A more direct intercourse took place between you. I need not apologize for the solicitude which I entertained for your safety. He that gifted me with perception of excellence, compelled me to love it. In the midst of danger and pain, my contemplations have ever been cheered by your image. Every object in competition with you, was worthless and trivial. No price was too great by which your safety could be purchased. For that end, the sacrifice of ease, of health, and even of life, would cheerfully have been made by me. What wonder then, that I scrutinized the sentiments and deportment of this man with ceaseless vigilance; that I watched your words and your looks when he was present; and that I extracted cause for the deepest inquietudes, from every token which you gave of having put your happiness into this man's keeping?

"I was cautious in deciding. I recalled the various conversations in which the topics of love and marriage had been discussed. As a woman, young, beautiful, and independent, it behoved you to have fortified your mind with just principles on this subject. Your principles were eminently just. Had not their rectitude and their firmness been attested by your treatment of that specious seducer Dashwood?[1] These principles, I was prone to believe, exempted you from danger in this new state of things. I was not the last to pay my homage to the unrivalled capacity, insinuation, and eloquence of this man. I have disguised, but could never stifle the conviction, that his eyes and voice had a witchcraft in them, which rendered him truly formidable: but I reflected on the ambiguous expression of his countenance—an ambiguity which you were the first to remark; on the cloud which obscured his character; and on the suspicious nature of that concealment which he studied; and concluded you to be safe. I denied the obvious construction to appearances. I referred your conduct to some principle which had not been hitherto disclosed, but which was reconcileable with those already known.

"I was not suffered to remain long in this suspence. One evening, you may recollect, I came to your house, where it was my purpose, as usual, to lodge, somewhat earlier than ordinary. I spied a light in your chamber as I approached from the outside, and on inquiring of Judith, was informed that you were writing. As your kinsman and friend, and fellow-lodger, I thought I had a right to be familiar. You were in your chamber, but your employment and the time were such as to make it no infraction of decorum to follow you thither. The spirit of mischievous gaiety[2] possessed me. I

---

[1] "Specious seducer Dashwood": Pleyel compares Carwin to Francis Dashwood (1708–1781), a notorious English rake and founder of an upper-class private "Hellfire Club" rumored to commit various pseudopagan rituals and immoral acts.

[2] "Mischievous gaiety": Pleyel's assumption that he has the right to sneak up and silently observe Clara's writing mirrors Carwin's.

proceeded on tiptoe. You did not perceive my entrance; and I advanced softly till I was able to overlook your shoulder.

"I had gone thus far in error, and had no power to recede. How cautiously should we guard against the first inroads of temptation! I knew that to pry into your papers was criminal; but I reflected that no sentiment of yours was of a nature which made it your interest to conceal it. You wrote much more than you permitted your friends to peruse. My curiosity was strong, and I had only to throw a glance upon the paper, to secure its gratification. I should never have deliberately committed an act like this. The slightest obstacle would have repelled me; but my eye glanced almost spontaneously upon the paper. I caught only parts of sentences; but my eyes comprehended more at a glance, because the characters were short-hand. I lighted on the words *summer-house, midnight,* and made out a passage which spoke of the propriety and of the effects to be expected from *another* interview. All this passed in less than a moment. I then checked myself, and made myself known to you, by a tap upon your shoulder.

"I could pardon and account for some trifling alarm; but your trepidation and blushes were excessive. You hurried the paper out of sight, and seemed too anxious to discover whether I knew the contents to allow yourself to make any inquiries. I wondered at these appearances of consternation, but did not reason on them until I had retired. When alone, these incidents suggested themselves to my reflections anew.

"To what scene, or what interview, I asked, did you allude? Your disappearance on a former evening, my tracing you to the recess in the bank, your silence on my first and second call, your vague answers and invincible embarrassment, when you, at length, ascended the hill, I recollected with new surprize. Could this be the summer-house alluded to? A certain timidity and consciousness had generally attended you, when this incident and this recess had been the subjects of conversation. Nay, I imagined that the last time that adventure was mentioned, which happened in the presence of Carwin, the countenance of the latter betrayed some emotion. Could the interview have been with him?

"This was an idea calculated to rouse every faculty to contemplation. An interview at that hour, in this darksome retreat, with a man of this mysterious but formidable character; a clandestine interview, and one which you afterwards endeavoured with so much solicitude to conceal! It was a fearful and portentous[3] occurrence. I could not measure his power, or fathom his designs. Had he rifled from you the secret of your love, and reconciled you to concealment and nocturnal meetings? I scarcely ever spent a night of more inquietude.

"I knew not how to act. The ascertainment of this man's character and views seemed to be, in the first place, necessary. Had he openly preferred his suit to you, we should have been impowered to make direct inquiries; but since he had chosen this obscure path, it seemed reasonable to infer that his character was exceptionable. It, at least, subjected us to the necessity of resorting to other means of information. Yet the improbability that you should commit a deed of such rashness, made me reflect anew

---

[3] "Portentous": ominous, threatening, having the quality of an omen or portent.

upon the insufficiency of those grounds on which my suspicions had been built, and almost to condemn myself for harbouring them.

"Though it was mere conjecture that the interview spoken of had taken place with Carwin, yet two ideas occurred to involve me in the most painful doubts. This man's reasonings might be so specious, and his artifices so profound, that, aided by the passion which you had conceived for him, he had finally succeeded; or his situation might be such as to justify the secrecy which you maintained. In neither case did my wildest reveries suggest to me, that your honor had been forfeited.

"I could not talk with you on this subject. If the imputation was false, its atrociousness would have justly drawn upon me your resentment, and I must have explained by what facts it had been suggested. If it were true, no benefit would follow from the mention of it. You had chosen to conceal it for some reasons, and whether these reasons were true or false, it was proper to discover and remove them in the first place. Finally, I acquiesced in the least painful supposition, trammelled as it was with perplexities, that Carwin was upright, and that, if the reasons of your silence were known, they would be found to be just.

Chapter XIV

"THREE days have elapsed since this occurrence. I have been haunted by perpetual inquietude. To bring myself to regard Carwin without terror, and to acquiesce in the belief of your safety, was impossible. Yet to put an end to my doubts, seemed to be impracticable. If some light could be reflected on the actual situation of this man, a direct path would present itself. If he were, contrary to the tenor of his conversation, cunning and malignant, to apprize you of this, would be to place you in security. If he were merely unfortunate and innocent, most readily would I espouse his cause; and if his intentions were upright with regard to you, most eagerly would I sanctify your choice by my approbation.

"It would be vain to call upon Carwin for an avowal of his deeds. It was better to know nothing, than to be deceived by an artful tale. What he was unwilling to communicate, and this unwillingness had been repeatedly manifested, could never be extorted from him. Importunity might be appeased, or imposture effected by fallacious representations. To the rest of the world he was unknown. I had often made him the subject of discourse; but a glimpse of his figure in the street was the sum of their knowledge who knew most. None had ever seen him before, and received as new, the information which my intercourse with him in Valencia,[1] and my present intercourse, enabled me to give.

"Wieland was your brother. If he had really made you the object of his courtship, was not a brother authorized to interfere and demand from him the confession of his views? Yet what were the grounds on which I had reared this supposition? Would they justify a measure like this? Surely not.

"In the course of my restless meditations, it occurred to me, at length, that my duty required me to speak to you, to confess the indecorum of which I had been guilty, and to state the reflections to which it had led me. I was prompted by no mean or selfish views. The heart within my breast was not more precious than your safety: most cheerfully would I have interposed my life between you and danger. Would you cherish resentment at my conduct? When acquainted with the motive which produced it, it would not only exempt me from censure, but entitle me to gratitude.

"Yesterday had been selected for the rehearsal of the newly-imported tragedy. I promised to be present. The state of my thoughts but little qualified me for a performer or auditor in such a scene; but I reflected that, after it was finished, I should return home with you, and should then enjoy an opportunity of discoursing with you fully on this topic. My resolution was not formed without a remnant of doubt, as to its propriety. When I left this house to perform the visit I had promised, my mind was full of apprehension and despondency. The dubiousness of the event of our conversation, fear that my interference was too late to secure your peace, and the uncertainty to which hope gave birth, whether I had not erred in believing you devoted to this man, or, at least, in imagining that he had obtained your consent to

---

[1] "In Valencia": Pleyel refers to his first meeting with Carwin in Spain, which he described in Chapter 7. See notes 7.8–7.12.

midnight conferences, distracted me with contradictory opinions, and repugnant emotions.

"I can assign no reason for calling at Mrs. Baynton's. I had seen her in the morning, and knew her to be well. The concerted hour had nearly arrived, and yet I turned up the street which leads to her house, and dismounted at her door. I entered the parlour and threw myself in a chair. I saw and inquired for no one. My whole frame was overpowered by dreary and comfortless sensations. One idea possessed me wholly; the inexpressible importance of unveiling the designs and character of Carwin, and the utter improbability that this ever would be effected. Some instinct induced me to lay my hand upon a newspaper. I had perused all the general intelligence it contained in the morning, and at the same spot. The act was rather mechanical than voluntary.

"I threw a languid glance at the first column that presented itself. The first words which I read, began with the offer of a reward of three hundred guineas[2] for the apprehension of a convict under sentence of death, who had escaped from Newgate prison in Dublin. Good heaven! how every fibre of my frame tingled when I proceeded to read that the name of the criminal was Francis Carwin![3]

"The descriptions of his person and address were minute. His stature, hair, complexion, the extraordinary position and arrangement of his features, his aukward and disproportionate form, his gesture and gait, corresponded perfectly with those of our mysterious visitant. He had been found guilty in two indictments. One for the murder of the Lady Jane Conway, and the other for a robbery committed on the person of the honorable Mr. Ludloe.[4]

---

[2] "Three hundred guineas": a guinea is a British gold coin, worth slightly more than a pound sterling (21 shillings as opposed to 20). The reward is enormous; typically £40 was offered to catch a felon and £40–50 was an annual wage for many artisan laborers at this time.

[3] "Newgate prison in Dublin . . . Francis Carwin!": the passage provides Carwin's first name, as well the claim that he was in an Irish jail. Neither *Wieland* nor *Memoirs of Carwin* ever returns to this claim and thus the reader never learns whether it is true or false.

[4] "Murder of the Lady Jane Conway . . . Mr. Ludloe": the first mention of the character Ludloe, who will play an important role as Carwin's elite patron in the novel's backstory and *Memoirs of Carwin*. The newspaper article's assertion that Carwin murdered "Lady Jane" Conway seems to mysteriously connect Carwin to the Conway subplot, but in a manner that is never explained or resolved. See notes 4.2–4.6 for Clara's initial explanation of the Conway backstory. In Chapter 4, Major Stuart referred to his daughter Louisa's mother, who appeared to be "of no mean birth" (26) by the same name (27–28), but here a Conway figure is given the name Jane, with at least some implication that this can be understood as Louisa's mother. If "Jane" refers to Louisa's mother and the earlier usage of "Louisa" for the mother is a slip of Brown's pen or has another explanation, then the newspaper article is implicitly a false accusation, for Clara previously explained that Louisa Conway's mother died serenely "under my aunt's protection" (see note 4.3). In Carwin's confession in Chapter 23 (see note 23.4) and in Chapter 27, the reader learns that the information in the newspaper article was planted by Ludloe as part of his "persecutions" of Carwin. The theme of wrongful incrimination and pursuit by a higher-status individual seeking revenge is a motif that Brown repeatedly draws from William Godwin's *Caleb Williams* (1794), a key precedent for Brown's novel-writing. For more of Brown's use of this motif, see the Introduction.

"I repeatedly perused this passage. The ideas which flowed in upon my mind, affected me like an instant transition from death to life. The purpose dearest to my heart was thus effected, at a time and by means the least of all others within the scope of my foresight. But what purpose? Carwin was detected. Acts of the blackest and most sordid guilt had been committed by him. Here was evidence which imparted to my understanding the most luminous certainty. The name, visage, and deportment, were the same. Between the time of his escape, and his appearance among us, there was a sufficient agreement. Such was the man with whom I suspected you to maintain a clandestine correspondence. Should I not haste to snatch you from the talons of this vulture? Should I see you rushing to the verge of a dizzy precipice, and not stretch forth a hand to pull you back? I had no need to deliberate. I thrust the paper in my pocket, and resolved to obtain an immediate conference with you. For a time, no other image made its way to my understanding. At length, it occurred to me, that though the information I possessed was, in one sense, sufficient, yet if more could be obtained, more was desirable. This passage was copied from a British paper; part of it only, perhaps, was transcribed. The printer was in possession of the original.

"Towards his house I immediately turned my horse's head. He produced the paper, but I found nothing more than had already been seen. While busy in perusing it, the printer stood by my side. He noticed the object of which I was in search. 'Aye,' said he, 'that is a strange affair. I should never have met with it, had not Mr. Hallet[5] sent to me the paper, with a particular request to republish that advertisement.'

"Mr. Hallet! What reasons could he have for making this request? Had the paper sent to him been accompanied by any information respecting the convict? Had he personal or extraordinary reasons for desiring its republication? This was to be known only in one way. I speeded to his house. In answer to my interrogations, he told me that Ludloe had formerly been in America, and that during his residence in this city, considerable intercourse had taken place between them. Hence a confidence arose, which has since been kept alive by occasional letters. He had lately received a letter from him, enclosing the newspaper from which this extract had been made. He put it into my hands, and pointed out the passages which related to Carwin.

"Ludloe confirms the facts of his conviction and escape; and adds, that he had reason to believe him to have embarked for America. He describes him in general terms, as the most incomprehensible and formidable among men; as engaged in schemes, reasonably suspected to be, in the highest degree, criminal, but such as no human intelligence is able to unravel: that his ends are pursued by means which leave it in doubt whether he be not in league with some infernal spirit: that his crimes have hitherto been perpetrated with the aid of some unknown but desperate accomplices:

---

[5] "Mr. Hallet": the first mention of Clara's maternal relation, the magistrate who will be the first on the ensuing scene of Clara's distress in Chapter 17. If Hallet knows Ludloe and Carwin has links to the Conways, then the pre-existing links between Carwin and the Wielands are closer than they have appeared thus far.

that he wages a perpetual war against the happiness of mankind, and sets his engines of destruction[6] at work against every object that presents itself.

"This is the substance of the letter. Hallet expressed some surprize at the curiosity which was manifested by me on this occasion. I was too much absorbed by the ideas suggested by this letter, to pay attention to his remarks. I shuddered with the apprehension of the evil to which our indiscreet familiarity with this man had probably exposed us. I burnt with impatience to see you, and to do what in me lay to avert the calamity which threatened us. It was already five o'clock. Night was hastening, and there was no time to be lost. On leaving Mr. Hallet's house, who should meet me in the street, but Bertrand, the servant whom I left in Germany. His appearance and accoutrements bespoke him to have just alighted from a toilsome and long journey. I was not wholly without expectation of seeing him about this time, but no one was then more distant from my thoughts. You know what reasons I have for anxiety respecting scenes with which this man was conversant.[7] Carwin was for a moment forgotten. In answer to my vehement inquiries, Bertrand produced a copious packet. I shall not at present mention its contents, nor the measures which they obliged me to adopt. I bestowed a brief perusal on these papers, and having given some directions to Bertrand, resumed my purpose with regard to you. My horse I was obliged to resign to my servant, he being charged with a commission that required speed. The clock had struck ten, and Mettingen was five miles distant.[8] I was to journey thither on foot. These circumstances only added to my expedition.

"As I passed swiftly along, I reviewed all the incidents accompanying the appearance and deportment of that man among us. Late events have been inexplicable and mysterious beyond any of which I have either read or heard. These events were coeval[9] with Carwin's introduction. I am unable to explain their origin and mutual dependance; but I do not, on that account, believe them to have a supernatural original. Is not this man the agent? Some of them seem to be propitious; but what should I think of those threats of assassination with which you were lately alarmed? Bloodshed is the trade, and horror is the element of this man.[10] The process by which the sympathies of nature are extinguished in our hearts, by which evil is made

---

[6] "Perpetual war against the happiness of mankind . . . engines of destruction": this paragraph's language, transmitted from Ludloe's letter demonizing Carwin, resonates with the fear mongering of the contemporary Illuminati scare. For more on the novel's implicit commentary on this episode, see the Introduction and Illuminati debates in Related Texts.

[7] "Scenes with which this man was conversant": Pleyel's servant Bertrand has been doing Pleyel's business in Saxony and Lusatia, and bears news of Pleyel's fiancée Theresa de Stolberg. The contents of Bertrand's packet will be revealed in Chapter 21; see note 21.2.

[8] "Five miles distant": remarks on the location of Pleyel's property in Chapters 3 and 5 revealed that his house is about five miles from the Wieland estate. See notes 3.12 and 5.13. Note also that Pleyel has taken five hours to go through these papers.

[9] "Coeval": simultaneous with, going back to the same date.

[10] "Bloodshed is the trade, and horror is the element of this man": Pleyel assumes that the accusations against Carwin are true, but the line also echoes the generic language of contemporary discussions of gothic fiction.

our good, and by which we are made susceptible of no activity but in the infliction, and no joy but in the spectacle of woes, is an obvious process. As to an alliance with evil geniuses, the power and the malice of dæmons have been a thousand times exemplified in human beings. There are no devils but those which are begotten upon selfishness, and reared by cunning.[11]

"Now, indeed, the scene was changed. It was not his secret poniard[12] that I dreaded. It was only the success of his efforts to make you a confederate in your own destruction, to make your will the instrument by which he might bereave you of liberty and honor.

"I took, as usual, the path through your brother's ground. I ranged with celerity and silence along the bank. I approached the fence, which divides Wieland's estate from yours. The recess in the bank being near this line, it being necessary for me to pass near it, my mind being tainted with inveterate suspicions concerning you; suspicions which were indebted for their strength to incidents connected with this spot; what wonder that it seized upon my thoughts!

"I leaped on the fence; but before I descended on the opposite side, I paused to survey the scene. Leaves dropping with dew, and glistening in the moon's rays, with no moving object to molest the deep repose, filled me with security and hope. I left the station at length, and tended forward. You were probably at rest. How should I communicate without alarming you, the intelligence of my arrival? An immediate interview was to be procured. I could not bear to think that a minute should be lost by remissness or hesitation. Should I knock at the door? or should I stand under your chamber windows, which I perceived to be open, and awaken you by my calls?

"These reflections employed me, as I passed opposite to the summer-house. I had scarcely gone by, when my ear caught a sound unusual at this time and place. It was almost too faint and too transient to allow me a distinct perception of it. I stopped to listen; presently it was heard again, and now it was somewhat in a louder key. It was laughter; and unquestionably produced by a female voice. That voice was familiar to my senses. It was yours.

"Whence it came, I was at first at a loss to conjecture; but this uncertainty vanished when it was heard the third time. I threw back my eyes towards the recess. Every other organ and limb was useless to me. I did not reason on the subject. I did not, in a direct manner, draw my conclusions from the hour, the place, the hilarity which this sound betokened, and the circumstance of having a companion, which it no less incontestably proved. In an instant, as it were, my heart was invaded with cold, and the pulses of life at a stand.

---

[11] "Geniuses . . . dæmons . . . no devils but those which are begotten upon selfishness, and reared by cunning": Pleyel rejects the notions about supernatural, guardian spirits that have been evoked up to this point (see notes 5.17, 10.3), and accurately assumes that the mysterious events must involve trickery. In passages like this, the novel participates in the common late-Enlightenment mode of texts that demystify religious superstition and common frauds or "impostures."

[12] "Secret poniard": a poniard is generally a small, slim dagger, but sturdier than the penknives and stilettos that figure elsewhere in the text. The term is already somewhat archaic and exotic by the 1790s. *The Gentlemen's Compleat Military Dictionary* (Boston, 1759) defines poniard as "A sort of Short Sword used in *Spain* and *Italy*."

"Why should I go further? Why should I return? Should I not hurry to a distance from a sound, which, though formerly so sweet and delectable, was now more hideous than the shrieks of owls?

"I had no time to yield to this impulse. The thought of approaching and listening occurred to me. I had no doubt of which I was conscious. Yet my certainty was capable of increase. I was likewise stimulated by a sentiment that partook of rage. I was governed by an half-formed and tempestuous resolution to break in upon your interview, and strike you dead with my upbraiding.

"I approached with the utmost caution. When I reached the edge of the bank immediately above the summer-house, I thought I heard voices from below, as busy in conversation. The steps in the rock are clear of bushy impediments. They allowed me to descend into a cavity beside the building without being detected. Thus to lie in wait could only be justified by the momentousness of the occasion."

Here Pleyel paused in his narrative, and fixed his eyes upon me. Situated as I was, my horror and astonishment at this tale gave way to compassion for the anguish which the countenance of my friend betrayed. I reflected on his force of understanding. I reflected on the powers of my enemy. I could easily divine the substance of the conversation that was overheard. Carwin had constructed his plot in a manner suited to the characters of those whom he had selected for his victims. I saw that the convictions of Pleyel were immutable. I forbore to struggle against the storm, because I saw that all struggles would be fruitless. I was calm; but my calmness was the torpor of despair, and not the tranquillity of fortitude. It was calmness invincible by any thing that his grief and his fury could suggest to Pleyel. He resumed—

"Woman! wilt thou hear me further? Shall I go on to repeat the conversation? Is it shame that makes thee tongue-tied? Shall I go on? or art thou satisfied with what has been already said?"

I bowed my head. "Go on," said I. "I make not this request in the hope of undeceiving you. I shall no longer contend with my own weakness. The storm is let loose, and I shall peaceably submit to be driven by its fury.[13] But go on. This conference will end only with affording me a clearer foresight of my destiny; but that will be some satisfaction, and I will not part without it."

Why, on hearing these words, did Pleyel hesitate? Did some unlooked-for doubt insinuate itself into his mind? Was his belief suddenly shaken by my looks, or my words, or by some newly recollected circumstance? Whencesoever it arose, it could not endure the test of deliberation. In a few minutes the flame of resentment was again lighted up in his bosom. He proceeded with his accustomed vehemence—

"I hate myself for this folly. I can find no apology for this tale. Yet I am irresistibly impelled to relate it. She that hears me is apprized of every particular. I have only to repeat to her her own words. She will listen with a tranquil air, and the spectacle of her obduracy will drive me to some desperate act. Why then should I persist! yet persist I must."

---

[13] "I bowed my head . . . I shall peaceably submit to be driven by its fury": Clara's resignation before Pleyel's rage ("Woman!") is partly motivated by the dramatic circumstance, but also partly a performance of customary female obedience and deference toward male authority.

Again he paused. "No," said he, "it is impossible to repeat your avowals of love, your appeals to former confessions of your tenderness, to former deeds of dishonor, to the circumstances of the first interview that took place between you. It was on that night when I traced you to this recess. Thither had he enticed you, and there had you ratified an unhallowed compact by admitting him—

"Great God! Thou witnessedst the agonies that tore my bosom at that moment! Thou witnessedst my efforts to repel the testimony of my ears! It was in vain that you dwelt upon the confusion which my unlooked-for summons excited in you; the tardiness with which a suitable excuse occurred to you; your resentment that my impertinent intrusion had put an end to that charming interview: A disappointment for which you endeavoured to compensate yourself, by the frequency and duration of subsequent meetings.

"In vain you dwelt upon incidents of which you only could be conscious; incidents that occurred on occasions on which none beside your own family were witnesses. In vain was your discourse characterized by peculiarities inimitable of sentiment and language. My conviction was effected only by an accumulation of the same tokens. I yielded not but to evidence which took away the power to withhold my faith.

"My sight was of no use to me. Beneath so thick an umbrage,[14] the darkness was intense. Hearing was the only avenue to information, which the circumstances allowed to be open. I was couched within three feet of you. Why should I approach nearer? I could not contend with your betrayer. What could be the purpose of a contest? You stood in no need of a protector. What could I do, but retire from the spot overwhelmed with confusion and dismay? I sought my chamber, and endeavoured to regain my composure. The door of the house, which I found open, your subsequent entrance, closing, and fastening it, and going into your chamber, which had been thus long deserted, were only confirmations of the truth.

"Why should I paint the tempestuous fluctuation of my thoughts between grief and revenge, between rage and despair? Why should I repeat my vows of eternal implacability and persecution, and the speedy recantation of these vows?

"I have said enough. You have dismissed me from a place in your esteem. What I think, and what I feel, is of no importance in your eyes. May the duty which I owe myself enable me to forget your existence. In a few minutes I go hence. Be the maker of your fortune, and may adversity instruct you in that wisdom, which education was unable to impart to you."

Those were the last words which Pleyel uttered. He left the room, and my new emotions enabled me to witness his departure without any apparent loss of composure. As I sat alone, I ruminated on these incidents. Nothing was more evident than that I had taken an eternal leave of happiness. Life was a worthless thing, separate from that good which had now been wrested from me; yet the sentiment that now possessed me had no tendency to palsy my exertions, and overbear my strength. I noticed that the light was declining, and perceived the propriety of leaving this house. I placed myself again in the chaise, and returned slowly towards the city.

---

[14] "Umbrage": literally, shade or shadow caused by trees.

Chapter XV

BEFORE I reached the city it was dusk. It was my purpose to spend the night at Mettingen. I was not solicitous, as long as I was attended by a faithful servant, to be there at an early hour. My exhausted strength required me to take some refreshment. With this view, and in order to pay respect to one whose affection for me was truly maternal, I stopped at Mrs. Baynton's. She was absent from home; but I had scarcely entered the house when one of her domestics presented me a letter. I opened and read as follows:

"To Clara Wieland,

"What shall I say to extenuate the misconduct of last night? It is my duty to repair it to the utmost of my power, but the only way in which it can be repaired, you will not, I fear, be prevailed on to adopt. It is by granting me an interview, at your own house, at eleven o'clock this night. I have no means of removing any fears that you may entertain of my designs, but my simple and solemn declarations. These, after what has passed between us, you may deem unworthy of confidence. I cannot help it. My folly and rashness has left me no other resource. I will be at your door by that hour. If you chuse to admit me to a conference, provided that conference has no witnesses, I will disclose to you particulars, the knowledge of which is of the utmost importance to your happiness. Farewell.

CARWIN."

What a letter was this! A man known to be an assassin and robber; one capable of plotting against my life and my fame; detected lurking in my chamber, and avowing designs the most flagitious and dreadful, now solicits me to grant him a midnight interview! To admit him alone into my presence! Could he make this request with the expectation of my compliance? What had he seen in me, that could justify him in admitting so wild a belief? Yet this request is preferred with the utmost gravity. It is not accompanied by an appearance of uncommon earnestness. Had the misconduct to which he alludes been a slight incivility, and the interview requested to take place in the midst of my friends, there would have been no extravagance in the tenor of this letter; but, as it was, the writer had surely been bereft of his reason.

I perused this epistle frequently. The request it contained might be called audacious or stupid, if it had been made by a different person; but from Carwin, who could not be unaware of the effect which it must naturally produce, and of the manner in which it would unavoidably be treated, it was perfectly inexplicable. He must have counted on the success of some plot, in order to extort my assent. None of those motives by which I am usually governed would ever have persuaded me to meet any one of his sex, at the time and place which he had prescribed. Much less would I consent to a meeting with a man, tainted with the most detestable crimes, and by whose arts my own safety had been so imminently endangered, and my happiness irretrievably destroyed. I shuddered at the idea that such a meeting was possible. I felt some reluctance to approach a spot which he still visited and haunted.

Such were the ideas which first suggested themselves on the perusal of the letter. Meanwhile, I resumed my journey. My thoughts still dwelt upon the same topic. Gradually from ruminating on this epistle, I reverted to my interview with Pleyel. I recalled the particulars of the dialogue to which he had been an auditor. My heart sunk anew on viewing the inextricable complexity of this deception, and the inauspicious concurrence of events, which tended to confirm him in his error. When he approached my chamber door, my terror kept me mute. He put his ear, perhaps, to the crevice, but it caught the sound of nothing human. Had I called, or made any token that denoted some one to be within, words would have ensued; and as omnipresence was impossible, this discovery, and the artless narrative of what had just passed, would have saved me from his murderous invectives. He went into his chamber, and after some interval, I stole across the entry and down the stairs, with inaudible steps. Having secured the outer doors, I returned with less circumspection. He heard me not when I descended; but my returning steps were easily distinguished. Now he thought was the guilty interview at an end. In what other way was it possible for him to construe these signals?

How fallacious and precipitate was my decision! Carwin's plot owed its success to a coincidence of events scarcely credible. The balance was swayed from its equipoise by a hair. Had I even begun the conversation with an account of what befel me in my chamber, my previous interview with Wieland would have taught him to suspect me of imposture; yet, if I were discoursing with this ruffian, when Pleyel touched the lock of my chamber door, and when he shut his own door with so much violence, how, he might ask, should I be able to relate these incidents? Perhaps he had withheld the knowledge of these circumstances from my brother, from whom, therefore, I could not obtain it, so that my innocence would have thus been irresistibly demonstrated.

The first impulse which flowed from these ideas was to return upon my steps, and demand once more an interview; but he was gone: his parting declarations were remembered.

Pleyel, I exclaimed, thou art gone for ever! Are thy mistakes beyond the reach of detection? Am I helpless in the midst of this snare? The plotter is at hand. He even speaks in the style of penitence. He solicits an interview which he promises shall end in the disclosure of something momentous to my happiness. What can he say which will avail to turn aside this evil? But why should his remorse be feigned? I have done him no injury. His wickedness is fertile only of despair; and the billows of remorse will some time overbear him. Why may not this event have already taken place? Why should I refuse to see him?

This idea was present, as it were, for a moment. I suddenly recoiled from it, confounded at that frenzy which could give even momentary harbour to such a scheme; yet presently it returned. A length I even conceived it to deserve deliberation. I questioned whether it was not proper to admit, at a lonely spot, in a sacred hour, this man of tremendous and inscrutable attributes, this performer of horrid deeds, and whose presence was predicted to call down unheard-of and unutterable horrors.

What was it that swayed me? I felt myself divested of the power to will contrary to the motives that determined me to seek his presence. My mind seemed to be split into separate parts, and these parts to have entered into furious and implacable contention. These tumults gradually subsided. The reasons why I should confide in that interposition which had hitherto defended me; in those tokens of compunction which this letter contained; in the efficacy of this interview to restore its spotlessness to my character, and banish all illusions from the mind of my friend, continually acquired new evidence and new strength.

What should I fear in his presence? This was unlike an artifice intended to betray me into his hands. If it were an artifice, what purpose would it serve? The freedom of my mind was untouched, and that freedom would defy the assaults of blandishments or magic. Force was I not able to repel. On the former occasion my courage, it is true, had failed at the imminent approach of danger; but then I had not enjoyed opportunities of deliberation; I had foreseen nothing; I was sunk into imbecility by my previous thoughts; I had been the victim of recent disappointments and anticipated ills: Witness my infatuation in opening the closet in opposition to divine injunctions.

Now, perhaps, my courage was the offspring of a no less erring principle. Pleyel was for ever lost to me. I strove in vain to assume his person, and suppress my resentment; I strove in vain to believe in the assuaging influence of time, to look forward to the birth-day of new hopes, and the re-exaltation of that luminary, of whose effulgencies I had so long and so liberally partaken.[1]

What had I to suffer worse than was already inflicted?

Was not Carwin my foe? I owed my untimely fate to his treason. Instead of flying from his presence, ought I not to devote all my faculties to the gaining of an interview, and compel him to repair the ills of which he has been the author? Why should I suppose him impregnable to argument? Have I not reason on my side, and the power of imparting conviction? Cannot he be made to see the justice of unravelling the maze in which Pleyel is bewildered?

He may, at least, be accessible to fear. Has he nothing to fear from the rage of an injured woman? But suppose him inaccessible to such inducements; suppose him to persist in all his flagitious purposes; are not the means of defence and resistance in my power?

In the progress of such thoughts, was the resolution at last formed. I hoped that the interview was sought by him for a laudable end; but, be that as it would, I trusted

---

[1] "The re-exaltation of that luminary, of whose effulgencies I had … partaken": in other words, Clara hopes to be reunited with Pleyel, figured as a superior "light." "Luminary" is poetically the sun or moon, or a deity personifying them; "effulgence" is splendid radiance; neither is ordinary language in the 1790s. Clara's language in this chapter deifies Pleyel and demonizes Carwin. The contrast is also one of status and authority: after Clara accepts Pleyel's decision and "rage" in the previous chapter, she now begins to feel empowered to challenge Carwin, a lower-status male, and subject him to her own "rage."

that, by energy of reasoning or of action, I should render it auspicious, or, at least, harmless.

Such a determination must unavoidably fluctuate. The poet's chaos was no unapt emblem of the state of my mind. A torment was awakened in my bosom, which I foresaw would end only when this interview was past, and its consequences fully experienced. Hence my impatience for the arrival of the hour which had been prescribed by Carwin.

Meanwhile, my meditations were tumultuously active. New impediments to the execution of the scheme were speedily suggested. I had apprized Catharine of my intention to spend this and many future nights with her. Her husband was informed of this arrangement, and had zealously approved it. Eleven o'clock exceeded their hour of retiring. What excuse should I form for changing my plan? Should I shew this letter to Wieland, and submit myself to his direction? But I knew in what way he would decide. He would fervently dissuade me from going. Nay, would he not do more? He was apprized of the offences of Carwin, and of the reward offered for his apprehension. Would he not seize this opportunity of executing justice on a criminal?

This idea was new. I was plunged once more into doubt. Did not equity enjoin me thus to facilitate his arrest? No. I disdained the office of betrayer. Carwin was unapprized of his danger, and his intentions were possibly beneficent. Should I station guards about the house, and make an act, intended perhaps for my benefit, instrumental to his own destruction? Wieland might be justified in thus employing the knowledge which I should impart, but I, by imparting it, should pollute myself with more hateful crimes than those undeservedly imputed to me. This scheme, therefore, I unhesitatingly rejected. The views with which I should return to my own house, it would therefore be necessary to conceal. Yet some pretext must be invented. I had never been initiated into the trade of lying. Yet what but falsehood was a deliberate suppression of the truth? To deceive by silence or by words is the same.

Yet what would a lie avail me? What pretext would justify this change in my plan? Would it not tend to confirm the imputations of Pleyel? That I should voluntarily return to an house in which honor and life had so lately been endangered, could be explained in no way favorable to my integrity.

These reflections, if they did not change, at least suspended my decision. In this state of uncertainty I alighted at the *hut*. We gave this name to the house tenanted by the farmer and his servants, and which was situated on the verge of my brother's ground, and at a considerable distance from the mansion. The path to the mansion was planted by a double row of walnuts. Along this path I proceeded alone. I entered the parlour, in which was a light just expiring in the socket. There was no one in the room. I perceived by the clock that stood against the wall, that it was near eleven. The lateness of the hour startled me. What had become of the family? They were usually retired an hour before this; but the unextinguished taper, and the unbarred door were indications that they had not retired. I again returned to the hall, and passed from one room to another, but still encountered not a human being.

I imagined that, perhaps, the lapse of a few minutes would explain these appearances. Meanwhile I reflected that the preconcerted hour had arrived. Carwin was perhaps waiting my approach. Should I immediately retire to my own house, no one would be apprized of my proceeding. Nay, the interview might pass, and I be enabled to return in half an hour. Hence no necessity would arise for dissimulation.

I was so far influenced by these views that I rose to execute this design; but again the unusual condition of the house occurred to me, and some vague solicitude as to the condition of the family. I was nearly certain that my brother had not retired; but by what motives he could be induced to desert his house thus unseasonably, I could by no means divine. Louisa Conway, at least, was at home, and had, probably, retired to her chamber; perhaps she was able to impart the information I wanted.

I went to her chamber, and found her asleep. She was delighted and surprized at my arrival, and told me with how much impatience and anxiety my brother and his wife had waited my coming. They were fearful that some mishap had befallen me, and had remained up longer than the usual period. Notwithstanding the lateness of the hour, Catharine would not resign the hope of seeing me. Louisa said she had left them both in the parlour, and she knew of no cause for their absence.

As yet I was not without solicitude on account of their personal safety. I was far from being perfectly at ease on that head, but entertained no distinct conception of the danger that impended over them. Perhaps to beguile the moments of my long protracted stay, they had gone to walk upon the bank. The atmosphere, though illuminated only by the star-light, was remarkably serene. Meanwhile the desireableness of an interview with Carwin again returned, and I finally resolved to seek it.

I passed with doubting and hasty steps along the path. My dwelling, seen at a distance, was gloomy and desolate. It had no inhabitant, for my servant, in consequence of my new arrangement, had gone to Mettingen. The temerity of this attempt began to shew itself in more vivid colours to my understanding. Whoever has pointed steel is not without arms; yet what must have been the state of my mind when I could meditate, without shuddering, on the use of a murderous weapon, and believe myself secure merely because I was capable of being made so by the death of another? Yet this was not my state. I felt as if I was rushing into deadly toils,[2] without the power of pausing or receding.

---

[2] "Toils": traps or snares.

Chapter XVI

AS soon as I arrived in sight of the front of the house, my attention was excited by a light from the window of my own chamber. No appearance could be less explicable. A meeting was expected with Carwin, but that he pre-occupied my chamber, and had supplied himself with light, was not to be believed. What motive could influence him to adopt this conduct? Could I proceed until this was explained? Perhaps, if I should proceed to a distance in front, some one would be visible. A sidelong but feeble beam from the window, fell upon the piny copse which skirted the bank. As I eyed it, it suddenly became mutable, and after flitting to and fro,[1] for a short time, it vanished. I turned my eye again toward the window, and perceived that the light was still there; but the change which I had noticed was occasioned by a change in the position of the lamp or candle within. Hence, that some person was there was an unavoidable inference.

I paused to deliberate on the propriety of advancing. Might I not advance cautiously, and, therefore, without danger? Might I not knock at the door, or call, and be apprized of the nature of my visitant before I entered? I approached and listened at the door, but could hear nothing. I knocked at first timidly, but afterwards with loudness. My signals were unnoticed. I stepped back and looked, but the light was no longer discernible. Was it suddenly extinguished by a human agent? What purpose but concealment was intended? Why was the illumination produced, to be thus suddenly brought to an end? And why, since some one was there, had silence been observed?

These were questions, the solution of which may be readily supposed to be entangled with danger. Would not this danger, when measured by a woman's fears, expand into gigantic dimensions? Menaces of death; the stunning exertions of a warning voice; the known and unknown attributes of Carwin; our recent interview in this chamber; the pre-appointment of a meeting at this place and hour, all thronged into my memory. What was to be done?

Courage is no definite or stedfast principle. Let that man who shall purpose to assign motives to the actions of another, blush at his folly and forbear.[2] Not more presumptuous would it be to attempt the classification of all nature, and the scanning of supreme intelligence. I gazed for a minute at the window, and fixed my eyes, for a second minute, on the ground. I drew forth from my pocket, and opened, a penknife. This, said I, be my safe-guard and avenger. The assailant shall perish, or myself shall fall.

---

[1] "Flitting to and fro": another instance in which shimmering or uncertain light presages a dramatic encounter. For an early example, see note 2.5.

[2] "Assign motives to the actions of another . . . forbear": the futility of assigning simple, individualistic motives or causes to complex actions or events, and the related limitations of any individual's perspective, are principles that Brown constantly evokes and dramatizes in his fiction. For the development of this point in Brown's approach to fiction, see the Introduction and Brown's essays on novel writing in Related Texts.

I had locked up the house in the morning, but had the key of the kitchen door in my pocket. I, therefore, determined to gain access behind. Thither I hastened, unlocked and entered. All was lonely, darksome, and waste. Familiar as I was with every part of my dwelling, I easily found my way to a closet, drew forth a taper, a flint, tinder, and steel, and, in a moment as it were, gave myself the guidance and protection of light.

What purpose did I meditate? Should I explore my way to my chamber, and confront the being who had dared to intrude into this recess, and had laboured for concealment? By putting out the light did he seek to hide himself, or mean only to circumvent my incautious steps? Yet was it not more probable that he desired my absence by thus encouraging the supposition that the house was unoccupied? I would see this man in spite of all impediments; ere I died, I would see his face, and summon him to penitence and retribution; no matter at what cost an interview was purchased. Reputation and life might be wrested from me by another, but my rectitude and honor were in my own keeping, and were safe.

I proceeded to the foot of the stairs. At such a crisis my thoughts may be supposed at no liberty to range; yet vague images rushed into my mind, of the mysterious interposition which had been experienced on the last night. My case, at present, was not dissimilar; and, if my angel were not weary of fruitless exertions to save, might not a new warning be expected? Who could say whether his silence were ascribable to the absence of danger, or to his own absence?

In this state of mind, no wonder that a shivering cold crept through my veins; that my pause was prolonged; and, that a fearful glance was thrown backward.

Alas! my heart droops, and my fingers are enervated; my ideas are vivid, but my language is faint; now know I what it is to entertain incommunicable sentiments. The chain of subsequent incidents is drawn through my mind, and being linked with those which forewent, by turns rouse up agonies and sink me into hopelessness.

Yet I will persist to the end. My narrative may be invaded by inaccuracy and confusion; but if I live no longer, I will, at least, live to complete it. What but ambiguities, abruptnesses, and dark transitions, can be expected from the historian who is, at the same time, the sufferer of these disasters?

I have said that I cast a look behind. Some object was expected to be seen, or why should I have gazed in that direction? Two senses were at once assailed. The same piercing exclamation of *hold! hold!* was uttered within the same distance of my ear. This it was that I heard. The airy undulation, and the shock given to my nerves, were real. Whether the spectacle which I beheld existed in my fancy or without, might be doubted.

I had not closed the door of the apartment I had just left. The stair-case, at the foot of which I stood, was eight or ten feet from the door, and attached to the wall through which the door led. My view, therefore, was sidelong, and took in no part of the room.

Through this aperture was an head thrust and drawn back with so much swiftness, that the immediate conviction was, that thus much of a form, ordinarily invisible, had been unshrowded. The face was turned towards me. Every muscle was tense; the forehead and brows were drawn into vehement expression; the lips were stretched as in the act of shrieking, and the eyes emitted sparks, which, no doubt, if I had been unattended by a light, would have illuminated like the coruscations of a meteor. The sound and the vision were present, and departed together at the same instant; but the cry was blown into my ear, while the face was many paces distant.

This face was well suited to a being whose performances exceeded the standard of humanity, and yet its features were akin to those I had before seen. The image of Carwin was blended in a thousand ways with the stream of my thoughts. This visage was, perhaps, pourtrayed by my fancy. If so, it will excite no surprize that some of his lineaments[3] were now discovered. Yet affinities were few and unconspicuous, and were lost amidst the blaze of opposite qualities.

What conclusion could I form? Be the face human or not, the intimation was imparted from above. Experience had evinced the benignity of that being who gave it. Once he had interposed to shield me from harm, and subsequent events demonstrated the usefulness of that interposition. Now was I again warned to forbear. I was hurrying to the verge of the same gulf, and the same power was exerted to recall my steps. Was it possible for me not to obey? Was I capable of holding on in the same perilous career?[4] Yes. Even of this I was capable!

The intimation was imperfect: it gave no form to my danger, and prescribed no limits to my caution. I had formerly neglected it, and yet escaped. Might I not trust to the same issue? This idea might possess, though imperceptibly, some influence. I persisted; but it was not merely on this account. I cannot delineate the motives that led me on. I now speak as if no remnant of doubt existed in my mind as to the supernal origin of these sounds; but this is owing to the imperfection of my language, for I only mean that the belief was more permanent, and visited more frequently my sober meditations than its opposite. The immediate effects served only to undermine the foundations of my judgment and precipitate my resolutions.

I must either advance or return. I chose the former, and began to ascend the stairs. The silence underwent no second interruption. My chamber door was closed, but unlocked, and, aided by vehement efforts of my courage, I opened and looked in.

No hideous or uncommon object was discernible. The danger, indeed, might easily have lurked out of sight, have sprung upon me as I entered, and have rent me with his iron talons; but I was blind to this fate, and advanced, though cautiously, into the room.

Still every thing wore its accustomed aspect. Neither lamp nor candle was to be found. Now, for the first time, suspicions were suggested as to the nature of the light which I had seen. Was it possible to have been the companion of that supernatural visage; a meteorous refulgence[5] producible at the will of him to whom that visage belonged, and partaking of the nature of that which accompanied my father's death?

---

[3] "Lineaments": "distinctive features or characteristics" (*OED*).

[4] "Career": in this usage, path or rapid forward impulse.

[5] "Meteorous refulgence": sudden or rapidly passing light, likened to the trace of a meteor.

The closet was near, and I remembered the complicated horrors of which it had been productive. Here, perhaps, was inclosed the source of my peril, and the gratification of my curiosity. Should I adventure once more to explore its recesses? This was a resolution not easily formed. I was suspended in thought: when glancing my eye on a table, I perceived a written paper. Carwin's hand was instantly recognized, and snatching up the paper, I read as follows:—

"There was folly in expecting your compliance with my invitation. Judge how I was disappointed in finding another in your place. I have waited, but to wait any longer would be perilous. I shall still seek an interview, but it must be at a different time and place: meanwhile, I will write this—How will you bear—How inexplicable will be this transaction!—An event so unexpected—a sight so horrible!"

Such was this abrupt and unsatisfactory script. The ink was yet moist, the hand was that of Carwin. Hence it was to be inferred that he had this moment left the apartment, or was still in it. I looked back, on the sudden expectation of seeing him behind me.

What other did he mean? What transaction had taken place adverse to my expectations? What sight was about to be exhibited? I looked around me once more, but saw nothing which indicated strangeness. Again I remembered the closet, and was resolved to seek in that the solution of these mysteries. Here, perhaps, was inclosed the scene destined to awaken my horrors and baffle my foresight.

I have already said, that the entrance into this closet was beside my bed, which, on two sides, was closely shrouded by curtains. On that side nearest the closet, the curtain was raised. As I passed along I cast my eye thither. I started, and looked again. I bore a light in my hand, and brought it nearer my eyes, in order to dispel any illusive mists that might have hovered before them. Once more I fixed my eyes upon the bed, in hope that this more stedfast scrutiny would annihilate the object which before seemed to be there.

This then was the sight which Carwin had predicted! This was the event which my understanding was to find inexplicable! This was the fate which had been reserved for me, but which, by some untoward chance, had befallen on another!

I had not been terrified by empty menaces. Violation and death awaited my entrance into this chamber. Some inscrutable chance had led *her* hither before me, and the merciless fangs of which I was designed to be the prey, had mistaken their victim, and had fixed themselves in *her* heart. But where was my safety? Was the mischief exhausted or flown? The steps of the assassin had just been here; they could not be far off; in a moment he would rush into my presence, and I should perish under the same polluting and suffocating grasp!

My frame shook, and my knees were unable to support me. I gazed alternately at the closet door and at the door of my room. At one of these avenues would enter the exterminator of my honor and my life. I was prepared for defence; but now that danger was imminent, my means of defence, and my power to use them were gone. I was not qualified, by education and experience, to encounter perils like these: or, perhaps, I was powerless because I was again assaulted by surprise, and had not fortified my mind by foresight and previous reflection against a scene like this.

Fears for my own safety again yielded place to reflections on the scene before me. I fixed my eyes upon her countenance. My sister's well-known and beloved features could not be concealed by convulsion or lividness. What direful illusion led thee hither? Bereft of thee, what hold on happiness remains to thy offspring and thy spouse? To lose thee by a common fate would have been sufficiently hard; but thus suddenly to perish—to become the prey of this ghastly death! How will a spectacle like this be endured by Wieland? To die beneath his grasp would not satisfy thy enemy. This was mercy to the evils which he previously made thee suffer! After these evils death was a boon which thou besoughtest him to grant. He entertained no enmity against thee: I was the object of his treason; but by some tremendous mistake his fury was misplaced. But how comest thou hither? and where was Wieland in thy hour of distress?

I approached the corpse: I lifted the still flexible hand, and kissed the lips which were breathless. Her flowing drapery was discomposed. I restored it to order, and seating myself on the bed, again fixed stedfast eyes upon her countenance. I cannot distinctly recollect the ruminations of that moment. I saw confusedly, but forcibly, that every hope was extinguished with the life of *Catharine*. All happiness and dignity must henceforth be banished from the house and name of Wieland: all that remained was to linger out in agonies a short existence; and leave to the world a monument of blasted hopes and changeable fortune. Pleyel was already lost to me; yet, while Catharine lived life was not a detestable possession: but now, severed from the companion of my infancy, the partaker of all my thoughts, my cares, and my wishes, I was like one set afloat upon a stormy sea, and hanging his safety upon a plank; night was closing upon him, and an unexpected surge had torn him from his hold and overwhelmed him forever.

Chapter XVII

I HAD no inclination nor power to move from this spot. For more than an hour, my faculties and limbs seemed to be deprived of all activity. The door below creaked on its hinges, and steps ascended the stairs. My wandering and confused thoughts were instantly recalled by these sounds, and dropping the curtain of the bed, I moved to a part of the room where any one who entered should be visible; such are the vibrations of sentiment, that notwithstanding the seeming fulfilment of my fears, and increase of my danger, I was conscious, on this occasion, to no turbulence but that of curiosity.

At length he entered the apartment, and I recognized my brother. It was the same Wieland whom I had ever seen. Yet his features were pervaded by a new expression. I supposed him unacquainted with the fate of his wife, and his appearance confirmed this persuasion. A brow expanding into exultation I had hitherto never seen in him, yet such a brow did he now wear. Not only was he unapprized of the disaster that had happened, but some joyous occurrence had betided. What a reverse was preparing to annihilate his transitory bliss! No husband ever doated more fondly, for no wife ever claimed so boundless a devotion. I was not uncertain as to the effects to flow from the discovery of her fate. I confided not at all in the efforts of his reason or his piety. There were few evils which his modes of thinking would not disarm of their sting; but here, all opiates to grief, and all compellers of patience were vain. This spectacle would be unavoidably followed by the outrages of desperation, and a rushing to death.

For the present, I neglected to ask myself what motive brought him hither. I was only fearful of the effects to flow from the sight of the dead. Yet could it be long concealed from him? Some time and speedily he would obtain this knowledge. No stratagems could considerably or usefully prolong his ignorance. All that could be sought was to take away the abruptness of the change, and shut out the confusion of despair, and the inroads of madness: but I knew my brother, and knew that all exertions to console him would be fruitless.

What could I say? I was mute, and poured forth those tears on his account, which my own unhappiness had been unable to extort. In the midst of my tears, I was not unobservant of his motions. These were of a nature to rouse some other sentiment than grief, or, at least, to mix with it a portion of astonishment.

His countenance suddenly became troubled. His hands were clasped with a force that left the print of his nails in his flesh. His eyes were fixed on my feet. His brain seemed to swell beyond its continent. He did not cease to breathe, but his breath was stifled into groans. I had never witnessed the hurricane of human passions. My element had, till lately, been all sunshine and calm. I was unconversant with the altitudes and energies of sentiment, and was transfixed with inexplicable horror by the symptoms which I now beheld.

After a silence and a conflict which I could not interpret, he lifted his eyes to heaven, and in broken accents exclaimed, "This is too much! Any victim but this, and thy will be done. Have I not sufficiently attested my faith and my obedience? She that is gone, they that have perished, were linked with my soul by ties which only thy command would have broken; but here is sanctity and excellence surpassing human. This workmanship is thine, and it cannot be thy will to heap it into ruins."

Here suddenly unclasping his hands, he struck one of them against his forehead, and continued—"Wretch! who made thee quick sighted in the councils of thy Maker? Deliverance from mortal fetters is awarded to this being, and thou art the minister of this decree."

So saying, Wieland advanced towards me. His words and his motions were without meaning, except on one supposition. The death of Catharine was already known to him, and that knowledge, as might have been suspected, had destroyed his reason. I had feared nothing less; but now that I beheld the extinction of a mind the most luminous and penetrating that ever dignified the human form,[1] my sensations were fraught with new and insupportable anguish.

I had not time to reflect in what way my own safety would be effected by this revolution, or what I had to dread from the wild conceptions of a madman. He advanced towards me. Some hollow noises were wasted by the breeze. Confused clamours were succeeded by many feet traversing the grass, and then crowding into the piazza.

These sounds suspended my brother's purpose, and he stood to listen. The signals multiplied and grew louder; perceiving this, he turned from me, and hurried out of my sight. All about me was pregnant with motives to astonishment. My sister's corpse, Wieland's frantic demeanour, and, at length, this crowd of visitants so little accorded with my foresight, that my mental progress was stopped. The impulse had ceased which was accustomed to give motion and order to my thoughts.

Footsteps thronged upon the stairs, and presently many faces shewed themselves within the door of my apartment. These looks were full of alarm and watchfulness. They pryed into corners as if in search of some fugitive; next their gaze was fixed upon me, and betokened all the vehemence of terror and pity. For a time I questioned whether these were not shapes and faces like that which I had seen at the bottom of the stairs, creatures of my fancy or airy existences.

My eye wandered from one to another, till at length it fell on a countenance which I well knew. It was that of Mr. Hallet.[2] This man was a distant kinsman of my mother, venerable for his age, his uprightness, and sagacity. He had long discharged the functions of a magistrate and good citizen. If any terrors remained, his presence was sufficient to dispel them.

He approached, took my hand with a compassionate air, and said in a low voice. "Where, my dear Clara, are your brother and sister?" I made no answer, but pointed to the bed. His attendants drew aside the curtain, and while their eyes glared with horror at the spectacle which they beheld, those of Mr. Hallet overflowed with tears.

---

[1] "Extinction of a mind the most luminous and penetrating that ever dignified the human form": as she did earlier with regard to Pleyel, Clara seems to rationalize her brother's actions, even as she acknowledges their literal insanity.

[2] "Hallet": the maternal relation with whom Pleyel discussed Carwin and Ludloe in Chapter 14. See note 14.5.

After considerable pause, he once more turned to me. "My dear girl, this sight is not for you. Can you confide in my care, and that of Mrs. Baynton's? We will see performed all that circumstances require."

I made strenuous opposition to this request. I insisted on remaining near her till she were interred. His remonstrances, however, and my own feelings, shewed me the propriety of a temporary dereliction. Louisa stood in need of a comforter, and my brother's children of a nurse. My unhappy brother was himself an object of solicitude and care. At length, I consented to relinquish the corpse, and go to my brother's, whose house, I said, would need mistress, and his children a parent.

During this discourse, my venerable friend struggled with his tears, but my last intimation called them forth with fresh violence. Meanwhile, his attendants stood round in mournful silence, gazing on me and at each other. I repeated my resolution, and rose to execute it; but he took my hand to detain me. His countenance betrayed irresolution and reluctance. I requested him to state the reason of his opposition to this measure. I entreated him to be explicit. I told him that my brother had just been there, and that I knew his condition. This misfortune had driven him to madness, and his offspring must not want a protector. If he chose, I would resign Wieland to his care; but his innocent and helpless babes stood in instant need of nurse and mother, and these offices I would by no means allow another to perform while I had life.

Every word that I uttered seemed to augment his perplexity and distress. At last he said, "I think, Clara, I have entitled myself to some regard from you. You have professed your willingness to oblige me. Now I call upon you to confer upon me the highest obligation in your power. Permit Mrs. Baynton to have the management of your brother's house for two or three days; then it shall be yours to act in it as you please. No matter what are my motives in making this request: perhaps I think your age, your sex, or the distress which this disaster must occasion, incapacitates you for the office. Surely you have no doubt of Mrs. Baynton's tenderness or discretion."

New ideas now rushed into my mind. I fixed my eyes stedfastly on Mr. Hallet. "Are they well?" said I. "Is Louisa well? Are Benjamin, and William, and Constantine, and Little Clara,[3] are they safe? Tell me truly, I beseech you!"

"They are well," he replied; "they are perfectly safe."

"Fear no effeminate weakness in me: I can bear to hear the truth. Tell me truly, are they well?"

He again assured me that they were well.[4]

"What then," resumed I, "do you fear? Is it possible for any calamity to disqualify me for performing my duty to these helpless innocents? I am willing to divide the

---

[3] "Benjamin . . . William . . . Constantine . . . Little Clara": named here only, the children of Catherine and Theodore were first mentioned by Clara at the beginning of Chapter 4.

[4] "Assured me that they were well": In *Macbeth* IV.iii.176–206, as the messenger Ross attempts to avoid telling MacDuff that his wife and children are dead, he repeatedly but unconvincingly claims "they were well" before finally revealing that MacDuff's family was "savagely slaughter'd" by a "tyrant."

care of them with Mrs. Baynton; I shall be grateful for her sympathy and aid; but what should I be to desert them at an hour like this!"

I will cut short this distressful dialogue. I still persisted in my purpose, and he still persisted in his opposition. This excited my suspicions anew; but these were removed by solemn declarations of their safety. I could not explain this conduct in my friend; but at length consented to go to the city, provided I should see them for a few minutes at present, and should return on the morrow.

Even this arrangement was objected to. At length he told me they were removed to the city. Why were they removed, I asked, and whither? My importunities would not now be eluded. My suspicions were roused, and no evasion or artifice was sufficient to allay them. Many of the audience began to give vent to their emotions in tears. Mr. Hallet himself seemed as if the conflict were too hard to be longer sustained. Something whispered to my heart that havoc had been wider than I now witnessed. I suspected this concealment to arise from apprehensions of the effects which a knowledge of the truth would produce in me. I once more entreated him to inform me truly of their state. To enforce my entreaties, I put on an air of insensibility. "I can guess," said I, "what has happened—They are indeed beyond the reach of injury, for they are dead! Is it not so?" My voice faltered in spite of my courageous efforts.

"Yes," said he, "they are dead! Dead by the same fate, and by the same hand, with their mother!"

"Dead!" replied I; "what, all?"

"All!" replied he: "he spared *not one!*"

Allow me, my friends, to close my eyes upon the after-scene. Why should I protract a tale which I already begin to feel is too long? Over this scene at least let me pass lightly. Here, indeed, my narrative would be imperfect. All was tempestuous commotion in my heart and in my brain. I have no memory for ought but unconscious transitions and rueful sights. I was ingenious and indefatigable in the invention of torments. I would not dispense with any spectacle adapted to exasperate my grief. Each pale and mangled form I crushed to my bosom. Louisa, whom I loved with so ineffable a passion, was denied to me at first, but my obstinacy conquered their reluctance.

They led the way into a darkened hall. A lamp pendant from the ceiling was uncovered, and they pointed to a table. The assassin had defrauded me of my last and miserable consolation. I sought not in her visage, for the tinge of the morning, and the lustre of heaven. These had vanished with life; but I hoped for liberty to print a last kiss upon her lips. This was denied me; for such had been the merciless blow that destroyed her, that not a *lineament remained!*

I was carried hence to the city. Mrs. Hallet was my companion and my nurse. Why should I dwell upon the rage of fever, and the effusions of delirium? Carwin was the phantom that pursued my dreams, the giant oppressor under whose arm I was for ever on the point of being crushed. Strenuous muscles were required to hinder my flight, and hearts of steel to withstand the eloquence of my fears. In vain I called upon them to look upward, to mark his sparkling rage and scowling contempt. All I sought was to fly from the stroke that was lifted. Then I heaped upon my guards the most vehement reproaches, or betook myself to wailings on the haplessness of my condition.

This malady, at length, declined, and my weeping friends began to look for my restoration. Slowly, and with intermitted beams, memory revisited me. The scenes that I had witnessed were revived, became the theme of deliberation and deduction, and called forth the effusions of more rational sorrow.

Chapter XVIII

I HAD imperfectly recovered my strength, when I was informed of the arrival of my mother's brother, Thomas Cambridge.[1] Ten years since, he went to Europe, and was a surgeon in the British forces in Germany, during the whole of the late war.[2] After its conclusion, some connection that he had formed with an Irish officer, made him retire into Ireland. Intercourse had been punctually maintained by letters with his sister's children, and hopes were given that he would shortly return to his native country, and pass his old age in our society. He was now in an evil hour arrived.

I desired an interview with him for numerous and urgent reasons. With the first returns of my understanding I had anxiously sought information of the fate of my brother. During the course of my disease I had never seen him; and vague and unsatisfactory answers were returned to all my inquiries. I had vehemently interrogated Mrs. Hallet and her husband, and solicited an interview with this unfortunate man; but they mysteriously insinuated that his reason was still unsettled, and that his circumstances rendered an interview impossible. Their reserve on the particulars of this destruction, and the author of it, was equally invincible.

For some time, finding all my efforts fruitless, I had desisted from direct inquiries and solicitations, determined, as soon as my strength was sufficiently renewed, to pursue other means of dispelling my uncertainty. In this state of things my uncle's arrival and intention to visit me were announced. I almost shuddered to behold the face of this man. When I reflected on the disasters that had befallen us, I was half unwilling to witness that dejection and grief which would be disclosed in his countenance. But I believed that all transactions had been thoroughly disclosed to him, and confided in my importunity to extort from him the knowledge that I sought.

I had no doubt as to the person of our enemy; but the motives that urged him to perpetrate these horrors, the means that he used, and his present condition, were totally unknown. It was reasonable to expect some information on this head, from my uncle. I therefore waited his coming with impatience. At length, in the dusk of the evening, and in my solitary chamber, this meeting took place.

This man was our nearest relation, and had ever treated us with the affection of a parent. Our meeting, therefore, could not be without overflowing tenderness and gloomy joy. He rather encouraged than restrained the tears that I poured out in his arms, and took upon himself the task of comforter. Allusions to recent disasters could not be long omitted. One topic facilitated the admission of another. At length, I mentioned and deplored the ignorance in which I had been kept respecting my

---

[1] "Thomas Cambridge": the maternal uncle who witnessed the elder Wieland's alleged spontaneous combustion in Chapter 2. As a surgeon and man of science, Cambridge rejects any supernatural explanation for past events. From here on, the figures supervising Clara are identified with the maternal side of the family (Cambridge and Hallet) or fulfill a maternal function (Baynton).

[2] "The late war": The Seven Years War (1756–1763). If Cambridge left for Germany ten years ago to serve in "the whole of the late war," then this action is set in 1766 or 1767, ten years after the war began. For the initial establishment of the novel's chronology, see note 0.3.

brother's destiny, and the circumstances of our misfortunes. I entreated him to tell me what was Wieland's condition, and what progress had been made in detecting or punishing the author of this unheard-of devastation.

"The author!" said he; "Do you know the author?"

"Alas!" I answered, "I am too well acquainted with him. The story of the grounds of my suspicions would be painful and too long. I am not apprized of the extent of your present knowledge. There are none but Wieland, Pleyel, and myself, who are able to relate certain facts."

"Spare yourself the pain," said he. "All that Wieland and Pleyel can communicate, I know already. If any thing of moment has fallen within your own exclusive knowledge, and the relation be not too arduous for your present strength, I confess I am desirous of hearing it. Perhaps you allude to one by the name of Carwin. I will anticipate your curiosity by saying, that since these disasters, no one has seen or heard of him. His agency is, therefore, a mystery still unsolved."

I readily complied with his request, and related as distinctly as I could, though in general terms, the events transacted in the summer-house and my chamber. He listened without apparent surprize to the tale of Pleyel's errors and suspicions, and with augmented seriousness, to my narrative of the warnings and inexplicable vision, and the letter found upon the table. I waited for his comments.

"You gather from this," said he, "that Carwin is the author of all this misery."

"Is it not," answered I, "an unavoidable inference? But what know you respecting it? Was it possible to execute this mischief without witness or coadjutor? I beseech you to relate to me, when and why Mr. Hallet was summoned to the scene, and by whom this disaster was first suspected or discovered. Surely, suspicion must have fallen upon some one, and pursuit was made."

My uncle rose from his seat, and traversed the floor with hasty steps. His eyes were fixed upon the ground, and he seemed buried in perplexity. At length he paused, and said with an emphatic tone, "It is true; the instrument is known. Carwin may have plotted, but the execution was another's. That other is found, and his deed is ascertained."

"Good heaven!" I exclaimed, "what say you? Was not Carwin the assassin? Could any hand but his have carried into act this dreadful purpose?"

"Have I not said," returned he, "that the performance was another's? Carwin, perhaps, or heaven, or insanity, prompted the murderer; but Carwin is unknown. The actual performer[3] has, long since, been called to judgment and convicted, and is, at this moment, at the bottom of a dungeon loaded with chains."

I lifted my hands and eyes. "Who then is this assassin? By what means, and whither was he traced? What is the testimony of his guilt?"

---

[3] "Carwin, perhaps, or heaven, or insanity . . . actual performer": Cambridge refuses to speculate on Theodore's motivation, even as he places responsibility for the murders squarely on Theodore's shoulders. Here and in Chapter 20, Cambridge repeatedly deflates Clara's attempts to blame Carwin for Theodore's actions.

"His own, corroborated with that of a servant-maid who spied the murder of the children from a closet where she was concealed. The magistrate returned from your dwelling to your brother's. He was employed in hearing and recording the testimony of the only witness, when the criminal himself, unexpected, unsolicited, unsought, entered the hall, acknowledged his guilt, and rendered himself up to justice.

"He has since been summoned to the bar. The audience was composed of thousands whom rumours of this wonderful event had attracted from the greatest distance. A long and impartial examination was made, and the prisoner was called upon for his defence. In compliance with this call he delivered an ample relation of his motives and actions." There he stopped.

I besought him to say who this criminal was, and what the instigations that compelled him. My uncle was silent. I urged this inquiry with new force. I reverted to my own knowledge, and sought in this some basis to conjecture. I ran over the scanty catalogue of the men whom I knew; I lighted on no one who was qualified for ministering to malice like this. Again I resorted to importunity. Had I ever seen the criminal? Was it sheer cruelty, or diabolical revenge that produced this overthrow?

He surveyed me, for a considerable time, and listened to my interrogations in silence. At length he spoke: "Clara, I have known thee by report, and in some degree by observation. Thou art a being of no vulgar sort. Thy friends have hitherto treated thee as a child. They meant well, but, perhaps, they were unacquainted with thy strength. I assure myself that nothing will surpass thy fortitude.

"Thou art anxious to know the destroyer of thy family, his actions, and his motives. Shall I call him to thy presence, and permit him to confess before thee? Shall I make him the narrator of his own tale?"

I started on my feet, and looked round me with fearful glances, as if the murderer was close at hand. "What do you mean?" said I; "put an end, I beseech you, to this suspence."

"Be not alarmed; you will never more behold the face of this criminal, unless he be gifted with supernatural strength, and sever like threads the constraint of links and bolts. I have said that the assassin was arraigned at the bar, and that the trial ended with a summons from the judge to confess or to vindicate his actions. A reply was immediately made with significance of gesture, and a tranquil majesty, which denoted less of humanity than god-head. Judges, advocates and auditors were panic-struck and breathless with attention. One of the hearers faithfully recorded the speech. There it is," continued he, putting a roll of papers in my hand, "you may read it at your leisure."

With these words my uncle left me alone. My curiosity refused me a moment's delay. I opened the papers, and read as follows.

Chapter XIX

"THEODORE WIELAND,[1] the prisoner at the bar, was now called upon for his defence. He looked around him for some time in silence, and with a mild countenance. At length he spoke:

"It is strange; I am known to my judges and my auditors. Who is there present a stranger to the character of Wieland? who knows him not as an husband—as a father—as a friend? yet here am I arraigned as criminal. I am charged with diabolical malice; I am accused of the murder of my wife and my children!

"It is true, they were slain by me; they all perished by my hand. The task of vindication is ignoble. What is it that I am called to vindicate? and before whom?

"You know that they are dead, and that they were killed by me. What more would you have? Would you extort from me a statement of my motives? Have you failed to discover them already? You charge me with malice; but your eyes are not shut; your reason is still vigorous; your memory has not forsaken you. You know whom it is that you thus charge. The habits of his life are known to you; his treatment of his wife and his offspring is known to you; the soundness of his integrity, and the unchangeableness of his principles, are familiar to your apprehension; yet you persist

---

[1] "Theodore Wieland": the only appearance of Theodore's first or "Christian" name, which Clara never uses (see note 3.1). Brown seems to have selected the name with at least some degree of irony in mind on several levels, given that Theodore is a murderer and maniac. Etymologically, the name signifies "gift of god," or "divine gift" (from Greek *theos* or god; and *doros* or gift). The name may wryly and polemically echo that of Theodore Dwight (1764–1846) or, more likely, a composite of Theodore and his brother Timothy Dwight (1752–1817), both personally known to Brown and his associates as partisan Federalists. The Dwights attacked and were attacked in turn as major contributors to the Illuminati hysteria, and, as historian Robert Imholt puts it, "to attack one Dwight was to attack them both." For more on their contribution to this atmosphere, see the Illuminati debates in Related Texts. The name does not appear in the preliminary "outline" for Wieland (which includes lists of names, and most of the names finally used in the novel) and thus seems to have been selected late in the process of composition.

Theodore and Timothy Dwight, grandsons of late-Calvinist theologian and philosopher Jonathan Edwards, were twin pillars of conservative institutional power and cultural orthodoxy in New England and New York society of the period. Theodore was an attorney, historian, and later a member of Congress, and Timothy a Congregationalist minister, theologian, neo-classical poet, and then president of Yale University (1795–1817). Although their patrician conservatism did not rule out enlightened abolitionist activities during the 1780s and early 1790s, when their circles began to overlap with Brown's in New York, the Dwights became ideologically polarized as counterrevolutionary extremists in the crisis atmosphere of 1797–1801 and became icons of that moment's "paranoid" style of reactionary and xenophobic polemics, fear-mongering, and religious-political posturing. Timothy was famously dubbed by his opponents the Federalist "Pope" of Connecticut and cultivated a public air of patrician severity. Notably, in the context of Brown's novel, he also suffered emotional-physical breakdowns after conversion experiences and religiously inspired episodes of ascetic self-discipline, which repeated those suffered by his grandfather Jonathan Edwards. His lifelong eye problems and sensitivity to light, for example, apparently originated in such episodes. See Kafer, "The Making of Timothy Dwight: A Connecticut Morality Tale" and Imholt, "Timothy Dwight, Federalist Pope of Connecticut."

in this charge! You lead me hither manacled as a felon; you deem me worthy of a vile and tormenting death!

"Who are they whom I have devoted to death? My wife—the little ones, that drew their being from me—that creature who, as she surpassed them in excellence, claimed a larger affection than those whom natural affinities bound to my heart. Think ye that malice could have urged me to this deed? Hide your audacious fronts from the scrutiny of heaven. Take refuge in some cavern unvisited by human eyes. Ye may deplore your wickedness or folly, but ye cannot expiate it.

"Think not that I speak for your sakes. Hug to your hearts this detestable infatuation. Deem me still a murderer, and drag me to untimely death. I make not an effort to dispel your illusion: I utter not a word to cure you of your sanguinary[2] folly: but there are probably some in this assembly who have come from far: for their sakes, whose distance has disabled them from knowing me, I will tell what I have done, and why.

"It is needless to say that God is the object of my supreme passion. I have cherished, in his presence, a single and upright heart. I have thirsted for the knowledge of his will. I have burnt with ardour to approve my faith and my obedience.

"My days have been spent in searching for the revelation of that will; but my days have been mournful, because my search failed. I solicited direction: I turned on every side where glimmerings of light could be discovered. I have not been wholly uninformed; but my knowledge has always stopped short of certainty. Dissatisfaction has insinuated itself into all my thoughts. My purposes have been pure; my wishes indefatigable; but not till lately were these purposes thoroughly accomplished, and these wishes fully gratified.

"I thank thee, my father, for thy bounty; that thou didst not ask a less sacrifice than this; that thou placedst me in a condition to testify my submission to thy will![3] What have I withheld which it was thy pleasure to exact? Now may I, with dauntless and erect eye, claim my reward, since I have given thee the treasure of my soul.

"I was at my own house: it was late in the evening: my sister had gone to the city, but proposed to return. It was in expectation of her return that my wife and I delayed going to bed beyond the usual hour; the rest of the family, however, were retired.

"My mind was contemplative and calm; not wholly devoid of apprehension on account of my sister's safety. Recent events, not easily explained, had suggested the existence of some danger; but this danger was without a distinct form in our imagination, and scarcely ruffled our tranquillity.

---

[2] "Sanguinary": overconfident or rash, but also bloody.

[3] "Submission to thy will!": the theme of a father demonstrating obedience to the divine by murdering family members most clearly recalls the story of the patriarch Abraham and his willingness to sacrifice his son Isaac (Genesis 22:1–15). In Abraham's story, however, the divine injunction is only a test and the child is spared. A well-known early work of Christoph Martin Wieland, *Der Geprüfte Abraham* [Abraham Tested] (1753), develops this theme. At least three English editions, all titled *The Trial of Abraham*, appeared from the 1760s to the 1790s.

"Time passed, and my sister did not arrive;[4] her house is at some distance from mine, and though her arrangements had been made with a view to residing with us, it was possible that, through forgetfulness, or the occurrence of unforeseen emergencies, she had returned to her own dwelling.

"Hence it was conceived proper that I should ascertain the truth by going thither. I went. On my way my mind was full of these ideas which related to my intellectual condition. In the torrent of fervid conceptions, I lost sight of my purpose. Some times I stood still; some times I wandered from my path, and experienced some difficulty, on recovering from my fit of musing, to regain it.

"The series of my thoughts is easily traced. At first every vein beat with raptures known only to the man whose parental and conjugal love is without limits, and the cup of whose desires, immense as it is, overflows with gratification. I know not why emotions that were perpetual visitants should now have recurred with unusual energy. The transition was not new from sensations of joy to a consciousness of gratitude. The author of my being was likewise the dispenser of every gift with which that being was embellished. The service to which a benefactor like this was entitled, could not be circumscribed. My social sentiments were indebted to their alliance with devotion for all their value. All passions are base, all joys feeble, all energies malignant, which are not drawn from this source.

"For a time, my contemplations soared above earth and its inhabitants. I stretched forth my hands; I listed my eyes, and exclaimed, O! that I might be admitted to thy presence; that mine were the supreme delight of knowing thy will, and of performing it! The blissful privilege of direct communication with thee,[5] and of listening to the audible enunciation of thy pleasure!

"What task would I not undertake, what privation would I not cheerfully endure, to testify my love of thee? Alas! thou hidest thyself from my view: glimpses only of thy excellence and beauty are afforded me. Would that a momentary emanation from thy glory would visit me! that some unambiguous token of thy presence would salute my senses!

"In this mood, I entered the house of my sister. It was vacant. Scarcely had I regained recollection of the purpose that brought me hither. Thoughts of a different tendency had such absolute possession of my mind, that the relations of time and space were almost obliterated from my understanding. These wanderings, however, were restrained, and I ascended to her chamber.

"I had no light, and might have known by external observation, that the house was without any inhabitant. With this, however, I was not satisfied. I entered the room, and the object of my search not appearing, I prepared to return.

---

[4] "My sister did not arrive": Wieland went to Clara's house, where Carwin was waiting to meet her, because she had not returned to his house, where she had arranged to stay. Clara was delayed because she was in Philadelphia speaking with Pleyel. These events transpire during Chapters 12–16.

[5] "Blissful privilege of direct communication with thee": Theodore says aloud that he wants to speak with the divine. Carwin would have heard this, since he is hiding in the house. Carwin is adept at overhearing bits of the Wielands' speech and quickly extrapolating ways to use the information they reveal to influence them through his ventriloquism.

"The darkness required some caution in descending the stair. I stretched my hand to seize the balustrade by which I might regulate my steps. How shall I describe the lustre, which, at that moment, burst upon my vision!

"I was dazzled. My organs were bereaved of their activity. My eye-lids were half-closed, and my hands withdrawn from the balustrade. A nameless fear chilled my veins, and I stood motionless. This irradiation did not retire or lessen. It seemed as if some powerful effulgence[6] covered me like a mantle.

"I opened my eyes and found all about me luminous and glowing. It was the element of heaven that flowed around. Nothing but a fiery stream was at first visible; but, anon, a shrill voice from behind called upon me to attend.

"I turned: It is forbidden to describe what I saw: Words, indeed, would be wanting to the task. The lineaments of that being, whose veil was now lifted, and whose visage beamed upon my sight, no hues of pencil or of language can pourtray.

"As it spoke, the accents thrilled to my heart. 'Thy prayers are heard. In proof of thy faith, render me thy wife. This is the victim I chuse. Call her hither, and here let her fall.'—The sound, and visage, and light vanished at once.

"What demand was this? The blood of Catharine was to be shed! My wife was to perish by my hand! I sought opportunity to attest my virtue. Little did I expect that a proof like this would have been demanded.

"My wife! I exclaimed: O God! substitute some other victim. Make me not the butcher of my wife. My own blood is cheap. This will I pour out before thee with a willing heart; but spare, I beseech thee, this precious life, or commission some other than her husband to perform the bloody deed.

"In vain. The conditions were prescribed; the decree had gone forth, and nothing remained but to execute it. I rushed out of the house and across the intermediate fields, and stopped not till I entered my own parlour.

"My wife had remained here during my absence, in anxious expectation of my return with some tidings of her sister. I had none to communicate. For a time, I was breathless with my speed: This, and the tremors that shook my frame, and the wildness of my looks, alarmed her. She immediately suspected some disaster to have happened to her friend, and her own speech was as much overpowered by emotion as mine.

"She was silent, but her looks manifested her impatience to hear what I had to communicate. I spoke, but with so much precipitation as scarcely to be understood; catching her, at the same time, by the arm, and forcibly pulling her from her seat.

"Come along with me: fly: waste not a moment: time will be lost, and the deed will be omitted. Tarry not; question not; but fly with me!

"This deportment added afresh to her alarms. Her eyes pursued mine, and she said, 'What is the matter? For God's sake what is the matter? Where would you have me go?'

"My eyes were fixed upon her countenance while she spoke. I thought upon her virtues; I viewed her as the mother of my babes; as my wife: I recalled the purpose for

---

[6] "Effulgence": splendid radiance, light that shines forth brilliantly; the term was often used in early modern religious discourse in relation to the glory, or glowing, of the divine.

which I thus urged her attendance. My heart faltered, and I saw that I must rouse to this work all my faculties. The danger of the least delay was imminent.

"I looked away from her, and again exerting my force, drew her towards the door— 'You must go with me—indeed you must.'

"In her fright she half-resisted my efforts, and again exclaimed, 'Good heaven! what is it you mean? Where go? What has happened? Have you found Clara?'

"'Follow me, and you will see,' I answered, still urging her reluctant steps forward.

"'What phrenzy has seized you? Something must needs have happened. Is she sick? Have you found her?'

"'Come and see. Follow me, and know for yourself.'

"Still she expostulated and besought me to explain this mysterious behaviour. I could not trust myself to answer her; to look at her; but grasping her arm, I drew her after me. She hesitated, rather through confusion of mind than from unwilling-ness to accompany me. This confusion gradually abated, and she moved forward, but with irresolute footsteps, and continual exclamations of wonder and terror. Her interrogations of what was the matter? and whither was I going? were ceaseless and vehement.

"It was the scope of my efforts not to think; to keep up a conflict and uproar in my mind in which all order and distinctness should be lost; to escape from the sensations produced by her voice. I was, therefore, silent. I strove to abridge this interval by my haste, and to waste all my attention in furious gesticulations.

"In this state of mind we reached my sister's door. She looked at the windows and saw that all was desolate—'Why come we here? There is no body here. I will not go in.'

"Still I was dumb; but opening the door, I drew her into the entry. This was the allotted scene; here she was to fall. I let go her hand, and pressing my palms against my forehead, made one mighty effort to work up my soul to the deed.

"In vain; it would not be; my courage was appalled; my arms nerveless: I muttered prayers that my strength might be aided from above. They availed nothing.

"Horror diffused itself over me. This conviction of my cowardice, my rebellion, fas-tened upon me, and I stood rigid and cold as marble. From this state I was somewhat relieved by my wife's voice, who renewed her supplications to be told why we came hither, and what was the fate of my sister.

"What could I answer? My words were broken and inarticulate. Her fears naturally acquired force from the observation of these symptoms; but these fears were mis-placed. The only inference she deduced from my conduct was, that some terrible mishap had befallen Clara.

"She wrung her hands, and exclaimed in an agony, 'O tell me, where is she? What has become of her? Is she sick? Dead? Is she in her chamber? O let me go thither and know the worst!'

"This proposal set my thoughts once more in motion. Perhaps what my rebellious heart refused to perform here, I might obtain strength enough to execute elsewhere.

"'Come then,' said I, 'let us go.'

"'I will, but not in the dark. We must first procure a light.'

"'Fly then and procure it; but I charge you, linger not. I will await for your return.'

"While she was gone, I strode along the entry. The fellness of a gloomy hurricane but saintly resembled the discord that reigned in my mind. To omit this sacrifice must not be; yet my sinews had refused to perform it. No alternative was offered. To rebel against the mandate was impossible; but obedience would render me the executioner of my wife. My will was strong, but my limbs refused their office.

"She returned with a light; I led the way to the chamber; she looked round her; she lifted the curtain of the bed; she saw nothing.

"At length, she fixed inquiring eyes upon me. The light now enabled her to discover in my visage what darkness had hitherto concealed. Her cares were now transferred from my sister to myself, and she said in a tremulous voice, 'Wieland! you are not well: What ails you? Can I do nothing for you?'

"That accents and looks so winning should disarm me of my resolution, was to be expected. My thoughts were thrown anew into anarchy. I spread my hand before my eyes that I might not see her, and answered only by groans. She took my other hand between her's, and pressing it to her heart, spoke with that voice which had ever swayed my will, and wasted away sorrow.

"'My friend! my soul's friend! tell me thy cause of grief. Do I not merit to partake with thee in thy cares? Am I not thy wife?'

"This was too much. I broke from her embrace, and retired to a corner of the room. In this pause, courage was once more infused into me. I resolved to execute my duty. She followed me, and renewed her passionate entreaties to know the cause of my distress.

"I raised my head and regarded her with stedfast looks. I muttered something about death, and the injunctions of my duty. At these words she shrunk back, and looked at me with a new expression of anguish. After a pause, she clasped her hands, and exclaimed—

"'O Wieland! Wieland! God grant that I am mistaken; but surely something is wrong. I see it: it is too plain: thou art undone—lost to me and to thyself.' At the same time she gazed on my features with intensest anxiety, in hope that different symptoms would take place. I replied to her with vehemence—

"'Undone! No; my duty is known, and I thank my God that my cowardice is now vanquished, and I have power to fulfil it. Catharine! I pity the weakness of thy nature: I pity thee, but must not spare. Thy life is claimed from my hands: thou must die!'

"Fear was now added to her grief. 'What mean you? Why talk you of death? Bethink yourself, Wieland: bethink yourself, and this fit will pass. O why came I hither! Why did you drag me hither?'

"'I brought thee hither to fulfil a divine command. I am appointed thy destroyer, and destroy thee I must.' Saying this I seized her wrists. She shrieked aloud, and endeavoured to free herself from my grasp; but her efforts were vain.

"'Surely, surely Wieland, thou dost not mean it. Am I not thy wife? and wouldst thou kill me? Thou wilt not; and yet—I see—thou art Wieland no longer! A fury resistless and horrible possesses thee—Spare me—spare—help—help—'

"Till her breath was stopped she shrieked for help—for mercy. When she could speak no longer, her gestures, her looks appealed to my compassion. My accursed hand was irresolute and tremulous. I meant thy death to be sudden, thy struggles to be brief. Alas! my heart was infirm; my resolves mutable. Thrice I slackened my grasp, and life kept its hold, though in the midst of pangs. Her eye-balls started from their sockets. Grimness and distortion took place of all that used to bewitch me into transport, and subdue me into reverence.

"I was commissioned to kill thee, but not to torment thee with the foresight of thy death; not to multiply thy fears, and prolong thy agonies. Haggard, and pale, and lifeless, at length thou ceasedst to contend with thy destiny.

"This was a moment of triumph. Thus had I successfully subdued the stubbornness of human passions: the victim which had been demanded was given: the deed was done past recal.

"I lifted the corpse in my arms and laid it on the bed. I gazed upon it with delight. Such was the elation of my thoughts, that I even broke into laughter. I clapped my hands and exclaimed, 'It is done! My sacred duty is fulfilled! To that I have sacrificed, O my God! thy last and best gift, my wife!'

"For a while I thus soared above frailty. I imagined I had set myself forever beyond the reach of selfishness; but my imaginations were false. This rapture quickly subsided. I looked again at my wife. My joyous ebullitions vanished, and I asked myself who it was whom I saw? Methought it could not be Catharine. It could not be the woman who had lodged for years in my heart; who had slept, nightly, in my bosom; who had borne in her womb, who had fostered at her breast, the beings who called me father; whom I had watched with delight, and cherished with a fondness ever new and perpetually growing: it could not be the same.

"Where was her bloom! These deadly and blood-suffused orbs but ill resemble the azure and exstatic tenderness of her eyes. The lucid stream that meandered over that bosom, the glow of love that was wont to sit upon that cheek, are much unlike these livid stains and this hideous deformity. Alas! these were the traces of agony; the gripe of the assassin had been here!

"I will not dwell upon my lapse into desperate and outrageous sorrow. The breath of heaven that sustained me was withdrawn, and I sunk into *mere man*. I leaped from the floor: I dashed my head against the wall: I uttered screams of horror: I panted after torment and pain. Eternal fire, and the bickerings of hell, compared with what I felt, were music and a bed of roses.

"I thank my God that this degeneracy was transient, that he deigned once more to raise me aloft. I thought upon what I had done as a sacrifice to duty, and *was calm*. My wife was dead; but I reflected, that though this source of human consolation was closed, yet others were still open. If the transports of an husband were no more, the feelings of a father had still scope for exercise. When remembrance of their mother should excite too keen a pang, I would look upon them, and *be comforted*.

"While I revolved these ideas, new warmth flowed in upon my heart—I was wrong. These feelings were the growth of selfishness. Of this I was not aware, and to dispel the mist that obscured my perceptions, a new effulgence and a new mandate were necessary.

"From these thoughts I was recalled by a ray that was shot into the room. A voice spake like that which I had before heard—'Thou hast done well; but all is not done—the sacrifice is incomplete—thy children must be offered—they must perish with their mother!—'"

Chapter XX

WILL you wonder that I read no farther? Will you not rather be astonished that I read thus far? What power supported me through such a task I know not. Perhaps the doubt from which I could not disengage my mind, that the scene here depicted was a dream, contributed to my perseverance. In vain the solemn introduction of my uncle, his appeals to my fortitude, and allusions to something monstrous in the events he was about to disclose; in vain the distressful perplexity, the mysterious silence and ambiguous answers of my attendants, especially when the condition of my brother was the theme of my inquiries, were remembered. I recalled the interview with Wieland in my chamber, his preternatural[1] tranquillity succeeded by bursts of passion and menacing actions. All these coincided with the tenor of this paper.

Catharine and her children, and Louisa were dead. The act that destroyed them was, in the highest degree, inhuman. It was worthy of savages trained to murder, and exulting in agonies.

Who was the performer of the deed? Wieland! My brother! The husband and the father! That man of gentle virtues and invincible benignity! placable and mild—an idolator of peace! Surely, said I, it is a dream. For many days have I been vexed with frenzy. Its dominion is still felt; but new forms are called up to diversify and augment my torments.

The paper dropped from my hand, and my eyes followed it. I shrunk back, as if to avoid some petrifying influence that approached me. My tongue was mute; all the functions of nature were at a stand, and I sunk upon the floor lifeless.

The noise of my fall, as I afterwards heard, alarmed my uncle, who was in a lower apartment, and whose apprehensions had detained him. He hastened to my chamber, and administered the assistance which my condition required. When I opened my eyes I beheld him before me. His skill as a reasoner as well as a physician, was exerted to obviate the injurious effects of this disclosure; but he had wrongly estimated the strength of my body or of my mind. This new shock brought me once more to the brink of the grave, and my malady was much more difficult to subdue than at first.

I will not dwell upon the long train of dreary sensations, and the hideous confusion of my understanding. Time slowly restored its customary firmness to my frame, and order to my thoughts. The images impressed upon my mind by this fatal paper were somewhat effaced by my malady. They were obscure and disjointed like the parts of a dream. I was desirous of freeing my imagination from this chaos. For this end I questioned my uncle, who was my constant companion. He was intimidated by the issue of his first experiment, and took pains to elude or discourage my inquiry. My impetuosity some times compelled him to have resort to misrepresentations and untruths.

---

[1] "Preternatural": primarily "unnatural; abnormal, exceptional, unusual," but also, in some usages, "supernatural" (*OED*).

Time effected that end, perhaps, in a more beneficial manner. In the course of my meditations the recollections of the past gradually became more distinct. I revolved them, however, in silence, and being no longer accompanied with surprize, they did not exercise a death-dealing power. I had discontinued the perusal of the paper in the midst of the narrative; but what I read, combined with information elsewhere obtained, threw, perhaps, a sufficient light upon these detestable transactions; yet my curiosity was not inactive. I desired to peruse the remainder.

My eagerness to know the particulars of this tale was mingled and abated by my antipathy to the scene which would be disclosed. Hence I employed no means to effect my purpose. I desired knowledge, and, at the same time, shrunk back from receiving the boon.

One morning, being left alone, I rose from my bed, and went to a drawer where my finer clothing used to be kept. I opened it, and this fatal paper saluted my sight. I snatched it involuntarily, and withdrew to a chair. I debated, for a few minutes, whether I should open and read. Now that my fortitude was put to trial, it failed. I felt myself incapable of deliberately surveying a scene of so much horror. I was prompted to return it to its place, but this resolution gave way, and I determined to peruse some part of it. I turned over the leaves till I came near the conclusion. The narrative of the criminal was finished. The verdict of *guilty* reluctantly pronounced by the jury, and the accused interrogated why sentence of death should not pass. The answer was brief, solemn, and emphatical.

"No. I have nothing to say. My tale has been told. My motives have been truly stated. If my judges are unable to discern the purity of my intentions, or to credit the statement of them, which I have just made; if they see not that my deed was enjoined by heaven; that obedience was the test of perfect virtue, and the extinction of selfishness and error, they must pronounce me a murderer.

"They refuse to credit my tale; they impute my acts to the influence of dæmons; they account me an example of the highest wickedness of which human nature is capable; they doom me to death and infamy. Have I power to escape this evil? If I have, be sure I will exert it. I will not accept evil at their hand, when I am entitled to good; I will suffer only when I cannot elude suffering.

"You say that I am guilty. Impious and rash! thus to usurp the prerogatives of your Maker! to set up your bounded views and halting reason, as the measure of truth!

"Thou, Omnipotent and Holy! Thou knowest that my actions were conformable to thy will. I know not what is crime; what actions are evil in their ultimate and comprehensive tendency or what are good. Thy knowledge, as thy power, is unlimited. I have taken thee for my guide, and cannot err. To the arms of thy protection, I entrust my safety. In the awards of thy justice, I confide for my recompense.

"Come death when it will, I am safe. Let calumny and abhorrence pursue me among men; I shall not be defrauded of my dues. The peace of virtue, and the glory of obedience, will be my portion hereafter."

Here ended the speaker. I withdrew my eyes from the page; but before I had time to reflect on what I had read, Mr. Cambridge entered the room. He quickly perceived how I had been employed, and betrayed some solicitude respecting the condition of my mind.

His fears, however, were superfluous. What I had read, threw me into a state not easily described. Anguish and fury, however, had no part in it. My faculties were chained up in wonder and awe. Just then, I was unable to speak. I looked at my friend with an air of inquisitiveness, and pointed at the roll. He comprehended my inquiry, and answered me with looks of gloomy acquiescence. After some time, my thoughts found their way to my lips.

"Such then were the acts of my brother. Such were his words. For this he was condemned to die: To die upon the gallows! A fate, cruel and unmerited! And is it so?" continued I, struggling for utterance, which this new idea made difficult; "is he—dead!"

"No. He is alive. There could be no doubt as to the cause of these excesses. They originated in sudden madness; but that madness continues, and he is condemned to perpetual imprisonment."

"Madness, say you? Are you sure? Were not these sights, and these sounds, really seen and heard?"

My uncle was surprized at my question. He looked at me with apparent inquietude. "Can you doubt," said he, "that these were illusions? Does heaven, think you, interfere for such ends?"

"O no; I think it not. Heaven cannot stimulate to such unheard-of outrage. The agent was not good, but evil."

"Nay, my dear girl," said my friend, "lay aside these fancies. Neither angel nor devil had any part in this affair."[2]

"You misunderstand me," I answered; "I believe the agency to be external and real, but not supernatural."

"Indeed!" said he, in an accent of surprize. "Whom do you then suppose to be the agent?"

"I know not. All is wildering conjecture. I cannot forget Carwin.[3] I cannot banish the suspicion that he was the setter of these snares. But how can we suppose it to be madness? Did insanity ever before assume this form?"

"Frequently. The illusion, in this case, was more dreadful in its consequences, than any that has come to my knowledge; but, I repeat that similar illusions are not rare. Did you never hear of an instance which occurred in your mother's family?"[4]

---

[2] "Neither angel nor devil had any part in this affair": Cambridge definitively rejects supernatural influences in the murders.

[3] "Carwin": As she struggles to account for the "monstrous" and "criminal" events revealed by the court papers, a traumatized Clara seems to reflexively displace or extenuate Theodore's responsibility by blaming Carwin. Her maternal uncle, surgeon Thomas Cambridge, characterized earlier in this chapter as "a reasoner as well as a physician" will repeatedly explain Theodore's emotional breakdown in rational and clinical terms but, through the remainder of this chapter and to the end of her narrative, Clara will refuse to accept explanations that affirm Theodore's primary responsibility in murdering his family.

[4] "Your mother's family": Although Clara has concentrated on the paternal, German side of her family history, Cambridge reveals a history of emotional disturbance on the maternal, British side as well.

"No. I beseech you relate it. My grandfather's death I have understood to have been extraordinary, but I know not in what respect. A brother, to whom he was much attached, died in his youth, and this, as I have heard, influenced, in some remarkable way, the fate of my grandfather; but I am unacquainted with particulars."

"On the death of that brother," resumed my friend, "my father was seized with dejection, which was found to flow from two sources. He not only grieved for the loss of a friend, but entertained the belief that his own death would be inevitably consequent on that of his brother. He waited from day to day in expectation of the stroke which he predicted was speedily to fall upon him. Gradually, however, he recovered his cheerfulness and confidence. He married, and performed his part in the world with spirit and activity. At the end of twenty-one years it happened that he spent the summer with his family at an house which he possessed on the sea coast in Cornwall.[5] It was at no great distance from a cliff which overhung the ocean, and rose into the air to a great height. The summit was level and secure, and easily ascended on the land side. The company frequently repaired hither in clear weather, invited by its pure airs and extensive prospects. One evening in June my father, with his wife and some friends, chanced to be on this spot. Every one was happy, and my father's imagination seemed particularly alive to the grandeur of the scenery.

"Suddenly, however, his limbs trembled and his features betrayed alarm. He threw himself into the attitude of one listening. He gazed earnestly in a direction in which nothing was visible to his friends. This lasted for a minute; then turning to his companions, he told them that his brother had just delivered to him a summons, which must be instantly obeyed. He then took an hasty and solemn leave of each person, and, before their surprize would allow them to understand the scene, he rushed to the edge of the cliff, threw himself headlong, and was seen no more.

"In the course of my practice in the German army, many cases, equally remarkable, have occurred, Unquestionably the illusions were maniacal, though the vulgar thought otherwise. They are all reducible to one class,* and are not more difficult of explication and cure than most affections of our frame."

*Mania Mutabilis. See Darwin's Zoonomia, vol. ii, Class III.1.2, where similar cases are stated.[6]

---

[5] "Cornwall": a county in England, at the end of the peninsula forming the island's southwestern tip. The coastline features high cliffs like the one in this scene.

[6] "Mania Mutabilis . . . stated": to identify this form of mental disturbance, Cambridge refers to one of the period's key medical-biological works, Erasmus Darwin's *Zoönomia; or, The Laws of Organic Life* (1794). *Mania mutabilis*, mutable or changeable madness, is Darwin's category in which one mistakes "imaginations for realities." The disease is closely related, in this system, to *somnambulismus* or sleepwalking, which Brown used for his novel *Edgar Huntly*, and to *spes religiosa* or "superstitious hope," another form of delusion related to religious and superstitious thinking.

Erasmus Darwin (1731–1802; grandfather of scientists Charles Darwin and Francis Dalton) was an influential physician, naturalist, and poet whose work played a central role in progressive, late-Enlightenment intellectual circles in England and North America. Darwin's medical and scientific theories were important sources for Brown and his New York circle. Brown's closest friend, physician and poet Elihu Hubbard Smith, corresponded with Darwin and arranged for the first

This opinion my uncle endeavoured, by various means, to impress upon me. I listened to his reasonings and illustrations with silent respect. My astonishment was great on finding proofs of an influence of which I had supposed there were no examples; but I was far from accounting for appearances in my uncle's manner. Ideas thronged into my mind which I was unable to disjoin or to regulate. I reflected that this madness, if madness it were, had affected Pleyel and myself as well as Wieland. Pleyel had heard a mysterious voice. I had seen and heard. A form had showed itself to me as well as to Wieland. The disclosure had been made in the same spot. The appearance was equally complete and equally prodigious in both instances. Whatever supposition I should adopt, had I not equal reason to tremble? What was my security against influences equally terrific and equally irresistible?

It would be vain to attempt to describe the state of mind which this idea produced. I wondered at the change which a moment had affected in my brother's condition. Now was I stupified with tenfold wonder in contemplating myself. Was I not likewise transformed from rational and human into a creature of nameless and fearful attributes? Was I not transported to the brink of the same abyss? Ere a new day should come, my hands might be embrued in blood, and my remaining life be consigned to a dungeon and chains.

With moral sensibility like mine, no wonder that this new dread was more insupportable than the anguish I had lately endured. Grief carries its own antidote along with it. When thought becomes merely a vehicle of pain, its progress must be stopped. Death is a cure which nature or ourselves must administer: To this cure I now looked forward with gloomy satisfaction.

My silence could not conceal from my uncle the state of my thoughts. He made unwearied efforts to divert my attention from views so pregnant with danger. His efforts, aided by time, were in some measure successful. Confidence in the strength of my resolution, and in the healthful state of my faculties, was once more revived. I was able to devote my thoughts to my brother's state, and the causes of this disastrous proceeding.

My opinions were the sport of eternal change. Some times I conceived the apparition to be more than human. I had no grounds on which to build a disbelief. I could not deny faith to the evidence of my religion; the testimony of men was loud and unanimous: both these concurred to persuade me that evil spirits existed, and that their energy was frequently exerted in the system of the world.

These ideas connected themselves with the image of Carwin. Where is the proof, said I, that dæmons may not be subjected to the controul of men? This truth may be distorted and debased in the minds of the ignorant. The dogmas of the vulgar, with regard to this subject, are glaringly absurd; but though these may justly be neglected by the wife, we are scarcely justified in totally rejecting the possibility that men may obtain supernatural aid.

U.S. edition of *Zoönomia* in 1796 with T. & J. Swords, the same printers who published Brown's *Wieland,* his feminist dialogue *Alcuin,* and other works by Smith and the New York circle. For more on Darwin and *Zoönomia,* see the excerpt in Related Texts.

The dreams of superstition are worthy of contempt. Witchcraft, its instruments and miracles, the compact ratified by a bloody signature, the apparatus of sulpherous smells and thundering explosions, are monstrous and chimerical.[7] These have no part in the scene over which the genius[8] of Carwin presides. That conscious beings, dissimilar from human, but moral and voluntary agents as we are, some where exist, can scarcely be denied. That their aid may be employed to benign or malignant purposes, cannot be disproved.

Darkness rests upon the designs of this man. The extent of his power is unknown; but is there not evidence that it has been now exerted?

I recurred to my own experience. Here Carwin had actually appeared upon the stage; but this was in a human character. A voice and a form were discovered; but one was apparently exerted, and the other disclosed, not to befriend, but to counteract Carwin's designs. There were tokens of hostility, and not of alliance, between them. Carwin was the miscreant whose projects were resisted by a minister of heaven. How can this be reconciled to the stratagem which ruined my brother? There the agency was at once preternatural and malignant.

The recollection of this fact led my thoughts into a new channel. The malignity of that influence which governed my brother had hitherto been no subject of doubt. His wife and children were destroyed; they had expired in agony and fear; yet was it indisputably certain that their murderer was criminal? He was acquitted at the tribunal of his own conscience; his behaviour at his trial and since, was faithfully reported to me; appearances were uniform; not for a moment did he lay aside the majesty of virtue; he repelled all invectives by appealing to the deity, and to the tenor of his past life; surely there was truth in this appeal: none but a command from heaven could have swayed his will; and nothing but unerring proof of divine approbation could sustain his mind in its present elevation.

---

[7] "Monstrous and chimerical": Clara recites a list of generic devices in the period's (German) gothic writing that were often singled out as silly and unbelievable. Although this list could be applied to most of the period's terrific writing, it may also refer to Leonhard Wächter (pseud. Veit Weber, 1762–1837), *The Sorcerer: A tale. from the German of Veit Weber.* (London: J. Johnson, 1795), originally published as *Die Teufelsbeschwörung* [*The Summoning of the Devil*]. Printed in English by Wollstonecraft's progressive publisher, *The Sorceror* tells the story of a man who murders a child, after tricking the youth into believing that he has accidentally summoned a demon using his father's mystical apparatus. The man then convinces the dead child's father to believe this account so that the father will commit suicide and leave his wealth to the charlatan. *The Sorcerer* combines this demystification of gothic elements with lengthy critiques of the institution of marriage by the chief female character, a move that links gothic terror to heterosexual matrimony.

[8] "Genius": Clara disparages the trickery of ordinary gothic stage-scenery but, when it comes to Carwin, she continues to invoke the kinds of mysterious supernatural spirits she has mentioned earlier as daemons, geniuses, and angels. See notes 5.17, 10.3.

Chapter XXI

SUCH, for some time, was the course of my meditations. My weakness, and my aversion to be pointed at as an object of surprize or compassion, prevented me from going into public. I studiously avoided the visits of those who came to express their sympathy, or gratify their curiosity. My uncle was my principal companion. Nothing more powerfully tended to console me than his conversation.

With regard to Pleyel, my feelings seemed to have undergone a total revolution. It often happens that one passion supplants another. Late disasters had rent my heart, and now that the wound was in some degree closed, the love which I had cherished for this man seemed likewise to have vanished.

Hitherto, indeed, I had had no cause for despair. I was innocent of that offence which had estranged him from my presence. I might reasonably expect that my innocence would at some time be irresistably demonstrated, and his affection for me be revived with his esteem. Now my aversion to be thought culpable by him continued, but was unattended with the same impatience. I desired the removal of his suspicions, not for the sake of regaining his love, but because I delighted in the veneration of so excellent a man, and because he himself would derive pleasure from conviction of my integrity.

My uncle had early informed me that Pleyel and he had seen each other, since the return of the latter from Europe. Amidst the topics of their conversation, I discovered that Pleyel had carefully omitted the mention of those events which had drawn upon me so much abhorrence. I could not account for his silence on this subject. Perhaps time or some new discovery had altered or shaken his opinion. Perhaps he was unwilling, though I were guilty, to injure me in the opinion of my venerable kinsman. I understood that he had frequently visited me during my disease, had watched many successive nights by my bedside, and manifested the utmost anxiety on my account.

The journey which he was preparing to take, at the termination of our last interview, the catastrophe of the ensuing night induced him to delay. The motives of this journey I had, till now, totally mistaken.[1] They were explained to me by my uncle, whose tale excited my astonishment without awakening my regret. In a different state of mind, it would have added unspeakably to my distress, but now it was more a source of pleasure than pain. This, perhaps, is not the least extraordinary of the facts contained in this narrative. It will excite less wonder when I add, that my indifference was temporary, and that the lapse of a few days shewed me that my feelings were deadened for a time, rather than finally extinguished.

Theresa de Stolberg was alive. She had conceived the resolution of seeking her lover in America. To conceal her flight, she had caused the report of her death to be propagated. She put herself under the conduct of Bertrand, the faithful servant of Pleyel.

---

[1] "Totally mistaken": after her confrontation with Pleyel at his home at the end of Chapter 14, Clara assumed that Pleyel planned to leave Philadelphia because he had lost faith in her, when they could have been destined for marriage. As she puts it two paragraphs farther on, "I had mistaken the heroism of friendship for the frenzy of love."

The pacquet which the latter received from the hands of his servant, contained the tidings of her safe arrival at Boston, and to meet her there was the purpose of his journey.[2]

This discovery had set this man's character in a new light. I had mistaken the heroism of friendship for the phrenzy of love. He who had gained my affections, may be supposed to have previously entitled himself to my reverence; but the levity which had formerly characterized the behaviour of this man, tended to obscure the greatness of his sentiments. I did not fail to remark, that since this lady was still alive, the voice in the temple which asserted her death, must either have been intended to deceive, or have been itself deceived. The latter supposition was inconsistent with the notion of a spiritual, and the former with that of a benevolent being.

When my disease abated, Pleyel had forborne his visits, and had lately set out upon this journey. This amounted to a proof that my guilt was still believed by him. I was grieved for his errors, but trusted that my vindication would, sooner or later, be made.

Meanwhile, tumultuous thoughts were again set afloat by a proposal made to me by my uncle. He imagined that new airs would restore my languishing constitution, and a varied succession of objects tend to repair the shock which my mind had received. For this end, he proposed to me to take up my abode with him in France or Italy.

At a more prosperous period, this scheme would have pleased for its own sake. Now my heart sickened at the prospect of nature. The world of man was shrouded in misery and blood, and constituted a loathsome spectacle. I willingly closed my eyes in sleep, and regretted that the respite it afforded me was so short. I marked with satisfaction the progress of decay in my frame, and consented to live, merely in the hope that the course of nature would speedily relieve me from the burthen. Nevertheless, as he persisted in his scheme, I concurred in it merely because he was entitled to my gratitude, and because my refusal gave him pain.

No sooner was he informed of my consent, than he told me I must make immediate preparation to embark, as the ship in which he had engaged a passage would be ready to depart in three days. This expedition was unexpected. There was an impatience in his manner when he urged the necessity of dispatch that excited my surprize. When I questioned him as to the cause of this haste, he generally stated reasons which, at that time, I could not deny to be plausible; but which, on the review, appeared insufficient. I suspected that the true motives were concealed, and believed that these motives had some connection with my brother's destiny.

I now recollected that the information respecting Wieland which had, from time to time, been imparted to me, was always accompanied with airs of reserve and mysteriousness. What had appeared sufficiently explicit at the time it was uttered, I now remembered to have been faltering and ambiguous. I was resolved to remove my doubts, by visiting the unfortunate man in his dungeon.

---

[2] "The pacquet . . . his journey": Bertrand arrived in Philadelphia to deliver this packet in Chapter 14. See note 14.7.

Heretofore the idea of this visit had occurred to me; but the horrors of his dwelling-place, his wild yet placid physiognomy, his neglected locks, the fetters which constrained his limbs, terrible as they were in description, how could I endure to behold!

Now, however, that I was preparing to take an everlasting farewell of my country, now that an ocean was henceforth to separate me from him, how could I part without an interview? I would examine his situation with my own eyes. I would know whether the representations which had been made to me were true. Perhaps the sight of the sister whom he was wont to love with a passion more than fraternal, might have an auspicious influence on his malady.

Having formed this resolution, I waited to communicate it to Mr. Cambridge. I was aware that, without his concurrence, I could not hope to carry it into execution, and could discover no objection to which it was liable. If I had not been deceived as to his condition, no inconvenience could arise from this proceeding. His consent, therefore, would be the test of his sincerity.

I seized this opportunity to state my wishes on this head. My suspicions were confirmed by the manner in which my request affected him. After some pause, in which his countenance betrayed every mark of perplexity, he said to me, "Why would you pay this visit? What useful purpose can it serve?"

"We are preparing," said I, "to leave the country forever: What kind of being should I be to leave behind me a brother in calamity without even a parting interview? Indulge me for three minutes in the sight of him. My heart will be much easier after I have looked at him, and shed a few tears in his presence."

"I believe otherwise. The sight of him would only augment your distress, without contributing, in any degree, to his benefit."

"I know not that," returned I. "Surely the sympathy of his sister, proofs that her tenderness is as lively as ever, must be a source of satisfaction to him. At present he must regard all mankind as his enemies and calumniators. His sister he, probably, conceives to partake in the general infatuation, and to join in the cry of abhorrence that is raised against him. To be undeceived in this respect, to be assured that, however I may impute his conduct to delusion, I still retain all my former affection for his person, and veneration for the purity of his motives, cannot but afford him pleasure. When he hears that I have left the country, without even the ceremonious attention of a visit, what will he think of me? His magnanimity may hinder him from repining, but he will surely consider my behaviour as savage and unfeeling. Indeed, dear Sir, I must pay this visit. To embark with you without paying it, will be impossible. It may be of no service to him, but will enable me to acquit myself of what I cannot but esteem a duty. Besides," continued I, "if it be a mere fit of insanity that has seized him, may not my presence chance to have a salutary influence? The mere sight of me, it is not impossible, may rectify his perceptions."

"Ay," said my uncle, with some eagerness; "it is by no means impossible that your interview may have that effect; and for that reason, beyond all others, would I dissuade you from it."

I expressed my surprize at this declaration. "Is it not to be desired that an error so fatal as this should be rectified?"

"I wonder at your question. Reflect on the consequences of this error. Has he not destroyed the wife whom he loved, the children whom he idolized? What is it that enables him to bear the remembrance, but the belief that he acted as his duty enjoined? Would you rashly bereave him of this belief? Would you restore him to himself, and convince him that he was instigated to this dreadful outrage by a perversion of his organs, or a delusion from hell?

"Now his visions are joyous and elate.[3] He conceives himself to have reached a loftier degree of virtue, than any other human being. The merit of his sacrifice is only enhanced in the eyes of superior beings, by the detestation that pursues him here, and the sufferings to which he is condemned. The belief that even his sister has deserted him, and gone over to his enemies, adds to his sublimity of feelings, and his confidence in divine approbation and future recompense.

"Let him be undeceived in this respect, and what floods of despair and of horror will overwhelm him! Instead of glowing approbation and serene hope, will he not hate and torture himself? Self-violence, or a phrenzy far more savage and destructive than this, may be expected to succeed. I beseech you, therefore, to relinquish this scheme. If you calmly reflect upon it, you will discover that your duty lies in carefully shunning him."

Mr. Cambridge's reasonings suggested views to my understanding, that had not hitherto occurred. I could not but admit their validity, but they shewed, in a new light, the depth of that misfortune in which my brother was plunged. I was silent and irresolute.

Presently, I considered, that whether Wieland was a maniac, a faithful servant of his God, the victim of hellish illusions, or the dupe of human imposture, was by no means certain.[4] In this state of my mind it became me to be silent during the visit that I projected. This visit should be brief; I should be satisfied merely to snatch a look at him. Admitting that a change in his opinions were not to be desired, there was no danger from the conduct which I should pursue, that this change should be wrought.

But I could not conquer my uncle's aversion to this scheme. Yet I persisted, and he found that to make me voluntarily relinquish it, it was necessary to be more explicit than he had hitherto been. He took both my hands, and anxiously examining my countenance as he spoke, "Clara," said he, "this visit must not be paid. We must hasten with the utmost expedition from this shore. It is folly to conceal the truth from you, and since it is only by disclosing the truth that you can be prevailed upon to lay aside this project, the truth shall be told.

"O my dear girl!" continued he with increasing energy in his accent, "your brother's phrenzy is, indeed, stupendous and frightful. The soul that formerly actuated

---

[3] "Elate": proud, lofty.

[4] "Whether Wieland was a maniac, a faithful servant of God, the victim of hellish illusions, or the dupe of human imposture, was by no means certain": Clara again seems to fall back on interpretations of Theodore's murders that extenuate his agency and responsibility, tending to blame others for his acts.

his frame has disappeared. The same form remains; but the wise and benevolent Wieland is no more. A fury that is rapacious of blood, that lifts his strength almost above that of mortals, that bends all his energies to the destruction of whatever was once dear to him, possesses him wholly.

"You must not enter his dungeon; his eyes will no sooner be fixed upon you, than an exertion of his force will be made. He will shake off his fetters in a moment, and rush upon you. No interposition will then be strong or quick enough to save you.

"The phantom that has urged him to the murder of Catharine and her children is not yet appeased. Your life, and that of Pleyel, are exacted from him by this imaginary being. He is eager to comply with this demand. Twice he has escaped from his prison. The first time, he no sooner found himself at liberty, than he hasted to Pleyel's house. It being midnight, the latter was in bed. Wieland penetrated unobserved to his chamber, and opened his curtain. Happily, Pleyel awoke at the critical moment, and escaped the fury of his kinsman, by leaping from his chamber-window into the court. Happily, he reached the ground without injury. Alarms were given, and after diligent search, your brother was found in a chamber of your house, whither, no doubt, he had sought you.

"His chains, and the watchfulness of his guards, were redoubled; but again, by some miracle, he restored himself to liberty. He was now incautiously apprized of the place of your abode: and had not information of his escape been instantly given, your death would have been added to the number of his atrocious acts.

"You now see the danger of your project. You must not only forbear to visit him, but if you would save him from the crime of embruing[5] his hands in your blood, you must leave the country. There is no hope that his malady will end but with his life, and no precaution will ensure your safety, but that of placing the ocean between you.

"I confess I came over with an intention to reside among you, but these disasters have changed my views. Your own safety and my happiness require that you should accompany me in my return, and I entreat you to give your cheerful concurrence to this measure."

After these representations from my uncle, it was impossible to retain my purpose. I readily consented to seclude myself from Wieland's presence. I likewise acquiesced in the proposal to go to Europe; not that I ever expected to arrive there, but because, since my principles forbad me to assail my own life, change had some tendency to make supportable the few days which disease should spare to me.[6]

What a tale had thus been unfolded! I was hunted to death, not by one whom my misconduct had exasperated, who was conscious of illicit motives, and who sought his end by circumvention and surprise; but by one who deemed himself commissioned for this act by heaven, who regarded this career of horror as the last refinement

---

[5] "Embruing": staining or defiling.

[6] "Few days which disease should spare me": Although she will not commit suicide, Clara assumes her depression will lead to her death during a long and arduous Atlantic crossing, which required about two months in this period.

of virtue, whose implacability was proportioned to the reverence and love which he felt for me, and who was inaccessible to the fear of punishment and ignominy!

In vain should I endeavour to stay his hand by urging the claims of a sister or friend: these were his only reasons for pursuing my destruction. Had I been a stranger to his blood; had I been the most worthless of human kind; my safety had not been endangered.

Surely, said I, my fate is without example. The phrenzy which is charged upon my brother, must belong to myself. My foe is manacled and guarded; but I derive no security from these restraints. I live not in a community of savages; yet, whether I sit or walk, go into crouds, or hide myself in solitude, my life is marked for a prey to inhuman violence; I am in perpetual danger of perishing; of perishing under the grasp of a brother!

I recollected the omens of this destiny; I remembered the gulf to which my brother's invitation had conducted me; I remembered that, when on the brink of danger, the author of my peril was depicted by my fears in his form: Thus realized, were the creatures of prophetic sleep, and of wakeful terror![7]

These images were unavoidably connected with that of Carwin. In this paroxysm of distress, my attention fastened on him as the grand deceiver; the author of this black conspiracy; the intelligence that governed in this storm.

Some relief is afforded in the midst of suffering, when its author is discovered or imagined; and an object found on which we may pour out our indignation and our vengeance. I ran over the events that had taken place since the origin of our intercourse with him, and reflected on the tenor of that description which was received from Ludloe. Mixed up with notions of supernatural agency, were the vehement suspicions which I entertained, that Carwin was the enemy whose machinations had destroyed us.

I thirsted for knowledge and for vengeance.[8] I regarded my hasty departure with reluctance, since it would remove me from the means by which this knowledge might be obtained, and this vengeance gratified. This departure was to take place in two days. At the end of two days I was to bid an eternal adieu to my native country. Should I not pay a parting visit to the scene of these disasters? Should I not bedew with my tears the graves of my sister and her children? Should I not explore their desolate habitation, and gather from the sight of its walls and furniture food for my eternal melancholy?

This suggestion was succeeded by a secret shuddering. Some disastrous influence appeared to overhang the scene. How many memorials should I meet with serving to recall the images of those I had lost!

---

[7] "Thus realized . . . prophetic sleep . . . wakeful terror!": Clara recalls and acknowledges her earlier intuitions that Theodore was dangerous, in the dream she had in Chapter 7 (see note 7.2), and when she assumed he was hiding in her closet and about to attack her in Chapter 9 (see note 9.8).

[8] "Carwin . . . I thirsted for knowledge and for vengeance": again Clara's "paroxysm of distress" is converted into a pattern of revenge. Brown's novels often, as in this passage, emphasize the Woldwinite theme that revenge is an unenlightened, irrational passion that backfires on those who give in to it.

I was tempted to relinquish my design, when it occurred to me that I had left among my papers a journal of transactions in short-hand. I was employed in this manuscript on that night when Pleyel's incautious curiosity tempted him to look over my shoulder. I was then recording my adventure in *the recess,* an imperfect sight of which led him into such fatal errors.

I had regulated the disposition of all my property. This manuscript, however, which contained the most secret transactions of my life, I was desirous of destroying. For this end I must return to my house, and this I immediately determined to do.

I was not willing to expose myself to opposition from my friends, by mentioning my design; I therefore bespoke the use of Mr. Hallet's chaise, under pretence of enjoying an airing, as the day was remarkably bright.

This request was gladly complied with, and I directed the servant to conduct me to Mettingen. I dismissed him at the gate, intending to use, in returning, a carriage belonging to my brother.

Chapter XXII

THE inhabitants of the HUT received me with a mixture of joy and surprize. Their homely welcome, and their artless sympathy, were grateful to my feelings. In the midst of their inquiries, as to my health, they avoided all allusions to the source of my malady. They were honest creatures,[1] and I loved them well. I participated in the tears which they shed when I mentioned to them my speedy departure for Europe, and promised to acquaint them with my welfare during my long absence.

They expressed great surprize when I informed them of my intention to visit my cottage. Alarm and foreboding overspread their features, and they attempted to dissuade me from visiting an house which they firmly believed to be haunted by a thousand ghastly apparitions.

These apprehensions, however, had no power over my conduct. I took an irregular path which led me to my own house. All was vacant and forlorn. A small enclosure, near which the path led, was the burying-ground belonging to the family. This I was obliged to pass. Once I had intended to enter it, and ponder on the emblems and inscriptions which my uncle had caused to be made on the tombs of Catharine and her children; but now my heart faltered as I approached, and I hastened forward, that distance might conceal it from my view.

When I approached the recess, my heart again sunk. I averted my eyes, and left it behind me as quickly as possible. Silence reigned through my habitation, and a darkness, which closed doors and shutters produced. Every object was connected with mine or my brother's history. I passed the entry, mounted the stair, and unlocked the door of my chamber. It was with difficulty that I curbed my fancy and smothered my fears. Slight movements and casual sounds were transformed into beckoning shadows and calling shapes.

I proceeded to the closet. I opened and looked round it with fearfulness. All things were in their accustomed order. I sought and found the manuscript where I was used to deposit it. This being secured, there was nothing to detain me; yet I stood and contemplated awhile the furniture and walls of my chamber. I remembered how long this apartment had been a sweet and tranquil asylum; I compared its former state with its present dreariness, and reflected that I now beheld it for the last time.

Here it was that the incomprehensible behaviour of Carwin was witnessed: this the stage on which that enemy of man shewed himself for a moment unmasked.

---

[1] "HUT . . . artless sympathy . . . honest creatures": Clara's language here seems to reemphasize her unquestioned sense of class privilege. The uneducated groundskeepers on the Wieland estate are neither named, individualized, or considered to rise above the status of "creatures" to merit consideration as fellow humans. In the next paragraph she speaks condescendingly of their naive ideas about "ghastly apparitions," even as she herself indulges notions of spirits aiding Carwin. A "hut" in this period is a primitive dwelling of turf, mud, and branches; in the early U.S. up to the period of the Civil War, slave dwellings were often referred to as huts. For Clara's earlier and related reflections on laborers at Mettingen, see notes 6.1 and 6.4. It is also possible that the term alludes to the Moravian leanings of her mother, echoing early Moravian events at Herrnhut on the Zinzendorf estate (see note 1.20).

Here the menaces of murder were wasted to my ear; and here these menaces were executed.

These thoughts had a tendency to take from me my self-command. My feeble limbs refused to support me, and I sunk upon a chair. Incoherent and half-articulate exclamations escaped my lips. The name of Carwin was uttered, and eternal woes, woes like that which his malice had entailed upon us, were heaped upon him. I invoked all-seeing heaven to drag to light and to punish this betrayer, and accused its providence for having thus long delayed the retribution that was due to so enormous a guilt.

I have said that the window shutters were closed. A feeble light, however, found entrance through the crevices. A small window illuminated the closet, and the door being closed, a dim ray streamed through the key-hole. A kind of twilight was thus created, sufficient for the purposes of vision; but, at the same time, involving all minuter objects in obscurity.

This darkness suited the colour of my thoughts. I sickened at the remembrance of the past. The prospect of the future excited my loathing. I muttered in a low voice, Why should I live longer? Why should I drag a miserable being? All, for whom I ought to live, have perished. Am I not myself hunted to death?

At that moment, my despair suddenly became vigorous. My nerves were no longer unstrung. My powers, that had long been deadened, were revived. My bosom swelled with a sudden energy, and the conviction darted through my mind, that to end my torments was, at once, practicable and wise.

I knew how to find way to the recesses of life. I could use a lancet[2] with some skill, and could distinguish between vein and artery. By piercing deep into the latter, I should shun the evils which the future had in store for me, and take refuge from my woes in quiet death.

I started on my feet, for my feebleness was gone, and hasted to the closet. A lancet and other small instruments were preserved in a case which I had deposited here. Inattentive as I was to foreign considerations, my ears were still open to any sound of mysterious import that should occur. I thought I heard a step in the entry. My purpose was suspended, and I cast an eager glance at my chamber door, which was open. No one appeared, unless the shadow which I discerned upon the floor, was the outline of a man. If it were, I was authorized to suspect that some one was posted close to the entrance, who possibly had overheard my exclamations.

My teeth chattered, and a wild confusion took place of my momentary calm. Thus it was when a terrific visage had disclosed itself on a former night. Thus it was when the evil destiny of Wieland assumed the lineaments of something human. What horrid apparition was preparing to blast my sight?

Still I listened and gazed. Not long, for the shadow moved; a foot, unshapely and huge, was thrust forward; a form advanced from its concealment, and stalked into the room. It was Carwin!

---

[2] "Lancet": a surgical instrument, "usually with two edges and a point like a lance, used for bleeding, opening abscesses, etc." (*OED*).

While I had breath I shrieked. While I had power over my muscles, I motioned with my hand that he should vanish. My exertions could not last long; I sunk into a fit.

O that this grateful oblivion had lasted for ever! Too quickly I recovered my senses. The power of distinct vision was no sooner restored to me, than this hateful form again presented itself, and I once more relapsed.

A second time, untoward nature recalled me from the sleep of death. I found myself stretched upon the bed. When I had power to look up, I remembered only that I had cause to fear. My distempered fancy fashioned to itself no distinguishable image. I threw a languid glance round me; once more my eyes lighted upon Carwin.

He was seated on the floor, his back rested against the wall, his knees were drawn up, and his face was buried in his hands. That his station was at some distance, that his attitude was not menacing, that his ominous visage was concealed, may account for my now escaping a shock, violent as those which were past. I withdrew my eyes, but was not again deserted by my senses.

On perceiving that I had recovered my sensibility, he lifted his head. This motion attracted my attention. His countenance was mild, but sorrow and astonishment sat upon his features. I averted my eyes and feebly exclaimed—"O! fly—fly far and for ever!—I cannot behold you and live!"

He did not rise upon his feet, but clasped his hands, and said in a tone of deprecation—"I will fly. I am become a fiend, the sight of whom destroys. Yet tell me my offence! You have linked curses with my name; you ascribe to me a malice monstrous and infernal. I look around; all is loneliness and desert! This house and your brother's are solitary and dismantled! You die away at the sight of me! My fear whispers that some deed of horror has been perpetrated; that I am the undesigning cause."

What language was this? Had he not avowed himself a ravisher? Had not this chamber witnessed his atrocious purposes? I besought him with new vehemence to go.

He lifted his eyes—"Great heaven! what have I done? I think I know the extent of my offences. I have acted, but my actions have possibly effected more than I designed. This fear has brought me back from my retreat. I come to repair the evil of which my rashness was the cause, and to prevent more evil. I come to confess my errors."

"Wretch!" I cried when my suffocating emotions would permit me to speak, "the ghosts of my sister and her children, do they not rise to accuse thee? Who was it that blasted the intellects of Wieland? Who was it that urged him to fury, and guided him to murder? Who, but thou and the devil, with whom thou art confederated?"

At these words a new spirit pervaded his countenance. His eyes once more appealed to heaven. "If I have memory, if I have being, I am innocent. I intended no ill; but my folly, indirectly and remotely, may have caused it; but what words are these! Your brother lunatic! His children dead!"

What should I infer from this deportment? Was the ignorance which these words implied real or pretended?—Yet how could I imagine a mere human agency in these events? But if the influence was preternatural or maniacal in my brother's case, they must be equally so in my own. Then I remembered that the voice exerted, was to save me from Carwin's attempts. These ideas tended to abate my abhorrence of this man, and to detect the absurdity of my accusations.

"Alas!" said I, "I have no one to accuse. Leave me to my fate. Fly from a scene stained with cruelty; devoted to despair."

Carwin stood for a time musing and mournful. At length he said, "What has happened? I came to expiate my crimes: let me know them in their full extent. I have horrible forebodings! What has happened?"

I was silent; but recollecting the intimation given by this man when he was detected in my closet, which implied some knowledge of that power which interfered in my favor, I eagerly inquired, "What was that voice which called upon me to hold when I attempted to open the closet? What face was that which I saw at the bottom of the stairs? Answer me truly."

"I came to confess the truth. Your allusions are horrible and strange. Perhaps I have but faint conceptions of the evils which my infatuation has produced; but what remains I will perform. It was *my voice* that you heard! It was *my face* that you saw!"

For a moment I doubted whether my remembrance of events were not confused. How could he be at once stationed at my shoulder and shut up in my closet? How could he stand near me and yet be invisible? But if Carwin's were the thrilling voice and the fiery visage which I had heard and seen, then was he the prompter of my brother, and the author of these dismal outrages.

Once more I averted my eyes and struggled for speech. "Begone! thou man of mischief! Remorseless and implacable miscreant! begone!"

"I will obey," said he in a disconsolate voice; "yet, wretch as I am, am I unworthy to repair the evils that I have committed? I came as a repentant criminal. It is you whom I have injured, and at your bar am I willing to appear, and confess and expiate my crimes. I have deceived you: I have sported with your terrors: I have plotted to destroy your reputation. I come now to remove your errors; to set you beyond the reach of similar fears; to rebuild your fame as far as I am able.

"This is the amount of my guilt, and this the fruit of my remorse. Will you not hear me? Listen to my confession, and then denounce punishment. All I ask is a patient audience."

"What!" I replied, "was not thine the voice that commanded my brother to imbrue his hands in the blood of his children—to strangle that angel of sweetness his wife? Has he not vowed my death, and the death of Pleyel, at thy bidding? Hast thou not made him the butcher of his family; changed him who was the glory of his species into worse than brute; robbed him of reason, and consigned the rest of his days to fetters and stripes?"

Carwin's eyes glared, and his limbs were petrified at this intelligence. No words were requisite to prove him guiltless of these enormities: at the time, however, I was nearly insensible to these exculpatory tokens. He walked to the farther end of the room, and having recovered some degree of composure, he spoke—

"I am not this villain; I have slain no one; I have prompted none to slay; I have handled a tool of wonderful efficacy without malignant intentions, but without caution; ample will be the punishment of my temerity, if my conduct has contributed to this evil." He paused.—

I likewise was silent. I struggled to command myself so far as to listen to the tale which he should tell. Observing this, he continued—

"You are not apprized of the existence of a power which I possess. I know not by what name[3] to call it.* It enables me to mimic exactly the voice of another, and to modify the sound so that it shall appear to come from what quarter, and be uttered at what distance I please.

"I know not that every one possesses this power. Perhaps, though a casual position of my organs in my youth shewed me that I possessed it, it is an art which may be taught to all. Would to God I had died unknowing of the secret! It has produced nothing but degradation and calamity.

* *Biloquium,* or ventrilocution. Sound is varied according to the variations of direction and distance. The art of the ventriloquist consists in modifying his voice according to all these variations, without changing his place. See the work of the Abbe de la Chappelle,[4] in which are accurately recorded the performances of one of these artists, and some ingenious, though unsatisfactory speculations are given on the means by which the effects are produced. This power is, perhaps, given by nature, but is doubtless improvable, if not acquirable, by art. It may, possibly, consist in an unusual flexibility or exertion of the bottom of the tongue and the uvula. That speech is producible by these alone must be granted, since anatomists mention two instances of persons speaking without a tongue. In one case, the organ was originally wanting, but its place was supplied by a small tubercle, and the uvula was perfect. In the other, the tongue was destroyed by disease, but probably a small part of it remained.

This power is difficult to explain, but the fact is undeniable. Experience shews that the human voice can imitate the voice of all men and of all inferior animals. The sound of musical instruments, and even noises from the contact of inanimate substances, have been accurately imitated. The mimicry of animals is notorious; and Dr. Burney (Musical Travels)[5] mentions one who imitated a flute and violin, so as to deceive even his ears.

---

[3] "By what name": Carwin begins his confession, which will continue through the next two chapters, by revealing his ventriloquistic abilities. In the prequel *Memoirs of Carwin*, he already refers to this practice as "biloquism" (the term is a neologism, Brown's invention). In an intertextual sense, then, this may be another instance of Carwin's tactical imposture.

[4] "Abbe de la Chappelle": Jean Baptiste de la Chapelle (1710–1792), author of the first comprehensive treatise on ventriloquism, *Le Ventriloque, ou l'engastrimythe* (The Ventriloquist, or the belly-talker; 1772). The book provides an encyclopedic, skeptical and debunking account of lore on ventriloquism, from the biblical episode in which the Witch of Endor claims to communicate with a spirit for King Saul in 1 Samuel 28 to eighteenth-century tricksters. Brown seems to draw on the article "Ventriloquism" in the 1798 Philadelphia printing of *Encyclopædia: or a Dictionary of Arts, Sciences, and Miscellaneous Literature* (Thomas Dobson's U.S. printing of the third edition of the *Britannica*; vol. 18, 639–41) which summarizes la Chapelle and adds accounts of other ventriloquistic pranks used for petty frauds or deceptions like Carwin's. Brown reviewed this edition in the May 1799 issue of his circle's *Monthly Magazine.*

[5] "Dr. Burney (Musical Travels)": Charles Burney (1726–1814), English music historian and father of Fanny Burney, a novelist read attentively by Brown and his circle. In *The Present State of Music In Germany, The Netherlands, And United Provinces. Or, The Journal of a Tour Through Those Countries, Undertaken To Collect Materials for a General History Of Music* (London: Becket, 1773), Burney relates a visit to a synagogue of German Jews in Amsterdam, where he hears the singers replicating the sound of an organ and then mentions other instances of the human voice mimicking musical instruments.

"For a time the possession of so potent and stupendous an endowment elated me with pride. Unfortified by principle, subjected to poverty, stimulated by headlong passions, I made this powerful engine subservient to the supply of my wants, and the gratification of my vanity. I shall not mention how diligently I cultivated this gift, which seemed capable of unlimited improvement; nor detail the various occasions on which it was successfully exerted to lead superstition, conquer avarice, or excite awe.

"I left America, which is my native soil, in my youth. I have been engaged in various scenes of life, in which my peculiar talent has been exercised with more or less success. I was finally betrayed by one who called himself my friend, into acts which cannot be justified, though they are susceptible of apology.

"The perfidy of this man compelled me to withdraw from Europe. I returned to my native country, uncertain whether silence and obscurity would save me from his malice. I resided in the purlieus[6] of the city. I put on the garb and assumed the manners of a clown.

"My chief recreation was walking. My principal haunts were the lawns and gardens of Mettingen. In this delightful region the luxuriances of nature had been chastened by judicious art, and each successive contemplation unfolded new enchantments.[7]

"I was studious of seclusion: I was satiated with the intercourse of mankind, and discretion required me to shun their intercourse. For these reasons I long avoided the observation of your family, and chiefly visited these precincts at night.

"I was never weary of admiring the position and ornaments of *the temple*. Many a night have I passed under its roof, revolving no pleasing meditations. When, in my frequent rambles, I perceived this apartment was occupied, I gave a different direction to my steps. One evening, when a shower had just passed, judging by the silence that no one was within, I ascended to this building. Glancing carelessly round, I perceived an open letter on the pedestal. To read it was doubtless an offence against politeness. Of this offence, however, I was guilty.

"Scarcely had I gone half through when I was alarmed by the approach of your brother. To scramble down the cliff on the opposite side was impracticable. I was unprepared to meet a stranger. Besides the aukwardness attending such an interview in these circumstances, concealment was necessary to my safety. A thousand times had I vowed never again to employ the dangerous talent which I possessed; but such was the force of habit and the influence of present convenience, that I used this method of arresting his progress and leading him back to the house, with his errand, whatever it was, unperformed. I had often caught parts, from my station below, of your conversation in this place, and was well acquainted with the voice of your sister.

"Some weeks after this I was again quietly seated in this recess. The lateness of the hour secured me, as I thought, from all interruption. In this, however, I was

---

[6] "Purlieus": "an outlying district of a city or town; a suburb. Also: a poor or disreputable area of a city, town, or district; a slum" (*OED*).

[7] "Judicious art . . . contemplation . . . enchantments": Carwin's first attachment to Mettingen is based on the claims of sensibility that Clara attached to the estate's gardens in Chapter 5 (see notes 5.15, 6.3). This is where Clara first glimpses Carwin in Chapter 6.

mistaken, for Wieland and Pleyel, as I judged by their voices, earnest in dispute, ascended the hill.

"I was not sensible that any inconvenience could possibly have flowed from my former exertion; yet it was followed with compunction, because it was a deviation from a path which I had assigned to myself. Now my aversion to this means of escape was enforced by an unauthorized curiosity, and by the knowledge of a bushy hollow on the edge of the hill, where I should be safe from discovery. Into this hollow I thrust myself.

"The propriety of removal to Europe was the question eagerly discussed. Pleyel intimated that his anxiety to go was augmented by the silence of Theresa de Stolberg. The temptation to interfere in this dispute was irresistible. In vain I contended with inveterate habits. I disguised to myself the impropriety of my conduct, by recollecting the benefits which it might produce. Pleyel's proposal was unwise, yet it was enforced with plausible arguments and indefatigable zeal. Your brother might be puzzled and wearied, but could not be convinced. I conceived that to terminate the controversy in favor of the latter was conferring a benefit on all parties. For this end I profited by an opening in the conversation, and assured them of Catharine's irreconcilable aversion to the scheme, and of the death of the Saxon baroness. The latter event was merely a conjecture, but rendered extremely probable by Pleyel's representations. My purpose, you need not be told, was effected.

"My passion for mystery, and a species of imposture, which I deemed harmless, was thus awakened afresh. This second lapse into error made my recovery more difficult. I cannot convey to you an adequate idea of the kind of gratification which I derived from these exploits; yet I meditated nothing. My views were bounded to the passing moment, and commonly suggested by the momentary exigence.

"I must not conceal any thing. Your principles teach you to abhor a voluptuous temper; but, with whatever reluctance, I acknowledge this temper to be mine. You imagine your servant Judith to be innocent as well as beautiful; but you took her from a family where hypocrisy, as well as licentiousness, was wrought into a system. My attention was captivated by her charms, and her principles were easily seen to be flexible.

"Deem me not capable of the iniquity of seduction. Your servant is not destitute of feminine and virtuous qualities; but she was taught that the best use of her charms consists in the sale of them. My nocturnal visits to Mettingen were now prompted by a double view, and my correspondence with your servant gave me, at all times, access to your house.

"The second night after our interview,[8] so brief and so little foreseen by either of us, some dæmon of mischief seized me. According to my companion's report, your

---

[8] "Our interview": Carwin refers to the encounter with Judith that marked Clara's first awareness of him. See notes 6.4–6.5. Carwin's reference, in the previous paragraph, to multiple "nocturnal visits" implies that Carwin and Judith were already engaged in their affair when that meeting occurred. Clara never disputes Carwin's claim that her servant is dishonest and sexually permissive, even though she vigorously seeks to defend herself when Pleyel makes analogous accusations against her.

perfections were little less than divine. Her uncouth but copious narratives converted you into an object of worship. She chiefly dwelt upon your courage, because she herself was deficient in that quality. You held apparitions and goblins in contempt. You took no precautions against robbers. You were just as tranquil and secure in this lonely dwelling, as if you were in the midst of a crowd.

"Hence a vague project occurred to me, to put this courage to the test. A woman capable of recollection in danger, of warding off groundless panics, of discerning the true mode of proceeding, and profiting by her best resources, is a prodigy. I was desirous of ascertaining whether you were such an one.

"My expedient was obvious and simple: I was to counterfeit a murderous dialogue; but this was to be so conducted that another, and not yourself, should appear to be the object. I was not aware of the possibility that you should appropriate these menaces to yourself.[9] Had you been still and listened, you would have heard the struggles and prayers of the victim, who would likewise have appeared to be shut up in the closet, and whose voice would have been Judith's. This scene would have been an appeal to your compassion; and the proof of cowardice or courage which I expected from you, would have been your remaining inactive in your bed, or your entering the closet with a view to assist the sufferer. Some instances which Judith related of your fearlessness and promptitude made me adopt the latter supposition with some degree of confidence.

"By the girl's direction I found a ladder, and mounted to your closet window. This is scarcely large enough to admit the head, but it answered my purpose too well.

"I cannot express my confusion and surprize at your abrupt and precipitate flight. I hastily removed the ladder; and, after some pause, curiosity and doubts of your safety induced me to follow you. I found you stretched on the turf before your brother's door, without sense or motion. I felt the deepest regret at this unlooked-for consequence of my scheme. I knew not what to do to procure you relief. The idea of awakening the family naturally presented itself. This emergency was critical, and there was no time to deliberate. It was a sudden thought that occurred. I put my lips to the key-hole, and founded an alarm which effectually roused the sleepers. My organs were naturally forcible, and had been improved by long and assiduous exercise.

"Long and bitterly did I repent of my scheme. I was somewhat consoled by reflecting that my purpose had not been evil, and renewed my fruitless vows never to attempt such dangerous experiments. For some time I adhered, with laudable forbearance, to this resolution.

"My life has been a life of hardship and exposure. In the summer I prefer to make my bed of the smooth turf, or, at most, the shelter of a summer-house suffices. In all my rambles I never found a spot in which so many picturesque beauties and rural delights were assembled as at Mettingen. No corner of your

[9] "Appropriate these menaces to yourself": in Carwin's performance, the endangered female was ostensibly Judith, not Clara, but he underestimated the panic and confusion his prank would cause.

little domain unites fragrance and secrecy in so perfect a degree as the recess in the bank. The odour of its leaves, the coolness of its shade, and the music of its water-fall, had early attracted my attention. Here my sadness was converted into peaceful melancholy—here my slumbers were sound, and my pleasures enhanced.[10]

"As most free from interruption, I chose this as the scene of my midnight interviews with Judith. One evening, as the sun declined, I was seated here, when I was alarmed by your approach. It was with difficulty that I effected my escape unnoticed by you.

"At the customary hour, I returned to your habitation, and was made acquainted by Judith, with your unusual absence. I half suspected the true cause, and felt uneasiness at the danger there was that I should be deprived of my retreat; or, at least, interrupted in the possession of it. The girl, likewise, informed me, that among your other singularities, it was not uncommon for you to leave your bed, and walk forth for the sake of night-airs and starlight contemplations.

"I desired to prevent this inconvenience. I found you easily swayed by fear. I was influenced, in my choice of means, by the facility and certainty of that to which I had been accustomed. All that I forsaw was, that, in future, this spot would be cautiously shunned by you.

"I entered the recess with the utmost caution, and discovered, by your breathings, in what condition you were. The unexpected interpretation which you placed upon my former proceeding, suggested my conduct on the present occasion. The mode in which heaven is said by the poet, to interfere for the prevention of crimes,* was somewhat analogous to my province, and never failed to occur to me at seasons like this. It was requisite to break your slumbers, and for this end I uttered the powerful monosyllable, 'hold! hold!' My purpose was not prescribed by duty, yet surely it was far from being atrocious and inexpiable. To effect it, I uttered what was false, but it was well suited to my purpose. Nothing less was intended than to injure you. Nay, the evil resulting from my former act, was partly removed by assuring you that in all places but this you were safe.

---

* ——Peeps through the blanket of the dark and cries
Hold! Hold![11] ——SHAKESPEARE.

---

[10] "My pleasures enhanced": since Carwin has essentially been living in this "recess" since his arrival at Mettingen, he tends to resort to ventriloquism whenever the Wielands come close by and might discover where he has been sleeping.

[11] "Hold! Hold!": Carwin recalls *Macbeth* I.v.50–54. Lady Macbeth speaks these words as she hopes that no divine spirit will witness or intervene to stop her plan to assassinate Duncan: "Come, thick night / And pall thee in dunnest smoke of hell, / That my keen knife see not the wound it makes, / Nor heaven peep through the blanket of the dark, / To cry 'Hold, hold!'" The citation exemplifies the ambiguous or double-tongued nature of many of Carwin's statements: even his attempts to prevent violence refer to acts of violence. The passage may also prefigure Clara's ambiguous role in Theodore's final moments, in Chapter 26.

Chapter XXIII

"MY morals will appear to you far from rigid, yet my conduct will fall short of your suspicions. I am now to confess actions less excusable, and yet surely they will not entitle me to the name of a desperate or sordid criminal.

"Your house was rendered, by your frequent and long absences, easily accessible to my curiosity. My meeting with Pleyel was the prelude to direct intercourse with you. I had seen much of the world, but your character exhibited a specimen of human powers that was wholly new to me. My intercourse with your servant furnished me with curious details of your domestic management. I was of a different sex: I was not your husband; I was not even your friend; yet my knowledge of you was of that kind, which conjugal intimacies can give, and, in some respects, more accurate. The observation of your domestic was guided by me.

"You will not be surprised that I should sometimes profit by your absence, and adventure to examine with my own eyes, the interior of your chamber. Upright and sincere, you used no watchfulness, and practised no precautions. I scrutinized every thing, and pried every where. Your closet was usually locked, but it was once my fortune to find the key on a bureau. I opened and found new scope for my curiosity in your books. One of these was manuscript, and written in characters which essentially agreed with a short-hand system which I had learned from a Jesuit missionary.[1]

"I cannot justify my conduct, yet my only crime was curiosity.[2] I perused this volume with eagerness. The intellect which it unveiled, was brighter than my limited and feeble organs could bear. I was naturally inquisitive as to your ideas respecting my deportment, and the mysteries that had lately occurred.

"You know what you have written. You know that in this volume the key to your inmost soul was contained. If I had been a profound and malignant impostor, what plenteous materials were thus furnished me of stratagems and plots!

"The coincidence of your dream in the summer-house with my exclamation, was truly wonderful. The voice which warned you to forbear was, doubtless, mine; but mixed by a common process of the fancy, with the train of visionary incidents.

---

[1] "Jesuit missionary": the Jesuits, or Society of Jesus, are a Roman Catholic religious order founded in 1534, during the Counter-Reformation, whose missionary work played a significant role in early modern colonial expansion and the political-religious struggles it entailed. Jesuits were instrumental in the European penetration of Japan, China, India, and Latin America, and developed a reputation for political intrigue, conspiratorial guile, and scholarly rigor. "Jesuitical" became synonymous with deceitful, equivocal, or cunning. Under political pressure, the order was suppressed in 1767 in France, Portugal, parts of Italy, and the Spanish Empire. The order was reestablished in 1814 as part of the counterrevolutionary restoration in post-Napoleonic Europe, after which it assumed a more conventional profile. Given this timeline, Carwin encountered the Jesuits at the moment they were being suppressed worldwide as a conspiratorial menace. Carwin will refer in greater detail to the Jesuits and their colonial social engineering in *Memoirs of Carwin*.

[2] "My only crime was curiosity": a keyword and frequent source of motivation for Brown's characters. For an earlier instance in this novel, see note 1.12.

"I saw in a stronger light than ever, the dangerousness of that instrument which I employed, and renewed my resolutions to abstain from the use of it in future; but I was destined perpetually to violate my resolutions. By some perverse fate, I was led into circumstances in which the exertion of my powers was the sole or the best means of escape.

"On that memorable night on which our last interview took place, I came as usual to Mettingen. I was apprized of your engagement at your brother's, from which you did not expect to return till late. Some incident suggested the design of visiting your chamber. Among your books which I had not examined, might be something tending to illustrate your character, or the history of your family. Some intimation had been dropped by you in discourse, respecting a performance of your father, in which some important transaction in his life was recorded.

"I was desirous of seeing this book; and such was my habitual attachment to mystery, that I preferred the clandestine perusal of it. Such were the motives that induced me to make this attempt. Judith had disappeared, and finding the house unoccupied, I supplied myself with a light, and proceeded to your chamber.

"I found it easy, on experiment, to lock and unlock your closet door without the aid of a key. I shut myself in this recess, and was busily exploring your shelves, when I heard some one enter the room below. I was at a loss who it could be, whether you or your servant. Doubtful, however, as I was, I conceived it prudent to extinguish the light. Scarcely was this done, when some one entered the chamber. The footsteps were easily distinguished to be yours.

"My situation was now full of danger and perplexity. For some time, I cherished the hope that you would leave the room so long as to afford me an opportunity of escaping. As the hours passed, this hope gradually deserted me. It was plain that you had retired for the night.

"I knew not how soon you might find occasion to enter the closet. I was alive to all the horrors of detection, and ruminated without ceasing, on the behaviour which it would be proper, in case of detection, to adopt. I was unable to discover any consistent method of accounting for my being thus immured.

"It occurred to me that I might withdraw you from your chamber for a few minutes, by counterfeiting a voice from without. Some message from your brother might be delivered, requiring your presence at his house. I was deterred from this scheme by reflecting on the resolution I had formed, and on the possible evils that might result from it. Besides, it was not improbable that you would speedily retire to bed, and then, by the exercise of sufficient caution, I might hope to escape unobserved.

"Meanwhile I listened with the deepest anxiety to every motion from without. I discovered nothing which betokened preparation for sleep. Instead of this I heard deep-drawn sighs, and occasionally an half-expressed and mournful ejaculation. Hence I inferred that you were unhappy. The true state of your mind with regard to Pleyel your own pen had disclosed; but I supposed you to be framed of such materials, that, though a momentary sadness might affect you, you were impregnable to any permanent and heartfelt grief. Inquietude for my own safety was, for a moment, suspended by sympathy with your distress.

"To the former consideration I was quickly recalled by a motion of yours which indicated I knew not what. I fostered the persuasion that you would now retire to bed; but presently you approached the closet, and detection seemed to be inevitable. You put your hand upon the lock. I had formed no plan to extricate myself from the dilemma in which the opening of the door would involve me. I felt an irreconcilable aversion to detection. Thus situated, I involuntarily seized the door with a resolution to resist your efforts to open it.

"Suddenly you receded from the door. This deportment was inexplicable, but the relief it afforded me was quickly gone. You returned, and I once more was thrown into perplexity. The expedient that suggested itself was precipitate and inartificial. I exerted my organs and called upon you to *hold*.

"That you should persist in spite of this admonition, was a subject of astonishment.[3] I again resisted your efforts; for the first expedient having failed, I knew not what other to resort to. In this state, how was my astonishment increased when I heard your exclamations!

"It was now plain that you knew me to be within. Further resistance was unavailing and useless. The door opened, and I shrunk backward. Seldom have I felt deeper mortification, and more painful perplexity. I did not consider that the truth would be less injurious than any lie which I could hastily frame. Conscious as I was of a certain degree of guilt, I conceived that you would form the most odious suspicions. The truth would be imperfect, unless I were likewise to explain the mysterious admonition which had been given; but that explanation was of too great moment, and involved too extensive consequences to make me suddenly resolve to give it.

"I was aware that this discovery would associate itself in your mind, with the dialogue formerly heard in this closet. Thence would your suspicions be aggravated, and to escape from these suspicions would be impossible. But the mere truth would be sufficiently opprobrious, and deprive me for ever of your good opinion.

"Thus was I rendered desperate, and my mind rapidly passed to the contemplation of the use that might be made of previous events. Some good genius would appear to you to have interposed to save you from injury intended by me. Why, I said, since I must sink in her opinion, should I not cherish this belief? Why not personate an enemy, and pretend that celestial interference has frustrated my schemes? I must fly, but let me leave wonder and fear behind me. Elucidation of the mystery will always be practicable. I shall do no injury, but merely talk of evil that was designed, but is now past.

"Thus I extenuated my conduct to myself, but I scarcely expect that this will be to you a sufficient explication of the scene that followed. Those habits which I have imbibed, the rooted passion which possesses me for scattering around me amazement and fear, you enjoy no opportunities of knowing. That a man should wantonly impute to himself the most flagitious designs, will hardly be credited, even though

---

[3] "Astonishment": Carwin recounts his second incorrect expectation of Clara's actions. The first was described in Chapter 22 (note 22.9).

you reflect that my reputation was already, by my own folly, irretrievably ruined; and that it was always in my power to communicate the truth, and rectify the mistake.

"I left you to ponder on this scene. My mind was full of rapid and incongruous ideas. Compunction, self-upbraiding, hopelessness, satisfaction at the view of those effects likely to flow from my new scheme, misgivings as to the beneficial result of this scheme took possession of my mind, and seemed to struggle for the mastery.

"I had gone too far to recede. I had painted myself to you as an assassin and rav-isher, withheld from guilt only by a voice from heaven. I had thus reverted into the path of error, and now, having gone thus far, my progress seemed to be irrevocable. I said to myself, I must leave these precincts for ever. My acts have blasted my fame in the eyes of the Wielands. For the sake of creating a mysterious dread, I have made myself a villain. I may complete this mysterious plan by some new imposture, but I cannot aggravate my supposed guilt.

"My resolution was formed, and I was swiftly ruminating on the means for execut-ing it, when Pleyel appeared in sight. This incident decided my conduct. It was plain that Pleyel was a devoted lover, but he was, at the same time, a man of cold resolves and exquisite sagacity. To deceive him would be the sweetest triumph I had ever en-joyed. The deception would be momentary, but it would likewise be complete. That his delusion would so soon be rectified, was a recommendation to my scheme, for I esteemed him too much to desire to entail upon him lasting agonies.

"I had no time to reflect further, for he proceeded, with a quick step, towards the house. I was hurried onward involuntarily and by a mechanical impulse. I followed him as he passed the recess in the bank, and shrowding myself in that spot, I coun-terfeited sounds which I knew would arrest his steps.

"He stopped, turned, listened, approached, and overheard a dialogue whose pur-pose was to vanquish his belief in a point where his belief was most difficult to vanquish. I exerted all my powers to imitate your voice, your general sentiments, and your language. Being master, by means of your journal, of your personal history and most secret thoughts, my efforts were the more successful. When I reviewed the tenor of this dialogue, I cannot believe but that Pleyel was deluded. When I think of your character, and of the inferences which this dialogue was intended to suggest, it seems incredible that this delusion should be produced.

"I spared not myself. I called myself murderer, thief, guilty of innumerable perjuries and misdeeds: that you had debased yourself to the level of such an one, no evidence, methought, would suffice to convince him who knew you so thoroughly as Pleyel; and yet the imposture amounted to proof which the most jealous scrutiny would find to be unexceptionable.

"He left his station precipitately and resumed his way to the house. I saw that the detection of his error would be instantaneous, since, not having gone to bed, an immediate interview would take place between you. At first this circumstance was considered with regret; but as time opened my eyes to the possible consequences of this scene, I regarded it with pleasure.

"In a short time the infatuation which had led me thus far began to subside. The remembrance of former reasonings and transactions was renewed. How often I had repented this kind of exertion; how many evils were produced by it which I had not foreseen; what occasions for the bitterest remorse it had administered, now passed through my mind. The black catalogue of stratagems was now increased. I had inspired you with the most vehement terrors: I had filled your mind with faith in shadows and confidence in dreams: I had depraved the imagination of Pleyel: I had exhibited you to his understanding as devoted to brutal gratifications and consummate in hypocrisy. The evidence which accompanied this delusion would be irresistible to one whose passion had perverted his judgment, whose jealousy with regard to me had already been excited, and who, therefore, would not fail to overrate the force of this evidence. What fatal act of despair or of vengeance might not this error produce?

"With regard to myself, I had acted with a phrenzy that surpassed belief. I had warred against my peace and my fame: I had banished myself from the fellowship of vigorous and pure minds: I was self-expelled from a scene which the munificence of nature had adorned with unrivalled beauties, and from haunts in which all the muses and humanities had taken refuge.

"I was thus torn by conflicting fears and tumultuous regrets. The night passed away in this state of confusion; and next morning in the gazette left at my obscure lodging, I read a description and an offer of reward for the apprehension of my person. I was said to have escaped from an Irish prison, in which I was confined as an offender convicted of enormous and complicated crimes.[4]

"This was the work of an enemy, who, by falsehood and stratagem, had procured my condemnation. I was, indeed, a prisoner, but escaped, by the exertion of my powers, the fate to which I was doomed, but which I did not deserve. I had hoped that the malice of my foe was exhausted; but I now perceived that my precautions had been wise, for that the intervention of an ocean was insufficient for my security.

"Let me not dwell on the sensations which this discovery produced. I need not tell by what steps I was induced to seek an interview with you, for the purpose of disclosing the truth, and repairing, as far as possible, the effects of my misconduct. It was unavoidable that this gazette would fall into your hands, and that it would tend to confirm every erroneous impression.

"Having gained this interview, I purposed to seek some retreat in the wilderness, inaccessible to your inquiry and to the malice of my foe, where I might henceforth employ myself in composing a faithful narrative of my actions. I designed it as my vindication from the aspersions that had rested on my character, and as a lesson to mankind on the evils of credulity on the one hand, and of imposture on the other.

"I wrote you a billet, which was left at the house of your friend, and which I knew would, by some means, speedily come to your hands. I entertained a faint hope that

---

[4] "Complicated crimes": Caleb Williams, in William Godwin's 1794 novel known by the same name, is likewise pursued and persecuted by a higher-rank figure who spreads false rumors to incriminate him. The implication here is that the "enemy" by whom Carwin is pursued is his former patron Ludloe, mentioned as the source of the article in Chapter 14. For the first discussion of this newspaper announcement, see notes 14.2–14.4.

my invitation would be complied with. I knew not what use you would make of the opportunity which this proposal afforded you of procuring the seizure of my person; but this fate I was determined to avoid, and I had no doubt but due circumspection, and the exercise of the faculty which I possessed, would enable me to avoid it.

"I lurked, through the day, in the neighbourhood of Mettingen: I approached your habitation at the appointed hour: I entered it in silence, by a trap-door which led into the cellar. This had formerly been bolted on the inside, but Judith had, at an early period in our intercourse, removed this impediment. I ascended to the first floor, but met with no one, nor any thing that indicated the presence of an human being.

"I crept softly up stairs, and at length perceived your chamber door to be opened, and a light to be within. It was of moment to discover by whom this light was accompanied. I was sensible of the inconveniencies to which my being discovered at your chamber door by any one within would subject me; I therefore called out in my own voice, but so modified that it should appear to ascend from the court below, 'Who is in the chamber? Is it Miss Wieland?'

"No answer was returned to this summons. I listened, but no motion could be heard. After a pause I repeated my call, but no less ineffectually.

"I now approached nearer the door, and adventured to look in. A light stood on the table, but nothing human was discernible. I entered cautiously, but all was solitude and stillness.

"I knew not what to conclude. If the house were inhabited, my call would have been noticed; yet some suspicion insinuated itself that silence was studiously kept by persons who intended to surprize me. My approach had been wary, and the silence that ensued my call had likewise preceded it; a circumstance that tended to dissipate my fears.

"At length it occurred to me that Judith might possibly be in her own room. I turned my steps thither; but she was not to be found. I passed into other rooms, and was soon convinced that the house was totally deserted. I returned to your chamber, agitated by vain surmises and opposite conjectures. The appointed hour had passed, and I dismissed the hope of an interview.

"In this state of things I determined to leave a few lines on your toilet, and prosecute my journey to the mountains. Scarcely had I taken the pen when I laid it aside, uncertain in what manner to address you. I rose from the table and walked across the floor. A glance thrown upon the bed acquainted me with a spectacle to which my conceptions of horror had not yet reached.

"In the midst of shuddering and trepidation, the signal of your presence in the court below recalled me to myself. The deed was newly done: I only was in the house: what had lately happened justified any suspicions, however enormous. It was plain that this catastrophe was unknown to you: I thought upon the wild commotion which the discovery would awaken in your breast: I found the confusion of my own thoughts unconquerable, and perceived that the end for which I sought an interview was not now to be accomplished.

"In this state of things it was likewise expedient to conceal my being within. I put out the light and hurried down stairs. To my unspeakable surprize, notwithstanding every motive to fear, you lighted a candle and proceeded to your chamber.

"I retired to that room below from which a door leads into the cellar. This door concealed me from your view as you passed. I thought upon the spectacle which was about to present itself. In an exigence so abrupt and so little foreseen, I was again subjected to the empire of mechanical and habitual impulses. I dreaded the effects which this shocking exhibition, bursting on your unprepared senses, might produce.

"Thus actuated, I stept swiftly to the door, and thrusting my head forward, once more pronounced the mysterious interdiction. At that moment, by some untoward fate, your eyes were cast back, and you saw me in the very act of utterance. I fled through the darksome avenue at which I entered, covered with the shame of this detection.

"With diligence, stimulated by a thousand ineffable emotions, I pursued my intended journey. I have a brother whose farm is situated in the bosom of a fertile desert, near the sources of the Leheigh,[5] and thither I now repaired.

---

[5] "A fertile desert, near the sources of the Leheigh": desert, in this sense, is a relatively uninhabited wilderness area. The sources of the Lehigh River are in the Pocono Mountains of northeastern Pennsylvania, about ninety miles due north of Philadelphia. This is the area of the early Moravian settlements Nazareth and Bethlehem, Pennsylvania (see note 1.20).

Chapter XXIV

"DEEPLY did I ruminate on the occurrences that had just passed. Nothing excited my wonder so much as the means by which you discovered my being in the closet. This discovery appeared to be made at the moment when you attempted to open it. How could you have otherwise remained so long in the chamber apparently fearless and tranquil? And yet, having made this discovery, how could you persist in dragging me forth: persist in defiance of an interdiction so emphatical and solemn?

"But your sister's death was an event detestable and ominous. She had been the victim of the most dreadful species of assassination. How, in a state like yours,[1] the murderous intention could be generated, was wholly inconceivable.

"I did not relinquish my design of confessing to you the part which I had sustained in your family, but I was willing to defer it till the task which I had set myself was finished. That being done, I resumed the resolution. The motives to incite me to this continually acquired force. The more I revolved the events happening at Mettingen, the more insupportable and ominous my terrors became. My waking hours and my sleep were vexed by dismal presages and frightful intimations.

"Catharine was dead by violence. Surely my malignant stars had not made me the cause of her death; yet had I not rashly set in motion a machine, over whose progress I had no controul, and which experience had shewn me was infinite in power? Every day might add to the catalogue of horrors of which this was the source, and a seasonable disclosure of the truth might prevent numberless ills.

"Fraught with this conception, I have turned my steps hither. I find your brother's house desolate: the furniture removed, and the walls stained with damps. Your own is in the same situation. Your chamber is dismantled and dark, and you exhibit an image of incurable grief, and of rapid decay.

"I have uttered the truth. This is the extent of my offences. You tell me an horrid tale of Wieland being led to the destruction of his wife and children, by some mysterious agent. You charge me with the guilt of this agency; but I repeat that the amount of my guilt has been truly stated. The perpetrator of Catharine's death was unknown to me till now; nay, it is still unknown to me."

At that moment, the closing of a door in the kitchen was distinctly heard by us. Carwin started and paused. "There is some one coming. I must not be found here by my enemies, and need not, since my purpose is answered."

I had drunk in, with the most vehement attention, every word that he had uttered. I had no breath to interrupt his tale by interrogations or comments. The power that he spoke of was hitherto unknown to me: its existence was incredible; it was susceptible of no direct proof.

He owns that his were the voice and face which I heard and saw. He attempts to give an human explanation of these phantasms; but it is enough that he owns

---

[1] "In a state like yours": that is, among privileged, well-to-do members of the gentry class.

himself to be the agent; his tale is a lie, and his nature devilish. As he deceived me, he likewise deceived my brother, and now do I behold the author of all our calamities![2]

Such were my thoughts when his pause allowed me to think. I should have bad him begone if the silence had not been interrupted; but now I feared no more for myself; and the milkiness of my nature was curdled into hatred and rancour. Some one was near, and this enemy of God and man might possibly be brought to justice. I reflected not that the preternatural power which he had hitherto exerted, would avail to rescue him from any toils in which his feet might be entangled. Meanwhile, looks, and not words of menace and abhorrence, were all that I could bestow.

He did not depart. He seemed dubious, whether, by passing out of the house, or by remaining somewhat longer where he was, he should most endanger his safety. His confusion increased when steps of one barefoot were heard upon the stairs. He threw anxious glances sometimes at the closet, sometimes at the window, and sometimes at the chamber door, yet he was detained by some inexplicable fascination. He stood as if rooted to the spot.

As to me, my soul was bursting with detestation and revenge. I had no room for surmises and fears respecting him that approached. It was doubtless a human being, and would befriend me so far as to aid me in arresting this offender.

The stranger quickly entered the room. My eyes and the eyes of Carwin were, at the same moment, darted upon him. A second glance was not needed to inform us who he was. His locks were tangled, and fell confusedly over his forehead and ears. His shirt was of coarse stuff, and open at the neck and breast. His coat was once of bright and fine texture, but now torn and tarnished with dust. His feet, his legs, and his arms were bare. His features were the seat of a wild and tranquil solemnity, but his eyes bespoke inquietude and curiosity.

He advanced with firm step, and looking as in search of some one. He saw me and stopped. He bent his sight on the floor, and clenching his hands, appeared suddenly absorbed in meditation. Such were the figure and deportment of Wieland! Such, in his fallen state, were the aspect and guise of my brother!

Carwin did not fail to recognize the visitant. Care for his own safety was apparently swallowed up in the amazement which this spectacle produced. His station was conspicuous, and he could not have escaped the roving glances of Wieland; yet the latter seemed totally unconscious of his presence.

Grief at this scene of ruin and blast was at first the only sentiment of which I was conscious. A fearful stillness ensued. At length Wieland, lifting his hands, which were locked in each other, to his breast, exclaimed, "Father! I thank thee. This is thy guidance. Hither thou hast led me, that I might perform thy will: yet let me not err: let me hear again thy messenger!"

---

[2] "Devilish . . . author of all our calamities!": Clara again succumbs to anger and vengeful demonization, dismissing Theodore's part in the events. The final encounter that begins at this point will immediately confront her with the limitations of this perspective.

He stood for a minute as if listening; but recovering from his attitude, he continued—
"It is not needed. Dastardly wretch! thus eternally questioning the behests of thy Maker!
weak in resolution! wayward in faith!"

He advanced to me, and, after another pause, resumed: "Poor girl! a dismal fate has
set its mark upon thee. Thy life is demanded as a sacrifice. Prepare thee to die. Make
not my office difficult by fruitless opposition. Thy prayers might subdue stones; but
none but he who enjoined my purpose can shake it."

These words were a sufficient explication of the scene. The nature of his phrenzy, as
described by my uncle, was remembered. I who had sought death, was now thrilled
with horror because it was near. Death in this form, death from the hand of a brother,
was thought upon with undescribable repugnance.

In a state thus verging upon madness, my eye glanced upon Carwin. His astonishment appeared to have struck him motionless and dumb. My life was in danger,
and my brother's hand was about to be embrued in my blood. I firmly believed that
Carwin's was the instigation. I could rescue me from this abhorred fate; I could dissipate this tremendous illusion; I could save my brother from the perpetration of new
horrors, by pointing out the devil who seduced him; to hesitate a moment was to
perish. These thoughts gave strength to my limbs, and energy to my accents: I started
on my feet.

"O brother! spare me, spare thyself: There is thy betrayer. He counterfeited the
voice and face of an angel, for the purpose of destroying thee and me. He has this
moment confessed it. He is able to speak where he is not. He is leagued with hell, but
will not avow it; yet he confesses that the agency was his."

My brother turned slowly his eyes, and fixed them upon Carwin. Every joint in the
frame of the latter trembled. His complexion was paler than a ghost's. His eye dared
not meet that of Wieland, but wandered with an air of distraction from one space
to another.

"Man," said my brother, in a voice totally unlike that which he had used to me,
"what art thou? The charge has been made. Answer it. The visage—the voice—at the
bottom of these stairs—at the hour of eleven—To whom did they belong? To thee?"

Twice did Carwin attempt to speak, but his words died away upon his lips. My
brother resumed in a tone of greater vehemence—

"Thou falterest; faltering is ominous; say yes or no: one word will suffice; but
beware of falsehood. Was it a stratagem of hell to overthrow my family? Wast thou
the agent?"

I now saw that the wrath which had been prepared for me was to be heaped upon
another. The tale that I heard from him, and his present trepidations, were abundant
testimonies of his guilt. But what if Wieland should be undeceived! What if he shall
find his acts to have proceeded not from an heavenly prompter, but from human
treachery! Will not his rage mount into whirlwind? Will not he tare limb from limb
this devoted wretch?

Instinctively I recoiled from this image, but it gave place to another. Carwin may
be innocent, but the impetuosity of his judge may misconstrue his answers into
a confession of guilt. Wieland knows not that mysterious voices and appearances

were likewise witnessed by me. Carwin may be ignorant of those which misled my brother. Thus may his answers unwarily betray himself to ruin.

Such might be the consequences of my frantic precipitation, and these, it was necessary, if possible, to prevent. I attempted to speak, but Wieland, turning suddenly upon me, commanded silence, in a tone furious and terrible. My lips closed, and my tongue refused its office.

"What art thou?" he resumed, addressing himself to Carwin. "Answer me; whose form—whose voice—was it thy contrivance? Answer me."

The answer was now given, but confusedly and scarcely articulated. "I meant nothing—I intended no ill—if I understand—if I do not mistake you—it is too true—I did appear—in the entry—did speak. The contrivance was mine, but—"

These words were no sooner uttered, than my brother ceased to wear the same aspect. His eyes were downcast: he was motionless: his respiration became hoarse, like that of a man in the agonies of death. Carwin seemed unable to say more. He might have easily escaped, but the thought which occupied him related to what was horrid and unintelligible in this scene, and not to his own danger.

Presently the faculties of Wieland, which, for a time, were chained up, were seized with restlessness and trembling. He broke silence. The stoutest heart would have been appalled by the tone in which he spoke. He addressed himself to Carwin.

"Why art thou here? Who detains thee? Go and learn better. I will meet thee, but it must he at the bar of thy Maker. There shall I bear witness against thee."

Perceiving that Carwin did not obey, he continued; "Dost thou wish me to complete the catalogue by thy death? Thy life is a worthless thing. Tempt me no more. I am but a man, and thy presence may awaken a fury which may spurn my controul. Begone!"

Carwin, irresolute, striving in vain for utterance, his complexion pallid as death, his knees beating one against another, slowly obeyed the mandate and withdrew.

Chapter XXV

A FEW words more and I lay aside the pen for ever. Yet why should I not relinquish it now? All that I have said is preparatory to this scene, and my fingers, tremulous and cold as my heart, refuse any further exertion. This must not be. Let my last energies support me in the finishing of this task. Then will I lay down my head in the lap of death. Hushed will be all my murmurs in the sleep of the grave.

Every sentiment has perished in my bosom. Even friendship is extinct. Your love for me[1] has prompted me to this task; but I would not have complied if it had not been a luxury thus to feast upon my woes. I have justly calculated upon my remnant of strength. When I lay down the pen the taper of life will expire: my existence will terminate with my tale.

Now that I was left alone with Wieland, the perils of my situation presented themselves to my mind. That this paroxysm should terminate in havock and rage it was reasonable to predict. The first suggestion of my fears had been disproved by my experience. Carwin had acknowledged his offences, and yet had escaped. The vengeance which I had harboured had not been admitted by Wieland, and yet the evils which I had endured, compared with those inflicted on my brother, were as nothing. I thirsted for his blood, and was tormented with an insatiable appetite for his destruction; yet my brother was unmoved, and had dismissed him in safety. Surely thou wast more than man, while I am sunk below the beasts.[2]

Did I place a right construction on the conduct of Wieland? Was the error that misled him so easily rectified? Were views so vivid and faith so strenuous thus liable to fading and to change? Was there not reason to doubt the accuracy of my perceptions? With images like these was my mind thronged, till the deportment of my brother called away my attention.

I saw his lips move and his eyes cast up to heaven. Then would he listen and look back, as if in expectation of some one's appearance. Thrice he repeated these gesticulations and this inaudible prayer. Each time the mist of confusion and doubt seemed to grow darker and to settle on his understanding. I guessed at the meaning of these tokens. The words of Carwin had shaken his belief, and he was employed in summoning the messenger who had formerly communed with him, to attest the value of those new doubts. In vain the summons was repeated, for his eye met nothing but vacancy, and not a sound saluted his ear.

He walked to the bed, gazed with eagerness at the pillow which had sustained the head of the breathless Catharine, and then returned to the place where I sat. I had no power to list my eyes to his face: I was dubious of his purpose: this purpose might aim at my life.

---

[1] "Your love for me": a suggestion that it is a surviving family member, possibly Thomas Cambridge, who has asked Clara to compose a memoir of these events. See notes 1.2 and 26.3.

[2] "Thirsted for his blood . . . below the beasts": Clara is ashamed to realize that she has succumbed to an irrational obsession with revenge, when even her brother, in his deluded state, has not done so. By the end of this chapter, Clara will refer to her vengeful outbursts as a delusive "phrenzy" (169). For previous emphasis on the irrationality of revenge motivation, see note 21.8.

Alas! nothing but subjection to danger, and exposure to temptation, can show us what we are. By this test was I now tried, and found to be cowardly and rash. Men can deliberately untie the thread of life, and of this I had deemed myself capable; yet now that I stood upon the brink of fate, that the knife of the sacrificer was aimed at my heart, I shuddered and betook myself to any means of escape, however monstrous.

Can I bear to think—can I endure to relate the outrage which my heart meditated? Where were my means of safety? Resistance was vain. Not even the energy of despair could set me on a level with that strength which his terrific prompter had bestowed upon Wieland. Terror enables us to perform incredible feats; but terror was not then the state of my mind; where then were my hopes of rescue?

Methinks it is too much. I stand aside, as it were, from myself; I estimate my own deservings; a hatred, immortal and inexorable, is my due. I listen to my own pleas, and find them empty and false: yes, I acknowledge that my guilt surpasses that of all mankind: I confess that the curses of a world, and the frowns of a deity, are inadequate to my demerits. Is there a thing in the world worthy of infinite abhorrence? It is I.

What shall I say! I was menaced, as I thought, with death, and, to elude this evil, my hand was ready to inflict death upon the menacer. In visiting my house, I had made provision against the machinations of Carwin. In a fold of my dress an open penknife was concealed.[3] This I now seized and drew forth. It lurked out of view; but I now see that my state of mind would have rendered the deed inevitable if my brother had lifted his hand. This instrument of my preservation would have been plunged into his heart.

O, insupportable remembrance! hide thee from my view for a time; hide it from me that my heart was black enough to meditate the stabbing of a brother! a brother thus supreme in misery; thus towering in virtue!

He was probably unconscious of my design, but presently drew back. This interval was sufficient to restore me to myself. The madness, the iniquity of that act which I had purposed rushed upon my apprehension. For a moment I was breathless with agony. At the next moment I recovered my strength, and threw the knife with violence on the floor.

The sound awoke my brother from his reverie. He gazed alternately at me and at the weapon. With a movement equally solemn he stooped and took it up. He placed the blade in different positions, scrutinizing it accurately, and maintaining, at the same time, a profound silence.

---

[3] "Penknife was concealed": Carwin's entry earlier prevented Clara from looking for a lancet with which to commit suicide (see note 22.2), but she has apparently picked up or brought a penknife for defensive purposes as well. Clara's writerly association with the penknife was established in the first bedroom assault scene in Chapter 10 (see note 10.7). Shifts in Clara's behavior may suggest that some degree of change in her thinking and assumptions has occurred between the two scenes of bedroom violence: whereas in the first incident she conventionally contemplates suicide rather than self-defense against a male attacker, she now seriously considers self-defense, albeit with guilty misgivings. For her reflections on the first incident, see note 10.8.

Again he looked at me, but all that vehemence and loftiness of spirit which had so lately characterized his features, were flown. Fallen muscles, a forehead contracted into folds, eyes dim with unbidden drops, and a ruefulness of aspect which no words can describe, were now visible.

His looks touched into energy the same sympathies in me, and I poured forth a flood of tears. This passion was quickly checked by fear, which had now, no longer my own, but his safety for their object. I watched his deportment in silence. At length he spoke:

"Sister," said he, in an accent mournful and mild, "I have acted poorly my part in this world. What thinkest thou? Shall I not do better in the next?"

I could make no answer. The mildness of his tone astonished and encouraged me. I continued to regard him with wistful and anxious looks.

"I think," resumed he, "I will try. My wife and my babes have gone before. Happy wretches! I have sent you to repose, and ought not to linger behind."

These words had a meaning sufficiently intelligible. I looked at the open knife in his hand and shuddered, but knew not how to prevent the deed which I dreaded. He quickly noticed my fears, and comprehended them. Stretching towards me his hand, with an air of increasing mildness: "Take it," said he: "Fear not for thy own sake, nor for mine. The cup is gone by, and its transient inebriation is succeeded by the soberness of truth.

"Thou angel whom I was wont to worship! fearest thou, my sister, for thy life? Once it was the scope of my labours to destroy thee, but I was prompted to the deed by heaven; such, at least, was my belief. Thinkest thou that thy death was sought to gratify malevolence? No. I am pure from all stain. I believed that my God was my mover!

"Neither thee nor myself have I cause to injure. I have done my duty, and surely there is merit in having sacrificed to that, all that is dear to the heart of man. If a devil has deceived me, he came in the habit of an angel. If I erred, it was not my judgment that deceived me, but my senses. In thy sight, being of beings! I am still pure. Still will I look for my reward in thy justice!"

Did my ears truly report these sounds? If I did not err, my brother was restored to just perceptions. He knew himself to have been betrayed to the murder of his wife and children, to have been the victim of infernal artifice; yet he found consolation in the rectitude of his motives. He was not devoid of sorrow, for this was written on his countenance; but his soul was tranquil and sublime.

Perhaps this was merely a transition of his former madness into a new shape. Perhaps he had not yet awakened to the memory of the horrors which he had perpetrated. Infatuated wretch that I was! To set myself up as a model by which to judge of my heroic brother! My reason taught me that his conclusions were right; but conscious of the impotence of reason over my own conduct; conscious of my cowardly rashness and my criminal despair, I doubted whether any one could be stedfast and wise.

Such was my weakness, that even in the midst of these thoughts, my mind glided into abhorrence of Carwin, and I uttered in a low voice, O! Carwin! Carwin! What hast thou to answer for?

My brother immediately noticed the involuntary exclamation: "Clara!" said he, "be thyself. Equity used to be a theme for thy eloquence. Reduce its lessons to practice, and be just to that unfortunate man.[4] The instrument has done its work, and I am satisfied.

"I thank thee, my God, for this last illumination! My enemy is thine also. I deemed him to be man, the man with whom I have often communed; but now thy goodness has unveiled to me his true nature. As the performer of thy behests, he is my friend."

My heart began now to misgive me. His mournful aspect had gradually yielded place to a serene brow. A new soul appeared to actuate his frame, and his eyes to beam with preternatural lustre. These symptoms did not abate, and he continued:

"Clara! I must not leave thee in doubt. I know not what brought about thy interview with the being whom thou callest Carwin. For a time, I was guilty of thy error, and deduced from his incoherent confessions that I had been made the victim of human malice. He left us at my bidding, and I put up a prayer that my doubts should be removed. Thy eyes were shut, and thy ears sealed to the vision that answered my prayer.

"I was indeed deceived. The form thou hast seen was the incarnation of a dæmon. The visage and voice which urged me to the sacrifice of my family, were his. Now he personates a human form: then he was invironed with the lustre of heaven.—

"Clara," he continued, advancing closer to me, "thy death must come. This minister is evil, but he from whom his commission was received is God. Submit then with all thy wonted resignation to a decree that cannot be reversed or resisted. Mark the clock.[5] Three minutes are allowed to thee, in which to call up thy fortitude, and prepare thee for thy doom." There he stopped.

Even now, when this scene exists only in memory, when life and all its functions have sunk into torpor, my pulse throbs, and my hairs uprise: my brows are knit, as then; and I gaze around me in distraction. I was unconquerably averse to death; but death, imminent and full of agony as that which was threatened, was nothing. This was not the only or chief inspirer of my fears.

For him, not for myself, was my soul tormented. I might die, and no crime, surpassing the reach of mercy, would pursue me to the presence of my Judge; but my assassin would survive to contemplate his deed, and that assassin was Wieland!

Wings to bear me beyond his reach I had not. I could not vanish with a thought. The door was open, but my murderer was interposed between that and me. Of self-defence I was incapable. The phrenzy that lately prompted me to blood was gone; my state was desperate; my rescue was impossible.

---

[4] "Be just to that unfortunate man": Theodore argues against revenge, reinforcing earlier reflections on this theme. See notes 21.8, 25.2.

[5] "Mark the clock": The obsession with obeying divine injunctions at a precise time recalls the elder Wieland's anxious focus on religious devotion and obedience at noon and midnight, measured by the same clock that is in Clara's bedroom now. See notes 1.19 and 6.10.

The weight of these accumulated thoughts could not be borne. My sight became confused; my limbs were seized with convulsion; I spoke, but my words were half-formed:—

"Spare me, my brother! Look down, righteous Judge! snatch me from this fate! take away this fury from him, or turn it elsewhere!"

Such was the agony of my thoughts, that I noticed not steps entering my apartment. Supplicating eyes were cast upward, but when my prayer was breathed, I once more wildly gazed at the door. A form met my sight: I shuddered as if the God whom I invoked were present. It was Carwin that again intruded, and who stood before me, erect in attitude, and stedfast in look!

The sight of him awakened new and rapid thoughts. His recent tale was remembered: his magical transitions and mysterious energy of voice: Whether he were infernal or miraculous, or human, there was no power and no need to decide. Whether the contriver or not of this spell, he was able to unbind it, and to check the fury of my brother. He had ascribed to himself intentions not malignant. Here now was afforded a test of his truth. Let him interpose, as from above; revoke the savage decree which the madness of Wieland has assigned to heaven, and extinguish for ever this passion for blood!

My mind detected at a glance this avenue to safety. The recommendations it possessed thronged as it were together, and made but one impression on my intellect. Remoter effects and collateral dangers I saw not. Perhaps the pause of an instant had sufficed to call them up. The improbability that the influence which governed Wieland was external or human; the tendency of this stratagem to sanction so fatal an error, or substitute a more destructive rage in place of this; the sufficiency of Carwin's mere muscular forces to counteract the efforts, and restrain the fury of Wieland, might, at a second glance, have been discovered; but no second glance was allowed. My first thought hurried me to action, and, fixing my eyes upon Carwin I exclaimed—

"O wretch! once more hast thou come? Let it be to abjure thy malice; to counterwork this hellish stratagem; to turn from me and from my brother, this desolating rage!

"Testify thy innocence or thy remorse: exert the powers which pertain to thee, whatever they be, to turn aside this ruin. Thou art the author of these horrors! What have I done to deserve thus to die? How have I merited this unrelenting persecution? I adjure thee, by that God whose voice thou hast dared to counterfeit, to save my life!

"Wilt thou then go? leave me! Succourless!"

Carwin listened to my intreaties unmoved, and turned from me. He seemed to hesitate a moment: then glided through the door. Rage and despair stifled my utterance. The interval of respite was passed; the pangs reserved for me by Wieland, were not to be endured; my thoughts rushed again into anarchy. Having received the knife from his hand, I held it loosely and without regard; but now it seized again my attention; and I grasped it with force.

He seemed to notice not the entrance or exit of Carwin. My gesture and the murderous weapon appeared to have escaped his notice. His silence was unbroken; his eye, fixed upon the clock for a time, was now withdrawn; fury kindled in every feature; all that was human in his face gave way to an expression supernatural and tremendous. I felt my left arm within his grasp.—

Even now I hesitated to strike. I shrunk from his assault, but in vain.—

Here let me desist. Why should I rescue this event from oblivion? Why should I paint this detestable conflict? Why not terminate at once this series of horrors?— Hurry to the verge of the precipice, and cast myself for ever beyond remembrance and beyond hope?

Still I live: with this load upon my breast; with this phantom to pursue my steps; with adders lodged in my bosom, and stinging me to madness: still I consent to live!

Yes, I will rise above the sphere of mortal passions: I will spurn at the cowardly re-morse that bids me seek impunity in silence, or comfort in forgetfulness. My nerves shall be new strung to the task. Have I not resolved? I will die. The gulph before me is inevitable and near. I will die, but then only when my tale is at an end.

Chapter XXVI

MY right hand, grasping the unseen knife, was still disengaged. It was lifted to strike. All my strength was exhausted, but what was sufficient to the performance of this deed. Already was the energy awakened, and the impulse given, that should bear the fatal steel to his heart, when—Wieland shrunk back: his hand was withdrawn. Breathless with affright and desperation, I stood, freed from his grasp; unassailed; untouched.

Thus long had the power which controuled the scene forborne to interfere; but now his might was irresistible, and Wieland in a moment was disarmed of all his purposes. A voice, louder than human organs could produce, shriller than language can depict, burst from the ceiling, and commanded him—to *hold!*

Trouble and dismay succeeded to the stedfastness that had lately been displayed in the looks of Wieland. His eyes roved from one quarter to another, with an expression of doubt. He seemed to wait for a further intimation.

Carwin's agency was here easily recognized. I had besought him to interpose in my defence. He had flown. I had imagined him deaf to my prayer, and resolute to see me perish: yet he disappeared merely to devise and execute the means of my relief.

Why did he not forbear when this end was accomplished? Why did his misjudging zeal and accursed precipitation overpass that limit? Or meant he thus to crown the scene, and conduct his inscrutable plots to this consummation?

Such ideas were the fruit of subsequent contemplation. This moment was pregnant with fate. I had no power to reason. In the career of my tempestuous thoughts, rent into pieces, as my mind was, by accumulating horrors, Carwin was unseen and unsuspected. I partook of Wieland's credulity, shook with his amazement, and panted with his awe.

Silence took place for a moment; so much as allowed the attention to recover its post. Then new sounds were uttered from above.

"Man of errors! cease to cherish thy delusion: not heaven or hell, but thy senses have misled thee to commit these acts. Shake off thy phrenzy, and ascend into rational and human. Be lunatic no longer."

My brother opened his lips to speak. His tone was terrific and faint. He muttered an appeal to heaven. It was difficult to comprehend the theme of his inquiries. They implied doubt as to the nature of the impulse that hitherto had guided him, and questioned whether he had acted in consequence of insane perceptions.

To these interrogatories the voice, which now seemed to hover at his shoulder, loudly answered in the affirmative. Then uninterrupted silence ensued.

Fallen from his lofty and heroic station; now finally restored to the perception of truth; weighed to earth by the recollection of his own deeds; consoled no longer by a consciousness of rectitude, for the loss of offspring and wife—a loss for which he was indebted to his own misguided hand; Wieland was transformed at once into the *man of sorrows!*[1]

---

[1] "*Man of sorrows!*": Isaiah 53:3, "He is despised and rejected of men; a man of sorrows; and acquainted with grief."

He reflected not that credit should be as reasonably denied to the last, as to any former intimation; that one might as justly be ascribed to erring or diseased senses as the other. He saw not that this discovery in no degree affected the integrity of his conduct; that his motives had lost none of their claims to the homage of mankind; that the preference of supreme good, and the boundless energy of duty, were undiminished in his bosom.

It is not for me to pursue him through the ghastly changes of his countenance. Words he had none. Now he sat upon the floor, motionless in all his limbs, with his eyes glazed and fixed; a monument of woe.

Anon a spirit of tempestuous but undesigning activity seized him. He rose from his place and strode across the floor, tottering and at random. His eyes were without moisture, and gleamed with the fire that consumed his vitals. The muscles of his face were agitated by convulsion. His lips moved, but no sound escaped him.

That nature should long sustain this conflict was not to be believed. My state was little different from that of my brother. I entered, as it were, into his thought. My heart was visited and rent by his pangs—Oh that thy phrenzy had never been cured! that thy madness, with its blissful visions, would return! or, if that must not be, that thy scene would hasten to a close! that death would cover thee with his oblivion!

What can I wish for thee? Thou who hast vied with the great preacher of thy faith in sanctity of motives, and in elevation above sensual and selfish! Thou whom thy fate has changed into paricide and savage! Can I wish for the continuance of thy being? No.

For a time his movements seemed destitute of purpose. If he walked; if he turned; if his fingers were entwined with each other; if his hands were pressed against opposite sides of his head with a force sufficient to crush it into pieces; it was to tear his mind from self-contemplation; to waste his thoughts on external objects.

Speedily this train was broken. A beam appeared to be darted into his mind, which gave a purpose to his efforts. An avenue to escape presented itself; and now he eagerly gazed about him: when my thoughts became engaged by his demeanour, my fingers were stretched as by a mechanical force, and the knife, no longer heeded or of use, escaped from my grasp, and fell unperceived on the floor. His eye now lighted upon it; he seized it with the quickness of thought.

I shrieked aloud, but it was too late. He plunged it to the hilt in his neck; and his life instantly escaped with the stream that gushed from the wound. He was stretched at my feet; and my hands were sprinkled with his blood as he fell.[2]

Such was thy last deed, my brother! For a spectacle like this was it my fate to be reserved! Thy eyes were closed—thy face ghastly with death—thy arms, and the spot

---

[2] "My hands were sprinkled with his blood as he fell": a detail that may hint that Clara participates in responsibility for this catastrophic outcome. Brown may have taken the device of an emblematic knife circulating suspensefully in a bedroom with three people from the climactic passage in Carl Grosse, *The Dagger* (London: Vernor & Hood, 1795). Grosse was also the author of *Horrid Mysteries* (London: Minerva Press, 1796; trans. Peter Will), an Illuminati novel that belongs to the State Romance genre of political plots.

where thou liedest, floated in thy life's blood! These images have not, for a moment, forsaken me. Till I am breathless and cold, they must continue to hover in my sight.

Carwin, as I said, had left the room, but he still lingered in the house. My voice summoned him to my aid; but I scarcely noticed his re-entrance, and now faintly recollect his terrified looks, his broken exclamations, his vehement avowals of innocence, the effusions of his pity for me, and his offers of assistance.

I did not listen—I answered him not—I ceased to upbraid or accuse. His guilt was a point to which I was indifferent. Ruffian or devil, black as hell or bright as angels, thenceforth he was nothing to me. I was incapable of sparing a look or a thought from the ruin that was spread at my feet.

When he left me, I was scarcely conscious of any variation in the scene. He informed the inhabitants of the hut of what had passed, and they flew to the spot. Careless of his own safety, he hasted to the city to inform my friends of my condition.

My uncle speedily arrived at the house. The body of Wieland was removed from my presence, and they supposed that I would follow it; but no, my home is ascertained; here I have taken up my rest, and never will I go hence, till, like Wieland, I am borne to my grave.

Importunity was tried in vain: they threatened to remove me by violence—nay, violence was used; but my soul prizes too dearly this little roof to endure to be bereaved of it. Force should not prevail when the hoary locks and supplicating tears of my uncle were ineffectual. My repugnance to move gave birth to ferociousness and phrenzy when force was employed, and they were obliged to consent to my return.

They besought me—they remonstrated—they appealed to every duty that connected me with him that made me, and with my fellow-men—in vain. While I live I will not go hence. Have I not fulfilled my destiny?

Why will ye torment me with your reasonings and reproofs? Can ye restore to me the hope of my better days? Can ye give me back Catharine and her babes? Can ye recall to life him who died at my feet?

I will eat—I will drink—I will lie down and rise up at your bidding—all I ask is the choice of my abode. What is there unreasonable in this demand? Shortly will I be at peace. This is the spot which I have chosen in which to breathe my last sigh. Deny me not, I beseech you, so slight a boon.

Talk not to me, O my revered friend! of Carwin. He has told thee his tale, and thou exculpatest him[3] from all direct concern in the fate of Wieland. This scene of havock was produced by an illusion of the senses. Be it so: I care not from what source these disasters have flowed; it suffices that they have swallowed up our hopes and our existence.

---

3 "His tale . . . thou exculpatest him": since Clara's uncle Cambridge, her primary companion and guardian after the catastrophe, previously told her that he does not view Carwin as the primary cause of Wieland's madness, and because she emphasizes Cambridge's familiarity with Carwin's tale in the next, final chapter, this passage hints that he may be the "friend" and relative who has asked Clara to write her memoir. If so, Cambridge may intend the memoir as a public document of an extraordinary case of emotional illness and possible claim for the inheritability of madness.

What his agency began, his agency conducted to a close. He intended, by the final effort of his power, to rescue me and to banish his illusions from my brother. Such is his tale, concerning the truth of which I care not. Henceforth I foster but one wish—I ask only quick deliverance from life and all the ills that attend it.—

Go wretch! torment me not with thy presence and thy prayers.—Forgive thee? Will that avail thee when thy fateful hour shall arrive? Be thou acquitted at thy own tribunal, and thou needest not fear the verdict of others. If thy guilt be capable of blacker hues, if hitherto thy conscience be without stain, thy crime will be made more flagrant by thus violating my retreat. Take thyself away from my sight if thou wouldest not behold my death!

Thou art gone! murmuring and reluctant! And now my repose is coming—my work is done!

Chapter XXVII

[Written three years after the foregoing, and dated at Montpellier.[1]]

I IMAGINED that I had forever laid aside the pen; and that I should take up my abode in this part of the world, was of all events the least probable. My destiny I believed to be accomplished, and I looked forward to a speedy termination of my life with the fullest confidence.

Surely I had reason to be weary of existence, to be impatient of every tie which held me from the grave. I experienced this impatience in its fullest extent. I was not only enamoured of death, but conceived, from the condition of my frame, that to shun it was impossible, even though I had ardently desired it; yet here am I, a thousand leagues from my native soil, in full possession of life and of health, and not destitute of happiness.

Such is man. Time will obliterate the deepest impressions. Grief the most vehement and hopeless, will gradually decay and wear itself out. Arguments may be employed in vain: every moral prescription may be ineffectually tried: remonstrances, however cogent or pathetic, shall have no power over the attention, or shall be repelled with disdain; yet, as day follows day, the turbulence of our emotions shall subside, and our fluctuations be finally succeeded by a calm.

Perhaps, however, the conquest of despair was chiefly owing to an accident which rendered my continuance in my own house impossible. At the conclusion of my long, and as I then supposed, my last letter to you, I mentioned my resolution to wait for death in the very spot which had been the principal scene of my misfortunes. From this resolution my friends exerted themselves with the utmost zeal and perseverance to make me depart. They justly imagined that to be thus surrounded by memorials of the fate of my family, would tend to foster my disease. A swift succession of new objects, and the exclusion of every thing calculated to remind me of my loss, was the only method of cure.

I refused to listen to their exhortations. Great as my calamity was, to be torn from this asylum was regarded by me as an aggravation of it. By a perverse constitution of mind, he was considered as my greatest enemy who sought to withdraw me from a scene which supplied eternal food to my melancholy, and kept my despair from languishing.

In relating the history of these disasters I derived a similar species of gratification. My uncle earnestly dissuaded me from this task; but his remonstrances were as fruitless on

---

[1] "Montpellier": a city in the Languedoc region of southern France, near the Mediterranean. In the novel's coda, Clara has left the colonies to live in the region where the Albigensian and Camisard religious wars occurred (see notes 1.10, 1.13). In one sense, then, her relocation brings the Wieland family story back where it began, to the old and still prerevolutionary world that continues to be riven by politico-religious and imperial conflict. In another sense, which will be reinforced by the reintroduction of the Conway subplot in this final chapter, this displacement never leaves the theater of Anglo-French war and class conflict with which the narrative began (see note 0.3).

this head as they had been on others. They would have withheld from me the implements of writing; but they quickly perceived that to withstand would be more injurious than to comply with my wishes. Having finished my tale, it seemed as if the scene were closing. A fever lurked in my veins, and my strength was gone. Any exertion, however slight, was attended with difficulty, and, at length, I refused to rise from my bed.

I now see the infatuation and injustice of my conduct in its true colours. I reflect upon the sensations and reasonings of that period with wonder and humiliation.[2] That I should be insensible to the claims and tears of my friends; that I should overlook the suggestions of duty, and fly from that post in which only I could be instrumental to the benefit of others; that the exercise of the social and beneficent affections, the contemplation of nature and the acquisition of wisdom should not be seen to be means of happiness still within my reach, is, at this time, scarcely credible.

It is true that I am now changed; but I have not the consolation to reflect that my change was owing to my fortitude or to my capacity for instruction. Better thoughts grew up in my mind imperceptibly. I cannot but congratulate myself on the change, though, perhaps, it merely argues a fickleness of temper, and a defect of sensibility.

After my narrative was ended I betook myself to my bed, in the full belief that my career in this world was on the point of finishing. My uncle took up his abode with me, and performed for me every office of nurse, physician and friend. One night, after some hours of restlessness and pain, I sunk into deep sleep. Its tranquillity, however, was of no long duration. My fancy became suddenly distempered, and my brain was turned into a theatre of uproar and confusion. It would not be easy to describe the wild and phantastical incongruities that pestered me. My uncle, Wieland, Pleyel and Carwin were successively and momently discerned amidst the storm. Sometimes I was swallowed up by whirlpools, or caught up in the air by half-seen and gigantic forms, and thrown upon pointed rocks, or cast among the billows. Sometimes gleams of light were shot into a dark abyss, on the verge of which I was standing, and enabled me to discover, for a moment, its enormous depth and hideous precipices. Anon, I was transported to some ridge of Ætna, and made a terrified spectator of its fiery torrents and its pillars of smoke.[3]

However strange it may seem, I was conscious, even during my dream, of my real situation. I knew myself to be asleep, and struggled to break the spell, by muscular

---

[2] "Infatuation and injustice . . . wonder and humiliation": in retrospect, Clara acknowledges the self-destructive tendency of her behavior at Mettingen, and observes that her almost suicidal focus on grief and blame caused her to ignore the opportunities for survival and recovery.

[3] "Some ridge of Ætna . . . smoke": Mount Etna in Sicily is a continually active volcano frequently referenced in classical and modern texts. In many accounts, for example, the pre-Socratic philosopher Empedocles died by throwing himself into Mount Etna. Major modern treatments of this scenario, such as German poet Friedrich Hölderlin's play *Death of Empedocles* (1798), written the same year as *Wieland*, make Etna's barren, scorched landscape an emblem of self-scrutiny and despair after the close of the revolutionary era. Here a rationalistic interpretation of the connection between dream and reality is provided when the real fire in Clara's bedroom is translated as the dream of Etna's fires.

exertions. These did not avail, and I continued to suffer these abortive creations till a loud voice, at my bed side, and some one shaking me with violence, put an end to my reverie. My eyes were unsealed, and I started from my pillow.

My chamber was filled with smoke, which, though in some degree luminous, would permit me to see nothing, and by which I was nearly suffocated. The crackling of flames, and the deafening clamour of voices without, burst upon my ears. Stunned as I was by this hubbub, scorched with heat, and nearly choaked by the accumulating vapours, I was unable to think or act for my own preservation; I was incapable, indeed, of comprehending my danger.

I was caught up, in an instant, by a pair of sinewy arms, borne to the window, and carried down a ladder which had been placed there. My uncle stood at the bottom and received me. I was not fully aware of my situation till I found myself sheltered in the *Hut,* and surrounded by its inhabitants.

By neglect of the servant, some unextinguished embers had been placed in a barrel in the cellar of the building. The barrel had caught fire; this was communicated to the beams of the lower floor, and thence to the upper part of the structure. It was first discovered by some persons at a distance, who hastened to the spot and alarmed my uncle and the servants. The flames had already made considerable progress, and my condition was overlooked till my escape was rendered nearly impossible.

My danger being known, and a ladder quickly procured, one of the spectators ascended to my chamber, and effected my deliverance in the manner before related.

This incident, disastrous as it may at first seem, had, in reality, a beneficial effect upon my feelings. I was, in some degree, roused from the stupor which had seized my faculties. The monotonous and gloomy series of my thoughts was broken. My habitation was levelled with the ground, and I was obliged to seek a new one. A new train of images, disconnected with the fate of my family, forced itself on my attention, and a belief insensibly sprung up, that tranquillity, if not happiness, was still within my reach. Notwithstanding the shocks which my frame had endured, the anguish of my thoughts no sooner abated than I recovered my health.

I now willingly listened to my uncle's solicitations to be the companion of his voyage. Preparations were easily made, and after a tedious passage, we set our feet on the shore of the ancient world. The memory of the past did not forsake me; but the melancholy which it generated, and the tears with which it filled my eyes, were not unprofitable. My curiosity was revived, and I contemplated, with ardour, the spectacle of living manners and the monuments of past ages.

In proportion as my heart was reinstated in the possession of its ancient tranquillity, the sentiment which I had cherished with regard to Pleyel returned. In a short time he was united to the Saxon woman, and made his residence in the neighbourhood of Boston. I was glad that circumstances would not permit an interview to take place between us. I could not desire their misery; but I reaped no pleasure from reflecting on their happiness. Time, and the exertions of my fortitude, cured me, in some degree, of this folly. I continued to love him, but my passion was disguised to myself; I considered it merely as a more tender species of friendship, and cherished it without compunction.

Through my uncle's exertions a meeting was brought about between Carwin and Pleyel, and explanations took place which restored me at once to the good opinion of the latter. Though separated so widely our correspondence was punctual and frequent, and paved the way for that union which can only end with the death of one of us.

In my letters to him I made no secret of my former sentiments. This was a theme on which I could talk without painful, though not without delicate emotions. That knowledge which I should never have imparted to a lover, I felt little scruple to communicate to a friend.

A year and an half elapsed when Theresa was snatched from him by death, in the hour in which she gave him the first pledge of their mutual affection.[4] This event was borne by him with his customary fortitude. It induced him, however, to make a change in his plans. He disposed of his property in America, and joined my uncle and me, who had terminated the wanderings of two years at Montpellier, which will henceforth, I believe, be our permanent abode.

If you reflect upon that entire confidence which had subsisted from our infancy between Pleyel and myself; on the passion that I had contracted, and which was merely smothered for a time; and on the esteem which was mutual, you will not, perhaps, be surprized that the renovation of our intercourse should give birth to that union which at present subsists. When the period had elapsed necessary to weaken the remembrance of Theresa, to whom he had been bound by ties more of honor than of love, he tendered his affections to me. I need not add that the tender was eagerly accepted.

Perhaps you are somewhat interested in the fate of Carwin. He saw, when too late, the danger of imposture. So much affected was he by the catastrophe to which he was a witness, that he laid aside all regard to his own safety. He sought my uncle, and confided to him the tale which he had just related to me. He found a more impartial and indulgent auditor in Mr. Cambridge, who imputed to maniacal illusion the conduct of Wieland, though he conceived the previous and unseen agency of Carwin, to have indirectly but powerfully predisposed to this deplorable perversion of mind.

It was easy for Carwin to elude the persecutions of Ludloe. It was merely requisite to hide himself in a remote district of Pennsylvania. This, when he parted from us, he determined to do. He is now probably engaged in the harmless pursuits of agriculture, and may come to think, without insupportable remorse, on the evils to which his fatal talents have given birth. The innocence and usefulness of his future life may, in some degree, atone for the miseries so rashly or so thoughtlessly inflicted.

More urgent considerations hindered me from mentioning, in the course of my former mournful recital, any particulars respecting the unfortunate father of Louisa Conway.[5] That man surely was reserved to be a monument of capricious fortune. His southern journies being finished, he returned to Philadelphia. Before he reached the city he left the highway, and alighted at my brother's door. Contrary to his expectation,

---

[4] "The first pledge of their mutual affection": Theresa de Stolberg dies in childbirth.

[5] "The unfortunate father of Louisa Conway": Clara will conclude her narrative by returning to the Conway subplot first introduced in Chapter 4 (see notes 4.2, 4.5–4.6, and 14.4).

no one came forth to welcome him, or hail his approach. He attempted to enter the house, but bolted doors, barred windows, and a silence broken only by unanswered calls, shewed him that the mansion was deserted.

He proceeded thence to my habitation, which he found, in like manner, gloomy and tenantless. His surprize may be easily conceived. The rustics who occupied the hut told him an imperfect and incredible tale. He hasted to the city, and extorted from Mrs. Baynton a full disclosure of late disasters.

He was inured to adversity, and recovered, after no long time, from the shocks produced by this disappointment of his darling scheme. Our intercourse did not terminate with his departure from America. We have since met with him in France, and light has at length been thrown upon the motives which occasioned the disappearance of his wife, in the manner which I formerly related to you.

I have dwelt upon the ardour of their conjugal attachment, and mentioned that no suspicion had ever glanced upon her purity. This, though the belief was long cherished, recent discoveries have shewn to be questionable. No doubt her integrity would have survived to the present moment, if an extraordinary fate had not befallen her.

Major Stuart had been engaged, while in Germany, in a contest of honor with an Aid de Camp of the Marquis of Granby.[6] His adversary had propagated a rumour injurious to his character. A challenge was sent; a meeting ensued; and Stuart wounded and disarmed the calumniator. The offence was atoned for, and his life secured by suitable concessions.[7]

Maxwell, that was his name,[8] shortly after, in consequence of succeeding to a rich inheritance, sold his commission and returned to London. His fortune was speedily

---

[6] "An Aid de Camp of the Marquis of Granby": an aide-de-camp is an officer, usually a colonel or lieutenant, serving as assistant to a general or other senior military commander. John Manners, Marquess of Granby (1721–1770), was a British general active in the German theater of the Seven Years War. He was commander in Westphalia and at the Battle of Minden, when Major Stuart served in Germany, according to Chapter 4's account of Stuart's background (see note 4.5).

[7] "Challenge . . . suitable concessions": Stuart and the aide-de-camp Maxwell (named in the next paragraph) arrange a duel and perform its ritual of elite male honor and revenge; they will subsequently arrange a second duel before which Maxwell pays to have Stuart assassinated. The entire conflict between Stuart and Maxwell will be played out according to backward-looking codes of patriarchal honor and revenge, and Stuart's wife will be sacrificed to these codes as a mere side effect of the transaction between elite men.

In many Woldwinite and other novels of this era, dueling, already archaic in this period, serves as an example of the decadence of the old regime and its values, as a regressive, irrational old-regime determination of justice by force, rather than modern, middle-class adjudication through law. In his *Enquiry Concerning Political Justice* (1793), a crucial text for Brown (see Related Texts), William Godwin writes that dueling "was originally invented by barbarians for the gratification of revenge" (Book II, ch.2, appendix II, "Of Dueling").

[8] "Maxwell, that was his name": both Maxwell and Stuart are the names of Scottish clans that were part of the Jacobite uprising against English authority in 1745 and have complexly interrelated histories. Thus, while both characters serve in the imperial army, the cause for their duel over honor may rest in the residue of defeat and betrayal of their Scottish ethnic background. Although Maxwell lives in London, like Carwin he may be a backcountry immigrant to the metropolis.

augmented by an opulent marriage. Interest was his sole inducement to this marriage, though the lady had been swayed by a credulous affection. The true state of his heart was quickly discovered, and a separation, by mutual consent, took place. The lady withdrew to an estate in a distant county, and Maxwell continued to consume his time and fortune in the dissipation of the capital.

Maxwell, though deceitful and sensual, possessed great force of mind and specious accomplishments. He contrived to mislead the generous mind of Stuart, and to regain the esteem which his misconduct, for a time, had forfeited. He was recommended by her husband to the confidence of Mrs. Stuart. Maxwell was stimulated by revenge, and by a lawless passion, to convert this confidence into a source of guilt.

The education and capacity of this woman, the worth of her husband, the pledge of their alliance which time had produced, her maturity in age and knowledge of the world—all combined to render this attempt hopeless. Maxwell, however, was not easily discouraged. The most perfect being, he believed, must owe his exemption from vice to the absence of temptation. The impulses of love are so subtile, and the influence of false reasoning, when enforced by eloquence and passion, so unbounded, that no human virtue is secure from degeneracy. All arts being tried, every temptation being summoned to his aid, dissimulation being carried to its utmost bound, Maxwell, at length, nearly accomplished his purpose. The lady's affections were withdrawn from her husband and transferred to him. She could not, as yet, be reconciled to dishonor. All efforts to induce her to elope with him were ineffectual. She permitted herself to love, and to avow her love; but at this limit she stopped, and was immoveable.

Hence this revolution in her sentiments was productive only of despair. Her rectitude of principle preserved her from actual guilt, but could not restore to her her ancient affection, or save her from being the prey of remorseful and impracticable wishes. Her husband's absence produced a state of suspense. This, however, approached to a period, and she received tidings of his intended return. Maxwell, being likewise apprized of this event, and having made a last and unsuccessful effort to conquer her reluctance to accompany him in a journey to Italy, whither he pretended an invincible necessity of going, left her to pursue the measures which despair might suggest. At the same time she received a letter from the wife of Maxwell, unveiling the true character of this man, and revealing facts which the artifices of her seducer had hitherto concealed from her. Mrs. Maxwell had been prompted to this disclosure by a knowledge of her husband's practices, with which his own impetuosity had made her acquainted.

This discovery, joined to the delicacy of her scruples and the anguish of remorse, induced her to abscond. This scheme was adopted in haste, but effected with consummate prudence. She fled, on the eve of her husband's arrival, in the disguise of a boy, and embarked at Falmouth[9] in a packet bound for America.

---

[9] "Falmouth": a port in Cornwall, near the southwestern tip of England. This is the same region where Clara's maternal grandfather committed suicide by leaping off a cliff, an incident recounted in Chapter 20 (see notes 20.4–20.6).

The history of her disastrous intercourse with Maxwell, the motives inducing her to forsake her country, and the measures she had taken to effect her design, were related to Mrs. Maxwell, in reply to her communication. Between these women an ancient intimacy and considerable similitude of character subsisted. This disclosure was accompanied with solemn injunctions of secrecy, and these injunctions were, for a long time, faithfully observed.

Mrs. Maxwell's abode was situated on the banks of the Wey.[10] Stuart was her kinsman; their youth had been spent together; and Maxwell was in some degree indebted to the man whom he betrayed, for his alliance with this unfortunate lady. Her esteem for the character of Stuart had never been diminished. A meeting between them was occasioned by a tour which the latter had undertaken, in the year after his return from America, to Wales and the western countries. This interview produced pleasure and regret in each. Their own transactions naturally became the topics of their conversation; and the untimely fate of his wife and daughter were related by the guest.

Mrs. Maxwell's regard for her friend, as well as for the safety of her husband, persuaded her to concealment; but the former being dead, and the latter being out of the kingdom, she ventured to produce Mrs. Stuart's letter, and to communicate her own knowledge of the treachery of Maxwell. She had previously extorted from her guest a promise not to pursue any scheme of vengeance; but this promise was made while ignorant of the full extent of Maxwell's depravity, and his passion refused to adhere to it.

At this time my uncle and I resided at Avignon.[11] Among the English resident there, and with whom we maintained a social intercourse, was Maxwell. This man's talents and address rendered him a favorite both with my uncle and myself. He had even tendered me his hand in marriage; but this being refused, he had sought and obtained permission to continue with us the intercourse of friendship. Since a legal marriage was impossible, no doubt, his views were flagitious. Whether he had relinquished these views I was unable to judge.

He was one in a large circle at a villa in the environs, to which I had likewise been invited, when Stuart abruptly entered the apartment. He was recognized with genuine satisfaction by me, and with seeming pleasure by Maxwell. In a short time, some affair of moment being pleaded, which required an immediate and exclusive interview, Maxwell and he withdrew together. Stuart and my uncle had been known to each other in the German army;[12] and the purpose contemplated by the former in this long and hasty journey, was confided to his old friend.

---

[10] "Wey": The river Wey is a tributary of the Thames in Southern England, just southwest of London.

[11] "Avignon": a city in southern France, not far from Montpellier but in a different administrative division on the east side of the Rhone River. Before 1789 and the onset of the French Revolution, and thus while Clara and her uncle Cambridge live there, Avignon was not part of France, but belonged to the Papacy. It was the seat of an alternative pope or "antipope" during a period of schism in the Church, and later a site of prolonged Inquisition.

[12] "Known to each other in the German army": more professional and family connections reinforce the sense that the Stuarts, Maxwells, Cambridges, Wielands, and Pleyels are all interrelated the sprawling military-colonial apparatus of the British Empire.

A defiance was given and received, and the banks of a rivulet, about a league from the city, was selected as the scene of this contest. My uncle, having exerted himself in vain to prevent an hostile meeting, consented to attend them as a surgeon.—Next morning, at sun-rise, was the time chosen.

I returned early in the evening to my lodgings. Preliminaries being settled between the combatants, Stuart had consented to spend the evening with us, and did not retire till late. On the way to his hotel he was exposed to no molestation, but just as he stepped within the portico, a swarthy and malignant figure started from behind a column, and plunged a stiletto into his body.

The author of this treason could not certainly be discovered; but the details communicated by Stuart, respecting the history of Maxwell, naturally pointed him out as an object of suspicion. No one expressed more concern, on account of this disaster, than he; and he pretended an ardent zeal to vindicate his character from the aspersions that were cast upon it. Thenceforth, however, I denied myself to his visits; and shortly after he disappeared from this scene.

Few possessed more estimable qualities, and a better title to happiness and the tranquil honors of long life; than the mother and father of Louisa Conway: yet they were cut off in the bloom of their days; and their destiny was thus accomplished by the same hand. Maxwell was the instrument of their destruction, though the instrument was applied to this end in so different a manner.

I leave you to moralize on this tale. That virtue should become the victim of treachery is, no doubt, a mournful consideration; but it will not escape your notice, that the evils of which Carwin and Maxwell were the authors, owed their existence to the errors of the sufferers. All efforts would have been ineffectual to subvert the happiness or shorten the existence of the Stuarts, if their own frailty had not seconded these efforts. If the lady had crushed her disastrous passion in the bud, and driven the seducer from her presence, when the tendency of his artifices was seen; if Stuart had not admitted the spirit of absurd revenge, we should not have had to deplore this catastrophe. If Wieland had framed juster notions of moral duty, and of the divine attributes; or if I had been gifted with ordinary equanimity or foresight, the double-tongued[13] deceiver would have been baffled and repelled.

---

[13] "Double-tongued": the novel's final sentence provides the second occurrence of this keyword, mirroring its prefatory appearance in the poetic epigraph on the title page (see note on the title page).

RELATED TEXTS

1. Charles Brockden Brown, "Walstein's School of History. From the German of Krants of Gotha." *The Monthly Magazine and American Review* 1:5 (August–September 1799)

Published in August–September 1799, at the height of Brown's novelistic phase, "Walstein's School of History" is an important fictionalized essay in which Brown articulates his plan for novel writing, identifying both the rationale for his novels and the themes and techniques he will use to construct them.

Along with "The Difference Between History and Romance," which develops further remarks on the close relation of historical and "romance" narratives that is a central point in this essay, this is a key document for understanding Brown's aims and methods in writing fiction. It also arguably establishes Brown as the first modern U.S. literary critic, in the sense of one who explores how texts construct meaning and function in society rather than simply asserting the relative merits of literary productions judged against an imaginary standard of excellence.

The essay's theory of novel writing is similar to ideas about the relation of history and literature raised by the English Woldwinites (see Godwin's remarks on literature in Related Texts and in his unpublished 1797 essay "Of History and Romance"), but is presented within a fictional framework that alludes primarily to the late-1790s wave, in English-speaking literary circles, of German literary and cultural sources. This frame concerns the literary productions of Walstein, a professor of history at Jena, a center of intellectual culture in Germany, and of his leading student Engel. Brown's choice of the name Walstein likely refers to the work of Friedrich Schiller (1759–1805), a professor of history and philosophy at Jena and a major figure of the late Enlightenment, whose progressive fictions, histories, dramas, and doctrines about art were well known to Brown and his friends. Schiller's 1791–1793 History of the Thirty Years War, *for example, appeared in English translation in 1799; "Walstein" is an alternative English spelling in the period for Wallenstein, a general that Schiller writes about in that history and in several plays; and the setting in Jena and Weimar recalls several 1799* Monthly Magazine *articles by Brown and his circle on Schiller and August von Kotzebue (1761–1819), another contemporary German writer associated with these cities and their cultural institutions.*

Just as Brown uses living German writers for character names in Wieland, *this essay similarly draws on recognizable names. The name Engel, given to the pupil of Walstein discussed in the second part of the piece, seems to reference Johann Jakob Engel (1741–1802), a poet, dramatist, and philosopher, who taught in Saxony before becoming a professor in Berlin for moral philosophy, logic, and history, advisor to Frederick the Great, and a contributor to Schiller's magazine* Die Horen *(after initially opposing Schiller's tempestuous Sturm und Drang style of writing). Engel was known as an inspiring, if not entirely original or complex, teacher and writer, whose style conveyed current arguments about sympathy and history in ways that made these topics approachable for nonelite audiences. The story of "Olivo Ronsica" that Engel writes, in this fictional frame, is in fact a summary of the plot of Brown's Philadelphia novel* Arthur Mervyn, *first part* (1799), *here transposed to Weimar during the chaos and disease created by the Thirty Years War (1618–1648). In an anagrammatical fashion, Engel's title "Olivo Ronsica" may echo that of C.M Wieland's novel,* (Der Sieg der Natur über die Schwärmerei oder Die Abenteuer des) Don Silvio von Rosalva (1764), *published in English in 1773 as* Reason Triumphant over Fancy; or the Adventures of Don Silvio of Rosalva.

Brown derives the essay's approach to novel writing from primarily British Woldwinite models, but the Schillerian frame implicitly joins these two related currents of late-Enlightenment thinking about progressive historical and fictional story telling. Walstein provides a first model for the progressive novel by combining history and romance in such a way as to promote "moral and political" engagement while rejecting universal truths: the novel provides models for benevolent action and makes its readers active observers of the social world around them. Walstein's fictions concern classical or elite figures such as the Roman statesman and orator Cicero (who struggled to defend the Roman Republic and who is emphasized in Wieland *and other texts reprinted here) and Portugal's Marquis of Pombal (a modernizing Enlightenment reformer mentioned in* Memoirs of Carwin, *who struggled against old-regime aristocratic and religious forces in eighteenth-century Portugal). Engel modernizes Walstein's model by focusing on ordinary, nonelite person-ages (as the novelist Richardson has done with his* Clarissa*), arguing that a romance, to be effective in today's world, must be addressed to a wide popular audience and draw its characters and dilemmas not from the elite, but from the same lower-status groups (women, laborers, servants, etc.) that will read and be moved by the work. Engel insists that history and romance alike should address issues and situations familiar to their modern audiences, notably the common inequalities arising from sex and property. Thus, Engel's modern ro-mances will insert ordinary individuals like "Olivo Ronsica," or Brown's novelistic charac-ters, into situations of stress resulting from contemporary tensions and inequalities related to money and other property relations, and erotic desire and other forms of personal relations. Finally, Engel adds that a thrilling style is also necessary if modern fictions are to hold their reader's interest and move them toward progressive values and behaviors.*

*****

Walstein was professor of history at Jena, and, of course, had several pupils. Nine of them were more assiduous in their attention to their tutor than the others. This circumstance came at length to be noticed by each other, as well as by Walstein, and naturally produced good-will and fellowship among them. They gradually sepa-rated themselves from the negligent and heedless crowd, cleaved to each other, and frequently met to exchange and compare ideas. Walstein was prepossessed in their favour by their studious habits, and their veneration for him. He frequently admit-ted them to exclusive interviews, and, laying aside his professional dignity, conversed with them on the footing of a friend and equal.

Walstein's two books were read by them with great attention. These were justly to be considered as exemplifications of his rules, as specimens of the manner in which history was to be studied and written.

No wonder that they found few defects in the model; that they gradually adopted the style and spirit of his composition, and, from admiring and contemplating, should, at length, aspire to imitate. It could not but happen, however, that the criterion of excellence would be somewhat modified in passing through the mind of each; that each should have his peculiar modes of writing and thinking.

All observers, indeed, are, at the first and transient view, more affected by resemblances than differences. The works of Walstein and his disciples were hastily ascribed to the same hand. The same minute explication of motives, the same indissoluble and well-woven tissue of causes and effects, the same unity and coherence of design, the same power of engrossing the attention, and the same felicity, purity, and compactness of style, are conspicuous in all.

There is likewise evidence, that each had embraced the same scheme of accounting for events, and the same notions of moral and political duty. Still, however, there were marks of difference in the different nature of the themes that were adopted, and of the purpose which the productions of each writer seemed most directly to promote.

We may aim to exhibit the influence of some moral or physical cause, to enforce some useful maxim, or illustrate some momentous truth. This purpose may be more or less simple, capable of being diffused over the surface of an empire or a century, or of shrinking into the compass of a day, and the bounds of a single thought.

The elementary truths of morals and politics may merit the preference: our theory may adapt itself to, and derive confirmation from whatever is human. Newton and Xavier, Zengis and William Tell,[1] may bear close and manifest relation to the system we adopt, and their fates be linked, indissolubly, in a common chain.

The physician may be attentive to the constitution and diseases of man in all ages and nations. Some opinions, on the influence of a certain diet, may make him eager to investigate the physical history of every human being. No fact, falling within his observation, is useless or anomalous. All sensibly contribute to the symmetry and firmness of some structure which he is anxious to erect. Distances of place and time, and diversities of moral conduct, may, by no means, obstruct their union into one homogeneous mass.

I am apt to think, that the moral reasoner may discover principles equally universal in their application, and giving birth to similar coincidence and harmony among characters and events. Has not this been effected by Walstein?

Walstein composed two works. One exhibited, with great minuteness, the life of Cicero; the other, that of the Marquis of Pombal.[2] What link did his reason

---

[1] "Newton . . . Xavier . . . Zengis . . . Tell": Isaac Newton (1642–1727), the mathematician and physicist who first described the laws of gravitation; Francis Xavier (1506–1552), cofounder of the Jesuit order and Catholic missionary who died trying to extend Jesuit institutions to China; Genghis Khan (c. 1162–1227), architect of the Mongol Empire; William Tell, a legendary hero of Swiss independence supposed to have lived in the fourteenth century (new versions of the Tell legend proliferated in the Romantic era).

[2] "Cicero . . . Pombal": for Brown's wider interest in the Roman statesman and orator Cicero, see Related Texts. Pombal is Sebastião José de Carvalho e Melo, Marquis of Pombal (1699–1782), who directed the Portuguese government as an enlightened prime minister, 1750–1777. For references to Pombal and his struggles against the Jesuits, see Part 6 of *Memoirs of Carwin*.

discover, or his fancy create between times, places, situations, events, and characters so different? He reasoned thus:—

Human society is powerfully modified by individual members. The authority of individuals sometimes flows from physical incidents; birth, or marriage, for example. Sometimes it springs, independently of physical relation, and, in defiance of them, from intellectual vigour. The authority of kings and nobles exemplifies the first species of influence. Birth and marriage, physical, and not moral incidents, entitle them to rule.

The second kind of influence, that flowing from intellectual vigour, is remarkably exemplified in Cicero and Pombal. In this respect they are alike.

The mode in which they reached eminence, and in which they exercised power, was different, in consequence of different circumstances. One lived in a free, the other in a despotic state. One gained it from the prince, the other from the people. The end of both, for their degree of virtue was the same, was the general happiness. They promoted this end by the best means which human wisdom could suggest. One cherished, the other depressed the aristocracy. Both were right in their means as in their end; and each, had he exchanged conditions with the other, would have acted like that other.

Walstein was conscious of the uncertainty of history. Actions and motives cannot be truly described. We can only make approaches to the truth. The more attentively we observe mankind, and study ourselves, the greater will this uncertainty appear, and the farther shall we find ourselves from truth.

This uncertainty, however, has some bounds. Some circumstances of events, and some events, are more capable of evidence than others. The same may be said of motives. Our guesses as to the motives of some actions are more probable than the guesses that relate to other actions. Though no one can state the motives from which any action has flowed, he may enumerate motives from which it is quite certain, that the action did *not* flow.

The lives of Cicero and Pombal are imperfectly related by historians. An impartial view of that which history has preserved makes the belief of their wisdom and virtue more probable than the contrary belief.

Walstein desired the happiness of mankind. He imagined that the exhibition of virtue and talents, forcing its way to sovereign power, and employing that power for the national good, was highly conducive to their happiness.

By exhibiting a virtuous being in opposite conditions, and pursuing his end by the means suited to his own condition, he believes himself displaying a model of right conduct, and furnishing incitements to imitate that conduct, supplying men not only with knowledge of just ends and just means, but with the love and the zeal of virtue.

How men might best promote the happiness of mankind in given situations, was the problem that he desired to solve. The more portraits of human excellence he was able to exhibit the better; but his power in this respect was limited. The longer his life and his powers endured the more numerous would his portraits become. Futurity, however, was precarious, and, therefore, it behoved him to select, in the first place, the most useful theme.

His purpose was not to be accomplished by a brief or meagre story. To illuminate the understanding, to charm curiosity, and sway the passions, required that events should be copiously displayed and artfully linked, that motives should be vividly depicted, and scenes made to pass before the eye. This has been performed. Cicero is made to compose the story of his political and private life from his early youth to his flight from Astura, at the coalition of Antony and Octavius. It is addressed to Atticus, and meant to be the attestor of his virtue, and his vindicator with posterity.[3]

The style is energetic, and flows with that glowing impetuosity which was supposed to actuate the writer. Ardent passions, lofty indignation, sportive elegance, pathetic and beautiful simplicity, take their turns to control his pen, according to the nature of the theme. New and striking portraits are introduced of the great actors on the stage. New lights are cast upon the principal occurrences. Everywhere are marks of profound learning, accurate judgment, and inexhaustible invention. Cicero here exhibits himself in all the forms of master, husband, father, friend, advocate, pro-consul, consul, and senator.

To assume the person of Cicero, as the narrator of his own transactions, was certainly an hazardous undertaking. Frequent errors and lapses, violations of probability, and incongruities in the style and conduct of this imaginary history with the genuine productions of Cicero, might be reasonably expected, but these are not found. The more conversant we are with the authentic monuments, the more is our admiration at the felicity of this imposture enhanced.

The conspiracy of Cataline is here related with abundance of circumstances not to be found in Sallust.[4] The difference, however, is of that kind which result from a deeper insight into human nature, a more accurate acquaintance with the facts, more correctness of arrangement, and a deeper concern in the progress and issue of the story. What is false, is so admirable in itself, so conformable to Roman modes and sentiments, so self-consistent, that one is almost prompted to accept it as the gift of inspiration.

The whole system of Roman domestic manners, of civil and military government, is contained in this work. The facts are either collected from the best antiquarians, or artfully deduced from what is known, or invented with a boldness more easy to admire than to imitate. Pure fiction is never employed but when truth was unattainable.

The end designed by Walstein, is no less happily accomplished in the second, than in the first performance. The style and spirit of the narrative is similar; the same skill in the exhibition of characters and deduction of events, is apparent; but events and characters are wholly new. Portugal, its timorous populace, its besotted monks, its

---

[3] "Astura . . . Atticus": for all of these allusions to details concerning Cicero's political execution in 43 B.C.E., see Brown's "Death of Cicero" in Related Texts.

[4] "Conspiracy of Cataline . . . Sallust": Sallust (86–34 B.C.E.) is a Roman historian, along with Cicero the best-known source for information on a conspiracy in 64–62, led by Catiline Lucius Sergius Catalina, 108–62 B.C.E.), to overthrow the Roman government. Cicero was Catiline's greatest political opponent, and his Cataline orations (63 B.C.E.) present the conspirator as the embodiment of the vices that were weakening the Roman Republic.

jealous and effeminate nobles, and its cowardly prince, are vividly depicted. The narrator of this tale is, as in the former instance, the subject of it. After his retreat from court, Pombal consecrates his leisure to the composition of his own memoirs.

Among the most curious portions of this work, are those relating to the constitution of the inquisition, the expulsion of the Jesuits, the earthquake, and the conspiracy of Daveiro.[5]

The Romish religion, and the feudal institutions, are the causes that chiefly influence the modern state of Europe. Each of its kingdoms and provinces exhibits the operations of these causes, accompanied and modified by circumstances peculiar to each. Their genuine influence is thwarted, in different degrees, by learning and commerce. In Portugal, they have been suffered to produce the most extensive and unmingled mischiefs. Portugal, therefore, was properly selected as an example of moral and political degeneracy, and as a theatre in which virtue might be shewn with most advantage, contending with the evils of misgovernment and superstition.

In works of this kind, though the writer is actuated by a single purpose, many momentous and indirect inferences will flow from his story. Perhaps the highest and lowest degrees in the scale of political improvement have been respectively exemplified by the Romans and the Portuguese. The pictures that are here drawn, may be considered as portraits of the human species, in two of the most remarkable forms.

There are two ways in which genius and virtue may labour for the public good: first by assailing popular errors and vices, argumentatively and through the medium of books; secondly, by employing legal or ministerial authority to this end.

---

[5] "Inquisition . . . Jesuits . . . earthquake. . . Daveiro": allusions to the primary struggles of Pombal's administration. Pombal is generally known as an enlightened reformer who was hated by the older nobility as the son of a country squire. Throughout his administration he fought to wrest political power from the Catholic Church and its Inquisition, which had played a dominant role in Portuguese and Iberian affairs for two hundred years and was synonymous with superstition and tyranny. Pombal's struggles against the Jesuits, the Catholic order founded by Xavier (see note 1), led to their expulsion from Portugal and Portuguese colonies in 1767. The Great Lisbon Earthquake of 1755 amplified political tensions in Portugal, posed major problems for Portuguese colonialism, and became an Enlightenment cause célèbre in debunking myths about a benevolent deity, for example in Voltaire's widely read "Poem on the Lisbon Disaster " (1755) and his parable of enlightened education in *Candide* (1759).

The conspiracy of D'Aveiro refers to the Távora Affair, a political scandal that enveloped the Portuguese court following the earthquake. After the earthquake demolished the Royal Palace, King Joseph I and his court, including Pombal, were installed in a tent city outside Lisbon. After a failed assassination attempt there on the King in September 1758, Pombal's investigation revealed that the noble Távora family, who were plotting to make the Duke d'Aveiro king and diminish Pombal's power, had hired the assassins. D'Aveiro and the male Távoras were executed; the Jesuits were also implicated and publicly denounced as conspirators in the assassination plot, one of the key findings that led to their expulsion from Portuguese territories a few years later. Historians commonly understand the affair as an incident that Pombal used to diminish the authority of old aristocratic families and their allies in the church.

The last was the province which Cicero and Pombal assumed. Their fate may evince the insufficiency of the instrument chosen by them, and teach us, that a change of national opinion is the necessary prerequisite of revolutions.

———————

Engel, the eldest of Walstein's pupils, thought, like his master, that the narration of public events, with a certain license of invention, was the most efficacious of moral instruments. Abstract systems, and theoretical reasonings, were not without their use, but they claimed more attention than many were willing to bestow. Their influence, therefore, was limited to a narrow sphere. A mode by which truth could be conveyed to a great number, was much to be preferred.

Systems, by being imperfectly attended to, are liable to beget error and depravity. Truth flows from the union and relation of many parts. These parts, fallaciously connected and viewed separately, constitute error. Prejudice, stupidity, and indolence, will seldom afford us a candid audience, are prone to stop short in their researches, to remit, or transfer to other objects their attention, and hence to derive new motives to injustice, and new confirmations in folly from that which, if impartially and accurately examined, would convey nothing but benefit.

Mere reasoning is cold and unattractive. Injury rather than benefit proceeds from convictions that are transient and faint; their tendency is not to reform and enlighten, but merely to produce disquiet and remorse. They are not strong enough to resist temptation and to change the conduct, but merely to pester the offender with dissatisfaction and regret.

The detail of actions is productive of different effects. The affections are engaged, the reason is won by incessant attacks; the benefits which our system has evinced to be possible, are invested with a seeming existence; and the evils which error was proved to generate, exchange the fleeting, misty, and dubious form of inference, for a sensible and present existence.

To exhibit, in an eloquent narration, a model of right conduct, is the highest province of benevolence. Our patterns, however, may be useful in different degrees. Duties are the growth of situations. The general and the statesman have arduous duties to perform; and, to teach them their duty, is of use: but the forms of human society allow few individuals to gain the station of generals and statesmen. The lesson, therefore, is reducible to practice by a small number; and, of these, the temptations to abuse their power are so numerous and powerful, that a very small part, and these, in a very small degree, can be expected to comprehend, admire, and copy the pattern that is set before them.

But though few may be expected to be monarchs and ministers, every man occupies a station in society in which he is necessarily active to evil or to good. There is a sphere of some dimensions, in which the influence of his actions and opinions is felt. The causes that fashion men into instruments of happiness or misery, are numerous, complex, and operate upon a wide surface. Virtuous activity may, in a thousand ways, be thwarted and diverted by foreign and superior influence. It may seem best to purify the fountain, rather than filter the stream; but the latter is, to a certain degree, within our power, whereas, the former is impracticable. Governments and general education, cannot be rectified, but individuals may be somewhat fortified against their influence. Right intentions may be instilled into them, and some good may be done by each within his social and domestic province.

The relations in which men, unendowed with political authority, stand to each other, are numerous. An extensive source of these relations, is property. No topic can engage the attention of man more momentous than this. Opinions, relative to property, are the immediate source of nearly all the happiness and misery that exist among mankind. If men were guided by justice in the acquisition and disbursement, the brood of private and public evils would be extinguished.

To ascertain the precepts of justice, and exhibit these precepts reduced to practice, was, therefore, the favorite task of Engel. This, however, did not constitute his whole scheme. Every man is encompassed by numerous claims, and is the subject of intricate relations. Many of these may be comprised in a copious narrative, without infraction of simplicity or detriment to unity.

Next to property, the most extensive source of our relations is sex. On the circumstances which produce, and the principles which regulate the union between the sexes, happiness greatly depends. The conduct to be pursued by a virtuous man in those situations which arise from sex, it was thought useful to display.

Fictitious history has, hitherto, chiefly related to the topics of love and marriage. A monotony and sentimental softness have hence arisen that have frequently excited contempt and ridicule. The ridicule, in general, is merited; not because these topics are intrinsically worthless or vulgar, but because the historian was deficient in knowledge and skill.

Marriage is incident to all; its influence on our happiness and dignity, is more entire and lasting than any other incident can possess. None, therefore, is more entitled to discussion. To enable men to evade the evils and secure the benefits of this state, is to consult, in an eminent degree, their happiness.

A man, whose activity is neither aided by political authority nor by the *press,* may yet exercise considerable influence on the condition of his neighbours, by the exercise of intellectual powers. His courage may be useful to the timid or the feeble, and his knowledge to the ignorant, as well as his property to those who want. His benevolence and justice may not only protect his kindred and his wife, but rescue the victims of prejudice and passion from the yoke of those domestic tyrants, and shield the powerless from the oppression of power, the poor from the injustice of the rich, and the simple from the stratagems of cunning.

Almost all men are busy in acquiring subsistence or wealth by a fixed application of their time and attention. Manual or mental skill is obtained and exerted for this end. This application, within certain limits, is our duty. We are bound to chuse that species of industry which combines most profit to ourselves with the least injury to others; to select that instrument which, by most speedily supplying our necessities, leaves us at most leisure to act from the impulse of benevolence.

A profession, successfully pursued, confers power not merely by conferring property and leisure. The skill which is gained, and which, partly or for a time, may be exerted to procure subsistence, may, when this end is accomplished, continue to be exerted for the common good. The pursuits of law and medicine, enhance our power over the liberty, property, and health of mankind. They not only qualify us for imparting benefit, by supplying us with property and leisure, but by enabling us to obviate, by intellectual exertions, many of the evils that infest the world.

Engel endeavored to apply these principles to the choice of a profession, and to point out the mode in which professional skill, after it has supplied us with the means of subsistence, may be best exerted in the cause of general happiness.

Human affairs are infinitely complicated. The condition of no two beings is alike. No model can be conceived, to which our situation enables us to conform. No situation can be imagined perfectly similar to that of an actual being. This exact similitude is not required to render an imaginary portrait useful to those who survey it. The usefulness, undoubtedly, consists in suggesting a mode of reasoning and acting somewhat similar to that which is ascribed to a feigned person; and, for this end, some similitude is requisite between the real and imaginary situation; but that similitude is not hard to produce. Among the incidents which invention will set before us, those are to be culled out which afford most scope to wisdom and virtue, which are most analogous to facts, which most forcibly suggest to the reader the parallel between his state and that described, and most strongly excite his desire to act as the feigned personages act. These incidents must be so arranged as to inspire, at once, curiosity and belief, to fasten the attention, and thrill the heart. This scheme was executed in the life of "Olivo Ronsica."

Engel's principles inevitably led him to select, as the scene and period of his narrative, that in which those who should read it, should exist. Every day removed the reader farther from the period, but its immediate readers would perpetually recognize the objects, and persons, and events, with which they were familiar.

Olivo is a rustic youth, whom domestic equality, personal independence, agricultural occupations, and studious habits, had endowed with a strong mind, pure taste, and unaffected integrity. Domestic revolutions oblige him to leave his father's house in search of subsistence. He is destitute of property, of friends, and of knowledge of the world. These are to be acquired by his own exertions, and virtue and sagacity are to guide him in the choice and the use of suitable means.

Ignorance subjects us to temptation, and poverty shackles our beneficence. Olivo's conduct shews us how temptation may be baffled, in spite of ignorance, and benefits be conferred in spite of poverty.

He bends his way to Weimar. He is involved, by the artifices of others, and, in consequence of his ignorance of mankind, in many perils and perplexities. He forms a connection with a man of a great and mixed, but, on the whole, a vicious character. Semlits is introduced to furnish a contrast to the simplicity and rectitude of Olivo, to exemplify the misery of sensuality and fraud, and the influence which, in the present system of society, vice possesses over the reputation and external fortune of the good.

Men hold external goods, the pleasures of the senses, of health, liberty, reputation, competence, friendship, and life, partly by virtue of their own wisdom and activity.

This, however, is not the only source of their possession. It is likewise dependent on physical accidents, which human foresight cannot anticipate, or human power prevent. It is also influenced by the conduct and opinions of others.

There is no external good, of which the errors and wickedness of others may not deprive us. So far as happiness depends upon the retention of these goods, it is held at the option of another. The perfection of our character is evinced by the transient or slight influence which privations and evils have upon our happiness, on the skillfulness of those exertions which we make to avoid or repair disasters, on the diligence and success with which we improve those instruments of pleasure to ourselves and to others which fortune has left in our possession.

Richardson has exhibited in Clarissa,[6] a being of uncommon virtue, bereaved of many external benefits by the vices of others. Her parents and lover conspire to destroy her fortune, liberty, reputation, and personal sanctity.

More talents and address cannot be easily conceived, than those which are displayed by her to preserve and to regain these goods. Her efforts are vain. The cunning and malignity with which she had to contend, triumphed in the contest.

Those evils and privations she was unable to endure. The loss of fame took away all activity and happiness, and she died a victim to errors, scarcely less opprobrious and pernicious, than those of her tyrants and oppressors. She misapprehended the value of parental approbation and a fair fame. She depreciated the means of usefulness and pleasure of which fortune was unable to deprive her.

Olivo is a different personage. His talents are exerted to reform the vices of others, to defeat their malice when exerted to his injury, to endure, without diminution of his usefulness or happiness, the injuries which he cannot shun.

Semlits is led, by successive accidents, to unfold his story to Olivo, after which, they separate. Semlits is supposed to destroy himself, and Olivo returns into the country.

A pestilential disease, prevalent throughout the north of Europe, at that time (1630), appears in the city. To ascertain the fate of one connected, by the ties of kindred and love, with the family in which Olivo resides, and whose life is endangered by residence in the city, he repairs thither, encounters the utmost perils, is seized with the reigning malady, meets, in extraordinary circumstances, with Semlits, and is finally received into the house of a physician, by whose skill he is restored to health, and to whom he relates his previous adventures.

---

[6] "Richardson . . . Clarissa": novelist Samuel Richardson (1689–1761) and his best-known work, *Clarissa; or, the History of a Young Lady* (1748), one of the most significant English-language novels of the eighteenth century. This multivolume epistolary novel was a landmark presentation of new models of selfhood and virtue, and inaugurated a new subgenre of "seduction" narratives that explored women's lives for decades to come, for example in the popular best-sellers of the early American Republic. Brown's comments here suggest that Richardson placed too much emphasis on psychologized, inner standards of "virtue" that fetishize traditional categories such as piety and sexual chastity, for example, and not enough emphasis on the modernizing social empowerment of women in the public sphere.

He resolves to become a physician, but is prompted by benevolence to return, for a time, to the farm which he had lately left. The series of ensuing events, are long, intricate, and congruous, and exhibit the hero of the tale in circumstances that task his fortitude, his courage, and his disinterestedness.

Engel has certainly succeeded in producing a tale, in which are powerful displays of fortitude and magnanimity; a work whose influence must be endlessly varied by varieties of character and situation of the reader, but, from which, it is not possible for any one to rise without some degree of moral benefit, and much of that pleasure which always attends the emotions of curiosity and sympathy.

2. Charles Brockden Brown, "The Difference Between History and Romance." *The Monthly Magazine and American Review* 2:4 (April 1800)

Together with "Walstein's School of History," and appearing just a few months after it, this essay outlines the basic interrelation of history and fiction writing that Brown assumes in his novels and later historical writings, and helps explain how the novels are intended to educate readers and move them to greater awareness of their social surroundings. Likening the social relations investigated by historians and romancers to the material relations studied by key early modern scientists such as Isaac Newton (mathematician and physicist who first outlined the theory of gravity), Carl Linnaeus (founder of modern biological taxonomy and ecology), or William Herschel (astronomer who discovered infrared radiation and pioneered advanced telescope technologies such as interferometry), Brown argues that novelists and historians alike are, or should be, social scientists who use narrative to explore their social order and its history, and to educate their readers about it.

The essay rejects the common notion that history and fiction are different because one deals with factual and the other with fictional materials. Rather, Brown argues, history and fiction are best understood as two sides of one coin: history describes and documents the results of actions, while fiction investigates the possible conditions and motives that cause these actions. Whereas the historian establishes facts about events and behaviors, the "romancer" is more concerned with asking why and how the events and behaviors took place. Thus the writing of romance (Brown's kind of novel) deals in conjecture about the causes and consequences of social actions and events. This imaginative conjecture is useful because it helps clarify the ways in which seemingly unique or personal events and acts (such as the crisis of the Wieland family) are actually conditioned, although not narrowly determined, by larger social forces.

The difference between history as documentation and romance as interpretation also allows Brown to develop an implicit distinction between "romance" and "novel." Brown's definition here situates romance as the kind of narrative that educates readers and helps them grasp the social processes in which they are embedded. Unlike the nineteenth century's contrast between realism and romance, where romance allows the imaginative flight of fancy from the mundane world (this is the way romance is understood in Nathaniel Hawthorne's prefaces of the 1850s, for example), Brown situates the "novel" as a fiction that seeks to amuse a passive reader, and "romance" as a fiction that seeks to train the reader as an active interpreter and interrogator of society. When Brown writes in this novel's "Preface" that his fiction dramatizes a social crisis and responses to it "in the spirit of salutary emulation," he is therefore indicating that he has designed the work as a romance, not a novel.

Most basically, then, Brown's ideas about "the difference between history and romance" imply that Clara Wieland's or Frank Carwin's tales should be read as part of an exploration of the causes of contemporary events and behaviors, rather than simply as "terrific" tales of sensational wonder (see the excerpt from "Terrific Novels" for Brown's definition of that variety of narrative).

*****

History and romance are terms that have never been very clearly distinguished from each other. It should seem that one dealt in fiction, and the other in truth; that one is a picture of the *probable* and certain, and the other a tissue of untruths; that one describes what *might* have happened, and what has *actually* happened, and the other what never had existence.

These distinctions seem to be just; but we shall find ourselves somewhat perplexed, when we attempt to reduce them to practice, and to ascertain, by their assistance, to what class this or that performance belongs.

Narratives, whether fictitious or true, may relate to the processes of nature, or the actions of men. The former, if not impenetrable by human faculties, must be acknowledged to be, hitherto, very imperfectly known. Curiosity is not satisfied with viewing facts in their disconnected state and natural order, but is prone to arrange them anew, and to deviate from present and sensible objects, into speculations on the past or future; it is eager to infer from the present state of things, their former or future condition.

The observer or experimentalist, therefore, who carefully watches, and faithfully enumerates the appearances which occur, may claim the appellation of historian. He who adorns these appearances with cause and effect, and traces resemblances between the past, distant, and future, with the present, performs a different part. He is a dealer, not in certainties, but probabilities, and is therefore a romancer.

An historian will relate the noises, the sights, and the smells that attend an eruption of Vesuvius. A romancer will describe, in the first place, the *contemporary* ebullitions and inflations, the combustion and decomposition that take place in the bowels of the earth. Next he will go to the origin of things, and describe the centrical, primary, and secondary orbs composing the universe, as masses thrown out of an immense volcano called *chaos.* Thirdly, he will paint the universal dissolution that is hereafter to be produced by the influence of volcanic or internal fire.

An historian will form catalogues of stars, and mark their positions at given times. A romancer will arrange them in *clusters* and dispose them in *strata,* and inform you by what influences the orbs have been drawn into sociable knots and circles.

An electrical historian will describe appearances that happen when hollow cylinders of glass and metal are placed near each other, and the former is rubbed with a cloth. The romancer will replenish the space that exists between the sun and its train of planetary orbs, with a fluid called electrical; and describe the modes in which this fluid finds its way to the surface of these orbs through the intervenient atmosphere.

Historians can only differ in degrees of diligence and accuracy, but romancers may have more or less probability in their narrations. The same man is frequently both historian and romancer in the compass of the same work. Buffon,[1] Linneus, and Herschel, are examples of this union. Their observations are as diligent as their theories are adventurous. Among the historians of nature, Haller[2] was, perhaps, the most diligent: among romancers, he that came nearest to the truth was Newton.

It must not be denied that, though history be a term commonly applied to a catalogue of natural appearances, as well as to the recital of human actions, romance is chiefly limited to the latter. Some reluctance may be felt in calling Buffon and Herschel romancers, but that name will be readily conferred on Quintus Curtius and Sir Thomas More.[3] There is a sufficient analogy, however, between objects and modes, in the physical and intellectual world, to justify the use of these distinctions in both cases.

Physical objects and appearances sometimes fall directly beneath our observation, and may be truly described. The duty of the *natural* historian is limited to this description. *Human* actions may likewise be observed, and be truly described. In this respect, the actions of *voluntary* and *involuntary* agents, are alike, but in other momentous respects they differ.

Curiosity is not content with noting and recording the *actions* of men. It likewise seeks to know the *motives* by which the agent is impelled to the performance of these actions; but motives are modifications of thought which cannot be subjected to the senses. They cannot be certainly known. They are merely topics of conjecture. Conjecture is the weighing of probabilities; the classification of probable events, according to the measure of probability possessed by each.

Actions of different men, or performed at different times, may be alike; but the motives leading to these actions must necessarily vary. In guessing at these motives, the knowing and sagacious will, of course, approach nearer to the truth than the ignorant and stupid; but the wise and the ignorant, the sagacious and stupid, when busy in assigning motives to actions, are not *historians* but *romancers*.

---

[1] "Buffon": Georges-Louis Leclerc, Compte de Buffon (1707–1788), French biologist and writer whose work on natural history was an important precedent for Darwin's theory of natural selection. Buffon is best know in a U.S. context as one of the scientists addressed in Thomas Jefferson's *Notes on the State of Virginia* (first published in Paris, 1784).

[2] "Haller": Albrecht von Haller (1708–1777), Swiss physiologist and botanist, and a leading contributor to both fields during the Enlightenment. He was notable for the immense number of his scientific publications, hence the "diligent" reputation to which Brown refers.

[3] "Quintus Curtius . . . More": two writers of more hypothetical works that may be contrasted with the scientific work of the previously mentioned figures. Quintus Curtius Rufus was a Roman historian of the first century B.C.E.; his only surviving work is two books of a history of Alexander the Great that are notable for speculating about unknowable aspects of Alexander's character. Thomas More (1478–1535) is the English statesman best known for writing the political allegory *Utopia* (1516), a work referenced as a "political romance" in Part 9 of *Memoirs of Carwin*.

The motive is the cause, and therefore the antecedent of the action; but the action is likewise the cause of subsequent actions. Two contemporary and (so to speak) adjacent actions may both be faithfully described, because both may be witnessed; but the connection between them, that quality which constitutes one the effect of the other, is mere matter of conjecture, and comes with the province, not of *history*, but *romance*.

The description of human actions is of moment merely as they are connected with motives and tendencies. The delineation of tendencies and motives implies a description of the action; but the action is describable without the accompanyment of tendencies and motives.

An action may be simply described, but such descriptions, though they alone be historical, are of no use as they stand singly and disjoined from tendencies and motives, in the page of the historian or the mind of the reader. The writer, therefore, who does not blend the two characters, is essentially defective. It is true, that facts simply described, may be connected and explained by the reader; and that the describer may, at least, claim the merit of supplying the builder with materials. The merit of him who drags stones together, must not be depreciated; but must not be compared with him who hews these stones into just proportions, and piles them up into convenient and magnificent fabrics.

That which is done beneath my own inspection, it is possible for me certainly to know and exactly to record; but that which is performed at a distance, either in time or place, is the theme of foreign testimony. If it be related by me, I relate not what I have witnessed, but what I derived from others who were witnesses. The subject of my senses is merely the existence of the record, and not the deed itself which is recorded. The truth of the action can be weighed in no scales but those of probability.

A voluntary action is not only connected with cause and effect, but is itself a series of motives and incidents subordinate and successive to each other. Every action differs from every other in the number and complexity of its parts, but the most simple and brief is capable of being analyzed into a thousand subdivisions. If it be witnessed by others, probabilities are lessened in proportion as the narrative is circumstantial.

These principles may be employed to illustrate the distinction between history and romance. If history relate what is true, its relations must be limited to what is known by the testimony of our senses. Its sphere, therefore, is extremely narrow. The facts to which we are immediate witnesses, are, indeed, numerous; but time and place merely connect them. Useful narratives must comprise facts linked together by some other circumstance. They must, commonly, consist of events, for a knowledge of which the narrator is indebted to the evidence of others. This evidence, though accompanied with different degrees of probability, can never give birth to certainty. How wide, then, if romance be the narrative of mere probabilities, is the empire of romance? This empire is absolute and undivided over the motives and tendencies of human actions. Over actions themselves, its dominion, though not unlimited, is yet very extensive.

X.

3. Two Statements on the Modern Novel

a) Charles Brockden Brown, "Romances." *The Literary Magazine and American Register* 3:16 (January 1805)

In this article on "romances," which in this case means the novel-like narratives that flourished from the Middle Ages to the 1600s, Brown reiterates the need for contemporary forms of art to focus on themes that are relevant for contemporary audiences. Works of the past may have been tremendous achievements, but their usefulness for the modern reader is limited because new historical conditions demand new ideas and modes of behavior. Brown's argument here suggests that there is no unchanging or eternal, transhistorical standard for values, ideas, or behaviors. The lessons of one age may not be useful for another. Like his contemporaries William Godwin and Thomas Paine, Brown remains skeptical about worshipping past forms of art, society, and government.

*****

A tale, agreeable to truth and nature or, more properly speaking, agreeable to *our own* conceptions of truth and nature, may be long, but cannot be tedious. Cleopatra and Cassandra by no means referred to an ideal world; they referred to the manners and habits of the age in which they were written; names and general incidents only were taken from the age of Alexander and Caesar. In that age, therefore, they were not tedious, but the more delighted was the reader the longer the banquet was protracted. In after times, when taste and manners were changed, the tale became tedious, because it was deemed unnatural and absurd, and it would have been condemned as tedious, and treated with neglect, whether it filled ten pages or ten volumes.

Cleopatra and Cassandra are no greater violations of historical veracity and probability, and no more drawn from an ideal world, than Johnson's Rasselas, Hawkesworth's Almoran and Hamet, or Fenelon's Telemachus.[1] In all these, names and incidents, and some machinery, are taken from a remote age and nation, but the manners and sentiments are modeled upon those of the age in which the works were written, as those of the Scuderis[2] were fashioned upon the habits of their own age. The present unpopularity of the romances of the fifteenth and sixteenth centuries is not owing to

---

[1] "Rasselas . . . Almoran and Hamet . . . Telemachus": popular adventure tales of the eighteenth century: Samuel Johnson, *The History of Rasselas* (1759); John Hawkesworth, *Almoran and Hamet* (1761); and François Fenelon's *The Adventures of Telemachus, Son of Ulysses* (1699). Hawkesworth was Samuel Johnson's successor at the London *Gentlemen's Magazine* and was also well known as editor of James Cook's account of his South Sea voyages (1773), noted in *Memoirs of Carwin*.

[2] "Scuderis": Georges (1601–1667) and Madeleine (1607–1701) de Scudéry, a brother and sister who were popular romancers throughout seventeenth-century Europe. Madeleine was considered the better of the two writers, and the lengthy, baroque narratives that she produced from the 1640s to the 1670s were widely influential, parodied, and taken as models for traditional "romance" writing well into the next century. Her romance *Clelia*, which appeared in ten volumes, 1648–1651, figures as a significant reference in Brown's novel *Stephen Calvert* (1799–1800).

the satires of Cervantes or of Boileau,[3] but to the gradual revolution of human manners and national taste.

The "*Arabian Nights*" delight us in childhood, and so do the chivalrous romances; but, in riper age, if enlightened by education, we despise what we formerly revered. Individuals, whose minds have been uncultivated, continue still their attachment to those marvelous stories. And yet, must it not be ascribed rather to change of manners than to any other cause, that we neglect and disrelish works which give infinite delight to sir Philip Sidney, sir Walter Raleigh, and sir Thomas More,[4] to Sully and Daubigne:[5] men whose knowledge of Augustan models, and delight in them, was never exceeded, and the general vigor and capacity of whose minds has never been surpassed.

The works that suited former ages are now exploded by us. The works that are now produced, and which accommodate themselves to our habits and taste, would have been utterly neglected by our ancestors: and what is there to hinder the belief, that they, in their turn, will fall into oblivion and contempt at some future time. We naturally conceive our own habits and opinions the standard of rectitude; but their rectitude, admitting our claim to be just, will not hinder them from giving way to others, and being exploded in their turn.

b) Charles Brockden Brown, excerpt from "Terrific Novels." *The Literary Magazine and American Register* 3:19 (April 1805)

This passage illustrates Brown's criticism of conventional gothic style and helps explain, by contrast, how his own use of the gothic is oriented toward the representation of modern life. Today the term "gothic" generally describes narratives that use the supernatural to excite fear and suspense in their audience. But in this essay, Brown judges such narratives by their motivation rather than by their form, themes, or effect on their audience. Brown calls novels that use sensational devices of mystery simply to create suspense "terrific" ones

---

[3] "Cervantes . . . Boileau": Miguel de Cervantes (1547–1616), whose modernizing novel *Don Quixote* (1605) includes a humorous polemic against earlier "romance" styles; and Nicolas Boileau-Despréaux (1636–1711), who struggled to reform verse styles in seventeenth-century France.

[4] "Sidney . . . Raleigh . . . More": three staples of sixteenth-century English letters and court culture (all knighted by British monarchs): Sidney was author of *Astrophel and Stella* and "A Defence of Poesie" in the 1580s; Raleigh, primarily known as a colonial adventurer, also wrote important poetry in the 1570s and 1580s; More's best-known work is *Utopia* (1516), which Brown references in *Memoirs of Carwin* and "The Difference Between History and Romance," both included in Related Texts.

[5] "Sully and Daubigne": Maximilien de Béthune, duc de Sully (1560–1641), a finance minister to king Henry IV of France, who published widely read memoirs (1662) and religious-utopian tracts (1638); and Théodore-Agrippa d'Aubigné (1552–1630), another political figure at the court of Henry IV who published widely read histories and tragedies in the 1610s and 1620s. Both were Huguenots whose political and literary careers were entwined with the Reformation-era Catholic-Protestant struggles in France. Brown's point in identifying this series of names is primarily that these are all elite-courtly writers. All of these names represent a pre-Enlightenment world of monarchical cultural production that is out of keeping with the needs and purposes of more modern readers in the Revolutionary age.

because they are intended to generate sensations of terror, rather than a sense of excel-lence. In keeping with his general emphasis on the development of modern forms suited to modern social conditions, Brown criticizes conventional gothic's emphasis on premodern superstitions rather than the anxieties and stresses of contemporary life. As opposed to castles, monks, and superstitions, Brown's version of the gothic, in Wieland *and his other novels, highlights scenarios and themes that his readers might actually experience: mental illness or psychological symptoms in conditions of extreme anxiety and stress such as the threat of rape, somnambulism, bankruptcy, impoverishment; vulnerability to illnesses like yellow fever; and so on.*

*****

The Castle of Otranto laid the foundation of a style of novel writing, which was carried to perfection by Mrs. Radcliff,[6] and which may be called the *terrific style.* The great talents of Mrs. Radcliff made some atonement for the folly of this mode of composition, and gave some importance to exploded fables and childish fears, by the charms of sentiment and description; but the multitude of her imitators seem to have thought that description and sentiment were impertinent intruders, and by lowering the mind somewhat to its ordinary state, marred and counteracted those awful feelings, which true genius was properly employed in raising. They endeavor to keep the reader in a constant state of tumult and horror, by the powerful engines of trap-doors, back stairs, black robes, and pale faces: but the solution of the enigma is ever too near at hand, to permit the indulgence of supernatural appearances. A well-written scene of a party at snap-dragon would exceed all the fearful images of these books. There is, besides, no *keeping* in the author's design: fright succeeds to fright, and danger to danger, without permitting the unhappy reader to draw his breath, or to repose for a moment on subjects of character or sentiment.

4. Three Texts on Cicero

a) Charles Brockden Brown, "On the Merits of Cicero." *The Literary Magazine and American Register* 3:20 (May 1805)

The writings of Marcus Tullius Cicero (106–43 B.C.E.) are among the most studied and canonized texts in European cultural history. Cicero was a Roman orator, writer, and statesman well known for his central role in political struggles over the status of the Roman Republic during Julius Caesar's dictatorship and in the civil wars leading to the Republic's end. His name is synonymous with the classical tradition in rhetoric and, in many accounts, his political execution in 43 B.C.E. stands as the end date of the Republic

---

[6] "Otranto . . . Mrs. Radcliff": Horace Walpole's *The Castle of Otranto* (1764), generally understood as the novel that inaugurates the gothic genre; and Ann Radcliffe (1764–1823), the preeminent author of gothic romances during the 1790s. Her best-known titles are *The Mystery of Udolpho* (1794) and *The Italian* (1796).

and the beginning of the Roman Empire. Cicero's writings were an important cal point in elite eighteenth-century education (when rhetoric was still an essential part of training for political leadership) and debates about Cicero's character functioned as coded political arguments throughout the period. By having Theodore Wieland idealize Cicero in Chapters 3–4 of his novel, installing a bust of Cicero on a pedestal in the temple formerly used for Protestant worship by his father, Brown uses recent writing on Cicero as a way to locate the Wieland family, and Theodore in particular, in terms of the period's politically coded responses to the classical tradition.

These debates generally contrast "Tory" or elite-conservative idealizations of Cicero as a model of patrician virtue, with dissenting positions that discredit Cicero by emphasizing his selfish desire for celebrity, for example, rather than a virtuous concern for the collective public good. These attacks are intended to debunk nostalgic myths of ancient Roman virtue that were generated in the eighteenth century to justify the political ideology of elite Republicanism, which highlights the importance of rule by leisured, "gentlemen" whose wealth makes them ostensibly "free" from being influenced by economic concerns in their political decision making. In these dissenting versions of Cicero's life, it is not a single man, such as the tyrannical or absolutist Caesar, who destroys the Republic (a scenario in which Cicero appears as a heroic patriot), but the combined failings of the patrician leadership class that undermine an earlier and more just balance of power (a scenario that emphasizes Cicero's personal shortcomings as representative of his class). After Cambridge don Conyers Middleton published his idealizing account, The History of the Life of Marcus Tullius Cicero *(1741), a new wave of critical studies appeared to challenge and rebut him. Colley Cibber's* The Character and Conduct of Cicero, Considered *(1747) and critical annotated translations by scholars such as William Guthrie and William Melmoth, for example (all republished through the rest of the century),[1] recognize Cicero's accomplishments while also strategically deploring his shortcomings and many vices, especially his oft-noted vanity and love of fame. These debates continue into the Revolutionary era in writers and works familiar to Brown, such as Adam Ferguson's* The History of the Progress and Termination of the Roman Republic *(1783), which adopts the critical position.*

During the 1790s in the U.S., these debates were adapted and transformed into a contrast between conservative, Federalist and Augustan idealizations of Cicero, and new versions, such as the Brown texts included here, of the dissenting accounts that had developed throughout the century. John Adams, for example, president of the U.S. and leader of the Federalist party when Wieland *appeared in 1798, famously idealized Cicero as the highest example of civic and patrician values.[2] Brown, on the other hand, like Franklin before him, maintains a modernizing position that discourages excessive or*

---

[1] Guthrie's *Cicero's Epistles to Atticus, with Notes, Historical, Explanatory, and Critical, Translated by William Guthrie, Esq. In Two Volumes* (London: T. Waller, 1752); and William Melmoth, *The Letters of Marcus Tullius Cicero to Several of his Friends: With Remarks. In Three Volumes* (London: J. Dodsley, 1753).

[2] For more on these Cicero debates, see Ward "The Tory View of Roman History"; Farrell, "John Adams' Autobiography: The Ciceronian Paradigm and the Quest for Fame"; and Smith, "Elizabeth Montagu's Study of Cicero's Life."

nostalgic idealization of the classical tradition in political thinking and education.³ In the American context, these Cicero debates act as an allegorical surrogate for arguments over which social group(s) have the most legitimacy to assume authority over the early American republic: the close-knit elite families who were already established as a quasi-aristocracy by the 1770s or the more heterogeneous ensembles of mercantile and artisan groups emerging as a political force in the century's last decades.

In the antithetically titled "On the Merits of Cicero," Brown rehearses the kinds of dissenting complaints about Cicero developed earlier in the century, and sets them in an intentionally deidealizing, unclassical setting, as the narrator muses on Cicero's demerits and deficiencies over his breakfast coffee. Brown's narrator has just read passages from "On Bearing Pain," the second of Cicero's "Tusculan Disputations," and finds a great deal to criticize, especially since he has a toothache. Contrasted with even the modest struggles of everyday life, the narrator finds Cicero's philosophizing in that text irritatingly inconsequential and, even in rhetorical terms, full of unpersuasive, contradictory, and useless arguments. The narrator confesses that his comments may seem "severe," but goes on to present even more extensive, ad hominem *criticisms, agreeing with earlier critics such as Cibber and Guthrie, that the orator was ruled by vanity, and compares badly with his friend Atticus, who is often cited in the dissenting tradition as a foil to Cicero's shortcomings.⁴*

*****

For the Literary Magazine.

ON THE MERITS OF CICERO.

I HAVE contrived to read the greater part of the works of Cicero through, merely by taking up the volume, at any odd, unoccupied moment, during the intervals, for instance, between my two dishes of coffee, or three pieces of bread, at breakfast. This morning I opened at the second Tusculan, and being somewhat in a sulky mood, by reason of some little domestic inconvenience not worth relating, I failed to discover all that wisdom and eloquence, of which I usually find a rich repast in these volumes. On the contrary, I really conceived a notion, from this dialogue, that Cicero, however great in other respects, was, upon the whole, both in theory and practice, but a poor *philosopher.*

---

³ See, for example, "Substitutes for Classical Education" (*Monthly Magazine*, March 1798) and a number of related arguments from 1805, published and likely written by Brown in his *Literary Magazine*, such as "Classical Learning" (April 1805); "The Women of the Romans" (May 1805); and "Classical Learning No Anti-Christian Tendency" (September 1805).

⁴ In keeping with this tradition of critical Cicero reception, Brown published a companion piece, not included here, that praises Atticus (as an implicit foil to Cicero) for avoiding party entanglements: "The Character of Atticus" *Literary Magazine* (May 1806), 332–33. In the classical tradition, Atticus is usually portrayed not as a patriot or political hero, but as an Epicurean who stands apart from political affairs.

It was, indeed, somewhat unlucky that I just now lighted on this dialogue, which attempts to prove, *that pain is no evil*, for I had, at that moment, just escaped from the twinges of a tooth-ache, from which I had reason to expect but a short respite, and which would effectually mar the pleasures of a scheme to which I had intended to devote the ensuing day.

The orator appears to me to begin with a pompous maxim, which he cannot support, and has not the candour to resign. In endeavouring to maintain it, he falls into pitiful evasions, substitutes brilliancy of expression for solidity of argument, and, in fact, deserts the ground on which he had first set out.

This dialogue is, indeed, a complete chaos; a confused collection of assertions, not merely without proof, but absolutely contradictory to each other; a useless detail of all the philosophical opinions then known; a compilation of stories, either real or fictitious, whence no consequence can be inferred, because we are in the dark with respect to the point from which the speaker sets out, as well as that to which he intends to conduct us; and a series of repetitions, which all the eloquence of *Cicero* cannot prevent from being tedious. In short, there is in it a total want of order, which is unavoidable where an author neither defines his terms, divides his subject, nor arranges his ideas.

All this is certainly very severe; but it must be acknowledged to be just, if he seriously meant to maintain the extravagant opinion, *that pain is no evil*. It has, however, been imagined, by some, that this intention was only to expose to contempt the pompous maxims and futile reasoning of some of the philosophers of his age. To me, I confess, this ridicule is not very obvious; but to his contemporaries, who knew the persons, and had attended the lessons of those to whom he alluded, it might be sufficiently apparent.

The vanity which Cicero betrays in quoting his own verses, and then making his auditor enquire whose they were, and in the immediate conviction which the latter is made to express, is very reprehensible. Vanity was a defect in the character of Cicero too prominent ever to be entirely concealed; the manner in which it here obtrudes itself may be ridiculous; but, in other parts of his writings, it appears in a very offensive point of view, and particularly in his letter to Lucceius, where he acknowledges that he writes what he was ashamed to speak; and plainly requests that historian to applaud his public conduct, even beyond what he might think it deserved, and to indulge his friendship, though at the expence of truth.

Vanity alone, in the degree in which it tyrannized over Cicero, and which overwhelmed him with so many fantastic miseries and mortifications, is sufficient to disprove his title to the name of a practical philosopher, or *wise man*. His lamentations on his banishment, and on the death of his daughter, with the strange means he proposed to consecrate her memory, and the exultations expressed on his recal, and in the review of his consulship, are equally unmanly and extravagant.

In truth, I am strongly inclined to think that, taking all circumstances into view, the wisest man of Cicero's time was Atticus. Atticus, it appears, was far from being void of patriotism and benevolence, but these passions led him to benefit his countrymen, his friends, and himself, by means far more efficacious than those adopted by the Ciceros and Brutuses of the age, and he appears to have been quite superior to the meretricious charms of power or popularity.

b) Charles Brockden Brown, "Ciceronians." *The Literary Magazine and American Register* 3:21 (June 1805)

Published one month after "On the Merits of Cicero," in the next issue of Brown's Literary Magazine, *"Ciceronians" moves from commentary on Cicero and his writings to more allegorical remarks on the way his works are received and used by those who overidealize him. The text begins by emphasizing Cicero's oft-cited vanity and goes on to develop the implicit argument that the meaning or value of literary monuments is not unchanging and determined according to ideal or absolute standards, but the product of real circumstances that change over historical time as texts are read in different settings and put to different uses. This claim about the varying utility of historical models for contemporary purposes was charted by Brown much earlier, as seen by the prior Related Texts. Cicero's works, he argues, have the particular status they hold for us partly because of the historical circumstances of their reception, for example the fact that most of the works of his peers have simply not survived, forcing greater attention on Cicero's works as some of the few that have. The latter part of the piece presents a criticism of present-day Cicero-worship at the end of the Revolutionary era with an invented parable about a brotherhood of "Ciceronians" who revere this "demon of eloquence" in a quasireligious manner; treasure his texts as sacred relics; and, like the character Theodore Wieland, institutionalize their idealization through the tools and practices of literary and textual scholarship. Closely related critical accounts of the quasireligious institutionalization of literary canons are developed in Brown's* Historical Sketches, *a historical fiction that he was writing in 1805–1806, simultaneously with "Ciceronians."*

****

For the Literary Magazine.

CICERONIANS.

THE ruling passion of Cicero was undoubtedly the love of fame. To this he was ready to sacrifice every other consideration. The images of future glory seem to have always occupied his fancy, and he wrote and spoke, doubtless, in some degree, for the sake of present and temporary purposes, but chiefly for the sake of a lasting reputation with posterity.

The order of sublunary things seems frequently adapted to disconcert and baffle human efforts and designs; but the fate of Cicero may, I think, be quoted as an exception to this rule, for no man has ever probably enjoyed, in a higher degree, the good of which he was so ambitious.

In the first place, the monuments of his genius have been preserved in a more entire and perfect state than those of almost any other ancient writer. Few writers have been more voluminous and versatile than he. He tried almost all the forms of composition: speeches, dialogues, essays, letters; and in every one of them numerous and extensive specimens of his powers still remain. He has been eminently fortunate in the nature

205

and relative value of what has escaped the ravages of time. Not only the largest, but likewise the most valuable, portions of his works are preserved. What is lost would, perhaps, have added nothing to the fame of his wisdom or eloquence.

Before the extinction of learning in the Roman empire, and long after the great change in its religion, Cicero continued to be regarded with an admiration next to idolatrous. The most eloquent of the Latin fathers drew their sentiments and doctrines from a very different source,[5] but, in all matters relative to language and rhetoric, Cicero was the master whom they served with the most superstitious fidelity.

After the revival of the Roman language, in modern times, Cicero's good fortune manifested itself not only in the preservation of so many of his own works, but likewise in the total destruction of the works of those who were his rivals while he lived. All the dialogists, letter writers, and orators of the same age have perished, and have thus enabled Cicero to monopolize all the fame which they might have otherwise shared with him.

It is difficult for us of the present times to conceive the degree of reverence which was paid by mankind, in the fourteenth, fifteenth, and sixteenth centuries, to the ancients in general, but more particularly to Cicero.

The votaries of Cicero were called Ciceronians, and formed a sort of fraternity, in which, strictly speaking, Cicero was a divinity, an object of worship.

They did not put up prayers to Cicero as to a saint or martyr.—They did not believe in his powers of protection or intercession. In this sense they were not his worshippers; but they deserved this name, inasmuch as they devoted all their studious and contemplative hours to his works; as they conceived all his opinions, moral, political, and critical, to be infallibly true, and his language to be the only medium through which a reasonable being ought to convey his thoughts.

They were, says an authentic historian, willing to deprive themselves of every pleasure, for his sake. They fled from the society of the living, as if they were themselves already dead; buried themselves in the grave of their study, and refrained from every kind of reading, except the works of Cicero, with as religious a care as Pythagoras abstained from the use of flesh. Their libraries were only diversified by the different editions of the works of Cicero. Their histories were only those of his life; and their epics only frigid narratives of his consulship; the painters and drawings in their galleries were only his portraits and actions. They had his head engraved on their seals, as well as on their hearts. By day and by night Cicero was the only object of their enquiries and conversations. They preferred the honour of collecting certain words, and arranging a round and nicely cadenced period, in his manner, to the performance of the most generous action. When, at length, their painful vigils had attenuated their bodies with illness, they died contented, since they had augmented the number of the martyrs of Cicero, and appeared in their last agony to be less pleased with the hope of the presence of God, than of meeting with this demon of eloquence.

---

[5] "Latin fathers . . . different source": in other words, the early Christian church "fathers," writing in Latin, who based their doctrines on Biblical sources. The "Church fathers" are the theologians and leaders of the early Christian church, especially in its first five centuries.

To retrieve a single sentence of his writing, whether it was only a *vale*, or a *mi amice*,[6] gave birth to the utmost exultation, and was celebrated with festivals and banquets. Many of them took the greatest delight in transcribing all his works with their own hand, and some happy memories thought the noblest achievement of human nature consisted in getting the whole of them by rote. In some instances, a kind of worship was paid to him; that is, a building was erected, in the temple fashion, in which a fraternity of classical devotees assembled, on stated days, when certain portions of his works were read, and voices and instruments joined in echoing his praise, in presence of his statue.

R.

c) Charles Brockden Brown, "Death of Cicero, A Fragment." From volume III of *Edgar Huntly; or, Memoirs of a Sleep-Walker*, second printing, c. January 1800

Cicero's death in December 43 B.C.E. was part of the civil wars and political struggles following the assassination of Julius Caesar in March 44 B.C.E. He was not one of the conspirators who killed Caesar to defend the Republic against dictatorship (the group led by Brutus and his brother-in-law Cassius), but sided with these anti-Caesar "Liberators" against Octavian and Marc Antony in the three-sided civil war that followed. He was effectively the public face of the anti-Caesar coalition and wrote a series of speeches (the Philippics*) in their defense. When Antony's forces gained the upper hand, Cicero was proscribed as an "enemy of the state," hunted down, and executed. The story of his final days is one of the most frequently retold and reinvented episodes of Cicero's larger legend. For centuries, "The Death of Cicero" served as a rhetorical exercise in the classical and medieval world, and orators used it as a topic with which to develop, practice, and teach their skills, so much so that the actual historical circumstances of the event are difficult to sort out in the aftermath of centuries of invention, embellishment, and reinvention.[7]*

Brown's tale on Cicero's death, along with another tale of governmental force set in the Roman world, "Thessalonica: A Roman Story," seems to have been written in 1799, and uses the classical materials of this episode, along with eighteenth-century Cicero debates, to articulate a modern parable for the Revolutionary age. The tale did not appear in the New York Monthly Magazine *that Brown was editing at this time ("Thessalonica" appeared in that magazine in May 1799). Rather, it was first published as a supplementary text, added to a second printing of the third (final) volume only (that is, the first two volumes were not yet reprinted) of Brown's novel* Edgar Huntly; or, Memoirs of a Sleep-Walker, *when that volume appeared, most likely in January 1800. The simplest explanation for the decision to include it along with a new printing of that novel, which is built around settler-Indian violence on the Pennsylvania frontier and seems to have little evident connection with the Cicero story, is that it was intended to fill out the third volume,*

---

[6] "Vale or mi amice": "Farewell" or "my friend."

[7] See Roller, "*Color*-Blindness: Cicero's Death, Declamation, and the Production of History."

which otherwise was far shorter than the other two. The tale is given its own pagination *in that first printing, apart from the pagination of the novel, another indication that it was likely a last-minute addition, meant to fill out available space in the volume and possibly provide an incentive for new purchases. In no later edition does the story appear paired with* Edgar Huntly.

Whatever the reason for the location of this initial printing, it seems clear that the tale is primarily related to Brown's commentary on the contemporary reception and significance of Cicero, and classical exemplars generally, in Wieland, *"Walstein's School of History," and pieces such as "Ciceronians" and "On the Merits of Cicero." Like most of Brown's narratives, "Death of Cicero" is a first-person memoir that prompts reflections on the ways that individuals respond to damaging circumstances and are shaped by the society in which they live, and that highlights the limited, perspectival nature of interpretation and history writing. The tale closely follows the theory of romance writing elaborated in "Walstein's School of History" and "The Difference Between History and Romance," and may be read as an example of the kind of fictitious history envisioned in those essays. The narrator is Tiro (Marcus Tullius Tiro, c. 103–4 B.C.E.), a well-known figure who was first Cicero's slave, then remained at his side as an emancipated servant and secretary after 53 B.C.E., and is thought to have played a central role in collecting and publishing Cicero's writings after his death. Tiro addresses the narrative to Atticus (Titus Pomponius Atticus, 112–32 B.C.E.), a close friend and correspondent of Cicero's, who is often contrasted favorably with Cicero in the dissenting tradition of eighteenth-century debates.*

As the narrator Tiro reviews Cicero's indecisive, unheroic, and mainly self-concerned behavior during his final hours, and as he vacillates between idealizing his master as a public savior of the Republic and criticizing him as a self-destructive private individual (while incidentally absorbing the Roman elite's prejudices and assumptions), his account of the event repeats and amplifies the eighteenth-century Cicero debates that Brown has used to build his tale. When he has Tiro point out Cicero's "perverse" behavior and pose rhetorical questions that highlight it—"Why do I calumniate the memory of Cicero? Arraign the wisdom of his conduct, and the virtue of this motives?"—Brown aligns his tale with critical interpretations of Cicero's character and implicitly argues against nostalgic uses of history as models for contemporary behavior.[8] In addition, since the iconography of the Roman Republic was so crucial for the latter-day "civic republicanism" of the Atlantic Revolutionary era, such a deflationary account of a hero of elite republican ideology constitutes an indirect criticism of the high-republican discourses of the U.S. leadership in the 1790s.

While most of the details in the narrative are drawn from familiar classical sources,[9] it is notable that Brown emphasizes the class and caste differences that separate the wealthy patrician Cicero from the slaves and servants who attend him, for example by

---

[8] For a discussion of the tale's critical thrust, see Scheiding, "'Plenum exemplorum est historia': Rewriting Exemplary History in Charles Brockden Brown's 'Death of Cicero.'"

[9] The most commonly cited sources in death-of-Cicero traditions, chronologically, are Livy, Seneca the Elder, Appian, Plutarch, and Dio Cassius; additional classical and modern variants abound. For a discussion of the tradition see Roller.

emphasizing the way the party travels between four of Cicero's villas. The two characters Brown seems to have invented, Chlorus and the nameless slave who reveals Cicero's whereabouts, are both lower-caste characters, and of course it is notable that Brown has chosen the former slave Tiro as his narrator. A traditional element of the story maintains that Cicero's slaves protected him and refused to share information about his hiding place, which was revealed instead by Philologus, a freed slave of Cicero's brother Quintus. Brown changes this element of the story, however, and makes a disgruntled slave, formerly a slave under the family of the earlier Roman dictator Sulla, the source of the information that leads Cicero's pursuers to him. This vengeful slave and his link to the despot Sulla seem to be Brown's invention and his primary modification of the familiar narrative.[10] In changing this detail, Brown's implication may be that the indirect fruits of patrician despotism are coming home to roost for Cicero, for the "perverse and malignant" character of the slave who will give up his whereabouts is presumably the result of cruel treatment while the property of Sulla, a famously ruthless and intimidating figure. The legacy of Sulla weakened the Republic, and now Cicero and others of his class, who are complicit in that decline, are powerless to stop Rome's slide into dictatorship.

****

DEATH OF CICERO,
A FRAGMENT.

TIRO TO ATTICUS.

THE task of relating the last events in the life of my beloved master, has fallen upon me. His last words reminded me of the obligation, which I had long since assumed, of conveying to his Atticus a faithful account of his death. Having performed this task, life will cease to be any longer of value.

Having parted with his brother,[11] he went on board a vessel which lay at anchor in the road. The master was a Cyprian, ignorant of the Roman language; a stupid

---

[10] Cicero's first judicial speech, the speech that first established his reputation as a speaker in defense, the *pro Sexto Roscio Amerino*, defended a young man who had been accused by close associates of Sulla. This willingness to challenge Sulla's circle has always been recognized as a very bold move on the young Cicero's part. Possibly, therefore, Brown's decision to end Cicero's career with a reference to his indirect imbrication in Sulla's corruptions is intentional dramatic irony.

[11] "Parted with this brother": in most accounts, Cicero receives news of the proscriptions at his villa at Tusculum (near present-day Frascati) where he is staying with his younger brother, Quintus Tullius Cicero, also a writer and statesman, and Quintus's son. Quintus had accompanied both Caesar and Cicero on military expeditions and administrative appointments. He was proscribed along with Cicero and executed shortly after him.

and illiterate sailor, whose provincial jargon was luckily understood and spoken by *Chlorus*, who was by birth a Cnidian. He served us as interpreter.[12]

He was a stranger to the affairs of Italy, and his knowledge was so extremely limited, that he had never heard even the name of my master. This ignorance we were careful not to remove; and finding him unengaged, and merely waiting till some one should offer him a cargo, I tendered him a large sum if he would set sail immediately. This incident determined our course. No great deviation from his usual route was necessary to carry us to Tarsus, and there my master would not only be under the protection of Cassius, but in the midst of his Cilician clients.[13] His ancient subjects would not fail to receive, with joy and gratitude, a patron from whom they had received so many benefits, and in case of any adverse fortune, their mountains would afford him concealment and security.

The vessel was small and crazy. It afforded wretched accommodation, but it behoved us to submit to every inconvenience, and to console ourselves with the hope that the voyage would be short. We had scarcely got on board, however, and made our bargain with the master when the wind, which had lately been propitious, changed to the southeast, and with this wind, the master declared it impossible to move from our present station.

This was an untoward event. Our safety depended upon the expedition with which we should fly from the shores of Italy. Our foot-steps would be diligently traced, and another hour might bring the blood-hounds within view.

One expedient was obvious. The search might be eluded, or, at least prolonged, by leaving this spot. It was possible to move by the help of oars along the coast. Further south, the country near the sea was still more desolate and woody than here, and we might be concealed in some obscure and unfrequented bay, till the wind should once more become favourable.

---

[12] "Cyprian . . . Cnidian . . . interpreter": although a former slave himself, Tiro assumes the Roman elite's sense of superiority and entitlement, looking down on the "provincial jargon" of a low-status foreigner from a subjugated territory. The servant or slave Chlorus is Brown's invention, not a historically attested character. His origins in either Knidos (Latin *Cnidus*), a small city on Cyprus (an island in the eastern Mediterranean), or more likely the much larger city with the same name on the Turkish coast not far from Cyprus, explain why he speaks the boat-captain's Cyprian dialect. A person from the city-state on the mainland would probably be referred to as a Cnidian, whereas one from the town on Cyprus would more likely refer to himself as a Cypriote or Cyprian.

[13] "Tarsus . . . Cassius . . . Cilician clients": Cilicia was a Roman province in the southeastern coastal region of present-day Turkey, near the island of Cyprus; Tarsus was its capital and major port. It later became part of Armenia, or the Kingdom of Cilician Armenia. Cicero can travel to that area and enjoy the protection of Cassius (85–42 B.C.E.), a leader of the anti-Caesar conspiracy who, at this time, had fled to the province of Syria (where he was earlier governor), which borders on Cilicia. Cicero has "clients" and "subjects" in Cilicia because he previously served there as proconsul, or imperial administrator, in 51–50, seven years prior to the time of the narrative, and oversaw the final Cilician war to subdue the region's last elements of resistance to Roman rule. From an eighteenth-century perspective, but quite anachronistically, Cicero's reputation as a republican patriot is complicated and limited by his participation in the machinery of imperial rule.

Additional rewards and promises induced the captain to adopt this scheme. The wind and the turbulence of the waves increased. My master had always an antipathy to voyages by sea, owing, probably, to the deadly sickness, with which the tossing of the billows never failed to afflict him. This sickness speedily came on, and added to the pent-up air, filthiness and inconvenience of the ship, plunged him into new impatience and dejection. He frequently declared his resolution to go on shore, and offer to his enemies a life which was a burden to him, and relinquished his design not till I had employed the most pathetic and vehement remonstrances.

We had not gone two leagues before night came on. This for a time suspended our toils. We came to anchor near the shore, and being somewhat sheltered from the wind, by the direction of the shore, the sea became more calm, and my master's sickness disappeared. Still he was unwilling to pass the night on board the vessel, and ordered us to land.

This proceeding was imminently dangerous. I endeavoured to convince him of this danger. The town of Circoeum[14] was two or three miles distant, but the huts of which it consisted would afford him accommodation little better than that which the ship afforded. He would unavoidably be recognized by the inhabitants, and if they had not yet heard of the proscription, his appearance among them would lead them to suspect the truth, and what reliance could be placed upon their fidelity? This town might contain some tenant or retainer of Cæsar, or it might at this moment be visited by the messengers of Anthony, at least, his appearance there would shortly be known, and would afford to his pursuers a new clue, by which they may be aided in their search. The same hazards would accompany his entrance into any of the neighbouring farmhouses.

These reasonings made him give up his resolution of going to Circoeum, but he retained his determination to land. If he should pass the night in the open air, though the ground was covered with snow, it was better than to breathe the poisonous atmosphere of the ship, and remain cooped up with the Cyprian and his crew.

Since he would not give up this design, I endeavoured to find reasons for approving it. One danger against which it was needful to provide, was the suspicion of the sailors. The grief and dejection of my master, our impatience be gone from Italy, and the secret and abrupt manner of our embarkation, could not but excite their notice and make them busy at conjecture. They would be still more at a loss to conceive why, when a town was so near, we should prefer to spend the night on board their vessel, and the shelter of a tree or a rock, with the fire which might easily be kindled, were, in truth, not less safe or commodious than continuance in the ship. Preparations, were, therefore, made to land.

My caution led me to go on shore before him, that any danger which impended might be seasonably descried. Wandering over the strand, a small hut was discovered

---

[14] "Circoeum": Circeii (modern Cape Circeo), a settlement at a promontory about halfway between Rome and Naples on the western coast of Italy. Cicero's group has traveled on land from the villa at Tusculum to another villa on the coast at Astura, just southwest of Rome (present-day Torre Astura), before sailing southward to Circoeum, and then on to Formia, another coastal town where Cicero owns a villa.

which appeared to have been formerly inhabited by fishermen. This was a season when the net was idle, and this hut was therefore deserted. The walls and roof were broken, but a good fire might render it tenable for a few hours. Here my master consented to repose himself.

The ground within the hut, as well as without, was covered with snow.[15] This was removed and a kind of bed of withered sticks and dried leaves was provided for him. On this he lay down, and the servants seated themselves around him. He did not endeavour to sleep, but supporting his head upon his elbow, and fixing his eyes, in a thoughtful mood, upon the fire, he delivered himself up to meditation. A pause of general and mournful silence ensued.

Every one's eyes were fixed upon those venerable features. To behold one, so illustrious, one that had so lately governed the destinies of mankind, seated on the pinnacle of human greatness, and encompassed with all the goods of fortune, thus reduced to the condition of a fugitive and out-law, stretched upon the bare earth, in this wretched hovel, affected all of us alike. Every bosom seemed swell with the same sentiment, and required the relief of tears. Chlorus set us the example of this weakness, and not one of us but sobbed aloud.

His attention was recalled by this sound. He lifted his head, and looked upon us by turns with an air of inexpressible benignity. My friends, said he, at length, be not discomposed. My life has been sufficiently long, since I have lived to reap the rewards of virtue. Those evils must indeed be great, which would not be compensated by these proofs of your affection. I need extort from you no other testimony of the equity and kindness of my treatment of you, than the fidelity and tenderness with which you have adhered to me in my distress. This is a consolation of which it is not in the power of the tyrants to bereave me. Let their executioners come: I am willing to die.

These words only heightened the emotions which they were intended to suppress. I desired for my own sake, to change or to terminate this scene, and to reflect that my duty forbade me to sit here in inactivity, when surrounded by so many dangers. None of us had eaten a morsel since we left Astura. Our master was too much absorbed in reflections connected with his fallen fortunes, to think of food. It was our duty to contend with his indifference or aversion, in this respect, as well as to supply our exhausted strength, and prepare for the hardships which we were yet to endure.

I determined, therefore, to go, with two or three companions, to Circoeum and purchase necessaries, as well as ascertain what danger was to be dreaded from this quarter. My master was careless of necessity or danger, and the task of consulting and deciding for the welfare of himself and his servants, had entirely devolved upon me. This charge, it behoved me to perform with circumspection and zeal.

We set out, and crossing an angle of the forest, quickly reached the village. The utmost caution was necessary to be used, since many of the servants of Cicero, and particularly myself, were nearly as well known, especially in this district, as our lord. Chlorus was least liable to be detected, in consequence of having spent the greater

---

[15] "Snow": the date is December 6, 43 B.C.E.

part of his life at the Cuman Villa.[16] He might be effectually disguised, likewise, by mimicking the accents of a Cyprian sailor, and pretending that he came from the vessel. Chlorus went forward, while I and Sura remained at a distance, awaiting his return. He came back in a short time, and with some tokens of alarm. He had crept into a tavern, and after purchasing some bread and dried fruits, had joined a knot of persons who were earnestly engaged in conversation in the portico. One appeared to be a stranger, who had just arrived, and was telling his news to the rest. The coalition of the tyrants was the theme of his discourse. Pœdius, the consul, was said to be included in the sentence of proscription, and a tumult was affirmed to have been raised, on this account, in the city. The populace had aided the magistrate in arresting the emisaries from the armies, and the senate had created Pœdius dictator.[17]

After listening some time, Chlorus ventured to slide into the company, and inquired, in his broken Latin, of what proscription they were talking. The traveller repeated his news with great vivacity, and mentioned, among a thousand incredible circumstances, that the army of Brutus had revolted, and that diligent search was making for the Ciceros. He had just passed near Astura, and was told that a troop had been there, hunting for the fugitives, and finding them to have lately fled, they had dispersed themselves over the country, and he was sure they could not escape. Hearing this, Chlorus withdrew, and hastened to communicate his tidings to me.

The revolt of the Macedonian army was sufficiently probable. This was mournful news, but it shewed with new force the propriety of taking refuge in Asia, rather than in Greece.[18] The last tale was no less probable, and convinced us that no time was to be lost in leaving this fatal shore.

To leave it, however, was not in our power. The present state of the wind imprisoned us in this spot. To change it for another would merely multiply our perils. Here we must remain till it should please Jove to give us a prosperous gale, or till our enemies should trace us to our covert. It only remained for us to hasten back to the hut, and defend our master at the expense of our own lives.

We returned. No interruption or intrusion had been experienced during our absence. On entering the hovel, I found my master in profound sleep. His features were

---

[16] "Cuman Villa": in other words, Chlorus is a servant or slave assigned to another of Cicero's villas, this one at Cumae, just north of Naples and farther away from Circoeum. Astura is only a few miles to the north, and the local inhabitants will therefore recognize servants from that estate.

[17] "Pœdius dictator": Quintus Pedius, a nephew of Caesar, was an ally and cousin of Octavian, Caesar's heir. After Caesar's death, an army commanded by Octavian and Pedius seized Rome and Pedius was left in charge while Octavian set off to ally himself with Antony against Brutus. Pedius authorized the proscription against the anti-Caesar faction, including Cicero, which was then called the Lex Pedia, or Pedian Law.

[18] "Macedonian army . . . Asia . . . Greece": in December 43, armies led by Octavian and Antony are traveling to Macedonia (northern Greece) to battle armies led by anti-Caesarians Brutus and Cassius (Cicero's allies). Ten months later, in October 42, the anti-Caesarians will be defeated in Macedonia (Brutus and Cassius will commit suicide) and Tiro is already hearing rumors (in the previous paragraph) that Brutus' legions there are in revolt. With Greece an unlikely refuge, therefore, asylum in the Asian provinces currently dominated by Cassius becomes Cicero's best option.

tranquil and placid, and his anxieties were, for a while, entirely firgotten. The head and fruits we had brought were shared among our companions, and we continued to watch during the night.

Anxious attention was paid to the state of the air, and fruitless wishes and repinings were whispered by one to another. The morning light returned. The enemy was still distant, but the sky was as untoward as ever.

At length, my master awoke of his own accord. After noticing the day-light, and recollecting his situation, he turned me, and said: Well, my dear Tiro, what is now to be done? I will tell thee what; we will go on board; the Cyprian shall ply his oars and carry us to Formia, and there will I wait for my release.

He noticed the down-cast eyes and mournful looks, which these words occasioned. No one seemed inclined to move to such a purpose. He looked around him, and continued in the same tone; What else, my friends, would you purpose to be done? How unworthy of the saviour of Rome and of Italy is it to be thus clinging to a wretched life, and skulking from ungrateful foes, among rocks and woods? No: I have done my part: All that remains is to die with firmness and with dignity.

Hitherto, I have been the fool of passion and inconstancy. My purposes have wavered from day to day, but it is time to shake off this irresolution and trample on this cowardice. I am now resolved, and will be gone to Formia this moment.

With these words he rose from the ground, and put on an air of sternness and command, which left me no power to expostulate. We obeyed him in silence, and once more put ourselves on board the vessel. The crew were still asleep, but being roused by our arrival, were prevailed upon to row along the shore towards Formia.

My master seemed to have retrieved his wonted tranquillity, in consequence of having formed his ultimate resolution. He was still, for the most part, wrapt in meditation. He forebore to converse with me, but sat upon the deck, with his eyes fixed upon the water, which was now less turbulent than on the former day, and did not occasion sickness.

My own thoughts were occupied in devising some means of escape. We were now approaching Sicily, and it was possible that some conveyance could be gained to that island.[19] This however must be found after our arrival at Formia, for beyond this the Cyprian refused to go, under pretence, which indeed, was probably true, of being unacquainted with the coast. Neither was I totally without hope that the wind would suddenly change, and permit us to leave the coast. On this event, I did not fear to obtain Cicero's concurrence, with a scheme so conducive to his safety. To despair of himself or the republic while the seas were open, and while Cassius was in arms, and furnished with the wealth of all the Asiatic provinces, was unworthy of his understanding and his virtue.

His purpose to go to any one of his villas was pregnant with danger. These places would be searched, by his enemies. As long as he remained in Italy, it was expedient

---

[19] "Sicily": the emphasis on possible refuge in Sicily seems to rest on the fact that Cicero served there as quaestor (a kind of treasurer) early in his career, successfully defended that province from the plunder and extortion of the governor Gaius Verres in the 70s, and consequently had a large number of supporters on the island throughout has career.

to conceal himself in unsuspected corners. Could not such be found, where he might remain unmolested for years.

I now reflected that Formia being situated within a mile of the sea, might be the best asylum to which he could betake himself. A ship might be provided, ready to profit by the first wind, to sail away to Sicily, while, in the mean time, my master might be effectually secreted in some part of his dominion.[20] The subterranean vaults, constructed preserve wine and other provisions, on this estate, might afford him concealment till the opportunity of escape should offer.

While brooding over these images, we came in sight of Formia. It was now time to mention to him this scheme. He received it with disapprobation—I am too old, said he, to undergo once more the hardships and hazards of a camp. I have witnessed long enough the ingratitude and perfidy of mankind. I am tired of the spectacle, and am determined to close my eyes upon it forever.

It shall never be said, that Marcus Cicero fled from the presence of tyrants, that he saved the miserable remnant of his old age, by making himself an exile from his country. I tell thee, Tiro, I am too old to become the sport of fortune, and the follower of armies. Cassius and Brutus are young, they are inured to war; it is their element. They fight for liberty and glory, which their age will permit them to enjoy for many years to come; but as to me, I have reached the verge of the grave already, and should I elude my enemies, and reach Rhodes[21] or Tarsus in safety, I should only have reserved myself for a speedy and ignoble death. No: Here shall be the end of my wanderings.

I will go to my house. I will pass my time without anxiety or fear. When the executioners of Antony arrive, they will find their victim prepared. My resolution continued he, with some impatience, is taken. It is to no purpose to harass me with arguments and remonstrances, for I shall never swerve from it.

I was not totally discouraged by these declarations. I confided in my power to vanquish this resolution, as soon as the means of escape should be provided. Till then it was indeed useless to contend with his despair. His imagination saw nothing but cowardice and degradation, in hiding himself in vaults and pits. That he who was so long at the head of the Roman state, should seek his safety in shifts and stratagems like these, was ignominious and detestable. Death was not so terrible that it should be shunned, life was not so dear that it should be preserved at this price.

He proceeded to his house with an air of fearlessness and confidence. It was far from certain, that it was not occupied already by assassins, expecting and waiting his approach; of this, however, he testified no apprehension. As soon as he entered the porch, his arrival was rumoured through the building, and his servants hurried from

---

[20] "Formia. . . his dominion": after landing at Formia, ten miles farther south along the coast from Cape Circeo, the group will take refuge at Cicero's villa there, still well north of the villa at Cumae mentioned earlier. The implication throughout, with references to Cicero's multiple estates, large land-holdings, slaves, and servants, seems to be on Cicero's great wealth as a member of the Republic's ruling class.

[21] "Rhodes": another city in the east, on an island of the same name off the southwest coast of present-day Turkey.

all quarters to welcome him. Their looks betrayed anxiety as well as joy. It was easy to perceive that they were not unapprised of the dangers which encompassed their master, and that his appearance among them had been unexpected. He greeted and smiled upon each, and then retired to his chamber, whither he would not allow any one to follow him.

It was now time to adopt those measures on which my thoughts had been engaged. As soon as I parted from my master, I took Glauco the steward aside. I told him what had lately happened, and what I now designed to do, and desired his assistance to procure a vessel which might carry us without delay to Sicily.

I found that there was need of the utmost expedition, for Glauco informed me that, not many hours before, a troop of twenty horse-men, had come hither. They rode furiously into the court, and without inquiry or permission, rushed into the house. They entered every apartment, and not finding their victim, indulged their resentment in imprecations on the upstart of Arpinum,[22] and in striking their swords against the furniture and pictures. Two busts, of Brutus and Ahala,[23] which stood in the library, they overturned upon the pavement.

The servants, affrighted at the stern and sullen visages of these intruders, fled from their presence. After lingering for some time in the house, they mounted their horses and disappeared.

These tidings shewed me the magnitude and nearness of the danger. Not a moment should be wasted in deliberation or uncertainty. It was possible that the assassins might not speedily return, and the interval was to be employed in procuring the means of flight. The sea was to be crossed, and Cajeta was a league distant. At Cajeta only was it possible to find a vessel, suited to our purpose.

I now called some of the most faithful servants together, and charged them guard the safety of their master, till Glauco and I should return, which should be in less than an hour. We were going, I told them, to Cajeta, in hopes of finding some immediate conveyance from this shore, and would return with the utmost expedition.

We set out, selecting the fleetest horses to carry us. Three barks were seen in the bay, Glauco imagined that he saw on one the stern and beak which is peculiar to Sicily. To this we immediately transported ourselves. Happily his penetration had not been

---

[22] "Upstart of Arpinum": Arpinum (modern Arpino), just southeast of Rome, was Cicero's birthplace.

[23] "Busts, of Brutus and Ahala": the two legendary tyrannicides and defenders of the early Roman Republic; Lucius Junius Brutus (a founder of the Republic and one of the first consuls in 509 B.C.E.), who led the revolt against the last Tarquinian king; and Gaius Servilius Ahala, who in legend saved Rome by killing would-be king Spurius Maelius in 439 B.C.E. with a hidden dagger. Cicero's ally Brutus led the anti-Caesar conspirators because he could claim to be descended from these two king-killers on the two sides of his family. In the 1790s, after Jacques-Louis David's epochal painting of Brutus, *Lictors Returning to Brutus the Body of his Sons* (1789), and the influential 1790 Parisian revival of Voltaire's play *Brutus* (originally 1730), which was performed with iconic twin busts of Voltaire and Brutus on stage to frame the actors, this elder Brutus was commonly understood as an symbol of revolutionary valor.

deceived, and the Sicilian readily consented to take us on board, and proceed immediately to Sicily.

By exerting themselves with energy, they might bring the vessel in a short time to the shore nearest to my master's house. This was better than to bring him to Cajeta, where it would be impossible for him to escape observation, and to which he could come only by a public road, thronged and obstructed with passengers.

I left Glauco on board the vessel, to hasten the motions of the sailors and to direct them to the proper place. Meanwhile, I mounted my horse and rode back to Formia. The vessel would be ready to receive us by the time that we should reach the shore.

The domestics, whom I had posted in the atrium, were still assembled and received me with joy, but one event had taken place in my absence which filled me with foreboding and anxiety. A slave who wrought in the fields, who formerly belonged to the Cornelian family,[24] and whose temper was remarkably perverse and malignant, had withdrawn himself immediately after my master's arrival. Glauco had frequently complained of the turbulent and worthless character of this slave, and had exhorted Cicero to part with him. In the multiplicity of more momentous concerns this affair had been overlooked by my master, and he still continued in the family.

It was now suggested to me that he had gone in order to recall the soldiers, and to avenge himself in this manner, for the punishments which his refractory and rebellious conduct had frequently incurred. This new danger was an additional incitement to my diligence. I went to my master's chamber and found him asleep. This was no time to be scrupulous or tardy. I awakened him.

On recovering his recollection, and finding me beside him, with every mark of trepidation and dismay, and silent, from my uncertainty in what manner to address him, he suspected that I brought fatal tidings. He looked at me without emotion, and said:

How is it with thee, my Tiro? With me, all is well. I have slept soundly, and am prepared to meet the worst. Thou wouldst tell me that they are coming. I rejoice to hear it: the sooner they arrive and execute the will of Anthony and his Octavius,[25] the better.

Saying this, he half rose from the couch, and stretching his feet towards the stove, he continued: Thanks to Jove, that, at a time like this, nothing but my feet are cold. I have done with hope and with fear, and Cæsar's ministers shall find that my heart's blood has lost none of its warmth. He may deface and mangle this frame, but my spirit shall be found invincible.

---

[24] "Cornelian family": the family of Lucius Cornelius Sulla (138–78 B.C.E.), whose temporary dictatorships and military march on Rome during earlier civil wars, only a generation in the past, prepared the decline of the Republic.

[25] "His Octavius": this usage of "Octavius" is a knowing, pointed detail on Brown's part, and fitting language for an enemy of Octavian to use. For referring to Caesar's heir as Octavius rather than Octavian (even worse, as Antony's Octavius) is implicitly an insult and a way of refusing to recognize his legitimacy. Cicero did, in fact, sometimes refuse to refer to him as "Octavian(us)," because the young Octavius only assumed the name after being formally adopted in Julius Caesar's will, whereupon, by Roman custom, he became "Gaius Julius Caesar Octavianus."

I could no longer forbear, but while the tears flowed down my cheeks, I pulled him by the arm towards the door, and exclaimed: We have found a vessel that will carry us to Sicily. She lies at this moment near the shore ready to receive us. Hasten, I beseech you, beyond the reach of the tyrants. Why would you glut the vengeance of Anthony, and not rather live to raise up the republic?

He shook his head, and resisting my efforts: It is too late, said he: I never can die in a fitter season and place than the present, and hence I will not move.

O! Heaven! Does Cicero love his enemies better than his friends? Is he willing to sacrifice his country to parricides and traitors? Shall he seek death because, while he lives, liberty is not extinguished; because the triumph of the wicked can only be completed by his death?

Has Antony merited so well at your hands, that you are willing to die, that his ambition may be fully gratified? Is this the issue of your warfare? After contending with his treason so long, do you now fall of your own accord at his feet, put the poniard in his hand and call upon him to strike? Thus will mankind regard your conduct when the means of escape are offered you, when the arms and treasures of Sicily and Greece and Asia are ready to be put into your hand, you reject the gift, you abandon the cause of your country, of liberty, of your friends; you invite infamous assassins to your bosom; you die at the moment when your life is of most value to mankind, and nothing but your death is wanting to ensure the destruction of Rome.

O! let it not be said that in his last hours, Marcus Cicero was a recreant and coward. That so illustrious a life was closed with infamy, that his eulogies on liberty, his efforts for the salvation of Rome, the claims of gratitude and friendship were forgotten or despised. That mankind called on their deliverer, that armies and provinces were offered to be employed by him in the rescue of his country, and the ruin of tyrants, in vain.

The road is open and direct, there is nothing to create momentary hindrance or delay. In a few hours, he may laugh at the impotent resentment of Antony; and arm himself to punish the ingratitude and perfidy of Cæsar—But no, he will thrust himself within their grasp; he will patiently wait till their assassins have leisure to execute their sentence; he will beg them to except his homage, and since his death is indispensable to their success, he will stretch out his neck to receive it.

Perceiving that my master's resolution began to faulter, I redoubled my remonstrances, I called up the images of his brother, his son and his nephew, of Cassius and Brutus and Pompeius.[26] I painted the effect which the tidings of his death would produce in them; their transports of grief awakened not so much by the injury redounding to the common cause, as by the infatuation and folly to which his death must be ascribed. With their humiliation and terror, I contrasted the

---

[26] "Pompeius": Gnaeus Pompeius Magnus (Pompey the Great, c.106–48 B.C.E.), a general who opposed Caesar before the assassination and, along with his son (who will be mentioned shortly), raised armies to struggle against him, but was defeated and executed by Caesar two years before the present narrative.

exultation of his enemies, to whose malice he was thus making himself a voluntary victim. What indignities would not be heaped upon his lifeless remains! How would Fulvia and Anthony feast their eyes upon his head, which, torn from the trunk, will be carried to their toilets, and how will the folly of inviting their revenge and crouching to the stroke of their assassins be made the endless theme of ridicule and mockery?—[27]

At this moment, the servants entered the chamber with a litter. I had given previous directions to this effect. I had resolved if persuasion should prove inefficacious, to carry him away by force. One of the bearers was Chlorus, whose looks betokened the deepest consternation, and by his eyes and gestures besought me to use dispatch. I made a sign to the attendants, who approached their master with diffidence and reverence and prepared to remove him from his couch to the litter.

I renewed my supplications and remonstrances, which he listened in silence, and though his looks testified reluctance and perplexity, he made no resistance. He was placed in the litter. I led the way into the garden. Chlorus had now an opportunity to whisper me that the soldiers had scented their prey anew and were hastening to the house. This intelligence induced me to strike into an obscure path which led through a wood and to quicken the pace of my companions.

The litter was surrounded by sixteen domestics well armed. They were all faithful to their trust. Most of them were grey with age, but vigorous and resolute. All of them had been, during many years, personal attendants on their lord, and were eager to shed their blood in his defence; I was not without hope that should we be overtaken and attacked, such resistance might be made, as, at least, to secure the retreat of my master to the shore.

We had now accomplished half the journey, and were inspired with new confidence in our good fortune. Turning an angle, however, a band of men appeared in sight. They discovered us in a moment, and shouting aloud, made towards us with the utmost expedition. There was now room but for one choice. Fly, said I, to those that bore the litter, fly with your burden to the shore and leave us to contend with these miscreants.

The enemy had been discovered by my master as soon as by us. He now raised himself up, and exclaimed in a tone of irresistable authority; No: I charge you stir not a step. Set down the litter and await their coming. Put up your swords, continued he, turning to the rest, who had, in imitation of my example unsheathed their weapons: Put up your swords. By the duty which you owe me, I command you to forbear.

---

[27] "Fulvia and Anthony . . . mockery": in keeping with the brutal traditions of Sulla, who has displayed the heads of his enemies in the Forum, Antony will have Cicero's severed head and hands (whether only the right hand or both hands is a detail that varies in different accounts) nailed to the Rostrum as public evidence of his defeat. In many versions, Antony's wife Fulvia then pierces the tongue in Cicero's head with her hairpins, in order to insult his eloquence and power with words. Fulvia was formerly married to Cicero's bitter opponent Clodius (see note 28), and was personally targeted by Cicero in his *Second Philippic*, so she has many reasons to detest him.

With whatever sternness these commands were delivered, they would not have made me hesitate or faulter. I was prepared to conduct myself, not agreeable to his directions, but to the exigencies of the time; I was willing to preserve his life even at the hazard of offending him beyond forgiveness; but my companions were endowed with less firmness.

Go on, said I, to the bearers, heed not the words of a desperate man. It is your duty to save him, though you forfeit your lives by your disobedience—They once more stooped to raise up the vehicle, but were again forbidden. What! said he, am I fallen so low as to be trampled on by slaves? Desist, this moment! Appalled and confounded by the energy of his accents, they let fall the litter, and stood with their eyes down-cast and motionless.

The delay which this altercation produced, rendered his escape impossible. The veteran and well-accoutred band that was approaching, left us no hope of victory. All that I had meditated, was to retard their progress so long that my master might reach the ship in safety. For this end, we were to lay down our own lives, but as long as he continued in this spot all opposition would be fruitless.

To stay and behold violence committed on that venerable head was not in my power. I went forward to meet the assassins. It was not, however, till I had discerned the person of their leader that I had any hopes of diverting them from their design. He was a tribune in the army of Cæsar, and his name was Popilius Lænas.

This man had been formerly accused of murdering his wife's brother. This brother had considerable property to which Lænas expected to succeed, but on some dissention between them, the brother had selected a new heir and Lænas was said to have gratified his vengeance by his death. His wife and children were among his accusers, and there was too much reason to believe the truth of the accusation.

In this extremity he besought Cicero to be his advocate. Lænas had been active in the Clodian tumults, had sided with Milo and the Senate, and had, consequently, promoted the interests of my master.[28] This service was now his plea, and, joined with unwearied importunities, accomplished his end. Cicero was an enthusiast in gratitude, and was not used to scrutinize suspiciously or weigh accurately, this kind of merit. Benefits received from others were, if possible, repaid an hundred fold. He made himself the advocate of a cause, which, without his assistance, would doubtless have been desperate, and Lænas

---

[28] "Clodian tumults . . . Milo . . . interests of my master": Publius Clodius Pulcher (92–52 B.C.E.) touched off a scandal in 62 when he disguised himself as a woman to enter Caesar's home while a liturgy forbidden to men was being performed there (possibly in order to have an affair with Caesar's wife). This caused a break between Clodius and Cicero, previously allies, because Cicero was the only witness to contradict Clodius' testimony that he had been away from Rome that day. Clodius then became a bitter antagonist who was instrumental in having Cicero banished to Thessalonica in Greece, confiscating his property, and burning down Cicero's Roman mansion on the Palatine hill, all in 58. After Cicero's return from banishment, he unsuccessfully attempted to defend Milo (Titus Annius Milo) after Milo had his slaves murder Clodius in the year 52 (Cicero's *Pro Milone* oration). Antony's wife Fulvia was formerly married to Clodius, another reason she despises Cicero (see note 27). The defeat in the Milo case is the only defeat that is certainly known in the extant record of Cicero's defenses.

was acquitted. His vows of gratitude and service were unbounded, and now that I discovered him at the head of Cæsar's executioners was scarcely credible.[29]

After a moments pause, I advanced towards him, and offered him my hand. He rejected it with scorn and rage, and thrusting me aside, Out of the way, villain, said he, and thank my mercy that you do not share the fate of the traitor you serve.

His followers surrounded me with drawn swords, and looking at the tribune, seemed to wait only for his signal to put me to death. Come on, he cried; Our prize is in view. Cut down every one that opposes, but leave the peaceable alone. They left me and hastened towards the litter.

My eyes followed them instinctively. Shuddering and a cold dew invaded my limbs. With the life of Cicero, methought, was entwined the existence of Rome. The stroke by which one was severed, would be no less fatal to the other. It was indeed true that liberty would be extinguished by his death, and then only would commence the reign of Anthony, and the servitude of mankind.

Would no effort avail to turn aside the stroke? Should I stand a powerless spectator of the deed? Might I not save myself at least the ignominy and horror of witnessing the fall of my master, by attacking his assassins or falling on my own sword?

These impulses of grief, were repressed by the remembrance of the duties, which his death would leave to be performed by me and of the promises by which I was bound.

During these thoughts my eyes were fixed upon the litter. My master, perceiving the approach of the tribune, held forth his head, as if to facilitate the assassin's office. His posture afforded a distinct view of his countenance, which was more thoughtful and serene than I had seen it during our flight from . . .

The eyes of the ruffians sparkled with joy at sight of their victim. They contended which should be foremost in guilt. The domestics, struck with consternation, looked

---

[29] "Scarely credible": in some accounts, Cicero had earlier saved Gaius Popilius Laenas by defending him in court against murder charges, and thus Tiro can hardly believe that Laenas now seeks to profit from Cicero's death in this manner. The bitter irony of this situation, as well as the reference to the Milo case, may recall Cicero's decision to defend another likely guilty party, Cluentius, from charges of family murder in his *Pro Cluentio*, the text that Theodore and Pleyel discuss in Chapter 4 of *Wieland*. From the point of view of eighteenth-century Cicero debates, none of these are honorable cases. They display a Cicero acting in his own self-interest or narrowly defined factional interests, rather than in a way that might promote justice or the common good of the Republic. In the critical Cicero commentary in his *Travels in the two Sicilies* . . . (London: Nichols, 1790), a text that was consulted by Brown's friend Elihu Hubbard Smith in 1798, Henry Swinburne (1743–1803) suggests that Laenas was also motivated to kill Cicero in order to punish him for his cynical treatment of his former ward and wife Publilia. In 46, a heavily indebted Cicero had divorced his first wife Terentia to marry his 15-year-old ward Publilia, a wealthy heiress. After he paid off creditors with Publilia's money, Cicero divorced her as well, and Swinburne suggests that she may have been related to Laenas (vol. 4, 347–54).

Although Brown uses it in his tale, the Popilius Laenas case is almost certainly an addition to the historical record, an invention by later declaimers to make the circumstances of Cicero's death more dramatic. Seneca the Elder is the earliest source that refers to this trial and he himself already doubts its historicity (*Controversiae* 7.2.8).

upon each other in silence. The soldiers, full of eagerness secure the reward which Anthony had promised for the head of his enemy, were too much occupied to speak to each other, or to heed any foreign object.

One blow severed the devoted head! No sooner had it fallen, than the troop set up an horrid shout of exultation. Lænas grasped the hair and threw the head into a large bag, held open by one of his companions for that purpose.

Come, lads, he cried: Post we, with our prize, with all speed to Rome? Anthony will pay us well for this service—So saying, they hastened away with as much expedition as they came.

All passed in a moment. Nothing but the headless trunk, stretched upon the floor of the litter, which floated in blood, remained. I approached the vehicle without being fully conscious of my movements, and gazed upon the mutilated figure. My thoughts were at a stand, as well as my power of utterance suspended. My heart seemed too small to embrace the magnitude of this calamity. It was not a single man who had fallen, or whose violent catastrophe was the theme of everlasting regret. The light of the world was extinguished, and the hopes of human kind brought to an end.

My mind gradually recovered some degree of activity. I mused upon the events that led to this disaster. It seemed as if the most flagitious folly, had given birth to this insupportable evil. Nothing was easier than to have fled to the shore; to have embarked in the Sicilian vessel, and quickly to have moved ourselves beyond the reach of our enemies. At one time, I loaded myself with the most vehement upbraidings: Why did I not exert myself to hinder him from leaving the Cyprian barque? Had we proceeded to Cajeta, without delay, we might have put ourselves on board the Agrigentine,[30] and set danger at defiance. The Cyprian refused to proceed, but menaces would have been successful where rewards had failed. He and his feeble crew, would have easily been mastered by our superior number.

But was not Cicero himself the author of his evil destiny? Irresolute, desponding or perverse, he thwarted or frustrated the measures conducive to his safety. More sensible to the stings of ingratitude and his personal humiliation, than to the claims of his fellow citizens; prone to despair of liberty, though the richest and most populous portion of the empire was still faithful to its cause; though veteran armies and illustrious officers were still ranged under its banners in Sicily, Greece and Asia, he lingered on this fatal shore, and threw himself before the executioner.

There were a thousand recesses on this desolate coast, and caverns in the Apenine,[31] and unsuspected retreats on his own estate, where he might have been effectually concealed, till Cassius and Pompey[32] had restored the republic, till the pursuit of his

---

[30] "The Agrigentine": that is, the ship from Agrigentum, a city on the southwest coast of Sicily.

[31] "The Apenine": the Apennine mountain range that runs the length of the Italian peninsula.

[32] "Pompey": Sextus Pompeius Magnus Pius (Sextus Pompey, c.67–35 B.C.E.), the son of the Pompeius (Pompey the Great) mentioned earlier (see note 26). After fighting Caesar in Spain with his father, who was executed there after capture by Caesar, this Pompey became the last leader of opposition to the Triumvirate of Antony, Octavian, and Lepidus and thus, along with Cassius, the last military survivor of the anti-Caesar coalition and defender of Cicero's cause.

enemies had slackened, and time and his faithful servants had supplied the means of his escape. Had he even permitted the generous sacrifice which his attendants were zealous to make, and profited by the interval, which their contest with the ruffians would have afforded, to reach the shore; had he looked, with a stern eye, on the tribune and his followers, and rebuked them with the eloquence whose force had been so long irresistable; had he called up the memory of past benefits, and thundered indignation in the ears of the apostate Lænas, who knows but the blood-hounds would have been eluded or baffled, or disarmed of their sanguinary purpose? They were wretches, incited by the lust of gain, void of enmity to Cicero, or love of his oppressors. The bribe with which Anthony had bought their zeal, might have easily been doubled by Cicero, to purchase their connivance at his flight. The hope of promotion in the legions of the east, might have changed them into guardians of our safety, and companions of our voyage. Thus had the magnanimity of Marcus snatched him from worse perils, and kept him from despairing of his life, and his cause, though labouring under a greater weight of years, encompassed by enemies more numerous and more triumphant: lonely, succourless, in chains and immured in a dungeon!

But why do I calumniate the memory of Cicero? Arraign the wisdom of his conduct, and the virtue of his motives? Had he not lived long enough for felicity and usefulness? Was there cowardice or error in refusing to mingle in the tumults of war? In resigning to younger hands, innured to military offices, the spear and the shield? Is it more becoming the brave to struggle for life; to preserve the remnant which infirmity and old age had left, than serenely to wait for death, and encounter it with majestic composure? Is it dishonourable to mourn over the triumph of ambition, and the woes of our country? To be impatient of life, when divorced from liberty, and fated to contemplate the ruin of those schemes, on which his powers had incessantly been exercised, and whose purpose was the benefit of mankind?

Yes. The close of thy day was worthy its beginning and its progress. Thou diest with no stain upon thy virtue. The termination of thy course was coeval with the ruin of thy country. Thy hand had upheld the fabric of its freedom and its happiness, as long as human force was adequate to that end. It fell, because the seeds of dissolution had arrived at maturity, and the basis and structure were alike dissolved. It fell, and thou wast crushed in its ruins.

5. Charles Brockden Brown, Letter to Samuel Miller of June 20, 1803

In Chapter 8 of Wieland, *in an answer to questions about his experiences in Spain, Frank Carwin offers a response that downplays national differences (between Protestant and Catholic states, for example) and instead envisions England and Spain together as part of a single historical narrative concerning the development of modern Europe: "they were formerly provinces of the same civil, and till lately, of the same religious, Empire" (62). Carwin's answer seems to minimize the significance of the nation-state as a basic unit of analysis and to imply instead a long-duration, empire-centered, and nonnationalistic conception of history. Similarly, in part 6 of* Memoirs of Carwin, *when he (naively) imagines a possible utopian colonization scheme, Carwin dismisses any focus on isolated states in order to speak generally (and critically) of the European and Atlantic world as "those fragments of Roman and Gothic barbarism, which cover the face of what are called the civilized nations" (256).*

Brown develops this long, cosmopolitan, and critical view of European, Atlantic, and global world history in the following letter, which he wrote to his friend Samuel Miller (1769–1850), in June 1803, five years after Wieland *but just four months before he would begin publishing* Memoirs of Carwin *from a manuscript first drafted in August 1798. In 1803, Miller was a Presbyterian minister working in New York (in 1813 he would become a professor at Princeton Theological Seminary) and wrote Brown as a former associate from the New York circle of the late 1790s, the setting in which Brown had written* Wieland *and his other best-known novels. At this time, Miller was working on his own best-known book,* A Brief Retrospective of the Eighteenth Century *(New York, 1803), and asked Brown to summarize his ideas about the most important developments of the previous century.*

Brown's response to Miller argues that the most important transformations that occurred in the eighteenth century were the critique and rejection of theism; the continual expansion of a Europe-centered, commercial world-system based on colonialism and imperialism; and the ever-more-rapid proliferation of print culture and informational media (in continual expansion since mechanical printing was first developed in the 1430s), which he suggests is sure to generate unforeseeable changes. The perspective Brown offers may surprise readers who expect a more conventional emphasis on national and political events such as, for example, the American or French revolutions. Brown bypasses such perspectives, however, and presents eighteenth-century developments as the world-systemic outcomes of centuries of socioeconomic, political, and ideological struggles and technical innovations. By extension, he seems to be championing analytical models that propose a global perspective on cultural development, a view similar to Goethe's pronouncement of the advent of "world literature."

In a more detailed version of the long-duration view of history suggested by his character Carwin, Brown's letter maintains that economically based imperial networks and large-scale sociocultural transformations, not individual states or isolated political and other phenomena, supply the key data for understanding historical relations and the forces that transform them. For example, he begins by arguing that the Christian religious schisms and wars of the Reformation, which play such a central role in Wieland family history, should be viewed in connection with the continuing importance of interstate structures inherited from the Roman Empire, and that the shift from state polytheism to state Christianity in the Empire and Middle Ages, or from Catholic to Protestant models in early modern Europe, are merely "nominal" changes of label that do not fundamentally change these underlying structures. Although many conventional histories concentrate on these religious or political transitions and period-divisions, Brown argues that they should not distract us from understanding the deeper political, socioeconomic, ideological, and informational relations that bind the Mediterranean, European, and now Atlantic and global worlds into coherent systems over time, beyond the boundaries of individual states, policies, or religions.

From his vantage point in 1803, Brown accurately suggests that an era of globalized commercial, geopolitical, and informational development rapidly approaching will dwarf the circumatlantic world systems of early-modern European empires. Brown's critical remarks and predictions concerning new stages of imperialism—in the passage where he suggests that "the same sort of community of knowledge, power & hate will reign throughout the Globe, which now exists among Europeans & their progeny"—seem prescient, and they prefigure the geopolitical commentary he develops in nonfictional forms in his historical "Annals of Europe and America" (published 1807–1810 in his final magazine, the American Register*) and several political pamphlets (1803, 1809).*

These themes surface again in the later episodes of Memoirs of Carwin *(likely written after the narrative began to be serialized in October 1803), when the mysterious colonization schemes that Carwin and Ludloe hint at seem to center on extending idealized European political models into new and unknown territories in the Pacific, presented in that fiction as a possibly high-minded but decidedly ominous undertaking. Brown likewise developed antiutopian models of worldwide colonial violence in the pseudohistorical fictions called the* Historical Sketches, *also written in the 1803–1806 period when he edited the Philadelphia* Literary Magazine, *and in other fictional fragments and sketches. As one of Brown's clearest expositions of his ideas on history, religion, and imperialism, this letter to Miller is a key link between the systematic reading of early modern European history implied in the back stories of* Wieland *(and Brown's other novels), and the critical depictions of colonial and imperial dynamics in* Memoirs of Carwin *and other later fictions, political pamphlets, and historical writings.*[1]

*****

Philad. June 20. 1803

My dear friend

The inclosed has been the result of several attempts. It is jejune & unsatisfactory, & nothing but your repeated wishes can induce me to send it to you. My wish to oblige you has made me contend with a great many untoward circumstances in my situation, which forbid me to comment or speculate on such subjects, but you will see, on reading the enclosed, that the <u>wish</u>, is all I have to give.

I ardently wish for a mind sufficiently disengaged for such a task, but I have it not. I cannot command it.

---

[1] The manuscript of the letter is held by Princeton University; the transcription, by John R. Holmes and Edwin Saeger, is the first state of the text that will be part of *The Letters and Selected Poetry of Charles Brockden Brown*, the first volume of the edition of Brown's nonnovelistic writings now in preparation at the Charles Brockden Brown Electronic Archive and Scholarly Edition, in collaboration with Kent State University Press. The address leaf of the letter reads: "Rev.[d] Samuel Millar / Liberty Street / New York / Mail." The letter's informal spelling, syntax, and punctuation have not been altered.

I hope that your gloomy prognostics, respecting the fate of your work, may not be realized. Barren wishes, indeed, may evince regard for you, but, alas, there is not a single circumstance in my situation enabling me to be a useful, a serviceable friend to your undertakings.[2]

My best regards to Mrs. M. & to your brother.[3]
Adieu

C. B. Brown

The <u>reformation</u> in religion, as it is called, was one of the most important revolutions which has occurred in Europe since the fall of the Roman Empire.

The destruction of this empire, was, indeed, rather nominal than real, since the Bishop of Rome succeeded the ancient emperors in one of their most important attributes or characters, that of the Pontifex Maximus,[4] & since, in this character,

---

[2] "My situation . . . your undertakings": Brown seems to be saying that he is overwhelmed with present challenges and changes, and does not have the time to help Miller with his book project by developing a more adequate response to Miller's question. In June 1803, Brown was 32 years old and an internationally renowned writer (already translated into French and German) without regular income. He had recently (in January and March 1803) published two important political pamphlets arguing for the acquisition of the Louisiana Territory; was planning with his friend Thomas Pym Cope to write an abolitionist *History of Slavery* (as of February 1803); coping with large shipping losses in his family mercantile firm; translating and annotating a major study of North American geology and geography by French writer Constantin Volney (published early 1804); negotiating with printers and backers in order to start his own magazine, which would begin publication in October 1803 as *The Literary Magazine and American Register*; and trying to maintain a respectable economic profile in order to court Elizabeth Linn, a Presbyterian minister's daughter he would marry in November 1804.

[3] "Mrs. M. and your brother": Miller's spouse and brother are Sarah Sergeant Miller (1778–1861), daughter of Princeton attorney Jonathan Dickinson Sergeant, a member of the Revolutionary Continental Congress; and Dr. Edward Miller (1760–1812), a physician. Along with Samuel Mitchill (1764–1831), another New York physician and member of Brown's New York circle, and Brown's closest friend Elihu Hubbard Smith, Edward Miller was a cofounder and coeditor of the New York circle's *Medical Repository*. He was present, with Brown, at Elihu Hubbard Smith's death from yellow fever in September 1798, in the apartment they all shared on Pine Street in New York.

[4] "Pontifex Maximus": originally, the presiding member of the Roman *Collegium Pontificum* or College of Pontiffs, the governing body of the highest-ranking priests of the Roman polytheistic state religion. Julius Caesar, for example, held this office while head of the Roman state. The authority of the office under the Republic and Empire was transferred to the Roman Catholic Bishop of Rome (the Pope) around 440 C.E. by Pope Leo I. Brown's secularist argument sets aside conventional distinctions between state and religious institutions in order to emphasize the ways that Roman Catholicism perpetuated the administrative power and state bureaucracy of the Roman Empire until the fifteenth century. His argument draws on enlightened genealogies of religion such as Edward Gibbon's *Decline and Fall of the Roman Empire* (1776–1788) and Scottish-school histories of classical and civil society; for example, Adam Ferguson's *An Essay on the History of Civil Society* (1767) and *The History of the Progress and Termination of the Roman Republic* (1783).

they exercised a much more absolute authority over more extensive & distant regions than was ever exercised by Trajan, Constantine or Justinian.[5] The Reformation may be considered as the defection of certain provinces of this empire & the effort by intrigues, arms & controversial writings, of Rome & her votaries to regain these provinces, which began in the Sixteenth, were far from having terminated at the opening of the Eighteenth century. The western nations of Europe were, at this period, engaged in a ruinous war,[6] in part of the consequence of this great scism. The great object which ingaged the attention of speculative men was the merits and demerits of different schemes of christianity, & kings & ministers were fully occupied in destroying or supporting the claims to civil authority founded upon these differences.

In the progress of this century, things insensibly assumed a new appearance. The mind of man is ever restless & each successive age producing a new object to exercise ambition & curiosity. Having exausted the great questions which divided protestants & Romanists, a controversy gradually arose as to the truth of religion, & more especially of Christianity itself. As the inhabitants of Europe were engaged in other earlier ages, & in discussing the respective merits of christianity & paganism & afterwards of the merits of different schemes or systems of Christianity, they came, in the Eighteenth century to discuss the truth of any form whatsoever of religion. In place of ancient denomination, mankind began to assume the distinctions of christians & infidels, or religionists & atheists. From enquiring how the scriptures ought to be interpreted, & which among the successors of christ deserve to be held in reverence as infallible teaching, the questions now were whether Christ himself ever existed; whether the history of his life possessed any historical credibility, & even whether there were any grounds for the existance or commonly recieved attributes of GOD himself.

On these great questions the human understanding has been employed with extraordinary zeal, & they have been investigated in a manner of which no former age affords an example. All the arguments historical, metaphysical, & moral, respecting religion, & particularly christianity, have received a thorough discussion.[7]

This age has likewise been eminently distinguished from all others by the progress the European or Christian nations have made towards that political ascendency over the Earth to which they are destined to arrive. The three great departments of the civilized world are China, India & Europe. The latter has diffused itself over nearly the whole of the Western hemisphere, unpreoccupied before except the Savages, &

---

[5] "Trajan, Constantine or Justinian": Trajan (Emperor 98–117 C.E.), Constantine I (Emperor 306–37), and Justinian I (Eastern Emperor, 527–65) are cited as especially significant and influential Roman Emperors by way of emphasizing the political hegemony of the Papacy.

[6] "A ruinous war": the Thirty Years War (1618–1648), which led to the inception of the modern European nation-state system, and which Brown refers to in a related way in his essay on novel writing, "Walstein's School of History." In both essays, Brown characterizes this war and its geopolitical implications as a key turning point in early modern history before the era of the American and French revolutions.

[7] "A thorough discussion": Samuel Miller is a Presbyterian minister, and thus Brown's argument that the rejection of theism is the most significant development of the previous century necessarily has a polite but polemical edge.

the extensive continent of Indoostan, peopled by a race of equally numerous, much more ancient, & in some respect more civilized than the European race, may safely be said, at present, to be a conquered & subjected nation. During the two former ages, the progress of Europeans in the east was restricted by the efforts of each other. They sought for commercial rather than territorial empire in Asia. The Duch have long possessed as absolute an authority in the most important of the Indian Isles,[8] as their commercial views would admit, but not till the close of the 18th century were any important territorial acquisitions made, by any nation of Europe, on the continent. Lately, however, the removal of their great rivals the French, have given the English room for territorial acquisition.[9]

We cannot imagine any obstacle to their universal conquest of India, & such is the nature of human affairs, that India cannot possibly be the limit of these conquests. They must necessarily extend themselves beyond the Indian borders, & penetrate the regions that lie North East & West.

The eighteenth century will likewise be ever memorable for the colonization of New Holland.[10] This is the only considerable portion of the globe that remained till lately unexplored & unclaimed by European Nations. Now the world may be said to be subjected to this race. The Barbarous part of it is in a fair way of being subduced by Colonies, & the civilized by conquest. On an impartial survey of the globe we inhabit every dispassionate observer must percieve that the last age has forwarded in a wonderful & unexampled degree the progress of mankind to that state in which the most distant parts will become members of the same vast community.

There are, indeed, no natural indications that war & political division will either cease or diminish, but those political & commercial relations that have hitherto extended to a small portion of the world, there is abundant reason to think will speedily embrace the whole. All parts of America will bear a certain similarity to each other & some, if I may so speak, into commercial & political contact, not only among themselves, but with either extremity of the old world. Spanish & English Russians & French or their descendants will occupy America from pale to pale, will spread themselves over New Holland, & over either peninsula of India; will pervade Tartary, Persia, China, Arabia & Africa, & the same sort of community of knowledge, power & hate will reign throughout the Globe, which now exists among Europeans & their progeny.

Great effects are ascribed to the discovery of the art of printing. This age is distinguished from former ones by the extraordinary prevalence of this art. The number

---

[8] "Indian Isles": Dutch East India, present-day Indonesia.

[9] "Territorial acquisition": the Seven Years War (1756–1763), the worldwide war fought in Europe, Africa, India, North America (the French and Indian War), and the Philippines, during which England wrested control of India from France. This war forms the general backdrop for the lives of characters in both *Wieland* (1798) and *Edgar Huntly* (1799).

[10] "New Holland": present-day Australia. The name New Holland was used 1644–1824. Mysterious colonization schemes concerning New Holland figure in the plot of Brown's fictional fragment "Signior Adini" (c. 1793–1796) and possibly in the South Sea projects discussed in *Memoirs of Carwin* (1798–1805).

of authours & annual publications are probably ten fold greater at the close than at the opening of the century. Works, printed in small portions & periodically, that is, yearly, monthly, weekly or dayly, have multiplied beyond all example. The effects of this increase of publication, must be considerable, though it requires the utmost sagacity & most extensive knowledge, truly to estimate these effects.

It surprises that so little knowledge of the world at large has been gained by European nations, during a century so active & enlightened. We have already said that the Hindoos & Chinese are two, out of three, great divisions into which the human race, the civilized part of them, may be divided. The ascendency of the English in India afforded them the best opportunity imaginable for gaining a perfect knowledge of that country, & yet, compared with such opportunities, our knowledge is extremely limited. But it is in relation to China that our ignorance is most opprobrious.

There is a constant commercial intercourse maintained between Europe & China, & numerous agents of this commerce reside permanently in the latter empire. These however are confined to the suburbs of a single Sea-port,[11] & their minds are entirely engrossed by objects very different from the manners & opinions of the Chineze.

The Dutch & English governments have sent ambassadors to China. These were of course permitted to pass through the heart of the country to the capital. These, however, were subjected to the disadvantages of passing hastily & in one line thro' the country. This circumstance would be important if the country passed through were of narrow dimensions, but it is enhanced by the consideration that China is broader than Europe, that it is divided into a great number of provinces, each of which is equal in extent to European Kingdoms, & that, therefore, the accounts of an ambassador, however diligent & watchful, resemble what a Chinese envoy would be enabled to give of Spain, Germany & Poland, by travelling post from Liverpool to London.[12]

In truth, the last century cannot be said to have added any thing to our knowledge of China. In the Seventeenth century much was written & published by Romish Missionaries, respecting China,[13] to which, however vague, fallacious & unsatisfactory, the age under review, has added nothing worthy of mention.

---

[11] "A single Sea-port": present-day Guangzhou, then transliterated as Canton, was the Chinese port open to European commerce in the eighteenth century.

[12] "Liverpool to London": Brown's description of the limitations of Dutch and English legations to China during the eighteenth century summarizes the article "Some Particulars respecting the late Embassy of the Dutch East-India Company" which appeared in the Brown-edited *Monthly Magazine, and American Review* (May 1799, 148–150).

[13] "Romish Missionaries . . . China": that is, the writings that emerged from the Jesuit missions in China. The Jesuits were the first European institution to penetrate China. Francis Xavier, one of the founders of the Jesuits, was the first to attempt this and died in the attempt, on Shangchuan Island off China, in 1552. Later generations of Jesuits continued these efforts and established substantial relations with the Chinese court in Beijing; they dreamed of founding a Sino-Christian civilization that would rival the Roman-Christian civilization of Europe. The early Jesuits and their theocratic colonization schemes are referenced in *Wieland, Memoirs of Carwin*, and "Walstein's School of History."

Two very important Kingdoms of Asia, Corea & Japan have been altogether unvisited & undescribed, by any rational traveller, during this century. Some very important projects have lately been set afoot in Russia,[14] which will probably unfold the present state of these remote countries, to the present age in a very satisfactory manner.

6. Charles Brockden Brown, *Memoirs of Carwin the Biloquist. The Literary Magazine and American Register* (November 1803 to March 1805)

The unfinished Memoirs of Carwin the Biloquist *is best known as a prequel to* Wieland *that explains how, prior to the novel's events at Mettingen, Frank Carwin discovered his ventriloquistic abilities, left his backwoods Pennsylvania home for Philadelphia, met his elite patron Ludloe, traveled to Ireland and Europe under Ludloe's guidance, and learned of Ludloe's shadowy affairs. In Chapters 14, 23, and 27 of* Wieland, *Clara Wieland reports a newspaper announcement in which Ludloe accuses Carwin of crimes, and explains, after Carwin's confession and her uncle Cambridge's communications with the ventriloquist, that the newspaper report was an attempt to pursue and persecute Carwin. All of these narrative elements seem to draw openly from the basic scenario of William Godwin's* Things as They Are; or, The Adventures of Caleb Williams *(1794), the novel of social injustice that Godwin published as the fictional emplotment of the political principles organized in his* Enquiry Concerning Political Justice *(1793). Godwin's novel supplies the theme of an initially fascinating elite patron who exemplifies the violence and inequalities of the social order as he pursues a lower-status assistant whose curiosity has led him to discover the patron's secret activities. Godwin's writings were key sources for Brown and his closest associates in the New York circle (see the Godwin excerpts here in Related Texts).*

Brown began working on the narrative and probably finished or at least drafted a great deal of it in August 1798, even as he was finishing Wieland. *Work broke off during the New York yellow fever epidemic of September 1798,[1] however, and Brown did not find an occasion to publish or continue the story until 1803, when he started his* Literary Magazine *in Philadelphia and decided to serialize the narrative in monthly installments in that setting. Since the first seven of ten installments were published continuously, before a one-month break in May–July 1804 and a further six-month break before the final two episodes in February–March 1805, scholars generally assume that the first seven install-*

---

[14] "Projects . . . in Russia": Brown included numerous articles on recent developments in Russia in the New York *Monthly Magazine*. See, for example "Remarks upon the Russian Empire" (April 1800, 253–55) and "Account of the Political Journals, &c. in Russia" (October 1800, 308–11).

[1] As of 8 August 1798, Elihu Hubbard Smith's *Diary* reports "Read Brown's 'Carwin' as far as he has written it" and on September 4 Brown notes in a letter to William Dunlap (1766–1839) that he has stopped work on the narrative: "I have written something of the history of Carwin which I will send. I have desisted for the present from the prosecution of this plan . . . ." And on September 14, five days before Smith dies of yellow fever, Dunlap reports "Afternoon read CB Brown's beginning for the Life of Carwin—as far as he has gone he has done well: he has taken up the schemes of the Illuminati." For a discussion of the composition process, see the Cowie, "Historical Essay," in the 1977 Kent State Bicentennial edition of *Wieland* and *Carwin*.

ments correspond to material from August 1798, and that the remaining installments were developed in 1804–1805. There is no information to help us understand exactly what portions were completed in 1798 and whether they were revised as part of the later serialization, however. This is significant because it reminds us that the work may serve as a link between the novelistic projects of the 1798–1801 period and the fictional narratives, political pamphlets, and historical "Annals" of the 1803–1809 years.

Besides the details that link Carwin's patron Ludloe with the Illuminati scare of 1798–1801, the narrative is notable for the way it inscribes Carwin and his travels within a cosmopolitan, global understanding of European and world history that was already hinted at in Wieland. *In its concluding references to Pacific explorations, far-flung colonization projects, and political struggles over the theocratic colonization schemes of the Jesuits, for example,[2] the narrative seems to connect with the global view of world history Brown sketched out in his June 1803 letter to Samuel Miller (included in Related Texts). In addition, the brief discussion of marriage as an oppressive institution in part 7 is a striking element of the text that connects this publication with Brown's discussion of the relation between property and sex-gender as far back as his Wollstonecraftian dialogue* Alcuin *(1798) and "Walstein's School of History" (1799).*

After its first appearance, Memoirs of Carwin *was reprinted in two collections of Brown's miscellaneous writings in the nineteenth century (1815, 1822[3]), but not again until scholar Fred Lewis Pattee published the first combined edition of* Wieland *and* Carwin *in 1926. Since that time, it has become common to print both narratives in the same volume, although Carwin's memoir is usually edited into a continuous form. In order to give the reader a taste of the original, the text that follows preserves the divisions between the serialized installments. These ten parts are not necessarily where Brown might have drawn eventual chapter divisions had the narrative been completed and published separately, but they allow the reader to experience the serialized form that Brown originally gave the text.[4]*

---

[2] For more on this aspect of Carwin's memoir, see Hsu, "Democratic Expansionism in Memoirs of Carwin"; Kazanjian, "Charles Brockden Brown's Biloquial Nation: National Culture and White Settler Colonialism in *Memoirs of Carwin the Biloquist*"; and Leask, "Irish Republicans and Gothic Eleutherarchs: Pacific Utopias in the Writings of Theobald Wolfe Tone and Charles Brockden Brown."

[3] These were Dunlap's *Life of Charles Brockden Brown* (Philadelphia: James P. Parke, 1815) and, in England, Henry Colburn's *Carwin the Biloquist and other American Tales and Pieces* (London: Henry Colburn, 1822). The Colburn printing divided the narrative into five chapters. For the text's history, see the Historical and Textual essays in the 1977 Kent State Bicentennial edition.

[4] The installments originally appeared as follows:
  1. *Literary Magazine (LM)* 1.2 (November 1803): 100–104.
  2. *LM* 1.3 (December 1803): 181–85.
  3. *LM* 1.4 (January 1804): 255–59.
  4. *LM* 1.5 [incorrectly labeled "4"] (February 1804), 332–35.
  5. *LM* 1.6 (March 1804): 412–16.
  6. *LM* 2.7 (April 1804): 3–7.
  7. *LM* 2.8 (May 1804): 89–93.
  8. *LM* 2.10 (July 1804): 248–52.
  9. *LM* 3.17 (February 1805): 110–14, and "Notes from the Editor," 160.
  10. *LM* 3.18 (March 1805): 210–14.

*****

MEMOIRS OF CARWIN THE BILOQUIST

I

I WAS the second son of a farmer, whose place of residence was a western district of Pennsylvania. My eldest brother seemed fitted by nature for the employment to which he was destined. His wishes never led him astray from the hay-stack and the furrow. His ideas never ranged beyond the sphere of his vision, or suggested the possibility that to-morrow could differ from to-day. He could read and write, because he had no alternative between learning the lesson prescribed to him and punishment. He was diligent, as long as fear urged him forward, but his exertions ceased with the cessation of this motive. The limits of his acquirements consisted in signing his name, and spelling out a chapter in the bible.

My character was the reverse of his. My thirst of knowledge was augmented in proportion as it was supplied with gratification. The more I heard or read, the more restless and unconquerable my curiosity[5] became. My senses were perpetually alive to novelty, my fancy teemed with visions of the future, and my attention fastened upon every thing mysterious or unknown.

My father intended that my knowledge should keep pace with that of my brother, but conceived that all beyond the mere capacity to write and read was useless or pernicious. He took as much pains to keep me within these limits, as to make the acquisitions of my brother come up to them, but his efforts were not equally successful in both cases. The most vigilant and jealous scrutiny was exerted in vain: Reproaches and blows, painful privations and ignominious penances had no power to slacken my zeal and abate my perseverance. He might enjoin upon me the most laborious tasks, set the envy of my brother to watch me during the performance, make the most diligent search after my books, and destroy them without mercy, when they were found; but he could not outroot my darling propensity. I exerted all my powers to elude his watchfulness. Censures and stripes[6] were sufficiently unpleasing to make me strive to avoid them. To effect this desirable end, I was incessantly employed in the invention of stratagems and the execution of expedients.

My passion was surely not deserving of blame, and I have frequently lamented the hardships to which it subjected me; yet, perhaps, the claims which were made upon my ingenuity and fortitude were not without beneficial effects upon my character.

This contention lasted from the sixth to the fourteenth year of my age. My father's opposition to my schemes was incited by a sincere though unenlightened desire for

---

[5] "Curiosity": an important keyword suggesting both the search for enlightenment and the risk of badly regulated or undisciplined energies in Brown's and Woldwinite novels of the period. See *Wieland* notes 1.12, 23.2.

[6] "Stripes": marks from caning or whipping.

my happiness. That all his efforts were secretly eluded or obstinately repelled, was a source of the bitterest regret. He has often lamented, with tears, what he called my incorrigible depravity, and encouraged himself to perseverance by the notion of the ruin that would inevitably overtake me if I were allowed to persist in my present career. Perhaps the sufferings which arose to him from the disappointment, were equal to those which he inflicted on me.[7]

In my fourteenth year, events happened which ascertained my future destiny. One evening I had been sent to bring cows from a meadow, some miles distant from my father's mansion. My time was limited, and I was menaced with severe chastisement if, according to my custom, I should stay beyond the period assigned.

For some time these menaces rung in my ears, and I went on my way with speed. I arrived at the meadow, but the cattle had broken the fence and escaped.[8] It was my duty to carry home the earliest tidings of this accident, but the first suggestion was to examine the cause and manner of this escape. The field was bounded by cedar railing. Five of these rails were laid horizontally from post to post. The upper one had been broken in the middle, but the rest had merely been drawn out of the holes on one side, and rested with their ends on the ground. The means which had been used for this end, the reason why one only was broken, and that one the uppermost, how a pair of horns could be so managed as to effect that which the hands of man would have found difficult, supplied a theme of meditation.

Some accident recalled me from this reverie, and reminded me how much time had thus been consumed. I was terrified at the consequences of my delay, and sought with eagerness how they might be obviated. I asked myself if there were not a way back shorter than that by which I had come. The beaten road was rendered circuitous by a precipice that projected into a neighbouring stream, and closed up a passage by which the length of the way would have been diminished one half: at the foot of the cliff the water was of considerable depth, and agitated by an eddy. I could not estimate the danger which I should incur by plunging into it, but I was resolved to make the attempt. I have reason to think, that this experiment, if it had been tried, would have proved fatal, and my father, while he lamented my untimely fate, would have been wholly unconscious that his own unreasonable demands had occasioned it.

I turned my steps towards the spot. To reach the edge of the stream was by no means an easy undertaking, so many abrupt points and gloomy hollows were interposed. I had frequently skirted and penetrated this tract, but had never been so completely

---

[7] "Sufferings . . . equal to those he inflicted on me": Carwin's rejection of paternalist authority as flawed, tyrannical, and backward is a common motif in writings of the Revolutionary age and Brown's novels. The rural protagonist of *Arthur Mervyn* (1799–1800), for example, struggles with his father in a similar way. Possibly as a consequence of his laboring-class origins, Carwin is never tempted by nostalgia concerning paternalist or pastoral ideals like those of the Wielands.

[8] "Cattle . . . escaped": this paragraph, which connects an episode of cowherding and mysterious loss or theft of cattle with the beginnings of Carwin's exploits, seems to renew the initial association of Hermes and Carwin established in *Wieland* (see note 6.5). Since Hermes stole cattle from Apollo on the day he was born and protected the heifer-nymph Io for Zeus, he is commonly depicted as a rustic but cunning cowherd in visual representations of these episodes.

entangled in the maze as now: hence I had remained unacquainted with a narrow pass, which, at the distance of an hundred yards from the river, would conduct me, though not without danger and toil, to the opposite side of the ridge.

This glen was now discovered, and this discovery induced me to change my plan. If a passage could be here effected, it would be shorter and safer than that which led through the stream, and its practicability was to be known only by experiment. The path was narrow, steep, and overshadowed by rocks. The sun was nearly set, and the shadow of the cliff above, obscured the passage almost as much as midnight would have done: I was accustomed to despise danger when it presented itself in a sensible form, but, by a defect common in every one's education, goblins and spectres were to me the objects of the most violent apprehensions. These were unavoidably connected with solitude and darkness, and were present to my fears when I entered this gloomy recess.

These terrors are always lessened by calling the attention away to some indifferent object. I now made use of this expedient, and began to amuse myself by hallowing as loud as organs of unusual compass and vigour would enable me. I uttered the words which chanced to occur to me, and repeated in the shrill tones of a Mohock[9] savage. . . "Cow! cow! come home! home!". . . These notes were of course reverberated from the rocks which on either side towered aloft, but the echo was confused and indistinct.

I continued, for some time, thus to beguile the way, till I reached a space more than commonly abrupt, and which required all my attention. My rude ditty was suspended till I had surmounted this impediment. In a few minutes I was at leisure to renew it. After finishing the strain, I paused. In a few seconds a voice as I then imagined, uttered the same cry from the point of a rock some hundred feet behind me; the same words, with equal distinctness and deliberation, and in the same tone, appeared to be spoken. I was startled by this incident, and cast a fearful glance behind, to discover by whom it was uttered. The spot where I stood was buried in dusk, but the eminences were still invested with a luminous and vivid twilight. The speaker, however, was concealed from my view.

I had scarcely begun to wonder at this occurrence, when a new occasion for wonder, was afforded me. A few seconds, in like manner, elapsed, when my ditty was again rehearsed, with a no less perfect imitation, in a different quarter. . . . To this quarter I eagerly turned my eyes, but no one was visible. . . . The station, indeed, which this new speaker seemed to occupy, was inaccessible to man or beast.

If I were surprized at this second repetition of my words, judge how much my surprise must have been augmented, when the same calls were a third time repeated, and coming still in a new direction. Five times was this ditty successively resounded, at intervals nearly equal, always from a new quarter, and with little abatement of its original distinctness and force.

---

[9] "Mohock": Mohawk, referring to the indigenous peoples residing at that time mainly in northern New York and Canada. As members of the Iroquois Confederation, they were traditional enemies of the Lenape (Delaware) people.

A little reflection was sufficient to show that this was no more than an echo of an extraordinary kind. My terrors were quickly supplanted by delight. The motives to dispatch were forgotten, and I amused myself for an hour, with talking to these cliffs: I placed myself in new positions, and exhausted my lungs and my invention in new clamours.

The pleasures of this new discovery were an ample compensation for the ill treatment which I expected on my return. By some caprice in my father I escaped merely with a few reproaches. I seized the first opportunity of again visiting this recess, and repeating my amusement; time, and incessant repetition, could scarcely lessen its charms or exhaust the variety produced by new tones and new positions.

The hours in which I was most free from interruption and restraint were those of moonlight. My brother and I occupied a small room above the kitchen, disconnected, in some degree, with the rest of the house. It was the rural custom to retire early to bed and to anticipate the rising of the sun. When the moonlight was strong enough to permit me to read, it was my custom to escape from bed, and hie with my book to some neighbouring eminence, where I would remain stretched on the mossy rock, till the sinking or beclouded moon, forbade me to continue my employment. I was indebted for books to a friendly person in the neighbourhood, whose compliance with my solicitations was prompted partly by benevolence and partly by enmity to my father, whom he could not more egregiously offend than by gratifying my perverse and pernicious curiosity.

In leaving my chamber I was obliged to use the utmost caution to avoid rousing my brother, whose temper disposed him to thwart me in the least of my gratifications. My purpose was surely laudable, and yet on leaving the house and returning to it, I was obliged to use the vigilance and circumspection of a thief.

One night I left my bed with this view. I posted first to my vocal glen, and thence scrambling up a neighbouring steep, which overlooked a wide extent of this romantic country, gave myself up to contemplation, and the perusal of Milton's Comus.[10]

My reflections were naturally suggested by the singularity of this echo. To hear my own voice speak at a distance would have been formerly regarded as prodigious. To hear too, that voice, not uttered by another, by whom it might easily be mimicked, but by myself! I cannot now recollect the transition which led me to the notion of sounds, similar to these, but produced by other means than reverberation. Could I not so dispose my organs as to make my voice appear at a distance?

---

[10] "Milton's Comus": John Milton's *Comus: a Maske presented at Ludlow Castle* (1637) is an allegory of virtue and temptation, in which a Lady is separated from her brothers in a forest and encounters the carnival of Comus, a god of excess, who tries to tempt her to abandon virtue and indulge in sex and other exotic, sensual pleasures. Reading the poem at night, outside and alone, Carwin may be imaginatively wishing for a similar extraordinary encounter, likely with a different outcome. References to *Comus* introduce the concluding romance and erotic encounter in Brown's novel *Arthur Mervyn* (1800). Other references and details in the narrative, for example the names Ludlow and Damon, will continue to echo Milton.

From speculation I proceeded to experiment. The idea of a distant voice, like my own, was intimately present to my fancy. I exerted myself with a most ardent desire, and with something like a persuasion that I should succeed. I started with surprise, for it seemed as if success had crowned my attempts. I repeated the effort, but failed. A certain position of the organs took place on the first attempt, altogether new, unexampled and as it were, by accident, for I could not attain it on the second experiment.

You[11] will not wonder that I exerted myself with indefatigable zeal to regain what had once, though for so short a space, been in my power. Your own ears have witnessed the success of these efforts. By perpetual exertion I gained it a second time, and now was a diligent observer of the circumstances attending it. Gradually I subjected these finer and more subtle motions to the command of my will. What was at first difficult, by exercise and habit, was rendered easy. I learned to accommodate my voice to all the varieties of distance and directions.

It cannot be denied that this faculty is wonderful and rare, but when we consider the possible modifications of muscular motion, how few of these are usually exerted, how imperfectly they are subjected to the will, and yet that the will is capable of being rendered unlimited and absolute, will not our wonder cease?

We have seen men who could hide their tongues so perfectly that even an Anatomist, after the most accurate inspection that a living subject could admit, has affirmed the organ to be wanting, but this was effected by the exertion of muscles unknown and incredible to the greater part of mankind.

The concurrence of teeth, palate and tongue, in the formation of speech should seem to be indispensable, and yet men have spoken distinctly though wanting a tongue, and to whom, therefore, teeth and palate were superfluous. The tribe of motions requisite to this end, are wholly latent and unknown, to those who possess that organ.

I mean not to be more explicit. I have no reason to suppose a peculiar conformation or activity in my own organs, or that the power which I posses may not, with suitable directions and by steady efforts, be obtained by others, but I will do nothing to facilitate the acquisition. It is by far, too liable to perversion for a good man to desire to possess it, or to teach it to another.

There remained but one thing to render this instrument as powerful in my hands as it was capable of being. From my childhood, I was remarkably skilful at imitation. There were few voices whether of men or birds or beasts which I could not imitate with success. To add my ancient, to my newly acquired skill, to talk from a distance, and at the same time, in the accents of another, was the object of my endeavours, and this object after a certain number of trials, I finally obtained.

In my present situation every thing that denoted intellectual exertion was a crime, and exposed me to invectives if not to stripes. This circumstance induced me to be

---

[11] "You": a later remark to the narrative's unnamed addressee will hint that he or she is member of the Wieland circle such as Thomas Cambridge (see note 31). Like Clara Wieland and all of Brown's narrators, Carwin presents a memoir of his extraordinary experiences that will clarify events in retrospect and serve as an instructive example of ways that social circumstances and pressures shape character and behavior.

silent to all others, on the subject of my discovery. But, added to this, was a confused belief, that it might be made, in some way instrumental to my relief from the hardships and restraints of my present condition. For some time I was not aware of the mode in which it might be rendered subservient to this end.

II

MY father's sister was an ancient lady, resident in Philadelphia, the relict[12] of a merchant, whose decease left her the enjoyment of a frugal competence. She was without children, and had often expressed her desire that her nephew Frank, whom she always considered as a sprightly and promising lad, should be put under her care. She offered to be at the expense of my education, and to bequeath to me at her death her slender patrimony.

This arrangement was obstinately rejected by my father, because it was merely fostering and giving scope to propensities, which he considered as hurtful, and because his avarice desired that this inheritance should fall to no one but himself. To me, it was a scheme of ravishing felicity, and to be debarred from it was a source of anguish known to few. I had too much experience of my father's pertinaciousness ever to hope for a change in his views; yet the bliss of living with my aunt, in a new and busy scene, and in the unbounded indulgence of my literary passion, continually occupied my thoughts: for a long time these thoughts were productive only of despondency and tears.

Time only enhanced the desirableness of this scheme; my new faculty would naturally connect itself with these wishes, and the question could not fail to occur whether it might not aid me in the execution of my favourite plan.

A thousand superstitious tales were current in the family. Apparitions had been seen, and voices had been heard on a multitude of occasions. My father was a confident believer in supernatural tokens. The voice of his wife, who had been many years dead, had been twice heard at midnight whispering at his pillow. I frequently asked myself whether a scheme favourable to my views might not be built upon these foundations. Suppose (thought I) my mother should be made to enjoin upon him compliance with my wishes?

This idea bred in me a temporary consternation. To imitate the voice of the dead, to counterfeit a commission from heaven, bore the aspect of presumption and impiety. It seemed an offence which could not fail to draw after it the vengeance of the deity. My wishes for a time yielded to my fears, but this scheme in proportion as I meditated on it, became more plausible; no other occurred to me so easy and so efficacious. I endeavoured to persuade myself that the end proposed, was, in the highest degree praiseworthy, and that the excellence of my purpose would justify the means employed to attain it.

My resolutions were, for a time, attended with fluctuations and misgivings. These gradually disappeared, and my purpose became firm; I was next to devise the means of effecting my views, this did not demand any tedious deliberation. It was easy to

---

[12] "Relict": a widow or surviving partner; a survivor.

gain access to my father's chamber without notice or detection, cautious footsteps and the suppression of breath would place me, unsuspected and unthought of, by his bed side. The words I should use, and the mode of utterance were not easily settled, but having at length selected these, I made myself by much previous repetition, perfectly familiar with the use of them.

I selected a blustering and inclement night, in which the darkness was augmented by a veil of the blackest clouds. The building we inhabited was slight in its structure, and full of crevices through which the gale found easy way, and whistled in a thousand cadencies. On this night the elemental music was remarkably sonorous, and was mingled not unfrequently with *thunder heard remote.*[13]

I could not divest myself of secret dread. My heart faultered with a consciousness of wrong. Heaven seemed to be present and to disapprove my work; I listened to the thunder and the wind, as to the stern voice of this disapprobation. Big drops stood on my forehead, and my tremors almost incapacitated me from proceeding.

These impediments however I surmounted; I crept up stairs at midnight, and entered my father's chamber. The darkness was intense and I sought with outstretched hands for his bed. The darkness, added to the trepidation of my thoughts, disabled me from making a right estimate of distances: I was conscious of this, and when I advanced within the room, paused.

I endeavoured to compare the progress I had made with my knowledge of the room, and governed by the result of this comparison, proceeded cautiously and with hands still outstretched in search of the foot of the bed. At this moment lightning flashed into the room: the brightness of the gleam was dazzling, yet it afforded me an exact knowledge of my situation. I had mistaken my way, and discovered that my knees nearly touched the bedstead, and that my hands at the next step, would have touched my father's cheek. His closed eyes and every line in his countenance, were painted, as it were, for an instant on my sight.

The flash was accompanied with a burst of thunder, whose vehemence was stunning. I always entertained a dread of thunder, and now recoiled, overborne with terror. Never had I witnessed so luminous a gleam and so tremendous a shock, yet my father's slumber appeared not to be disturbed by it.

I stood irresolute and trembling; to prosecute my purpose in this state of mind was impossible. I resolved for the present to relinquish it, and turned with a view of exploring my way out of the chamber. Just then a light seen through the window, caught my eye. It was at first weak but speedily increased; no second thought was necessary to inform me that the barn, situated at a small distance from the house, and newly stored with hay, was in flames, in consequence of being struck by the lightning.

---

[13] "*Thunder heard remote*": from John Milton's *Paradise Lost* (1667), II.473–77. The terrific sound is heard when the assembled host of Pandaemonium, gathered as a voting revolutionary legislature (previously "enslaved" and subjected to "stripes, and arbitrary punishment"; II.333–34), rises from their seats, recognizing Satan's heroic leadership and efforts to seek "deliverance" for his fallen angels: "But they / Dreaded not more th' adventure than his voice / Forbidding, and at once with him they rose; / Their rising all at once was as the sound / Of thunder heard remote."

My terror at this spectacle made me careless of all consequences relative to myself. I rushed to the bed and throwing myself on my father, awakened him by loud cries. The family were speedily roused, and were compelled to remain impotent spectators of the devastation. Fortunately the wind blew in a contrary direction, so that our habitation was not injured.

The impression that was made upon me by the incidents of that night is indelible. The wind gradually rose into an hurricane; the largest branches were torn from the trees, and whirled aloft into the air; others were uprooted and laid prostrate on the ground. The barn was a spacious edifice, consisting wholly of wood, and filled with a plenteous harvest. Thus supplied with fuel, and fanned by the wind, the fire raged with incredible fury; meanwhile clouds rolled above, whose blackness was rendered more conspicuous by reflection from the flames: the vast volumes of smoke were dissipated in a moment by the storm, while glowing fragments and cinders were borne to an immense height, and tossed everywhere in wild confusion. Ever and anon the sable canopy that hung around us was streaked with lightning and the peals, by which it was accompanied, were deafening, and with scarcely any intermission.

It was, doubtless, absurd to imagine any connexion between this portentous scene and the purpose that I had meditated, yet a belief of this connexion, though wavering and obscure, lurked in my mind; something more than a coincidence merely casual, appeared to have subsisted between my situation, at my father's bed side, and the flash that darted through the window and diverted me from my design. It palsied my courage, and strengthened my conviction, that my scheme was criminal.

After some time had elapsed, and tranquility was, in some degree, restored in the family, my father reverted to the circumstances in which I had been discovered on the first alarm of this event. The truth was impossible to be told. I felt the utmost reluctance to be guilty of a falsehood, but by falsehood only could I elude detection. That my guilt was the offspring of a fatal necessity, that the injustice of others gave it birth and made it unavoidable, afforded me slight consolation. Nothing can be more injurous than a lie, but its evil tendency chiefly respects our future conduct. Its direct consequences may be transient and few, but it facilitates a repetition, strengthens temptation, and grows into habit. I pretended some necessity had drawn me from my bed, and that discovering the condition of the barn, I hastened to inform my father.

Some time after this, my father summoned me to his presence. I had been previously guilty of disobedience to his commands, in a matter about which he was usually very scrupulous. My brother had been privy to my offence, and had threatened to be my accuser. On this occasion I expected nothing but arraignment and punishment. Weary of oppression, and hopeless of any change in my father's temper and views, I had formed the resolution of eloping from his house, and of trusting, young as I was, to the caprice of fortune. I was hesitating whether to abscond without the knowledge of the family, or to make my resolutions known to them, and while I avowed my resolution, to adhere to it in spite of opposition and remonstrances, when I received this summons.

I was employed at this time in the field; night was approaching, and I had made no preparation for departure; all the preparation in my power to make, was indeed small; a few clothes made into a bundle, was the sum of my possessions. Time would have little influence in improving my prospects, and I resolved to execute my scheme immediately.

I left work intending to seek my chamber, and taking what was my own, to disappear forever. I turned a stile that led out of the field into a bye path, when my father appeared before me, advancing in an opposite direction; to avoid him was impossible, and I summoned my fortitude to a conflict with his passion.

As soon as we met, instead of anger and upbraiding, he told me, that he had been reflecting on my aunt's proposal, to take me under her protection, and had concluded that the plan was proper; if I still retained my wishes on that head, he would readily comply with them, and that, if I chose, I might set off for the city next morning, as a neighbour's waggon was preparing to go.

I shall not dwell on the rapture with which this proposal was listened to: it was with difficulty that I persuaded myself that he was in earnest in making it, nor could divine the reasons, for so sudden and unexpected a change in his maxims. . . . These I afterwards discovered. Some one had instilled into him fears, that my aunt exasperated at his opposition to her request, respecting the unfortunate Frank, would bequeath her property to strangers; to obviate this evil, which his avarice prompted him to regard as much greater than any mischief, that would accrue to me, from the change of my abode, he embraced her proposal.

I entered with exultation and triumph on this new scene; my hopes were by no means disappointed. Detested labour was exchanged for luxurious idleness. I was master of my time, and the chuser of my occupations. My kinswoman on discovering that I entertained no relish for the drudgery of colleges, and was contented with the means of intellectual gratification, which I could obtain under her roof, allowed me to pursue my own choice.

Three tranquil years passed away, during which, each day added to my happiness, by adding to my knowledge. My biloquial faculty was not neglected. I improved it by assiduous exercise; I deeply reflected on the use to which it might be applied. I was not destitute of pure intentions; I delighted not in evil; I was incapable of knowingly contributing to another's misery, but the sole or principal end of my endeavours was not the happiness of others.

I was actuated by ambition. I was delighted to possess superior power; I was prone to manifest that superiority, and was satisfied if this were done, without much solicitude concerning consequences. I sported frequently with the apprehensions of my associates, and threw out a bait for their wonder, and supplied them with occasions for the structure of theories. It may not be amiss to enumerate one or two adventures in which I was engaged.

III

I HAD taken much pains to improve the sagacity of a favourite Spaniel. It was my purpose, indeed, to ascertain to what degree of improvement the principles of reasoning and imitation could be carried in a dog. There is no doubt that the animal affixes distinct ideas to sounds. What are the possible limits of his vocabulary no one can tell. In conversing with my dog I did not use English words, but selected simple monosyllables. Habit likewise enabled him to comprehend my gestures. If I crossed my hands on my breast he understood the signal and laid down behind me. If I joined my hands and lifted them to my breast, he returned home. If I grasped one arm above the elbow he ran before me. If I lifted my hand to my forehead he trotted composedly behind. By one motion I could make him bark; by another I could reduce him to silence. He would howl in twenty different strains of mournfulness, at my bidding. He would fetch and carry with undeviating faithfulness.

His actions being thus chiefly regulated by gestures, that to a stranger would appear indifferent or casual, it was easy to produce a belief that the animal's knowledge was much greater than in truth, it was.

One day, in a mixed company, the discourse turned upon the unrivaled abilities of *Damon*.[14] Damon had, indeed, acquired in all the circles which I frequented, an extraordinary reputation. Numerous instances of his sagacity were quoted and some of them exhibited on the spot. Much surprise was excited by the readiness with which he appeared to comprehend sentences of considerable abstraction and complexity, though, he in reality, attended to nothing but the movements of hand or fingers with which I accompanied my words. I enhanced the astonishment of some and excited the ridicule of others, by observing that my dog not only understood English when spoken by others, but actually spoke the language himself, with no small degree of precision.

This assertion could not be admitted without proof; proof, therefore, was readily produced. At a known signal, Damon began a low interrupted noise, in which the astonished hearers clearly distinguished English words. A dialogue began between the animal and his master, which was maintained, on the part of the former, with great vivacity and spirit. In this dialogue the dog asserted the dignity of his species and capacity of intellectual improvement.[15] The company separated lost in wonder, but perfectly convinced by the evidence that had been produced.

---

[14] "*Damon*": the dog's name resonates on several levels. The classical reference is to Damon and Pythias, symbols of true companionship; they were philosophical comrades who opposed a tyrant and were pardoned after each demonstrated his willingness to sacrifice himself for the other. A Miltonic reference extends from this legend, for Milton allegorically titled his poem on death of his closest friend Charles Diodati "Epitaphium Damonis" (Elegy for Damon; 1639). Finally, since Carwin's tricks with this dog lead to speculation, two paragraphs on, about guardian spirits or "invisible beings," the name seems to echo the "daemon" spirits discussed several times in *Wieland*; see notes 5.17, 9.9, 10.3, 10.5, 14.11, 20.8.

[15] "Intellectual improvement": the spaniel magically articulates a standard list of Enlightenment demands for universal human rights. This performance may parody contemporary conspiratorial fantasies, since the argument for enlightenment, coming from a lowly dog, is remotely controlled by a ventriloquizing master with his own agenda. In fact, the character Ludloe will first hint at a mysterious conspiratorial project in the next scene. An account of a British theatrical ventriloquist who faked less interesting conversations with his pet parrot was published in the Philadelphia *Weekly Magazine* of July 7, 1798, shortly before *Wieland* appeared.

On a subsequent occasion a select company was assembled at a garden, at a small distance from the city. Discourse glided through a variety of topics, till it lighted at length on the subject of invisible beings. From the speculations of philosophers we proceeded to the creations of the poet. Some maintained the justness of Shakspear's delineations of aerial beings, while others denied it. By no violent transition, Ariel[16] and his songs were introduced, and a lady, celebrated for her musical skill, was solicited to accompany her pedal harp with the song of "Five fathom deep thy father lies"[17] . . . She was known to have set, for her favourite instrument, all the songs of Shakspeare.

My youth made me little more than an auditor on this occasion. I sat apart from the rest of the company, and carefully noted every thing. The track which the conversation had taken, suggested a scheme which was not thoroughly digested when the lady began her enchanting strain.

She ended and the audience were mute with rapture. The pause continued, when a strain was wafted to our ears from another quarter. The spot where we sat was embowered by a vine. The verdant arch was lofty and the area beneath was spacious.

The sound proceeded from above. At first it was faint and scarcely audible; presently it reached a louder key, and every eye was cast up in expectation of beholding a face among the pendant clusters. The strain was easily recognized, for it was no other than that which Ariel is made to sing when finally absolved from the service of the wizard.

> In the Cowslip's bell I lie,
> On the Bat's back I do fly . . .
> After summer merrily, &c.[18]

Their hearts palpitated as they listened: they gazed at each other for a solution of the mystery. At length the strain died away at distance, and an interval of silence was succeeded by an earnest discussion of the cause of this prodigy. One supposition only could be adopted, which was, that the strain was uttered by human organs. That the songster was stationed on the roof of the arbour, and having finished his melody had risen into the viewless fields of air.

---

[16] "Ariel": the airy spirit who is a bound servant to Prospero in Shakespeare's *The Tempest*.

[17] "Five fathom deep thy father lies": *The Tempest*, I.ii.397–405. These lyrics change Shakespeare's line, "full fathom five thy father lies." The spirit Ariel sings these lines on Prospero's orders (another sort of ventriloquistic command), to deceive Ferdinand after the storm. This father is not dead, and the assertion is an attempt to manipulate.

[18] "In the Cowslip's bell I lie . . . &c.": *The Tempest*, V.i. 88–94. Again, the lyrics are slightly changed but, as Carwin notes, the song conveys Ariel's pleasure at being liberated from Prospero's service: "Where the bee sucks, there suck I; / In a cowslip's bell I lie; / There I couch when owls do cry. / On the bat's back I do fly / After summer merrily / Merrily, merrily shall I live now / Under the blossom that hangs on the bough."

I had been invited to spend a week at this house:[19] this period was nearly expired when I received information that my aunt was suddenly taken sick, and that her life was in imminent danger. I immediately set out on my return to the city, but before my arrival she was dead.

This lady was entitled to my gratitude and esteem; I had received the most essential benefits at her hand.[20] I was not destitute of sensibility, and was deeply affected by this event: I will own, however, that my grief was lessened by reflecting on the consequences of her death, with regard to my own condition. I had been ever taught to consider myself as her heir, and her death, therefore, would free me from certain restraints.

My aunt had a female servant, who had lived with her for twenty years: she was married, but her husband, who as an artizan, lived apart from her: I had no reason to suspect the woman's sincerity and disinterestedness; but my aunt was no sooner consigned to the grave than a will was produced in which Dorothy was named her sole and universal heir.

It was in vain to urge my expectations and my claims. . . the instrument was legibly and legally drawn up. . . Dorothy was exasperated by my opposition and surmises, and vigorously enforced her title. In a week after the decease of my kinswoman, I was obliged to seek a new dwelling. As all my property consisted in my cloths and my papers, this was easily done.

My condition was now calamitous and forlorn. Confiding in the acquisition of my aunts' patrimony, I had made no other provision for the future; I hated manual labour, or any task of which the object was gain. To be guided in my choice of occupations by any motive but the pleasure which the occupation was qualified to produce, was intolerable to my proud, indolent, and restive temper.

This resource was now cut off; the means of immediate subsistence were denied me: If I had determined to acquire the knowledge of some lucrative art, the acquisition would demand time, and, meanwhile, I was absolutely destitute of support. My father's house was, indeed, open to me, but I preferred to stifle myself with the filth of the kennel, rather than to return to it.

Some plan it was immediately necessary to adopt. The exigence of my affairs, and this reverse of fortune, continually occupied my thoughts; I estranged myself from society and from books, and devoted myself to lonely walks and mournful meditation.

---

[19] "This house": Carwin now moves in higher social circles that allow him to become a guest at what seems to be an elite country home with gardens used for musical-conversational gatherings, presumably along the Schuylkill and much like the Wieland estate Mettingen where that novel's encounter will begin.

[20] "Essential benefits at her hand": after his experience of paternal tyranny and laboring dependence, Carwin has experienced an interlude of maternally coded benevolence and economically secure leisure, now lost with the death of his generous aunt.

One morning as I ranged along the bank of Schuylkill, I encountered a person, by name Ludloe,[21] of whom I had some previous knowledge. He was from Ireland; was a man of some rank and apparently rich: I had met with him before, but in mixed companies, where little direct intercourse had taken place between us. Our last meeting was in the arbour where Ariel was so unexpectedly introduced.

Our acquaintance merely justified a transient salutation; but he did not content himself with noticing me as I passed, but joined me in my walk and entered into conversation. It was easy to advert to the occasion on which we had last met, and to the mysterious incident which then occurred. I was solicitous to dive into his thoughts upon this head and put some questions which tended to the point that I wished.

I was somewhat startled when he expressed his belief, that the performer of this mystic strain was one of the company then present, who exerted, for this end, a faculty not commonly possessed. Who this person was he did not venture to guess, and could not discover, by the tokens which he suffered to appear, that his suspicions glanced at me. He expatiated with great profoundness and fertility of ideas, on the uses to which a faculty like this might be employed. No more powerful engine, he said, could be conceived, by which the ignorant and credulous might be moulded to our purposes; managed by a man of ordinary talents, it would open for him the straightest and surest avenues to wealth and power.

His remarks excited in my mind a new strain of thoughts. I had not hitherto considered the subject in this light, though vague ideas of the importance of this art could not fail to be occasionally suggested: I ventured to inquire into his ideas of the mode, in which an art like this could be employed, so as to effect the purposes he mentioned.

He dealt chiefly in general representations. Men, he said, believed in the existence and energy of invisible powers, and in the duty of discovering and conforming to their will. This will was supposed to be sometimes made known to them through the medium of their senses. A voice coming from a quarter where no attendant form

---

[21] "Ludloe": the character first mentioned in Chapter 14 of *Wieland* and identified in the course of the novel as a former patron who pursues Carwin and attempts to falsely incriminate him, much like the patron Falkland in William Godwin's novel *Caleb Williams* (1794). Beginning with this stroll along the Schuylkill, this "prequel" narrative begins to explain how that relationship developed. See *Wieland* notes 14.4, 14.5, 23.4. Additionally, the association with Ireland links Ludloe and his plot line to contemporary conservative fears about Irish subversion.

The name may have had several associations for Brown. Ludlow is a town in Shropshire, western England, and the location of Ludlow Castle, where Milton's *Comus* was first performed. Edmund Ludlow (spelled variously) was a rebel leader and military commander under Cromwell in the English Civil War (1642–1651), when he fought in Ireland. He was a republican (or Parliamentarian), a Calvinist predestinarian, and one of the fifty-nine judges who signed the warrant for the execution of British king Charles I. Under the late phase of Cromwell's rule, Ludlow was arrested for refusing to submit to government authority, went into hiding, and was later imprisoned. After the restoration of the monarchy in 1660, he escaped from imprisonment in England and lived in exile in Switzerland as an unpardoned regicide, a sort of failed conspirator.

could be seen would, in most cases, be ascribed to supernal agency, and a command imposed on them, in this manner, would be obeyed with religious scrupulousness. Thus men might be imperiously directed in the disposal of their industry, their property, and even of their lives. Men, actuated by a mistaken sense of duty, might, under this influence, be led to the commission of the most flagitious, as well as the most heroic acts: If it were his desire to accumulate wealth, or institute a new sect, he should need no other instrument.

I listened to this kind of discourse with great avidity, and regretted when he thought proper to introduce new topics. He ended by requesting me to visit him, which I eagerly consented to do. When left alone, my imagination was filled with the images suggested by this conversation. The hopelessness of better fortune, which I had lately harboured, now gave place to cheering confidence. Those motives of rectitude which should deter me from this species of imposture, had never been vivid or stable, and were still more weakened by the artifices of which I had already been guilty. The utility or harmlessness of the end, justified, in my eyes, the means.

No event had been more unexpected, by me, than the bequest of my aunt to her servant. The will, under which the latter claimed, was dated prior to my coming to the city. I was not surprised, therefore, that it had once been made, but merely that it had never been cancelled or superseded by a later instrument. My wishes inclined me to suspect the existence of a later will, but I had conceived that, to ascertain its existence, was beyond my power.

Now, however, a different opinion began to be entertained. This woman like those of her sex and class was unlettered and superstitious. Her faith in spells and apparitions, was of the most lively kind. Could not her conscience be awakened by a voice from the grave! Lonely and at midnight, my aunt might be introduced, upbraiding her for her injustice, and commanding her to attone for it by acknowledging the claim of the rightful proprietor.

True it was, that no subsequent will might exist, but this was the fruit of mistake, or of negligence. She probably intended to cancel the old one, but this act might, by her own weakness, or by the artifices of her servant, be delayed till death had put it out of her power. In either case a mandate from the dead could scarcely fail of being obeyed.[22]

I considered this woman as the usurper of my property. Her husband as well as herself, were laborious and covetous; their good fortune had made no change in their mode of living, but they were as frugal and as eager to accumulate as ever. In their hands, money was inert and sterile, or it served to foster their vices. To take it

---

[22] "A mandate from the dead could scarcely fail of being obeyed": Brown seems to draw on similar accounts of petty frauds and impostures that were given in contemporary discussions of ventriloquistic pranks. The schemer Louis Brabant, discussed as "a capital ventriloquist and cheat" in la Chapelle's *Le Ventriloque* (1772) and in *Encyclopædia* articles drawn from it, developed a comparable scheme in which, for example, he faked the voice of an heiress' dead father so the girl's mother would allow Brabant to marry her and inherit her fortune. For Brown's sources on ventriloquism, see *Wieland* note 22.4.

from them would, therefore, be a benefit both to them and to myself; not even an imaginary injury would be inflicted. Restitution, if legally compelled to it, would be reluctant and painful, but if enjoined by Heaven would be voluntary, and the performance of a seeming duty would carry with it, its own reward.

These reasonings, aided by inclination, were sufficient to determine me. I have no doubt but their fallacy would have been detected in the sequel, and my scheme have been productive of nothing but confusion and remorse. From these consequences, however, my fate interposed, as in the former instance, to save me.

Having formed my resolution, many preliminaries to its execution were necessary to be settled. These demanded deliberation and delay; meanwhile I recollected my promise to Ludlow, and paid him a visit. I met a frank and affectionate reception. It would not be easy to paint the delight which I experienced in this man's society. I was at first oppressed with the sense of my own inferiority in age, knowledge and rank. Hence arose numberless reserves and incapacitating diffidences; but these were speedily dissipated by the fascinations of this man's address. His superiority was only rendered, by time, more conspicuous, but this superiority, by appearing never to be present to his own mind, ceased to be uneasy to me. My questions required to be frequently answered, and my mistakes to be rectified; but my keenest scrutiny, could detect in his manner, neither arrogance nor contempt. He seemed to talk merely from the overflow of his ideas, or a benevolent desire of imparting information.

IV

MY visits gradually became more frequent. Meanwhile my wants increased, and the necessity of some change in my condition became daily more urgent. This incited my reflections on the scheme which I had formed. The time and place suitable to my design, were not selected without much anxious inquiry and frequent waverings of purpose. These being at length fixed, the interval to elapse, before the carrying of my design into effect, was not without perturbation and suspense. These could not be concealed from my new friend and at length prompted him to inquire into the cause.

It was not possible to communicate the whole truth; but the warmth of his manner inspired me with some degree of ingenuousness. I did not hide from him my former hopes and my present destitute condition. He listened to my tale with no expressions of sympathy, and when I had finished, abruptly inquired whether I had any objection to a voyage to Europe? I answered in the negative. He then said that he was preparing to depart in a fortnight and advised me to make up my mind to accompany him.

This unexpected proposal gave me pleasure and surprize, but the want of money occurred to me as an insuperable objection. On this being mentioned, Oho! said he, carelessly, that objection is easily removed, I will bear all expenses of your passage myself.

The extraordinary beneficence of this act as well as the air of uncautiousness attending it, made me doubt the sincerity of his offer, and when new declarations removed this doubt, I could not forbear expressing at once my sense of his generosity and of my own unworthiness.

He replied that generosity had been expunged from his catalogue as having no meaning or a vicious one. It was the scope of his exertions to be just. This was the sum of human duty, and he that fell short, ran beside, or outstripped justice was a criminal. What he gave me was my due or not my due. If it were my due, I might reasonably demand it from him and it was wicked to withhold it. Merit on one side or gratitude on the other, were contradictory and unintelligible.

If I were fully convinced that this benefit was not my due and yet received it, he should hold me in contempt. The rectitude of my principles and conduct would be the measure of his approbation, and no benefit should he ever bestow which the receiver was not entitled to claim, and which it would not be criminal in him to refuse.

These principles were not new from the mouth of Ludloe, but they had, hitherto, been regarded as the fruits of a venturous speculation in my mind. I had never traced them into their practical consequences, and if his conduct on this occasion had not squared with his maxims, I should not have imputed to him inconsistency. I did not ponder on these reasonings at this time: objects of immediate importance engrossed my thoughts.

One obstacle to this measure was removed. When my voyage was performed how should I subsist in my new abode? I concealed not my perplexity and he commented on it in his usual manner. How did I mean to subsist, he asked, in my own country? The means of living would be, at least, as much within my reach there as here. As to the pressure of immediate and absolute want, he believed I should be exposed to little hazard. With talents such as mine, I must be hunted by a destiny peculiarly malignant, if I could not provide myself with necessaries wherever my lot were cast.

He would make allowances, however, for my diffidence and self-distrust, and would obviate my fears by expressing his own intentions with regard to me. I must be apprized, however, of his true meaning. He laboured to shun all hurtful and vitious things, and therefore carefully abstained from making or confiding in *promises*. It was just to assist me in this voyage, and it would probably be equally just to continue to me similar assistance when it was finished. That indeed was a subject, in a great degree, within my own cognizance. His aid would be proportioned to my wants and to my merits, and I had only to take care that my claims were just, for them to be admitted.

This scheme could not but appear to me eligible. I thirsted after an acquaintance with new scenes; my present situation could not be changed for a worse; I trusted to the constancy of Ludloe's friendship; to this at least it was better to trust than to the success of my imposture on Dorothy, which was adopted merely as a desperate expedient: finally I determined to embark with him.

In the course of this voyage my mind was busily employed. There were no other passengers beside ourselves, so that my own condition and the character of Ludloe, continually presented themselves to my reflections. It will be supposed that I was not a vague or indifferent observer.

There were no vicissitudes in the deportment or lapses in the discourse of my friend. His feelings appeared to preserve an unchangeable tenor, and his thoughts and words always to flow with the same rapidity. His slumber was profound and his wakeful hours serene. He was regular and temperate in all his exercises and gratifications. Hence were derived his clear perceptions and exuberant health.

This treatment of me, like all his other mental and corporal operations, was modelled by one inflexible standard. Certain scruples and delicacies were incident to my situation.[23] Of the existence of these he seemed to be unconscious, and yet nothing escaped him inconsistent with a state of absolute equality.

I was naturally inquisitive as to his fortune and the collateral circumstances of his condition. My notions of politeness hindered me from making direct inquiries. By indirect means I could gather nothing but that his state was opulent and independent, and that he had two sisters whose situation resembled his own.

Though, in conversation, he appeared to be governed by the utmost candour; no light was let in upon the former transactions of his life. The purpose of his visit to America I could merely guess to be the gratification of curiosity.

My future pursuits must be supposed chiefly to occupy my attention. On this head I was destitute of all stedfast views. Without profession or habits of industry or sources of permanent revenue, the world appeared to me an ocean on which my bark was set afloat, without compass or sail. The world into which I was about to enter, was untried and unknown, and though I could consent to profit by the guidance I was unwilling to rely on the support of others.

This topic being nearest my heart, I frequently introduced into conversation with my friend; but on this subject he always allowed himself to be led by me, while on all others, he was zealous to point the way. To every scheme that I proposed he was sure to cause objections. All the liberal professions were censured as perverting the understanding, by giving scope to the sordid motive of gain, or embuing the mind with erroneous principles. Skill was slowly obtained, and success, though integrity and independence must be given for it, dubious and instable. The mechanical trades were equally obnoxious; they were vitious by contributing to the spurious gratifications of the rich and multiplying the objects of luxury; they were destruction to the intellect and vigour of the artizan; they enervated his frame and brutalized his mind.

When I pointed out to him the necessity of some species of labour, he tacitly admitted that necessity, but refused to direct me in the choice of a pursuit, which though not free from defect should yet have the fewest inconveniences. He dwelt on the fewness of our actual wants, the temptations which attend the possession of wealth, the benefits of seclusion and privacy, and the duty of unfettering our minds from the prejudices which govern the world.

His discourse tended merely to unsettle my views and increase my perplexity. This effect was so uniform that I at length desisted from all allusions to this theme and endeavoured to divert my own reflections from it. When our voyage should be finished, and I should actually tread this new stage, I believed that I should be better qualified to judge of the measures to be taken by me.

---

[23] "Certain scruples and delicacies were incident to my situation": despite Ludloe's seemingly egalitarian and open treatment, Carwin needs to behave in a deferential manner because of his poverty and dependence on Ludloe's higher rank and status.

At length we reached Belfast. From thence we immediately repaired to Dublin. I was admitted as a member of his family. When I expressed my uncertainty as to the place to which it would be proper for me to repair, he gave me a blunt but cordial invitation to his house. My circumstances allowed me no option and I readily complied. My attention was for a time engrossed by a diversified succession of new objects. Their novelty however disappearing, left me at liberty to turn my eyes upon myself and my companion, and here my reflections were supplied with abundant food.

His house was spacious and commodious, and furnished with profusion and elegance. A suit of apartments was assigned to me, in which I was permitted to reign uncontrolled and access was permitted to a well furnished library. My food was furnished in my own room, prepared in the manner which I had previously directed. Occasionally Ludloe would request my company to breakfast, when an hour was usually consumed in earnest or sprightly conversation. At all other times he was invisible, and his apartments, being wholly separate from mine, I had no opportunity of discovering in what way his hours were employed.

He defended this mode of living as being most compatible with liberty. He delighted to expatiate on the evils of cohabitation. Men, subjected to the same regimen, compelled to eat and sleep and associate at certain hours, were strangers to all rational independence and liberty. Society would never be exempt from servitude and misery, till those artificial ties which held human beings together under the same roof were dissolved. He endeavoured to regulate his own conduct in pursuance of these principles, and to secure to himself as much freedom as the present regulations of society would permit. The same independence which he claimed for himself he likewise extended to me. The distribution of my own time, the selection of my own occupations and companions should belong to myself.

But these privileges, though while listening to his arguments I could not deny them to be valuable, I would have willingly dispensed with. The solitude in which I lived became daily more painful. I ate and drank, enjoyed clothing and shelter, without the exercise of forethought or industry; I walked and sat, went out and returned for as long and at what seasons I thought proper, yet my condition was a fertile source of discontent.

I felt myself removed to a comfortless and chilling distance from Ludloe. I wanted to share in his occupations and views. With all his ingenuousness of aspect and overflow of thoughts, when he allowed me his company, I felt myself painfully bewildered with regard to his genuine condition and sentiments.

He had it in his power to introduce me to society, and without an introduction, it was scarcely possible to gain access to any social circle or domestic fireside. Add to this, my own obscure prospects and dubious situation. Some regular intellectual pursuit would render my state less irksome, but I had hitherto adopted no scheme of this kind.

V

TIME tended, in no degree, to alleviate my dissatisfaction. It increased till the determination became at length formed of opening my thoughts to Ludloe. At the next breakfast interview which took place, I introduced the subject, and expatiated without reserve, on the state of my feelings. I concluded with intreating him to point out some path in which my talents might be rendered useful to himself or to mankind.

After a pause of some minutes, he said, What would you do? You forget the immaturity of your age. If you are qualified to act a part in the theatre of life, step forth; but you are not qualified. You want knowledge, and with this you ought previously to endow yourself. . . . Means, for this end, are within your reach. Why should you waste your time in idleness, and torment yourself with unprofitable wishes? Books are at hand. . . books from which most sciences and languages can be learned. Read, analise, digest; collect facts, and investigate theories: ascertain the dictates of reason, and supply yourself with the inclination and the power to adhere to them. You will not, legally speaking, be a man in less than three years. Let this period be devoted to the acquisition of wisdom. Either stay here, or retire to an house I have off the banks of Killarney,[24] where you will find all the conveniences of study.

I could not but reflect with wonder at this man's treatment of me. I could plead none of the rights of relationship; yet I enjoyed the privileges of a son.[25] He had not imparted to me any scheme, by pursuit of which I might finally compensate him for the expense to which my maintainance and education would subject him. He gave me reason to hope for the continuance of his bounty. He talked and acted as if my fortune were totally disjoined from his; yet was I indebted to him for the morsel which sustained my life. Now it was proposed to withdraw myself to studious leisure, and romantic solitude. All my wants, personal and intellectual, were to be supplied gratuitously and copiously. No means were prescribed by which I might make compensation for all these benefits. In conferring them he seemed to be actuated by no view to his own ultimate advantage. He took no measures to secure my future services.

I suffered these thoughts to escape me, on this occasion, and observed that to make my application successful, or useful, it was necessary to pursue some end. I must look forward to some post which I might hereafter occupy beneficially to myself or others; and for which all the efforts of my mind should be bent to qualify myself.

These hints gave him visible pleasure; and now, for the first time, he deigned to advise me on this head. His scheme, however, was not suddenly produced. The way to it was circuitous and long. It was his business to make every new step appear to be suggested by my own reflections.[26] His own ideas were the seeming result of the moment, and sprung out of the last idea that was uttered. Being hastily taken up,

---

[24] "Killarney": Killarney is a town in Kerry County, southwest Ireland, at this time a remote area of the country. Large estates, ruined castles, and abbeys are located on the banks of scenic lakes there, hence the "romantic solitude" Carwin refers to in the next paragraph.

[25] "Privileges of a son": Ludloe's mysterious wealth and benevolence imply the authority of a father or traditional landed gentry, but his assertions about enlightened ideas and behaviors leave Carwin wondering what sort of obligation and conditions this largesse will entail.

[26] "His scheme . . . my own reflections": in the following paragraphs, Carwin will explain how, although Ludloe pretends that he is speaking sincerely, everything he does is intended to involve Carwin in a premeditated scheme "to fit me for his purpose."

they were, of course, liable to objection. These objections, sometimes occurring to me and sometimes to him, were admitted or contested with the utmost candour. One scheme went through numerous modifications before it was proved to be ineligible, or before it yielded place to a better. It was easy to perceive, that books alone were insufficient to impart knowledge: that man must be examined with our own eyes to make us acquainted with their nature: that ideas collected from observation and reading, must correct and illustrate each other: that the value of all principles, and their truth, lie in their practical effects. Hence, gradually arose, the usefulness of travelling, of inspecting the habits and manners of a nation, and investigating, on the spot, the causes of their happiness and misery. Finally, it was determined that Spain was more suitable than any other, to the views of a judicious traveller.

My language, habits, and religion were mentioned as obstacles to close and extensive views; but these difficulties successively and slowly vanished. Converse with books, and natives of Spain, a steadfast purpose and unwearied diligence would efface all differences between me and a Castilian[27] with respect to speech. Personal habits, were changeable, by the same means. The bars to unbounded intercourse, rising from the religion of Spain being irreconcilably opposite to mine, cost us no little trouble to surmount, and here the skill of Ludloe was eminently displayed.

I had been accustomed to regard as unquestionable, the fallacy of the Romish faith. This persuasion was habitual and the child of prejudice, and was easily shaken by the artifices of this logician. I was first led to bestow a kind of assent on the doctrines of the Roman church; but my convictions were easily subdued by a new species of argumentation, and, in a short time, I reverted to my ancient disbelief, so that, if an exterior conformity to the rights of Spain were requisite to the attainment of my purpose, that conformity must be dissembled.

My moral principles had hitherto been vague and unsettled. My circumstances had led me to the frequent practice of insincerity; but my transgressions as they were slight and transient, did not much excite my previous reflections, or subsequent remorse. My deviations, however, though rendered easy by habit, were by no means sanctioned by my principles. Now an imposture, more profound and deliberate, was projected; and I could not hope to perform well my part, unless steadfastly and thoroughly persuaded of its rectitude.

My friend was the eulogist of sincerity. He delighted to trace its influence on the happiness of mankind; and proved that nothing but the universal practice of this virtue was necessary to the perfection of human society. His doctrine was splendid and beautiful. To detect its imperfections was no easy task;[28] to lay the foundations of

---

[27] "Castilian": native of Castile, in central and northern Spain.

[28] "His doctrine . . . to detect its imperfections was no easy task": emphasizing themes of benevolence, rationality, and sincerity, Ludloe's claimed principles align him on one level with the Woldwinite ideas of Godwin, Wollstonecraft, and others (see the excerpts from these writers in Related Texts, for example Godwin on sincerity). On another level, Carwin is pointing out that Ludloe has not revealed his own motives and "schemes," for example, and seems to be cultivating Carwin only because he suspects that Carwin possesses a rare ventriloquial talent.

virtue in utility, and to limit, by that scale, the operation of general principles; to see that the value of sincerity, like that of every other mode of action, consisted in its tendency to good, and that, therefore the obligation to speak truth was not paramount or intrinsical: that my duty is modelled on a knowledge and foresight of the conduct of others; and that, since men in their actual state, are infirm and deceitful, a just estimate of consequences may sometimes make dissimulation my duty were truths that did not speedily occur. The discovery, when made, appeared to be a joint work. I saw nothing in Ludlow but proofs of candour, and a judgment incapable of bias.

The means which this man employed to fit me for his purpose, perhaps owed their success to my youth and ignorance. I may have given you exaggerated ideas of his dexterity and address. Of that I am unable to judge. Certain it is, that no time or reflection has abated my astonishment at the profoundness of his schemes, and the perseverance with which they were pursued by him. To detail their progress would expose me to the risk of being tedious, yet none but minute details would sufficiently display his patience and subtlety.

It will suffice to relate, that after a sufficient period of preparation and arrangements being made for maintaining a copious intercourse with Ludloe, I embarked for Barcelona. A restless curiosity and vigorous application have distinguished my character in every scene. Here was spacious field for the exercise of all my energies. I sought out a preceptor in my new religion. I entered into the hearts of priest and confessors, the *hidalgo*[29] and the peasant, the monk and the prelate, the austere and voluptuous devotee[30] were scrutinized in all their forms.

Man was the chief subject of my study, and the social sphere that in which I principally moved; but I was not inattentive to inanimate nature, nor unmindful of the past. If the scope of virtue were to maintain the body in health, and to furnish its highest enjoyments to every sense, to increase the number, and accuracy, and order of our intellectual stores, no virtue was ever more unblemished than mine. If to act upon our conceptions of right, and to acquit ourselves of all prejudice and selfishness in the formation of our principles, entitle us to the testimony of a good conscience, I might justly claim it.

I shall not pretend to ascertain my rank in the moral scale. Your notions of duty differ widely from mine. If a system of deceit, pursued merely from the love of truth; if voluptuousness, never gratified at the expense of health, may incur censure, I am censurable. This, indeed, was not the limit of my deviations. Deception was often unnecessarily practised, and my biloquial faculty did not lie unemployed. What has happened to yourselves[31] may enable you, in some degree, to judge of the scenes in which

---

[29] "*Hidalgo*": a traditional Spanish title for men of the lower nobility or gentry; loosely, "gentleman."

[30] "The austere and voluptuous devotee": that is, pious, religiously observant women (devotees) who might be either prudish because of their faith, or open to illicit sexual affairs nevertheless. Carwin acknowledges in the next paragraph that he has indulged in such affairs.

[31] "What has happened to yourselves": the comment suggests that the narrative's addressee is a member of the Wieland family, possibly the physician Thomas Cambridge, and that, like Clara's narrative, this memoir is one element of wider attempts to understand the events that occurred at Mettingen. Clara's narrative suggested that Cambridge became familiar with Carwin's story, possibly via a memoir such as this one. See *Wieland* note 26.3.

my mystical exploits engaged me. In none of them, indeed, were the effects equally disastrous, and they were, for the most part, the result of well digested projects.

To recount these would be an endless task. They were designed as mere specimens of power, to illustrate the influence of superstition: to give sceptics the consolation of certainty: to annihilate the scruples of a tender female, or facilitate my access to the bosoms of courtiers and monks.

The first achievement of this kind took place in the convent of the Escurial.[32] For some time the hospitality of this brotherhood allowed me a cell in that magnificent and gloomy fabric. I was drawn hither chiefly by the treasures of Arabian literature, which are preserved here in the keeping of a learned Maronite, from Lebanon.[33] Standing one evening on the steps of the great altar, this devout friar expatiated on the miraculous evidences of his religion; and, in a moment of enthusiasm, appealed to San Lorenzo, whose martyrdom was displayed before us. No sooner was the appeal made than the saint, obsequious to the summons, whispered his responses from the shrine, and commanded the heritic to tremble and believe. This event was reported to the convent. With whatever reluctance, I could not refuse my testimony to its truth, and its influence on my faith was clearly shewn in my subsequent conduct.

A lady of rank, in Seville,[34] who had been guilty of many unauthorized indulgences,[35] was, at last, awakened to remorse, by a voice from Heaven, which she imagined had commanded her to expiate her sins by an abstinence from all food for thirty days. Her friends found it impossible to outroot this persuasion, or to overcome her resolution even by force. I chanced to be one in a numerous company where she was present. This fatal illusion was mentioned, and an opportunity afforded to the lady of defending her scheme. At a pause in the discourse, a voice was heard from the ceiling, which confirmed the truth of her tale; but, at the same time revoked the command and, in consideration of her faith, pronounced her

---

[32] "Escurial": El Escorial, or San Lorenzo de Escorial, is an immense palace-church complex near Madrid built 1563–1584 by Philip II of Spain, then the most powerful monarch and colonial ruler in Europe, and a deeply mystic (from Brown's perspective, superstitious) Catholic. An architectural marvel—built in the shape of a grid to memorialize the way its patron Saint Lawrence, San Lorenzo, was martyred by being roasted on a grill—now listed as a United Nations World Heritage Site, it contains a royal burial palace, a cathedral, a monastery, a school, and the renowned library that attracts Carwin. Spain reached the peak of its world-systemic power under Philip II and the Escorial Palace condenses the massive economic force, political hegemony, and religious-ideological weaponry of the Spanish Empire into a single edifice ("this magnificent and gloomy fabric"). Carwin's efforts to examine "specimens of power" explore it as a realm of political-religious intrigue and pious fraud.

[33] "A learned Maronite . . . Lebanon": Maronites are members of an eastern or Syriac branch of Christianity centered in the Levant (present-day Lebanon, Syria, Cyprus, Israel, and Palestinian territories). The friar is thus a "heretic" in this Counter-Reformation milieu, easily tricked into accepting Roman Catholicism after an experience of Carwin's ventriloquism.

[34] "Seville": the cultural center of southern Spain. After his reported visits to Barcelona in Catalonia (near Valencia and Sagunto on the Mediterranean coast, where he met Pleyel in Chapter 7 of *Wieland*) and to the region around Madrid in central Spain, an incident in Seville shifts Carwin to another major city in the region.

[35] "Unauthorized indulgences": sexual adventures.

absolution. Satisfied with this proof, the auditors dismissed their unbelief, and the lady consented to eat.

In the course of a copious correspondence with Ludlow, the observations I had collected were given. A sentiment, which I can hardly describe, induced me to be silent on all adventures connected with my bivocal projects. On other topics, I wrote fully, and without restraint. I painted, in vivid hues, the scenes with which I was daily conversant, and pursued, fearlessly, every speculation on religion and government that occurred. This spirit was encouraged by Ludloe, who failed not to comment on my narrative, and multiply deductions from my principles.

He taught me to ascribe the evils that infest society to the errors of opinion. The absurd and unequal distribution of power and property gave birth to poverty and riches, and these were the sources of luxury and crimes. These positions were readily admitted; but the remedy for these ills, the means of rectifying these errors were not easily discovered. We have been inclined to impute them to inherent defects in the moral constitution of men: that oppression and tyranny grow up by a sort of natural necessity, and that they will perish only when the human species is extinct. Ludloe laboured to prove that this was, by no means, the case: that man is the creature of circumstances: that he is capable of endless improvement: that his progress has been stopped by the artificial impediment of government: that by the removal of this, the fondest dreams of imagination will be realized.

From detailing and accounting for the evils which exist under our present institutions, he usually proceeded to delineate some scheme of Utopian felicity, where the empire of reason should supplant that of force; where justice should be universally understood and practised; where the interest of the whole and of the individual should be seen by all to be the same; where the public good should be the scope of all activity; where the tasks of all should be the same, and the means of subsistence equally distributed.

No one could contemplate his pictures without rapture. By their comprehensiveness and amplitude they filled the imagination. I was unwilling to believe that in no region of the world, or at no period could these ideas be realized. It was plain that the nations of Europe were tending to greater depravity, and would be the prey of perpetual vicissistude. All individual attempts at their reformation would be fruitless. He therefore who desired the diffusion of right principles, to make a just system be adopted by a whole community, must pursue some extraordinary method.

In this state of mind I recollected my native country, where a few colonists from Britain had sown the germe of populous and mighty empires. Attended, as they were, into their new abode, by all their prejudices, yet such had been the influence of new circumstances, of consulting for their own happiness, of adopting simple forms of government, and excluding nobles and kings from their system, that they enjoyed a degree of happiness far superior to their parent state.

To conquer the prejudices and change the habits of millions, are impossible. The human mind, exposed to social influences, inflexibly adheres to the direction that is given to it; but for the same reason why men, who begin in error will continue, those who commence in truth, may be expected to persist. Habit and example will operate with equal force in both instances.

Let a few, sufficiently enlightened and disinterested, take up their abode in some unvisited region. Let their social scheme be founded in equity, and how small soever their original number may be, their growth into a nation is inevitable. Among other effects of national justice, was to be ranked the swift increase of numbers. Exempt from servile obligations and perverse habits, endowed with property, wisdom, and health, hundreds will expand, with inconceivable rapidity into thousands and thousands, into millions; and a new race, tutored in truth, may, in a few centuries, overflow the habitable world.

Such were the visions of youth![36] I could not banish them from my mind. I knew them to be crude; but believed that deliberation would bestow upon them solidity and shape. Meanwhile I imparted them to Ludloe.

VI

IN answer to the reveries and speculations which I sent to him respecting this subject, Ludloe informed me, that they had led his mind into a new sphere of meditation. He had long and deeply considered in what way he might essentially promote my happiness. He had entertained a faint hope that I would one day be qualified for a station like that to which he himself had been advanced. This post required an elevation and stability of views which human beings seldom reach, and which could be attained by me only by a long series of heroic labours. Hitherto every new stage in my intellectual progress had added vigour to his hopes, and he cherished a stronger belief than formerly that my career would terminate auspiciously. This, however, was necessarily distant. Many preliminaries must first be settled; many arduous accomplishments be first obtained; and my virtue be subjected to severe trials. At present it was not in his power to be more explicit; but if my reflections suggested no better plan, he advised me to settle my affairs in Spain, and return to him immediately. My knowledge of this country would be of the highest use, on the supposition of my ultimately arriving at the honours to which he had alluded; and some of these preparatory measures could be taken only with his assistance, and in his company.

This intimation was eagerly obeyed, and, in a short time, I arrived at Dublin. Meanwhile my mind had copious occupation in commenting on my friend's letter. This scheme, whatever it was, seemed to be suggested by my mention of a plan of colonization, and my preference of that mode of producing extensive and permanent

---

[36] "Unvisited region . . . visions of youth!": Carwin imagines a utopian colony that might grow in number until it becomes a world empire, and implies retrospectively that this was a naive fantasy. By time of Mary Shelley's *Frankenstein; or, The Modern Prometheus* (1818), this kind of scenario is transformed into the nightmare that Victor Frankenstein imagines the creature will accomplish if he is allowed a female mate. Brown developed his own scenarios of nightmarish imperialist expansion and authoritarian religious-political systems in several prose fragments and the late, unpublished historical fiction called the *Historical Sketches*.

effects on the condition of mankind. It was easy therefore to conjecture that this mode had been pursued under some mysterious modifications and conditions.

It had always excited my wonder that so obvious an expedient had been overlooked. The globe which we inhabit was very imperfectly known. The regions and nations unexplored, it was reasonable to believe, surpassed in extent, and perhaps in populousness, those with which we were familiar. The order of Jesuits had furnished an example of all the errors and excellencies of such a scheme. Their plan was founded on erroneous notions of religion and policy, and they had absurdly chosen a scene* within reach of the injustice and ambition of an European tyrant.[38]

It was wise and easy to profit by their example. Resting on the two props of fidelity and zeal, an association might exist for ages in the heart of Europe, whose influence might be felt and might be boundless, in some region of the southern hemisphere; and by whom a moral and political structure might be raised, the growth of pure wisdom, and totally unlike those fragments of Roman and Gothic barbarism, which cover the face of what are called the civilized nations. The belief now rose in my mind that some such scheme had actually been prosecuted, and that Ludloe was a coadjutor. On this supposition, the caution with which

*Paraguay.[37]

---

[37] "Paraguay": Carwin's reference to events in Paraguay, in central South America, is to the Jesuit Reductions, attempts to organize indigenous South-American peoples into semi-independent, theocratic social experiments called "*Reducciones de Indios*" or "Reductions of Indians," i.e., their "reduction" or conversion into subjects of Christian monarchies. On the one hand, these efforts were typically colonialist in that they sought to "civilize" native peoples by subjecting them to imperially imposed Christianity. On the other, they angered imperial administrations in Spain and Portugal because they tended to remove the indigenous peoples from the economic machinery that enriched the metropolitan colonizers. These struggles between the Jesuits and Spanish-Portuguese imperial administrations in Paraguay, in which the Guarani Indians of that region were the chief victims, erupted into the brief "War of the Seven Reductions" or "Guarani War" in 1756, which belongs to the larger realm of the Seven Years War. In that conflict's major engagement, more than fifteen hundred Guaranis were massacred, as opposed to three casualties among the combined Spanish-Portuguese force. For the brief mention of Carwin's interaction with the Jesuits in *Wieland*, see the novel's note 23.1.

[38] "Within reach of the injustice and ambition of an European tyrant": the Jesuit Reductions were one of the major factors leading to the suppression of the Jesuit order in a complex context of Euro-colonial political-religious struggle that culminated precisely when Carwin says he encountered the Jesuits in the 1760s (see *Wieland* note 23.1). The "European tyrant" that the Jesuits came up against in the 1760s was the Enlightened Portuguese autocrat Sebastião José de Carvalho e Melo, Marquis of Pombal (1699–1782), who Brown discusses in his key essay on novel writing, "Walstein's School of History." As Brown notes in that essay, Pombal was well known for his agency in the "expulsion of the Jesuits" from Portugal and for his influence in wider efforts to suppress the order as part of modernizing bureaucratic reforms. Pombal was a key coordinator of anti-Jesuit activities, developing linked efforts in Portugal, England, and Austria, and launching elaborate conspiracy theories about the Jesuits' lust for power. Ironically, ultrareactionary propagandists like Jesuit Augustin Barruel (the greatest of the Illuminati fantasists) reversed the accusations and regarded Pombal himself as an agent of (anti-Christian) conspiracy.

he approached to his point, the arduous probation which a candidate for a part on this stage must undergo, and the rigours of that test by which his fortitude and virtue must be tried, were easily explained. I was too deeply imbued with veneration for the effects of such schemes, and too sanguine in my confidence in the rectitude of Ludloe, to refuse my concurrence in any scheme by which my qualifications might at length be raised to a due point.

Our interview was frank and affectionate. I found him situated just as formerly. His aspect, manners, and deportment were the same. I entered once more on my former mode of life, but our intercourse became more frequent. We constantly breakfasted together, and our conversation was usually prolonged through half the morning.

For a time our topics were general. I thought proper to leave to him the introduction of more interesting themes: this, however, he betrayed no inclination to do. His reserve excited some surprise, and I began to suspect that whatever design he had formed with regard to me, had been laid aside. To ascertain this question, I ventured, at length, to recall his attention to the subject of his last letter, and to enquire whether subsequent reflection had made any change in his views.

He said that his views were too momentous to be hastily taken up, or hastily dismissed; the station, my attainment of which depended wholly on myself, was high above vulgar heads, and was to be gained by years of solicitude and labour. This, at least, was true with regard to minds ordinarily constituted; I, perhaps, deserved to be regarded as an exception, and might be able to accomplish in a few months that for which others were obliged to toil during half their lives.

Man, continued he, is the slave of habit. Convince him today that his duty leads straight forward: he shall advance, but at every step his belief shall fade; habit will resume its empire, and to-morrow he shall turn back, or betake himself to oblique paths.

We know not our strength till it be tried. Virtue, till confirmed by habit, is a dream. You are a man imbued by errors, and vincible by slight temptations. Deep enquiries must bestow light on your opinions, and the habit of encountering and vanquishing temptation must inspire you with fortitude. Till this be done, you are unqualified for that post, in which you will be invested with divine attributes, and prescribe the condition of a large portion of mankind.

Confide not in the firmness of your principles, or the stedfastness of your integrity. Be always vigilant and fearful. Never think you have enough of knowledge, and let not your caution slumber for a moment, for you know not when danger is near.

I acknowledged the justice of his admonitions, and professed myself willing to undergo any ordeal which reason should prescribe. What, I asked, were the conditions, on the fulfilment of which depended my advancement to the station he alluded to? Was it necessary to conceal from me the nature and obligations of this rank?

These enquiries sunk him more profoundly into meditation than I had ever before witnessed. After a pause, in which some perplexity was visible, he answered:

I scarcely know what to say. As to promises, I claim them not from you. We are now arrived at a point, in which it is necessary to look around with caution, and that consequences should be fully known. A number of persons are leagued together for an

257

end of some moment.[39] To make yourself one of these is submitted to your choice. Among the conditions of their alliance are mutual fidelity and secrecy.

Their existence depends upon this: their existence is known only to themselves. This secrecy must be obtained by all the means which are possible. When I have said thus much, I have informed you, in some degree, of their existence, but you are still ignorant of the purpose contemplated by this association, and of all the members, except myself. So far no dangerous disclosure is yet made: but this degree of concealment is not sufficient. Thus much is made known to you, because it is unavoidable. The individuals which compose this fraternity are not immortal, and the vacancies occasioned by death must be supplied from among the living. The candidate must be instructed and prepared, and they are always at liberty to recede. Their reason must approve the obligations and duties of their station, or they are unfit for it. If they recede, one duty is still incumbent upon them: they must observe an inviolable silence. To this they are not held by any promise. They must weigh consequences, and freely decide; but they must not fail to number among these consequences their own death.

Their death will not be prompted by vengeance. The executioner will say, he that has once revealed the tale is likely to reveal it a second time; and, to prevent this, the betrayer must die. Nor is this the only consequence: to prevent the further revelation, he, to whom the secret was imparted, must likewise perish. He must not console himself with the belief that his trespass will be unknown. The knowledge cannot, by human means, be withheld from this fraternity. Rare, indeed, will it be that his purpose to disclose is not discovered before it can be effected, and the disclosure prevented by his death.

Be well aware of your condition. What I now, or may hereafter mention, mention not again. Admit not even a doubt as to the propriety of hiding it from all the world. There are eyes who will discern this doubt amidst the closest folds of your heart, and your life will instantly be sacrificed.

At present be the subject dismissed. Reflect deeply on the duty which you have already incurred. Think upon your strength of mind, and be careful not to lay yourself under impracticable obligations. It will always be in your power to recede. Even after you are solemnly enrolled a member, you may consult the dictates of your own understanding, and relinquish your post; but while you live, the obligation to be silent will perpetually attend you.

We seek not the misery or death of any one, but we are swayed by an immutable calculation. Death is to be abhorred, but the life of the betrayer is productive of more

---

[39] "A number of persons are leagued together for an end of some moment": after steadily building hints, Ludloe now speaks openly about a secret organization that is something like a Masonic order or the Illuminati. Note that Brown never uses the term "Illuminati" in either *Wieland* or this narrative. Nevertheless, Ludloe's discussion of a secret "brotherhood," enlightened themes, and air of sinister gravity constitute unmistakable allusions to the type of scenario that was repeated endlessly, parodied, and often reversed in the 1797–1801 wave of publications concerning supposed threats of subversion against established government and religion. For more, see the Illuminati debates in Related Texts.

evil than his death: his death, therefore, we chuse, and our means are instantaneous and unerring.

I love you. The first impulse of my love is to dissuade you from seeking to know more. Your mind will be full of ideas; your hands will be perpetually busy to a purpose into which no human creature, beyond the verge of your brotherhood, must pry. Believe me, who have made the experiment, that compared with this task, the task of inviolable secrecy, all others are easy. To be dumb will not suffice; never to know any remission in your zeal or your watchfulness will not suffice. If the sagacity of others detect your occupations, however strenuously you may labour for concealment, your doom is ratified, as well as that of the wretch whose evil destiny led him to pursue you.

Yet if your fidelity fail not, great will be your recompense. For all your toils and self-devotion, ample will be the retribution. Hitherto you have been wrapt in darkness and storm; then will you be exalted to a pure and unruffled element. It is only for a time that temptation will environ you, and your path will be toilsome. In a few years you will be permitted to withdraw to a land of sages, and the remainder of your life will glide away in the enjoyments of beneficence and wisdom.

Think deeply on what I have said. Investigate your own motives and opinions, and prepare to submit them to the test of numerous hazards and experiments.

Here my friend passed to a new topic. I was desirous of reverting to this subject, and obtaining further information concerning it, but he assiduously repelled all my attempts, and insisted on my bestowing deep and impartial attention on what had already been disclosed. I was not slow to comply with his directions. My mind refused to admit any other theme of contemplation than this.

As yet I had no glimpse of the nature of this fraternity. I was permitted to form conjectures, and previous incidents bestowed but one form upon my thoughts. In reviewing the sentiments and deportment of Ludloe, my belief continually acquired new strength. I even recollected hints and ambiguous allusions in his discourse, which were easily solved, on the supposition of the existence of a new model of society, in some unsuspected corner of the world.

I did not fully perceive the necessity of secrecy; but this necessity perhaps would be rendered apparent, when I should come to know the connection that subsisted between Europe and this imaginary colony. But what was to be done? I was willing to abide by these conditions. My understanding might not approve of all the ends proposed by this fraternity, and I had liberty to withdraw from it, or to refuse to ally myself with them. That the obligation of secrecy should still remain, was unquestionably reasonable.

It appeared to be the plan of Ludloe rather to damp than to stimulate my zeal. He discouraged all attempts to renew the subject in conversation. He dwelt upon the arduousness of the office to which I aspired, the temptations to violate my duty with which I should be continually beset, the inevitable death with which the slightest breach of my engagements would be followed, and the long apprenticeship which it would be necessary for me to serve, before I should be fitted to enter into this conclave.

Sometimes my courage was depressed by these representations. . . . My zeal, however, was sure to revive; and at length Ludloe declared himself willing to assist me in the accomplishment of my wishes. For this end, it was necessary, he said, that I should be informed of a second obligation, which every candidate must assume. Before any one could be deemed qualified, he must be thoroughly known to his associates. For this end, he must determine to disclose every fact in his history, and every secret of his heart. I must begin with making these confessions, with regard to my past life, to Ludloe, and must continue to communicate, at stated seasons, every new thought, and every new occurrence, to him. This confidence was to be absolutely limitless: no exceptions were to be admitted, and no reserves to be practised; and the same penalty attended the infraction of this rule as of the former. Means would be employed, by which the slightest deviation, in either case, would be detected, and the deathful consequence would follow with instant and inevitable expedition. If secrecy were difficult to practise, sincerity, in that degree in which it was here demanded, was a task infinitely more arduous, and a period of new deliberation was necessary before I should decide. I was at liberty to pause: nay, the longer was the period of deliberation which I took, the better; but, when I had once entered this path, it was not in my power to recede. After having solemnly avowed my resolution to be thus sincere in my confession, any particle of reserve or duplicity would cost me my life.

This indeed was a subject to be deeply thought upon. Hitherto I had been guilty of concealment with regard to my friend. I had entered into no formal compact, but had been conscious to a kind of tacit obligation to hide no important transaction of my life from him. This consciousness was the source of continual anxiety. I had exerted, on numerous occasions, my bivocal faculty, but, in my intercourse with Ludloe, had suffered not the slightest intimation to escape me with regard to it. This reserve was not easily explained. It was, in a great degree, the product of habit; but I likewise considered that the efficacy of this instrument depended upon its existence being unknown. To confide the secret to one, was to put an end to my privilege: how widely the knowledge would thenceforth be diffused, I had no power to foresee.

Each day multiplied the impediments to confidence. Shame hindered me from acknowledging my past reserves. Ludloe, from the nature of our intercourse, would certainly account my reserve, in this respect, unjustifiable, and to excite his indignation or contempt was an unpleasing undertaking. Now, if I should resolve to persist in my new path, this reserve must be dismissed: I must make him master of a secret which was precious to me beyond all others; by acquainting him with past concealments, I must risk incurring his suspicion and his anger. These reflections were productive of considerable embarrassment.

There was, indeed, an avenue by which to escape these difficulties, if it did not, at the same time, plunge me into greater. My confessions might, in other respects, be unbounded, but my reserves, in this particular, might be continued. Yet should I not expose myself to formidable perils? Would my secret be for ever unsuspected and undiscovered?

When I considered the nature of this faculty, the impossibility of going farther than suspicion, since the agent could be known only by his own confession, and even this confession would not be believed by the greater part of mankind, I was tempted to conceal it.

In most cases, if I had asserted the possession of this power, I should be treated as a liar; it would be considered as an absurd and audacious expedient to free myself from the suspicion of having entered into compact with a dæmon, or of being myself an emissary of the grand foe. Here, however, there was no reason to dread a similar imputation, since Ludloe had denied the preternatural pretensions of these airy sounds.

My conduct on this occasion was nowise influenced by the belief of any inherent sanctity in truth. Ludloe had taught me to model myself in this respect entirely with a view to immediate consequences. If my genuine interest, on the whole, was promoted by veracity, it was proper to adhere to it; but, if the result of my investigation were opposite, truth was to be sacrificed without scruple.

VII

MEANWHILE, in a point of so much moment, I was not hasty to determine. My delay seemed to be, by no means, unacceptable to Ludloe, who applauded my discretion, and warned me to be circumspect. My attention was chiefly absorbed by considerations connected with this subject, and little regard was paid to any foreign occupation or amusement.

One evening, after a day spent in my closet, I sought recreation by walking forth. My mind was chiefly occupied by the review of incidents which happened in Spain. I turned my face toward the fields, and recovered not from my reverie, till I had proceeded some miles on the road to Meath.[40] The night had considerably advanced, and the darkness was rendered intense, by the setting of the moon. Being somewhat weary, as well as undetermined in what manner next to proceed, I seated myself on a grassy bank beside the road. The spot which I had chosen was aloof from passengers, and shrouded in the deepest obscurity.

Some time elapsed, when my attention was excited by the slow approach of an equipage.[41] I presently discovered a coach and six horses, but unattended, except by coachman and postillion, and with no light to guide them on their way. Scarcely had they passed the spot where I rested, when some one leaped from beneath the hedge, and seized the head of the fore-horses. Another called upon the coachman to stop, and threatened him with instant death if he disobeyed. A third drew open the coach-door, and ordered those within to deliver their purses. A shriek of terror showed me that a lady was within, who eagerly consented to preserve her life by the loss of her money.

To walk unarmed in the neighbourhood of Dublin, especially at night, has always been accounted dangerous. I had about me the usual instruments of defence. I was desirous of rescuing this person from the danger which surrounded her, but was

---

[40] "Road to Meath": County Meath is northwest of Dublin, where Carwin is staying with Ludloe.

[41] "Equipage": in this usage, "a carriage and horses, with the attendant servants" (*OED*).

somewhat at a loss how to effect my purpose. My single strength was insufficient to contend with three ruffians. After a moment's debate, an expedient was suggested, which I hastened to execute.

Time had not been allowed for the ruffian who stood beside the carriage to receive the plunder, when several voices, loud, clamorous, and eager, were heard in the quarter whence the traveller had come. By trampling with quickness, it was easy to imitate the sound of many feet. The robbers were alarmed, and one called upon another to attend. The sounds increased, and, at the next moment, they betook themselves to flight, but not till a pistol was discharged. Whether it was aimed at the lady in the carriage, or at the coachman, I was not permitted to discover, for the report affrighted the horses, and they set off at full speed.

I could not hope to overtake them: I knew not whither the robbers had fled, and whether, by proceeding, I might not fall into their hands. . . . These considerations induced me to resume my feet, and retire from the scene as expeditiously as possible. I regained my own habitation without injury.

I have said that I occupied separate apartments from those of Ludloe. To these there were means of access without disturbing the family. I hasted to my chamber, but was considerably surprized to find, on entering my apartment, Ludloe seated at a table, with a lamp before him.

My momentary confusion was greater than his. On discovering who it was, he assumed his accustomed looks, and explained appearances, by saying, that he wished to converse with me on a subject of importance, and had therefore sought me at this secret hour, in my own chamber. Contrary to his expectation, I was absent. Conceiving it possible that I might shortly return, he had waited till now. He took no further notice of my absence, nor manifested any desire to know the cause of it, but proceeded to mention the subject which had brought him hither. These were his words.

You have nothing which the laws permit you to call your own. Justice entitles you to the supply of your physical wants, from those who are able to supply them; but there are few who will acknowledge your claim, or spare an atom of their superfluity to appease your cravings. That which they will not spontaneously give, it is not right to wrest from them by violence. What then is to be done?

Property is necessary to your own subsistence. It is useful, by enabling you to supply the wants of others. To give food, and clothing, and shelter, is to give life, to annihilate temptation, to unshackle virtue, and propagate felicity. How shall property be gained?

You may set your understanding or your hands at work. You may weave stockings, or write poems, and exchange them for money; but these are tardy and meagre schemes. The means are disproportioned to the end, and I will not suffer you to pursue them. My justice will supply your wants.

But dependance on the justice of others is a precarious condition. To be the object is a less ennobling state than to be the bestower of benefit. Doubtless you desire to be vested with competence and riches, and to hold them by virtue of the law, and not at the will of a benefactor. . . .He paused as if waiting for my assent to his positions. I readily expressed my concurrence, and my desire to pursue any means compatible with honesty. He resumed.

There are various means, besides labour, violence, or fraud. It is right to select the easiest within your reach. It happens that the easiest is at hand. A revenue of some thousands a year, a stately mansion in the city, and another in Kildare,[42] old and faithful domestics, and magnificent furniture, are good things. Will you have them?

A gift like that, replied I, will be attended by momentous conditions. I cannot decide upon its value, until I know these conditions.

The sole condition is your consent to receive them. Not even the airy obligation of gratitude will be created by acceptance. On the contrary, by accepting them, you will confer the highest benefit upon another.

I do not comprehend you. Something surely must be given in return.

Nothing. It may seem strange that, in accepting the absolute controul of so much property, you subject yourself to no conditions; that no claims of gratitude or service will accrue; but the wonder is greater still. The law equitably enough fetters the gift with no restraints, with respect to you that receive it; but not so with regard to the unhappy being who bestows it. That being must part, not only with property but liberty. In accepting the property, you must consent to enjoy the services of the present possessor. They cannot be disjoined.

Of the true nature and extent of the gift, you should be fully apprized. Be aware, therefore, that, together with this property, you will receive absolute power over the liberty and person of the being who now possesses it. That being must become your domestic slave; be governed, in every particular, by your caprice.

Happily for you, though fully invested with this power, the degree and mode in which it will be exercised will depend upon yourself. . . . You may either totally forbear the exercise, or employ it only for the benefit of your slave. However injurious, therefore, this authority may be to the subject of it, it will, in some sense, only enhance the value of the gift to you.

The attachment and obedience of this being will be chiefly evident in one thing. Its duty will consist in conforming, in every instance, to your will. All the powers of this being are to be devoted to your happiness; but there is one relation between you, which enables you to confer, while exacting, pleasure. . . . This relation is *sexual*. Your slave is a woman; and the bond, which transfers her property and person to you, is . . . *marriage*.[43]

My knowledge of Ludloe, his principles, and reasonings, ought to have precluded that surprise which I experienced at the conclusion of his discourse. I knew that he regarded the present institution of marriage as a contract of servitude, and the terms of it unequal and unjust. When my surprise had subsided, my thoughts turned upon the nature of his scheme. After a pause of reflection, I answered:

---

[42] "Kildare": County Kildare, southwest of Dublin.

[43] "Attachment and obedience . . . slave . . . *marriage*": throughout this passage, Ludloe articulates and endorses the Woldwinite critique of marriage as an unfair, contractually bound relationship that subordinates women in a state of quasislavery and sexual exploitation. These arguments on marriage, the relation of sex and property, and women's subordination are developed at greater length in Brown's Wollstonecraftian dialogue *Alcuin* (1798), and implicitly dramatized in the lives of female characters throughout Brown's novels.

Both law and custom have connected obligations with marriage, which, though heaviest on the female, are not light upon the male. Their weight and extent are not immutable and uniform; they are modified by various incidents, and especially by the mental and personal qualities of the lady.

I am not sure that I should willingly accept the property and person of a woman decrepid with age, and enslaved by perverse habits and evil passions: whereas youth, beauty, and tenderness would be worth accepting, even for their own sake, and disconnected with fortune.

As to altar vows, I believe they will not make me swerve from equity. I shall exact neither service nor affection from my spouse. The value of these, and, indeed, not only the value, but the very existence, of the latter depends upon its spontaneity. A promise to love tends rather to loosen than strengthen the tie.

As to myself, the age of illusion is past. I shall not wed, till I find one whose moral and physical constitution will make personal fidelity easy. I shall judge without mistiness or passion, and habit will come in aid of an enlightened and deliberate choice.

I shall not be fastidious in my choice. I do not expect, and scarcely desire, much intellectual similitude between me and my wife. Our opinions and pursuits cannot be in common. While women are formed by their education, and their education continues in its present state, tender hearts and misguided understandings are all that we can hope to meet with.

What are the character, age, and person of the woman to whom you allude? and what prospect of success would attend my exertions to obtain her favour?

I have told you she is rich. She is a widow, and owes her riches to the liberality of her husband, who was a trader of great opulence, and who died while on a mercantile adventure to Spain. He was not unknown to you. Your letters from Spain often spoke of him. In short, she is the widow of Bennington, whom you met at Barcelona. She is still in the prime of life; is not without many feminine attractions; has an ardent and credulent[44] temper; and is particularly given to devotion. This temper it would be easy to regulate according to your pleasure and your interest, and I now submit to you the expediency of an alliance with her.

I am a kinsman, and regarded by her with uncommon deference; and my commendations, therefore, will be of great service to you, and shall be given.

I will deal ingenuously with you. It is proper you should be fully acquainted with the grounds of this proposal. The benefits of rank, and property, and independence, which I have already mentioned as likely to accrue to you from this marriage, are solid and valuable benefits; but these are not the sole advantages, and to benefit you, in these respects, is not my whole view.

No. My treatment of you henceforth will be regulated by one principle. I regard you only as one undergoing a probation or apprenticeship; as subjected to trials of your sincerity and fortitude. The marriage I now propose to you is desirable, because it will make you independent of me. Your poverty might create an unsuitable bias in

---

[44] "Credulent": gullible, disposed to believe what she is told.

favour of proposals, one of whose effects would be to set you beyond fortune's reach. That bias will cease, when you cease to be poor and dependent.

Love is the strongest of all human delusions. That fortitude, which is not subdued by the tenderness and blandishments of woman, may be trusted; but no fortitude, which has not undergone that test, will be trusted by us.

This woman is a charming enthusiast.[45] She will never marry but him whom she passionately loves. Her power over the heart that loves her will scarcely have limits. The means of prying into your transactions, of suspecting and sifting your thoughts, which her constant society with you, while sleeping and waking, her zeal and watchfulness for your welfare, and her curiosity, adroitness, and penetration will afford her, are evident. Your danger, therefore, will be imminent. Your fortitude will be obliged to have recourse, not to flight, but to vigilance. Your eye must never close.

Alas! what human magnanimity can stand this test! How can I persuade myself that you will not fail? I waver between hope and fear. Many, it is true, have fallen, and dragged with them the author of their ruin, but some have soared above even these perils and temptations, with their fiery energies unimpaired, and great has been, as great ought to be, their recompence.

But you are doubtless aware of your danger. I need not repeat the consequences of betraying your trust, the rigour of those who will judge your fault, the unerring and unbounded scrutiny to which your actions, the most secret and indifferent, will be subjected.

Your conduct, however, will be voluntary. At your own option be it, to see or not to see this woman. Circumspection, deliberation, forethought, are your sacred duties and highest interest.

VIII

LUDLOE'S remarks on the seductive and bewitching powers of women, on the difficulty of keeping a secret which they wish to know, and to gain which they employ the soft artillery of tears and prayers, and blandishments and menaces, are familiar to all men, but they had little weight with me, because they were unsupported by my own experience. I had never had any intellectual or sentimental connection with the sex. My meditations and pursuits had all led a different way, and a bias had gradually been given to my feelings, very unfavourable to the refinements of love. I acknowledge, with shame and regret, that I was accustomed to regard the physical and sensual consequences of the sexual relation as realities, and every thing intellectual, disinterested, and heroic, which enthusiasts connect with it as idle dreams. Besides, said I, I am yet a stranger to the secret, on the preservation of which so much stress is laid, and it will be optional with me to receive it or not. If, in the progress of my

---

[45] "Enthusiast": primarily, someone who indulges in excessive religious emotionality or, as Ludloe put it five paragraphs earlier, "is particularly given to devotion." The implication here is that Bennington's "warm imagination" (266) makes her prone to illusions of romantic love as well. Carwin will shortly describe those who fall in love as "enthusiasts."

acquaintance with Mrs. Benington, I should perceive any extraordinary danger in the gift, cannot I refuse, or at least delay to comply with any new conditions from Ludloe? Will not his candour and his affection for me rather commend than disapprove my diffidence? In fine, I resolved to see this lady.

She was, it seems, the widow of Benington, whom I knew in Spain. This man was an English merchant settled at Barcelona, to whom I had been commended by Ludloe's letters, and through whom my pecuniary supplies were furnished. . . . Much intercourse and some degree of intimacy had taken place between us, and I had gained a pretty accurate knowledge of his character. I had been informed, through different channels, that his wife was much his superior in rank, that she possessed great wealth in her own right, and that some disagreement of temper or views occasioned their separation. She had married him for love, and still doated on him: the occasions for separation having arisen, it seems, not on her side but on his. As his habits of reflection were nowise friendly to religion, and as hers, according to Ludloe, were of the opposite kind, it is possible that some jarring had arisen between them from this source. Indeed, from some casual and broken hints of Benington, especially in the latter part of his life, I had long since gathered this conjecture. . . . Something, thought I, may be derived from my acquaintance with her husband favourable to my views.

I anxiously waited for an opportunity of acquainting Ludloe with my resolution. On the day of our last conversation, he had made a short excursion from town, intending to return the same evening, but had continued absent for several days. As soon as he came back, I hastened to acquaint him with my wishes.

Have you well considered this matter, said he. Be assured it is of no trivial import. The moment at which you enter the presence of this woman will decide your future destiny. Even putting out of view the subject of our late conversations, the light in which you shall appear to her will greatly influence your happiness, since, though you cannot fail to love her, it is quite uncertain what return she may think proper to make. Much, doubtless, will depend on your own perseverance and address, but you will have many, perhaps insuperable obstacles to encounter on several accounts, and especially in her attachment to the memory of her late husband. As to her devout temper, this is nearly allied to a warm imagination in some other respects, and will operate much more in favour of an ardent and artful lover, than against him.

I still expressed my willingness to try my fortune with her.

Well, said he, I anticipated your consent to my proposal, and the visit I have just made was to her. I thought it best to pave the way, by informing her that I had met with one for whom she had desired me to look out. You must know that her father was one of these singular men who set a value upon things exactly in proportion to the difficulty of obtaining or comprehending them. His passion was for antiques, and his favourite pursuit during a long life was monuments in brass, marble, and parchment, of the remotest antiquity. He was wholly indifferent to the character or conduct of our present sovereign and his ministers, but was extremely solicitous about the name and exploits of a king of Ireland that lived two or three centuries before the flood. He felt no curiosity to know who was the father of his wife's child, but would travel a thousand miles, and consume months, in investigating which son of Noah it was that first landed on the coast of Munster.[46] He would give a hundred guineas from the mint for a piece of old decayed copper no bigger than his nail, provided it had aukward characters upon it, too much defaced to be read. The whole stock of a great bookseller was, in his eyes, a cheap exchange for a shred of parchment, containing half a homily written by St. Patrick. He would have gratefully given all his patrimonial domains to one who should inform him what pendragon[47] or druid it was who set up the first stone on Salisbury plain.[48]

This spirit, as you may readily suppose, being seconded by great wealth and long life, contributed to form a very large collection of venerable lumber, which, though beyond all price to the collector himself, is of no value to his heiress but so far as it is marketable. She designs to bring the whole to auction, but for this purpose a catalogue and description are necessary. Her father trusted to faithful memory, and to vague and scarcely legible memorandums, and has left a very arduous task to any one who shall be named to the office. It occurred to me, that the best means of promoting your views was to recommend you to this office.

You are not entirely without the antiquarian frenzy yourself. The employment, therefore, will be somewhat agreeable to you for its own sake. It will entitle you to become an inmate of the same house, and thus establish an incessant intercourse between you, and the nature of the business is such, that you may perform it in what time, and with what degree of diligence and accuracy you please.

I ventured to insinuate that, to a woman of rank and family, the character of a hireling was by no means a favourable recommendation.

He answered, that he proposed, by the account he should give of me, to obviate every scruple of that nature. Though my father was no better than a farmer, it is not absolutely certain but that my remoter ancestors had princely blood in their veins: but as long as proofs of my low extraction did not impertinently intrude themselves, my silence, or, at most, equivocal surmises, seasonably made use of, might secure me from all inconveniences on the score of birth. He should represent me, and I was such, as his friend, favourite, and equal, and my passion for antiquities should be my principal inducement to undertake this office, though my poverty would make no objection to a reasonable pecuniary recompense.

Having expressed my acquiescence in his measures, he thus proceeded: My visit was made to my kinswoman, for the purpose, as I just now told you, of paving your way into her family; but, on my arrival at her house, I found nothing but disorder and alarm. Mrs. Benington, it seems, on returning from a longer ride than customary, last Thursday evening, was attacked by robbers. Her attendants related an imperfect tale of somebody advancing at the critical moment to her rescue. It seems, however, they

---

[46] "Noah . . . Munster": *Lebor Gabála Érenn* (Book of the Conquests of Ireland) is an eleventh-century text that recounts the mythological five invasions of Ireland before the arrival of the Celts. The first occurs when Noah's son Bith and grandaughter Cesair land in Munster shortly before the Flood.

[47] "Pendragon": head dragon, a title given to the legendary kings of ancient Britain, such as King Arthur.

[48] "Salisbury plain": the site of Stonehenge, in Wiltshire, southern England.

did more harm than good; for the horses took to flight and overturned the carriage, in consequence of which Mrs. Benington was severely bruised. She has kept her bed ever since, and a fever was likely to ensue, which has only left her out of danger to-day.

As the adventure before related, in which I had so much concern, occurred at the time mentioned by Ludloe, and as all other circumstances were alike, I could not doubt that the person whom the exertion of my mysterious powers had relieved was Mrs. Benington: but what an ill-omened interference was mine! The robbers would probably have been satisfied with the few guineas in her purse, and, on receiving these, would have left her to prosecute her journey in peace and security, but, by absurdly offering a succour, which could only operate upon the fears of her assailants, I endangered her life, first by the desperate discharge of a pistol, and next by the fright of the horses. . . .My anxiety, which would have been less if I had not been, in some degree, myself the author of the evil, was nearly removed by Ludloe's proceeding to assure me that all danger was at an end, and that he left the lady in the road to perfect health. He had seized the earliest opportunity of acquainting her with the purpose of his visit, and had brought back with him her cheerful acceptance of my services. The next week was appointed for my introduction.

With such an object in view, I had little leisure to attend to any indifferent object. My thoughts were continually bent upon the expected introduction, and my impatience and curiosity drew strength, not merely from the character of Mrs. Benington, but from the nature of my new employment. Ludloe had truly observed, that I was infected with somewhat of this antiquarian mania myself, and I now remembered that Benington had frequently alluded to this collection in possession of his wife. My curiosity had then been more than once excited by his representations, and I had formed a vague resolution of making myself acquainted with this lady and her learned treasure, should I ever return to Ireland. . . . Other incidents had driven this matter from my mind.

Meanwhile, affairs between Ludloe and myself remained stationary. Our conferences, which were regular and daily, related to general topics, and though his instructions were adapted to promote my improvement in the most useful branches of knowledge, they never afforded a glimpse towards that quarter where my curiosity was most active.

The next week now arrived, but Ludloe informed me that the state of Mrs. Benington's health required a short excursion into the country, and that he himself proposed to bear her company. The journey was to last about a fortnight, after which I might prepare myself for an introduction to her.

This was a very unexpected and disagreeable trial to my patience. The interval of solitude that now succeeded would have passed rapidly and pleasantly enough, if an event of so much moment were not in suspense. Books, of which I was passionately fond, would have afforded me delightful and incessant occupation, and Ludloe, by way of reconciling me to unavoidable delays, had given me access to a little closet, in which his rarer and more valuable books were kept.

All my amusements, both by inclination and necessity, were centered in myself and at home. Ludloe appeared to have no visitants, and though frequently abroad, or at least secluded from me, had never proposed my introduction to any of his friends, except Mrs. Benington. My obligations to him were already too great to allow me to lay claim to new favours and indulgences, nor, indeed, was my disposition such as to make society needful to my happiness. My character had been, in some degree, modelled by the faculty which I possessed. This deriving all its supposed value from impenetrable secrecy, and Ludloe's admonitions tending powerfully to impress me with the necessity of wariness and circumspection in my general intercourse with mankind, I had gradually fallen into sedate, reserved, mysterious, and unsociable habits. My heart wanted not a friend.

In this temper of mind, I set myself to examine the novelties which Ludloe's private book-cases contained. 'Twill be strange, thought I, if his favourite volumes do not show some marks of my friend's character. To know a man's favourite or most constant studies cannot fail of letting in some little light upon his secret thoughts, and though he would not have given me the reading of these books, if he had thought them capable of unveiling more of his concerns than he wished, yet possibly my ingenuity may go one step farther than he dreams of. You shall judge whether I was right in my conjectures.

IX

THE books which composed this little library were chiefly the voyages and travels of the missionaries of the sixteenth and seventeenth centuries. Added to these were some works upon political economy and legislation. Those writers who have amused themselves with reducing their ideas to practice, and drawing imaginary pictures of nations or republics, whose manners or government came up to their standard of excellence, were, all of whom I had ever heard, and some I had never heard of before, to be found in this collection. A translation of Aristotle's republic,[49] the political romances of sir Thomas Moore, Harrington, and Hume,[50] appeared to have been much read, and Ludlow had not been sparing of his marginal comments. In these writers he appeared to find nothing but error and absurdity; and his notes were introduced for no other end than to point out groundless principles and false conclusions. . . . The style of these remarks was already familiar to me. I saw nothing new in them, or different from the strain of those speculations with which Ludlow was accustomed to indulge himself in conversation with me.

---

[49] "Aristotle's republic": the reference seems to be to Aristotle's *Politics*, his major treatise on political economy, which examines the grounds of political and economic theory, contrasts the organizational assumptions and implications of an Athenian style constitution (from Brown's eighteenth-century perspective a "republican" model) with those of democracy, oligarchy, and kingship, and develops a critical examination of Plato's *Republic*.

[50] "Political romances of sir Thomas Moore, Harrington, and Hume": interrelated early modern and Enlightenment English speculations on republican theory and ideal forms of government, allegorically presented as island nations where systems of sociopolitical organization can be established without outside interference. The "romances" in question are *Utopia* (1516) by Thomas More (1478–1535); *The Commonwealth of Oceana* (1656) by James Harrington (1611–1677), and the "Idea of a Perfect Commonwealth" (1754) by David Hume (1711–1776).

After having turned over the leaves of the printed volumes, I at length lighted on a small book of maps, from which, of course, I could reasonably expect no information, on that point about which I was most curious. It was an atlas, in which the maps had been drawn by the pen. None of them contained any thing remarkable, so far as I, who was indeed a smatterer in geography, was able to perceive, till I came to the end, when I noticed a map, whose prototype I was wholly unacquainted with. It was drawn on a pretty large scale, representing two islands, which bore some faint resemblance, in their relative proportions, at least, to Great Britain and Ireland. In shape they were widely different, but as to size there was no scale by which to measure them. From the great number of subdivisions, and from signs, which apparently represented towns and cities, I was allowed to infer, that the country was at least as extensive as the British isles. This map was apparently unfinished, for it had no names inscribed upon it.

I have just said, my geographical knowledge was imperfect. Though I had not enough to draw the outlines of any country by memory, I had still sufficient to recognize what I had before seen, and to discover that none of the larger islands in our globe re-sembled the one before me. Having such and so strong motives to curiosity, you may easily imagine my sensations on surveying this map. Suspecting, as I did, that many of Ludlow's intimations alluded to a country well known to him, though unknown to others, I was, of course, inclined to suppose that this country was now before me.

In search of some clue to this mystery, I carefully inspected the other maps in this collection. In a map of the eastern hemisphere I soon observed the outlines of is-lands, which, though on a scale greatly diminished, were plainly similar to that of the land above described.

It is well known that the people of Europe are strangers to very nearly one half of the surface of the globe*. From the south pole up to the equator, it is only the small space occupied by southern Africa and by South America with which we are

* The reader must be reminded that the incidents of this narrative are supposed to have taken place before the voyages of Bougainville and Cook.[51] — EDITOR.

---

[51] "Before the voyages of Bougainville and Cook": this editorial note tells the reader that the events in Carwin's prequel take place before 1766, the year when the first of these famous voyages of Pacific exploration began, and situates Ludloe's mysterious island projects in the context of the period's early South Pacific colonial expeditions. Along with chronological landmarks in *Wieland,* this detail confirms that the main narrative of that novel is set in the late 1760s–early 1770s. See *Wieland* notes 0.3, 18.2.

After serving in the French Army during the Seven Years War, Louis-Antoine de Bougainville (1729–1811) commanded an expedition that circumnavigated the globe beginning in 1766. His well-known *Voyage autour du monde* (1771) is the first Western description of the Tahitian islanders' lifestyle.

British explorer James Cook (1728–1779) served in British Navy during the Seven Years War, op-erating in the same North American theater of operations as Bougainville, and later led three South Pacific expeditions beginning in 1768. He was the first European to circumnavigate Australia (then New Holland), one of the first to cross and chart the Antarctic Circle, and was killed in a struggle with Hawaiian islanders.

Both are veterans of the military struggle for imperial dominance between England and France, who went on to play crucial roles in consolidating the global reach of their rival commercial and colonial empires.

acquainted. There is a vast extent, sufficient to receive a continent as large as North America, which our ignorance has filled only with water. In Ludlow's maps nothing was still to be seen, in these regions, but water, except in that spot where the transverse parallels of the southern tropic and the 150th degree east longitude intersect each other.[52] On this spot were Ludlow's islands placed, though without any name or inscription whatever.

I needed not to be told that this spot had never been explored by any European voyager, who had published his adventures. What authority had Ludlow for fixing a habitable land in this spot? and why did he give us nothing but the courses of shores and rivers, and the scite of towns and villages, without a name?

As soon as Ludlow had set out upon his proposed journey of a fortnight, I unlocked his closet, and continued rummaging among these books and maps till night. By that time I had turned over every book and almost every leaf in this small collection, and did not open the closet again till near the end of that period. Meanwhile I had many reflections upon this remarkable circumstance. Could Ludlow have intended that I should see this atlas? It was the only book that could be styled a manuscript on these shelves, and it was placed beneath several others, in a situation far from being obvious and forward to the eye or the hand. Was it an oversight in him to leave it in my way, or could he have intended to lead my curiosity and knowledge a little farther onward by this accidental disclosure? In either case how was I to regulate my future deportment toward him? Was I to speak and act as if this atlas had escaped my attention or not? I had already, after my first examination of it, placed the volume exactly where I found it. On every supposition I thought this was the safest way, and unlocked the closet a second time, to see that all was precisely in the original order. . . . How was I dismayed and confounded on inspecting the shelves to perceive that the atlas was gone. This was a theft, which, from the closet being under lock and key, and the key always in my own pocket, and which, from the very nature of the thing stolen, could not be imputed to any of the domestics. After a few moments a suspicion occurred, which was soon changed into certainty by applying to the housekeeper, who told me that Ludlow had returned, apparently in much haste, the evening of the day on which he had set out upon his journey, and just after I had left the house, that he had gone into the room where this closet of books was, and, after a few minutes' stay, came out again and went away. She told me also, that he had made general enquiries after me, to which she had answered, that she had not seen me during the day, and supposed that I had spent the whole of it abroad. From this account it was plain, that Ludlow had returned for no other purpose but to remove this book out of my reach. But if he had a double key to this door, what should hinder his having access, by the same means, to every other locked up place in the house?

This suggestion made me start with terror. Of so obvious a means for possessing a knowledge of every thing under his roof, I had never been till this moment aware. Such is the infatuation which lays our most secret thoughts open to the world's

---

[52] "That spot . . . intersect each other": on later maps, the spot where the Tropic of Capricorn crosses 150 degrees east longitude is located in Queensland, northeast Australia.

scrutiny. We are frequently in most danger when we deem ourselves most safe, and our fortress is taken sometimes through a point, whose weakness nothing, it should seem, but the blindest stupidity could overlook.

My terrors, indeed, quickly subsided when I came to recollect that there was nothing in any closet or cabinet of mine which could possibly throw light upon subjects which I desired to keep in the dark. The more carefully I inspected my own drawers, and the more I reflected on the character of Ludlow, as I had known it, the less reason did there appear in my suspicions; but I drew a lesson of caution from this circumstance, which contributed to my future safety.

From this incident I could not but infer Ludlow's unwillingness to let me so far into his geographical secret, as well as the certainty of that suspicion, which had very early been suggested to my thoughts, that Ludlow's plans of civilization had been carried into practice in some unvisited corner of the world. It was strange, however, that he should betray himself by such an inadvertency. One who talked so confidently of his own powers, to unveil any secret of mine, and, at the same time, to conceal his own transactions, had surely committed an unpardonable error in leaving this important document in my way. My reverence, indeed, for Ludlow was such, that I sometimes entertained the notion that this seeming oversight was, in truth, a regular contrivance to supply me with a knowledge, of which, when I came maturely to reflect, it was impossible for me to make any ill use. There is no use in relating what would not be believed; and should I publish to the world the existence of islands in the space allotted by Ludlow's maps to these *incognitæ*,[53] what would the world answer? That whether the space described was sea or land was of no importance. That the moral and political condition of its inhabitants was the only topic worthy of rational curiosity. Since I had gained no information upon this point; since I had nothing to disclose but vain and fantastic surmises; I might as well be ignorant of every thing. Thus, from secretly condemning Ludlow's imprudence, I gradually passed to admiration of his policy. This discovery had no other effect than to stimulate my curiosity; to keep up my zeal to prosecute the journey I had commenced under his auspices.

I had hitherto formed a resolution to stop where I was in Ludlow's confidence: to wait till the success should be ascertained of my projects with respect to Mrs. Benington, before I made any new advance in the perilous and mysterious road into which he had led my steps. But, before this tedious fortnight had elapsed, I was grown extremely impatient for an interview, and had nearly resolved to undertake whatever obligation he should lay upon me.

This obligation was indeed a heavy one, since it included the confession of my vocal powers. In itself the confession was little. To possess this faculty was neither laudable nor culpable, nor had it been exercised in a way which I should be very much ashamed to acknowledge. It had led me into many insincerities and artifices, which, though not justifiable by any creed, was entitled to some excuse, on the score of youthful ardour and temerity. The true difficulty in the way of these confessions was the not having made them already. Ludlow had long been entitled to this confidence,

---

[53] "*Incognitæ*": unknown or unexplored regions, usually given as terrae incognitae.

and, though the existence of this power was venial or wholly innocent, the obstinate concealment of it was a different matter, and would certainly expose me to suspicion and rebuke. But what was the alternative? To conceal it. To incur those dreadful punishments awarded against treason in this particular. Ludlow's menaces still rung in my ears, and appalled my heart. How should I be able to shun them? By concealing from every one what I concealed from him? How was my concealment of such a faculty to be suspected or proved? Unless I betrayed myself, who could betray me?

In this state of mind, I resolved to confess myself to Ludlow in the way that he required, reserving only the secret of this faculty. Awful, indeed, said I, is the crisis of my fate. If Ludlow's declarations are true, a horrid catastrophe awaits me: but as fast as my resolutions were shaken, they were confirmed anew by the recollection—Who can betray me but myself? If I deny, who is there can prove? Suspicion can never light upon the truth. If it does, it can never be converted into certainty. Even my own lips cannot confirm it, since who will believe my testimony?

By such illusions was I fortified in my desperate resolution. Ludlow returned at the time appointed. He informed me that Mrs. Benington expected me next morning. She was ready to depart for her country residence, where she proposed to spend the ensuing summer, and would carry me along with her. In consequence of this arrangement, he said, many months would elapse before he should see me again. You will indeed, continued he, be pretty much shut up from all society. Your books and your new friend will be your chief, if not only companions. Her life is not a social one, because she has formed extravagant notions of the importance of lonely worship and devout solitude. Much of her time will be spent in meditation upon pious books in her closet. Some of it in long solitary rides in her coach, for the sake of exercise. Little will remain for eating and sleeping, so that unless you can prevail upon her to violate her ordinary rules for your sake, you will be left pretty much to yourself. You will have the more time to reflect upon what has hitherto been the theme of our conversations. You can come to town when you want to see me. I shall generally be found in these apartments.

In the present state of my mind, though impatient to see Mrs. Benington, I was still more impatient to remove the veil between Ludlow and myself. After some pause, I ventured to enquire if there was any impediment to my advancement in the road he had already pointed out to my curiosity and ambition.

He replied, with great solemnity, that I was already acquainted with the next step to be taken in this road. If I was prepared to make him my confessor, as to the past, the present, and the future, *without exception or condition*, but what arose from defect of memory, he was willing to receive my confession.

I declared myself ready to do so.

I need not, he returned, remind you of the consequences of concealment or deceit. I have already dwelt upon these consequences. As to the past, you have already told me, perhaps, all that is of any moment to know. It is in relation to the future that caution will be chiefly necessary. Hitherto your actions have been nearly indifferent to the ends of your future existence. Confessions of the past are required, because they are an earnest of the future character and conduct. Have you then—but this is too abrupt. Take an hour to reflect and deliberate. Go by yourself; take yourself to severe task, and make up your mind with a full, entire, and unfailing resolution; for the moment in which you assume this new obligation will make you a new being. Perdition or felicity will hang upon that moment.

This conversation was late in the evening. After I had consented to postpone this subject, we parted, he telling me that he would leave his chamber door open, and as soon as my mind was made up I might come to him.

**

[Later in this same issue, the "Notes from the Editor" includes this announcement:]

The writer of the Memoirs of Carwin was influenced to discontinue the publication of that work from a persuasion that the narrative was of too grave and argumentative a cast to be generally amusing. He has, however, received so many and such urgent intreaties to resume the story that he should not be justified in suppressing it any longer. Hereafter it will be continued with regularity.

X

I RETIRED accordingly to my apartment, and spent the prescribed hour in anxious and irresolute reflections. They were no other than had hitherto occurred, but they occurred with more force than ever. Some fatal obstinacy, however, got possession of me, and I persisted in the resolution of concealing *one thing*. We become fondly attached to objects and pursuits, frequently for no conceivable reason but the pain and trouble they cost us. In proportion to the danger in which they involve us do we cherish them. Our darling potion is the poison that scorches our vitals.

After some time, I went to Ludloe's apartment. I found him solemn, and yet benign, at my entrance. After intimating my compliance with the terms prescribed, which I did, in spite of all my labour for composure, with accents half faultering, he proceeded to put various questions to me, relative to my early history.

I knew there was no other mode of accomplishing the end in view, but by putting all that was related in the form of answers to questions; and when meditating on the character of Ludloe, I experienced excessive uneasiness as to the consummate art and penetration which his questions would manifest. Conscious of a purpose to conceal, my fancy invested my friend with the robe of a judicial inquisitor, all whose questions should aim at extracting the truth, and entrapping the liar.

In this respect, however, I was wholly disappointed. All his inquiries were general and obvious.—They betokened curiosity, but not suspicion; yet there were moments when I saw, or fancied I saw, some dissatisfaction betrayed in his features; and when I arrived at that period of my story which terminated with my departure, as his companion, for Europe, his pauses were, I thought, a little longer and more museful than I liked. At this period, our first conference ended. After a talk, which had commenced at a late hour, and had continued many hours, it was time to sleep, and it was agreed that next morning the conference should be renewed.

On retiring to my pillow, and reviewing all the circumstances of this interview, my mind was filled with apprehension and disquiet. I seemed to recollect a thousand things, which showed that Ludloe was not fully satisfied with my part in this interview. A strange and nameless mixture of wrath and of pity appeared, on recollection, in the glances which, from time to time, he cast upon me. Some emotion played upon his features, in which, as my fears conceived, there was a tincture of resentment and ferocity. In vain I called my usual sophistries to my aid. In vain I pondered on the inscrutable nature of my peculiar faculty. In vain I endeavoured to persuade myself, that, by telling the truth, instead of entitling myself to Ludloe's approbation, I should only excite his anger, by what he could not but deem an attempt to impose upon his belief an incredible tale of impossible events. I had never heard or read of any instance of this faculty. I supposed the case to be absolutely singular, and I should be no more entitled to credit in proclaiming it, than if I should maintain that a certain billet of wood possessed the faculty of articulate speech. It was now, however, too late to retract. I had been guilty of a solemn and deliberate concealment. I was now in the path in which there was no turning back, and I must go forward.

The return of day's encouraging beams in some degree quieted my nocturnal terrors, and I went, at the appointed hour, to Ludloe's presence. I found him with a much more cheerful aspect than I expected, and began to chide myself, in secret, for the folly of my late apprehensions.

After a little pause, he reminded me, that he was only one among many, engaged in a great and arduous design. As each of us, continued he, is mortal, each of us must, in time, yield his post to another.—Each of us is ambitious to provide himself a successor, to have his place filled by one selected and instructed by himself. All our personal feelings and affections are by no means intended to be swallowed up by a passion for the general interest; when they can be kept alive and be brought into play, in subordination and subservience to the *great end*, they are cherished as useful, and revered as laudable; and whatever austerity and rigour you may impute to my character, there are few more susceptible of personal regards than I am.

You cannot know, till *you* are what *I* am, what deep, what all-absorbing interest I have in the success of my tutorship on this occasion. Most joyfully would I embrace a thousand deaths, rather than that you should prove a recreant. The consequences of any failure in your integrity will, it is true, be fatal to yourself: but there are some minds, of a generous texture, who are more impatient under ills they have inflicted upon others, than of those they have brought upon themselves; who had rather perish, themselves, in infamy, than bring infamy or death upon a benefactor.

Perhaps of such noble materials is your mind composed. If I had not thought so, you would never have been an object of my regard, and therefore, in the motives that shall impel you to fidelity, sincerity, and perseverance, some regard to my happiness and welfare will, no doubt, have place.

And yet I exact nothing from you on this score. If your own safety be insufficient to controul you, you are not fit for us. There is, indeed, abundant need of all possible inducements to make you faithful. The task of concealing nothing from me must be easy. That of concealing every thing from others must be the only arduous one. The *first* you can hardly fail of performing, when the exigence requires it, for what motive can you possibly have to practice evasion or disguise with me? You have surely committed no crime; you have neither robbed, nor murdered, nor betrayed. If you have, there is no room for the fear of punishment or the terror of disgrace to step in, and make you hide your guilt from me. You cannot dread any further disclosure, because I can have no interest in your ruin or your shame: and what evil could ensue the confession of the foulest murder, even before a bench of magistrates, more dreadful than that which will inevitably follow the practice of the least concealment to me, or the least undue disclosure to others?

You cannot easily conceive the emphatical solemnity with which this was spoken. Had he fixed piercing eyes on me while he spoke; had I perceived him watching my looks, and labouring to penetrate my secret thoughts, I should doubtless have been ruined: but he fixed his eyes upon the floor, and no gesture or look indicated the smallest suspicion of my conduct. After some pause, he continued, in a more pathetic tone, while his whole frame seemed to partake of his mental agitation.

I am greatly at a loss by what means to impress you with a full conviction of the truth of what I have just said. Endless are the sophistries by which we seduce ourselves into perilous and doubtful paths. What we do not see, we disbelieve, or we heed not. The sword may descend upon our infatuated head from above, but we who are, meanwhile, busily inspecting the ground at our feet, or gazing at the scene around us, are not aware or apprehensive of its irresistible coming. In this case, it must not be seen before it is felt, or before that time comes when the danger of incurring it is over. I cannot withdraw the veil, and disclose to your view the exterminating angel. All must be vacant and blank, and the danger that stands armed with death at your elbow must continue to be totally invisible, till that moment when its vengeance is provoked or unprovokable. I will do my part to encourage you in good, or intimidate you from evil. I am anxious to set before you all the motives which are fitted to influence your conduct; but how shall I work on your convictions?

Here another pause ensued, which I had not courage enough to interrupt. He presently resumed.

Perhaps you recollect a visit which you paid, on Christmas day, in the year——, to the cathedral church at Toledo.[54] Do you remember?

A moment's reflection recalled to my mind all the incidents of that day. I had good reason to remember them. I felt no small trepidation when Ludloe referred me to that day, for, at the moment, I was doubtful whether there had not been some bivocal agency exerted on that occasion. Luckily, however, it was almost the only similar occasion in which it had been wholly silent.

I answered in the affirmative. I remember them perfectly.

And yet, said Ludloe, with a smile that seemed intended to disarm this declaration of some of its terrors, I suspect your recollection is not as exact as mine, nor, indeed, your knowledge as extensive. You met there, for the first time, a female, whose nomi-

---

[54] "Toledo": the city in central Spain, near Madrid.

nal uncle, but real father, a dean of that ancient church, resided in a blue stone house, the third from the west angle of the square of St. Jago.

All this was exactly true.

This female, continued he, fell in love with you. Her passion made her deaf to all the dictates of modesty and duty, and she gave you sufficient intimations, in subsequent interviews at the same place, of this passion; which, she being fair and enticing, you were not slow in comprehending and returning. As not only the safety of your intercourse, but even of both your lives, depended on being shielded even from suspicion, the utmost wariness and caution was observed in all your proceedings. Tell me whether you succeeded in your efforts to this end.

I replied, that, at the time, I had no doubt but I had.

And yet, said he, drawing something from his pocket, and putting it into my hand, there is the slip of paper, with the preconcerted emblem inscribed upon it, which the infatuated girl dropped in your sight, one evening, in the left aisle of that church. That paper you imagined you afterwards burnt in your chamber lamp. In pursuance of this token, you deferred your intended visit, and next day the lady was accidentally drowned, in passing a river. Here ended your connexion with her, and with her was buried, as you thought, all memory of this transaction.

I leave you to draw your own inference from this disclosure. Meditate upon it when alone. Recal all the incidents of that drama, and labour to conceive the means by which my sagacity has been able to reach events that took place so far off, and under so deep a covering. If you cannot penetrate these means, learn to reverence my assertions, that I cannot be deceived; and let sincerity be henceforth the rule of your conduct towards me, not merely because it is right, but because concealment is impossible.

We will stop here. There is no haste required of us. Yesterday's discourse will suffice for to-day, and for many days to come. Let what has already taken place be the subject of profound and mature reflection. Review, once more, the incidents of your early life, previous to your introduction to me, and, at our next conference, prepare to supply all those deficiencies occasioned by negligence, forgetfulness, or design on our first. There must be some. There must be many. The whole truth can only be disclosed after numerous and repeated conversations. These must take place at considerable intervals, and when *all* is told, then shall you be ready to encounter the final ordeal, and load yourself with heavy and terrific sanctions.

I shall be the proper judge of the completeness of your confession.—Knowing previously, and by unerring means, your whole history, I shall be able to detect all that is deficient, as well as all that is redundant. Your confessions have hitherto adhered to the truth, but deficient they are, and they must be, for who, at a single trial, can detail the secrets of his life? whose recollection can fully serve him at an instant's notice? who can free himself, by a single effort, from the dominion of fear and shame? We expect no miracles of fortitude and purity from our disciples. It is our discipline, our wariness, our laborious preparation that creates the excellence we have among us. We find it not ready made.

I counsel you to join Mrs. Bennington without delay. You may see me when and as often as you please. When it is proper to renew the present topic, it shall be renewed.

Till then we will be silent.—Here Ludloe left me alone, but not to indifference or vacuity. Indeed I was overwhelmed with the reflections that arose from this conversation. So, said I, I am still saved, if I have wisdom enough to use the opportunity, from the consequences of past concealments. By a distinction which I had wholly overlooked, but which could not be missed by the sagacity and equity of Ludloe, I have praise for telling the truth, and an excuse for withholding some of the truth. It was, indeed, a praise to which I was entitled, for I have made no *additions* to the tale of my early adventures. I had no motive to exaggerate or dress out in false colours. What I sought to conceal, I was careful to exclude entirely, that a lame or defective narrative might awaken no suspicions.

The allusion to incidents at Toledo confounded and bewildered all my thoughts. I still held the paper he had given me. So far as memory could be trusted, it was the same which, an hour after I had received it, I burnt, as I conceived, with my own hands. How Ludloe came into possession of this paper; how he was apprised of incidents, to which only the female mentioned and myself were privy; which she had too good reason to hide from all the world, and which I had taken infinite pains to bury in oblivion, I vainly endeavoured to conjecture.

[*Memoirs of Carwin* breaks off here.]

7. The Yates and Beadle Family Murders

7a. Anonymous, "An Account of a Murder, Committed by Mr. J—— Y——, Upon his Family, in December, A.D. 1781. *The New York Weekly Magazine; or Miscellaneous Repository*, July 20 & 27, 1796

In December 1781, James Yates murdered his family in rural upstate New York. Yates had moved to that area from Westchester County, downstate near New York City, and was perhaps the son of loyalist Richard Yates and related to other loyalist families in the New York region. On January 7, 1782, the New York Gazette and Weekly Mercury *carried a small announcement explaining that James Yates had been committed to jail for murdering his wife, four children, and livestock in Rensselaer County's "Tomhanick," where the Tomhannock Creek flows into the Hoosick River, in present-day Schaghticoke, near the Vermont and Massachusetts borders.*

The murder apparently did not create significant public interest at that time, despite a February 1782 notice in the Massachusetts Spy *which wrongly claimed that Yates was a member of the ecstatic Shakers (a Protestant group related to the Quakers and "French Prophets" that figure in the background of the elder Wieland) and "was tempted to this horrid Deed by the Spirit which so manifestly actuates the whole Society." The Yates murders resurfaced fourteen years later when "An Account of a Murder, Committed by Mr. J— Y—" was published in the* New York Weekly Magazine, *July 20 and 27, 1796, and reprinted in the* Philadelphia Minerva *August 20 and 27, 1796. Judging from the article's timing, location, and internal evidence, it seems probable that this account was authored by either Margaretta V. Bleecker Faugères or Anthony Bleecker, or some combination of the two.*

After Yates' confession in December 1781, he was held for a few days at the home of Ann Eliza Bleecker (1752–1783), poet and author of the popular and sensational captivity narrative The History of Maria Kittle *(serialized 1790–1791, book publication 1797). She is the "Mrs. Bl—r" mentioned in this account. Bleecker was known for her mainly pastoral poetry, which appeared first in the* New-York Magazine *during 1790–1791 and in book form as* The Posthumous Works of Ann Eliza Bleecker *(1793), printed by T. and J. Swords. Bleecker's daughter Margaretta V. Bleecker Faugères was responsible for bringing all of Bleecker's work into print after her mother's death, and Faugères used the opportunity of her mother's growing reputation to include her own poetry and writing with the book publication of her mother's poetry. Faugères may have been able to secure publication with New York journals and printers through her first cousin Anthony Bleecker, a wealthy merchant and minor poet, who may be the "Anna" that introduces the account, since it was conventional practice in the early Republic for men to use woman's names as pseudonyms in print. Anthony Bleecker had contact with the* New York Weekly Magazine *and Swords (the printer favored by Brown's circle) both directly and through his Manhattan literary and business associates. It is impossible to determine the degree of editorial intervention or revision, by either Margaretta or Anthony, of what is presumably a story originally based on Ann Eliza Bleecker's personal knowledge.*

Brown would have known this account and the individuals responsible for it because he was an active reader and writer for the journals involved; Anthony Bleecker was an occasional member of Brown's circle; and Faugères' husband was a French immigrant physician who, like Brown's close friend Elihu Hubbard Smith, died of yellow fever while tending to the sick during the New York yellow fever outbreak that occurred in September 1798, shortly after Brown finished Wieland.

Similarities between elements of this text and Theodore Wieland's murders—the imagined divine commands and relays of patriarchal force, the inner struggles of the murderer, the disfigurement of a victim, and efforts at self-vindication—make "An Account" a clear primary source for Brown. Brown's early "outline" and notes for Wieland[1] *include details that correspond to the Yates murders but that do not appear in the final novel; for example, the way the murderous father kills livestock in both scenarios. While the account of the Yates incident seems factually correct, it also reads as a successful piece of fiction or fictionalized reportage that repeats the primary emphases in Ann Eliza Bleecker's work: it presents the reader with an idealized vision of rural harmony interrupted by inexplicable violence, which leaves the narrator unable to shake off traumatic memories. Bleecker's* Maria Kittle *was a fictionalized account of her own involvement in an Indian raid and captivity. "An Account" echoes the captivity genre when Yates dashes his child's head against the wall (a recurring but probably fantastical element of the period's Indian raid and captivity genre) and with Yates' initial idea of blaming the murders on a warpath raid and feared ethno-racial others.*

The writer seems ambivalent about assigning interpretations to or closely examining the murders. On the one hand, Yates is presented as simply insane, but the piece ends by undermining

---

[1] Brown Family Papers, Notebook 24, Historical Society of Pennsylvania; the relevant pages of this notebook are transcribed and photographically reproduced in the Kent State Bicentennial edition of *Wieland.*

the spirit of Enlightenment rationality and skepticism, for it resurrects ideas of insanity caused by demonic intervention and concludes with a pseudo-Biblical adage warning that human reason should be constrained within conventional limits. Instead of "Dare to know!"—the motto that German philosopher Immanuel Kant gave to the Enlightenment, this popular account of a sensational murder counsels the reader to hold fast to traditional modes of thinking, lest "open" minds also open the door to satanic invasions. Brown's Wieland *can be read as a pointed rebuttal of the kinds of assumptions that produce such claims.*

Except for the remarks in the Massachusetts Spy *that targeted Shakers, there was little attempt to contextualize the murders with political and social history. Yet in upstate New York in the 1780s, land disputes over the accumulation of property and an estate system that was virtually neo-feudal were intense. Shortly before Yates' murders, loyalist families had fled the region as American Tories were rounded up and their land confiscated. If Yates was indeed the son of loyalist Richard Yates, he had likely recently witnessed local "patriots" seizing his father's property for private gain. In this light, Yates' attack on his "idols" might be read as a grotesque internalization and outward projection of the violence done to his family by local partisans. Ann Eliza Bleecker herself championed the notion that social events could be internalized, and later wrote in a letter that her neighbor "the poor Mrs. F was lately delivered of a child who is a terror to every one that sees it. It seems that she was so struck at the sight of James Yates' murdered family, that it made too fatal an impression."*

Beyond this account, the historical record concerning Yates after the murders is sparse. He petitioned the courts for release from jail in 1787 and 1788, arguing that he had come to his senses. These pleas were unsuccessful and he may have died in prison.[2]

*****

To the *Editor* of the *New-York Weekly Magazine*.

Sir,

THE inclosed Account I transmit to you for publication, at the particular request of a friend who is well acquainted with the circumstances that gave rise to it.— It is drawn up by a female hand, and she here relates respecting Mr. Y—— what she knew of him herself, and what she had heard of him in her father's family, where he had been an occasional visitant; as I have no reason to believe that this transaction has ever appeared in print, you will be pleased to give it a place among your original compositions.

ANNA.

New-York, *May 17, 1796.*

---

[2] For more on the Yeats (and Beadle) cases in relation to *Wieland*, see Axelrod, *Charles Brockden Brown: An American Tale*; Kafer, *Charles Brockden Brown's Revolution*; Fitzgerald, *Wieland's Crime: A Source and Analogue Study of the Foremost Novel of the Father of American Literature*; Hughes, "'Wonderfully Cruel Proceedings': The Murderous Case of James Yates"; and Williams, "Writing under the Influence: An Examination of *Wieland*'s 'Well Authenticated Facts' and the Depiction of Murderous Fathers in Post-Revolutionary Print Culture."

AN ACCOUNT

OF A MURDER COMMITTED BY MR. J— Y—, UPON

HIS FAMILY, IN DECEMBER, A.D. 1781.

THE unfortunate subject of my present essay, belonged to one of the most respectable families in this state; he resided a few miles from Tomhanick, and though he was not in the most affluent circumstances, he maintained his family (which consisted of a wife and four children,) very comfortably.—From the natural gentleness of his disposition, his industry, sobriety, probity and kindness, his neighbours universally esteemed him, and until the fatal night when he perpetrated the cruel act, none saw cause of blame in him.

In the afternoon preceding that night, as it was Sunday and there was no church near, several of his neighbours with their wives came to his house for the purpose of reading the scripture and singing psalms; he received them cordially, and when they were going to return home in the evening, he pressed his sister and her husband, who came with the others, to stay longer; at his very earnest solicitation they remained until near nine o'clock, during which time his conversation was grave as usual, but interesting and affectionate: to his wife, of whom he was very fond, he made use of more than commonly endearing expressions, and caressed his little ones alternately:—he spoke much of his domestic felicity, and informed his sister, that to render his wife more happy, he intended to take her to New-Hampshire the next day; "I have just been refitting my sleigh," said he, "and we will set off by day-break."—After singing another hymn, Mr. and Mrs. J—s—n departed.

"They had no sooner left us (said he upon his examination) than taking my wife upon my lap, I opened the Bible to read to her—my two boys were in bed—one five years old, the other seven; —my daughter Rebecca, about eleven, was sitting by the fire, and my infant aged about six months was slumbering at her mother's bosom.—Instantly a new light shone into the room, and upon looking up I beheld two Spirits, one at my right hand and the other at my left;—he at the left bade me destroy all my *idols*, and begin by casting the Bible into the fire;—the other Spirit dissuaded me, but I obeyed the first, and threw the book into the flames. My wife immediately snatched it out, and was going to expostulate, when I threw it in again and held her fast until it was entirely consumed:—then filled with the determination to persevere, I flew out of the house, and seizing an axe which lay by the door, with a few strokes demolished my sleigh, and running to the stable killed one of my horses—the other I struck, but with one spring he got clear of the stable.—My spirits were now high, and I hasted to the house to inform my wife of what I had done. She appeared terrified, and begged me to sit down; but the good angel whom I had obeyed stood by me and bade me go on, "You have more idols, (said he) look at your wife and children." I hesitated not a moment, but rushed to the bed where my boys lay, and catching the eldest in my arms, I threw him with such violence against the wall, that he expired without a groan!—his brother was still asleep—I took him by the feet, and dashed his skull in pieces against the fire-place!—Then looking round, and perceiving that my wife and daughters were fled, I left the dead where they lay, and went in pursuit of the living, taking up the axe again.—A slight snow had fallen

281

that evening, and by its light I descried my wife running towards her father's (who lived about a half mile off) encumbered with her babe; I ran after her, calling upon her to return, but she shrieked and fled faster, I therefore doubled my pace, and when I was within thirty yards of her, threw the axe at her, which hit her upon the hip!— the moment that she felt the blow she dropped the child, which I directly caught up, and threw against the log-fence—I did not hear it cry—I only heard the lamentations of my wife, of whom I had now lost sight; but the blood gushed so copiously from her wound that it formed a distinct path along the snow. We were now within sight of her father's house, but from what cause I cannot tell, she took an opposite course, and after running across an open field several times, she again stopped at her own door; I now came up with her—my heart bled to see her distress, and all my *natural feelings* began to revive; I forgot my duty, so powerfully did her moanings and pleadings affect me, "Come then, my love (said I) we have one child left, let us be thankful for that—what is done is right—we must not repine, come let me embrace you—let me know that you do indeed love me." She encircled me in her trembling arms, and pressed her quivering lips to my cheek.—A voice behind me, said, "This is also an idol!"—I broke from her instantly, and wrenching a stake from the garden fence, with one stroke leveled her to the earth! and lest she should only be stunned, and might, perhaps recover again, I repeated my blows, till I could not distinguish one feature of her face!!! I now went to look after my last sublunary treasure, but after calling several times without receiving any answer, I returned to the house again; and in the way back picked up the babe and laid it on my wife's bosom.—I then stood musing a minute—during which interval I though I heard the suppressed sobbings of some one near the barn, I approached it in silence, and beheld my daughter Rebecca endeavouring to conceal herself among the hay-stacks.—

At the noise of my feet upon the dry corn stalks—she turned hastily round and seeing me exclaimed, "O father, my dear father, spare me, let me live—let me live,—I will be a comfort to you and my mother—spare me to take care of my little sister Diana—do—do let me live."—She was my darling child, and her fearful cries pierced me to the soul—the tears of *natural pity* fell as plentifully down my cheeks, as those of terror did down her's, and methought that to destroy *all* my idols, was a hard task—I again relapsed at the voice of complaining; and taking her by the hand, led her to where her mother lay; then thinking that if I intended to retain her, I must make some other severe sacrifice, I bade her sing and dance—She complied, terribly situated as she was,—but I was not acting in the line of my duty—I was convinced of my error, and catching up a hatchet that stuck in a log, with one well aimed stroke cleft her forehead in twain—she fell—and no sign of retaining life appeared.

I then sat down on the threshold, to consider what I had best do—"I shall be called a murderer (said I) I shall be seized—imprisoned—executed, and for what?—for destroying my idols—for obeying the mandate of my father—no, I will put all the dead in the house together, and after setting fire to it, run to my sister's and say the Indians have done it—"I was preparing to drag my wife in, when the idea struck me that I was going to tell a *horrible lie*;" and how will that accord with my profession?

(asked I.) No, let me speak the truth, and declare the good motive for my actions, be the consequences what they may."

His sister, who was the principal evidence against him, stated—that she had scarce got home, when a message came to Mr. J—n, her husband, informing him that his mother was ill, and wished to see him; he accordingly set off immediately, and she not expecting him home again till the next day, went to bed—there being no other person in the house. About four in the morning she heard her brother Y— call her, she started up and bade him come in. "I will not (returned he) for I have committed the unpardonable sin—I have burnt the Bible." She knew not what to think, but rising hastily opened the door which was only latched, and caught hold of his hand: let me go, Nelly (said he) my hands are wet with blood—the blood of my Elizabeth and her children.—She saw the blood dripping from his fingers, and her's chilled in the veins, yet with a fortitude unparalleled she begged him to enter, which—as he did, he attempted to seize a case knife, that by the light of a bright pine-knot fire, he perceived lying on the dresser—she prevented him, however, and tearing a trammel from the chimney, bound him with it to the bed post—fastening his hands behind him—She then quitted the house in order to go to his, which as she approached she heard the voice of loud lamentation, the hope that it was some one of the family who had escaped the effects of her brother's frenzy, subdued the fears natural to such a situation and time, she quickened her steps, and when she came to the place where Mrs. Y— lay, she perceived that the moans came from Mrs. Y—'s aged father, who expecting that his daughter would set out upon her journey by day break, had come at that early hour to bid her farewell.

They alarmed their nearest neighbours immediately, who proceeded to Mrs. J—n's, and there found Mr. Y— in the situation she had left him; they took him from hence to Tomhanick, where he remained near two days—during which time Mr. W—tz—l (a pious old Lutheran, who occasionally acted as a preacher) attended upon him, exhorting him to pray and repent; but he received the admonitions with contempt, and several times with ridicule, refusing to confess his error or *join* in prayer—I say *join* in prayer, for he would not kneel when the rest did, but when they arose he would prostrate himself and address his "father," frequently saying "my father, thou knowest that it was in obedience to they commands, and for thy glory that I have done this deed." Mrs. Bl—r, at whose house he then was, bade some one ask him who his father was?—he made no reply—but pushing away the person who stood between her and himself, darted at her a look of such indignation as thrilled horror to her heart—his speech was connected, and he told his tale without variation; he expressed much sorrow for the loss of his dear family, but consoled himself with the idea of having performed his duty—he was taken to ALBANY and there confined as a lunatic in the goal, from which he escaped twice, once by the assistance of Aqua Fortis, with which he opened the front door.

I went in 1782 with a little girl, by whom Mr. Bl—r had sent him some fruit; he was then confined in dungeon, and had several chains on—he appeared to be much affected at her remembrance of him, and put up a pious ejaculation for her and her family—since then I have received no accounts respecting him.

The cause for his wonderfully cruel proceedings is beyond the conception of human beings—the deed so unpremeditated, so unprovoked, that we do not hesitate to pronounce it the effect of insanity—yet upon the other hand, when we reflect upon the equanimity of his temper, and the comfortable situation in which he was, and no visible circumstance operating to render him frantic, we are apt to conclude, that he was under a strong delusion of Satan. But what avail our conjectures, perhaps it is best that some things are concealed from us, and the only use we can now make of our knowledge of this affair, is to be humble under a scene of human frailty to renew our petition, "Lead us not into temptation."
May, 27, 1796.

7b. Anonymous, Account of the Beadle Murders, *Connecticut Journal* December 19, 1783

James Yates was not the only patriarchal family murderer whose story circulated in Brown's milieu in the 1790s. On December 11, 1782, Wethersfield, Connecticut retail merchant William Beadle murdered his wife and four children after long premeditation, apparently after drugging them, and then committed suicide. The incident received more printed commentary, over the next two decades, than any previous American murder. Local reportage and dismay at the horror of the event, in newspaper accounts and broadsides reprinted throughout the region, was amplified by clerical commentary that focused on Beadle's dedication to Deism,[3] the belief in a God who is largely absent after the creation of the world and does not stand as omniscient and omnipresent moral arbiter, leaving the consideration of ethical behavior to humanity's rational contemplation. Deism was especially influential in America among the elite collegians, professionals, and educated artisans of Brown's generation, through writings such as Thomas Paine's The Age of Reason *(1794), and it posed a dual threat to the period's ministerial elites, who struggled on the one hand to secure extragovernmental authority over their congregations and, more widely, the early American republic, and on the other to consolidate their prestige and cultural power as educators (for more on the period's ministerial elites, see the Illuminati scare debates here in Related Texts). Thus Yale president Timothy Dwight, in his polemical poem* The Triumph of Infidelity *(1787), references Beadle as if to cement an equation between religious skepticism, nonconformity, and the slide into irrational murder. Clearly this, too, is a scenario that is rejected in Brown's* Wieland.

The following anonymous newspaper account of the incident, which was reprinted as a broadside in Providence, Rhode Island, and redated January 1, 1783, popularizes this reactionary ministerial framing, presenting the murders as a consequence of Beadle's supposed free-thinking and Deism, and demonizing Enlightenment thinking as the reduction of souls to mere "machines." Beadle's insanity is presented as a sort of logical "practice" entailed by "his new theoretic system" and "mischievous error." The account notes his

---

[3] See, for example, James Dana, *Dr. Dana's Discourse on the Tragical Exit of William Beadle and his Family* (New-Haven: T. & S. Green, 1783).

"declining business" as a trader but makes no effort to explore circumstances or behaviors beyond his exemplarity as a manifestation of the dangers posed by Enlightenment's critique of religion. Despite the contrasting theist and Deist mindsets of Yates and Beadle, both invoke fundamentally patriarchal models of authority, force, and naturalized social violence.

✶✶✶✶✶

Hartford, December 17 [1783]

The following contains all the particulars of an unhappy affair which lately happened at Wethersfield, which have as yet come to hand:

On the morning of the 11th instant, about Wethersfield, a deed was perpetrated, of the most extraordinary and astonishing nature:—William Beadle, a native of South-Britain, who has resided in that town nearly ten, and in America, about twenty years, who became acquainted with, and married (at Fairfield, in this State, about 14 years since) an amiable woman, of a reputable family, by whom he had four lovely and promising children, one son and three daughters, whose education he superintended with great care and seeming solicitude, and was apparently an affectionate husband—His business, which was that of a trader, declining some years since, he betook himself more to books than usual, and was unhappily fond of those esteemed Deistical; of late he rejected all Revelation, as imposition, and (as he expresses himself) "renounced all the popular religions of the world, he intended to die a proper Deist." Having discarded all ideas of moral good and evil, he considered himself, and all the human race, as mere machines; and that he had a right to dispose of his own and the lives of his family. In letters and papers he left, addressed to sundry persons of his acquaintance, wrote a short time before his death, he declares he has had in contemplation for three years past the awful tragedy he now proceeds to act with all imaginable deliberation and composure of mind.

About sun-rise he sent his maid (the only person of the family who survived) with a letter to a friend in the neighborhood, therein announcing his dreadful purpose, and declaring that before his friend should read the letter he and his family should enter into a happier state, and desiring him to call upon two persons and come to his house, gently to alarm the neighbours, and advise them to be as collected in their minds and reason as he was. Upon receipt of this line, the house was instantly opened; but too late! All was over—He had made ready the knife, the ax and pistols, as weapons of death; the latter he made use of upon himself, the two former upon his family; these instruments he had carried with him to his bed chamber for some weeks under pretence of defending against thieves.—With the utmost secrecy, unperceived by any, he destroyed a worthy and beautiful wife, in the midst of life, and four pleasant children, sleeping in their beds, the eldest about 12 years of age, who the evening preceding were like olive branches around his table—He closed the awful scene by destroying himself. Some circumstances render it probable that he had given an opiate to the family before they retired to rest.

Speaking of this catastrophe in one of his letters, he says, "I mean to close the eyes of six persons through perfect humanity and the most endearing fondness and friendship; for never mortal father felt more of those tender ties than myself." Having become reduced in some degree in his circumstances, he rejected his former ideas of divine Revelation and belief of a future state of misery: He adopted this new theoretic system which he now put in practice.

The Jury of inquest, were of opinion, that he was of sound mind, and returned their verdict accordingly. 'Tis difficult to determine where distraction begins. 'Tis very evident he was rational on every other subject; on this no one conversed with him.

On Thursday the body of this man was buried without any marks of respect; and on Friday the unfortunate woman, with her children by her side, were interred in one grave, with every mark of respect. When a sermon was preached, suitable to the occasion, to a large concourse of people, and grief mingled with pity, displayed itself in every countenance, on the unusual and melancholy occasion.

The humane and benevolent, while they execrate the deed and detest the direful principles productive of such effects, cannot fail to weep over the victims who fell a sacrifice to such mischievous error.

7c. Stephen Mix Mitchell, excerpts from *A Narrative of the Life of William Beadle*. Windsor, VT: Spooner, 1795 (first published 1783)

Outside the kinds of ministerial and reactionary arguments that presented Beadle's breakdown as a result of Deism and late-Enlightenment thinking, the Beadle murders seem to have been noted primarily for their spectacular potential as a chilling narrative of family murders and suicide, as the kind of "horror" tale that allows a fascinated audience to both recognize and deny the violence and sinister potentials that may lurk within conventional structures of family and social life, and that allows writers and printers to realize a quick profit.[4] It is noteworthy that one of these later elaborations of the Beadle narrative, Stephen Mix Mitchell's 1783 account, reproduced below from the 1795 reprinting that Brown may have read before composing Wieland, *seems to locate the root of Beadle's turmoil in socioeconomic crisis and one man's financial fall from a relative standard of wealth. Stephen Mix Mitchell (1743–1835) was an attorney and county court judge from Wethersfield, the town where the Beadle incident occurred. He had been a delegate to the Continental Congress, was a member of the Connecticut state legislature when he wrote this account, and later became a Justice on the state's Supreme Court.*

Mitchell's narrative amplifies and capitalizes on the story's shock value. But it also transforms the ministerial focus on Beadle's religious questioning of a provident god into a more sociologically attuned reflection on a man who has apparently been formed by economic and personal insecurity (born a bastard or "natural son" of "some gentleman"), and by a series of life experiences that convey him from a metropolitan center of colonial commerce

---

[4] For more on the Beadle murders and their development as sensationalist narratives, see Halttunen, "Early American Murder Narratives: The Birth of Horror" and *Murder Most Foul*; and the previously mentioned Williams, "Writing under the Influence."

in London to the administrative bureaucracy of slave colonies on the Caribbean periphery, and thence, at the end of the Seven Years War, to North American colonies where he hoped to make his fortune as a storekeeper and petty merchant. Mitchell explains that Beadle built up a respectable amount of capital after relocating to North America, but then saw it evaporate when colonial currencies lost their value as a result of the American Revolutionary war, and remained embittered by a humiliating loss of class status despite his lifelong efforts. In this parable of social crisis and decline, then, the suggestion may be that Beadle's collapse was a manifestation of psychic distress brought on by economic turbulence tied to colonialism and the violent political and economic transformations of the British Empire. Like Yates, Beadle may be using religious ideas as a means of responding to social, economic, and political stresses. His actions appear as a "barbaric" message in deeds, conveying a savage negation, possibly, of that which he cannot articulate due to implied pressure in the 1780s to support American rebellion against British rule, or of that for which he tragically lacks a language.

*****

A LETTER from a Gentleman in Weathersfield, to his Friend—containing a Narrative of the Life of William Beadle, *(so far as it is known) and the Particulars of the Massacre of Himself and Family.*

"Sir,

"IT is not strange that reports various and contradictory, should have circulated on so interesting and terrible a subject, that of a man's consigning himself to the grave himself and family, in a moment of apparent ease and tranquility. The agitation of mind, which must be the consequence of being near such a scene of horror, will sufficiently apologize for not answering your request for the particulars o'er this. Our ignorance of the history of this man at first precluded a possibility of giving you satisfaction on this head. Perhaps no one in this town had more favorable opportunities of obtaining the particulars of his history: Yet I could never induce him to mention a single syllable relating to his age, parentage, or early occupation. To have asked him directly would have been rude, when he evidently meant to be silent on these subjects.—My conjecture was, however, that he was the natural son of some gentleman in England, and that he had been brought up in or near London, and had been about the court. Since his decease, have been able to learn from undoubted authority, that he was born in the county of Essex, in a village not far from London. As to his business in youth, am still left in the dark, but find he has once mentioned to a gentleman, some incidents which happened to him while in company with his father, and that he very early became acquainted with a club in London who were Deists, where 'tis probable he received the first rudiments in those principles. While in England, where he left a mother and sister, he sustained a fair character for integrity and honesty. In the year 1755, he went out to the island of Barbadoes, in the family of Charles Pintold, Esq. Governor of that island, where he tarried six years, then returned to England, purchased some merchandize, and from thence came to New York, in the year 1762—and immediately removed to Stratford in this state—from thence to Darby—and then to Fairfield, where he married and dwelt some years.—By this time he had acquired about twelve hundred pounds property, with which he removed to this town, about ten years since, where he resided until his death.—His business was that of retailing. He formerly credited his goods; but since his residence in this town, he has refused to give any credit, intending to keep his property within his own reach, believing it always secure while his eye was upon it. While he added considerable to his stock, none of which he ever vested in real estate; the continental currency taught him, that wealth could take to itself wings and fly away, notwithstanding all his vigilance.

"When the war commenced he had on hand a very handsome assortment of goods for a country store, which he sold for the currency of the country, without any advance in the price; the money he laid by, waiting and expecting the time would soon arrive, when he might therewith replace his goods, resolving not to part with it until it should be in as good demand as when received by him. His expectations from this quarter daily lessening, finally lost all hope, and was thrown into a state little better than despair, as appears from his writings. He adopted a plan of the most rigid family oeconomy; but still kept up the outward appearance of his former affluence—and even to the last, entertained his friend with his usual decent hospitality. Although nothing appeared in his outward deportment, which evinced, the uncommon pride of his heart; yet his writings showed clearly that he determined not to bear the mortification of being thought by his friends poor and dependant. On this subject he expresses himself in the following extraordinary manner: "If a man, who has once lived well, meant well, and done well, falls by unavoidable accident into poverty, and then submits to be laughed at, despised and tramped on by a set of mean wretches, as far below him as the moon is below the sun: I say, if such a man submits, he must become meaner than meanness itself—and I sincerely with he might have ten years added to his natural life to punish him for his folly."

"He fixed upon the night succeeding the 18th of November for the execution of his nefarious purpose, and procured a supper of oysters, of which the family eat very plentifully; that evening he writes as follows: "I have prepared a noble supper of oysters, that my flock and I may eat and drink together, thank God and die." After supper he sent the maid with a studied errand to a friend's house at some distance, directing her to stay until she obtained an answer to an insignificant letter he wrote his friend, intending that she should not return that evening. She did however return, which perhaps disconcerted him, and prevented him for that time.—The next day he carried his pistols to a smith, for repair; it may be, the ill condition of his pistols might be an additional reason for the delay.

"On the evening of the 10th of December, some persons were with him at his house, to whom he appeared as cheerful and serene as usual; he attended to the little affairs of his family, as if nothing uncommon was in contemplation. The company left him about nine o'clock in the evening, when he was urgent as usual for their stay; whether he slept that night is uncertain—but it is to be believed he went to bed. The children and maid slept in one chamber: In the grey of the morning on the 11th of December, he went to their bed-chamber, awaked the maid, and ordered her to arise gently, without disturbing the children; when she came down stairs he gave her a line to the family physician, who lived at the distance of a quarter of a mile; ordered her to carry it immediately—at the same time declaring Mrs Beadle had been ill all night, and directing her to stay until the physician should come with her; this he repeated sundry times with a degree of ardor. There is much reason to believe he had murdered Mrs Beadle before he awaked the maid. Upon the maid's leaving the house, he immediately proceeded to execute his purpose on the children and himself. It appears he had for some time before carried to his bed every night an axe and a carving knife: He smote his wife and each of the children with an axe on the side of the head as they lay sleeping in their beds; the woman had two wounds in the head—the skull of each of them was fractured; he then with the carving knife cut their throats from ear to ear; the woman and little boy were partly drawn over the side of their beds, as if to prevent the bedding from being besmeared with blood; the three daughters were taken from their beds and laid upon the floor side by side, like three lambs, before their throats were cut; they were covered with a blanket, and the woman's face with an handkerchief.—He then proceeded to the lower floor of the house, leaving marks of his footsteps in blood on the stairs, carrying with him the axe and knife—the latter he laid upon the table in the room where he was found, reeking with the blood of his family.—Perhaps he had thoughts he might use it against himself if his pistols should fail; it appears he then seated himself in a Windsor chair; with his arms supported by the arms of the chair, he fixed the muzzles of the pistols into his two ears, and fired them at the same instant: The balls went through the head in transverse directions. Although the neighbors were very near, and some of them awake, none heard the report of the pistols.

"The capital facts of the massacre you have seen in the public papers. A minute detail was too horrible to be given at first, until the mind (especially of the relatives of the unhappy woman) had been prepared by a summary narrative; and even now it is enough to give feelings to apathy itself, to relate the horrid tale.

"The letter to the physician obscurely announced the intentions of the man; the house was soon opened, but alas too late! The bodies were pale and motionless, swimming in their blood, and their faces white as mountain snow; yet life seemed to tremble at their lips; description can do no more than faintly ape and trifle with the real figure.

"Such a tragical scene filled every mind with the deepest distress; nature recoiled and was on the rack with distorting passions; the most poignant sorrow and tender pity for the lady and her innocent babes, who were the hapless victims of the brutal studied cruelty of a husband and father, in whose embraces they expected to find security, melted every heart.—Shocking effects of pride and false notions about religion.

"To paint the first transports this affecting scene produced, when the house was opened, is beyond my reach:—Multitudes of all ages and sexes were drawn together by the sad tale—the very inmost souls of the beholders were wounded at the sight, and torn by contending passions; silent grief, with marks of astonishment, were succeeded by furious indignation against the author of the affecting spectacle, which vented itself in incoherent exclamations. Some old soldiers accidentally passing through the town that morning, on their way from camp to visit their friends, led by curiosity turned in, to view the sad remains; on sight of the woman and her tender offspring, notwithstanding all their firmness, the tender sympathetic tear stealing gently down their furrowed cheeks, betrayed the anguish of their hearts—and on being showed the body of the sacrificer, they paused a moment, then muttering forth an oath or two of execration, with their eyes fixed on the ground in silent sorrow, they slowly went their way. So awful and terrible a disaster wrought wonderfully on the minds of the neighborhood; nature itself seemed ruffled, and refused the kind aid of sleep for a time.

"Near the close of the day, on the 12th of December, the bodies still being unburied, the people who had collected in great numbers, grew almost frantic with rage, and in manner demanded the body of the murderer; the law being silent on the subject, it was difficult to determine where decency required the body should be placed; many proposed it should be in an ignominious manner, where four roads met, without any coffin or insignia or respect, and perforated by a stake. Upon which a question arose where that place could be found, which might be unexceptionable to the neighborhood?—but no one would consent it should be near his house or land. After some consultation it was thought best to place it on the bank of the river, between high and low water mark:—The body was accordingly handed out at the window, and bound with cords on a sled, with the cloths on as it was found, and the bloody knife tied on his breast, without coffin or box, and the horse he usually rode was made fast to the sled—The horse unaccustomed to the draught, proceeded with great unsteadiness, sometimes running full speed, then stopping, followed by a multitude, until arriving at the water's edge, the body was tumbled into a hole dug for the purpose, like the carcase of a beast. Not many days after, there appeared an uneasiness in sundry persons, at placing the body so near a ferry much frequented; some threatnings were given out that the body should be taken up and exposed a second time to view. It was thought prudent the body should be removed, and secretly deposited in some obscure spot; it was accordingly removed with the utmost secrecy; notwithstanding which, some children accidentally discovered the place, and the early freshes having partly washed up the body, it has had a second remove to a place where it is hoped mankind will have no further vexation with it.

"On the 13th of December, the bodies of the murdered were interred in a manner much unlike that of the unnatural murderer.—The remains of the children were born by a suitable number of equal age, attended with a sad procession of youths of the town, all bathed in tears; side by side the hapless woman's corpse was carried in solemn procession to the parish church-yard, followed by a great concourse, who with affectionate concern and every token of respect, were anxious to express their heart-felt sorrows, in performing the last mournful duties.

[. . .]

It is doubtful whether any history of modern times can afford an instance of similar barbarity, even in the extreme distress of war. The ancients, encouraged by numerous examples, did, in hours of despair, destroy themselves, to avoid the shame of becoming captives to be led in triumph; and they commonly exercised it in those barbarous ages.

By this time your curiosity itself will be pleased to find me subscribing myself,

Your very humble servant,

Weathersfield, February, 1783

8. Elias (Élie) Marion, excerpts from *Prophetical Warnings of Elias Marion, heretofore One of the Commanders of the Protestants, that had taken Arms in the Cevennes: or, Discourses Uttered by him in London, under the Operation of the Spirit; and Faithfully taken in Writing, whilst they were spoken* (London: Ben. Bragge, 1707)

After French king Louis XIV revoked the Edict of Nantes, which had granted Protestants freedom to worship in France, and accelerated the decline of regional economies by increasing taxes, the rural Languedoc-Cévennes mountain region in southern France saw the rise of a violent peasant rebellion that combined armed resistance to the Catholic State with apocalyptic and messianic prophecies. In the late 1680s, itinerant preachers and local visionaries circulated apocalyptic prophecies that were revealed in convulsive, trance-like states. These ecstatic pronouncements foresaw the arrival of a messianic liberator, possibly linked to expectations that Protestant champion William of Orange might provide aid to the group. Even when expectations of a saving presence were disappointed, the prophets claimed that they were protected by angelic guardians. In an ensuing 1689 confrontation with state authorities, three hundred were killed after they shouted "back Satan" and opened their shirts to the militia, placing misguided faith in divine protection against bullets.

After this massacre the movement dissipated for a time, but was renewed, in the new years of the next century, in the form of a long and violent guerilla revolt (1702–1710) that included the murder of Catholic priests and armed resistance against the French monarchy. Known as Camisards, a term derived from the camise *(shirt or smock in the Occitaine dialect) that indicated the group's laboring-class, artisan, peasant affiliation, the Protestant rebels wore these distinctive shirts in lieu of uniforms. The revolt was led by charismatic religious teachers or "prophets," probably numbering about 100, and was only crushed after many atrocities. Although the visions of these self-styled prophets were not in ancient tongues, they were, however, usually pronounced in French, rather than in the regional occitane dialect,* langue d'oc *(from "oc," the local low-latin form for "yes"), ordinarily spoken by the prophets and their audience. The struggle became known to Atlantic reading audiences in works such Maximilien Mission's* Le Théâtre Sacré des Cévennes (The Sacred Theater of the Cévennes), *published in English as* A Cry From The Desert: Or, Testimonials of the Miraculous Things Lately Come to Pass In The

Cevennes, Verified Upon Oath, and by Other Proofs *(London: Ben Bragge, 1707).* *This tract was translated by John Lacey, one of the best known of the English Prophets group that emerged as the movement spread beyond southern France.*

Accounts of the group's prophecies and liberation struggle circulated and reached Anglophone audiences after a fraction of the Camisard Protestants, known in English as the "French Prophets" or "Cévenols" (from the Cévennes Mountains) fled to London in 1706, mainly under the leadership of Élie Marion (1678–1713). Acting from a new base in London, Marion and other Cévenol prophets held that the end of the world was near, warned that a vengeful God would punish all but a small group of the elect, who must prepare for suffering and emigration, and practiced "divine revelation" through dreams, visions, public speaking in tongues, and bodily writhing, all accepted as signs of an invasive spirit. The selections below from Marion's translated prophetical warnings illustrate the themes of millenarian revenge that characterize the group's rhetoric.

Quickly persecuted for spreading "terror" among the Queen's subjects in England, Marion and others were arrested in 1707 for blasphemy and sedition, and sentenced to the pillory. The authorities' main concern was probably for how the group quickly attracted English Prophets, followers from within London's artisan and plebian class who were themselves beginning to deliver visionary declarations. The group left England in 1710 and Marion died in Turkey in 1713.

The most significant material consequence of the group's English activities was the influence they had on the 1747 inception of the Shaker movement, which fused Quaker and French Prophet beliefs. Additionally, the French Prophets became a touchstone for English bourgeois and elite publicists such as Shaftesbury (Anthony Ashley Cooper, 1671–1713), who were anxious to validate their secular claims for an embodied sympathy and sensibility, against the damaging reputation of plebian "enthusiasm." In a closely related way, cosmopolitan advocates for a public sphere of rational questioning, such as Immanuel Kant, warned against religious fanatics (Schwärmerei) who justified actions based on the belief that God, or the Holy Spirit, is everywhere and can direct individuals privately.

These polemics against religious enthusiasm mistake, perhaps, the origin of the social inequality that gives rise to such movements. The French Prophets can be seen as an instance of frustrated modernity, whereby social groups who feel encouraged by emancipating historical movements find that their opportunities to realize new liberties have been blocked. This is what happened to the French Protestants who received religious toleration only to have it taken away from them. Similarly, enthusiastic forms of sacred feeling often emerge from lower-middle-class groups who feel that their economic security is made fragile or threatened by distant governmental actions.[1]

In Wieland, the tension between social equality and commonwealth on the one hand, and blocked advancement on the other, appears in two ways. The unnamed elder Wieland

---

[1] For more on the Camisard and French Prophet episodes, see Schwartz, *The French Prophets: The History of a Millenarian Group in Eighteenth-Century England;* Cosmos, *Huguenot Prophecy and Clandestine Worship in the Eighteenth Century: 'The Sacred Theatre of the Cévennes';* and Le Roy Ladurie, *The Peasants of Languedoc.*

first reads the warnings of the French and English Prophets in Chapter 1 because he is a struggling and exploited artisan, bound as an indentured apprentice; his social location makes him part of the Prophets' most receptive audience. His sense of impending divine punishment in Chapter 2 may, perhaps, be understood as a sign of guilt at having become financially secure after abandoning his efforts to spread social change through proselytizing. Secondly, the encounter between Carwin and the Wielands can likewise be read as a recurrence of plebian "prophet" resistance. As the Memoirs of Carwin *make clear, Carwin's life narrative is one of frustration at his inability to advance into the middle classes. His ventriloquism, while not literally involving trance-like speaking in tongues, is likened to such practices by Brown's descriptions of Carwin's bodily contortions and use of apocalyptic language. The collision between Clara's use of "sympathy" as a means of exculpating her own class-coded violence against Carwin, as well as her brother's, suggests that the social energies congealed within Marion's text, or related ones, can be used as a key context for deciphering the subterranean tensions of* Wieland.

Additionally, Brown was likely familiar with the French Prophets through more local sources, since, according to Benjamin Franklin's Autobiography, Franklin's first Philadelphia employer and later competition, printer Samuel Keimer, had "become one of the French Prophets and could act their enthusiastic Agitations." Keimer was imprisoned in London in 1713 for printing French Prophet material, but afterward published an attack on the group, Brand Pluck'd From The Burning: Exemplify'd in the Unparallel'd Case Of Samuel Keimer *(London: Boreham, 1718).*

*****

And at Midnight there was a Cry made, Behold, the Bridegroom comes; Go ye out to meet Him, Matt. Xxv. 6

Ezek. III. Ver. 17, 18, 19

Therefore hear the Word at my Mouth, and give them Warning, from Me. When I say unto the Wicked, Thou shalt surely die; and thou givest him not Warning, nor speakest to warn the Wicked from his wicked way, to save his Life: The same wicked Man shall die in his Iniquity: but his Blood will I require at thine hand. Yet if thou warn the Wicked, and he turn not from his Wickedness, nor from his wicked ways, he shall die in his Iniquity; but thou hast delivered thy Soul.

The Declaration of Elias Marion.

When the Spirit of God is about to seize me, I feel a great Heat in my Heart and the Parts adjacent; which sometimes has a shivering of my whole Body going before it: At other times I am seized all at once, without having any such preceeding Notice. As soon as I find my self seized, my Eyes are instantly shut up, and the Spirit causes in me great Agitations of Body, making me to put forth great Sighs and Throbbings, which are cut short, as if I were labouring for Breath. I have also frequently very hard

Shocks; but yet all this is without Pain, and without hindering me of the Freedom of thinking. I continue thus about a Quarter of an Hour, more or less, before I utter one Word. At last I feel that the Spirit forms in my Mouth the Words which he will have me to pronounce, which are almost always accompanied with some Agitations, or extraordinary Motions, or at least with a great Constraint. Sometimes it is so, that the first Word that I am to speak next, is already formed in my own Idea; but I am very often ignorant how that very Word will end which the Spirit has already begun. And it has happened sometimes, that when I thought I was going to pronounce a Word, or a Sentence, it proved to be only a meer inarticulate Sound that was formed by my Voice. During all the time of these Visits I always feel my Spirit extreamly enlarged toward my God.

   And now I do here protest and declare before that Supreme Being, that I am no way sollicited, prevailed upon, or seduced by any Person whatsoever, nor moved by any worldly Prospect, Design, Combination, Suggestion or Artifice, to pronounce one Word other than what the Spirit or the Angel of God does himself form, in making use of my Organs of Speech, as his Instrument. And to him in these Ecstacies I do intirely give up the Government of my Tongue, my Spirit being then imployed only in thinking upon God, and in being attentive to the Words which my Mouth doth then recite. I know that then a Foreign and Superior Power makes me speak. I meditate not, nor know at all before-hand the things that I my self am to speak. While I am speaking, my Spirit gives attention to what my Mouth does pronounce, as if it were a Discourse spoken by some other Person; and which, as such, does ordinarily leave Impressions more or less, lively upon my Memory. And by that means I have been enabled to know that these Warnings, which are here published, have been taken in Writing with all the Sincerity and Faithfulness, which a Work of that Nature is capable of; whereof I can give the most certain Testimony, because I have regularly, and almost always heard every several Warning read over in a few Hours, or perhaps Minutes after their having been delivered: That short time (especially when several Persons have been writing them) being necessary for reducing the several Copies into one; and not being capable much to weaken my Memory. I have never seen any thing in them that I could in the least suspect to have been put in by Fraud; much less has any thing of moment been thrust in, that has relation either to States, or Persons of an eminent Character, or to Religion.

   Lastly, I do declare, That for these Four last Years of my Life, I do know that I have been, and that I am yet in a State of Grace, of Comfort, and of Peace with my God; and I cannot but look upon my self as his Servant, being fully assured, that it is his Holy Spirit, or his Angel that speaks by me. For a further Satisfaction to the Publick, I think it necessary to declare, That I have been careful to take regularly my self, and as soon as I could, the Copy of every Warning, having always had the free use of the Originals.

ELIAS MARION

Written at London, March 31. 1707.

Warnings Pronounced by Elias Marion

I. *Wednesday Sept.* 18. 1706. D.P.

The Devil's Destruction is near. Oh the gracious Promises which I have for you! The Trumpet is ready to sound. Fire, Lightnings, and Thunderbolts are prepared for thine Enemies. Since there are many Persons who come only out of a Spirit of Curiosity, I will not have my Word manifested to such People. Prepare thy self to depart within a short time out of this Country, and go to thy Brethren, to fight there more than ever.

II. *Friday Sept.* 20. D.F.P.

My Child, I come with a Rod of Iron, to chastise the Wicked. Thou shalt soon see the Devil swallowed up in Victory. Thou shalt quickly depart out of this Country. Leave the World and the Devil, they join with one another. You are rejected, but I receive you. Ah what tumults are at hand! Every thing is making ready for Battle; but many will be faint-hearted. I have many things to communicate to you. Be not you affrighted. Let the World take its Course. Be not thou afraid; I will be with thee. The Time draws near wherein I must gather mine Elect. I will place them in a Corner, where they shall fight. The Devil rejoiceth, believing that he hath destroyed my People; but I assure thee he will work his own Destruction. Many strange things shall appear. The World shall be affrighted. I am coming to my People. Oh what Tempests are preparing for the Wicked! The Devil shall not rule any more over my People. I have chosen my Children for to fight. No Peace for the Wicked; He must be destroyed. Oh the Wonders that are preparing for my People! (Oh the great Wonders!) The Earth shall quake; the Earth shall open it self; and the Heavens shall guide my People; the World and the Devil shall be affrighted at their Coming.

IV. *Wednesday Sept.* 25. D.F.P.

Ah thou Tormentor of thine own Conscience! What will become of thee in a little Time? Thou wretched Persecutor! Thou hast destroyed my People; but I come (to destroy thee). Ah my dear Children! Ah my Child, I assure thee that there are many of thy Brethren, who are now suffering. O my Child, how should I forgive those that have persecuted my People? No, no my Child. All things do prepare for the Victory, which I have promised to my People. My Child, how great are the Sufferings of my poor People? I tell thee, many things are preparing.

VI. *Friday Sept* 27. F.

My Child, I have foretold thee often—If you knew the things that are preparing, you would be fill'd with Joy. You may with all assurance ask me whatever you would have. Do not forsake me. The Devil is troubled at my Coming; but I am ready for his Destruction. My Heart is fill'd with Joy to see my Children coming over to stand on my side. Every thing shall tremble at the Appearance of my Standards. Nothing shall resist my Word. The Devil is going to be destroy'd. Fear him not, any more. He shall have no more Power over thee. I have Victories in reserve for many. My Child, I have one thing to warn thee of; I will that thou abide for some time within doors. Do not yet manifest thy self to all, I will yet do before—I will visit thee. I will give thee notice of such things as are to happen to thee. 'Tis nothing, Fear not, my Child. I have some new work to give you in hand; I have some hidden things to discover to you. But be stedfast, my Children.

XI. *Tuesday Octob.* 22. P.

My Child have I not several times told thee that thou art to suffer much for my Name? I will yet stir up the Devil against thee. I will come very soon to avenge the Outrage done to my Glory. Ah my Child, terrible Judgments are preparing for the Wicked. The Devil is going to chained up with—Be not thou affrighted. I will that thou cry aloud against— I will send you double Strength to combat with the Devil and his Friends. My Child I have many things to say to you. Prepare your selves to receive them. Prepare to receive them, by Fasting and Prayer; and to cry out against those who—Terrible Judgments—I am weary of such a People. I will soon execute Vengeance upon them, and root them out. My Strength shall appear. My avenging Arm cometh to destroy the Wicked. Ah many Calamities will quickly fall upon the Earth—Upon the Wicked. Gnashing of Teeth. Total Destruction against the —There are many who betray their Conscience. They suspect themselves to be in wrong, and are so indeed. My Children, be stedfast to me. Let the World and the Devil take their Course. Their Efforts are coming to an End. My Judgments are ready, and Justice shall soon be done. One Moment is enough to destroy the Wicked, altho' they be many in number. O ye Despisers of my Word, ye shall be scourged. I will send one Messenger after another; one Express after another, for the Destruction of the Wicked. I leave thee my Blessing. Be thou comforted.

XII. *Wednesday Octob.* 23. D.P.

My Child, I assure thee that this Day there have been mischievous Contrivances plotting against you. But you have nothing to fear. I am with you. Perform my Will. Answer them it is my Will that you are doing. Let them go on. Yes, yes, I assure thee that wicked Counsels have been contriving against my Children. My Children, Prepare your selves, all of you, to draw still nearer and nearer to me. I have you in my Mind. I will never leave you. Prepare your selves by Fasting and Prayer. You have Enemies to fight with: You have Enemies to fight with, my Children.[. . .]

9. William Godwin, excerpts from *Enquiry Concerning Political Justice* (1793)

William Godwin (1756–1836) was at the center of British progressive culture and politics in the 1790s. His Political Justice *is a key work of the Woldwinite circle, the most*

9. William Godwin, excerpts from *Enquiry Concerning Political Justice* (1793)

complete articulation of its social principles and program. Along with Mary Wollstonecraft and Thomas Paine, Godwin was tremendously popular and influential among the college-educated young men who formed the core of Brown's associates. These writings operate as the common sense and moral compass for Brown's group, which corresponded with Godwin and Godwin's fellow traveler Thomas Holcroft as early as 1796.

Brown and his circle were familiar with Political Justice *in its successive editions. They could easily compare and contrast passages from expanded later editions with earlier material. With the exception of the first passage provided here, on the social function of literature, these excerpts follow the second (1796) edition in the Philadelphia printing by Bioren and Madan, the version that was most readily available to Brown during his novelistic years. The first edition sets forth Godwin's belief that reasonable conversation—rational discussion, dialogue, and learning—can generally impart truth to those who participate in it, and that this rationalizing spirit will spread outward from small communities that practice it to peacefully undermine the coercive practices of traditional states and governments, and the abusive superstition imposed by institutionalized religion.*

Literature plays a basic role in this gradual process of progressive action initiated through cultural practices, and Godwin assumes that the political purpose of fiction is to help educate readers about social relations so that they can overcome the retarding limits of traditional beliefs and behaviors that are merely reproduced and imposed by the status quo. Although Godwin removed this entire passage from later editions, he continued to reflect on the relation of literature and politics in his unpublished writings and, implicitly, in his fictions. His reticence to publish essays and make explicit public statements on the link between literature and politics may well be the result of increased repression and political prosecutions against free speech in Great Britain during the 1790s.

In a preview of the 1798 U.S. Alien and Sedition Acts, British state measures against democratic and dissenting writers resulted in several ideological trials that particularly targeted Godwin's circle. During a well known but possibly apocryphal exchange, British Prime Minister William Pitt is said to have argued that there was no need to suppress Political Justice *as he had suppressed Thomas Paine's* Rights of Man *(1791) because Godwin's large treatise was too expensive for laboring class militants to purchase.*

Consequently, Godwin and his closest associates, including Mary Wollstonecraft, responded to these pressures by shifting their writing away from explicitly political commentary and toward fiction. The removal of the passage about the political nature of literature after the first edition does not represent any fundamental shift in Godwin's thinking on this topic, in other words, but may be a safeguard against the risk of too openly advertising the purpose of his own literary practices. Contemporary readers understood "literature," of course, to mean print culture in general, all printed books, rather than belles lettres, "art," or the restricted realm of aesthetic distinction.

The remaining excerpts insist on several themes that are important in Brown's theory of novel writing and that are implicitly explored in Wieland: *the social degradation and psychic damage caused by inequalities of wealth; the obligation to struggle for social reform through rational improvements; the power of benevolence as it acts through associative sentiment; and the importance of intimate conversation and transparency of personal motivation in setting the stage for larger social and historical transformations.*

*****

First Edition (1793)

From *Book I. Of the Importance of Political Institutions; Chap. IV. Three Principle Causes of Moral Improvement; I. Literature.*

Few engines can be more powerful, and at the same time more salutary in their tendency, than literature. Without enquiring for the present into the cause of this phenomenon, it is sufficiently evident in fact, that the human mind is strongly infected with prejudice and mistake. The various opinions prevailing in different countries and among different classes of men upon the same subject, are almost innumerable; and yet of all these opinions only one can be true. Now the effectual way for extirpating these prejudices and mistakes seems to be literature.

Literature has reconciled the whole thinking world respecting the great principles of the system of the universe, and extirpated upon this subject the dreams of romance and the dogmas of superstition. Literature has unfolded the nature of the human mind, and Locke and others have established certain maxims respecting man, as Newton has done respecting matter, that are generally admitted for unquestionable. Discussion has ascertained with tolerable perspicuity the preference of liberty over slavery; and the Mainwarings, the Sibthorpes, and the Filmers, the race of speculative reasoners in favour of despotism, are almost extinct. Local prejudice had introduced innumerable privileges and prohibitions upon the subject of trade; speculation has nearly ascertained that perfect freedom is most favourable to her prosperity. If in many instances the collation of evidence have failed to produce universal conviction, it must however be considered, that it has not failed to produce irrefragable argument, and that falshood would have been much shorter in duration, if it had not been protected and inforced by the authority of political government.

Indeed, if there be such a thing as truth, it must infallibly be struck out by the collision of mind with mind. The restless activity of intellect will for a time be fertile in paradox and error; but these will be only diurnals, while the truths that occasionally spring up, like sturdy plants, will defy the rigour of season and climate. In proportion as one reasoner compares his deductions with those of another, the weak places of his argument will be detected, the principles he too hastily adopted will be overthrown, and the judgments, in which his mind was exposed to no sinister influence, will be confirmed. All that is requisite in these discussions is unlimited speculation, and a sufficient variety of systems and opinions. While we only dispute about the best way of doing a thing in itself wrong, we shall indeed make but a trifling progress; but, when we are once persuaded that nothing is too sacred to be brought to the touchstone of examination, science will advance with rapid strides. Men, who turn their attention to the boundless field of enquiry, and still more who recollect the innumerable errors and caprices of mind, are apt to imagine that the labour is without benefit and endless. But this cannot be the case, if truth at last have any real existence. Errors will, during the whole period of their reign, combat each other; prejudices that have passed unsuspected for ages, will have their era of detection; but, if in any science we discover one solitary truth, it cannot be overthrown.

Such are the arguments that may be adduced in favour of literature. But, even should we admit them in their full force, and at the same time suppose that truth is the omnipotent artificer by which mind can infallibly be regulated, it would yet by no means sufficiently follow that literature is alone adequate to all the purposes of human improvement. Literature, and particularly that literature by which prejudice is superseded, and the mind is strung to a firmer tone, exists only as the portion of a few. The multitude, at least in the present state of human society, cannot partake of its illuminations. For that purpose it would be necessary, that the general system of policy should become favourable, that every individual should have leisure for reasoning and reflection, and that there should be no species of public institution, which, having falshood for its basis, should counteract their progress. This state of society, if it did not precede the general dissemination of truth, would at least be the immediate result of it.

But in representing this state of society as the ultimate result, we should incur an obvious fallacy. The discovery of truth is a pursuit of such vast extent, that it is scarcely possible to prescribe bounds to it. Those great lines, which seem at present to mark the limits of human understanding, will, like the mists that rise from a lake, retire farther and farther the more closely we approach them. A certain quantity of truth will be sufficient for the subversion of tyranny and usurpation; and this subversion, by a reflected force, will assist our understandings in the discovery of truth. In the mean time, it is not easy to define the exact portion of discovery that must necessarily precede political melioration. The period of partiality and injustice will be shortened, in proportion as political rectitude occupies a principal share in our disquisition. When the most considerable part of a nation, either for numbers or influence, becomes convinced of the flagrant absurdity of its institutions, the whole will soon be prepared tranquilly and by a sort of common consent to supersede them.

*****

Second Edition (1796)

Book I: Of The Powers Of Man Considered In His Social Capacity; Chapter III. Spirit Of Political Institutions

Two of the greatest abuses relative to the interior policy of nations, which at this time prevail in the world, consist in the irregular transfer of property, either first by violence, or secondly by fraud. . . . First then it is to be observed that, in the most refined states of Europe, the inequality of property has risen to an alarming height. Vast numbers of their inhabitants are deprived of almost every accommodation that can render life tolerable or secure. Their utmost industry scarcely suffices for their support. . . . A perpetual struggle with the evils of poverty, if frequently ineffectual, must necessarily render many of the sufferers desperate. A painful feeling of their oppressed situation will itself deprive them of the power of surmounting it. The superiority of the rich, being thus unmercifully exercised, must inevitably expose them to reprisals; and the poor man will be induced to regard the state of society as a state of war, an unjust combination, not for protecting every man in his rights and securing to him the means of existence, but for engrossing all its advantages to a few favoured individuals, and reserving for the portion of the rest want, dependence and misery.

Chapter IV. The Characters Of Men Originate In Their External Circumstances

. . . I shall attempt to prove two things: first, that the actions and dispositions of mankind are the offspring of circumstances and events, and not of any original determination that they bring into the world; and, secondly, that the great stream of our voluntary actions essentially depends, not upon the direct and immediate impulses of sense, but upon the decisions of the understanding.

Chapter V. The Voluntary Actions Of Men Originate In Their Opinions

The corollaries respecting political truth, deducible from the simple proposition, which seems clearly established by the reasonings of the present chapter, that the voluntary actions of men are in all instances conformable to the deductions of their understanding, are of the highest importance. Hence we may infer what are the hopes and prospects of human improvement. The doctrine which may be founded upon these principles may perhaps best be expressed in the five following propositions: Sound reasoning and truth, when adequately communicated, must always be victorious over error: Sound reasoning and truth are capable of being so communicated: Truth is omnipotent: The vices and moral weakness of man are not invincible: Man is perfectible, or in other words susceptible of perpetual improvement.
[. . .]

Book 2. Principles of Society; Chapter IV: Of Personal Virtue and Duty

In the first sense I would define virtue to be any action or actions of an intelligent being proceeding from kind and benevolent intention, and having a tendency to contribute to general happiness. Thus defined, it distributes itself under two heads; and, in whatever instance either the tendency or the intention is wanting, the virtue is incomplete. An action, however pure may be the intention of the agent, the tendency of which is mischievous, or which shall merely be nugatory and useless in its character, is not a virtuous action. Were it otherwise, we should be obliged to concede the appellation of virtue to the most nefarious deeds of bigots, persecutors and religious assassins, and to the weakest observances of a deluded superstition. Still less does an action, the consequences of which shall be supposed to be in the highest degree beneficial, but which proceeds from a mean, corrupt and degrading motive, deserve the appellation of virtue. A virtuous action is that, of which both the motive and the tendency concur to excite our approbation.
[. . .]

Book IV, Chapter III, Appendix. Of the Connection Between Understanding and Virtue

A proposition which, however evident in itself, seems never to have been considered with the attention it deserves is that which affirms the connection between understanding and virtue. Can an honest ploughman be as virtuous as Cato? Is a man of weak intellects and narrow education as capable of moral excellence as the sublimest genius or the mind most stored with information and science?

To determine these questions it is necessary we should recollect the nature of virtue. Considered as a personal quality, it consists in the disposition of the mind, and may be defined a desire to promote the happiness of intelligent beings in general, the quantity of virtue being as the quantity of desire.

Book IV, Chapter VI. Of Sincerity

The powerful recommendations attendant upon sincerity are obvious. It is intimately connected with the general dissemination of innocence, energy, intellectual improvement, and philanthropy. [. . . .]

There is a further benefit that would result to me from the habit of telling every man the truth, regardless of the dictates of worldly prudence and custom. I should acquire a clear, ingenuous and unembarrassed air. . . . Sincerity would liberate my mind, and make the eulogiums I had occasion to pronounce, clear, copious and appropriate. Conversation would speedily exchange its present character of listlessness and insignificance, for a Roman boldness and fervour; and, accustomed, at first by the fortuitous operation of circumstances, to tell men of things it was useful for them to know, I should speedily learn to study their advantage, and never rest satisfied with my conduct till I had discovered how to spend the hours I was in their company in the way which was most rational and improving. [. . .]

What is it that, at this day, enables a thousand errors to keep their station in the world; priestcraft, tests, bribery, war, cabal and whatever else excites the disapprobation of the honest and enlightened mind? Cowardice; the timid reserve which makes men shrink from telling what they know; and the insidious policy that annexes persecution and punishment to an unrestrained and spirited discussion of the true interests of society. Men either refrain from the publication of unpalatable opinions because they are unwilling to make a sacrifice of their worldly prospects; or they publish them in a frigid and enigmatical spirit, stripped of their true character, and incapable of their genuine operation. If every man today would tell all the truth he knew, it is impossible to predict how short would be the reign of usurpation and folly.

Book VI. Effects of the Political Superintendence of Opinion; Chapter I. General Effects of the Political Superintendence of Opinion

The legitimate instrument of effecting political reformation is knowledge. Let truth be incessantly studied, illustrated and propagated, and the effect is inevitable. Let us not vainly endeavour, by laws and regulations, to anticipate the future dictates of the general mind, but calmly wait till the harvest of opinion is ripe. Let no new practice in politics be introduced, and no old one he anxiously superseded, till the alteration is called for by the public voice. The task which, for the present, should occupy the first rank in the thoughts of the friend of man is enquiry, communication, discussion.

[. . .]

10. Erasmus Darwin, excerpts from *Zoönomia; or, The Laws of Organic Life* (1794)

Erasmus Darwin (1731–1802) was an influential physician, naturalist, and poet whose importance has often been overshadowed by the achievements of his intellectually vibrant descendants, such as evolutionist Charles Darwin and eugenicist Francis Galton, both grandsons, as well as later descendants and their relations by marriage, including economist John Maynard Keynes. His medical writings are an important source for Brown's thinking about the mind and his representations of emotional disturbance. Additionally, for Brown, Darwin had the prestige of close association with literary figures to whom Brown looked for inspiration and emulation.

Darwin is mainly known for Zoönomia; or, The Laws of Organic Life *(1794–1796) and an earlier work on biology,* The Botanic Garden *(1791). Darwin's work popularized botanical classification. It extended earlier models proposed by the Swedish zoologist Carl Linnaeus (1707–1778) and was notable at the time for refusing to censor Linnaeus's sexualized language to patronize and "protect" female readers, as earlier English translators had done. Darwin combined arguments about the continuity of the natural and human worlds with politically progressive ideals about slavery and Revolutionary era politics, and his writings became key sources for Brown and his New York circle. They discussed and endorsed his progressive ideas about medicine, the body, the general relation of nature and society, and the use of poetry and literature to disseminate scientific, philosophical, and political ideas to a nonspecialized audience. Brown's friend Elihu Hubbard Smith corresponded with Darwin and published the first U.S. edition of* The Botanic Garden *in 1798, during the period when Brown was most closely associated with him. Smith wrote that* Zoönomia *was "the most masterly performance ever given the world on the subject of Medicine."[1]*

The following excerpts from Zoönomia *provide the medical-physiological understanding of mania that Brown utilizes in* Wieland *and in several other fictions and novels, notably* Edgar Huntly *(1799), that deploy madness and emotional breakdown as central themes. In explaining these phenomena as symptoms of emotional and physical processes, Darwin provides Brown with a late-eighteenth-century understanding of madness as the result of an imbalance of the senses, a view that Clara invokes when attempting to understand acts committed by her own family, but not, significantly, when discussing those of the*

---

[1] For Darwin's significance within Brown's entire circle, see Teute, "The Loves of the Plants; or, the Cross-Fertilization of Science and Desire at the End of the Eighteenth Century."

lower-status Carwin. In Zoönomia, *Darwin joins discussions of environmental causes for mental disturbances with a theory of biological generation that his grandson Charles Darwin viewed as the immediate source for naturalist Jean-Baptiste Lamarck's ideas that acquired traits and skills are passed on to following generations. In this manner, Darwin marks a transition in medical thinking concerning the etiology or causation of disease, moving away from Aristotelian and early modern notions of the body's four humors, and from the idea that madness is caused by demonic possession, to more modern ideas about biological, environmental and protoevolutionist causation.*

For Brown's circle, Darwin's ideas about the social conditions of physiology and illness connected with William Godwin's arguments that human behavior is preconditioned by society (see Godwin's comments in Related Texts). When these sources are combined, they form the outlines of an entire intellectual orientation that Brown would use to calibrate his own literary compass. Darwin's significance for Brown also results from his participation in an important group of scientists and thinkers in the English Midlands known as the Lunar Society. Another member of that circle was writer Robert Bage, whose novel Hermsprong; or, Man as He is Not *(1796) was one of a group of key Woldwinite sources and models for Brown at the moment when he was beginning his novelistic phase. Brown and his New York group planned, but never completed, a stage version of* Hermsprong. *That novel's status as a precursor for* Wieland *is apparent in its coded subtitle, which identifies it as another "man and society" narrative following Godwin's* Things as They Are; or, The Adventures of Caleb Williams *(1794). It also provides plot points for* Wieland *in the way that the central character Hermsprong unexpectedly appears on a manorial estate from the North American backwoods and creates transformations in the thinking of the estate's gentry inhabitants.*

Darwin explains mania mutabilis, *mutable or changing mania, as the radical transformation or changing of an individual's character and body based on deluded belief. His commentary here is an early attempt to formulate categories of obsession and obsessive-compulsive disorder, as well as rudiments of a theory of depression. Though Darwin's examples do not explicitly include a critique against religious belief and its institutionalized rituals as a maddening form of superstition, much of the period's sensational fiction seems to link the two, as Clara Wieland seems to do when she considers her father's spontaneous combustion from what is essentially a Darwinist perspective. The response of the surgeon Thomas Cambridge to Clara's downward spiral seems at least partly drawn from Darwin's clinical indications for treatment of* mania mutabilis, *for Cambridge follows Darwin in advising travel as a possible recuperative strategy. This detail may additionally suggest that Cambridge thinks that Clara shares in her family's disposition to mania.*

Brown was not the only writer who mined Darwin's description and analysis of mania mutabilis *for literary effect. William Wordsworth's "Goody Blake and Harry Gill," included in the* Lyrical Ballads *collection published with Samuel Taylor Coleridge in 1798, the same year as* Wieland, *is based on the case history of the Warwickshire farmer that Darwin discusses at the end of the passage excerpted here.*

The text used here is the second American edition (Philadelphia; Dobson, 1797), little changed from the first English edition (1794–1796), which was printed by London radical publisher Joseph Johnson (1738–1809), editor of the progressive Analytical Review *(1788–1798).*

*****

DISEASES [CLASS III. 1. 2.]

ORDO I.

Increased Volition.

GENUS II.

With increased Actions of the Organs of Sense.

IN every species of madness there is a peculiar idea of either of desire or aversion, which is perpetually excited in the mind with all its connections. In some constitutions this is connected with pleasurable ideas without the exertion of much muscular action, in others it produces violent muscular action to gain or avoid the object of it, in others it is attended with despair and inaction. Mania is the general word for the two former of these, and melancholia for the latter; but the species of them are as numerous as the desires and aversions of mankind.

In the present age the pleasurable insanities are most frequently induced by superstitious hopes of heaven, by sentimental love, and by personal vanity. The furious insanities by pride, anger, revenge, suspicion. And the melancholy ones by fear of poverty, fear of death, and fear of hell; with innumerable others [. . . .]

This idea, however, which induces madness or melancholy, is generally untrue; that is, the object of a mistaken fact.[. . .]

SPECIES.

1. *Mania mutabilis.* Mutable madness. Where the patients are liable to mistake ideas of sensation for those from irritation, that is imaginations for realities, if cured of one source of insanity, they are liable in a few months to find another source in some new mistaken or imaginary idea, and to act from this new idea. The idea belongs to delirium, when it is an imaginary or mistaken one; but it is the voluntary actions exerted in consequence of this mistaken idea, which constitute insanity.

In this disease the patient is liable carefully to conceal the object of his desire or aversion. But a constant inordinate suspicion of all people, and a carelessness of cleanliness, and of decency, are generally comitants of madness. Their designs cannot be counteracted, till you can investigate the delirious idea of object of their insanity; but as they are generally timid, they are therefore less to be dreaded.

Z.Z. called a young girl, one of his maid-servants, into the parlour, and, with cocked pistols in his hands, ordered her to strip herself naked; he then inspected her with some attention, and dismissed her untouched. Then he stripped two of his male servants in the same manner, to the great terror of the neighborhood. After he was secured, with much difficulty he was persuaded to tell me, that he had got the itch, and had examined some of his servants to find out from whom he had received it;

though at the same time there was not a spot to be seen on his hands, or other parts. The outrages in consequence of this false idea were in some measure to be ascribed to the pride occasioned by unrestrained education, affluent wealth, and dignified family.

[. . .]

I received good information of the truth of the following case, which was published a few years ago in the newspapers. A young farmer in Warwickshire, finding his hedges broke, and the sticks carried away during a frosty season, determined to watch for the thief. He lay many cold hours under a hay-stack, and at length an old woman, like a witch in a play, approached, and began to pull up the hedge; he waited she had tied up her bottle of sticks, and was carrying them off, that he might convict her of theft, and then springing from his concealment, he seized his prey with violent threats. After some altercation, in which her load was left upon the ground, she kneeled upon her bottle of sticks, and raising her arms to heaven beneath the bright moon then at the full, spoke to the farmer already shivering with cold, "Heaven grant, that thou mayest know again the blessing to be warm." He complained of cold all the next day, and wore an upper coat, and in a few days another, and in a fortnight took to his bed, always saying nothing made him warm, he covered himself with very many blankets, and ad a sieve over his face, as he lay; and from this one insane idea he kept his bed above twenty years for fear of the cold air, till at length he died.

[. . .]

When a person becomes insane, who has a family of small children to solicit his attention, the prognostic is very unfavourable; as it shews the maniacal hallucination to be more powerful than those ideas which generally interest us the most.

11. Christoph Martin Wieland, excerpt from "Answers and Counter-Questions to Some Doubts and Questions from a Curious World Citizen" (1783). Translation Joerg Meindl, with Anne Schwan

"Antworten und Gegenfragen auf einige Zweifel und Anfragen eines neugierigen Weltbürgers," *Teutsche Merkur*, 1783/I, 229–45 and 1783/II, 87–96. Edition used: *Sämmtliche Werke*, a facsimile reprint of the *Ausgabe letzter Hand* (Leipzig: Göschen, 1794–1811). Reprint ed. by Hamburger Stiftung zur Förderung von Wissenschaft und Kultur in Zusammenarbeit mit dem Wieland-Archiv und Dr Hans Radspieler, Hamburg, 1984. "Antworten und Gegenfragen": vol. IX, 28, 305–39.

Christoph Martin Wieland (1733–1813) was a prolific and highly influential German poet, novelist, editor, and translator. Anglophone reviewers in Brown's period routinely considered him the foremost living German literary figure, although his reputation dimmed throughout the nineteenth century relative to the rising consecrations of Schiller and Goethe. His translations of Shakespeare's plays (1762–1766) remained the authoritative versions into the early nineteenth century (eventually displaced by those of

August Wilhelm Schlegel, a shift that corresponds to the displacement of Enlightenment by Romantic literary fields), and his magazine Der Teutsche Merkur *(The German Mercury; 1773–1789) was an influential outlet for Enlightenment values. Throughout the 1780s, Wieland engaged in a series of polemics that defended the notion of enlightened cosmopolitanism against accusations that it was unpatriotic, merely subversive, and led to violence, and he confronted German-Austrian panic over the Illuminati after the group was banned in 1785 (Wieland's son-in-law and co-editor of the* Merkur, *Carl Leonhard Reinhold (1757–1823) had been a member).*[1]

In 1783, the Berlinische Monatsschrift (Berlin Monthly) *published an essay by Johann Friedrich Zöllner (1753–1804) on the desirability of civil marriages. The essay passingly asked the question, "What is Enlightenment?" Over the next few years, the question received several important responses, most notably those of Moses Mendelssohn (1729–1786) and Immanuel Kant (1724–1804). In the course of the debate, a distinction arose between "true" or "genuine" enlightenment and "relative" forms. Conservatives advocated "relative" enlightenment as a way of arguing that knowledge should be disseminated according to social rank. This would be a form of Enlightened Absolutism, in which the higher ranks would be free to think, while lower ones would be taught only what they needed to know in order to fulfill their function and maintain the economic and political status quo. Wieland refutes this notion by affirming a universal right to participate in the enlightenment without regard to social class, and he seeks to calm elite anxieties concerning the spread of the enlightenment. The primary worry in Wieland's immediate context was that progressive reform will lead a still largely agrarian population from questioning religious (Catholic) authority to interrogating the legitimacy of the existing aristocratic political order; or, in other words, that rural laborers will progress from the demand for free thought to insistence on social emancipation.*

The excerpt presented here, from one of Wieland's key contributions to this debate, is the first five paragraphs of an essay published in his Teutsche Merkur *in response to an anonymous pamphlet titled* Neugierden eines Weltbürgers. Oder Zweifel und Anfragen eines Menschenfreundes. Allen Staatsgrüblern zur beliebigen Prüfung und Beantwortung gewidmet *(Curiosities of a World Citizen; or, Doubts and Questions of a Philanthrope. Dedicated to All Those who Brood about the State, for Free Examination and Reply; 1782). As is typical of Wieland's overall liberal (as opposed to progressive) orientation, his essay-response encourages the inevitable enlightenment tendency to political and cultural questioning, while at the same time remaining extremely cautious about radical or accelerated social change, preferring gradual, if not imperceptible, reform. Wieland cautions his readers against violent or popular revolution by citing examples such as the protosocialist and visionary Anabaptist Rebellion (1534–1535) in the German city Münster, which was brutally suppressed after being led by Bernhard Knipperdolling (1495–1536), or the king-killing English Civil War (1642–1651) that was led by Oliver Cromwell (1599–1658).*

---

[1] For more on Wieland's role in Enlightenment debates, see Kleingeld, "Six Varieties of Cosmopolitanism in Late Eighteenth-Century Germany"; and Roehr, *A Primer on German Enlightenment.*

This debate about the need for equipoise in a democratizing time is also evident in Brown's novel Wieland. *The pastoral balance of the estate at Mettingen is disturbed when the backcountry Carwin, a sort of "illuminated farmer," to use Wieland's terminology, begins to challenge his exclusion from the debates of the gentrified Wielands. Often associated with will-o-the-wisp glimmers like those that Wieland associates here with popular enlightenment, Carwin's injection of doubt and uncertainty into Mettingen through his ventriloquism can be read as a dramatic version of the underlying question faced by all of the period's reforming elites, including the landed gentry who had led the American revolt against an imperial master and in the 1790s still held political power in the new U.S. nation–state. In the age of Enlightenment, can democratic urges be safely regulated in ways that prevent the arrival of a truly egalitarian society?*

*****

If there were yet any doubts as to whether there are indeed false world citizens who usurp this noble name without being legitimated by agreement between basic principles and ethos with those of the true Cosmopolitans, the anonymous author of "Curiosities of a World Citizen" (a pamphlet recently published on one and a half sheets)[2] would have relieved us from the trouble of having to remove from the world all doubts about the existence of such false brothers. This would-be world citizen may have directed his doubts and questions explicitly to those who brood about the State [*Staatsgrüblern*] for examination and answers. Some of these doubts, however, (and especially those that trouble this would-be world citizen the most) can be resolved solely through the use of simple human understanding without any of the nit-picking of those brooders. Therefore, I feel even more motivated to provide this would-be world citizen with such a modest service, especially since his doubts refer to issues on which his ideas differ very strongly from those of the true Cosmopolitans.

In times *when every man is brooding,* perhaps nothing is more natural than to probe those doctrines, which during the centuries when only monks were brooding were regarded as unquestioned truths, in order to reveal the record on which their unchallenged certainty is based. Common sense [*natürliche Verstand*], which teaches all human beings to recognize instinctively what is good or evil, is lethargic by itself; it is all-but-too easily contented and, under certain circumstances, may even be lulled for centuries. But once it is roused and intimidated, its suspicion will grow as large as its former certainty. It loses all respect and no longer trusts its best friends, or anything else any longer; it smells deceit and danger everywhere. Thus it illuminates every dark corner with its lamp, but it is as frightened of a light that is too blinding as it is of sacred darkness, because it senses that either way it will be in danger of being relieved of its———money. This suspicion must grow at the same rate that it realizes how certain people have taken advantage of its good-hearted

---

[2] *Neugierden eines Weltbürgers. Oder Zweifel und Anfragen eines Menschenfreundes. Allen Staatsgrüblern zur beliebigen Prüfung und Beantwortung gewidmet* (1782) [Curiosities of a World Citizen; or, Doubts and Questions of a Philanthrope. Dedicated to All Those who Brood about the State, for Free Examination and Reply].

trust and its untroubled slumbers. Added to this is a curious philosophy that constantly unsettles natural understanding with questions to which it has no other answer than, *"ask my Court Tutor."* Dissatisfied with this dismissal, this philosophy doubts and disputes everything: all those things which understanding has been forced to swallow as holy truth since childhood, by force-feeding, singing, preaching, and beatings. This is a philosophy that refuses to acknowledge reputation based on personality and status, privilege of age, or social rank that relieves its owner from any examination of his title; a philosophy that wants to uncover everything which is hidden and leaves nothing luminous untouched, nothing mysterious unexplained; a philosophy that cannot even be disposed of through *unshakeable proofs* because it always demands *proof of the proof.* In the end, things have even come so far that this philosophy, under the popular name of Enlightenment and liberation from the yoke of old prejudice, has extended its influence to all classes of a great nation, causing agitation in all heads, with the help of book-factories and printing presses. It is no surprise then that heads become dizzy from all the enlightenment and freedom to think, the envy of all human prestige, and the distrust of all super-human appearances. Indeed, nothing around us seems to hold steady any longer, and an *epidemic addiction to doubt* threatens the world with even worse conditions than those suffered when it blindly entrusted itself to the court Tutor and doubted its own senses, rather than its leaders' infallibility.

Obviously, a large part of Europe approaches these conditions at a rapid pace. The philosophy we have described, not satisfied with having nearly completely overtaken the higher classes, is on its way to those parts of the people that previously fared best with *bare belief.* What will be the natural outcome of this increasingly generalized spirit of agitation against all reputation, against everything that was honorable and untouchable to our fathers? The answer to this question seems to be more worthy of an academic award than some of the other issues that have occupied the dialectical skills of our finest thinkers in competitions. Soon these people will be done with religion and priesthood, and will move on to examinations that will not be to the taste of our worldly powers, however indifferent their present feeling of strength may make them. For they too eventually will be asked: On what grounds of power are you acting? By whom were you granted those powers and to whom are you accountable? On what do you base your privileges, your properties, and your entitlements? Was it from nature that you received those powers that force us down to the ground? Are you made from a more perfect matter than us? Do you have more senses, more hands, more feet, &c.? Or, what if all your privileges—as our philosophers are preaching from the rooftops—are solely based on a contract between us and you? What if everything you own is only entrusted to you, and if your status does not and cannot have any legal justification other than the conditional mandate which you have received from us—which can be revoked at any time, as soon as we find a better arrangement? How can you expect that people as enlightened as we are will grant you arbitrary and unlimited power over our persons, our property, and our earthly lives—over the most important thing in our lives, and the only thing that remains for us, after your philosophers have taught us that man's soul is in his blood? Before we obey your legislation, we want to examine whether these laws will make us happier. Before we grant our subsidies to you, we want to know how you reckon to use them for our benefit. Before we accept to be led to the slaughterhouse or exposed to the danger of having our fields devastated, our houses burnt, our women and daughters defiled, and our sons carried into serfdom as soldiers, we want to examine the question, whether it is in our interest for you to impose more or less tax on a couple of square miles.

I have no doubts whatsoever that our superiors should be capable of giving very valid answers to all these disrespectful questions, without even needing a club, a prison, or a fortress. But the history of ages past has taught me that it is still safer not to push the issue to such extremes, and that illuminated farmers [*illuminierte Bauern*] and passionate *Knipperdollings* and *Cromwells*, &c. are dangerous advocates of the rights of man. In a word, it is better to wait calmly for the beneficial outcomes that will undoubtedly be created among the peoples of the world by the inconspicuous growth of reason. This will be better than attempting to reach this point in time (which will undoubtedly still come) more quickly, by means whose ill-considered consequences would be worse and more destructive than the evils which one hopes to resolve thereby.

Heaven forbid that the idea of setting limits to the enlightenment of our times by any means other than those of wholesome reason and solid science should ever occur to those who have power over us! *True illumination* [*Wahre Erleuchtung*], regarding everything that concerns man in his essence, is our most important and most general interest; and *improvements* are its natural outcome. However, there are also will-o'-the-wisps whose deceptive gleam lures into the quagmire. To the weak eyes of a blind man who has regained his eyesight, even beneficial sunlight has to be introduced with great sensitivity and nearly imperceptible stages; and a light beam that is too powerful blinds even the eye that is accustomed to light. To set one half of the world on fire in order to provide beautiful, idyllic illumination for the other, is a project that is only possible in a head such as the one that arranged for Rome to be set on fire at all four corners in order to give more truth to a poetic painting of Troy in flames.[3]

[. . . .]

12. Gottfried Bürger's *Lenore*: William Taylor translation, "Lenora: A Ballad, from Bürger" (1796). *The Weekly Magazine of Original Essays, Fugitive Pieces, and Interesting Intelligence* (March 17, 1798). Reprinted from the London *Monthly Magazine*, March 1796

Written and first published in 1773–1774 by German poet Gottfried August Bürger (1747–1794), the ballad-poem Lenore *was literally and figuratively a sensation. It may*

---

[3] "A head . . . Troy in flames": that is, the Roman emperor Nero, whose name is synonymous with tyrannical and irrational cruelty. The analogy is an interesting one; to caution against the results of excessive popular rationalization from below, Wieland offers a name that signifies autocratic madness in rulers, or in other words reactive violence from above, and associates it with excessive or irrational aestheticization.

reasonably be considered one of the most influential, or at least noteworthy, poems of the Romantic period in Anglophone Atlantic culture. Brown and his circle read and compared several new translations of the poem that circulated through the English-speaking world in 1796–1798, and the poem is legible as the primary reference in Clara's evocation of an emotionally charged ballad in Chapter 6 of Wieland.

Bürger's poetry was popular in Germany, but by the 1790s his work was being criticized by figures such as Friedrich Schiller for failing to engage the higher functions of aesthetic imagination. Whatever the state of Bürger's reputation in Germany, a rising wave of Germanophile literary reception had great appeal for English-speaking audiences that were increasingly attuned to German poetry, drama, and fiction from the 1770s onward. Within this literary wave, which peaked in the years when Brown was working on Wieland *and his other novels, and which was commonly connected with progressive sentiment in the period's coded cultural polemics, Bürger's* Lenore *generated tremendous interest and functioned as the centerpiece of a powerful literary and cultural vogue. Four major English translations appeared in 1796 alone,[1] and the same English journals that were followed closely by Brown's circle, the* Monthly Review *and* Monthly Magazine, *eagerly dissected and compared the competing versions.[2]*

The poem conveys a terrifying tale of a bride-to-be who longs for her soldier-lover after he departs for battle. Distraught when her beloved does not return, Lenore renounces God and wishes for death. Unexpectedly the lover reappears that night and carries her away on horseback. Ghosts appear around them as they ride, the bridegroom's armor and flesh fall away to reveal a deathly skeleton, and the longed-for marriage bed is revealed as a graveyard plot.

In Bürger's 1773 German original and most English versions (except, notably, the Taylor version printed here), the lover is a cavalier who falls at the battle of Prague (May 6, 1757), during Prussian leader Frederick the Great's failed invasion of Saxony and Silesia in the Seven Years War. In the William Taylor[3] version favored by Brown's circle, however, the setting is shifted to the Third Crusade (1189–1192) and Richard the Lionheart's unsuccessful attempt to recapture the Holy Land from Saladin. Despite Taylor's alteration of the poem's dramatic setting and its verse form, his translation was widely considered

---

[1] The 1796 versions of the poem had their individual periodical and book publications, but interest was intense enough that they were also republished together with the German original in volumes that allowed readers to experience multiple versions together. See, for example, *Leonora. A ballad, translated from the German of Gottfried Augustus Bürger. By W. R. Spencer, Esq. H. J. Pye. J. T. Stanley, Esq. F.R.S. To which is added, the original text* (Vienna: R. Sammer, 1798).

[2] For discussions of the *Lenore* phenomenon and its role in the politically coded reception of the German literary wave of the late 1790s, see Mortensen, *British Romanticism and Continental Influences: Writing in an Age of Europhobia*; Jolles, *G. A. Bürger's Ballade Lenore in England*; and Herzfeld, *William Taylor of Norwich*.

[3] William Taylor was a key English mediator of German writing throughout the late 1790s. Taylor was a scholar and translator who published innumerable articles and reviews on German literature in English periodicals of the late 1790s, including influential accounts of individual volumes of C.M. Wieland's *Collected Works* as they appeared in German. See the discussions in Herzfeld, *William Taylor of Norwich* and Skokoe, *German Influence in the English Romantic Period, 1788–1818*.

the leading English version of the poem, and it connects the narrative with the Crusader setting evoked by Clara Wieland, albeit in inexact ways, since Clara's invented ballad and Taylor's Lenora *refer to two different Crusades.[4]*

Brown and his closest associates, the physician and writer Elihu Hubbard Smith and dramatist William Dunlap, studied the different 1796 translations, as well as their illustrations, such as the image by Beauclerk and Bartolozzi reproduced here. Brown and his friends were likely responsible for having the Taylor version from the March, 1796 London Monthly Magazine *(one of Taylor's two different versions in 1796) reprinted in the Philadelphia* Weekly Magazine *(which featured many pieces by Brown) in March 1798, at the time Brown was composing* Wieland. *Brown's circle was eager to circulate Bürger's work among themselves and, at this time, Elihu Hubbard Smith also transcribed another of Bürger's translated ballads,* The Lass of Fair Wone, *for a Connecticut friend.[5]*

The poem's initial publication came almost immediately after Johan Gottfried Herder's (1744–1803) call for the arts to reflect the native spirit of a national people's folk traditions, and at the same time as widespread fascination with the "Ossian" poems that Scot James Macpherson (1736–1796) began to publish in 1761 under the false claim that they were written by an ancient Celtic bard. Bürger gives his poem an air of "ancientness" by using the ballad form (possibly sourced from an English ballad Sweet William's Ghost, *which Bürger knew from Thomas Percy's 1765 collection* Reliques of Ancient English Poetry*) and rejecting themes of classical mythology and pastoral sentimentalism. In the English versions, this ancient or primitive quality is signified and intensified by the use of nonstandard "gothic" spelling. On the other hand, the poem also enacts modernizing energies with its contemporary subject matter and its emphasis on driving, vivid rhythms and overwrought language that aim to create sensationalized emotions and rising anxiety in the reader, rather than a detached sense of classical repose or rural harmony.*

The construction of an intensified state of mind through physicalized gothic themes appealed to an English and Anglophone arts community that lacked native models for this effect, since the initial 1760s recovery of the ballad form in England had not attempted to generate psychological tension. While the period's fascination with the ballad form was often tied to nationalist agendas, as was Herder's intention, the gothicized variant often undermines patriotic unity; Lenora *begins, after all, with imperialist troops returning in defeat.*

In this manner, by shifting an earlier set of concepts and artistic practices into a newer phase that produced a new set of meanings and implications, Lenore *became the match that lit the tinder for the ensuing wave of Anglophone Romantic poetry and prose. Records of the enthusiasm and emotionalized responses occasioned by the poem give us some idea of its impact.*

---

[4] Brown may also have had the Crusader reference in mind from a 1796 English translation of *The Black Valley*, a "terror" novel by Leonhard Wächter (pseud. Veit Weber). This tale, about German nobles at the time of "the conquest of Jerusalem by Godfrey of Bouillon," dramatizes a mixed-class and mixed-religion love affair in order to develop a lengthy critique of marriage as an institution of female servitude, a theme favored by Brown and Woldwinite writers such as Godwin, Wollstonecraft, and Holcroft, his primary literary models.

[5] See Smith's accounts, which compare the different translations, repeatedly praising the William Taylor *Monthly Magazine* version and finding William Spencer's version inferior, in *The Diary of Elihu Hubbard Smith*, pages 228, 266, 294, 316, 350, 404.

For example, when this Taylor version was read aloud at an Edinburgh social gathering in 1794, one of the audience described it to Scottish writer Walter Scott and Scott became so electrified that he stayed awake an entire night making his own translation, William and Helen, *which then became his first publication. Perhaps in relation to such responses, Brown introduces Clara's ballad, in Chapter 6 of* Wieland, *at a critical moment in her story, in the pause between her first, eroticized and unsettling glimpse of the stranger Carwin, and her first horrified experience of the mysterious voices that have previously affected her brother and Pleyel. By introducing the ballad at a moment when Clara undergoes intensified and over-whelming emotional and physical responses, Brown links the reader's experience to the newest sensational effects of literature and provides a foreshadowing frame for Clara's later "fall" after deathly revelations that transform the physical state of her loved ones.*[6]

*****

LENORA
A Ballad, from Bürger

[The following translation (made some years since) of a celebrated piece, of which other versions have appeared, and are now on the point of appearance, possesses so much peculiar and intrinsic merit, that we are truly happy in being permitted to present it to our Readers.]

At break of day, with frightful dreams
Lenora struggled sore:
My William, art thou slaine, say'd she,
Or dost thou love no more?

He went abroade with Richard's host,
The Paynim foes to quell;
But he no word to her had writt,
An he were sick or well.

With sowne of trump, and beat of drum,
His felow-soldyers come;
Their helmes bydeckt with oaken boughs,
They seeke their long'd-for home.

And ev'ry roade, an ev'ry lane
Was full of old and young,
To gaze at the rejoicing band,
To hail with gladsome toung.

"Thank God!" their wives and children saide,
"Welcome!" the brides did saye:
But greete or kiss Lenora gave
To none upon that daye.

She askte of all the passing traine,
For him she wisht to see:
But none of all the passing traine
Could tell if lived hee.

---

[6] The poem and its "spectre bridegroom" motif were echoed, transformed, and satirized in countless new forms throughout the nineteenth century. Over the next generation, in England and Europe, it appeared as Matthew Lewis' "Alonzo the Brave and the Fair Imogene" (in *The Monk*, 1795); James Harris' "The Daemon Lover" (1812); William Harrison Ainsworth's "The Spectre Bride" (1822), and Alexander Push-kin's "Zenikh" (Bridegroom, 1825); in the U.S. as Washington Irving's "The Spectre Bridegroom" (1819), Nathaniel Hawthorne's "The Wedding Knell" (1836), and Edgar Allan Poe's "Lenore" (1831) and "The Raven" (1844); and in musical forms such as Anton Dvorak's dramatic cantata, *The Spectre's Bride* (1885).

And when the soldyers all were bye,
She tore her raven haire,
And cast herself upon the growne
In furious despaire.

Her mother ran and lyfte her up,
And clasped in her arme,
"My child, my child, what dost thou ail?
God shield thy life from harm!"

"O mother, mother! William's gone!
What's all besyde to me?
There is no mercye, sure, above!
All, all were spar'd but hee!"

"Kneel downe, thy paternoster saye,
'Twill calm they troubled spright;
The Lord is wyse, the Lord is good;
What hee hath done is right."

"O mother, mother! say not so;
Most cruel is my fate:
I prayde, and prayde; but watte avayl'd?
'Tis now, alas! Too late."

"Our Heavenly Father, if we praye,
Will help a suff'ring childe:
Go take the holy sacrament;
So shall they grief grow milde."

"O mother, what I feel within,
No sacrament can staye;
No sacrament can teche the dead
To bear the sight of daye."

"May be, among the heathen folk
Thy William false doth prove,
And puts away his faith and troth,
And takes another love.

Then wherefore sorrow for his loss?
Thy moans are all in vain:
And when his soul and body parte,
His falsehode brings him paine."

"O mother, mother! Gone is gone:
My hope is all forlorn;
The grave mie onlye safeguarde is—
O, had I ne'er been borne!

Go out, go out, my lampe of life;
In grislie darkness die:
There is no mercye, sure, above!
For ever let me lie."

"Almighty God! O do not judge
My poor unhappy childe;
She knows not what her lips pronounce,
Her anguish makes her wilde.

My girl, forget thine earthly woe,
And think on God and bliss;
For so, at least, shall not thy soule
Its heavenly bridegroom miss."

"O mother, mother! what is blisse,
And what the fiendis celle?
With him 'tis heaven any where,
Without my William, helle.

"Go out, go out, my lamp of life;
In endless darkness die:
Without him I must loathe the earth,
Without him scorne the skye."

And so despaire did rave and rage
Athwarte her boiling veins;
Against the Providence of God
She hurlde her impious strains.

She bet her breaste, and wrung her hands,
And rollde her tearlesse eye,
From rise of morne, till the pale stars
Again did seeke the skye.

When harke! abroade she hearde the trampe
Of nimble-hoofed steed;
She hearde a knighte with clank alighte,
And climb the staire in speede.

And soon she herde a tinkling hande,
That twirled at the pin;
And thro' her door, that open'd not,
These words were breathed in.

"What ho! what ho! thy dore undoe;
Art watching or asleepe?
My love, dost yet remember mee,
And dost thou laugh or weep?"

"Ah! William here so late at night!
Oh! I have watche and wak'd:
Whence dost thou come? For thy return
My hearte has sorely ak'd."

"At midnight only we may ride;
I come o'er land and sea:
I mounted late, but soone I go;
Aryse, and come with me."

"O William, enter first my bowre,
And give me one embrace:
The blasts athwarte the hawthorne hiss;
Awayte a little space."

"Tho' blasts athwarte the hawthorn hiss,
I may not harboure here;
My spurre is sharpe, my courser pawes,
My houre of flighte is nere.

All as thou lyest upon thy couch,
Aryse, and mount behinde;
To-night we'le ride a thousand miles,
The bridal bed to finde."

"How, ride to-night a thousand miles?
Thy love thou dost bemocke:
Eleven is the stroke that still
Rings on within the clocke."

"Looke up; the moone is bright, and we
Outstride the earthlie men:
I'll take thee to the bridal bed,
And night shall end but then."

"And where is, then, thy house and home;
And where thy bridal bed?"
" 'Tis narrow, silent, chilly, dark;
Far hence I rest my head."

"And is there any room for mee,
Wherein that I may creepe?"
"There room enough for thee and mee,
Wherein that we may sleepe.

All as thou ly'st upon thy couch,
Aryse, no longer stop;
The wedding guests thy coming waite,
The chamber dore is ope."

All in her sarke, as there she lay,
Upon his horse she sprung;
And with her lily hands so pale
About her William clung.

And hurry-skurry forth they go,
Unheeding wet or dry;
And horse and rider snort and blow,
And sparkling pebbles fly.

How swift the flood, the mead, the wood,
Aright, aleft, are gone!
The bridges thunder as they pass,
But earthly sowne is none.

Tramp, tramp, across the land they speede;
Splash, splash, across the see:
"Hurrah! the dead can ride apace;
Dost feare to ride with mee?

The moone is bryghte, and blue the nyghte;
Dost quake the blast to stem?
Dost shudder, mayde, to seeke the dead?"
"No, no, but what of them?"

How glumlie sownes yon dirgye song!
Night-ravens flappe the wing,
What knell doth slowlie toll ding-dong?
The psalmes of death who sing?

It creeps, the swarthie funeral traine,
The corse is onn the beere;
Like croke of todes from lonely moores,
The chaunte doth meet the eere."

"Go, bear her corse when midnight's past,
With song, and tear, and wayle;
I've gott my wife, I take her home,
My bowre of wedlocke hayl.

Lead forth, O clarke, the chaunting quire,
To swell our nuptial song:
Come, preaste, and reade the blessing soone;
For bed, for bed we long."

They heede his calle, and husht the sowne;
The biere was seene no more;
And followde him ore feeld and flood
Yet faster than before.

Halloo! halloo! away they goe,
Unheeding wet or drye;
And horse and rider snort and blowe,
And sparkling pebbles flye.

How swifte the hill, how swifte the dale,
Aright, aleft, are gone!
By hedge and tree, by thorpe and towne,
They gallop, gallop on.

Tramp, tramp, across the land they speede;
Splash, splash, acrosse the see:
"Hurrah! the dead can ride apace;
Dost fear to ride with me?

Look up, look up, and airy crewe
In roundel daunces reele:
The moone is bryghte, and blue the nyghte,
Mayst dimlie see them wheele.

Come to, some to, ye gostlie crew,
Come to, and follow mee,
And daunce for us the wedding daunce,
When we in bed shall be."

And brush, brush, brush, the gostlie crew
Come wheeling ore their heads,
All rustling like the wither'd leaves
That wyde the whirlwind spreads.

Halloo! halloo! away they go,
Unheeding wet or dry;
And horse and rider snort and blowe,
And sparkling pebbles flye.

And all that in the moonshyne lay,
Behynde them fled afar;
And backwarde scudded overhead
The sky and every star.

Tramp, tramp, across the lande they speede;
Splash, splash, across the see:
"Hurrah! the dead can ride apace;
Dost fear to ride with mee?

I weene the cock prepares to crowe;
The sand will soone be runne:
I snuffe the earlye morning aire;
Downe, downe! our worke is done.

The dead, the dead can ryde apace;
Oure wed-bed here is fit:
Our race is ridde, oure journey ore,
Our endlesse union knit."

And lo! an yren-grated grate
Soon biggens to their viewe:
He crackte his whyppe; the clangynge boltes,
The doores asunder flewe.

They pass, and 'twas on graves they trode;
"'Tis hither we are bounde:"
And many a tombstone ghostlie white
Lay inn the moonshyne round.

And when hee from his steede alytte,
His armour black as cinder,
Did moulder, moulder all awaye,
As were it made of tinder.

His head became a naked skull;
Nor haire nor eyne had hee:
His body grew a skeleton,
Whilome so blythe of blee.

And att his dry and boney heele
No spur was left to be;
And inn his witherde hande you might
The scythe and hour-glasse see.

And lo! his steede did thin to smoke,
And charnel fires outbreathe;
And pal'd, and bleach'd, then vanish'd quite
The mayde from underneathe.

And hollow howlings hung in aire,
And shrekes from vaults arose.
Then knew the mayde she mighte no more
Her living eyes unclose.

But onwarde to the judgement seat,
Thro' myste and moonlight dreare,
The ghostlie crews their flyghte persewe,
And hollowe inn her eare:—

"Be patient; tho' thyne herte should breke,
Arrayne not Heven's decree;
Thou nowe art of thie bodie refte,
Thie soule forgiven bee!"

12b. Diana Beauclerk and Francesco Bartolozzi, engraving of Lenore and the Spectre Bride-groom, from *Leonora. Translated from the German of Gottfried Augustus Bürger, by W.R. Spencer, Esq. with Designs by the Right Honourable Lady Diana Beauclerc.* London: T. Bensley, 1796.

12b. Diana Beauclerk and Francesco Bartolozzi, engraving of Lenore and the Spectre Bridegroom

In his diary entry for May 9, 1797, Brown's friend Elihu Hubbard Smith notes that he viewed a new edition of "Spencer's Translation of Buerger's Lenora—with it's fine engravings." Smith saw the book while he was in Philadelphia on a trip to attend a meeting of abolitionist societies, and on a day largely spent in socializing with Brown, Dunlap, their friend Thomas Pym Cope, and other Philadelphians. Although Smith's comments about Lenore *consistently favor the Taylor translation provided here, they also reveal how the group participated in the* Lenore *phenomenon by comparing different text versions and their visual illustrations.*

This engraving of the ballad's concluding scene, in which the Spectre Bridegroom reveals his deathly purpose, was the work of illustrator Diana Beauclerk, a figure connected in a number of ways with the period's gothic wave, and Francesco Bartolozzi, one of the period's leading engravers and a notable figure in his own right. Artist and poet William Blake illustrated another of the 1796 Lenore *translations (the J. T. Stanley version), but Beauclerk's drawings are remarkable for the way they connect the poem's overwrought atmosphere of physicalized intensity to popular gothic and horror thematics. Additionally, the image brings out the erotic charge commonly associated with the poem, which Brown may reference as well with his decision to place Clara's evocation of the ballad just after her initial encounter with Carwin. It may also be read as an image of how Brown imagines Clara's mental state in the novel's final chapters.*

Diana Beauclerk (1734–1808, born Diana Spencer), was an English aristocrat who pursued a relatively independent career as a painter and illustrator working along the faultlines between literary and visual cultures. Besides her drawings for this edition of Lenore, *she worked closely with Horace Walpole, author of the early gothic novel* The Castle of Otranto *(1764). Walpole spent years redesigning his villa at Strawberry Hill near London as a rambling, pseudo-Gothic architectural fantasy, and one tower in the building was designed to showcase Beauclerk's illustrations for his play* The Mysterious Mother *(1768).*

Francesco Bartolozzi (1725–1815) was the foremost London engraver of the 1790s, before he ended his career after 1802 as director of the National Academy in Lisbon. After early training in Venice and Rome, his London years were notable for important technical innovations and collaborations with the leading painters and illustrators of the period, including Beauclerk, Angelica Kaufmann, and others. In his novel Ormond, *published in January 1799 just months after* Wieland, *Brown names Bartolozzi as one of the artists who train Stephen Dudley, the father of that novel's central figure Constantia Dudley.*

13. Horror Novel, State Romance, and the German Literary Wave

13a. Peter Will, "Preface of the Translator," from *The Victim of Magical Delusion; or, The Mystery of the Revolution of P——L: A Magico-Political Tale. Founded on Historical Facts, and Translated from the German of Cajetan Tschink. By P. Will* (London: G. and J. Robinson, 1795). Original title: *Geschichte eines Geistersehers: Aus den Papieren des Mannes mit der*

Eisernen Larve [*The Tale of a Ghost-seer: From the Papers of the Man with the Iron Mask*] (1790–1793)

Peter Will, a Lutheran minister at the Savoy Chapel in London, played an important role in the gothic and horror wave of the late 1790s as translator and promoter of a series of novels and other works that participated in the progressive attack on monarchical and religious institutions of the old regime. Will's polemical prefaces and afterwords, included in a series of novelistic works that debunk supernatural illusions and defend Illuminati and Masonic networks against conservative demonization (see the Illuminati debates in Related Texts), had wide currency in the 1790s and were well known to Brown and his circle.

Whereas the translations and articles of William Taylor of Norwich, the most visible English face of the 1790s German wave (author of the influential version of Bürger's Lenore *included in Related Texts), presented German productions in relatively scholarly and intellectualized terms, Will embraced the tools of popular culture to bring forward-looking political perspectives to a wide audience of readers who might be influenced ideologically as they consumed thrilling narratives. While Taylor wrote for the nonconformist but mainstream* Monthly Review, *Will worked with the Minerva Press, the English house that was committed to publishing sensational fiction and that would publish the first British editions of Brown's novels* Ormond *(1800);* Arthur Mervyn *(1803);* Edgar Huntly *(1803); and* Jane Talbot *(1804), Minerva did not publish the British edition of Brown's* Wieland, *however. Will's translations were often condemned for stylistic irregularities and vulgarities, as examples of what was dubbed "The Terrorist System of Novel-Writing"[1] (hence his defensive stance in the final paragraph of this "Preface"), but their popularizing tendency gave them wide currency. Thus when Jane Austen mocks excessively "horrid" " gothic novels in her* Northanger Abbey *(written 1798, published 1803), Will's translation of* Horrid Mysteries *for Minerva Press is one of the titles singled out.*

Will's packaging and presentation of Cajetan Tschink's "magico-political" tale The Victim of Magical Delusion, *is a good example of his literary activism. The "Preface" situates the novel and its implications in ways that are clearly relevant to Brown's* Wieland, *bringing Tschink's work into view for English reading audiences. German writer Cajetan Tschink (1763–1812) had initially entered the Carmelite order, before studying philosophy at Jena and teaching in what is today the Czech Republic. His fictional and nonfictional writings are skeptical explanations of the natural causes and technically produced effects of what seem to be magic and witchcraft. Tschink's concern was to rescue those who might be easily manipulated by phantasmagoric performances from willingly assenting to their own subordination. Following Tschink, Will's approach is frankly political. Rather than presenting the novel in terms of suspenseful plot points concerning love, courtship, and adventure, he invites his readers to participate in an attack on supernatural delusions, superstitions, and other fraudulent manifestations of the power of backward looking cultural institutions in the revolutionary age.*

Will's particular target in this "Preface" is the use of religious superstition or delusion as a political tool. In passages not included here, the "Preface" provides concrete examples of the role of religious or pseudoreligious delusions in current State scandals involving Prussian

---

[1] See "A Letter to the Editor," London *Monthly Magazine* 4.21 (August 1797), 102–4; reprinted in Norton, *Gothic Readings: The First Wave, 1764–1840.*

Minister of Finance Johann Wöllner, who manipulated Frederick II of Prussia by posing as a mystical seer, and in the 1795 case of self-styled prophet and London antimonarchy activist Richard Brothers, who was condemned as criminally insane after he preached that he would soon be accepted as "Revealed Prince" and ruler of the world.

*****

The sources from which we derive the knowledge of what is good and true, originate from Sensation, Experience, Reflection, Reasoning, and from the genuine accounts we receive of the observations and the experience of others; and we cannot miss the road leading the Sanctuary of Truth, if we make a proper use of *all* these different Sources of Knowledge. If we, however, conceive an exclusive attachment to *one* of them, and for instance, confine ourselves merely to sensation and experience, if we desire to *see* and to *feel* those things which cannot be perceived by the senses, but are known to us only through the medium of our understanding; if we, for example, are not satisfied with what the contemplation of nature, and the gospel teach us of God, but desire to have an immediate, and physical communion with the invisible; we then cannot avoid the deviations of fanaticism, and are easily led to confound our *feelings* and *ideas* with external effects; the effects of our souls with effects produced by superior beings; we believe that we see, hear, and perceive what exists no where but in our imagination; we stray from ourselves and from the objects around us, to a world of ideas which is the workmanship of our fancy, and are misled by the vivacity and strength of our feelings, and mistake for *reality*, what is merely *ideal*. Thus we dream while we are awake, and sooner or later, find ourselves woefully deceived. All pretended apparitions, every imaginary communion with superior beings, the belief in witches, sorcerers, and in the secret power of magical spells, owe their existence to this species of fanaticism, which has always given ample scope for preying on the weakness and ignorance of the sensitive and credulous; to those who, by their superior power of reasoning, by a more intimate knowledge of nature, and the human heart, have been able to avail themselves of the predominant propensity to the wonderful, which exercises an almost uncontroulled sway over people who in their search of Truth and Knowledge, are guided only by their senses, and by experience, which commonly are chosen by those who are addicted to laziness, and indolence, destitute of a proper knowledge of Nature and Religion, disinclined to, or incapable of thinking and investigating, ruled by wild irregular passions, and endowed with a lively and prolific imagination.

This has been the chief reason that the numberless hordes of impostors, who at all times have invaded the kingdom of truth and human felicity, have found it very easy to succeed in their attempts when playing off their fanatical engines for the sake of lucre or ambition, or with the view of carrying some political end. This sort of fanaticism and fanatical illusion, has never been more predominant in civilized Europe, than in the middle centuries, and raged with unabated fury till the immortal Wickliff,[2]

---

[2] "Wickliff": John Wycliffe (c.1320s–1384), one of the earliest English religious reformers and opponents of Catholic state power. His name has many variant spellings.

Luther, and their fellow labourers began to combat the prevailing religious errors, and restored reason, that overflowing source of knowledge and happiness, to her sacred rights. We should however, be mistaken if we were to imagine, that since the reformation, fanaticism has entirely lost its powerful influence on the human mind, for alas! modern history furnishes us with but too many facts which serve to prove undeniably, that this baneful foe to human happiness still counts many votaries.[. . .]

13b. Friedrich Schiller, excerpts from *The Ghost-Seer; or Apparitionist: An Interesting Fragment, Found Among the Papers of Count O******, from the German of Schiller. (New York: T. and J. Swords, 1796), Tr. Daniel Boileau

Friedrich Schiller (1759–1805), active from the 1780s to the 1800s as a poet, playwright, aesthetic philosopher, and historian, stands today as one of the major literary figures of the German eighteenth century. His plays, especially the 1781 Die Räuber *(The Robbers) epitomize the German* Sturm und Drang *(Storm and Stress) movement that flourished from the 1760s to the early 1780s. These works emphasize extreme states of individual emotion as a counterweight to an Enlightenment rationality that is perceived as a failure insofar as it has not overcome aristocratic despotism. The movement blends into and can be read as part of the ensuing rise of the gothic* Schauerroman *(horror or sensational novel).*

Schiller's reputation in the eighteenth-century Anglophone world was greater than that of Johann Wolfgang von Goethe, who today is perceived as the central cultural figure of the age. Goethe's sensibility-novel The Sorrows of Young Werther *(1774) did not create as great a vogue for "Wertherism" among English readers as it did on the Continent, perhaps because, as many reviewers noted, the English translations of the novel were inferior and ineffective. In the revolutionary period, and especially during the German wave of 1796–1802 that is registered in so many ways by Brown's* Wieland, *Schiller's plays and Bürger's poetry (see Related Texts) carried the banner for German literary sensationalism.*

Der Geisterseher (The Ghost-Seer) was first serialized from 1786 to 1789, with a title that refers to philosopher Immanuel Kant's early treatise, Dreams of a Spirit-Seer (Geisterseher), Illustrated by Dreams of Metaphysics *(1766). It tells the story of a German Prince in Venice who encounters a mysterious figure, The Arminian [sic], who possesses otherwise secret information about the Prince and seems to be part of a conspiracy to convert the Protestant aristocrat to Catholicism. The story balances a cautionary tale illustrating the dangers of religious enthusiasm and naïve belief in the occult against incendiary rumors about political manipulations and international plots by conspiratorial secret societies. The postscript's mention of the Illuminati is one of the earliest English-language references to the society and predates Augustin Barruel's and John Robison's alarmist accounts of the society (for more on the Illuminati scare, see Related Texts).*

The context of The Ghost-Seer *involves conflicts over religion and political authority in post-Seven Years War Germany. The Prince, likely from one of the smaller principates around Saxony, is caught in the larger contest between Protestant Prussia and Catholic Habsburg Austria, even though he initially seems unaware of his location within the larger historical tumult. The parts of the tale that Schiller wrote indicate the Prince's struggle to explain obscure events and his vacillation between Enlightenment skepticism and a backward belief in magical supernaturalism, associated with the Catholic Inquisition. The mysterious Arminian appears as a Levantine stranger during Venice's Carnival, but the reader learns that this is only his most recent masqueraded identity. The shadowy figure seems almost omnipotent; he easily manipulates events and intervenes to shape the thought processes of the young Prince.*

In the 1790s, The Ghost-Seer *sparked a series of similar tales of State Romance that combine gothic themes with anxieties about clandestine networks seeking to overthrow a weak state: the best known are Cajetan Tschink's* The Victim of Magical Delusion; or the Mystery of the Revolution Of P——L. A Magico-Political Tale *(1793); Jean Paul's* Invisible Lodge *(1793); C.M. Wieland's* Peregrinus Proteus *(1791); Ludwig Tieck's* William Lovell *(1795); and Carl Grosse's* The Genius *(1791–95; translated as* Horrid Mysteries*).³ These stories and the short-lived subgenre that they form need to be read as the conflicted expression of subterranean desires for the French Revolution's sweeping-away of the ancien regime by writers who were impatient with their own German regions' inability to accomplish these transformations for themselves.*

Although Schiller never completed the tale, he published three book editions, each different, in 1789, 1792, and 1798; other writers attempted to continue and supplement the tale in later versions.⁴ The metaphysical discussion between the Arminian and the Prince on the nature of evil (a theme evidenced in The Robbers*), which became known as the "Philosophical Dialogue," was modified several times and in later versions is often printed as an appendix to the main narrative.⁵*

The earliest English version of The Ghost-Seer *was republished serially in New York in 1795–1796 under the title* The Apparitionist, *and read with great interest by Brown's New York circle, who compared it favorably with Tschink's* The Victim of Magical Delusion.⁶ *Brown's closest friend, physician and writer Elihu Hubbard Smith, played a key role in*

---

³ Other popular tales following Schiller's *The Ghost-Seer* are K.F. Kahlert's *Der Geisterbanner, eine Wundergeschichte* (The Necromancer, a Tale of Marvel; 1790); G. Bücher's *Der Geisterseher. Eine venetianische Geschichte wundervollen Inhalts* (The Ghost-Seer: A Venetian Tale with a Wondrous Content; 1793); and E. Bornschein's *Moritz Graf von Portokar oder zwei Jahre aus dem Leben eines Geistersehers* (Moritz, Lord of Potokar, or Two Years from the Life of a Ghost-Seer; 1800).

⁴ After serialization in Schillers' journal *Thalia* (1787–1789), the first book edition was *Der Geisterseher: Eine Geschichte aus den Memoires des Grafen von O*** (The Ghost-Seer: A Tale from the Memoirs of the Count of O**; Leipzig: bei Georg Joachim Göschen, 1789). The most popular continuation was the six-hundred page narrative written and published anonymously by Ernst Friedrich Follenius as *Friedrich Schillers Geisterseher. Aus den Memoires des Grafen von O*** (Leipzig, 1796–1798), which ends with the imprisonment and confession of the Arminian.

⁵ The entire serial version, including the fullest text of the "Philosophical Dialogue," made up the first (1789) book edition. The second edition in 1792 shortened the Philosophical Dialogue significantly, and the third and final, 1798 edition cut the Dialogue even further. In many English versions of the novel, one of the shorter variants of the Dialogue appears as Part II, "Fourth Letter, June 12th."

⁶ The text that became available to Brown and his circle first appeared in 1795 as *The Ghost-Seer; or Apparitionist (London: Vernor & Hood, 1795;* Tr. Daniel Boileau*)*. A second English version, including parts of the Follenius additions, appeared in 1800 as *The Armenian or, the ghost seer. A history founded on fact. Translated . . . by the Rev. W. Render* (London: C. Whittingham, for H.D. Symonds, 1800).

arranging for a New York book edition in 1796 with T. & J. Swords, the same firm that printed Wieland *and other works by Brown, Smith, and their associates. Smith carried the novel on a trip home to Connecticut to convince a publisher there to reprint it as well. Three decades later, perceived links between Brown's work, Schiller, and the Godwin circle were strong enough that an 1831 British printing of* The Ghost-Seer *bound the novel together with Brown's novel* Edgar Huntly *and Mary Shelley's* Frankenstein *in a single combined edition.[7]*

Schiller's impact on Brown is clear. Besides their common late-Enlightenment emphasis on the demystification of superstition and "magical delusions," and their common efforts to "explode" backward-looking state-church alliances, several aspects of the character Theodore Wieland seem modeled on the Prince. The two share an intellectual formation that is dangerously dependent on an education that has been too limited, unsystematic, and isolated from wider experience with the world. Like the Prince, Wieland ultimately capitulates to a violent fantasy. Brown's character Carwin resembles the Arminian in his ability to disrupt and manipulate the Wielands with a few words and staged deceptions. In Memoirs of Carwin, *however, Carwin resembles the Prince as he is gradually entrapped by a mysterious member of a secret fraternity who seems to possess omniscient knowledge about him. Despite Carwin's functional similarity to Schiller's Arminian in* Wieland, *Brown seems to have abandoned Schiller's State Romance themes of intrigue about national politics, even as he retains* The Ghost-Seer's *fascination with conspiracy, its sharp tensions between a quasiaristocratic gentry and laboring peasantry or mercantile-bourgeois interests (like Jews, Armenians were a diasporic group that survived by developing international trade partnerships out of familial and ethnonational networks), and its contextual emphasis on a historical period and region notable for politico-religious violence.*

The novel's theatrical stagings of "ghost raising" also became connected with local New York popular culture in the late 1790s. When Swords re-advertised their edition of The Ghost-Seer *in 1799, they promoted it in light of a recent trick about raising ghosts that had apparently involved members of the city's elites.[8]*

*****

On my return to Courland in the year 17.., sometime about the Carnival, I visited the Prince of . . . . at Venice. We had been acquainted in the . . . . . . service,

---

[7] *The ghost-seer!* 2 volumes (London: Henry Colburn, 1831). Part I is bound with Shelley, *Frankenstein; or, The modern Prometheus*; part II with Brown, *Edgar Huntly; or, The Sleep Walker*. This combined edition was reprinted in Paris in 1832 (A. and W. Galignani).

[8] On February 11, 1799, the New York *Commercial Advertiser* published a short notice, with a hint of irony, explaining that "the attention of the city has been a good deal engaged for two days past about a story of raising GHOSTS; and respectable names have been mentioned as seeing and even conversing with them. The editor has taken pains to inquire particularly, and can assure his readers from the best authority, that there is nothing more in the affair, than a dextrous trick."

Three days later on February 14, T. & J. Swords seized the opportunity, printing a new advertisement for *The Ghost-Seer* in the city's *Mercantile Advertiser*, with the additional information that "this little volume illustrates, in a surprizing and fascinating manner, the trick recently played in this city, and which has, for three or four days, occupied so much of the pubic attention."

and we here renewed an intimacy which had been interrupted by the restoration of peace. As I wished to see the curiosities of this city, and as the Prince was waiting only for the arrival of remittances to return to his native country, he easily prevailed on me not to depart before him. We agreed not to separate during the time of our residence at Venice, and the Prince was so kind to accommodate me at his lodgings *at the Moor*.

As the small revenues of the Prince did not permit him to maintain the dignity of his rank, he lived at Venice *incognito*. Two noblemen, in whom he had entire confidence, composed all his retinue. He shunned expences, however, more from inclination than economy. He avoided all kinds of diversions, and though he was but thirty-five years old, he had resisted the numerous attractions of this voluptuous city. To the charms of the fair sex he was wholly indifferent. A settled gravity and a profound melancholy were the prominent features of his character. His passions were tranquil, but obstinate to excess. He formed his attachments with caution and timidity, but when once formed they were permanent and cordial. In the midst of a tumultuous crowd he walked alone. Occupied by his own visionary ideas, he was often a stranger to the world about him. Sensible of the deficiency of his own judgment, he was apt to give an unwarranted preference to the judgment of others. Though far from being weak, no man was more liable to be governed. When conviction, however, had once entered his mind, he became firm and decisive; equally courageous to combat an acknowledged prejudice or to die for a new one.

As he was the third Prince of his house, he had no expectation of acquiring the sovereignty. His ambition had never been awakened; his passions had taken another turn. He read much, but without discrimination. As his education had been neglected, and as he had early entered the career of arms, his understanding had never come to maturity. Hence the knowledge he afterwards acquired, served but to increase the chaos of his ideas, because it was built on an unstable foundation.

Like the rest of his family he professed the Protestant religion, because he was born in it. Enquiry or investigation he had never attempted, although at one period of his life he had been an enthusiast. It is necessary to observe that he had never been a freemason.

∗∗∗∗∗

"Let us go!" said the Prince, addressing himself to us. The Jailor came in. "We have done," said the Prince to him. "As for you," turning to the prisoner, "you shall hear farther from me."—

"I am tempted to ask your Highness the last question you proposed to the Conjurer," said I to the Prince, when we were alone. "Do you believe the second Ghost to have been a real one?"

"I believe it! no, not now, most assuredly."

"Not now! Then you have once believed it?"—

"I confess I was tempted for a moment to believe it to have been something more than the contrivance of a Juggler."—

"And I could wish to see the man, who under further circumstances would not have formed the same supposition. But what reasons have you for altering your opinion? What the prisoner has related of the Arminian ought to increase, rather than diminish your belief in his supernatural power."—

"What this wretch has related of him!" said the Prince, interrupting me very gravely. "I hope" continued he, "you have not now any doubt that we have had to with a villain."—

"No; but must his evidence on that account . . . ."—

"The evidence of a villain! Suppose I had no other reason for doubt, the evidence of such a person can be of no weight against common sense, and established truth. Does a man who has already deceived me several times, and whose trade it is to deceive, does he deserve to be heard in a cause in which the unsupported testimony of even the most sincere adherent to truth could not be received? Ought we believe a man who perhaps never once spoke truth for its own sake? Does such a man deserve credit, when he appears as evidence against human reason and the eternal laws of nature? Would it not be as absurd as to admit the accusation of a person notoriously infamous, against unblemished and reproachless innocence?"—

"But what motives could he have for giving so great a character to a man whom he has so many reasons to hate?"—

"I am not to conclude that he can have no motives for doing this, because I am unable to comprehend them. Do I know who has bribed him to deceive me? I confess I cannot penetrate the whole contexture of his plan; but he has certainly done a material injury to the cause he contends for, by shewing himself at least an impostor, and perhaps something worse."

*****

[The Prince explains that he considers all of the narrative's events, including the panto-mime play, the séances, and the Sicilian's confession, to be stage managed by the Arminian in order to trick the Prince. Schiller's tale ends after the Prince's speech, but the book publication contains the following note about the tale's continuation by others.]

*****

THE translator of this Fragment, which ends with the above reflections of Count O. . . . . . ., in order to remove the uncertainty in which the reader is left, as to the conclusion of these extraordinary adventures, and particularly with a view to explain some allusions in the concluding paragraph, has thought it necessary to subjoin a few particulars, in addition to what appears in the original.

The *Ghost-Seer* was first published in a German periodical work of the name of *Thalia* in detached parts. It appeared at a time when the sect of the *Illuminated*, as it is called, was beginning to extend itself very rapidly in Germany. These people, it is well known, were accustomed to seduce the ignorant and superstitious, by extravagant and incredible tales of supernatural powers and appearances. This story being calculated in some measure, to expose these miraculous accounts would, of course, be received with avidity; the editor was therefore induced to publish the most interesting part in a small volume by itself; and it is from such a separate edition that the present translation has been made.

The conclusion of these adventures is related, though very imperfectly, in the periodical work above-mentioned. It is principally to be gathered from a very long correspondence between the Prince and Count O . . . . chiefly on metaphysical subjects [. . .]

It appears, however, from the sequel, that the person so often mentioned in the preceding work, under the name of the *Arminian*, was a Roman Catholic Priest. In his attempts upon the Prince, he acted under the influence and direction of the Holy Inquisition. The design of this venerable and enlightened body was to gain him over to the Catholic religion, in order to make him at some future period, the instrument of disseminating it among his subjects. Among the unaccountable absurdities in human nature it may be remarked, that the zeal for making proselytes will frequently urge men to the commission of acts, which are directly inconsistent with the doctrines they are labouring to propagate. [. . . .]

Insnared in this manner . . . the Prince was soon completely perverted. He embraced the Catholic faith, and under the ridiculous pretense of gaining millions of deluded Protestants to the true Church, he was brought to consent to the murder of the Prince who barred his ascent to the throne. The attempt however did not succeed, and the same persons who engaged him in the crime, inflicted his punishment. To avoid the danger of discovery, they dispatched him by poison, and he died in the bitterest agonies of contrition and remorse.

FINIS.

14. Illuminati Debates

The Illuminati scare that began in 1797 and spread rapidly through the Atlantic world was a concerted, remarkably effective effort by ultraconservative propagandists to demonize the French Revolution and, by extension, the Enlightenment (or Illumination, an early synonym for Enlightenment) ideas that had driven a major wave of progressive change in all fields over the previous generation. In the United States, the scare also became an effort, by mainly conservative ministers, to reassert their authority by supporting the ruling Federalist Party's attempt to safeguard its diminishing power in a time of domestic and international challenges. Our discussion in what follows focuses primarily on the panic, Brown's response to it, and the role that it played in the counterrevolutionary turn of the late 1790s, illustrated by the Dwight-Ogden debate excerpted here.

The Illuminati Scare

The eruption of elite reactionary panic in the Illuminati scare is still studied today as a classic case and precedent for many episodes of antimodern political, religious, and cultural demonology that follow the age of democratic revolutions and extend to the present. Scapegoating, projection, and blame were not new strategies of panic in the 1790s, of course. Nor were fears of political conspiracy, which were widespread in early modern political thinking. But the way that these basic processes and themes were linked to fears of modernizing change and exploited as mass-political tools in the Illuminati scare is often understood as a landmark event that inaugurates new, postrevolutionary, and media-driven or spectacular forms of political demonology, and that sets the tone for new variations of xenophobic and racist activity in subsequent European and U.S. political history.[1]

Wieland *and Brown's other novels were written at the height of the Illuminati scare and respond to it in on several levels, most generally by foregrounding and consistently rejecting the fears of "foreign" subversive influence that are an important dimension of the larger Illuminati myth. As Brown was writing his novels, anti-Illuminati narratives were being used in the U.S. to aggravate an increasingly partisan crisis atmosphere generated by a threat of impending war against France in 1797, and by the repressive Alien and Sedition Acts (1798–1801), which targeted Irish and French immigrants as perceived subversives, and attempted to silence the opposition press (writing against the Anglophile Federalist administration of John Adams) by reviving old-regime definitions of political critique as unlawful sedition. These drew their inspiration from the similar 1795 British "Two Acts" introduced by the government after it had failed the year before to convict English radicals of treason.*

By 1800, however, the Illuminati panic had failed in the U.S. political sphere. The first-ever transfer of political power occurred with the rise of the Democratic-Republican party and, after his election as president, Thomas Jefferson (the primary political target of the U.S. anti-Illuminati tracts) pardoned those who had been convicted under the Alien and Sedition Acts and allowed the Acts to expire. The groups tarred by association with the Illuminati waged a successful counterattack in the press that mocked and discredited the clerical promoters of the panic.

---

[1] Scholarship on the episode develops concepts of "countersubversive" extremism, "political demonology," and, more locally, the "paranoid tradition" in U.S. politics. For historical perspectives on the relation of the Illuminati scare to modernization and postrevolutionary shifts, see Garrard, *Counter-Enlightenments: From the Eighteenth Century to the Present*; Koselleck, *Critique and Crisis: Enlightenment and the Pathogenesis of Modern Society*; Leinesch, "The Illusion of the Illuminati: The Counterconspiratorial Origins of Post-Revolutionary Conservatism"; McMahon, *Enemies of the Enlightenment: The French Counter-Enlightenment and the Making of Modernity*; Roberts, *The Mythology of the Secret Societies*. For the scare's impact in Brown's New York circle, see Waterman, *Republic of Intellect: The Friendly Club of New York City and the Making of American Literature*. A related body of scholarship builds on the work of Richard Hofstadter and focuses on the event as a precedent for later U.S. reactionary panics: see Hofstadter, *The Paranoid Style in American Politics and Other Essays*; Davis, *The Fear of Conspiracy: Images of Un-American Subversion from the Revolution to the Present*; Rogin, *Ronald Reagan, the Movie: And other Episodes in Political Demonology*; Stauffer, *New England and the Bavarian Illuminati*; Tise, *The American Counterrevolution: A Retreat from Liberty, 1783–1800*; Wood, "Conspiracy and the Paranoid Style: Causality and Deceit in the Eighteenth Century"; and White, "The Value of Conspiracy Theory."

The anti-Illuminati narrative and the myths that it created circulated in loose diatribes and rumors during the early years of the French Revolution, but took their canonical form with the antirevolutionary propaganda tracts of French Jesuit and monarchist Augustin Barruel (1741–1820). Barruel, *from a family of petty* noblesse de robe *(lesser aristocratic status achieved by rising through the judicial or administrative bureaucracies), was trained in the Jesuit order and first left France when the order was suppressed there in 1767. After Jesuit assignments in Germany and Austria, he returned to France when the order was entirely suppressed by Pope Clement XIV in 1773, and began a career as a propagandist for crown and altar. Barruel relocated to London after the French Revolution began and in 1793–1794 published French and English editions of his first antirevolutionary tract,* The History of the Clergy during the French Revolution. A Work Dedicated to the English Nation. *In 1797, still working from London, he published his best-known work,* Mémoires pour servir à l'histoire du Jacobinisme, *immediately translated as* Memoirs, illustrating the History of Jacobinism. *This work developed the anti-Illuminati narrative in its fullest form, in four books: I,* The Antichristian Conspiracy; *II,* The Antimonarchical Conspiracy; *III,* The Antisocial Conspiracy; *and IV, a historical appendix to* The Antisocial Conspiracy *that claimed to document conspiratorial activities of German Masonic lodge leaders such as Adam Weishaupt (1748–1830) and Adolf Knigge (1752–1796).[2] At the same time, the narrative was reiterated and circulated in Anglophone form by Edinburgh physicist and professor of philosophy John Robison (1739–1805). Like Barruel's* Memoirs, *Robison's* Proofs of a Conspiracy against all the Religions and Governments of Europe, carried on in the Secret Meetings of Free-Masons, Illuminati and Reading Societies, etc., collected from good authorities *(1797), was republished in several editions in England and the United States over the next four years. Together, these two books provided the basic scenario and ostensible evidence that was quoted, recirculated, and debated in innumerable forms in the following years, and which provides the basis for the two debates given here.*

The anti-Illuminati narratives of Barruel and Robison tell a simple story, although at great length and with great bombast. The "antichristian" and "antimonarchical" conspiracies of Barruel's books I and II are the Enlightenment itself, the influence of rationalizing ideas on religion and society developed throughout the eighteenth century. Barruel frames his critique of the old regime as a disastrous development and blames its influence in France on intellectuals from Voltaire to Diderot and the Encyclopedists, and in Germany on modernizing reforms initiated by Frederick the Great. These modernizing ideas, for Barruel, primarily encourage popular hatred against aristocrats and the rich, and have led to antireligious measures such as, notably, the suppression of the Jesuit order. The "antisocial" conspiracy of Barruel's books III and IV is the Masonic movement, and

---

[2] Internal conflicts between Knigge and Weishaupt were a key factor to the Illuminati's demise. When Knigge left the Illuminati in 1784, he may have been responsible for convincing the Bavarian Elector to ban the group. His popular *Über den Umgang mit Menschen* (1788) is ostensibly a manual of manners, but is also an early sociological study in managing human relations. The relation between the reality of secret societies and gothic fiction appears as this title was first translated as *Practical Philosophy of Social Life; or the Art of Conversing with Men* (1794) by Peter Will, who specialized in horror fiction (see the excerpt from Will in Related Texts).

particularly the Masonic lodge in Bavaria (southern Germany) known as the Illuminati. Barruel and Robison claim that this lodge, led by Weishaupt in its earlier development and Knigge in later forms, has been responsible for secretive, conspiratorial plots that have spread via the institutions of print culture; led to the French Revolution itself; and threaten to spread further, undermining church and state institutions (the old regimes) in other Christian and monarchical nations. Wieshaupt and Knigge were, in fact, dedicated to progressive change, and Weishaupt's "Illuminati" largely ceased to exist after Bavarian elector Karl Theodore banned it as seditious in 1784. Nevertheless, Barruel's narrative seizes on a minor incident from the period's enlightened lodge activism (widely publicized and allegorized in many forms throughout the late Enlightenment, for example Mozart's 1791 opera The Magic Flute *or the Masonic emblems on the Great Seal of the United States) and inflates it into an epic myth of conspiratorial terror.*

Like so many other sensational effects taken up in the Anglophone world in the 1790s, the Illuminati phenomenon began in Germany during the 1770s and 1780s. Although the order, its suppression, and ensuing print wars around it were real events, as opposed to literary movements, the entire episode deserves to be seen as an analogue to the contemporaneous rise of "Storm and Stress" (Sturm und Drang) *writing, involving the young Goethe and Schiller among others, and of the horror novels* (Schauerroman) *and State Romances, especially as the latter trends utilize the Illuminati legends as well. All of these trends follow a similar time sequence; and after their elaboration in Germany, all are eagerly transported into England in the early 1790s and the U.S. shortly thereafter.*

On May 1, 1776, Adam Weishaupt, the first lay professor of canon law at the University of Ingolstadt (1472–1800), formed a secret society of freethinkers dedicated to speeding the agendas of the rational Enlightenment throughout the globe.[3] Weishaupt initially called the group the Perfectibilists, but later changed it to the Illuminati Order. The Bavarian university lay on one of the fault lines of the seesaw between the Enlightenment and Counterreformation, and Weishaupt lived out these tensions. Raised by a progressive professor of law at Ingolstadt, Weishaupt quickly rose through the academic hierarchy in the university, which had been founded to advance Christian ideals. The suppression of the Jesuit order in 1773 made it possible for Weishaupt to be promoted to professor of canon law, the only professor in the university who did not have a Jesuit background. Undermined by the machinations of the remaining Jesuit faculty, Weishaupt formed the Illuminati. The group was organized on strictly hierarchical lines: the leaders of one cell initiated others, who remained ignorant about the identity of the group's other leaders, and seeded new cells in turn. Although Weishaupt despised the Jesuits, he followed their organizational system, with its network of spies, and he believed that the ends justified the means in spreading the ideals of the radical Enlightenment.

---

[3] For discussions of the historical Illuminati episode, its relation to wider Masonic and lodge elements of the late Enlightenment, and to the scare, see the previously mentioned studies by Koselleck, Leinesch, and Roberts, as well as Hofman, "Opinion, Illusion, and the Illusion of Opinion: Barruel's Theory of Conspiracy" and "The Origins of the Theory of the Philosophe Conspiracy"; as well as Luckert, *Jesuits, Freemasons, Illuminati, and Jacobins: Conspiracy Theories, Secret Societies, and Politics in Late Eighteenth-century Germany.*

Under Weishaupt's eccentric academic leadership, the group remained very small until it was reorganized by a Bavarian diplomat and a Hessian noble with contacts in Masonic circles. Thence the group spread through Germany, reaching a peak membership of perhaps two thousand, primarily civil servants, officers, minor nobles, publicists, and academics. Some of its more famous members were Goethe, Herder, and the reformist educationalist Johann Heinrich Pestalozzi (1746–1827), although it is unlikely that these participants were deeply involved. Increasingly concerned about its influence, the Bavarian Elector Karl Theodor banned the order in 1784–1785. At that point the Illuminati ceased to exist as a functioning group, only to return in ensuing print wars and the paranoid imagination of the late 1790s. The discovery and publication of the group's secret correspondence by the Bavarian authorities in the mid-1780s marked the first public scare concerning its activities, and Weishaupt, in exile at Gotha, one of the Saxon principates, spent the later 1780s writing public defenses of the organization.

Although the actual Illuminati were, in sum, a local episode in the period's vogue for lodge, club, salon, and other private association activism, the grand conspiracy theory put forward by Barruel and Robison, on the other hand (both working from England), blamed the French Revolution on progressive French intellectuals and members of this small band of German Masons in Berlin who trained French acolytes, and claimed that barbaric social violence was the preconcerted goal and outcome of enlightenment ideas and modernizing social reforms. It is not difficult to see how the scenario was built around basic structures of projection and scapegoating. Viewed historically and analytically, it appears as a fantastic reversal or inversion, a mirror image, of the actual historical situation in the 1790s, when the combined forces of monarchical Europe and its church institutions were focusing their economic, military, political, and ideological resources on the goal of violently crushing the French Revolution and the world view it represented.

In this manner the theory, beyond assigning an absurdly simple cause to complex and systemic historical transformations, projects the organizational and coercive energies of European monarchies onto the reform-minded Enlightenment, and demonizes its representatives as agents of a violence which is being planned and enacted by the monarchies themselves. However implausible, this narrative and its logic of projection and blame was eagerly embraced and amplified by conservatives who were grateful for any means of combating progressive ideas and condemning the social changes associated with the French and American revolutions. English figures such as Edmund Burke and elite U.S. Federalists such as President John Adams or Reverend Timothy Dwight (see excerpt) embraced the theory and used it to malign their political opponents as dangerous, godless extremists.

Shortly after the English publications of Barruel and Robison, the scare was brought to American shores primarily by a number of Congregationalist, New England ministers, including Timothy Dwight and Jedidiah Morse (1761–1826). On May 9, 1798, a day appointed by President Adams as a national fast day for repentance at the nation's "hazardous and afflictive position," Morse delivered the first of several sermons to his Boston congregation that inveighed against the Illuminati and attempted to associate the scare with the Democratic-Republican political party led by Jefferson. As a result of rebuttals like that of John Ogden, included here, however, the panic ebbed. These challenges also included published letters from the head of the Hamburg library Christopher Daniel

Ebeling (1741–1817), who denounced Robison's claims as riddled with inaccuracies and complained that because both Barruel and Robison did not know German, they were unfamiliar with the primary sources and context of the Illuminati debate in Germany and Austria.[4]

Debate and Response

   With an understanding of the basic argument and tendency of the anti-Illuminati scenario, it becomes possible to ask how Brown responds to it and how he develops commentary on the Illuminati scare in his novels and other writings. In his essayistic writings, Brown offers only a discreet rejection of the theory, making points that refer to his ideas on the relation of history and fiction writing. In the New York Monthly Magazine *of July, 1799, in his review of an anti-Illuminati oration, Brown points out the implausibility of assigning simple causes to complex events, observing how a grand conspiracy theory obscures thinking by explaining events with a simplistic and tendentious "plot" rather than necessary analysis. In the review's critical and dismissive synopsis of Barruel, Brown dryly observes, for example, how "the Romish religion, and hereditary despotism, were, in the eyes of one of his order and profession, virtue and duty."*[5] *In addition to his rejection of Barruel in this review, it is notable that nowhere in his writings, including* Wieland *and* Memoirs of Carwin, *does Brown use the word* Illuminati, *and nowhere does he discuss the historical episode or the scare that was built on it, as if to avoid becoming embroiled with reactionary claims concerning the Illuminati or any other specific group. Brown's avoidance of the word seems quite deliberate. Although his hundreds of periodical writings focus on a great many contemporary topics and events, he chooses never to adopt the terms or concerns of this reactionary scare.*

   In an "American Tale" like Wieland, *Brown seems to focus on the local dynamics of the scare in order to suggest how it precludes a clear or even remotely rational view of events. When Clara Wieland and Henry Pleyel suppose that the lower-status interloper Carwin is a dangerous foreigner, despite his subsequently revealed local origins, absorb misleading print material accusing him of crimes, and consistently and irrationally blame Carwin*

---

[4] Considered one of the first "Americanists" in Germany and author of internationally respected studies on American geography and history, the seven-volume *Erdbeschreibung und Geschichte von Amerika* (1793–1816), Ebeling already knew Morse, and had found wanting the geographical work on which Morse had mainly made his reputation. An outspoken and unapologetic defender of the cosmopolitan (and Protestant) Enlightenment, Ebeling was in frequent contact with a wide spectrum of American writers and scholars at the time. His work was mentioned frequently in U.S. newspapers and magazines in the 1790s, including the Brown-edited New York *Monthly Magazine*, and was thus familiar to members of Brown's circle, some of whom were collecting and then shipping over books and maps for Ebeling's collection in Hamburg, which became the most comprehensive library of Americana in Europe at that time. He also created an impressive collection of material relating to the United States for his alma mater, the University of Gottingen, which continues to hold the largest collection of American Studies in Germany today.

[5] See Brown's review of "An Oration, spoken at Hartford . . . by William Brown" in *Monthly Magazine* July 1799, 289–92. For more on this review's rejection of the anti-Illuminati theories, see Wood, "Conspiracy and the Paranoid Style: Causality and Deceit in the Eighteenth Century."

for traumatic events even though more plausible scenarios are repeatedly offered by Clara's uncle Thomas Cambridge, for example, one may plausibly read the novel as an allegory of the elite panic that gives shape to the anti-Illuminati myths.

The character Ludloe, Carwin's elite patron in Memoirs of Carwin, *represents an unfinished attempt to develop a character engaged in a secretive, utopian "fraternity" and his role in that narrative clearly alludes to contemporary concerns with the Illuminati and other secret societies. Ludloe's schemes apparently involve colonial projects like those of the Jesuits, however, rather than any attempt to subvert existing institutions in the Atlantic world, and connect that narrative more clearly to the anticolonial scenarios in Brown's historical fiction fragments (the* Historical Sketches *and other unfinished writings) than to the anti-Illuminati narratives that circulated after 1797.*

Timothy Dwight versus John Ogden (1798–1799)

The polemical exchange that follows, between Timothy Dwight and John Ogden, illustrates the ways that the Illuminati scare was received and debated in Brown's immediate context. The anti-Illuminati tract by Dwight begins from the Barruel-Robison narrative, accepting their claims of illicit conspiracies by Weishaupt and Knigge, and argues that extensions of their illuminating and cosmopolitanizing activities pose an immediate threat to U.S. society. The rebuttal from John Ogden points out the outlandish, improbable nature of the anti-Illuminati theories and defends progressive positions by identifying the partisan political and institutional motivations of those who use the Illuminati panic to consolidate their own power and positions in the nation's religious, political, and educational elite.

Timothy Dwight (1752–1817) was well known in the 1790s as a Congregationalist minister, theologian, neoclassical poet, and president of Yale University (1795–1817). Along with his brother, attorney Theodore Dwight (1764–1846), a possible source for the first name of Theodore Wieland, he was a pillar of the period's Federalist conservative orthodoxy and one of the most visible public amplifiers of the Illuminati scare in the early American republic. Although the Dwights' patrician conservatism did not rule out support for abolitionist activities during the 1780s and early 1790s, when their circles began to overlap with Brown's in New York, they became ideologically polarized as counterrevolutionary extremists in the crisis atmosphere of 1797–1801 and emerged as icons of that moment's "paranoid" style of reactionary, xenophobic polemics and religious-political posturing. Timothy was famously dubbed by his opponents the Federalist "Pope" of Connecticut.[6] John Cosens Ogden (1740–1800) was a Vermont Episcopalian minister who opposed conservative positions in the period's culture wars and acted as a supporter of democratic-republican interests. His last book was a commentary on the Moravian community that also figures in the early Wieland family history: An Excursion into Bethlehem and Nazareth in Pennsylvania, in the Year 1799, with a Succinct History of the Society of the United Brethren, commonly called Moravians *(Philadelphia, 1800).*

---

[6] See Kafer, "The Making of Timothy Dwight: A Connecticut Morality Tale" and Imholt, "Timothy Dwight, Federalist Pope of Connecticut."

Dwight's oration and pamphlet on the "Duty of Americans, at the Present Crisis" rehearses the basic anti-Illuminati scenario drawn from Barruel and Robison, arguing that enlightened thinking and social change represent dangerous forms of un-Christian subversion. In passages not included here, he attempts to associate these supposed threats with Thomas Jefferson and the Francophile Democratic-Republican Party that supported him. Rebutting Dwight's Barruel and Robison-inspired accusations, Ogden's pamphlet counters by ironically reversing and demystifying the basic conspiracy fantasy, identifying Dwight as one of a powerful group of interrelated conservative educational and political administrators that make up a counterrevolutionary "New-England Illuminati." Ogden points out that clerical ideologues like Dwight and his well-connected allies constitute a quasiaristocratic cabal that combines to found their own networks of wealthy private institutions, notably colleges and universities, in order to further the interests of their own family and class alliances, using their influence to monopolize power and educational opportunities that deliver credentials and contacts for career advancement, and to manipulate and dominate the far more numerous laboring and professional classes who stand to benefit from public institutions and progressive reforms.

*****

Timothy Dwight, *The Duty of Americans, at the Present Crisis, Illustrated in a Discourse, Preached on the Fourth of July, 1798; by the Reverend Timothy Dwight, D.D. President of Yale-College at the Request of the Citizens of New-Haven.* New Haven: Thomas and Samuel Green, 1798

While these measures were advancing the great design with a regular and rapid progress, Doctor Adam Weishaupt, professor of the Canon law in the University of Ingolstadt, a city of Bavaria (in Germany) formed, about the year 1777, the order of Illuminati. This order is professedly a higher order of Masons, originated by himself, and grafted on ancient Masonic Institutions. The secresy, solemnity, mysticism, and correspondence of Masonry, were in this new order preserved and enhanced; while the ardour of innovation, the impatience of civil and moral restraints, and the aims against government, morals, and religion, were elevated, expanded, and rendered more systematical, malignant, and daring.

In the societies of Illuminati doctrines were taught, which strike at the root of all human happiness and virtue; and every such doctrine was either expressly or implicitly involved in their system.

The being of God was denied and ridiculed.

Government was asserted to be a curse, and authority a mere usurpation.

Civil society was declared to be the only apostasy of man.

The possession of property was pronounced to be robbery.

Chastity and natural affection were declared to be nothing more than groundless prejudices.

Adultery, assassination, poisoning, and other crimes of the like infernal nature, were taught as lawful, and even as virtuous actions.

To crown such a system of falsehood and horror all means were declared to be lawful, provided the end was good.

In this last doctrine men are not only loosed from every bond, and from every duty; but from every inducement to perform any thing which is good, and, abstain from any thing which is evil; and are set upon each other, like a company of hellhounds to worry, rend, and destroy. Of the goodness of the end every man is to judge for himself; and most men, and all men who resemble the Illuminati, will pronounce every end to be good, which will gratify their inclinations. The great and good ends proposed by the Illuminati, as the ultimate objects of their union, are the overthrow of religion, government, and human society civil and domestic. These they pronounce to be so good, that murder, butchery, and war, however extended and dreadful, are declared by them to be completely justifiable, if necessary for these great purposes. With such an example in view, it will be in vain to hunt for ends, which can be evil.

Correspondent with this summary was the whole system. No villainy, no impiety, no cruelty, can be named, which was not vindicated; and no virtue, which was not covered with contempt.

The names by which this society was enlarged, and its doctrines spread, were of every promising kind. With unremitted ardour and diligence the members insinuated themselves into every place of power and trust, and into every literary, political and friendly society; engrossed as much as possible the education of youth, especially of distinction; became licensers of the press, and directors of every literary journal; waylaid every foolish prince, every unprincipled civil officer, and every abandoned clergyman; entered boldly into the desk, and with unhallowed hands, and satanic lips, polluted the pages of God; inlisted in their service almost all the booksellers, and of course the printers, of Germany; inundated the country with books, replete with infidelity, irreligion, immorality, and obscenity; prohibited the printing, and prevented the sale, of books of the contrary character; decried and ridiculed them when published in spite of their efforts; panegyrized and trumpeted those of themselves and their coadjutors; and in a word made more numerous, more diversified, and more strenuous exertions, than an active imagination would have preconceived.

[. . .]

For what end shall we be connected with men, of whom this is the character and conduct? Is it that we may assume the same character, and pursue the same conduct? Is it, that our churches may become temples of reason, our Sabbath a decade, and our psalms of praise Marseillois hymns?[7] Is it, that we may change our holy worship into a dance of Jacobin phrenzy, and that we may behold a strumpet personating a Goddess on the altars of JEHOVAH? Is it that we may see the Bible cast into a bonfire, the vessels of the sacramental supper borne by an ass in public procession,

---

[7] "Marseillois hymns": the "Marseillaise," the revolutionary anthem written in 1792, and today the national anthem of the French Republic. Conservative French regimes banned it several times in the early nineteenth century before it was permanently adopted as the national anthem in 1879.

and our children, either wheedled or terrified, uniting in the mob, chanting mockeries against God, and hailing in the sounds of Ca ira[8] the ruin of their religion, and the loss of their souls? Is it, that we may see our wives and daughters the victims of legal prostitution; soberly dishonoured; speciously polluted; the outcasts of delicacy and virtue, and the loathing of God and man? Is it, that we may see, in our public papers, a solemn comparison drawn by an American Mother club between the Lord Jesus Christ and a new Marat;[9] and the fiend of malice and fraud exalted above the glorious Redeemer?

Shall we, my brethren, become partakers of these sins? Shall we introduce them into our government, our schools, our families? Shall our sons become the disciples of Voltaire, and the dragoons of Marat[*]; or our daughters the concubines of the Illuminati?

[. . .]

*****

John Ogden. *A View of the New-England Illuminati; Who Are Indefatigably Engaged in Destroying the Religion and Government of the United States; Under a Feigned Regard for their Safety—And Under an Impious Abuse of True Religion.* Philadelphia: Printed by James Carey, No. 16, Chesnut-Street, 1799

WHILE clamours and prejudices are excited publicly and artfully against a large and respectable body of our fellow-citizens, under the pretext, that some are secretly embarked with a society in Europe, who are engaged in the destruction of religion and government in general, it is proper to present before the public a society which actually exists in the United States. This is more needful at this time, as these last are indefatigably engaged in destroying the religion and government of *this* country, under a feigned regard for their safety—and under an impious abuse of true religion.

These societies have passed without general scrutiny, until they have nearly destroyed our liberties and happiness at home, and contributed to plunge us into a share of the confusions of Europe.

These are the monthly meetings of the Clergy. As their design, tendency, and effect have been to destroy established law, morals, order, and universal toleration; they too

* See a four years Residence in France, lately published by Mr. Cornelius Davis of New-York. This is a most valuable and interesting work, and exhibits the French Revolution in a far more perfect light than any book I have seen. *It ought to be read by every American.*

---

[8] "Ca ira": the best-known popular song of the French Revolution. The title, repeated several times in each line of the chorus, means literally "it will go" or "it will work"; figuratively, "we will win."

[9] "Marat": Jean-Paul Marat (1743–1793), a Swiss-born physician, journalist, and political leader with the Jacobin faction during the French Revolution. His reputation as an extremist and his assassination in 1793 by Charlotte Corday are familiar commonplaces in revolutionary lore, in works such as painter Jacques-Louis David's *The Death of Marat* (1793).

bear near an affinity to the Illuminati Societies of Europe, not be viewed as part of the same: at least, if Professor *Robeson* and Abbé *Barruel* are to be believed, they must be *sister societies*. They have been known by the appellation of *Ministers' Meetings*—But I shall take the liberty of calling them the New-England Illuminati; leaving the reader to decide upon the propriety of the name.

These societies originated about thirty years ago; and were designed to increase the power and influence of the clergy. Success attending this confederacy, certain opulent and leading laymen have fostered and encouraged them, thereby forming that union of Church and State—of laymen and ecclesiastics—which have created an order equally formidable with that body of men in any country in Europe.

[. . .]

In this way Connecticut, especially, has become almost totally an ecclesiastical state, ruled by the *President* of the *College, as a Monarch*. The caution and politeness of the Governor of that state, the great age of many of the council, the respectful condescension of the members of the lower house, the submission of the clergy, the influence of *clubs*, of *uncles, brothers, cousins*, scribblers, and poets—of former and present pupils, have given him almost unlimited control.—Sufficient to undertake great duties, he does not consider the weight of cares, too difficult for his years, health, or inclination, but has assumed, among a passive people, the dignity of ruling with the united powers of an ecclesiastic and a politician.

[. . .]

To give the people of the United States a more perfect yet concise view of the proceedings of the Illuminati of Connecticut, and their adherents elsewhere, it is not amiss to recapitulate some things which relate to their arts, to secure religion, learning, the colleges, schools, and public property, to their uses. This is more important, as thereby they have called off the public attention from the schools and children of the yeomanry in general, to the promoting of the children of the Illuminati, and the colleges subservient to them.

A few clergymen artfully attempted to begin a college in Branford, in Connecticut, by depositing a few books. This design fell through, from want of consistency and property; and a new plan was adopted at Saybrook, which the government fostered; and it ended in Yale College. Mr. Yale, Governor of the East-India Company, and a churchman, liberally bestowed such benefactions as led the corporation to call it after his name, and write him a most flattering letter of thanks. Dean Berkley, afterwards Bishop of Coyne, in Ireland, gave an handsome farm on Rhode-Island, and a large library, to this college. The colony and state of Connecticut have erected three buildings and the chapel, and paid large annual sums to help it forward: but the illiberal and contracted doings of the clergy and corporation, caused the government and the generously disposed, to withhold their bounty. Five hundred pounds were left at one time, in this way, and given by a gentleman in England, to Cambridge College, in Massachusetts.

[. . .]

The sons and favourites of the Illuminati now hold seats in the Senate and House of Representatives in Congress.—They gained and hold their stations thereby: their efforts to gain a sedition law, and carry it into execution in their own state, is too evidently in order to check that *examination into their own affairs*, to which the people of Connecticut are prone, and from which they will not be deterred.

[. . .]

This gives a short view of a leading law character.—The head of the Illuminati, Doctor *Dwight*, a divine, who has made himself so conspicuous and has been so often animadverted upon publicly, that the nation are very generally acquainted with his character and proceedings.

In his sermon preached on the fourth day of July, 1798, in New-Haven, he has given us a perfect picture of the Illuminati of Connecticut, under his control, in the representation he has made of the Illuminati of Europe. To transcribe it might be useful; but the sermon is in the hands of so many, that it would be needless to swell this tract, by excerpts from it.

Birth, education, elevation, and connections have placed Doctor Dwight at the head of the Edwardean sect[10] and Illuminati. Active, persevering, and undaunted, he proceeds to direct all political, civil, and ecclesiastical affairs. Science, he forsakes, and her institutions he prostrates, to promote party, bigotry, and error. He is making great strides after universal control in Connecticut, New-England, and the United States, over religious opinions and politics. He is seeking the establish the Edwardean system of doctrines and discipline, from pride for his grandfather's (President Edwards') talents and fame; while few indeed of that deceased gentleman's descendents believe in his tenets. With a large salary, paid from the public bounty, he is maintained in his place, and excites and perpetuates party designs. For more than twenty years, he has been a writer in the newspapers upon many points, where he wished to forward alterations. He attacked the constitution of the college, while it was still directed by his predecessor, Dr. Stiles, and ecclesiastics only. Layman are now introduced, to little good purpose; and we must believe, without a violation of charity, that if a President had been elected who was not an Edwardean, he would have zealously sought to place that institution upon the same liberal foundation with other colleges.

Under his administration, and Illuminati influence, expecting favours from this nation, he has frequently disannulled the ties of religion, consanguinity, and friendship. Merit is neglected, and youth taught prejudices by him. These are circulated, to please the President of the College, and gain diplomas and flattering recommendations to schools and colleges.

[. . .]

---

[10] "Edwardean sect": in the passage that follows, Ogden builds on then commonly understood connections among the New England ministerial elite. Timothy Dwight was a grandson of late-Calvinist theologian and writer Jonathan Edwards (1703–1758), who also served briefly as first president of Princeton University.

BIBLIOGRAPHY AND WORKS CITED

I. Writings by Brown

Comprehensive bibliographies of Brown's writings and of recent scholarship on Brown are available at the Web site of The Charles Brockden Brown Electronic Edition and Scholarly Archive: http://www.brockdenbrown.ucf.edu

A. Novels

Brown, Charles Brockden. *Wieland; or The Transformation. An American Tale.* New York: Printed by T. & J. Swords for H. Caritat, 1798.

———. *Arthur Mervyn; or, Memoirs of the Year 1793.* Philadelphia: H. Maxwell, 1799.

———. *Edgar Huntly; or, Memoirs of a Sleep-Walker.* Philadelphia: H. Maxwell, 1799.

———. *Ormond; or The Secret Witness.* New York: Printed by G. Forman for H. Caritat, 1799.

———. *Memoirs of Stephen Calvert.* Published serially in *The Monthly Magazine*, vols. I–II (New York: T. & J. Swords, June 1799–June 1800).

———. *Arthur Mervyn; or, Memoirs of the Year 1793. Second Part.* New York: George F. Hopkins, 1800.

———. *Clara Howard; In a Series of Letters.* Philadelphia: Asbury Dickens, 1801.

———. *Jane Talbot; A Novel.* Philadelphia: John Conrad; Baltimore: M. & J. Conrad; Washington City: Rapin & Conrad, 1801.

———. *The Novels and Related Works of Charles Brockden Brown.* Bicentennial Edition. Six Volumes. Sydney J. Krause and S.W. Reid, eds. Kent, Ohio: Kent State UP, 1977–1987. *The Bicentennial Edition is the modern scholarly text of Brown's seven novels, plus the Wollstonecraftian dialogue* Alcuin *and* Memoirs of Carwin.

B. Essays and Uncollected Fiction

Brown, Charles Brockden. *Alcuin; A Dialogue.* New York: T. & J. Swords, 1798.

———. *Historical Sketches.* Short sections published in *The Literary Magazine and American Register*, 1805; most of the project appeared posthumously in the Allen & Dunlap biographies (1811–1815).

———. *Literary Essays and Reviews.* Alfred Weber and Wolfgang Schäfer, eds. Frankfurt: Peter Lang, 1992.

———. *Somnambulism and Other Stories.* Alfred Weber, ed. Frankfurt: Peter Lang, 1987.

———. *The Rhapsodist and Other Uncollected Writings.* Harry R. Warfel, ed. Delmar, NY: Scholar's Facsimiles and Reprints, 1977.

C. Periodicals and Pamphlets

The three periodicals that Brown edited include hundreds of his own articles and miscellaneous pieces in a variety of genres (essays, short fictions, reviews, dialogues, anecdotes, and other forms) and on a wide range of subjects, from literary and artistic culture to social and political questions, history, geopolitics, and different subfields of science. For a listing of these publications, consult the Comprehensive Bibliography at the web site of The Charles Brockden Brown Electronic Archive and Scholarly Edition.

Brown, Charles Brockden. *The Monthly Magazine and American Review.* Vols. I–III. New York: T. & J. Swords, April 1799–December 1800.

———. *An Address to the Government of the United States, on the Cession of Louisiana to the French.* Philadelphia: John Conrad, 1803.

———. *Monroe's Embassy, or, the Conduct of the Government, in Relation to Our Claims to the Navigation of the Mississippi [sic], Considered.* Philadelphia: John Conrad, 1803.

———. *The Literary Magazine and American Register.* Vols. I–VIII. Philadelphia: C. & A. Conrad, 1803–1806.

———. *The American Register, or General Repository of History, Politics, and Science.* Vols. I–VII. Philadelphia: C. & A. Conrad, 1807–1809.

———. *An Address to the Congress of the United States, on the Utility and Justice of Restrictions upon Foreign Commerce.* Philadelphia: C. & A. Conrad, 1809.

II. Biographies of Brown and Diaries of his Friends Smith, Dunlap, and Cope

Besides the published biographies, an important resource is the unfinished biographical study written 1910–1945 by Daniel Edwards Kennedy, now preserved at the Kent State Institute for Bibliography and Editing. The Smith and Dunlap diaries provide detailed reportage about Brown and his New York circle in the crucial period when Brown was writing his novels. Cope's diary documents Brown's never-accomplished plan, in 1803–1806, to write an abolitionist History of Slavery.

Allen, Paul. *The Life of Charles Brockden Brown.* Charles E. Bennett, ed. Delmar, NY: Scholar's Facsimiles and Reprints, 1975 (written 1811–14). *Allen's unfinished biography is the preliminary version of Dunlap's 1815* Life, *and remained unpublished until the late twentieth century. It prints miscellaneous fictional fragments and other texts by Brown not available elsewhere.*

———. *The Late Charles Brockden Brown.* Edited, with an Introduction, by Robert E. Hemenway and Joseph Katz. Columbia, SC: J. Faust, 1976. *This is a second facsimile edition of the unfinished Allen biography, with additional commentary and information on the circumstances surrounding the influential 1815 Dunlap version.*

Clark, David Lee. *Charles Brockden Brown: Pioneer Voice of America.* Durham: Duke UP, 1952.

Cope, Thomas P. *Philadelphia Merchant: The Diary of Thomas P. Cope, 1800–1851.* Edited and with an introduction and appendices by Eliza Cope Harrison. South Bend, IN: Gateway Editions, 1978.

Dunlap, William. *Diary of William Dunlap (1766–1839): The Memoirs of a Dramatist, Theatrical Manager, Painter, Critic, Novelist, and Historian.* 3 volumes. Dorothy C. Barck, ed. New York: The New-York Historical Society, 1930.

———. *The Life of Charles Brockden Brown.* 2 volumes. Philadelphia: James P. Parke, 1815. *A revision and extension of Allen, above. Together, Dunlap and Allen provide the only texts for the* Historical Sketches, *the complete version of* Alcuin, *and other pieces not available elsewhere.*

Kafer, Peter. *Charles Brockden Brown's Revolution and the Birth of American Gothic.* Philadelphia: U of Pennsylvania P, 2004.

Smith, Elihu Hubbard. *The Diary of Elihu Hubbard Smith (1771–1798).* James E. Cronin, ed. Philadelphia: American Philosophical Society, 1973.

Warfel, Harry R. *Charles Brockden Brown: American Gothic Novelist.* Gainesville: U of Florida P, 1949.

III. Brown, *Wieland,* and *Memoirs of Carwin* in the wider context of cultural and literary history

Amfreville, Marc. *Charles Brockden Brown: La part du doute.* Paris: Belin, 2000.

Axelrod, Alan. *Charles Brockden Brown, An American Tale.* Austin: U of Texas P, 1983.

Barnard, Philip. "Culture and Authority in Brown's *Historical Sketches.*" In Philip Barnard, Mark L. Kamrath, and Stephen Shapiro, eds. *Revising Charles Brockden Brown: Culture, Politics, and Sexuality in the Early Republic,* 310–31. Knoxville: U of Tennessee P, 2004.

Bell, Michael Davitt. "'The Double-Tongued Deceiver': Sincerity and Duplicity in the Novels of Charles Brockden Brown." *Early American Literature* 9.2 (1974): 143–63.

Bradfield, Scott. *Dreaming Revolution: Transgression in the Development of American Romance.* Iowa City: U of Iowa P, 1993.

Budick, Emily Miller. *Fiction and Historical Consciousness: The American Romance Tradition.* New Haven: Yale UP, 1989.

Cahill, Edward. "An Adventurous and Lawless Fancy: Charles Brockden Brown's Aesthetic State." *Early American Literature* 36.1 (2001): 31–70.

Chase, Richard. *The American Novel and Its Tradition.* New York: Doubleday, 1957.

Christophersen, Bill. *The Apparition in the Glass: Charles Brockden Brown's American Gothic.* Athens, GA: U of Georgia P, 1993.

Clark, David Lee. "Brockden Brown and the Rights of Women." *University of Texas Bulletin* 22.12 (1922): 1–48.

Clement, John. "Charles Brockden." *The Pennsylvania Magazine of History and Biography* 12.2 (1888): 185–93.

Cody, Michael. *Charles Brockden Brown and the Literary Magazine: Cultural Journalism in the Early American Republic.* Jefferson, NC: McFarland, 2004.

Crain, Caleb. *American Sympathy: Men, Friendship, and Literature in the New Nation.* New Haven: Yale UP, 2001.

Dauber, Kenneth. *The Idea of Authorship in America: Democratic Poetics from Franklin to Melville.* Madison: U of Wisconsin P, 1990.

Davidson, Cathy. *Revolution and the Word: The Rise of the Novel in America.* Expanded Edition. New York: Oxford UP, 2004.

Davis, Mike Lee. *Reading The Text That Isn't There: Paranoia in the Nineteenth-Century American Novel.* New York: Routledge, 2005.

Dawes, James. "Fictional Feeling: Philosophy, Cognitive Science, and the American Gothic." *American Literature* 76.3 (2004): 437–66.

DeGuzmán, María. *Spain's Long Shadow: The Black Legend, Off-Whiteness, and Anglo-American Empire.* Minneapolis: U of Minnesota P, 2005.

Delbourgo, James. *A Most Amazing Scene of Wonders: Electricity and Enlightenment in Early America.* Cambridge: Harvard UP, 2006.

Dillon, Elizabeth Maddock. *The Gender of Freedom: Fictions of Liberalism and the Literary Public Sphere.* Stanford: Stanford UP, 2004.

Dillon, James. "'The Highest Province of Benevolence': Charles Brockden Brown's Fictional Theory." *Studies in Eighteenth-Century Culture* 27 (1998): 237–58.

Doolen, Andy. *Fugitive Empire: Locating Early American Imperialism.* Minneapolis: U of Minnesota P, 2005.

Downes, Paul. *Democracy, Revolution, and Monarchism in Early American Literature.* Cambridge: Cambridge UP, 2002.

Doyle, Laura. *Freedom's Empire: Race and the Rise of the Novel in Atlantic Modernity, 1640–1940.* Durham: Duke UP, 2008.

Elliott, Emory. *Revolutionary Writers: Literature and Authority in the New Republic, 1725–1810.* New York: Oxford UP, 1982.

Emerson, Amanda. "The Early American Novel: Charles Brockden Brown's Fictitious Historiography." *Novel: A Forum on Fiction* 40.1–2 (2006): 125–50.

Fiedler, Leslie A. *Love and Death in the American Novel.* New York: Criterion Books, 1960.

Fleischmann, Fritz. *A Right View of the Subject: Feminism in the Works of Charles Brockden Brown and John Neal.* Erlangen: Palm & Enke, 1983.

Goddu, Teresa. *Gothic America: Narrative, History, and Nation.* New York: Columbia UP, 1997.

Grabo, Norman S. *The Coincidental Art of Charles Brockden Brown.* Chapel Hill: U of North Carolina P, 1981.

Hedges, William. "Charles Brockden Brown and the Culture of Contradictions." *Early American Literature* 9 (1974): 107–42.

Hinds, Elizabeth Jane Wall. *Private Property: Charles Brockden Brown's Gendered Economics of Virtue.* Newark: U of Delaware P, 1997.

Jordan, Cynthia S. *Second Stories: The Politics of Language, Form, and Gender in Early American Fictions.* Chapel Hill: U of North Carolina P, 1989.

Kindermann, Wolf. *Man Unknown to Himself: Kritische Reflexion der Amerikanischen Aufklärung: Crèvecoeur, Benjamin Rush, Charles Brockden Brown.* Tübingen: G. Narr, 1993.

Levine, Robert S. *Conspiracy and Romance: Studies in Brockden Brown, Cooper, Hawthorne, and Melville.* New York: Cambridge UP, 1989.

Lewis, Paul. "Charles Brockden Brown and the Gendered Canon of Early American Fiction." *Early American Literature* 31:2 (1996): 167–88.

Lewis, R.W.B. *The American Adam: Innocence, Tragedy and Tradition in the Nineteenth Century.* Chicago: U of Chicago P, 1955.

Limon, John. *The Place of Fiction in the Time of Science: A Disciplinary History of American Writing.* Cambridge: Cambridge UP, 1990.

Looby, Christopher. *Voicing America: Language, Literary Form, and the Origins of the United States.* Chicago: U of Chicago P, 1996.

Moses, Richard P. "The Quakerism of Charles Brockden Brown." *Quaker History* 75.1 (1986): 12–25.

Okun, Peter. *Crime and the Nation: Prison Reform and Popular Fiction in Philadelphia, 1786–1800.* New York: Routledge, 2002.

Patterson, Mark. *Authority, Autonomy, and Representation in American Literature, 1776–1865.* Princeton: Princeton UP, 1988.

Porte, Joel. "In the Hands of an Angry God: Religious Terror in Gothic Fiction." In G. R. Thompson, ed., *The Gothic Imagination: Essays in Dark Romanticism,* 42–64. Pullman: Washington State UP, 1974.

Reising, Russell. *Loose Ends: Closure and Crisis in the American Social Text.* Durham: Duke UP, 1997.

Ringe, Donald A. *Charles Brockden Brown.* Revised Edition. Boston: Twayne, 1991.

Rowe, John Carlos. *Literary Culture and U.S. Imperialism: From the Revolution to World War II.* New York: Oxford UP, 2000.

Ruttenberg, Nancy. *Democratic Personality: Popular Voice and the Trial of American Authorship.* Stanford: Stanford UP, 1998.

Samuels, Shirley. *Romances of the Republic: Women, the Family, and Violence in the Literature of the Early American Nation.* New York: Oxford UP, 1996.

Scheiding, Oliver. "'Plena exemplorum est historia': Rewriting Exemplary History in Charles Brockden Brown's 'Death of Cicero.'" In Bernd Engler and Oliver Scheiding, eds., *Re-Visioning the Past: Historical Self-Reflexivity in American Short Fiction,* 39–51. Trier: Wissenschaftlicher Verlag, 1998.

Shapiro, Stephen. *The Culture and Commerce of the Early American Novel: Reading the Atlantic World-System.* University Park: The Pennsylvania State UP, 2008.

Slawinski, Scott Paul. *Validating Bachelorhood: Audience, Patriarchy and Charles Brockden Brown's Editorship of the Monthly Magazine and American Review.* New York: Routledge, 2005.

Sutherland, Helen. "Varieties of Protestant Experience: Religion and the Doppelgänger in Hogg, Brown, and Hawthorne." *Studies in Hogg and His World* 16 (2005): 71–85.

Teute, Fredrika J. "A 'Republic of Intellect': Conversation and Criticism among the Sexes in 1790s New York." In Philip Barnard, Mark L. Kamrath, and Stephen

Shapiro, eds., *Revising Charles Brockden Brown: Culture, Politics, and Sexuality in the Early Republic,* 149–81. Knoxville: U of Tennessee P, 2004.

———. "The Loves of the Plants; or, the Cross-Fertilization of Science and Desire at the End of the Eighteenth Century." In Robert M. Maniquis, ed., *British Radical Culture of the 1790s,* 63–89. San Marino: Huntington Library, 2002.

Tompkins, Jane. *Sensational Designs: The Cultural Work of American Fiction, 1790–1860.* New York: Oxford UP, 1985.

Verhoeven, W. M. "Opening the Text: The Locked-Trunk Motif in Late Eighteenth-Century British and American Gothic Fiction." In Valeria Tinkler-Villani, Peter Davidson, and Jane Stevenson, eds., *Exhibited by Candlelight: Sources and Developments in the Gothic Tradition,* 205–19. Amsterdam: Rodopi, 1995.

Waterman, Bryan. *Republic of Intellect: The Friendly Club of New York City and the Making of American Literature.* Baltimore: Johns Hopkins UP, 2007.

Watts, Edward. *Writing and Postcolonialism in the Early Republic.* Charlottesville: UP of Virginia, 1998.

Watts, Steven. *The Romance of Real Life: Charles Brockden Brown and the Origins of American Culture.* Baltimore: Johns Hopkins UP, 1994.

Weyler, Karen A. *Intricate Relations: Sexual and Economic Desire in American Fiction, 1789–1814.* Iowa City: U of Iowa P, 2004.

Ziff, Larzer. *Writing in the New Nation: Prose, Print, and Politics in the Early United States.* New Haven: Yale UP, 1991.

IV. Discussions Primarily of *Wieland*

Achilles, Jochen. "Composite (Dis)Order: Cultural Identity in *Wieland, Edgar Huntly,* and *Arthur Gordon Pym.*" In Kevin L. Cope and Laura Morrow, eds., *Ideas, Aesthetics, and Inquires in the Early Modern Era,* 251–70. New York: AMS, 1997.

Alliata, Michela Vanon. "The Vertigo and the Abyss: Brown's Internalization of Gothic in *Wieland* and *Edgar Huntly.*" In Gigliola Nocera, ed., *America Today: Highways and Labyrinths,* 124–32. Siracusa, Italy: Grafià, 2003.

Barnes, Elizabeth. "Loving with a Vengeance: *Wieland,* Familicide and the Crisis of Masculinity in the Early Nation." In Milette Shamir and Jennifer Travis. eds., *Boys Don't Cry?: Rethinking Narratives of Masculinity and Emotion in the U.S.,* 44–63. New York: Columbia UP, 2002.

Bauer, Ralph. "Between Repression and Transgression: Rousseau's *Confessions* and Charles Brockden Brown's *Wieland.*" *American Transcendental Quarterly* 10 (1996): 311–29.

Baym, Nina. "A Minority Reading of *Wieland.*" In Bernard Rosenthal, ed., *Critical Essays on Charles Brockden Brown,* 87–103. Boston: G.K. Hall & Co., 1981.

Bradshaw, Charles C. "The New England Illuminati: Conspiracy and Causality in Charles Brockden Brown's *Wieland.*" *New England Quarterly* 76.3 (2003): 356–77.

Bredahl, A. Carl, Jr. "Transformation in *Wieland.*" *Early American Literature* 12 (1977): 177–92.

———. "The Two Portraits in *Wieland*." *Early American Literature* 16 (1981): 54–59.

Butler, Michael D. "Charles Brockden Brown's *Wieland*: Method and Meaning." *Studies in American Fiction* 4 (1976): 127–42.

Carballo, Robert. "Another Look at Shakespearean Tragedy as Proto-Text for *Wieland*." *Neohelicon* 22 (1995): 75–85.

Charras, Françoise. "Variations et anamorphoses sur le mode gothique: Les traductions en français de *Wieland* au XIXe siècle" [Variations and Anamorphoses on the Gothic Mode: French Translations of *Wieland* in the 19th Century]. *Profils Americains* 11 (1999): 191–212.

Christophersen, Bill. "Picking Up the Knife: A Psycho-Historical Reading of *Wieland*." *American Studies* 24 (1986): 115–26.

Clark, Michael. "Charles Brockden Brown's *Wieland* and Robert Proud's *History of Pennsylvania*." *Studies in the Novel* 20 (1988): 239–48.

Cowie, Alexander. "Historical Essay." In Charles Brockden Brown, *Wieland; or, The Transformation and Memoirs of Carwin the Biloquist. Vol. 1, The Novels and Related Works of Charles Brockden Brown. Bicentennial Edition,* 311–48. Kent: Kent State UP, 1977.

Crain, Caleb. "Introduction" and notes. In Charles Brockden Brown, *Wieland; or, The Transformation: An American Tale and Other Stories,* xi–xxiv. New York: Modern Library, 2002.

Dill, Elizabeth. "The Republican Stepmother: Revolution and Sensibility in Charles Brockden Brown's *Wieland*." *The Eighteenth-Century Novel* 2 (2002): 273–303.

Edwards, Justin D. *The Troubling Confessions of Charles Brockden Brown's* Wieland. Odense American Studies International Series, No. 64. Odense, Denmark: Center for American Studies, University of Southern Denmark, 2004.

Elliott, Emory. "Introduction" and notes. In Charles Brockden Brown, *Wieland; or, The Transformation and Memoirs of Carwin the Biloquist,* vii–xxx. New York: Oxford UP, 1994.

Fliegleman, Jay. "Introduction" and notes. In Charles Brockden Brown, *Wieland and Memoirs of Carwin the Biloquist,* vii–xlii. New York: Penguin Books, 1991.

Frank, John C. "The Wieland Family in Charles Brockden Brown." *Monatshefte* 42 (1950): 347–53.

Franklin, Wayne. "Tragedy and Comedy in Brown's *Wieland*." *Novel* 8 (1975): 147–63.

Fussell, Edwin Sill. "*Wieland*: A Literary and Historical Reading." *Early American Literature* 18.2 (Fall 1983): 171–86.

Gable, Jr., Harvey L. "*Wieland, Othello, Genesis,* and the Floating City: the Sources of Charles Brockden Brown's *Wieland*." *Papers on Language & Literature* 34 (1998): 301–18.

Galluzzo, Anthony. "*Carwin*'s Terrorist Aesthetic: Charles Brockden Brown's Aesthetics of Subversion." *Eighteenth-Century Studies* 4.2 (2009):255–71.

Garrow, Scott. "Character Formation in *Wieland*." *Southern Quarterly* 4 (1965–1966): 308–18.

Gilmore, Michael T. "Calvinism and Gothicism: The Example of Brown's *Wieland*." *Studies in the Novel* 98 (1977): 107–18.

Goddu, Teresa A. "Historicizing the American Gothic: Charles Brockden Brown's *Wieland.*" In Diane Long Hoeveler and Tamar Heller, eds., *Approaches to Teaching Gothic Fiction: The British and American Traditions,* 184–89. New York: Modern Language Association of America, 2003.

Greiner, Donald J. "Brown's Use of the Narrator in *Wieland*: An Indirect Plea for the Acceptance of Fiction." *College Language Association Journal* 13 (1969): 131–36.

Hagenbüchle, Roland. "American Literature and the Nineteenth-Century Crisis in Epistemology: The Example of Charles Brockden Brown." *Early American Literature* 23 (1988): 121–51.

Harris, Jennifer. "At One with the Land: The Domestic Remove—Charles Brockden Brown's *Wieland* and Matters of National Belonging." *Canadian Review of American Studies* 33.3 (2003): 189–210.

Hesford, Walter. "Do You Know the Author? The Question of Authorship in *Wieland.*" *Early American Literature* 17.3 (Winter 1982–1983): 239–48.

Hobson, Robert W. "Voices of Carwin and Other Mysteries in Charles Brockden Brown's *Wieland.*" *Early American Literature* 10 (1975): 307–9.

Hogsette, David S. "Textual Surveillance, Social Codes, and Sublime Voices: The Tyranny of Narrative in *Caleb Williams* and *Wieland.*" Transatlantic Romanticism: A Special Issue of *Romanticism on the Net* 38–39 (May–August 2005). http://www.erudit.org/revue/RON/2005/v/n38-39/011667ar.html

Hughes, Rowland. "'Wonderfully Cruel Proceedings': The Murderous Case of James Yates." *Canadian Review of American Studies* 38: 1 (2008), 43–62.

Jenkins, R. B. "Invulnerable Virtue in *Wieland* and 'Comus.'" *South Atlantic Bulletin* 38.2 (May 1973): 72–75.

Jordan, Cynthia S. "On Rereading *Wieland*: The Folly of Precipitate Conclusions." *Early American Literature* 16.2 (1981): 154–74.

Katz, Joseph. "Analytical Bibliography and Literary History: The Writing and Printing of *Wieland.*" *Proof* 1 (1971): 18–34.

Kirkham, E. Bruce. "A Note on *Wieland.*" *American Notes and Queries* 5.6 (1967): 86–87.

Kittel, Harald. "Free Indirect Discourse and the Experiencing Self in Eighteenth-Century American Autobiographical Fiction: The Narration of Consciousness in Charles Brockden Brown's *Wieland.*" *New Comparison* 9 (1990): 73–89.

Korobkin, Laura H. "Murder by Madman: Criminal Responsibility, Law, and Judgment in *Wieland.*" *American Literature* 72 (2000): 721–50.

Krause, Sidney J. "Romanticism in *Wieland*: Brown and the Reconciliation of Opposites." In Robert J. Demott and Sanford E. Marovitz, eds., *Artful Thunder: Versions of the Romantic Tradition in American Literature in Honor of Howard P. Vincent,* 13–24. Kent: Kent State UP, 1975.

Kreyling, Michael. "Construing Brown's *Wieland*: Ambiguity and Derridean 'Free-play.'" *Studies in the Novel* 14.1 (1982): 43–54.

Kutchen, Larry. "The 'Vulgar Thread of the Canvas': Revolution and the Picturesque in Ann Eliza Bleecker, Crevecoeur, and Charles Brockden Brown." *Early American Literature* 36 (2001): 395–426.

Lam, Bethany L. "Brown's *Wieland; or, The Transformation: an American Tale.*" *Explicator* 64.2 (Winter 2006): 78–81.

Litton, Alfred G. "The Failure of Rhetoric in Charles Brockden Brown's *Wieland.*" *Lamar Journal of the Humanities* 16 (1990): 23–40.

Lyttle, David. "The Case Against Carwin." *Nineteenth-Century Fiction* 26.3 (1971): 257–269.

Manly, William M. "The Importance of Point of View in Brockden Brown's *Wieland.*" *American Literature* 35.3 (1963): 311–21.

Manning, Susan L. "Enlightenment's Dark Dreams: Two Fictions of Henry Mackenzie and Charles Brockden Brown." *Eighteenth-Century Life* 21.3 (1997): 39–56.

Manuel Cuenca, Carme. "Charles Brockden Brown's *Wieland* or, Fiction as an Instrument of Salvation in Post-Revolutionary America." *Revista Alicantina de Estudios Ingleses* 12 (1999): 91–104.

Mulqueen, James E. "The Plea for a Deistic Education in Charles Brockden Brown's *Wieland.*" *Ball State University Forum* 10 (1969): 70–77.

Murley, Jane. "Ordinary Sinners and Moral Aliens: The Murder Narratives of Charles Brockden Brown and Edgar Allan Poe." In Margaret Sönser Breen, ed., *Understanding Evil: An Interdisciplinary Approach,* 181–200. New York: Rodopi, 2003.

Norwood, Lisa West. "'I May Be a Stranger to the Grounds of Your Belief': Constructing a Sense of Place in *Wieland.*" *Early American Literature* 38 (2003): 89–122.

O'Shaughnessy, Toni. "'An Imperfect Tale': Interpretive Accountability in *Wieland.*" *Studies in American Fiction* 18 (1990): 41–54.

Paryz, Marek. "Madness, Man and Social Order in Charles Brockden Brown's *Wieland.*" *American Studies* [Warsaw, Poland] 16 (1998): 31–47.

Patrick, Marietta S. "Romantic Iconography in *Wieland.*" *South Atlantic Review* 49.4 (1984): 65–74.

Pattee, Fred Lewis. "Introduction." In Charles Brockden Brown, *Wieland, or The Transformation together with Memoirs of Carwin the Biloquist, a Fragment,* ix–xlvi. New York: Harcourt, Brace, Jovanovich, 1926.

Prescott, Frederick C. "*Wieland* and *Frankenstein.*" *American Literature* 2 (1930): 192–73.

Pribeck, Thomas. "A Note on Depravity in *Wieland.*" *Philological Quarterly* 64.2 (1985): 273–79.

Ridgely, Joseph V. "The Empty World of *Wieland.*" In Kenneth H. Baldwin and David K. Kirby, eds., *Individual and Community: Variations on a Theme in American Fiction,* 3–16. Durham: Duke UP, 1975.

Rombes, Nicholas, Jr. "'All Was Lonely, Darksome, and Waste': *Wieland* and the Construction of the New Republic." *Studies in American Fiction* 22 (1994): 37–46.

Rosenthal, Bernard. "The Voices of *Wieland*" In Bernard Rosenthal, ed., *Critical Essays on Charles Brockden Brown,* 104–25. Boston: G.K. Hall & Co., 1981.

Russo, James. "The Chimeras of the Brain: Clara's Narrative in *Wieland.*" *Early American Literature* 16.1 (1981): 60–88.

Samuels, Shirley. "Wieland: Alien and Infidel." *Early American Literature* 25.1 (1990): 45–66.

Schneck, Peter. "Wieland's Testimony: Charles Brockden Brown and the Rhetoric of Evidence." *REAL: The Yearbook of Research in English and American Literature* 18 (2002): 167–213.

Schnell, Michael. "'The Sacredness of Conjugal and Parental Duties': the Family, the Twentieth-Century Reader, and *Wieland*." *Christianity & Literature* 44 (1995): 259–73.

Schreiber, Andrew J. "'The Arm Lifted Against Me': Love, Terror, and the Construction of Gender in *Wieland*." *Early American Literature* 26 (1991): 173–94.

Seed, David. "The Mind Set Free: Charles Brockden Brown's *Wieland*." In A. Robert Lee and Verhoeven, W. M., eds., *Making America/Making American Literature*, 105–22. Amsterdam: Rodopi, 1996.

Seltzer, Mark. "Saying Makes It So: Language and Event in Brown's *Wieland*." *Early American Literature* 8 (1978): 81–91.

Shelden, Pamela J. "The Shock of Ambiguity: Brockden Brown's *Wieland* and the Gothic Tradition." *DeKalb Literary Arts Journal* 10 (1977): 17–26.

Soldati, Joseph. "The Americanization of Faust: A Study of Charles Brockden Brown's *Wieland*." *ESQ* (Emerson Society Quarterly) 20 (1974): 1–14.

Stewart, Larry. "Charles Brockden Brown: Quantitative Analysis and Literary Interpretation." *Literary and Linguistic Computing* 18.2 (2003): 129–38.

Surratt, Marshall N. "'The Awe-Creating Presence of the Deity: Some Religious Sources for Charles Brockden Brown's *Wieland*." *Papers on Language and Literature* 33 (1997): 310–24.

Traister, Bryce. "Libertinism and Authorship in America's Early Republic." *American Literature* 72 (March 2000): 1–30.

Vickers, Anita M. "Patriarchal and Political Authority in *Wieland*." *AUMLA: Journal of the Australasian Universities Language and Literature Association* 90 (1998): 1–19.

Voloshin, Beverly R. "*Wieland*: 'Accounting for Appearances.'" *The New England Quarterly* 59.3 (1986): 341–57.

Wallach, Rick. "The Manner in Which Appearances are Solved: Narrative Semiotics in *Wieland, or the Transformation*." *South Atlantic Review* 64 (1999): 1–15.

Warfel, Harry R. "Charles Brockden Brown's German Sources." *Modern Language Quarterly* 1.3 (1940): 357–65.

Waterman, Bryan. "The Bavarian Illuminati, the Early American Novel, and Histories of the Public Sphere." *The William and Mary Quarterly* 62.1 (2005): 9–30.

Weldon, Roberta F. "Charles Brockden Brown's *Wieland*: A Family Tragedy." *Studies in American Fiction* 12.1 (1984): 1–11.

White, Ed. "Carwin the Peasant Rebel." In Philip Barnard, Mark L. Kamrath, and Stephen Shapiro, eds., *Revising Charles Brockden Brown: Culture, Politics, and Sexuality in the Early Republic*, 41–59. Knoxville: U of Tennessee P, 2004.

Whittier, John Greenleaf. "Fanaticism." In *The Complete Works of John Greenleaf Whittier in Seven Volumes*, vol. VII, 391–95. Boston: Houghton and Mifflin Co., 1892.

Williams, Daniel E. "Writing under the Influence: An Examination of *Wieland*'s 'Well Authenticated Facts' and the Depiction of Murderous Fathers in Post-Revolutionary Print Culture." *Eighteenth-Century Fiction* 15:3–4 (2003): 643–68.

Witherington, Paul. "Image and Idea in *Wieland* and *Edgar Huntly.*" *The Serif: Kent State University Library Quarterly* 3 (1966): 19–26.

Wolfe, Eric A. "Ventriloquizing Nation: Voice, Identity, and Radical Democracy in Charles Brockden Brown's *Wieland.*" *American Literature* 78 (2006): 431–57.

Woodward, Maureen L. "Female Captivity and the Deployment of Race in Three Early American Texts." *Papers on Language and Literature* 32.2 (1996): 115–46.

Ziaja-Buchholz, Miroslawa. "*Wieland: Or the Transformation* by Charles Brockden Brown: An Attempt at Interpretation." *American Studies* [Warsaw, Poland] 16 (1998): 23–29.

Ziff, Larzer. "A Reading of *Wieland.*" *PMLA* (*Publications of the Modern Language Association*) 77.1 (1962): 51–57.

V. Discussions Primarily of *Memoirs of Carwin*

Downes, Paul. "Constitutional Secrets: 'Memoirs of Carwin' and the Politics of Concealment." *Criticism* 39 (1997): 89–117.

Edwards, Justin D. "Engendering a New Republic: Charles Brockden Brown's *Alcuin, Carwin* and the Legal Fictions of Gender." *Nordic Journal of English Studies* 2.2 (2002): 279–302.

Hsu, Hsuan L. "Democratic Expansionism in Memoirs of Carwin." *Early American Literature* 35 (2000): 137–56.

Kazanjian, David. "Charles Brockden Brown's Biloquial Nation: National Culture and White Settler Colonialism in *Memoirs of Carwin the Biloquist.*" *American Literature* 73 (2001): 459–96.

Leask, Nigel. "Irish Republicans and Gothic Eleutherarchs: Pacific Utopias in the Writings of Theobald Wolfe Tone and Charles Brockden Brown." In Robert M. Maniquis, ed., *British Radical Culture of the 1790s,* 347–67. San Marino: Huntington Library, 2002.

VI. *Wieland*'s Atlantic and Early National Context

A. Anglophone Reception of German Literature, Culture, and History in the 1790s

Andriopoulos, Stefan. "Occult Conspiracies: Spirits and Secret Societies in Schiller's *Ghost-Seer.*" *New German Critique* 103, 35.1 (2008): 65–81.

Baker, George M. "Graf Friedrich von Stolberg in England." *Modern Language Notes* 21.8 (1906): 232–34.

Benton, Rita. "Ignace Joseph Pleyel." In Stanley Sadie, ed., *The New Grove Dictionary of Music and Musicians,* vol. 19, 918–19. New York: Grove, 2001.

Emerson, Oliver Farrar. *The Earliest English Translations of Bürger's Lenore: A Study in English and German Romanticism.* Cleveland: Western Reserve UP, 1915.

Herzfeld, Georg. *William Taylor of Norwich: A Study of the Influence of Modern German Literature in England* (1897). Translated by Astrid Wind; Edited with an Introduction by David Chandler; and with a Foreword by Frederick Burwick. A Romantic Circles Scholarly Resource: http://www.rc.umd.edu/reference/

Jolles, Evelyn B. *G. A. Bürger's Ballade Lenore in England.* Regensburg: Verlag Hans Carl, 1974.

Karr, David. "'Thoughts That Flash Like Lightning': Thomas Holcroft, Radical Theater, and the Production of Meaning in 1790s London." *The Journal of British Studies,* 40.3 (2001): 324–56.

Kleingeld, Pauline. "Six Varieties of Cosmopolitanism in Late Eighteenth-Century Germany." *Journal of the History of Ideas* 60.3 (July 1999): 505–24.

Kurrelmeyer, W. "Wieland's *Teutscher Merkur* and Contemporary English Journals." *PMLA (Papers of the Modern Language Association)* 38.4 (1923): 869–86.

Maertz, Gregory. "The Importation of German and Dissenting Voices in British Culture: Thomas Holcroft and the Godwin Circle." *1650–1850: Ideas, Aesthetics, and Inquiries in the Early Modern Era* III (1997): 271–300.

Mortensen, Peter. *British Romanticism and Continental Influences: Writing in an Age of Europhobia.* New York: Palgrave Macmillan, 2004.

Roehr, Sabine. *A Primer on German Enlightenment: With a Translation of Karl Leonhard Reinhold's The Fundamental Concepts and Principles of Ethics.* Columbia: U of Missouri P, 1995.

Skokoe, Frank Woodyer. *German Influence in the English Romantic Period, 1788–1818.* Cambridge: Cambridge UP, 1926.

Sutter, Paula. *Protestantism and Primogeniture in Early Modern Germany.* New Haven: Yale UP, 1989.

B. Family Murders; Spontaneous Combustion; Ventriloquism

Family murders:

Broderick, Warren F. "Fiction Based on 'Well-Authenticated Facts': Documenting the Birth of the American Novel." *The Hudson Valley Regional Review* 4.2 (1987): 1–37.

Cohen, Daniel A. "Homicidal Compulsion and the Conditions of Freedom: The Social and Psychological Origins of Familicide in America's Early Republic." *Journal of Social History* 28.4 (1995): 725–64.

Davis, David Brion. *Homicide in American Fiction, 1798–1860: A Study in Social Values.* Ithaca: Cornell UP, 1957.

Fitzgerald, Neil. *Wieland's Crime: A Source and Analogue Study of the Foremost Novel of the Father of American Literature.* Dissertation: Brown University, 1980.

Grasso, Christopher. "Deist Monster: On Religious Common Sense in the Wake of the American Revolution." *The Journal of American History* 95.1 (2008): 43–68.

Halttunen, Karen. "Early American Murder Narratives: The Birth of Horror." In Richard Wrightman Fox and T.J. Jackson Lears, eds., *The Power of Culture: Critical Essays in American History,* 67–102. Chicago: U of Chicago P, 1993.

————. *Murder Most Foul: The Killer and the American Gothic Imagination.* Cambridge: Harvard UP, 1998.

Hendrickson, James C. "A Note on *Wieland.*" *American Literature* 8.3 (1936): 305–6.

Spontaneous combustion:

Croft, Lee B. "Spontaneous Human Combustion in Literature: Some Examples of the Literary Use of Popular Mythology." *College Language Association Journal* 32 (1989): 335–47.

Heilbron, Joseph. "The Affair of the Countess Görlitz." *Proceedings of the American Philosophical Society* 138.2 (1994): 284–316.

Ventriloquism:

Connor, Steven. *Dumbstruck: A Cultural History of Ventriloquism.* New York: Oxford UP, 2000.

Davis, Charles B. *Ventriloquism: Identity and the Multiple Voice.* Dissertation: University of Washington, 1997.

Schmidt, Leigh Eric. "From Demon Possession to Magic Show: Ventriloquism, Religion, and the Enlightenment." *Church History* 67.2 (1998): 274–304.

C. Classical References: Cicero Debates in the Eighteenth Century; the Daemon of Socrates; Hermes

Brown, Norman O. *Hermes the Thief: The Evolution of a Myth.* Madison: U of Wisconsin P, 1947.

Destrée, Pierre and Nicholas D. Smith, eds. "Socrates' Divine Sign: Religion, Practice, and Value in Socratic Philosophy." Special issue of *APEIRON: A Journal for Ancient Philosophy and Science* 38.2 (2005).

Farrell, James M. "John Adams's Autobiography: The Ciceronian Paradigm and the Quest for Fame." *New England Quarterly* 62.4 (1989): 502–28.

————. "'Syren Tully' and the Young John Adams." *The Classical Journal* 87.4 (1992): 373–90.

Hamilton, W. "The Myth in Plutarch's *De Genio* (589F-592E)." *The Classical Quarterly* 28.3–4 (1934): 175–82.

Kerényi, Karl. *Hermes Guide of Souls: The Mythologem of the Masculine Source of Life.* Zürich: Spring Publications, 1976.

Rist, John M. "Plotinus and the 'Daimonion' of Socrates." *Phoenix* 17.1 (1963): 13–24.

Roller, Matthew B. "*Color*-Blindness: Cicero's Death, Declamation, and the Production of History." *Classical Philology* 92.2 (1997): 109–30.

Smith, Tania. "Elizabeth Montagu's Study of Cicero's Life: The Formation of an Eighteenth-Century Woman's Rhetorical Identity." *Rhetorica* 26.2 (2008): 165– 87.

Ward, Addison. "The Tory View of Roman History." *Studies in English Literature, 1500–1900* 4.3 (1964): 413–56.

Woodley, E. C. "Cicero's Pro Cluentio: An Ancient Cause Célèbre." *The Classical Journal* 42.7 (1947): 415–18.

D. The Illuminati Scare and the Counter-Enlightenment

Chandos, Michael Brown. "Mary Wollstonecraft; or, the Female Illuminati: The Campaign against Women and 'Modern Philosophy' in the Early Republic. *Journal of the Early Republic* 15 (1995): 389–424.

Davis, David Brion. *The Fear of Conspiracy: Images of Un-American Subversion from the Revolution to the Present.* Ithaca: Cornell UP, 1971.

Garrard, Graeme. *Counter-Enlightenments: From the Eighteenth Century to the Present.* New York: Routledge, 2006.

Hofman, Amos. "Opinion, Illusion, and the Illusion of Opinion: Barruel's Theory of Conspiracy." *Eighteenth-Century Studies* 27.1 (1993): 27–60.

———. "The Origins of the Theory of the Philosophe Conspiracy." *French History* 2.2 (1988): 152–72.

Hofstadter, Richard. *The Paranoid Style in American Politics and Other Essays.* New York: Knopf, 1966.

Koselleck, Reinhard. *Critique and Crisis: Enlightenment and the Pathogenesis of Modern Society.* Cambridge: MIT Press, 1988.

Leinesch, Michael. "The Illusion of the Illuminati: The Counterconspiratorial Origins of Post-Revolutionary Conservatism." In Wil Verhoeven, ed., *Revolutionary Histories: Translatlantic Cultural Nationalism, 1775–1815,* 152–65. New York: Palgrave, 2002.

Luckert, Steven. *Jesuits, Freemasons, Illuminati, and Jacobins: Conspiracy Theories, Secret Societies, and Politics in Late Eighteenth-century Germany.* Dissertation: University of New York at Binghamton, 1993.

McMahon, Darrin M. *Enemies of the Enlightenment: The French Counter-Enlightenment and the Making of Modernity.* New York: Oxford UP, 2001.

Roberts, J. M. *The Mythology of the Secret Societies.* London: Secker & Warburg, 1972.

Rogin, Michael Paul. *Ronald Reagan, the Movie: And other Episodes in Political Demonology.* Berkeley: U of California P, 1987.

Stauffer, Vernon L. *New England and the Bavarian Illuminati.* New York: Columbia UP, 1918.

White, Ed. "The Value of Conspiracy Theory." *American Literary History* 14.1 (2002): 1–31.

Wood, Gordon S. "Conspiracy and the Paranoid Style: Causality and Deceit in the Eighteenth Century." *William & Mary Quarterly* 39 (1982): 401–41.

E. Religious Wars, Religious Counterpublics, and Early Modern Empire

Barber, Malcolm. *The Cathars: Dualist Heretics in Languedoc in the High Middle Ages.* London: Longman, 2000.

Cosmos, Georgia. *Huguenot Prophecy and Clandestine Worship in the Eighteenth Century: 'The Sacred Theatre of the Cévennes.'* Aldershot: Ashgate, 2005.

Frey, Linda and Marsha Frey. *Societies in Upheaval: Insurrections in France, Hungary, and Spain in the Early Eighteenth Century.* New York: Greenwood Press, 1987.

Garrett, Clarke. *Respectable Folly: Millenarians and the French Revolution in France and England.* Baltimore: Johns Hopkins UP, 1975.

———. *Spirit Possession and Popular Religion: From the Camisards to the Shakers.* Baltimore: Johns Hopkins UP, 1987.

Juster, Susan. *Doomsayers: Anglo-American Prophecy in the Age of Revolution.* Philadelphia: U of Pennsylvania P, 2003.

Le Roy Ladurie, Emmanuel. *The Peasants of Languedoc.* Translated with an intro. by John Day. George Huppert, consulting editor. Urbana: U of Illinois P, 1974.

Pocock, J. G. A. "Enthusiasm: The Antiself of Enlightenment." *The Huntington Library Quarterly* 60.1–2, (1997): 7–28.

Schwartz, Hillel. *The French Prophets: The History of a Millenarian Group in Eighteenth-Century England.* Berkeley: U California P, 1980.

Taves, Ann. *Fits, Trances, and Visions: Experiencing Religion and Explaining Experience from Wesley to James.* Princeton: Princeton UP, 1999.

Walters, Kerry S. *Rational Infidels: The American Deists.* Durango: Longwood Academic, 1992.

F. Women, Patriarchy, and Sexuality in the Revolutionary Age and Early Republic

Block, Sharon. *Rape and Sexual Power in Early America.* Chapel Hill: U of North Carolina P, 2006.

Branson, Susan. *Those Fiery Frenchified Dames: Women and Political Culture in Early National Philadelphia.* Philadelphia: U of Pennsylvania P, 2001.

Daniels, Christine and Michael V. Kennedy, eds. *Over the Threshold: Intimate Violence in Early America.* New York: Routledge, 1999.

Fliegelman, Jay. *Prodigals and Pilgrims: The American Revolution Against Patriarchal Authority.* Cambridge: Cambridge UP, 1982.

Hoffman, Ronald and Peter J. Albert, eds. *Women in the Age of the American Revolution.* Charlottesville: U of Virginia P, 1989.

Kerber, Linda K. *Women of the Republic: Intellect and Ideology in Revolutionary America.* Chapel Hill: U of North Carolina P, 1997.

Lyons, Clare. *Sex Among the Rabble: An Intimate History of Gender & Power in the Age of Revolution, Philadelphia, 1730–1830.* Chapel Hill: U of North Carolina P, 2006.

Pateman, Carole. *The Sexual Contract.* Stanford: Stanford UP, 1988.

Stone, Lawrence. *The Family, Sex, and Marriage in England, 1500–1800.* New York: Harper & Row, 1977.

G. Revolution Debates and Counterrevolutionary Backlash in the American 1790s

Carter, Edward C., II. "A 'Wild Irishman' Under Every Federalist's Bed: Naturalization in Philadelphia, 1789–1806." *Proceedings of the American Philosophical Society* 133.2 (1989): 178–89.

Cotlar, Seth, "The Federalists' Transatlantic Cultural Offensive of 1798 and the Moderation of American Political Discourse." In Jeffrey L. Pasley, Andrew W. Robertson, and David Waldstreicher, eds., *Beyond the Founders: New Approaches to the Political History of the Early American Republic,* 274–99. Chapel Hill: U of North Carolina P, 2004.

Elkins, Stanley and Eric McKitrick. *The Age of Federalism: The Early American Republic, 1788–1800.* New York: Oxford UP, 1993.

Fitzmier, John R. *New England's Moral Legislator: Timothy Dwight, 1752–1817.* Bloomington: Indiana UP, 1998.

Fischer, David Hackett. *The Revolution of American Conservatism: The Federalist Party in the Era of Jeffersonian Democracy.* New York: Harper & Row, 1965.

Imholt, Robert J. "Timothy Dwight, Federalist Pope of Connecticut." *The New England Quarterly* 73.3 (2000): 386–411.

Kafer, Peter. "The Making of Timothy Dwight: A Connecticut Morality Tale." *The William and Mary Quarterly* 47.2 (1990): 189–209.

Kaplan, Catherine O'Donnell. *Men of Letters in the Early Republic: Cultivating Forms of Citizenship.* Chapel Hill: U of North Carolina P, 2008.

Kramnick, Isaac. *Republicanism and Bourgeois Radicalism: Political Ideology in Late Eighteenth-Century England and America.* Ithaca: Cornell UP, 1994.

Miller, John C. *Crisis in Freedom: The Alien and Sedition Acts.* Boston: Little, Brown, and Company, 1951.

Simpson, Lewis. "Federalism and the Crisis of Literary Order." *American Literature* 32 (1960/61): 253–66.

Tise, Larry E. *The American Counterrevolution: A Retreat from Liberty, 1783–1800.* Mechanicsburg, PA: Stackpole Books, 1998.

Trotsky, Leon. *History of the Russian Revolution.* New York: Anchor, 1989.

———. *The Permanent Revolution, and Results and Prospects.* New York: Pathfinder, 1978.

Wallerstein, Immanuel. *After Liberalism.* New York: New Press, 1995.

———. "The Bourgeois(ie) as Concept and Reality." *New Left Review* 167 (1988): 91–106.

White, Ed. *The Backcountry and the City: Colonization and Conflict in Early America.* Minneapolis: U of Minnesota P, 2005.

H. British Radical-Democratic Novel in the 1790s; Links between Woldwinites and Brown's Circle

Butler, Marilyn. *Jane Austen and the War of Ideas.* Oxford: Clarendon Press, 1975.

Clemit, Pamela. *The Godwinian Novel: The Rational Fictions of Godwin, Brockden Brown, Mary Shelley.* Oxford: Oxford UP, 1993.

Green, David Bonnell. "Letters of William Godwin and Thomas Holcroft to William Dunlap." *Notes and Queries* 3.10 (1956): 441–43.

Kelly, Gary. *The English Jacobin Novel 1780–1805.* Oxford: Oxford UP, 1976.

————. *English Fiction of the Romantic Period, 1789–1830*. London: Longman, 1989.

Pollin, Burton R. "Godwin's Letter to Ogilvie, Friend of Jefferson, and the Federalist Propaganda." *Journal of the History of Ideas* 28.3 (1967): 432–44.

Steinman, Lisa M. "Transatlantic Cultures: Godwin, Brown, and Mary Shelley." *Wordsworth Circle* 32.3 (2001): 126–30.

Tompkins, J. M. S. *The Popular Novel in England, 1770–1800*. Lincoln: U of Nebraska P, 1961.

I. Sensibility, Sentiment, and the Gothic

Barker-Benfield, G. J. *The Culture of Sensibility: Sex and Society in Eighteenth-Century Britain*. Chicago: U of Chicago P, 1992.

Barnes, Elizabeth. *States of Sympathy: Seduction and Democracy in the American Novel*. New York: Columbia UP, 1997.

Botting, Fred. *Gothic*. London: Routledge, 1995.

Burgett, Bruce. *Sentimental Bodies: Sex, Gender, and Citizenship in the Early Republic*. Princeton: Princeton UP, 1998.

Chapman, Mary and Glenn Hendler. *Sentimental Men: Masculinity and the Politics of Affect in American Culture*. Berkeley: U of California P, 1999.

Ellis, Markman. *The History of Gothic Fiction*. Edinburgh: Edinburgh UP, 2000.

Heiland, Donna. *Gothic and Gender: An Introduction*. Oxford: Blackwell Publishing, 2004.

Howard, June. "What Is Sentimentality." *American Literary History* 11.1 (1999): 63–81.

Johnson, Claudia L. *Equivocal Beings: Politics, Gender, and Sentimentality in the 1790s—Wollstonecraft, Burney, Radcliffe, Austin*. Chicago: U of Chicago P, 1995.

Jones, Chris. *Radical Sensibility: Literature and Ideas in the 1790s*. London: Routledge, 1993.

Kilgour, Maggie. *The Rise of the Gothic Novel*. London: Routledge, 1995.

McGann, Jerome. *The Poetics of Sensibility: A Revolution in Literary Style*. New York: Oxford UP, 1996.

Monleón, José B. *A Specter Is Haunting Europe: A Sociohistorical Approach to the Fantastic*. Princeton: Princeton UP, 1990.

Mullan, John. *Sentiment and Sociability: The Language of Feeling in the Eighteenth Century*. Oxford: Clarendon Press, 1988.

Norton, Rictor. *Gothic Readings: The First Wave, 1764–1840*. New York: Continuum, 2000.

Paulson, Ronald. *Representations of Revolution, 1789–1820*. New Haven: Yale UP, 1983.

Todd, Janet. *Sensibility: An Introduction*. London: Methuen, 1986.

Williams, Raymond. *The English Novel from Dickens to Lawrence*. London: Chatto and Windus, 1970.